EL OCEAN

UNMAPPED
TUNDRA

OAST

GLACIER

ICESCARP
ALPS

SKRAELINGS

SCARP
RREN

AVARINHEIM

FORTRESS RANGES

R. NORDRA

WILD DOG PLAINS

WIDOWMAKER SEA

SIGHOLT

HOLDHARD
PASS

S
NG

R. NORDRA

TAILEM
BEND

SMYRTON

SEAGRASS PLAINS

Starman

Tor Books by Sara Douglass

The Wayfarer Redemption

Enchanter

Starman

Starman

— BOOK THREE OF —
THE WAYFARER REDEMPTION

Sara Douglass

TOR®
fantasy

A TOM DOHERTY ASSOCIATES BOOK
NEW YORK

STARMAN

Copyright © 1996 by Sara Douglass Enterprises Pty Ltd.

First published in Australia in 1996. This edition first published in 1998 by HarperCollins*Publishers* Pty Limited.

A Tor Book
Published by Tom Doherty Associates, LLC
175 Fifth Avenue
New York, NY 10010

Tor® is a registered trademark of Tom Doherty Associates, LLC.

Library of Congress Cataloging-in-Publication Data

Douglass, Sara
    Starman / Sara Douglass.—1st Tor ed.
        p. cm.—(Wayfarer redemption ; bk. 3)
    ISBN 0-312-87888-5
    I. Title.

PR9619.3.D672 S73 2002
823'.914—dc21

                                                          2001059651

First Tor Edition: May 2002

Printed in the United States of America

0 9 8 7 6 5 4 3 2 1

Nothing but idiot gabble!
For the prophecy given of old
And then not understood,
Has come to pass as foretold;
Not let any man think for the public good,
But babble, merely for babble.
For I never whisper'd a private affair
Within the hearing of cat or mouse,
No, not to myself in the closet alone,
But I heard it shouted at once from the top of the house;
Everything came to be known.
Who told *him* we were there?

Not that gray old wolf, for he came not back
From the wilderness, full of wolves, where he used to lie;
He has gather'd the bones for his o'ergrown whelp to crack;
Crack them now for yourself, and howl, and die.

Alfred, Lord Tennyson,
from Part II.v of *Maud*

Contents

Contents

The Prophecy of the Destroyer

A day will come when born will be
Two babes whose blood will tie them.
That born to Wing and Horn will hate
The one they call the StarMan.
Destroyer! rises in the north
And drives his Ghostmen south;
Defenseless lie both flesh and field
Before Gorgrael's ice.
To meet this threat you must release
The StarMan from his lies,
Revive Tencendor, fast and sure
Forget the ancient war,
For if Plow, Wing and Horn can't find
The bridge to understanding,
Then will Gorgrael earn his name
And bring Destruction hither.
StarMan, listen, heed me well,
Your power will destroy you
If you should wield it in the fray
'Ere these prophecies are met:
The Sentinels will walk abroad
'Til power corrupt their hearts;
A child will turn her head and cry
Revealing ancient arts;
A wife will hold in joy at night
The slayer of her husband;
Age-old souls, long in cribs,
Will sing o'er mortal land;
The remade dead, fat with child
Will birth abomination;
A darker power will prove to be
The father of salvation.
Then waters will release bright eyes
To form the Rainbow Scepter.

StarMan, listen, for I know
That you can wield the scepter

To bring Gorgrael to his knees
And break the ice asunder.
But even with the power in hand
Your pathway is not sure:
A Traitor from within your camp
Will seek and plot to harm you;
Let not your Lover's pain distract
For this will mean your death;
Destroyer's might lies in his hate
Yet you must never follow;
Forgiveness is the thing assured
To save Tencendor's soul.

Starman

1

The Day of Power

It was a long day, the day Axis tried to kill Azhure, then married her. It was a day filled with power, and thus power found it easy to wrap and manipulate lives. The power of the Enchantress—untested and, for the moment, uncontrolled—had dominated the morning. Now, as the Enchantress smiled and kissed her new husband, it lay quiescent, waiting.

But as the gate that had imprisoned Azhure's power and identity had shattered that day, so had other gates shattered, and so other powers had moved—and not all of them welcomed by the Prophecy.

As the Enchantress leaned back from her husband, accepting the warmth and love of her friends and family about her, so power walked the land of Tencendor.

It would be a long day.

Axis pulled the Enchantress' ring from a small secret pocket in his breeches. He held it up so that all in the room could see it, then he slid the ring onto the heart finger of Azhure's left hand. It fit perfectly, made only for this woman, and for this finger.

"Welcome into the House of the Stars to stand by my side, Enchantress. May we walk together forever."

"Forever?" the GateKeeper said. "You and the Enchantress? For ever*? As you wish, StarMan, as you wish."*

She laughed, then, from one of the bowls on the table before her she lifted out two balls and studied them.

"Forever," she muttered, and placed them with the group of seven sparkling balls at the front of her table. The Greater. "Nine. Complete. The Circle is complete*! At last . . . at last!"*

She fell silent, deep in thought. Her fingers trembled. Already he had one child, and more to follow. And then . . . the other.

She held a hand over one of the bowls again, dipped it in sharply, and brought out four more balls. She dropped them into the pile of softly glowing golden balls which represented those who did not have to go through her Gate. The Lesser.

"Yet one *more!*" A spasm of pain crossed her face. Her hand lifted slowly, shaking, then she snarled and snatched a dull black ball from the pile of those who refused to go through her Gate.

She hissed, for the GateKeeper loathed releasing a soul without exacting fair price. "Does that satisfy your promise, WolfStar? *Does* it?"

She dropped it with the other four on the pile of the Lesser.

"Enough," she said in relief. "It is done. Enough."

Faraday tightened the girth on the donkey and checked the saddlebags and panniers. She did not carry much with her: the bowl of enchanted wood that the silver pelt had given her so long ago; the green gown that the Mother had presented to her; some extra blankets; a pair of sturdy boots should the weather break; and a few spare clothes.

It was not much for a widowed Queen, thought Faraday, fighting to keep her emotions under control. Where were the retainers? The gilded carriage and the caparisoned horses? The company of two white donkeys was paltry considering what she had done for Axis and for Tencendor—and what she would yet do.

Carriages and horses? What did she need with those? All she needed, all she wanted, was the love of a man who did not love her.

She thought about Azhure and Caelum, envying the woman yet sharing her joy in her son. Well, she thought, no matter. I am mother to forty-two-thousand souls. Surely their birthing will give me pain and joy enough.

The stables, as the rest of the palace of Carlon, were still and quiet. When she had left the Sentinels earlier Faraday had heard that the princes and commanders closest to Axis and Azhure had been called to the apartment where Faraday had left them.

"A wedding, I hope," Faraday murmured, and did not know whether to smile for Azhure's sake, or cry for her own.

She took a deep breath and steeled herself. She had her own role to play in the Prophecy and it would take her far from Carlon. Faraday could not wait to leave the palace and the city. There were no happy memories here. Even the recent eight days and nights she had spent at Axis' side had turned out to be nothing but a lie and a betrayal. It was their memory Faraday wanted to escape most of all.

Why had no one told her about Azhure? Everyone close to Axis—indeed, many distant from him—had known of his love for Azhure, yet none had thought to tell Faraday. Not even the Sentinels.

"You let me think that once Borneheld was dead Axis would be mine," she had cried to the Sentinels. "All I had to comfort me during that frightful marriage was the thought that one day my efforts for the Prophecy would be rewarded with Axis' love, and yet that comfort was a lie."

Ogden and Veremund hung their heads in shame, and when Yr stepped forward to comfort Faraday, she jerked away.

"Did *you* know?" Faraday shouted at Jack. "Did *you* know from the very beginning that I would lose Axis?"

"None of us know all of the twists and turns of the Prophecy, sweet girl," Jack replied, his face unreadable.

Faraday had stared flatly at him, almost tasting the lie he'd mouthed.

She signed. Her meeting with the Sentinels had not gone well. She now regretted the harsh words she'd lashed at them before she'd stalked out the door. Ogden and Veremund had scurried after her, their cheeks streaked with tears, asking her where she was going. "Into Prophecy—where you have thrust me," Faraday had snapped.

"Then take our donkeys and their bags and panniers," they'd begged.

Faraday nodded curtly. "If you wish."

Then she had left them standing in the corridor, as much victims of the Prophecy as she was.

Now all she knew was that she had to go east and that, sooner or later, she would have to begin the transfer of the seedlings from Ur's nursery in the Enchanted Woods beyond the Sacred Grove to this world.

Faraday gathered the leads of the placid donkeys and turned to the stable entrance. A heavily cloaked figure stood there, shrouded in shadows. Faraday jumped, her heart pounding.

"Faraday?" a soft voice asked, and she let out a breath in sheer relief. She'd thought that this dark figure might be the mysterious and dangerous WolfStar.

"Embeth! What are you doing down here? Why are you cloaked so heavily?"

Embeth tugged back the hood. Her face was pale and drawn, her eyes showing the strain of sleepless nights.

"You're leaving, Faraday?"

Faraday stared at the woman, remembering how Embeth, like the Sentinels, had urged her into the marriage with Borneheld. She also remembered that Embeth and Axis had been lovers for many years. Well could you dissuade me from Axis and urge me to Borneheld's bed, she thought sourly, when you had enjoyed Axis for so long.

But Faraday forced herself to remember that Embeth had been doing only what she thought best for a young girl untutored in the complexities of court intrigue. Embeth had known nothing of prophecies or of the maelstrom that had, even then, caught so many of its victims into its swirling dark outer edges.

"Yes. There is no place for me here, Embeth. I travel east," she replied, deliberately vague, letting Embeth think she was traveling back to her family home in Skarabost.

Embeth's hands twisted in front of her. "What of you and Axis?"

Faraday stared unbelievingly at her before she realized that Embeth probably had no knowledge of the day's events.

"I leave Axis to his lover, Embeth. I leave him to Azhure." Her voice was so soft that Embeth had to strain to hear it.

"Oh, Faraday," she said, hesitating only an instant before she stepped forward and hugged the woman tightly. "Faraday, I am sorry I did not tell you . . . about . . . well, about Azhure and her son. But I could not find the words, and after a few days I had convinced myself that you must have known. That Axis must have told you. But I saw your face yesterday when Axis acknowledged Azhure and named her son as his heir and I realized then that Axis had kept his silence. That everyone had. Faraday, please forgive me."

Faraday finally broke down into the tears she had not allowed herself since that appalling moment at the ceremony when she had realized the depth of Axis' betrayal. She sobbed, and Embeth hugged her fiercely. For a few minutes the two women stood in the dim stable, then Faraday pulled back and wiped her eyes, an unforced smile on her face.

"Thank you, Embeth. I needed that."

"If you are going east then you must be going past Tare," Embeth said. "Please, Faraday, let me come with you as far as Tare. There is no place here in Carlon for me anymore. Timozel has gone, only the gods know where, my other two children are far distant—both married now—and I do not think either Axis or Azhure would feel comfortable with my continuing presence."

As mine, Faraday thought. Discarded lovers are a source of some embarrassment.

"Judith still waits in Tare, and needs my company. And there are . . . other . . . reasons I should return home."

Faraday noted the older woman's hesitancy. "StarDrifter?" she asked.

"Yes," Embeth said after a moment's hesitation. "I was a fool to succumb to his well-practiced enticements, but the old comfortable world I knew had broken apart into so many pieces that I felt lost, lonely, unsure. He was an escape and I . . . I, as his son's former lover, was an irresistible challenge."

A wry grin crossed her face. "I fear I may have made a fool of myself, Faraday, and that thought hurts more than any other pain I have endured over the past months. StarDrifter only used me to sate his curiosity, he did not care for me. We did not even share the friendship that Axis and I did."

We have both been used and discarded by these damn SunSoar men, Faraday thought. "Well," she said, "as far as Tare, you say? How long will it take you to pack?"

To her surprise Embeth actually laughed. "As long as it takes me to saddle a horse. I have no wish to go back inside the palace. I already wear a serviceable dress and good boots, and should I require anything else then I have gold pieces in my purse. We shall not want for food along the way."

Faraday smiled. "We would not have wanted for food in any case." She patted one of the saddlebags.

Embeth frowned in puzzlement at the empty saddlebag, but Faraday only reached out her hand. "Come, let us both walk away from these SunSoar men. Let us find meaning for our lives elsewhere."

As Faraday and Embeth left the palace of Carlon, far to the north Timozel sat brooding on the dreary shores of Murkle Bay, To his right rose the cheerless Murkle Mountains that spread north for some fifty leagues along the western border of Aldeni. Relentless cold, dry winds blew off the Andeis Sea, making the all but impossible within the mountain range.

The darkness of the waters before Timozel reflected the blackness of his mind. If, far to the south, Embeth worried about her lost son, Timozel spared no thought for his mother—Gorgrael dominated his mind awake and asleep.

Over the past nine days Timozel had ridden as hard as he dared for the north. With each league farther away from Carlon and Faraday he could feel Gorgrael's grip clench tighter about his soul.

The horror Timozel had felt when Faraday dropped the pot and shattered the ties that bound him to her had dimmed, but had not completely left him. In those odd hours when he snatched some sleep, nightmares invariably claimed him and he always woke screaming. Three times this day he had dropped off in the saddle, only to find Gorgrael waiting for him in his dreams, his claws digging into Timozel's neck, his repulsive face bending close to Timozel's own. "Mine," the dream-Gorgrael would hiss. "Mine! You are *mine!*"

And with his every step farther north the more potent became the nightmares. If only he could turn his back on Gorgrael and ride for Carlon. Beg forgiveness from Faraday, find some way to reconstitute his vows of Championship. But Gorgrael's claws had sunk too deep.

Despair overwhelmed Timozel, and he wept, grieving for the boy he had once been, grieving for the pact he had been forced to make with Gorgrael, grieving for the loss of Faraday's friendship.

Beside him lay the cooling carcass of the latest horse he'd killed. The animal had staggered to a halt, stood a moment, and then sunk wearily to the sandy beach. This was the sixth horse he had literally ridden into the ground in recent days—and Timozel had slid his feet quickly from the stirrups and swung his leg over the horse's wither as it slumped to the ground, standing himself in one graceful movement.

As Timozel sat on the gritty beach, watching the gray waves, he wondered what to do next. How was he going to keep moving north now that this damned horse had died on him?

And what had driven him to the shores of Murkle Bay in the first place? It was many leagues to the west of where he should have been heading—Jervois Landing, then north into the Skraeling-controlled Ichtar through Gorken Pass and then north, north, north to Gorgrael's Ice Fortress. It would be a hard journey, perhaps months long, and only Timozel's determination and his bond to Gorgrael would see him through.

As each horse fell Timozel had stolen another one—not a difficult proposition in the well-populated regions of Avonsdaie. But he was unlikely to find a horse in the desolate regions surrounding Murkle Bay or in the mountains themselves.

He squared his shoulders. Well then, he would walk and Gorgrael—if he truly wanted Timozel—would no doubt provide.

But not today. Even his fear of Gorgrael-sent nightmares would not keep Timozel from sleep tonight. He shivered and pulled his cloak closer, shifting uncomfortably on the cold, damp sand. Somehow he would have to find enough fuel for a fire to keep him warm through the night. A rumble in his belly reminded him that he had not eaten in over two days, and he wondered if he could snatch a fish from Murkle Bay's depths.

His eyes narrowed as he gazed across the bay. What was that out to sea? Perhaps a hundred paces distant from the beach Timozel could see a small, dark hump bobbing in the waves. He'd heard stories of the whales that lived in the Andeis Sea and wondered if perhaps this dark shape was the back of one of the mammoth ocean fish that had strayed into Murkle Bay.

Timozel stared, blinking in the salty breeze. As the dark shape came closer Timozel leaped to his feet.

"What?" he hissed.

The hump had resolved itself into the silhouette of a heavily cloaked man rowing a tiny boat. He was making directly for Timozel.

Timozel's dull headache abruptly flared into white heat and he cried out, doubling over in agony. But the pain died as quickly as it had erupted and after catching his breath Timozel slowly straightened out. When he looked up again he saw that the man and his boat were almost to shore.

He shivered. The man was so tightly cloaked and hooded Timozel could not see his face, yet he knew that this was no ordinary fisherman. But what disturbed him most was that although the man made every appearance of rowing vigorously, the oars that dipped into the water never made a splash and the boat itself sailed as smoothly and as calmly as if it were pushed by some powerful underwater hand.

Magic! Timozel took a step back as the boat slipped smoothly ashore.

The man shipped his oars and stood up, wrapping his cloak about him. Timozel could *feel* but not *see* a smile on the man's face.

"Ah, Timozel," he said in a deeply musical voice, stepping smoothly out of the boat and striding across the sand that separated them. "How fortunate you should be waiting for me."

Sweat beaded in the palms of Timozel's hands and he had to force himself not to wipe them along his cloak. For the first time in nine days thoughts of Gorgrael slipped completely from his mind. He stared at the dark man who had halted some three or four paces in front of him.

"Timozel," the man said, and despite his fears Timozel relaxed slightly. How could a man with such a gentle voice harbor foul intent?

"Timozel. It is late and I would appreciate a place beside the warmth of your campfire for the night."

Startled, Timozel looked over his shoulder at where the man pointed. A bright fire leaped cheerfully into the darkness; a large rabbit sizzled on a spit and a pot steamed gently to one side of the coals.

"How . . . ?" Timozel began, doubt and fear resurfacing in his mind.

"Timozel," the man said, his voice slipping into an even deeper timber. "You must have lit the fire earlier and, in your exhaustion, forgotten the deed."

"Yes." Timozel's shoulders slumped in relief. "Yes, that must be it. Yes, my mind is so hazy."

Beneath his hood the Dark Man's smile broadened. Poor, troubled Timozel. His mind had been shadowed for so long that it was now an easy task to manipulate it.

"The rabbit smells good," he said, taking Timozel's arm. Surprisingly, all traces of Timozel's headache faded completely at the man's touch. "Shall we eat?"

An hour later Timozel sat before the fire, feeling more relaxed than he had in months. He no longer minded that his companion chose not to reveal his features. In these past months he had seen stranger creatures, like those feathered abominations that now crawled over the fouled palace of Carlon. His lip curled.

"You do not like what you have seen in Carlon, Timozel."

"Disgusting," Timozel said.

"Oh, absolutely."

Timozel shifted, his loathing of the Icarii rippling through his body. "Borneheld tried to stop them, but he failed."

The Dark Man shrugged. "Unfortunate."

"Treachery undid him."

"Of course."

"He *should* have won!" Timozel clenched his fists and stared across the fire at the cloaked man. "He *should* have. I had a vision—"

He stopped. Why had he mentioned that vision? Would this strange man laugh at him?

"Really?" The Dark Man's voice held no trace of derision; indeed, it held traces of awe. "You must be beloved of the immortals, Timozel, if you have been granted visions."

"But I fear the vision misled me."

"Well," the cloaked man said slowly, as if reluctant to speak, "I have traveled widely, Timozel, and I have seen many bizarre sights and heard even stranger stories. One of the things I have learned is that visions can sometimes be misunderstood, misinterpreted. Would you," his hands twisted nervously before him, "would you share your vision with me?"

Timozel considered the man through narrowed eyes. He had never shared the details of the vision with anyone—not even Borneheld, although Borneheld knew Artor had enabled Timozel to foresee his victory over Axis.

But Borneheld *hadn't* won, had he? And Artor seemed powerless in the face of the Forbidden invasion; even the Brother-Leader had gibbered impotently before Axis. Timozel dropped his gaze and rubbed his eyes. Perhaps the vision was worthless. A phantasm, nothing more.

"Tell me of the vision," the Dark Man whispered. Share.

Timozel hesitated.

"I want to hear of it." *Share*

"Perhaps I *will* tell you," Timozel said. "It came time and time again. Always the same. I rode a great and noble beast—it cried with such a voice that all before it quailed." As Timozel spoke he fell under the spell of the vision again, and his voice sped up, the words turning from his mouth. "I fought for a Great Lord, and in his name I commanded an army that undulated for leagues in every direction."

"Goodness," the Dark Man said. "A truly great vision."

"Hundreds of thousands screamed my name." Now Timozel leaned forward, his voice earnest. "They hurried to fulfill my every wish. The enemy quivered in terror; they could do nothing. Remarkable victories were mine for the taking . . . in the name of my Lord *I* was going to clear the filth that invaded Achar!"

"If you did that then your name would live in legend forever," the Dark Man said, and Timozel could hear the admiration in his voice.

"Yes! Yes, it would. Millions would thank me. I saw more—"

"Tell me!"

"I saw myself seated before a fire with my Lord, and Faraday at our side. The battles were over. All was well. I . . . I had found my destiny. I had found my light."

He dropped his face into his hands momentarily, and when he raised his eyes again the Dark Man could see they were reddened and lost. "But it was all a lie."

"How so?"

"Borneheld lies dead—I saw Axis tear his heart out myself. His armies are dead or have betrayed his name and fled to Axis. In any case, Borneheld would never give me command."

"He did not trust your vision. Perhaps that is why he lost," the stranger said, and Timozel nodded slowly.

"Now Faraday lies with Axis and becomes his wife, and we are all lost. Lost. And now . . . now . . ."

"Now?" the Dark Man asked. "Do you experience other visions? Dreams, perhaps?"

Timozel's eyes flared, his suspicions aroused. "How did you know?"

"Oh," the Dark Man soothed. "You have the look about you. The look of a man troubled by visions."

"It is not visions that wrap my thoughts now, but dark nightmares that ensorcel my soul!"

"Perhaps you have misinterpreted—"

"How can I misinterpret the fact that Gorgrael has his talons locked into my soul! It is over! *Finished!*"

He stopped, appalled. He had never, *never*, mentioned Gorgrael to another person before. How would Gorgrael punish him, now he had shared the secret?

The stranger did not seem overly perturbed by Timozel's mention of Gorgrael. "Ah yes, Gorgrael is a good and dear friend of mine."

Timozel recoiled in horror, almost falling backward in his haste to put more distance between himself and the cloaked man.

"Your friend?"

"Ah," the Dark Man said. "I fear you have fallen under the spell of the evil rumors about Gorgrael that sweep this land."

Timozel stared at him.

"Timozel, my friend, how can Gorgrael be evil and dark when he fights the same things that you do?"

"What do you mean?" How could that appalling creature *not* be evil and dark?

"Consider this, Timozel. Gorgrael and Borneheld fight-fought—for the same thing."

"*What?*" Perhaps he should slice this stranger's head off and be done with it, Timozel thought.

"Listen to me," the Dark Man said, his voice soothing, calming. "Gorgrael hates the Forbidden—the Icarii and the Avar—as Borneheld did. Gorgrael wants to see them destroyed as much as Borneheld did. Both shared the same purpose."

Timozel struggled with the stranger's words. Yes, it was true that Borneheld hated the Forbidden and ached for their destruction. And Gorgrael wants the same thing?

"He surely does," the Dark Man whispered. "He surely does."

"But the Prophecy says . . ." Timozel tried to remember exactly *what* it was that the Prophecy said.

"Bah!" The Dark Man grinned to himself under his hood. "The Prophecy is nothing but a tool of the Forbidden to cloud men's minds and blind them to their true Savior—Gorgrael."

"Yes . . . yes." Timozel thought it through. "That makes sense."

"And Gorgrael aches to kill Axis as much as Borneheld did."

"Axis." Now Timozel's voice was edged with unreasoning hatred.

"Who has brought the Forbidden back to crawl over Achar's lands, Timozel?"

"Axis!" Timozel hissed.

The Dark Man spoke very slowly, emphasizing every word. "Gorgrael is committed to killing Axis and ridding this fair land of the Forbidden. Is that not what *you* want?"

"Yes. Yes, that is what I want!"

"Gorgrael will help rescue Faraday from the foul clutches of Axis and the Forbidden."

"Faraday! He will help rescue Faraday?" Was there hope for Faraday yet?

"With your help, Timozel. With your help."

"With *my* help?" Could he redeem himself in Faraday's eyes?

"Ah, Timozel," the Dark Man said dejectedly. "Gorgrael is truly misunderstood and he fights for a true cause, but he is not a good war leader." He sighed, and Timozel leaned even closer, eager. "Timozel, he needs a war leader. He needs you and you need him. Together you can rid Achar of its foul corruption."

A small voice deep in Timozel's soul told him not to listen to this man, not to believe his smooth words. Had not Borneheld fought Gorgrael as well? Were not the Skraelings as evil as the Forbidden? But, caught as he was by the weight of the enchantments being woven about him and by the blackness that was eating into his soul, Timozel pushed those thoughts out of existence. Gorgrael would be the one to restore sanity and good health to Achar.

"He would give me command of his army?"

"Oh, surely. He knows that you are a great warrior."

Timozel sat back, enthralled. A command of his own, at last! Even Borneheld had not done that for him.

"Don't you see, Timozel?" the Dark Man asked, drawing the net of his lies closed. "Don't you *understand*? Gorgrael is the Great Lord of your visions. Fate must have sent me south to fetch you, to bring you north so that your Lord can give you control of his armies."

"Truly?" Perhaps there *was* still a chance the visions would be fulfilled.

That there was still a chance he could do some good. Yes, fate must have maneuvered this meeting.

"Very truly, Timozel."

Timozel thought about it, one thing gnawing at him. "But why has Gorgrael been disturbing my sleep with such dark dreams?"

The stranger reached out his hand and rested it on Timozel's shoulder. "The Forbidden are desperate to turn you from Gorgrael. They have been the instigators of those dreams, not Gorgrael. You will have no more bad dreams from now on."

Certainly not once I have a word with Gorgrael, the Dark Man thought. There had never been any need to disturb the boy's mind with such dreams— but Gorgrael was ever inclined to the melodramatic.

All doubts had gone from Timozel's mind now. At last he had found the right path. The visions *had* been true.

"Gorgrael will free Faraday from Axis' foul clutches?" he asked.

"Oh, assuredly," the Dark Man said. "Assuredly. He will be a master whom you will be proud to serve. You will sit by the fire with your Great Lord, Timozel, with Faraday by your side, sipping wine."

"Oh," Timozel breathed ecstatically, letting the vision engulf him.

"Now," the Dark Man rose with the Icarii grace that he could not completely repress, "why don't I take you to Great Lord? I have a boat, and in only a few short hours we shall reach his fortress. Your *savior's* fortress. Will you come?"

"Friend." Timozel stood by the Dark Man's side, shaking sand from his cloak. "You have not told me your name."

The Dark Man pulled his hood closer. "I have many names," he said quietly, "but you may call me Friend."

As Timozel climbed into the boat he realized how familiar Friend's voice sounded. Why? Who was he? Where had he heard the voice before?

"Timozel? Is anything the matter?"

Timozel stared at the man, then he shook himself and climbed in.

"No, Friend," he said. "Nothing's the matter."

Jayme abased himself before the icon of his beloved Artor the Plowman, the one true god of all Acharites—or at least, who *had* been until the setbacks of recent weeks.

Once the powerful Brother-Leader of the Seneschal, most senior mediator between Artor the Plowman and the hearts and souls of the Acharites, now Jayme mediated only between his own broken soul and the ghosts of his dreams and ambitions. He had once manipulated kings and peasants alike; now he manipulated little more than the buckles on his sandals. He had once resided in the great Tower of the Seneschal; now the Forbidden had reclaimed the Tower and burned the accumulated learning of over a thousand years. He had once sat easy with power, protected by the might of the military wing of the Seneschal, the Axe-Wielders and their BattleAxe. But now the remaining Axe-Wielders had cast aside their axes to serve the ghastly Forbidden, and their BattleAxe now claimed to be a Prince of the Forbidden. The BattleAxe. He had been as a son to Jayme, yet had betrayed both Jayme's love and the Seneschal in leading the Forbidden back into Achar.

Jayme had once enjoyed the friendship and support of his senior adviser, Moryson. But now Moryson had deserted him.

Slowly Jayme rose to his knees and stared about the chamber where he had been incarcerated for the past nine days. They had not left him much. A single wooden chair and a plain table. A bedroll and blanket. Nothing else. Axis believed Jayme might try to kill himself, and so guards had emptied the room of everything save what Jayme needed for basic comfort.

Twice a day guards came to bring him food and attend his needs, but otherwise Jayme had been left alone.

Apart from his two visitors. His eyes clouded as he remembered.

Two days after the death of Achar's hopes in the Chamber of the Moons, the Princess Rivkah had come to see him . . .

She entered the room silently and Jayme did not know she was there until he stood from his devotions before the sacred icon of Artor.

The moment Jayme turned and saw her his mouth went dry. He had never expected to be confronted by the woman he thought he and Moryson had murdered so many years previously.

For long minutes Rivkah just stood and stared at him. Jayme could not but help contrast her proud bearing with his own hunched and subservient posture. How is it, he thought, that the woman who did Achar and Artor so much wrong can stand there as if justice was on her side? How is it that she can stand there so beautiful and queenly when all Moryson and I deposited at the foot of the Icescarp Alps was a broken woman near death? *Artor, why did you let her survive? Artor? Artor? Are you there?*

"Why?" she eventually asked.

Surprising himself, Jayme actually replied in a moderately strong voice. "For the wrong that you did your husband and your country and your god, Rivkah. You did not deserve to live."

"*I* was the one wronged, Jayme," she said. "Yet you would that I had died a horrible death. You did not have the courage, as I remember, to put a knife through my throat."

"It was Moryson's idea," Jayme said. "He thought it best that you die in a place far enough removed from civilization that your bones would not corrupt Artor-fearing souls."

"Yet you let my son live."

"He was innocent of your evil—at least, that's what I thought at the time. I did not know then what it was that had put him in your belly. Knowing what I know now I *would* have put a knife to your throat, Rivkah. Well before you had a chance to give that abomination birth."

Rivkah's hands jerked slightly, the only sign she had been disturbed by Jayme's words. At that moment she longed to flee, so great was her loathing for him, but she had one more thing to ask.

"Why did you name my son Axis?"

Jayme blinked at her, surprised by the question, and fought to remember. He shrugged slightly.

"Moryson named him."

"But why *Axis?*"

"I do not know, Rivkah. It seemed a good enough name at the time. I could not have known then that he would prove to be the axis about which our entire world would turn and die."

Rivkah took a deep breath. "You denied me my son and warped his soul for almost thirty years, Jayme, while you left me to die a slow, lingering death." She stepped forward, and spat in Jayme's face. "They say that forgiveness is the beginning of healing, Jayme, but I find it impossible to forgive the wrong you have done myself, my son and his father."

She turned and strode to the door.

Just as she reached it Jayme spoke. Where the words came from he did not know, for the knowledge behind them and their sudden ferocity were not his.

"It is my understanding that the birdman you betrayed Searlas for has now betrayed and rejected you, Rivkah. You have been discarded, thrown aside because of your aging lines. Betrayal always returns to those who betray."

Rivkah turned and stared at him, appalled. This was not strictly correct, but it was close enough to the truth to hurt. Had the price for her betrayal of Searlas been the eventual death of StarDrifter's love for her? What price would she pay for the hurt she had caused Magariz so many years ago? She licked her lips and silently cursed her voice as it quavered.

"Then I am confident you will die a ghastly death, Jayme," she said.

Despite her brave words, Rivkah's entire body shuddered, and she flung the door open, running past the startled guard and down the corridor.

Jayme smiled, remembering Rivkah's agitation. But the smile died as he recalled his second visitor.

*   *   *

Jayme had heard Axis well before he entered the room.

Axis stood outside the closed door for several minutes, talking with the guard posted there. Jayme knew Axis was toying with him, letting the sound of his casual conversation outside increase Jayme's trepidation.

And his tactic worked. Jayme's stomach heaved as he heard the key in the lock.

"Jayme," Axis said flatly as he stepped inside the room.

Axis had always carried an aura of power as BattleAxe—now it was magnified ten times and carried with it infinite threat. Jayme opened his mouth to speak, but there was nothing to say.

"I have decided to put you on trial, Jayme. Rivkah has told me of your conversation," Axis said, "and of your wretched effort to lay the blame for her attempted murder at Moryson's feet. But it is not only the wrongs you have done me and my mother that you should answer for, Jayme, but the wrongs you have done the innocent people of Tencendor."

Jayme found his voice and his courage. "Yet how many innocent people have you murdered for your depraved purposes, Axis? Justice always seems to rest with the victor, does it not?"

Axis stabbed an accusing finger at the former Brother-Leader. "How many innocent people did I murder in the name of the Seneschal, Jayme? How many people, guilty of nothing save innocent questions, did you send your BattleAxe out after, to ride down into the earth? How many innocent people have I murdered? *You* tell *me*. *You* were the one who sent me out to murder them in the name of Artor!"

"I only did what Artor told me, Axis. I only did what was right for the Way of the Plow."

The anger faded from Axis' face and he stared incredulously at Jayme. "Have you never thought to question the world about you? Have you never thought to question the narrow and brutal Way of the Plow? Have you never stopped to think what beauty the Seneschal destroyed when it drove the Icarii and the Avar beyond the Fortress Ranges a thousand years ago? Have you never stopped to question *Artor*?"

"Axis," Jayme said, stepping forward. "What has happened to you? I thought I knew you, I thought I could trust you."

"You thought you could *use* me."

Axis stared at Jayme a moment longer, then turned for the door.

"I only used you for Artor's sake," Jayme said so softly that Axis barely heard him.

Axis looked around to his once-beloved Brother-Leader. "I shall spare no effort in dismantling the Seneschal, Jayme. I shall grind it and the cursed Way of the Plow into the dust where it belongs. I shall bury your hatreds and your bigotry and your unreasoning fears and I shall never, *never*, allow it or any like it to raise its deformed head in Tencendor again. Congratulations, Jayme. You will yet live to witness the complete destruction of the Seneschal."

Jayme's face was now completely white and his mouth trembled. He held out a hand. "Axis!"

But Axis was gone.

The memory of that visit disturbed Jayme so much that he abased himself once more before Artor's icon, seeking what comfort the crude figure could give him.

The guards had taken from his room the beautiful gold and enamel icon of Artor that had held pride of place in the center of the main wall. During the first two days of his captivity Jayme had laboriously carved out a life-sized outline of the great god into the soft plaster of the wall. Even though he had torn his nails with the effort, at least he had an icon to pray to.

He pressed his forehead to the floor.

The sound of noisy celebrations in the streets below finally roused him in the early evening. Curious despite his despondency, Jayme wandered over to the window.

Cheerful crowds thronged the streets and Jayme listened carefully, trying to make out what they shouted. Most held beakers of beer or ale, a few had goblets of wine. All were smiling.

"A toast to our lord and lady!" Jayme heard one stout fellow shout, and the crowd happily obliged.

"A marriage made in the stars, they say!" shouted another, and Jayme was horrified to see that it came from one of several winged creatures in the crowd.

He frowned. Had Axis married Faraday already?

A tiny piece of plaster fell to the floor behind him. Then another. Deep in concentration on the scene below him, Jayme did not hear.

"To Axis!"

"And to Azhure!"

Large cracks spread across the wall, and a piece of plaster the size of a man's fist bulged into the room.

"Azhure?" Jayme said. "Azhure?"

More plaster crumbled to the floor as further cracks and bulges raced across the wall, but Jayme was so engrossed in the crowd's celebrations he did not hear it.

"Who is this Azhure?" Now Jayme had both hands and face pressed to the window pane in an effort to catch the shouts of the crowd.

She is one of the many reasons for your death, fool.

Jayme whimpered in terror and his eyes refocused away from the street below him and onto the reflection in the glass.

Plaster fell to the floor in a torrent as the wall came alive behind him.

Jayme whimpered softly again, so horrified he could not move. His eyes remained glued to the terror in the reflection.

Nothing in his life could have prepared him for this, and yet he knew precisely what it was.

Artor, come to exact revenge for the failings of the Brother-Leader of his Seneschal.

"Beloved Lord," Jayme croaked.

In the reflection Jayme saw the wall ripple and a form bulge through, taking the shape of the icon Jayme had scratched in the plaster days ago.

It was too much, and Jayme screwed shut his eyes in terror.

Have you not the courage to face Me, Brother-Leader? Have you not the courage to face your Lord?

Jayme felt a powerful force seize control of his body. Suddenly he was spun around and slammed back against the window; he retained only enough power over his muscles to keep his eyelids tightly closed. Some part of his mind not yet completely numbed with terror hoped that Artor would use too much force and the window panes would crack behind him, allowing him to fall to a grateful death on the cobbles below.

But Artor knew His own power, and Jayme did not hit the glass with enough force to break it.

He was held there, his feet a handspan off the floor, and none of the crowd celebrating Axis and Azhure's marriage spared so much as a glance above to see Jayme pinned against the window as effectively as a cruel boy will pin an ant to a piece of paper.

The great god Artor the Plowman completed His transformation and stepped into the room. He was stunningly, furiously angry, and His wrath was a terrible thing to behold. Jayme had failed Him. The Seneschal was crumbling, and soon even those fragments that were left would be swept away in the evil wind that blew over the land of Achar. Day by day Artor could feel the loss of those souls who turned from the worship of Artor and the Way of the Plow to to the worship of other gods. *He* was the one true god, He *demanded* it, and Artor liked it not that those gods He had banished so long ago might soon walk this land again.

Jayme had failed Artor so badly and so completely that the god Himself had been forced from His heavenly kingdom to exact retribution from Brother-Leader Jayme for his pitiful failure to lead the Seneschal against the challenge of the StarMan.

What have you done, Jayme?

Jayme shuddered, and found that Artor had freed those muscles he needed to speak with. "I have done my best, Lord," he whispered.

Meet My eyes, Jayme, and know the god that you promised to serve.

Jayme tried to keep his eyes tightly shut, but the god's power tore them open—and Jayme screamed.

Standing before him was a man-figure, yet taller and more heavily muscle-bound than any man Jayme had ever seen before. Artor had chosen to reveal Himself in the symbolic attire of the plowman: the rough linen loincloth, the short leather cape thrown carelessly over His shoulders, its hood drawn close about Artor's face, and thick rope sandals. In one hand Artor held the traditional goad used to urge the plow team onward; the other hand He had clenched in the fist of righteous anger. Underneath the leather hood of His cape Artor had assumed the heavy, pitted features of a man roughened by years of tilling the soil, while His body was roped with the thick muscles needed to control the team and the cumbersome wheeled plow.

And underlying this immensely powerful and angry physical presence was the roiling fury of a god scorned and rejected by many of those who had once served Him.

Artor's eyes glittered with black rage. *Daily My power diminishes as the Seneschal crumbles into dust. Daily the souls of the Acharites are claimed by other, less deserving gods. For this I hold you responsible.*

"I could not have foreseen—" Jayme began, but Artor raised the goad menacingly above His head and took a powerful step forward, and Jayme fell into silence.

The power of the Mother threatens to spill over into this land as the bitch you failed to stop prepares to sow the seeds of the evil forest across Achar. The Star Gods now threaten to spread their cold light through this land again.

"I had not the knowledge or the power to stop these gods of whom you speak—"

Yet you incubated the egg that would hatch the traitorous viper. You nursed the viper to your—to My—bosom! You raised him, you taught him, you gave him the power and the means, and then you turned him loose to destroy all that I have worked to build.

"Axis! I could not have known that he—"

As the Brotherhood of the Seneschal falls to its knees so the worship of the Plow fades and I grow weak. Long-forgotten gods seek to take My place and banish Me from this land.

"Give me another chance and I will try to—"

But Artor did not want to hear empty excuses or useless promises. His judgment was final.

I shall seek out among those remaining to find one who will work My will for me. One who is still loyal. One who can steer the Plow that you have left to wheel out of control. Die, Jayme, and prepare to live your eternity within My eternal retribution. Feel My justice, Jayme! Feel it!

As Artor stepped forward, Jayme found breath enough for a last, pitiful shriek.

*   *   *

The guard standing outside the door thought he heard a cry, and he started to his feet. But the next moment a burst of fireworks lit the night sky and the guard relaxed, smiling. No doubt the noise had been the echo of the street celebrations below.

Another burst of fireworks exploded, drowning out the screams from the chamber as Artor exacted his divine retribution.

Faraday and Embeth, almost a league into the Plains of Tare, paused and looked back as the faint bursts of the fireworks reached them.

"He has married her," Faraday said tonelessly, "and now the people celebrate."

She turned the head of the donkey and urged it eastward.

Later that night, when the guard checked his prisoner, all he discovered was a pile of plaster by the far wall and a bloody body lying huddled underneath the locked window.

It looked suspiciously like . . . well, like it had been plowed.

2

The Song for Drying Clothes

Restoration of the royal apartments in the ancient palace of Carlon had been going on since Axis had defeated Borneheld, but the workmen doubled their efforts in the days after Axis married Azhure. Helping them—else how could so much work have been accomplished in so short a time?—were twelve of the best Icarii Enchanters who discovered the ancient lines and colors hidden behind a thousand years of veilings, and who directed the workmen and sewing women in the best and simplest ways to redecorate the chambers to suit the StarMan and the Enchantress.

The Icarii were amazed by the news that the Enchantress' ring had resurfaced to fit snugly on Azhure's finger—and yet, they said among themselves, who better to wear both ring and title than the woman who already commanded the Wolven and the Alaunt *and* the heart of the StarMan? Those who had seen her in the past few days had noted how the promise of strange power lay in the shadows of her eyes, and they wondered whether the ring had placed that power there, or whether the power released during her ordeal of her wedding day had called the ring to her.

None, whether Icarii or human, doubted that Azhure was a figure who could be as powerful as the StarMan, a legend in her own right.

Now Axis, Azhure and StarDrifter sat in their living chamber, Caelum playing quietly in a corner. On two walls windows stretched from the floor to the foot of a great jade dome, gauzy curtains billowing in the cool breeze of late afternoon. They had been there for some hours, and Azhure was clearly tired. Axis turned from her and addressed his father.

"These rooms are of Icarii origin, StarDrifter, and the Chamber of the

Moons is obviously patterned on the Star Gate. How so? I thought Carlon an entirely human affair."

StarDrifter, sprawled on his belly across a couch some paces away, his wings spreading across the floor on either side, shrugged his shoulders.

"The Icarii had to live somewhere, Axis. In the time of Tencendor gone, both human and Icarii must have lived in Carlon—it is a very ancient city."

He rolled over onto his back and stared at the ceiling. Both Axis and Azhure, wingless, wondered at StarDrifter's grace in rolling completely over without entangling himself in his wings.

"I have no doubt that Carlon would have been a popular residence for Icarii, Axis," StarDrifter continued, "as close as it is to the sacred Grail Lake and Spiredore." He paused, his face dreamy. "One could lift directly from those windows into the thermals rising off the great plains."

Azhure smiled briefly at Axis. StarDrifter looked far too lazy to do anything more than loll about the chamber. Her smile died as she shifted uncomfortably and pushed a pillow into the small of her back—every day the unborn twins grew larger and more cumbersome.

Axis looked at her, concerned. *We have tired you, beloved.*

"No," she said, although both StarDrifter and Axis could see the exhaustion tugging at her eyes. "No, I want to try again. Please, one more time before you go back down to your army."

Axis had belatedly realized how much time had elapsed since his defeat of Borneheld, and he was in the process of organizing a force to speed northward to bolster the defenses of Jervois Landing. Every hour brought them closer to autumn and Gorgrael's inevitable attack.

StarDrifter sat up, as concerned as Axis was with Azhure's condition. Faraday had obviously healed her back (and how much more desirable the woman was with her back clean and smooth and aching to be stroked, StarDrifter thought), but Azhure remained very weak from both the physical and emotional battering she had been forced to endure four days ago. Neither Axis nor StarDrifter was prepared to argue with Faraday's prediction that Azhure would have to rest until the birth of her children.

And yet how desperately I will need her against Gorgrael, Axis thought. How desperately I need her skill with both bow and command, her Alaunt, and her power. I can ill afford to lose her to a drawn-out recovery over the next few months. But how much less can I afford to lose her to inevitable death should I push her too hard now? Axis was still trying to come to terms with his guilt, not only over the events of a few days ago, but also over the fact that, unknown to him, Azhure had fought through the dreadful Battle of Bedwyr Fort while encumbered with such a difficult pregnancy. His hand tightened about hers as he realized his good fortune that Azhure had managed to survive the past weeks at all.

"Please," Azhure said. "One more time." She raised her free hand to brush some strands of hair from her forehead, and the Enchantress' ring glittered in the golden light of late afternoon.

Today was the first time Axis and StarDrifter had tried to teach Azhure the use of her Icarii power—but all in the room had been disheartened with the results, including Caelum who, wide-eyed, had watched the proceedings from his corner.

StarDrifter moved to a stool close to Azhure's side, remembering, in comparison, how easy he and MorningStar had found Axis to train. Azhure's father, WolfStar, must not have spent the time or the trouble training her as he had the young Axis. She had been completely ignored by WolfStar, and StarDrifter smoldered with anger thinking how WolfStar had abandoned Azhure to her awful fate in Smyrton.

As StarDrifter and MorningStar had once done for him, Axis now cupped Azhure's face gently in his hands.

"Hear the Star Dance," he said.

"Yes," she replied, barely audible.

At least hearing the Star Dance had been as easy for Azhure as it had for Axis—but then she had been hearing it for some time without being aware of what it actually was. Every time Axis had made love to her she'd heard it; sometimes when she had suckled Caelum; sometimes when she stood at an open window and let the wind rush about her; oftentimes at night when she dreamed of distant shorelines and the tug of strange tides at rocks and sand.

But Azhure also heard the Dark Music, the Dance of Death, the music renegade stars made when they left their assigned courses. Neither Axis nor StarDrifter, nor any other Icarii Enchanter, could routinely hear that music, although they recognized it if it was wielded by someone else. StarDrifter had heard its echo in the Chamber of the Moons the night Axis had battled Borneheld. Axis had witnessed two of the SkraeBolds use it at the gates of Gorkentown, and both he and StarDrifter recognized its presence the morning Azhure had used Dark Music to tear the Gryphon apart atop Spiredore.

Now Azhure put the ghastly discordant sounds of the Dark Music to the back of her mind and concentrated on the supremely beautiful Star Dance. All Icarii Enchanters wielded the power of the Star Dance by weaving fragments of its power into more manageable melodies, Songs, each with their own specific purpose.

Axis and StarDrifter had been trying to teach Azhure one or two of the more simple Songs. Songs so simple that all Icarii training as Enchanters mastered them within an hour or two. But they had been trying to teach Azhure for almost five hours now, and she had failed to grasp a single phrase.

Azhure closed her eyes and concentrated on the Song that Axis sang slowly for her. It was a Song for Drying Clothes, a ridiculously easy song requiring only the tiniest manipulation of power, yet it seemed totally beyond her ability.

Axis finished, and both he and StarDrifter held their breath.

Relax, beloved. It is a simple Song. Sing it for me.

Azhure sighed and began to sing. Axis and StarDrifter winced. Her voice was harsh, utterly toneless, and completely lacking any of the musical beauty that had, until now, come instinctively to any of Icarii blood, whether they were Enchanters or not.

Axis remembered how Azhure had tried to join in the Songs about the campfire on their trip down through the Icescarp Alps for the Beltide festivities. Then her voice had also been as completely toneless, as gratingly harsh, but Axis had felt sure that now that the block concealing Azhure's true identity and power had been removed her musical ability would naturally surface.

But apparently that was not to be. If Azhure had any power at all then obviously she would be unable to use the conduit of Song to manipulate it.

Unnoticed, Caelum tottered on unsteady baby legs to his parents' couch.

"Mama," he said, startling the other three. "Simple. See?"

And he hummed the Song for Drying Clothes as beautifully as Axis had.

Azhure opened her eyes, stared at her son, and burst into tears.

Axis glared the boy into silence and gathered Azhure into his arms. "Shush, sweetheart. I'm sure that—"

"No!" Azhure cried. "It's hopeless. I'll never be able to learn."

"Axis," StarDrifter said gently. "Perhaps the trouble is that, while Azhure is of SunSoar blood, the blood link is too far removed from either of us for us to be able to teach her."

The gift and powers of the Icarii Enchanters were passed on only through blood, from parent to child, and Enchanters could be trained only by one of their own House, or family, and usually only by someone of close blood relation. Normally it was a parent who trained a new Enchanter, although someone else of close blood link within the family could also assist. Thus Axis' grandmother, MorningStar, had been able to assist her son StarDrifter teach his son, Axis.

But WolfStar came from a generation of SunSoars four thousand years old. He had died, been entombed, walked through the Star Gate, and had then come back for purposes that neither Axis nor StarDrifter could yet fathom.

Axis stared at his father, then looked at his wife. "Azhure, StarDrifter could be right."

Azhure sat back. "Yet WolfStar could train both you and Gorgrael, Axis. You are as far removed from him in blood as *I* am from you."

"None of us knows how powerful WolfStar has become," StarDrifter said. "He obviously has the power to use whatever blood link there is, while neither Axis nor I can do that."

"Then perhaps Caelum can train me," Azhure said. "See how easily *he* has learned the Song for Drying Clothes!" Oh, how much it stung that she could not learn even a ridiculously mundane Song while a child less than a year old could do so! "And he is as closely blood-linked to me as WolfStar."

Surprised, for he had never thought of such a thing, Axis raised his eyebrows at StarDrifter in silent query. A child teach a parent? It had never been done before—but then never before had an Icarii Enchanter come to his or her powers *after* they had fathered or birthed a child.

Neither Axis nor StarDrifter liked the thought—a largely untrained child could do enormous damage to an equally untrained parent, but what harm could the Song for Drying Clothes cause? At most, it could cause a warm breeze to fill the room. And if Caelum *could* teach Azhure, then it would be best to find out now.

StarDrifter caught Axis' thoughts and nodded slightly.

Axis turned his gaze to his son, still cross at him for showing off in front of his mother. Even Caelum at his tender age should have had more sensitivity.

Well Caelum, would you like to try?

It was a thought that all in the room caught. The ability to hear and, eventually, speak with the mind voice was one of the earliest powers Azhure had demonstrated, and it was a skill she developed day by day. At least she had that much.

The child nodded soberly, ashamed for the hurt he had caused his mother.

Axis picked the baby up and sat him on his knee. The child reached out his chubby hands and Azhure, after a slight hesitation, took them in her own.

Again they went through the routine, Caelum using his mind voice to talk to Azhure—for it was easier for him than his still cumbersome tongue. Azhure closed her eyes and concentrated as hard as she could, and yet, when he had finished singing and it was her turn, all that issued forth from her mouth were such discordant notes that the three Enchanters' faces sank.

"Useless," Azhure said, and turned away from the others so they would not see her tears.

"Azhure," StarDrifter said. "No one knows how changed WolfStar was when he came *back* through the Star Gate. How his power was altered by his experiences beyond the Star Gate. It is more than conceivable that WolfStar has bequeathed you power through his blood that is different to any the Icarii have known previously. So different that you cannot be trained through traditional methods. You cannot even *use* your power in the traditional way. Axis—" His voice firmed. "Azhure obviously has power, we both witnessed her tear that Gryphon apart."

Axis nodded, and even Azhure wiped her eyes and stared at StarDrifter.

"We witnessed Azhure use power, Dark Music, to destroy the Gryphon that threatened her and Caelum, *but we did not hear her sing!*"

"Stars!" Axis said, shocked he hadn't remembered that himself.

StarDrifter suddenly laughed, his beautiful face joyous, and he deposited Caelum on the floor and seized Azhure's hands in his own. "Azhure! You have power, *magnificent* power, but it is so different to what any of us have experienced before that we do not know how to teach you. We probably *can't* teach you, anyway."

Azhure smiled as she absorbed what StarDrifter was saying. "Then what use is such *magnificent* power, StarDrifter, if the only time I can use it is when I am attacked by a Gryphon?"

Despite the concern evident in her words, Azhure's voice was more relaxed now and her tone lighter.

"Azhure," Axis said. "There are many reasons why you may be finding it so difficult to use your powers. StarDrifter has perhaps discovered the main one. But also you effectively blocked out your power for so many years that I am not surprised you find it almost impossible to call it willingly to you now."

Azhure reflected on his words, her smile losing some of its brilliance. Over the past few nights vaguely troubling dreams with even more troubling voices had disturbed her rest, but she could never remember the details when she woke. Were they a manifestation of her newly freed power bubbling uncontrolled to the surface? Perhaps she ought to talk to Axis about them—but all thoughts of dreams were forgotten with her husband's next words.

"And," Axis continued, "our unborn children may also be causing a block."

Three days ago Axis, according to the right and duty of every Icarii father, had awoken her twin babies. When he had done this for Caelum, calling the baby to awareness within her womb, it had been a joyous affair, but this awakening—the whole pregnancy—had been so different. The babes had witnessed what she and Axis had seen when he had forced Azhure to remember her mother's death and her subsequent physical and emotional torture at Hagen's hands. As she and Axis had endured the pain and the horror, so had her two unborn babies. Faraday had said that she thought the babies would be affected by the experience, although she did not know how. Now, both Azhure and Axis knew.

The awakening had been successful as the babies were now fully aware and active. But during the awakening, and in the days since, it had become painfully obvious that the twin babes distrusted and disliked their father. Azhure and Axis could feel their resentment every time Axis touched their mother; even now, cuddled together on the couch, both could feel the rising hostility from the twins. It made anything more intimate an impossibility; both Azhure's weak state and the twins' antagonism meant Axis and Azhure had yet to consummate their marriage. Axis had tried to harm the woman who carried them and, unlike Caelum, the twins were not prepared to forgive him. Yet even Azhure did not enjoy their affection; she sensed total disinterest seeping into her from the babies. They existed only for each other, their parents either untrusted or inconsequential.

Axis had not realized Azhure was pregnant for so long because he'd never felt the tug of the growing babies' blood. Even before the trauma of four days ago, he mused, the twins had been so self-absorbed that their SunSoar blood had not reached out beyond each other.

It made him wonder what kind of children he'd fathered.

The twins, as would be natural for children conceived of such powerful parents, would be Enchanters in their own right—even now they demonstrated their awakening powers in the womb. Azhure sighed. Since their awakening the twins had refused to listen to Axis on the five occasions he'd tried to teach them.

Were they somehow blocking Azhure's powers now?

Axis and Azhure glanced at each other, then at StarDrifter, letting him share their thoughts. They had told him of the problems with the twins and, unbelievably, when he had tried StarDrifter actually had more success communicating with the babies than Axis did. Azhure had not let StarDrifter touch her when she was pregnant with Caelum, but she knew that StarDrifter would undoubtedly be the Enchanter who conducted the majority of the twins' training while they were in the womb.

Now StarDrifter shook his head. "No, I don't think they would do that. Powerful as they might be, they aren't yet that powerful. And why would they want to block your power, in any case? No, Azhure. Unless you slip naturally into your powers, ease into them as time goes by, the only person who can teach you is WolfStar."

3

The Sentinels

Several floors below, the Sentinels sat in a circle, holding hands. They were silent as they remembered.

It had been a fine night, some three thousand years ago, when the Charonites had massed in the chamber below the well that led to the cave on the banks of the Nordra River.

The races of the Charonites and Icarii, both descended from the original Enchantress, had separated some twelve thousand years previously. As the Icarii loved the open sky and worshiped the stars, so they developed wings to give vent to their longings. But the Charonites were far more introspective, preferring the depths to the heights. Eventually they discovered and developed the UnderWorld and the waterways. They still studied the stars—and their very waterways reflected the music of the Star Dance—but they became increasingly reclusive, until even most of the Icarii doubted their existence.

Every few score years the Charonites gave vent to their urge to see once again the starlit night, to feel the soft wind of the OverWorld in their faces, to smell the scent of flowers and of the damp leaves that lined the floor of the forest, and to sail the lively waters of the Nordra, so different from the still waterways.

On this night, scores of Charonites sang and danced as they climbed the well leading to the OverWorld; the Charonites loved to dance and the figures carved about the walls of the well inspired them to ever more joyous efforts.

Once in the cave they lifted the flat-bottomed boats from their storage racks and, still laughing and singing, cast them into the water of the inlet that led to the Nordra as it flowed through the Avarinheim. The Avarinheim of three thousand years past was a much greater and more magical Avarinheim than the one that stood now; then the axes of the Seneschal had not wielded their destruction.

Five Charonites, lagging behind the others, seized the last and smallest boat and, singing, launched it into the water. They leaped in and worked their magic, and the boat glided effortlessly along the inlet, then slipped into the Nordra. The five were ecstatic with the feel of the soft night air and the immensity of the sky above them, and their singing increased in joy and reverence as their boat sailed farther down the Nordra.

Every so often a dark face peered at them from the forest that lined the Nordra—the Avar, woken from their slumber by the sounds of the Charonite merriment, crept from their sleeping skins to watch in awe as the Charonites slid past.

As the Charonites were wont to do, the five eventually moored their boat to a spotted willow that, heavy with age, drooped its branches deep into the water. Then they slipped ashore, planning to dance unrestrained along the corridors of the Avarinheim.

But sitting on the banks of the Nordra was a strange man—Icarii-featured but wingless—with a dismal face.

The five stopped to ask what was wrong, for although the Charonites preferred to keep their distance from other races, they were not an unkind people, and this man obviously needed their comfort.

The man sighed and spoke, and what he related wiped the joy from their faces. The man, this strange man, spoke of a time in the future.

"Tencendor will already wear the terrible legacy of a millennium of hatreds, but the Destroyer's one purpose will be to grind what is left of Tencendor into the dust. He hates, and his one desire is to give vent to his hate. To destroy."

The five, all thought of dance and song gone from their minds, asked the man how he knew these dreadful tidings.

"The burden of prophecy weighs heavily on my soul and it consumes my days and my nights," he said, and he stood up. "Soon I shall retire to solitude and commit what I have seen into words of power and magic."

The five stared solemnly at the Prophet, awed by the responsibility he had taken upon his shoulders.

The Prophet sighed again, and the five could see how much care and pain he labored under. They respected him deeply, although they did not envy him, for they of all races perhaps best understood the power and compulsions of prophesizing.

"Listen," he said, and then he intoned the Prophecy of the Destroyer.

The five moaned as they heard him speak, and leaned on each other's shoulders, and wept. They were accustomed to lives and thoughts of introspection and beauty and great mystery, but the Prophet's words destroyed the peace and harmony of their minds. How would they be able to resume their carefree existence after this? The words of the Prophecy would never leave them.

"The burden of a prophecy is a hard one to carry," one of the five said, and he took his wife's hand for comfort.

"That is so," the Prophet agreed.

Another of the five, one of two brothers, spoke. "And prophecies are terribly fragile. They prophesy only what might be, not what is certain."

"They can be easily bent out of shape," his brother added.

The youngest of the Charonites, a sensual and beautiful woman, now spoke. "And while the Prophecy indicates that this StarMan will reunite Tencendor, recreate its beauty despite the Destroyer's hate, his victory is not certain."

The Prophet waited.

Slowly the five spoke in turn.

"A prophecy is like . . ."

"A garden . . ."

"That is full of the promise of beauty . . ."

"And dreams never-ending . . ."

"But that can, if neglected . . ."

"Or left unattended . . ."

"Fall into barrenness . . ."

"And sorrow . . ."

"And despair . . ."

"And death."

The Prophet took a deep breath, and the younger woman realized for the first time what a handsome face he had.

The most experienced of the Charonites noted the Prophet's easy way with power, and thought he might not be all that he appeared, or that he might be more than he appeared. But he held his peace and, later, it would be he who would share most of the Prophet's secrets.

But for now the Prophet expelled his breath and spoke. "I need a gardener. Someone who is prepared to serve the Prophecy, and see to its needs. Someone who will wait for he who is to appear, and guide and guard his steps."

"I will do it," cried one of the Charonites, prepared to leave her life of contemplation for the service of the Prophecy.

"And I!"

"Both of us would serve," cried the brothers in unison.

"And I, too, would serve this Prophecy," said the last gravely, and the Prophet nodded.

"It was the power of the Prophecy that led me here this night to meet with you. You will be my Sentinels, and to you will I entrust the Prophecy over the coming ages."

The five never returned to their UnderWorld home. They stayed with the Prophet and accepted the secrets he entrusted to them and the transformations he wrought in them. They lost their previous identities and forms and became the Sentinels, and they became closer to each other than they had ever been before.

The other Charonites mourned them, but, with the other mystical races of Tencendor, they came to know of the Prophecy and understood the cause to which their brothers and sisters had been lost. They contemplated the mysteries that the Prophecy had created and prayed that the garden would survive the storm that would eventually engulf it.

Now the five Sentinels sat in their circle, hands tightly held, needing the contact and warmth and love. For three thousand years they had waited. Over the past two years they had guided and watched and waited for the Prophecy to work itself through. There had been times of warmth and laughter and there had been times of deep sadness and loss, but the Sentinels had been content, knowing that they did their best for the Prophet and the Prophecy.

"The Prophecy moves apace," Jack said into the silence.

"It slides to its conclusion," Yr responded, her voice sad. Of them all, perhaps Yr would lose the most in the coming months. She had been the freest, and she had enjoyed her freedom.

"And we slide to our—"

"Enough, Ogden!" Jack cautioned. "We all knew what our service to the Prophecy would entail and there is no need to voice our fate now. But the fact remains that, as soon as Axis moves north toward his confrontation with Gorgrael, we will have to begin our final duties."

There, the words were said.

Yr nodded jerkily, and a moment later the other three nodded.

"Faraday moves east," she said. "Axis prepares to move north, and Azhure . . . well, who knows what she will do."

The others thought silently on Azhure. Even Jack, who knew many things, had been stunned by the appearance of the Enchantress' ring and its choice of Azhure missing text believed the Wolven and the Alaunt had gravitated to Azhure because of her parentage . . . but now that he'd seen the ring on her finger Jack knew differently.

As the original Enchantress had acted only as custodian for the ring, so WolfStar had acted only as custodian for the Wolven and the Alaunt.

Now all had come home.

Had the Prophet known of this? The Prophecy itself gave no clues . . . *did it?*

The appearance of the ring had vastly increased the Sentinels' respect for Azhure—and for Axis. It would *only* have reappeared when the Circle was complete, and it marked both Axis and Azhure.

"Who knows what part she will play in the final act," Veremund said. "But whatever happens, let us hope Gorgrael never learns her true identity."

Again all were silent for some moments, then Yr spoke, realigning the subject back to *their* circle.

"As we are currently in Carlon, then I must go first."

Jack, his face unusually soft, nodded. "Yes, Yr. You will be first."

Yr's eyes filled with tears. "And now that the moment is here, I find my heart is full of regrets."

None of the others begrudged Yr her words. Regrets filled every one of them and they would not hesitate to voice them. But they would not let regrets stop them in their final service to the Prophecy and to Axis. Not when they had come this far.

"Many regrets."

4

Ice Fortress

For hours (or was it days?) Timozel sat knee to knee with Friend in the tiny boat, gliding smoothly and effortlessly over choppy gray waves and still, icy green waters alike. Friend kept up the pretense of rowing, but Timozel was sure some enchantment was being wielded. Who could row for hour after hour (day after day?) without tiring?

Friend had not said a word since he rowed out from the beach at Murkle Bay. But Timozel felt certain that within the shadows of the close hood Friend grinned maniacally at him. Timozel spent most of his time staring anywhere but at the darkness behind the man's black and gloomy hood.

After an unknowable time Timozel perceived that their boat glided through green and glassy waters so icy that great icebergs, only three or four to start with, jutted skyward. Soon Friend was maneuvering their tiny craft through a veritable forest of the ice mountains. To the south lay a grating ice pack, and beyond that a still and silent beach. Timozel twisted on his bench, anxiously peering this way and that, jumping every time a deep roll of thunder rumbled through the icy canyons toward them.

"Friend?" he asked, unable to keep his silence any longer. "Friend, what is that noise?"

Friend rowed in silence for a few more strokes, then spoke, startling Timozel, who had not expected a reply.

"The sound you hear is that of the great glacier of Talon Spike calving her icebergs into the ocean."

Timozel tried to remember the few rudimentary maps he had seen of the northern wastes. "We are in the Iskruel Ocean?"

"Assuredly, Timozel, assuredly. See, the icebears gambol, and to the south beyond the ice you can see the Icebear Coast."

Timozel twisted to where Friend had inclined his head. On the nearest berg a massive icebear stood watching them, her fur yellowed with age and the elements. One ear had been lost in a past dispute with another icebear over the carcass of a seal, and the loss gave her head a curiously lopsided charm. The bear's black eyes were uncomfortably all-knowing.

"We are almost there," the Dark Man said, his own eyes briefly meeting those of the icebear. "An hour or two, perhaps more, perhaps less. Gorgrael is close."

Timozel shivered and forgot the bear. "Gorgrael is close," he whispered. "Gorgrael is close."

He hoped Gorgrael would be all that his new friend had promised. He hoped Gorgrael would indeed prove to be the Great Lord of his visions. He hoped that in Gorgrael he would find the savior who would drive the Forbidden from Achar's fields and rescue Faraday from her fate at Axis' hands. If these hopes proved false, then Timozel knew he would go mad.

Gorgrael was keen to make a good first impression. Apart from the Dear Man, Timozel would be Gorgrael's first real visitor, and the arch-fiend of the Prophecy of the Destroyer was determined that Timozel should find his new master worthy of his service.

He stood in front of his (for once) brightly glowing fire, every sharp plane and angle in his warped furniture waxed and polished. The crystal—what was left of it—that Gorgrael had retrieved from Gorkenfort sat on the single flat surface of the sideboard. Wine glinted richly in the depths of the decanter. All Skraelings within his Ice Fortress had been banished to unseen rooms, and SkraeFear, representing the SkraeBolds, waited nervously in an anteroom to meet his new superior.

Gorgrael twisted his clawed hands as he watched with his mind's eye the Dear Man pilot his boat toward the Ice Fortress. So much depended on Timozel, and the Dear Man had recently convinced Gorgrael that gentle persuasion and seductive lies would more likely win Timozel's total support than the outright terror Gorgrael had been subjecting Timozel to in his dreams.

"After all," the Dear Man had said, "Timozel is an intelligent man. He deserves better than what you mete out to your SkraeBolds. Much better. Besides, better he work his heart out willingly for you than under duress."

Of course, Gorgrael reflected, Timozel would still need to have the ties that bound him to Gorgrael confirmed, and for that there would need to be a little pain. Just a little.

*   *   *

Friend had been rowing steadily northeast for some time when he suddenly shipped his oars and nodded to a spot behind Timozel.

"We walk from here," he said.

Timozel turned and stared. The little boat was drifting toward an ice-bound beach; he could see round pebbles and small rocks beneath a thin and treacherous layer of ice. Briefly he cast his eyes beyond the beach to the towering cliffs of ice that hid the land beyond, then looked back to Friend.

"We'll break our ankles within five steps on that footing, Friend. Do you know where you lead me?"

"Assuredly, sweet boy," Friend said. "I always know where I'm going."

As the boat crunched across the beach Friend rose and stepped past Timozel and out of the boat. "As this trusty boat has carried us through the treacherous waters of the Iskruel Ocean, then I am sure your feet will carry you safely across these shores."

Magic again, Timozel thought. Although he had been taught from birth by the Seneschal to loathe all manner of enchantments, Timozel was slowly coming to the understanding that perhaps the enchantments of the Forbidden could only be broken through similar magic; perhaps his visions were proof enough of that. He stepped carefully onto the ice-bound shoreline and found his booted feet gripped as surely as Friend had said they would. Well, whatever magic Friend had wrought to bring him to this remote spot seemed mild and harmless enough. Perhaps magic was only evil when used by the Forbidden and their spawn.

For some time they walked up the canyon, the ground rising and the walls narrowing as they proceeded. Timozel's breath came in short, sharp puffs that frosted heavily in the icy air. For the first time he noticed how cold it was and pulled his cloak closer about him. Friend's cloak billowed out as he strode several paces in front of Timozel, seemingly unconcerned by the cold. His features must be fully exposed as that cloak blows back, Timozel thought, and he tried to increase his pace so that he could catch the man and see his face.

But just as Timozel came within a pace of Friend, the ground rose sharply before them, and Timozel had to slow his pace and use both hands to steady himself as they climbed. The sky almost completely disappeared as the ice walls closed in; within minutes Timozel found that he was climbing almost vertically through a narrow icy chasm. Above him, Friend's boots sent a constant torrent of small rocks and slivers of ice cascading into his face and Timozel would have cursed, had he the breath.

Irritatingly, Friend whistled a silly ditty. Where does *he* find the breath? Timozel wondered as one of his hands slipped from its hold and he almost lost his footing. His heart pounded and Timozel felt sweat trickle down his face— he would die on the ice-covered rocks below if he fell down this chasm now. He gritted his teeth. If Friend could climb so effortlessly; then so could he.

As if he could feel Timozel's increased efforts, Friend called down reassurance. "Almost there, Timozel. Just a few more minutes."

That's what you said hours ago in the boat, Timozel thought.

The Dark Man laughed merrily. "Time means little to me, Timozel. But see, I have reached the top of this ice-pit."

Even as he spoke Friend's boots disappeared over the welcome lip of the cliff, and the next moment Timozel grasped the man's hand and let him pull him out of the chasm.

"See?" Friend cried. "The Ice Fortress!"

Timozel blinked and looked about him, narrowing his eyes. The sky was clear and the sunlight almost blinding as it glittered across the snow. They were standing on a flat, snow-covered plateau that stretched north and eastward from the ice cliffs bordering the Iskruel Ocean for what seemed like eternity.

"The Ice Fortress," Friend said again, pointing.

Perhaps half a league away to the east stood the Ice Fortress. It was constructed of jagged sheets of sheer ice that rose like perpendicular daggers toward the sky. It was massive, and Timozel guessed that it was twice the height and girth of the Tower of the Seneschal as it sat on the shores of the Grail Lake.

It was also very, very beautiful.

Shifting colors of mauve and pink shone as the sun struck the ice walls and reflected off on wildly divergent tangents.

"Beautiful," he whispered. "Beautiful."

"Of course!" Friend said, taking Timozel's arm and pulling him forward. "Of course. Did I not say that you would find Gorgrael worthy of your service? Could anyone as dark and as desperate as the Destroyer of the Forbidden's Prophecy live amid such beauty? No! Come."

The Ice Fortress was as beautiful inside as it was from the outside. There were none of the horrid writhing shapes beyond the corridor's ice walls that Timozel remembered from his nightmares and visions. All was calm, all was bright.

The corridor wound through the heart of the Ice Fortress, gentle pink light reflecting from unseen lamps. Gorgrael has done well, the Dark Man thought, very well indeed. He glanced at Timozel, who was walking steadily forward with a glazed expression on his face.

But that changed when they rounded a corner and Timozel found himself walking down the same stretch of corridor that he'd walked in his nightmares. He recognized it because there at the very end was the massive wooden door that his treacherous hand had knocked upon to summon Gorgrael.

"No!"

"Timozel, my man," the Dark Man said, his hand firm and reassuring on Timozel's shoulder. "What you dreamed was Forbidden-corrupted, not the truth. No one is more upset that you have been frightened than Gorgrael himself."

"Truly?" Timozel asked, desperate to believe Friend's explanation.

"Truly," the Dark Man soothed, wrapping Timozel's mind so tightly in enchantments that the man stood no chance of discerning truth from lies. "Very, *very* truly. Now, shall we go on?"

Gorgrael stood in the center of the room and extended his claws as the door opened and the Dear Man and Timozel stepped through. The man's face was pinched and white, despite the Dark Man's enchanted reassurances, and horror rippled across his features as he saw Gorgrael.

How could something this repulsive—so horribly malformed—be anything but an aberration?

In his nightmares, and in his enchanted vision when he had been forced to mortgage his soul to Gorgrael, Timozel had been brutally treated by the Destroyer.

But now the horror stepped forward, opening its taloned hands in welcome, dipping its tusked head almost in embarrassment that Timozel should find its form displeasing, spreading its wings behind it in unconscious imitation of the Icarii manner of abasement, and almost swallowing its overlarge tongue in an effort to twist its mouth in as close an imitation of a smile as it could get.

Timozel came close to fainting, and actually swayed slightly on his feet, but Friend grasped his elbow. "Steady, steady," he whispered. "Take courage. Think of this as a test. Do you have the courage to do what is needed to win both Achar and Faraday their freedom?"

"Yes," Timozel muttered. "Yes, I have the courage," and he straightened his back and squared his shoulders. "I have the courage," he said in a stronger voice.

"Timozel," Gorgrael said, and Timozel jumped slightly at the power and strength in Gorgrael's voice. He stared unflinching into the creature's silver eyes.

"Timozel, are you my man?"

"Do you fight to destroy the Forbidden?"

Gorgrael almost snarled. Who was this stripling to question *him*? But he felt the Dark Man's eyes on him, and he remembered their plan. "It is my name," he said in as soft a voice as he could manage. "The Destroyer. I live to destroy the Forbidden, the hateful Icarii and Avar."

"Will you free Achar?"

"I will drive the Forbidden from the land, yes."

Gorgrael would free Achar. Timozel only heard what he wanted to hear. He cleared his throat and spoke in a slightly stronger voice. "Do you seek to destroy Axis?"

Now Gorgrael could not help a small hiss and he flexed his clawed hands. "I will *shred* him!"

Timozel smiled, and for the first time he seemed comfortable. "Good. Will you free Faraday?"

Gorgrael smiled with an equal degree of chill. Faraday. Axis' Lover. The key to his destruction, and a woman Gorgrael had come to desire almost as much as he desired Axis' death.

"Will you help me free her, Timozel? Will you help me rescue Faraday?"

"Yes, yes and yes thrice over, Great Lord," he said. "You are all that Friend said you were." He paused. "My soul is yours."

Fool! Gorgrael thought. Your soul was mine from the moment Faraday broke your vows of Championship. But he ducked his head and simpered anyway. Time enough in the future for Timozel to realize exactly how deeply Gorgrael's claws were hooked into his soul.

"Then let us cement the bargain," Gorgrael whispered.

The Dark Man hurriedly stepped out of the way.

In the wink of an eye Gorgrael scurried the distance between himself and Timozel, his dreadful clawed hands and taloned wings extended. He was so quick that Timozel could not have moved, even had he wanted to.

All he had time for was a quick breath of surprise, a widening of the eyes, then Gorgrael was upon him.

With lightning-quick movements, Gorgrael shredded the clothes from Timozel's upper body, then knifed razor sharp claws deep into Timozel's chest.

Timozel opened his mouth to scream, but the pain was so great all that escaped his mouth was a harsh gurgle.

Gorgrael twisted his claws in deeper, then pulled Timozel next to him, their faces close in a frightful parody of a lover's embrace.

Timozel's eyes, open wide, were sightless with agony. His arms curled at his side, his hands crimped uselessly.

The Dark Man watched impassively. This had to be done, but he hoped that Gorgrael would be able to wield the enchantments so that Timozel would remember nothing of it afterward. Damn it, Gorgrael is enjoying this. Pity poor Faraday when Gorgrael finally has the chance to get his talons into her.

His claws scraping through bone and flesh, whimpering with pleasure, Gorgrael finally let a bolt of power flood through Timozel's body. If Timozel was to lead Gorgrael's army against Axis, then the man needed a well of power like those Gorgrael had given the SkraeBolds. It would contain only the minutest fraction of the power that Gorgrael himself commanded, but it would be more, far more than the SkraeBolds enjoyed. Timozel needed to be able to control the SkraeBolds as well.

"Feel it!" Gorgrael hissed ecstatically, wriggling and pulling Timozel more firmly against his own body. "Feel it!"

Somewhere in a dark corner of his mind that wasn't totally consumed by pain Timozel faintly heard Gorgrael's words, and, even more faintly, could feel something warm and dark writhing in his belly. Feel it.

This darkness suddenly, unbelievably, flared into such fire-barbed agony that Timozel finally found the breath to cry out. He arched his body, flung back his head and shrieked, and shrieked, and then shrieked once more.

"Yes!" Gorgrael groaned, then retracted his claws and let Timozel fall to the floor, dark blood streaming from the dreadful wounds in his chest.

Timozel drifted out of the blackness that had claimed him. He felt incredibly relaxed, and a feeling of such well-being flooded him that he tried to hold on to the blackness. He smiled, savoring the sensations. Not even Yr at her best had caused him to feel this satisfied, this replete.

The Dark Man caught Gorgrael's eye and nodded. *You have done better than I expected, my friend. You have excelled yourself. The man will do anything for you now. Anything.*

Gorgrael reflectively rubbed one of his tusks with a claw. *Good.*

Timozel stretched his body, turned his head, smiled, and opened his eyes.

Friend and Gorgrael were seated in grotesquely malcarved chairs before a roaring fire. Both held crystal glasses of wine. Both were gazing benignly at him.

Timozel smiled at them. "What happened?"

"I have accepted you into my service," Gorgrael said. "See?" He tapped his chest.

Timozel frowned, then realized that Gorgrael wanted him to look at his own chest. He raised himself onto his elbows, noting in some surprise that he only wore his breeches and boots.

On his chest was branded the outline of a clawed hand.

"My mark," Gorgrael said.

"Then I am proud to wear it, Great Lord," Timozel said boldly, and he rose to his feet. He had no memory of the assault that had put the mark there.

He felt incredibly well and powerful, and both Gorgrael and the Dark Man smiled at the expression of wonderment on Timozel's face.

"Already you feel the benefit of my power, Timozel," Gorgrael said, rising from his chair and moving to what Timozel, even in his sublime state, considered the ugliest sideboard he had ever seen. "Wine?"

Gorgrael held the decanter and shook it slightly in Timozel's direction.

"Yes," Timozel said. "Wine would be welcome." He wondered why he had ever feared this noble creature now standing before him. This was where he was meant to be. This was vision. This was destiny.

Gorgrael handed Timozel a glass of wine and waved him over to a table. "We must plan, Timozel, to bring Axis' evil house crashing about him and to restore Faraday to the light."

"With pleasure, Lord," Timozel said, taking a sip of the wine.

The Dark Man stood and the three toasted their future success.

Gorgrael was prepared to admit that the Dark Man had been right. He had over-reached himself by launching his attack on Gorkenfort two years ago. It had been precipitate and foolish. His SkraeBolds had badly mismanaged the attack on the Earth Tree Grove, as well as the battle above Gorkenfort where so many Skraelings had been destroyed by the emerald fire. But now Gorgrael felt that all the elements he needed to defeat Axis were firmly in his grasp. The last piece had been Timozel, and now Timozel stood here, so tightly bonded to Gorgrael's service that he would sell his soul . . . no! Gorgrael almost laughed out loud, Timozel would now gladly sell *Faraday's* soul to ensure his master's victory!

"Enough," he said, startling the other two. "We must plan. Timozel, let me tell you about the army you will command."

For the next hour Gorgrael spoke, and Timozel's excitement rose. What a force the Great Lord was handing him! Over the past year Gorgrael had been transforming his hordes. The Skraelings were no longer the misty wraiths Timozel had originally seen at Gorkenfort, vulnerable through their eyes. Now they were fully fleshed creatures, so totally encased in bony armor they would be near-impossible to kill.

The IceWorms had been bred larger, more numerous and more mobile.

"The weather is mine," Gorgrael said finally. "I now wield virtually total control over the ice and the wind."

The Dark Man nodded to himself. That was Gorgrael's Avar blood coming out in him; with that and his ability to wield the Dark Music, Gorgrael would be able to unleash a frozen hell over most of the northern half of Achar . . . Tencendor now. The Dark Man was pleased with Gorgrael's work in this area. Two years ago Gorgrael's control over the winter had been a haphazard and fragile affair. Now it was almost total.

"Then you would do well to send some of your ice south as soon as you can," Timozel said.

Gorgrael frowned. "Now?" He had thought Timozel would need at least a week or two to establish his control over the Skraeling force.

"Axis will be sending many of his army north soon, Great Lord. We are lucky that he has not already done so. If you send your ice south now—as far as the Western and Bracken Ranges if you can—then you will freeze those rivers that have caused you such trouble. And if the Nordra freezes, Axis will not be able to move his troops north faster than a crawl."

"Yes. Yes," Gorgrael said. "You make a good point."

Timozel watched his master. He vaguely remembered that once he had thought Gorgrael a creature so frightfully malformed, so disgusting, that his very appearance seemed the personification of evil. Now Gorgrael seemed noble, and his strange appearance only made him appear powerful, not ugly or frightful.

"And your ice spears, Master, why have you not used them again? You tried to murder Axis with them once outside the Barrows of the Enchanter-Talons, and you could perhaps have employed them to your advantage at Gorkenfort. If you use them again, I am confident they will create mayhem among Axis' force—and think how they could impale the Icarii Strike Force!"

Gorgrael looked embarrassed. "Ahem. Yes, well, I must admit, Timozel, that I badly overextended myself at the Ancient Barrows. I was not as powerful then as I am now. But I am afraid that I will not be able to use the ice spears again in any case, although they were such a pretty creation."

"But why, Great Lord, if your power is so much greater now?"

Gorgrael grinned to himself, and the Dark Man smiled too, knowing what Gorgrael was thinking of.

"Because I have one more secret to show you, Timozel. The weapon that will surely destroy Axis and his army."

He clicked his claws, and Timozel heard a movement in one of the darker corners of the room.

"I will give you an airborne force, Timozel, that will make the Icarii Strike Force seem pitiful indeed."

"The Gryphon!" Timozel suddenly remembered the dreadful winged creatures that had flown over Jervois Landing.

"Yes," Gorgrael said. "The Gryphon. Behold, my pet."

The Gryphon that now crawled on its belly toward them was much larger, her lion's body more powerfully built, than the original Gryphon Gorgrael and the Dark Man had created between them. As she approached Timozel she dipped her eagle's head in subservience.

The Dark Man managed to stop himself swearing in surprise. *This was not the Gryphon that he and Gorgrael had made!*

Gorgrael peered at the Dark Man slyly. "I lost another of the SkraeBolds in the WildDog Plains, Dear Man. With its decomposing flesh I made another Gryphon. Only larger, more powerfully built. More intelligent."

"And it breeds?" the Dark Man asked, his voice harsh.

"As do its pups," Gorgrael said, more than pleased at the Dark Man's surprise. "As do its pups."

He turned back to Timozel. "I will give you one of this creature's pups as your own. Go on, pat her head, scratch the back of her neck, she likes that. With one of these creatures as your mount you will be able to sail the thermals as easily as do the Icarii."

As Timozel bent down to the Gryphon fawning at his feet, Gorgrael took the Dark Man by the elbow and led him away a few steps, talking quietly.

"Perhaps there is something I should tell you, Dark Man."

Hearing the perverse pleasure in Gorgrael's voice, the Dark Man knew the news was going to be bad.

"Dear Man, I know you planned that the Gryphon should stop breeding after the second pack was whelped. I know you planned that the numbers of Gryphon would be limited."

Months ago Gorgrael and the Dark Man had created a Gryphon, a creature with the head of an eagle, the wings of a bird, and the body of a great cat. The Dark Man had infused deep enchantments into the making of the Gryphon; the single female had been created pregnant, and soon after she had been created she had whelped nine pups. And these nine pups had been born female and pregnant. After four months they too whelped, each bearing nine pups. But the Dark Man had thought he had manipulated the enchantments so that the breeding would stop there. He wanted Gorgrael to have a powerful air-borne force—and the eighty-two Gryphon created in this fashion would surely be that—but he did not intend that the breeding should continue.

"But the breeding *has* continued," Gorgrael hissed, and he felt the Dark Man twitch under his hand. "Already I have seven hundred and twenty-nine. And soon they will whelp. Each will whelp nine pregnant pups. Do you know how many that will be, Dear, Dear Man?"

The Dark Man was silent, almost overcome with horror.

"Over six and a half thousand. And in another four months those six and a half thousand will whelp—almost sixty thousand pups. And in four months those sixty thousand will—"

"Stop!" the Dark Man cried, and jerked his arm from Gorgrael's grasp.

"And not to forget, of course, the *second* Gryphon I created. She and hers have generated eighty-one Gryphon. In just over a month those eighty-one will become seven hundred and—"

"Yes, *yes!*" the Dark Man spat. "I understand!"

"No," Gorgrael said very, very softly. "I do not think you do. I am the Destroyer, Dear Man, and I *plan* to destroy. Whatever pretty enchantments Axis can throw my way, I will still destroy Tencendor. With the Gryphon breeding as they do, in less than a year there will be five-hundred thousand of them in the skies of Tencendor, Dear Man. Think of it. Five-hundred thousand. So what if my comely brother can stab one or two here or there? Or his army forty or fifty thousand? Even if one escapes, *one*, that one will breed nine, and those nine will whelp nine each, and . . . I need not continue. Even if *one* escapes, within two years at least sixty thousand will repopulate the skies of Tencendor."

Behind his hood the Dark Man stared at Gorgrael, appalled.

"So you see," Gorgrael said, "even if Axis destroyed me in battle, I have planned that he shall have nothing left to enjoy. Not even Axis can counter the virulence of the Gryphon. Eventually there will be nothing left of this green and pleasant land except the shadows of Gryphon wheeling and shrieking through the sky. They will blot out the sun and they will destroy and destroy and destroy until there is nothing—*nothing*—left!"

Oh Stars, thought the Dark Man, and felt the plans of three thousand years crumble to dust about him.

Gorgrael grinned triumphantly. At *last* he had bested the Dark Man. And if he could do that, then Gorgrael knew that he would best Axis.

5

A holy Crusade

Gilbert had known from the moment the Corolean transports disgorged their traitorous pirates into the seething mass that was the Battle of Bedwyr Fort that Borneheld was all but dead. Borneheld and his armies had failed to protect the Seneschal, and had failed in their supreme duty to Artor.

Not only would the beautiful Tower of the Seneschal now be overrun by Axis and the Forbidden, but Gilbert had realized that Carlon itself was lost. Sooner or later, Axis would seize the capital of Achar as well.

Gilbert had understood very clearly that his future lay as far away from Jayme, Borneheld and Carlon as he could get. He also knew that the future of the Seneschal and the Way of the Plow probably rested with him. Jayme had proved useless in massing the not inconsiderable resources of the Seneschal against Axis' forces; now the Brotherhood lay scattered among the ruins of Achar.

So Gilbert had backed silently away from Jayme and Moryson as they stood atop the parapets of Carlon, and sped down back stairs and corridors until he reached the home of one of his many cousins within the city. There he had begged a horse, clothes, supplies and a purse of gold coins and had ridden out of Carlon not five minutes before Borneheld and Gautier, fleeing from the battlefield, had ordered the gates sealed.

He rode hard and fast south, turning east after two days (fording the Nordra late one night and almost drowning in the process) to begin his long trek across the southern plains of Tare. He was not completely sure where he was going; he had a vague compulsion to travel east, perhaps to Arcness, maybe then north to Skarabost.

Each night Gilbert would pray to Artor for guidance. Surely Artor would not desert him or the Seneschal in this, its hour of greatest need?

It was now the third week of DeadLeaf-month, almost a month after the Battle of Bedwyr Fort, and Gilbert sat morosely by his tiny campfire, considering his future. It did not look very promising. From what he had heard from the occasional passing trader, many of whom had been returning to Nor from Carlon, Axis had destroyed the throne of Achar and had proclaimed himself StarMan of Tencendor. Gilbert snorted. StarMan of Tencendor? A gaudy title for the rebirth of an evil world.

He shivered in the cool night air and pulled his cloak tightly about him. Since he had escaped from Carlon he had not been able to travel very far; currently he was, at his best estimation, somewhere in the northern regions of Nor, or perhaps western Tarantaise.

He fingered his purse. He had carefully hoarded his coins, bargaining fiercely in the markets of the small towns he had passed through for food and supplies. He traveled as a minor nobleman—an easy disguise to assume, since Gilbert had originally come from one of the nobler families of Carlon—because in these eastern territories, where Axis armies and the Forbidden who traveled with him had already passed, it would not be very wise to be seen to be a Brother. Gilbert had also heard from the few merchants he had encountered that the names of old gods were now mouthed with increasing confidence across eastern Achar.

He leaned forward and prodded the bread he had baking in the coals. He had no life but that he had built for himself in the Seneschal. A young man, not yet thirty, Gilbert had risen quickly through the ranks of the Brotherhood. Six years ago Jayme had appointed him as his junior adviser, and Gilbert was not ashamed to admit to himself that his eye rested on the throne of the Brother-Leader itself. Jayme was old, as was Moryson, and who better to succeed Jayme than the talented younger adviser?

Of course, this possibility had been blown awry when this Destroyer had invaded from the north, and the BattleAxe had revealed his true colors and set about destroying both Achar and the Seneschal. Now Gilbert was left with little more than his broken ambitions to comfort him.

So Gilbert sat, desolately prodding the bread that seemed determined not to rise, until he gradually became aware that he was being watched.

For some time he continued to sit, absolutely still, his eyes on the now blackening bread, his ears straining. After long minutes of silence, Gilbert could stand it no longer.

"Who's there?" he called, injecting as much bravado into his voice as he could.

Silence still, then a small scratching noise as someone shifted a foot.

"Gilbert?" a thin, reedy voice quavered. "Gilbert?"

"Artor's arse!" Gilbert swore, so completely forgetting himself that he used an obscenity which until now he'd only heard soldiers mouth. "Moryson?"

"Aye, 'tis I," Moryson said, then shuffled into the light of the fire.

Gilbert's mouth dropped as he stared at the man who had been Jayme's senior adviser. Moryson looked even thinner and more fragile than usual, his clothes hanging tattered and dirty from his spare frame. A week-old stubble covered his cheeks, and his right hand trembled spasmodically as if he had damaged a nerve in his arm or neck.

"May I join you?" Moryson asked, looking as if he was about to fall, and Gilbert gestured to a spot by the fire.

Moryson sank down gratefully. "You are a hard man to catch, Gilbert."

Gilbert continued to stare. Moryson was the last person he would have expected to appear in this lonely night. "Why aren't you with—?"

"With Jayme?" Moryson's voice was stronger now that he'd taken the weight off his legs. "Why not? Because Jayme was ultimately a fool, Gilbert, and a loser. I may be old but I am not yet prepared to die."

Slowly Gilbert closed his mouth. Moryson was the last one he would have thought to desert Jayme. For perhaps forty years the pair had been inseparable, the friendship between them so deep and so strong—and so exclusive, Gilbert thought resentfully—that he would have wagered his own immortal soul on the fact that Moryson would elect to stay and share Jayme's fate.

"How did you escape Carlon?" Gilbert asked.

And why are you here, now?

Moryson coughed, a harsh guttural sound, and Gilbert passed across a waterskin.

Moryson took a deep draft, then wiped his mouth with his sleeve. "Thank you. I have not drunk in over a day. Well now, how did I escape? I saw you flee down the stairs as it became evident that Borneheld, the fool, had lost the battle with Axis. I knew why you left. There was nothing protecting Carlon now, and Axis would have little sympathy for you—nor for Jayme or myself.

"I tried to follow you down the stairs, but my legs are old and weak, and I lost you within minutes."

Gilbert frowned; surely he would have heard if Moryson had stumbled down the stairs after him?

"Jayme might choose to stay and confront his former BattleAxe, but I chose to leave and risk my life elsewhere," Moryson continued. "After I had lost you I fled to a small door I knew of, which opens onto Grail Lake. There I found a small boat moored. Exhausted, but frightened by the thought that soon Axis himself might come riding into Carlon, I rowed my way across the lake to a spot well north of the Tower of the Seneschal, then began my tedious flight."

Moryson's voice strengthened as he warmed to his tale. "For days I stumbled east, then southeast, desperate to avoid Axis and the Forbidden, snatching food where I could, rest where I dared. After a week I heard tell from a passing merchant, Dru-Beorh by name, that he had encountered you farther south in

Nor. I wondered if perhaps my future lay with you. Alone I could do nothing, but Gilbert, I thought, Gilbert must have a plan. I shall find Gilbert. So, here I am."

Gilbert just stared at the old man. Deprivation and fright have driven him senseless, he thought. How had he managed to survive this long?

"And what sort of plan did you think I might have in mind?" he asked. "What did you think I would be able to do for you?"

"I thought that you might know somewhere to hide," Moryson said, his voice slipping back into fragility. "I won't survive on my own, but, I thought, my old friend Gilbert will help me."

Old friend indeed, Gilbert thought angrily. Moryson and Jayme kept me at arm's length for years, never trusting me with their secret confidences, never truly thinking I was worthy of their regard. Yet now Moryson, frightened and directionless, dares to sit here and tell me that he is and has always been my friend.

"I thought perhaps we could find some of our scattered brethren," Moryson said. "Axis must have dispossessed dozens of Plow-Keepers as he rode through eastern Achar toward Carlon."

Gilbert finally noticed the blackened remains of the bread and busied himself pulling the loaf clear of the coals, thinking carefully as he did so. Moryson's vague words had given him the germ of an idea. He was right. There *must* be many Brothers of the Seneschal, scholars as well as the local Plow-Keepers—the Brothers who ministered within the villages—wandering as vaguely and with as little direction as he and Moryson Singly they could do nothing, but together . . .

"You have hit the matter on the head, Moryson," he said. "I intend to move eastward and gather what remnants of the Brotherhood remain."

"And then?" Moryson asked "What will we do then?"

"It is best that I wait until we are a dozen or so, Moryson," Gilbert replied smoothly, "and then I shall inform you of my plan."

Moryson nodded, his shoulders hunched Gilbert remembered Moryson as a strong and proud man, in spirit if not in body, but the man who now sat across the fire seemed shattered, almost servile.

Well, he thought, Moryson has had a bad few weeks, and has seen his life and his power destroyed. No wonder the old man now appears to want nothing more than a blanket-wrapped chair by a fire Gilbert smiled as he realized that the relationship between himself and Moryson had altered dramatically. Now he was the driving force, now he would say what was to be done and when, and Moryson would nod and agree and say that Gilbert knew best. Sitting about this fire were the two most senior members of the Seneschal remaining (for Axis had surely skewered Jayme by now), and of the two, Gilbert was the strongest. That makes me the leader of the Seneschal, he realized suddenly. *I am to all effects and purposes the Brother-Leader of the Seneschal!*

After gloating to himself for some minutes, Gilbert finally thought to carve up what was left of the bread and pass some to Moryson with some beef and a wizened apple. That should keep the old man alive until morning.

Once they had finished eating and as the fire died down, Gilbert led the nightly prayers to Artor. Even during the most harried days of his escape, Gilbert had never neglected his evening and dawn prayers to Artor. Of all the things that could be said about Gilbert, lack of dedication to his beloved god was not one of them.

Moryson and Gilbert were startled from their observances by a strange rhythmic thumping. It surrounded them, and the men exchanged puzzled and fearful glances as the noise grew louder.

"What is it?" Gilbert finally asked, not raising his voice above a whisper.

Moryson actually whimpered, and Gilbert glanced his way. If Moryson had seemed weak and fearful previously, now he was absolutely terrified. He had curled himself into as small a ball as possible, as if he could somehow burrow into the earth and escape whatever it was that came their way.

"What is it?" Gilbert hissed.

"Ahhh!" Moryson moaned, and wriggled some more, actually scraping at the earth with his fingers.

"Moryson!"

"Artor!" Moryson cried. "It is Artor!"

Gilbert stared at him wide-eyed. Artor? For an instant Gilbert's reaction vacillated between outright terror and transcendent ecstasy.

Ecstasy won.

"Artor!" he screamed and leaped to his feet. "Artor! It is I! Gilbert! Your true servant! What must I do to serve you? What is your desire?"

Damn fool, damn fool, damn fool, Moryson muttered over and over in his mind, not sure whether he referred to himself or Gilbert. Damn fool! He curled himself into an even tighter ball.

The strange thumping increased, now almost a thunder, and Gilbert could see a light in the distance. "Artor!" he screamed yet again.

As the light drew closer, Gilbert saw it emanated from two monstrous red bulls that were yoked to an equally monstrous plow. Behind strode Artor, one hand on the plow, the other raised to goad His team forward. The plowshare cut deep into the ground, making a rhythmic thump as it thudded through the earth. Behind Artor ran a wide and deep furrow, straight as an arrow, heading directly for Gilbert.

Breath steamed in great gouts from the flared nostrils of the bulls, and they flung their heads from side to side, rolling their furious eyes as if they wanted to trample all unbelievers and scorners in their path.

But Gilbert was neither an unbeliever nor a scorner, and he stood his ground confidently.

"Furrow wide, furrow deep!" he screamed as if he had suddenly become privy to the greatest secrets of life and death. He threw open his arms in an extravagant gesture of welcome and flung his head back. "Blessed Lord!"

My good, true son.

"Oh!" Gilbert could not believe himself to be so utterly blessed.

Artor halted His team not four or five paces from the ecstatic Gilbert and stepped out from behind the plow, appearing as He had before Jayme—a huge man muscled and scarred from a lifetime behind the plow. He pushed back His hood so that Gilbert might the more easily see the face of his god.

His muscles bunched and rolled as He strode forth, the goad still clasped in one hand.

Who is that who huddles in the dirt?

"It is but Moryson, Blessed Lord, a poor man who has been all but broken by the events of the past months," Gilbert said.

Fool, fool, fool, fool, Moryson droned over and over to himself, and somewhere in his terror-riddled mind he knew that he meant himself with that word. Fool to be here at this moment!

Artor had laid the blame for the Seneschal's loss squarely at Jayme's feet, and He lost interest in Moryson immediately. Sniveling cowards He had seen aplenty. What Artor needed now was a man who had soul and courage enough to restore Artor to His rightful place as supreme god of Achar. He seethed. Why, the viper had even changed the name of the land from the blessed Achar to the ancient and cursed Tencendor.

He turned His eyes back to Gilbert. *You are a man of true spirit. A man whom I can lean on. A man who can rebuild the Seneschal for Me.*

Gilbert fell to his knees and clasped his hands to his breast in adoration, tears in his eyes. At least Artor recognized his true worth.

For centuries Achar lay safe and pristine under My benevolence. Now it is befouled by the footsteps of the Forbidden and by worship of their frightful interstellar gods.

Artor did not like competition; the Seneschal had always disposed quickly and harshly of any who spoke of other ways and other gods.

The Way of the Plow sickens nigh unto death, and the Seneschal is grievously wounded. It will take commitment to ensure its survival and ultimate resurrection to all-consuming power. Are you committed, Gilbert?

"Yes," Gilbert all but shouted in an effort to convince his god.

I have a task for you, Gilbert.

"Anything!"

You know of this Faraday?

Gilbert blinked. Faraday? What could Artor want with—

DO YOU KNOW OF THIS FARADAY? Artor roared through his mind.

Gilbert cursed his hesitation. "Yes! Yes! I know her! She is married to Borneheld. Was, I suppose, if Borneheld is dead."

She is dangerous.

"She is but a woman."

Fool! Think not to contradict Me!

"She is dangerous, oh Blessed One."

Yes. She is dangerous. She must be found and she must be stopped.

"You have only to say the word, Lord, and she will die."

Artor laughed, and it was a terrible sound. *She will not be that easy, Gilbert, but she will be a good test of your commitment. She means to ride east, but her evil enchantments cloud my senses and I know not where she is. Your task is to find her and to stop her before she can replant the forests across good plow-land. If she completes that task then I . . . I . . .*

Gilbert sensed the god's feat. He did not know what Artor was talking about, and he could not see how Faraday could wield evil enchantments or why she was so dangerous. But that must be part of the test.

Then I am lost, the god whispered. *Then I am lost with that single act.* It worried Him greatly that He could not spy out Faraday with His power. It meant that the power of the Mother, which Faraday drew on, was growing stronger day by day.

The forest is evil, and it must be destroyed, never to rise again. Now Artor spoke from the Book of Field and Furrow, the holy text that He had given to mankind thousands of years ago. *Wood exists only to serve man, and it must never be allowed to grow wild and unrestrained, free to shelter dark spirits and wicked sprites.*

Gilbert experienced a rare flash of insight. "It is why we took the axe to the dark forest a thousand years ago, Blessed One. Should it spring to life again then the Way of the Plow will be strangled among its roots."

Yes. Yes, you will do well, good Gilbert. Make sure that you do well, Gilbert, for My wrath is a terrible thing.

Gilbert had every intention of doing well. How hard could it be to find Faraday and dispose of her? "I shall gather the remaining Plow-Keepers and Brothers together, Great Lord, all that I can find. The more eyes I have at my command the more likely it is that I can find the woman. And then when I find her, I will kill her."

Artor smiled. The fool had a lot to learn, but what he lost in naivety, he made up for in commitment and a singular adoration for Artor. There were not many like him left.

Good. I will direct homeless Brothers who still have the faith into your path. They will be your servants.

He touched Gilbert's forehead in benediction.

You will do well, Brother-Leader Gilbert. You have embarked on a Holy Crusade for My sake. Do well.

Then he vanished.

Moryson remained curled in a ball for almost an hour before he dared stand up. He could hardly believe that Artor had let him live. In his long, long life, this was the closest that Moryson had come to personal disaster. He looked around for the younger man.

Gilbert sat by the now dead fire, fervor shining bright in his eyes, planning his divine mission.

WolfStar huddled deep within the dark, dark night. Everything was going wrong. Gorgrael promised to fill the skies with ever-increasing numbers of Gryphon, and now Artor, curse His ravening immortal soul, walked Tencendor seeking vengeance. Had either of these two events been foreseen by prophecy? No, and no again.

"I must think," he muttered to himself. "I must think."

After some time the thought came to him. Azhure. Stars, but he needed Azhure. Tencendor needed Azhure.

6

Carlon

Axis rubbed his tired eyes and consciously worked to keep the deep uneasiness from showing on his face. He remembered Priam sitting in this very Privy Chamber, ragged lines of worry etching *his* face, as he shared his bad news with his commanders.

In the ten days since his marriage, Axis had finally begun sending troops northward to Jervois Landing. He supposed that Gorgrael would again attempt to break through into southern Tencendor with the main part of his force through Jervois Landing as he had last winter. The troops had embarked on river transports, normally the quickest and most efficient system of moving large numbers of troops and supplies. Normally.

"They have no way of breaking through?" Axis asked.

Belial gazed steadily at his friend. "The Nordra is completely frozen beyond the valley in the Western Ranges, Axis. No ship, no transport, can sail into Aldeni or Skarabost. The north is isolated."

"As are those troops currently in Jervois Landing, Axis," Magariz added.

Axis looked about the room, trying together his thoughts. The great Privy Chamber had not altered much since the days Axis had attended Priam's council here as BattleAxe of the Seneschal. But if the great Privy Chamber had not altered much in structure or hangings, it certainly had in the people grouped about the great circular table. Apart from Axis, Prince Tsgryn was the only one present who would have attended Priam's council. Duke Roland was still in Sigholt, slowly dying; the unlucky Earl Jorge had moved north to Jervois Landing with the first transports; and Baron Fulke was currently seeing to the last of the grape harvest in Romsdale.

Now Icarii Crest-Leaders shared the conference table with a Ravensbund

Chieftain and human princes. There were others, stranger, grouped about or under the table StarDrifter, not part of the conference, but present nevertheless. Azhure, looking slightly better but still weary, sat farther around the table. At her feet, and around the chamber, lay the fifteen great Alaunt hounds.

Come on, man, *think*, Axis berated himself. They wait on you. They believe in you.

But the truth was that Axis had not thought very much at all about what he would do once he had defeated Borneheld and proclaimed Tencendor. He had never really thought about how he was going to confront Gorgrael. Now it looked as though Gorgrael was going to force the issue, as though the final battle would be fought on Gorgrael's terms.

Axis roused himself, aware that the others were staring. "FarSight, is it possible to send your farflight scouts north to spy the danger?"

FarSight CutSpur, the senior Crest-Leader in the Icarii Strike Force, shook his dark head emphatically. "No, StarMan. No. The weather worsens hourly. Great winds of sleet and frost bear down from the north. If the farflight scouts actually survived the winds, then they would see nothing anyway."

Azhure spoke, her voice soft. "How many men do you have in Jervois Landing, Axis?"

"Over eight thousand. Five that Borneheld had left there, three from our own force. And one lonely wing of the Strike Force; they must be grounded if the weather at Jervois Landing is as bad as I fear."

Magariz and Belial exchanged glances.

"If Gorgrael attacks," Magariz said, "then they are lost. Eight thousand could not possibly hold out against the forces he could throw against them."

"Damn it, I know that!" Axis shouted. "But what can I *do*? I have no way of moving any more forces north quickly—even the Andeis Sea has succumbed to storms so violent that five ships have been lost this past week alone." He paused and calmed himself. "Gorgrael *will* strike," he resumed, "and he will strike soon All we can do is prepare as best we can."

"We move north?" Belial said.

Axis looked at him steadily, then gazed about the room, fixing the eyes of each of his commanders in turn. "We begin to prepare today."

He hesitated, then decided to voice his concern. "Truth to tell, my friends, I am unsure what to do. Where will Gorgrael strike? Jervois Landing, surely, but we will never be able to get there in time. Then where? If all of Aldeni is frozen he could mass his troops anywhere. I am loath to commit my force to any action or to any route north until I have a better idea what Gorgrael is going to do."

It was Ichtar all over again, Axis thought. If Gorgrael broke through Jervois Landing he would have the entire province of Aldini to roam in. And he would be only some fifty leagues from Carlon itself.

"Well, enough of my doubts" Axis spoke briskly, and more formally. "Princes

Belial, Magariz and Ysgryff and," he smiled slightly at his wife, "my Lady Azhure, Guardian of the East. Within three days I want from all of you a list of the resources that your provinces will be able to provide to support Tencendor's fight against Gorgrael. I want to know everything you've got, from food to wagons to fighting men to weapons to any *one* or any *thing* that can contribute to the war effort."

Magariz's mouth twitched, but his eyes were grave. "I do not need three days to compose a list, StarMan. My northern province can provide only one thing, but that in abundance—the enemy."

There was silence, then Axis spoke again.

"Sooner or later we will to have to ride into that icy hell above the Western Ranges," he said. "And I fear that there will be no glorious battle at the end of this march."

Especially if I cannot find the skills and the courage to wield enough of the Star Dance to use effective Songs of War, he thought, black despair threatening to overwhelm him.

"Eleven days ago, amid shouts of rejoicing, I proclaimed Tencendor. Ten days ago I married the woman I love more than life itself. But this has been a false summer, I think. Have we all celebrated too fast? Has darkness merely bided its time, waiting to catch us off guard?"

All that afternoon Azhure attended to her duties as Guardian of the East. Hers was a special responsibility, that of making sure that the integration of three races, three cultures, and three religions went smoothly and with the least rancor possible. It was a challenge that Azhure relished; she had spent time among all three races—Acharites (as the humans were still known), Avar and Icarii. Although the Avar still had not moved from their forest homelands, and probably would not until Faraday had planted the forest below the Fortress Ranges, Azhure had more than enough to do with the influx of Icarii into the southern lands of Tencendor. She was impatient with the paperwork that the scribes continually thrust her way; Azhure liked to hear a problem from all sides before making a decision that was best for the parties involved. She had got very used to the despairing cry of the scribes and administrators—"But it's never been done *that* way before!"—to which she always replied, with as much graciousness as she could, "Well, it's the way it's going to be done now."

In the early evening, Azhure wandered back to the royal apartments along the busy corridors of the palace. She hoped that Axis would soon return from his consultations with Belial and Magariz over preparations for their eventual march north. She needed to speak with him about what she had learned this afternoon and did not want to leave it for later that night as she was now so tired that she longed only for a simple meal and her bed.

Axis was still deeply worried about her health and, though they never spoke of it, both were extremely concerned over her continuing lack of control over her power. The morning after StarDrifter and Axis had tried to teach Azhure the Song for Drying Clothes, Carlon had awakened to a minor miracle.

The contents of every single laundry hamper in the city had been mysteriously emptied overnight, laundered, folded and stored.

There could be no explanation except that, somehow, Azhure had unconsciously used her power as she slept. She had no knowledge of how she had done it, and had become tearful when Axis had pressed her, and the matter of the clean clothes had been quietly dropped. But Azhure could feel Axis and StarDrifter's eyes on her occasionally, wondering. Wondering what? she thought. Wondering what might have happened if it had been a less innocuous Song? What if it had been the Song of Muddlement—would Carlon then have awoken with its population wandering the streets, dazed and disoriented?

Azhure sighed with relief when she reached the royal apartments; Axis was already there, and servants had just finished laying a meal for them on a low table in the Jade Chamber.

As they are, Azhure occasionally stole a glance at Axis, noting the lines of worry on his face. Some of them she knew were for her, but most were for the desperate situation faced by the troops currently at Jervois Landing. Axis worried for each soldier under his command; every time a man died Axis fretted. Could he have prevented it? Was the man's death the result of a bad decision on his part? Belial had told her of Axis' deep guilt after the loss of three hundred men at the Ancient Barrows when Gorgrael had rained down his cruel ice spears on them, and his even worse guilt after the disastrous loss of life in the battle for Gorkentown. Since she had been with him, Azhure had seen much of the same thing. Stars knows how he must be berating himself inside for not foreseeing the probable slaughter at Jervois Landing.

"Why do you smile?" Axis asked as he peeled back the purple skin of a juicy malayam fruit.

"I was thinking on the dismay of the scribes and recorders this afternoon. I do not, it seems, do things in the right order, at the right time, or use the correct bureaucratic procedure."

To her relief Axis laughed, his whole face lightening. "Then you are doing well, beloved, if you have already annoyed the bureaucrats."

They smiled at each other, then Azhure's expression became serious. "Axis. There is a matter that I ought to discuss with you. Do you mind?"

"Never fear to talk with me, Azhure. We have wasted months of our lives because we did not talk truthfully to each other."

"It is only a mundane matter, perhaps," she said, "but it needs to be aired. Dru-Beorh came to me this afternoon with some disturbing news." She paused. "He has seen both Moryson and Gilbert in his travels between here and Nor."

Axis grimaced. He should have known that their names would reemerge.

"They were both alone at the time he saw them, Moryson wandering south through the Plains of Tare, Gilbert traveling east through northern Nor. I thanked him for the information and said I would think further on it. Axis, Faraday was heading east when she left here. I cannot but think that perhaps she may encounter one of them."

Axis returned his eyes to the remains of the malayam fruit. After a moment he gave up all pretense at eating it and wiped his fingers on a napkin.

"I would give much to have those two locked securely in the palace dungeons, Azhure. Together with Jayme, they were directly responsible for many of the injustices that the Seneschal perpetuated. And that I helped perpetuate." Another guilt.

They both turned their minds to Jayme, and they shared their thoughts regarding his strange death. No one had been able to explain it, and while Axis had been pleased to see that Jayme had died in a manner befitting his crimes, he was unhappy that Jayme had escaped his trial. The guard had heard or seen nothing, and both Axis and Azhure could not help but feel that some dark enchantment had been at work in Jayme's death.

"Faraday?" Azhure prompted. "Do you think Faraday is in any danger? It is not only Gilbert and Moryson who concern me—there must be a number of Plow-Keepers wandering eastern Tencendor. They can be nothing but trouble."

Axis sipped some wine thoughtfully. He'd not had time to deal with the problem of the Seneschal and the Way of the Plow, and undoubtedly would not for many months to come. Despite the collapse of the Seneschal and the abandoning of Artor by so many people in these days of prophecy, Axis knew that in many villages the Plow-Keepers retained considerable power.

"Faraday?" Azhure asked yet again.

He started and smiled guiltily. "Sorry. Faraday . . ." Stars, another guilt, and the worst of all. She was, as Belial had once told him in anger, too wondrous a woman for him to have treated the way he had. "The east is massive. I doubt they will run into each other. And Faraday can look after herself, Azhure. She is infused with the power of the Mother and the Mother will aid her should she need it."

"I had thought that perhaps I could send a small unit of men to protect her."

"Would they find her? Would she welcome such company? And," the crux of the matter, "can we spare the men?"

"No. Perhaps you are right," Azhure said, worried nevertheless. Faraday had treated her with kindness, respect and friendship where Azhure had expected only bitterness and recrimination.

She forced her mind from Faraday for the moment. "Some Icarii are moving down from Talon Spike in small groups, Axis. Many of them are like children, so excited they know not what to see or do next."

"I hope they are not frightening the Acharites with their excitement."

"No. The majority still wait in Talon Spike, and RavenCrest, and I have asked that those who fly south restrain themselves. Most groups are flying to the Bracken Ranges where, so I am informed, there are ancient Icarii cities hidden under layers of dirt and boulders. Apparently, during the Wars of the Axe, when the Seneschal was succeeding in its bid to drive the Icarii from Achar, the Icarii Enchanters hid their cities in the Bracken Ranges with enchantments and, so they tell me, just a little dirt. Most of the Icarii efforts thus far have gone into dusting both enchantments and dirt from their ancient homes."

Axis smiled briefly, his eyes whimsical. "I would like to see these cities one day, but I do not know when. Not with the threat that seeps down from the north."

For some minutes Axis described the preparations that engulfed much of Carlon in getting some thirty-thousand men-at-arms ready for a march north. He had only succeeded in sending a fraction of his command north before the Nordra froze over. And for that, he thought grimly, I suppose I ought to be grateful. Better to have the majority here in Carlon where they will survive Gorgrael's inevitable attack on Jervois Landing.

"I wish," he concluded softly, taking her hand, "that you could travel north with me. And yet I am relieved that your pregnancy will force you to remain behind. At least something will be saved if disaster engulfs us in the north."

If disaster engulfs you in the north, my love, Azhure thought, I will have no reason left to live.

Azhure wished she could fight by Axis' side, but she knew that her physical state, while not desperate, was still sufficiently weak to cause concern. Each advancing day her unborn twins sapped more of her energy; Azhure had longed for Caelum to be born so that she could hold her wondrous son in her arms, but she longed for these twins to be born just so she could be freed of their encumbrance.

Axis watched her easy acceptance of his words with disquiet. The Azhure he had known would have fought bitterly to be allowed to ride at his side, pregnant or not. It was an indication of how deeply unwell she was that Azhure so meekly accepted the fact she would have to remain behind.

But Azhure had no intention of staying behind permanently, "Once they are born I will come," she said, squeezing his hand, "The birth is only three months away at the most. Then I will be free to join you."

If there is anything left to join, Axis thought to himself. If you still have a husband to join.

7

Timozel Plans

ver since Gorgrael had told him about his success with the Gryphon, the
Dear Man had disappeared. Gorgrael supposed that perhaps he was slightly
miffed at Gorgrael's achievements. But it did not matter, for now he had Timozel to talk to, and Timozel was such good company, not only because of his
intelligence, but because he was totally under the Destroyer's control.

Today was the last day that Timozel would spend at the Ice Fortress before
he joined the bulk of the Skraeling army north of Jervois Landing. He had
already begun to mold the Skraelings, relaying orders and receiving information
through the SkraeBolds and the Gryphon. Gorgrael hiccupped with pleasure
when he remembered how SkraeFear and his two remaining brothers had sulked
and brooded when introduced to Timozel, deeply resenting the loss of their
favored spot at Gorgrael's side. But Gorgrael had taught Timozel how best to
use his well of power, and Timozel had brooked no resentment nor resistance
from the SkraeBolds, all three now wore the welts to remind them that it was
not a good idea to cross Timozel.

Gorgrael looked fondly across the crazily canted table at his able lieutenant.
"What is it you plan, Timozel? How will you work my will?"

Timozel did not look up from the map he held straight with only the most
extreme difficulty, damn Gorgrael's preference for ridiculous angles and planes
in his furniture! "I will work your will to the best of my ability, Lord."

"Yes, yes." Gorgrael shifted impatiently. "But what is it you plan?"

Timozel tapped the map. "From the reports your Gryphon have brought
me, the force at Jervois Landing remains relatively small. The freezing of the
Nordra has effectively stopped Axis sending anymore troop transports north."
He paused. "I know Jervois Landing well. Now that the canals have been frozen

as solid as the Nordra the town's defenses are virtually nil. I shall overwhelm and crush Jervois Landing with little trouble."

"You won't attack through the WildDog Plains?"

"No." Both Timozel and Gorgrael were very reluctant, not only to split their force for a two-pronged attack through both Jervois Landing and the WildDog Plains, but to expose a Skraeling force to the powerful magic of Sigholt on the one flank and the Avarinheim on the other. Since he had been with Gorgrael, Timozel had learned a great deal about the magic of the land he and his master planned to invade. "No. We attack with full force at Jervois Landing. They won't even have time for final prayers before dying."

"And then you overrun Aldeni and Skarabost?" Gorgrael asked.

Timozel lifted his eyes from the map, and Gorgrael stilled at the cold light in them. "No."

Gorgrael was puzzled. "Well, straight to Carlon then. There is much beauty to destroy there."

The coldness deepened in Timozel's eyes. "No."

"Well, then, *what?*"

"Our main objective *must* be to destroy Axis' army. I have a better plan. Listen."

Gorgrael listened . . . and liked. It was a good plan, but better than that, it was a *tricky* plan. Timozel would do well, yes, indeed he would.

Spiredore

On the fourth day after she and Axis had discussed Faraday's safety, Azhure finally found herself with enough energy and free time to visit Spiredore. She had not been back to the tower across the Grail Lake since that dreadful morning when the Gryphon had attacked her and Caelum on its roof. But Azhure knew she would have to go back. She needed to speak to WolfStar, and she hoped he would appear to her in Spiredore again as he had two weeks ago. She also hoped she could learn more about the magic of Spiredore.

Azhure had been amazed to discover that Axis and StarDrifter, as every other Icarii Enchanter who entered the tower between the time it was reawoken and the time it was given to her, only saw a hollow shell with a plain staircase creeping about its walls to the roof. No one else had seen the crazy assemblage of balconies and intertwining stairs that she and Caelum had seen. Does Spiredore choose who will see its secrets? Azhure wondered as she sat in the bow of the small boat that Arne rowed for her.

"My Lady, are you well enough for this expedition?" Arne asked, barely out of breath despite his efforts. He was not sure if Axis knew what Azhure was doing and wondered if he should have told him. But Azhure was a grown woman and did not need Axis' permission for her actions. Arne's only real doubt was that Azhure looked so pale and thin despite her pregnancy that she might fall and injure herself inside the tower.

"I am well enough," Azhure said, her irritation at the question stilled by the genuine concern she knew lay behind it. "And besides, you do all the work."

"But you will be alone within the tower, my Lady."

Azhure bent down to pat the head of the great pale hound that rested in the belly of the boat. "I have Sicarius to watch over me, Arne. Should I suffer any mishap he will fetch help."

Arne nodded, satisfied.

When they docked at the small pier by Spiredore, Arne helped Azhure disembark. Then he sat to wait, watching as the white door closed behind Azhure and her hound.

The interior was exactly as Azhure remembered it. Now that sunlight suffused the atrium from windows set high overhead, she could see every detail of the stairwells and balconies that swirled to dizzying heights above her. Rooms, chambers, open spaces, all opened off balconies none of which were level with their neighbors. Again Azhure was struck by the beauty created by this chaos; she was sure there were secrets and mysteries within the rooms and stairwells that spiraled above her. Spiredore was alive with magic, and it was hers to discover as she willed.

For almost an hour Azhure wandered the ground-floor rooms, unwilling to climb any of the stairs lest she become lost and disoriented She had expected that once she was inside the tower WolfStar would appear as quickly and as mysteriously as he had that last time—but the rooms remained stubbornly empty and the stairwells disappointingly silent.

Finally, tired and dispirited, Azhure sank down onto the bare floor of one of the chambers.

Sicarius whined and pressed his head into her hands.

"Well, my fine fellow," Azhure said as she scratched the hound behind the ears. "Did WolfStar ever bring you here? Do you know how to find your former master?"

But the Alaunt remained as obstinately silent as Spiredore itself and Azhure sighed. Perhaps she should have brought Caelum. Perhaps the only reason WolfStar had come to her before was to see his grandson. But even as she thought this, Azhure realized WolfStar's interest in Caelum that night had been only tangential; his real focus had been her.

Azhure shifted her weight, uncomfortable on the hard floor, and thought that the answer *must* lie within her somewhere. Hadn't WolfStar told her that the tower had been built just for her? Well, here the tower stood, but the builders had forgotten to give her the key.

"Stop it, woman!" she said to herself, annoyed at her negative thoughts. WolfStar had also told her how to use this tower, hadn't he? Her brow creased as she tried to remember his exact words. So much had happened since that meeting to crowd out the memory of her conversation with him . . . so much . . . but just as Azhure thought she had indeed lost the memory forever WolfStar's words suddenly echoed around the chamber.

It is very simple. If you wander willy-nilly in Spiredore you will, as you thought, get completely lost. You must decide where you want to go before you start to climb the stairs, and then the stairs will take you to that place.

"Of course!" Azhure laughed, and struggled to her feet. "Of course! Thank you!" She patted the wall she had been resting against, then she walked as fast as she could back to the atrium and stared at the nearest staircase. Before she tested WolfStar's advice she leaned down to the hound. "Sicarius, should I become lost or disoriented in the stairs and chambers above, do you think you can understand enough of the magic of Spiredore to see me safely back to the door?"

The Alaunt gave a short, sharp bark in reply, and Azhure smiled. "Good. Well, Sicarius, shall we go see your former master?"

Azhure placed one hand firmly on the stair rail and with the other gathered up the skirts of the loose lavender gown she wore. She pictured WolfStar in her mind, the beautiful and powerful face, the copper curls, the golden wings.

"Take me to WolfStar SunSoar," she said, and began to climb.

With his power and experience, WolfStar felt Azhure move through the maze that was Spiredore, heard her call his name. He smiled in surprise, yet with deep pride, at her grasp of Spiredore's power. Nevertheless, WolfStar knew that it would be a disaster if she came to him in his present location, so he moved quickly to meet his daughter before she transferred out of Spiredore.

Azhure was finding the climb difficult and, as she grew more and more breathless, she wondered if she had understood WolfStar's words correctly. Surely even her climb to the rooftop had not taken her this long?

Beside her Sicarius climbed easily, his paws silent on the wooden treads.

"Stars, Sicarius," Azhure panted, pausing and resting her head on the railing. "I do not think even WolfStar is worth all this trouble."

"Then I am sorry for the effort I have caused you," a rich voice said above her, and Azhure started so violently she would have fallen had not WolfStar reached down a hand and steadied her.

"Come," he said, smiling, "there is a comfortable chamber just above. Two or three more steps and we are there."

Azhure blinked and looked past WolfStar. She could have sworn that before she had rested her head the stairway spiraled up into infinity, but now it ended in a landing not two or three steps ahead. Beyond this the door to a chamber stood invitingly open.

"Come," her father repeated, and Azhure let him lead her into the chamber. She sank down into a comfortable couch, richly embroidered and cushioned, and WolfStar, after patting and murmuring to the hound, walked to the window to stare over the Grail Lake toward Carlon while Azhure caught her breath.

She studied him curiously. He was as beautiful as she remembered, and she wondered why she had inherited none of his coloring or his Icarii bone structure.

"You know that I am your father?" WolfStar asked as he turned back into the chamber.

Azhure remembered their kiss, but she felt no shame. "I know that you are WolfStar SunSoar, come back through the Star Gate, and I know that you are my father. I know my mother's name was Niah, and that she was a Priestess in the Temple of the Stars." Azhure's voice became harsher as bitter resentments bubbled to the surface. "I know you got Niah pregnant and then abandoned her to her death. I know you thought so little of me that you let me linger under the appalling care of Hagen. I know you murdered MorningStar."

WolfStar stepped into the center of the room, his face tight with anger.

Azhure, angry herself, ignored the danger. "And I know that you are the Traitor who will betray Axis to Gorgrael—you probably already have."

"You know *nothing*! You have guessed my identity, and you have surmised that I came back through the Star Gate. You realize that I am your father, but the rest . . . *bah!*"

Azhure held his stare. She had not meant to accuse him so quickly, but she was tired and she was heartsick and here was the birdman who was at the root of all their problems. Did he think that she would fall into his arms weeping for joy once she had gleaned his identity?

"Then tell me why it is," she said, "that Niah and I were left to fend for ourselves. Niah died horribly, WolfStar—but perhaps you don't care about that—and I suffered many long years, lost, alone, despairing. Tell me why I should *not* accuse you?"

His eyes softened. "There are so many things that I cannot yet speak of, Azhure, and Niah's death and your life in Smyrron is one of them."

She turned her face away from him, tears of anger springing to her eyes.

"Azhure," he said, and she felt him sit down by her side. "You are my daughter and I think you know that I love you." He picked up her hand. "I did not willingly abandon either of you to . . . oh! By the Light of the Stars, Azhure! *What is this you wear?*"

His voice sounded tortured, and Azhure whipped her head about. WolfStar was staring at the ring on her finger, and he was trembling so badly that Azhure's arm also shook.

"WolfStar?"

"What is that you wear?" he whispered, his face colorless. He raised his great violet eyes to her own.

"It is the ring of the Enchantress, or so I am told. WolfStar? Why do you tremble so?"

"The Enchantress' ring," he said, his voice still soft. "I thought never to see this again. Azhure, how did you get this?"

His distress was catching, and Azhure had to lick her suddenly dry lips before continuing.

"Axis gave it to me. He was given it by the Ferryman, Orr." In the past days Axis had told her much of what had happened to him in the waterways. "And Orr said that—"

"That I gave it to him."

"Yes."

WolfStar took a deep breath and composed himself. He'd been driven by a powerful but little understood need to conceive Azhure with Niah, but until this moment he'd not realized the precise nature of what he'd seeded. Hesitantly he touched the ring.

"This ring is representative of great and unimaginable power." Reluctantly he let Azhure's hand go. He looked up and tried to smile but it was an abysmal failure. "When I gave it to Orr I thought never to see it again. To find it now on the finger of my own daughter is almost beyond my comprehension."

"Should I fear it, WolfStar?"

He lifted his hand and softly touched her cheek, wonder in his eyes. "No. No. The ring has chosen you, it has come home to you." *By the Stars!*, he thought, *the Circle has completed itself in my daughter!* "That is an unimaginable honor. Unimaginable. You need not fear it." Now his mouth did curl slightly, wonderingly. "It makes me fear *you*, though."

Azhure felt herself succumbing to WolfStar's immense appeal as he stroked her cheek and smiled into her eyes. She knew she should be angry with him, she knew she should hate him for abandoning Niah and herself to Hagen but her anger was fading with every stroke of his fingers. Again she understood why her mother must have yielded to him.

But while her anger faded, her curiosity and her desperation for answers still flared bright. "Who was the Enchantress, WolfStar, what power does her ring contain? And why did you tremble so when you spied it on my finger?"

"So many questions, Azhure."

A touch of determination hardened her voice. "I have almost thirty years of questions, WolfStar. These three will do to start with."

He sighed and dropped his hand. These three questions would not be the worst she would ask him.

"What do you know of the Enchantress? No, wait," he said quickly as he saw Azhure gesture in irritation. "I only ask this so that I do not repeat what you already know."

"That she was the mother from whom both Charomre and Icarii races sprang. That she was very powerful, the first of all the Enchanters. That this ring, which was hers, holds unknown powers. She used her power differently to other Enchanters—or Charonite mages, for all I know."

"The Enchantress was the Mother of Nations, yes."

Azhure blinked. The Ferryman had called her that when she had traveled with the Icarii and Raum to Talon Spike via the ancient Waterways.

"Not much is known about her. All we have now are legends . . . and this ring. She was a remarkable woman, and many of her powers and magic she passed on to her two youngest sons."

"Her youngest sons?"

WolfStar grinned. "The Enchantress did not favor her eldest son at all; it was he who fathered the Acharite race."

Azhure's mouth dropped open. "Do you mean that the Icarii, the Charonites and the Acharites *all* sprang from the one mother?"

WolfStar's grin became more feral. "The children of her unfavored eldest son became the toilers of the soil, while the children of those sons she did favor grew to hunt the mysteries of the universe."

Azhure wondered how the Acharites would react if they realized they sprang from the same source as the Icarii and Charonites "Are the Avar descended from her as well?"

"No. The Avar come from different stock altogether. Now, this ring. Again, like the Enchantress herself, what knowledge we have of this ring is ancient and riddled with mystery because of it." WolfStar knew far more than that about the ring, but it was not his place to tell Azhure. That right belonged to the . . . others. "It does not so much contain power itself as it represents power—unimaginable power. For many thousands of years it has manipulated as it sees fit to achieve its own ends, that is why I trembled so when I saw it on your finger. I, too, have been manipulated by this ring."

He was silent a moment. "You have, no doubt, heard the Icarii tell of my reign as Enchanter-Talon."

"Yes," Azhure whispered. Her father had hurled hundreds of innocent children to their deaths through the Star Gate in an effort to understand its mysteries. Eventually WolfStar's younger brother, CloudBurst, had assassinated him before WolfStar could murder the entire Icarii race. Of course, no one among the Icarii—or any other race that knew the story—had counted on WolfStar coming back through the Star Gate.

"My fascination was not only with the Star Gate, Azhure," and WolfStar's voice took on the quality of confession, "but also with this ring that my forebears had guarded for so many thousands of years. I know I cannot excuse what I did to those children, but the ring had haunted my dreams from childhood, and it drove me to maniacal deeds. It was the ring that whispered to me that I needed to sacrifice those children into the Star Gate . . . it was the ring that whispered to me that it wanted to be taken to the waterways, there to wait until it decided to move on again."

And was it the *ring* that sent me to Niah? WolfStar wondered. And whispered to me the name of the child she was to conceive?

Azhure's mind told her not to believe WolfStar, that he was merely using the ring as an excuse for his own inexcusable behavior, but her heart told her that he spoke the truth.

"Then it will only seek to use me," she said, horrified, twisting the ring off her hand. "It will use me and force me to do its will!"

"No!" WolfStar cried and clasped her hands between his to stop her pulling off the ring. "No! Legends said that one day the ring would seek out the hand of one who was fit to wear it—even the Enchantress was only a custodian, the ring was not truly hers. It has taken tens of thousands of years, but the ring has finally come home. Azhure, I trembled not only because I feared the power the ring represents, but also because I suddenly realized that I ought to fear you more."

Azhure was silent, staring at her father with great smoky eyes. Her entire body was still, her breathing so shallow that her breasts scarcely rose.

"Azhure, the ring has chosen you . . . and it is now subservient to you. It has chosen you as its home."

"But I do not know how to use it, or this power you say it represents," she said. "WolfStar, one of the reasons I came here today was to ask you how I can use my powers. You *must* teach me! Axis needs me!"

"One day I will teach you what I can, Azhure, but that day is not yet here." And what I *can* teach you is going to be little indeed, Azhure-heart.

"Damn you!" Azhure cried, and tore her hands from his. "I *need* to know!"

"Azhure, listen to me. This is not the time nor the place. No! *Listen* to me! I will not teach you, nor will any others, while you are pregnant with those twins—there are secrets you will learn that those babies should not know."

Azhure opened her mouth automatically to defend her twins, but closed it again as she remembered their continued antagonism to her and Axis. She rested a hand on her belly.

"And this is not the place to teach you," WolfStar continued. "There is one place that you can learn quickly and easily, a place where others can be involved in your teaching, a place where power is more likely to flare into life."

"The Island of Mist and Memory. Temple Mount."

"Yes. How did you know that?"

"Niah told me to go to Temple Mount . . . as she lay dying."

WolfStar ignored the hard edge of the last phrase, and his eyes dimmed in memory. "Ah . . . Niah." Perhaps Niah had known what WolfStar had only just come to understand. But then, she had been First, and perhaps the First was more intimately aware of the secrets of the gods than even he.

"Please," Azhure began. "Explain to me now why you treated us as you did."

"I cannot, Azhure," he said. "There are many things that must be explained, but I will need to wait until you are alone—" she knew he meant after she had given birth, "—and you are on the Island of Mist and Memory."

For some time Azhure sat half turned away from him. She had wanted to learn so much more from this meeting.

"All I have done has been for a purpose," WolfStar said eventually, understanding her hurt. "One day the reasons will become clear. But this I will tell you."

Azhure turned her eyes back to her father.

"I am not the Traitor that many think. The third verse of the Prophecy speaks of a Traitor, but I am not he."

"You seem to know your way about the Prophecy very well," Azhure said sharply.

"The Traitor has already made his move, Azhure. Fear not the people about either you or Axis. The Traitor is already with his master. He has already made his decision to betray, although he has not yet committed the final betrayal."

Azhure stared at WolfStar. *Who was the Traitor?* But WolfStar would not answer this unspoken query. He lifted his fingertips to her cheek again, the touch so light that Azhure could hardly feel it.

"Be assured, Azhure. You *will* find the answers you need to know on the Island. You think that you need to be by Axis' side, that you need to be there to fight for him, but the greatest service you can do for him now, as for yourself, is to spend time alone to accept and develop your power."

She nodded slightly, reluctantly. "I feel pulled in so many different directions. So many people, demanding different things from me. I *do* need time alone."

He leaned down and scratched Sicarius under the muzzle, then glanced back at Azhure. "You look very much like your mother, Azhure, and she was very, very desirable."

Later, as WolfStar sat huddled under the stars, he thought on the afternoon's encounter with his daughter. First Gorgrael and his Gryphon, then Artor, and now the Enchantress' ring resurfaces. Were things moving beyond his control?

Perhaps, but the fact that the ring had chosen Azhure gave him great hope for the future. Suddenly neither Artor nor a sky blackened with Gryphon seemed such an insurmountable threat.

9

Jervois Landing

For the past ten or eleven days an icy nightmare had closed about Jervois Landing. Nothing Jorge had seen before—not even the appalling conditions at Gorkenfort or the weather that Gorgrael had thrown their way last winter—had been this bad. The storm front, if such a mild expression could possibly describe what had descended on them, had moved into the town in an unbelievable two minutes. One minutes it had been cool and blustery, the clouds heavy with the promise of snow, the next . . . the next blew a wind so severe that only the strongest stone houses in the town were left standing. The wind carried with it ice and death, and everyone caught exposed to it had died; Jorge had lost over two thousand men in five minutes. The four Icarii scouts just returning to the town had fallen from the sky frozen solid.

When they hit the streets their bodies were shattered into such tiny pieces they were scattered away within moments.

Day after day Jorge and the remnants of his command had huddled by fires. No one was left manning the defenses of Jervois Landing—the system of canals that Borneheld had caused to be built—for none could survive in the open. And what defenses anyway? Jorge thought. The canals must have frozen within minutes of the storm's arrival. He grimaced under his blanket and crept an inch or two closer to the fire. Jervois Landing did not *have* defenses anymore.

The six thousand remaining men were, to the best of Jorge's knowledge, scattered throughout the town. He no longer sent men out into the streets to gather information, for that was far too cruel in this weather, so Jorge frankly had no idea about the state of his command.

The remaining eight Icarii were the most miserable of all. The Wing had arrived the day before the weather closed in, and now four of them were dead and the others cramped about what warmth the fires provided.

Jorge knew that his men all expected to die, because when he moved from group to group, trying to revive spirits, he found men praying, preparing their souls for the inevitable journey to the AfterLife. Some, but only a few, prayed to Artor. The Icarii prayed to their Star Gods, the few Ravensbund men in his command prayed to their own mysterious deities. But, to his surprise, Jorge found many men praying to Axis, the StarMan, invoking his name as a god. Some even prayed to Azhure, the woman who had ridden with Axis and whose reputation with the bow was almost as legendary as the Wolven itself and the ghost hounds that ran at her back.

Jorge had backed away, sickened, when he first heard a group of three soldiers praying in a low monotone to Axis. Had these men gone *mad*? Axis was a man like any other, was he not? Did a string of military victories qualify one for godlike status? Jorge had returned to his spot by the fire and sat for many hours, his thoughts in turmoil. Somehow this disturbed him even more than the Gorgrael-driven storm outside.

Had the world turned completely upside down? Did Axis now insist that his command worship him as a god?

Unknown to Jorge, Axis was not behind the actions of these men. He would have been confused and horrified had he known that many men within his command, and their wives and children, had begun, slowly and unconsciously, to perceive him as a god. The process had started a long time ago, among the three thousand who had followed Axis out of Gorkenfort to lead the Skraeling mass away from the fort so that Borneheld and the remaining soldiers could escape to Jervois Landing. They had seen him wield the emerald fire, and they had watched five magical winged creatures greet him at the foot of the Icescarp Alps. Once Axis' command had been ensconced in Sigholt the trend to understand Axis as something other than human or even mortal had continued apace. Surely no mere mortal could wield the power that he did? Surely no mortal power could command the winged creatures as Axis did? Surely no mortal could live in such a magical castle as Sigholt now showed itself to be? Then Axis had led his command south through Achar, defeating the murderer and usurper Borneheld, and had created for them the mighty realm of Tencendor. No mortal, many muttered, could have done all of this.

Slowly but surely, men and women everywhere were starting to worship Axis as their god of choice—the StarMan. Others preferred the calm beauty and the sure deadliness of the Enchantress.

Especially those who still recalled the ancient prayers to Lady Moon.

It was this trend, more than anything else, that had terrified Artor out of His heavenly kingdom and into flesh to try to stop the rot.

Jorge shivered and pulled his blanket closer and listened to the muttered prayers echo about him. Had he ever thought he'd live to see the day when the names of so *many* gods could be evoked by a force he led? Damn the impulse that had seen him volunteer to lead the command in Jervois Landing! Jorge had not wanted to linger in Carlon after the death of Borneheld, and Axis had granted his request to come farther north. Now the price of his impetuousness was apparently going to be death, and Jorge suddenly realized that he did not want to die. He might be close to seventy and he may have led a full life, but Jorge still had a lot that he wanted to do.

Jorge considered praying himself, but he did not know who to pray to. His lifelong devotion to Artor seemed inconsequential; of what use was a Plow-God here among the ice? Had Artor protected those who had called His name but had still died over the past two years? No, Artor was ineffectual, but Jorge was not yet ready to pray to any of the Star Gods, nor as he prepared to invoke the names of Axis or Azhure to his aid.

So he just sat.

And waited for death.

In the space of a heartbeat, the storm stopped. The sudden silence almost hurt the ears, but it did not cause any gladness. All knew what it meant.

Gorgrael was ready to attack.

High above circled the Gryphon. As soon as the winds had ceased the clouds too had faded away, as if they had needed the howling wind to exist themselves. Timozel had asked Gorgrael for a clear blue sky under which to conduct his massacre—as yet, he still preferred the sunshine to the gloom.

Now he sat on the Gryphon, his years of training as a horseman adapting easily to the creature's movements. The Gryphon dipped and soared, and *screamed with the voice of despair.* Timozel turned and to the west saw *a mighty army that undulated for leagues in every direction. He fought for a Great Lord, and in the name of that Lord he would . . .*

"Reap remarkable victories," Timozel whispered, caught in the recurring thrall of his vision. At last, he had found his appointed place. All would be well.

Timozel turned his head slightly. *Circle lower,* he commanded the creature, and the Gryphon gave a cry as she wheeled through the sky.

There. Timozel smiled in satisfaction. Below him lay the crippled town of Jervois Landing. Many of the buildings were slicked so deep with ice they were almost buried; when he peered closer Timozel could see at least three houses so completely iced over that they were closed to the outside world. His smile deepened. If any people had been inside those houses they would by now have frozen to death. He was well pleased.

Battalions of Skraelings were moving quickly south, outflanking the town. Timozel had spared only a quarter of his army for this attack; the rest of the

Skraeling mass he was already pushing south to their destination. Timozel was on a tight schedule; he needed to dispose of what pitiful force Axis had here in less than half a day, then move his army south and then . . . well, then move them to their hiding place. But he needed to get them there within ten days to be sure of avoiding the force that Axis was sure to send north once he heard of Jervois Landing's collapse.

Although Gorgrael could recloak the entire northern regions of this land in storms so devastating that no man could survive more than a few minutes, Timozel did not want Axis to face weather that severe. Bitter cold, surely, but nothing that would prevent him finally leading his army north. Timozel very, very much wanted Axis to get through.

We are ready. Timozel shared his thoughts not only with his subcommand— the SkraeBolds and the Skraelings of higher than average intelligence—but also with Gorgrael, eagerly following the course of the excitement with his mind's eye, deep within his Ice Fortress.

Privately, *very* privately, Timozel harbored resentment that Gorgrael should remain safely shrouded within his Fortress. Did he not want to face Axis himself? Or . . . was he afraid of him?

Timozel kept these thoughts very dark and very, very deep.

But he had better things to think of now, namely the killing that awaited him below.

Begin, he ordered.

Ninety IceWorms moved in first. Men in buildings closest to the northern outskirts of the town heard the sound first, a frightful slithering and screeching as the Worms hunched and scraped their way through the frozen streets.

No one assayed forth to attack them. Even if they had, archers would have lowered their bows in horror.

Like his Skraelings, Gorgrael had been working on the IceWorms over the past few months. In unrestrained narcissism, he had created all of his creatures with the huge silver eyes that he himself enjoyed.

The only problem, and it had been the problem that had largely frustrated Gorgrael's attempts to push south to this point, had been that all of his creatures, whether Skraeling or IceWorm or even SkraeBold, had been terribly vulnerable through their eyes.

Not so now. Now both Skraelings and IceWorms had their heads wrapped in bony armor that left only narrow slits over their eyes. Their vision was somewhat restricted, but it would take a skilled and extremely calm swordsman or archer to deliver a killing thrust.

Behind the IceWorms crept thousands of Skraelings, fully fleshed, equipped with bony protective armor, their mouths hanging open in delicious anticipation of the killing that awaited them.

Calmly, and with the most supreme confidence, the IceWorms crawled to the main buildings where most of the troops were likely to be located. Crouched behind one of the lower windows of the market hall where he was camped, Jorge was dry-mouthed with fear. He knew he was powerless to stop their attack; all he could do for his men was order them away from the windows and to the lower floors.

But what did it matter when it would delay their deaths but a few minutes?

He glanced behind him to the remainder of the Icarii wing. "Get out!" he rasped, "get back to Carlon. You alone will have a chance of escape. Tell your StarMan what you have seen here today. Go!" he shouted. "Do not linger!"

The Wing commander, RuffleCrest JoyFlight, signaled to the other seven Icarii. He did not share Jorge's belief that they would get back to Carlon. Surely Gorgrael would have Gryphon circling above—and RuffleCrest had seen what a Gryphon could do. But he nodded anyway. Perhaps one or two of them could get back.

They swiftly moved to a rear door and lifted on silent wings into the air. They blinked in the unexpected sunshine, circled for as long as they dared, noting the awesome forces that were crawling through the town and, farther west, through the northern Aldeni plains, then they bunched close together for protection and sped south.

To the north Timozel's eyes narrowed. So. He had expected such a foolish display of courage. Did they really expect to escape unscathed?

SkraeFear, who waited with one of the Skraeling units still outside Jervois Landing, screeched in his mind. *Let us destroy them, Lord Timozel! Or send the Gryphon! They can rip them to shreds in seconds!*

Fool! Timozel replied and drew on the well of power that Gorgrael had given him to wrap SkraeFear's mind and body with bands of cold steel. He could feel, if not hear, SkraeFear scream far below him. How had Gorgrael managed with such incompetents previously?

He touched the minds of a pack of thirty Gryphon circling to the west and directed them after the Icarii. *But I want one or two of them to escape,* he ordered, and he felt the Gryphon minds accept and agree. At least the Gryphon understood the principle of unquestioning obedience.

The Icarii birdwoman at RuffleCrest's wing felt rather than heard the Gryphon behind them. She wheeled to her left and dived with a wordless cry, and as the Gryphon pack struck the Icarii. Wing, the birdmen and -women broke formation, desperately trying to evade the Gryphon and, increasingly, engaged in useless battles for their own lives.

One after another they felt the Gryphon on their backs, felt the great legs wrap about their bodies, felt talons and razor-sharp beaks rip into flesh.

RuffleCrest felt the sudden rush of air and hot breath as a Gryphon fell through the air toward him, and he desperately twisted and dived, hoping that he would prove more agile than the creature behind him. He groped for an arrow from the quiver on his back, but just as his hand closed about the shaft of an arrow he was seized in the death grip of the Gryphon.

He screamed, but he could do nothing more. One arm was twisted and trapped beneath the body of the Gryphon as it clutched to his back—agony flared as the unnatural forces twisting his arm finally snapped both bone and tendon. His other hand grasped uselessly at one of the great paws that were wrapped about his chest and belly. His wings fluttered uselessly; the only thing that kept him in the air now were the powerful wings of the Gryphon.

To one side RuffleCrest could see another Gryphon clutching a birdwoman in a death grip. Even in the split second that his eyes remained on the woman the Gryphon's talons sheared through flesh and bone, and before his eyes the woman literally burst apart in a shower of blood and body parts.

The last thing he saw before he closed his eyes in horror was the carcass of his comrade falling through the sky.

The Gryphon tightened its grip, and RuffleCrest realized that at any heartbeat its talons would begin to tear him apart.

And indeed they did begin to tear, but they did not inflict fatal wounds. A whimper of pain escaped RuffleCrest as he felt the Gryphon's talons slice into the muscles of his chest and belly, but they did not penetrate to a to a killing depth. After raking him with its talons for several minutes, slowly, extending its enjoyment, the Gryphon unbelievably released him, and RuffleCrest fell almost a hundred paces through the air before he recovered enough to spread his wings and push himself as hard as he could for the south.

Five of the hellish creatures chased him and toyed with him for several leagues, RuffleCrest sobbing with fear, certain that at any moment one would strike and finish him.

But they didn't. Eventually they left him alone, and when RuffleCrest finally looked back it was to see that the sky behind him was empty of both Gryphon and Icarii.

He was the only one of his Wing who had survived.

Hugging his crippled arm to his chest, RuffleCrest slowly limped south. The flight would take him several days, and he would be almost dead from exhaustion and the spreading poison from his infected wounds when he finally reached safety.

In his more lucid moments, he wondered why he had been left alive.

Almost immediately after the Icarii had fled, the IceWorms staged an attack. Rearing their monstrous heads, they crashed through the upper windows of the

buildings that they ringed, heaving obscenely to disgorge their cargos of Skraelings directly into the buildings' upper levels.

At the same time the Skraeling units outside attacked the ground floors
through doors and windows. And, as the IceWorms, empty, their task done,
withdrew from the streets and joined their companions to the west, hundreds
of Gryphon exploded through windows.

The attacks by the IceWorms, Skraelings and Gryphon occurred so close
together that to Jorge it sounded like one continuous roar. He heard the windows in the upper levels of the market hall explode first, then, an instant later,
the screams of both wraiths and men as the ground-floor windows shattered.
Gripping his sword in hands so cold they were virtually numb, feeling the icy
air sear his lungs as he took a deep breath, Jorge stepped forward to meet the
first Skraeling who leaped his way.

May his Star Gods help him, Jorge thought as he kept the bony-armored
Skraelings at bay with well-placed strokes of his sword, desperately seeking an
opening for a killing thrust. Even Axis will be hard pressed to defeat such as
these.

And, even more worrying than their new appearance, where had they
learned their newfound discipline? Today's attack on Jervois Landing had been
well planned and well coordinated as no Skraeling attack had been previously.
What had they learned? Jorge wondered as his breath came in short gasps and
his arms began to tremble with weariness. And who have they learned it from?

Out of the corners of his eyes Jorge could see his men dying about him.
Gryphon were creeping down the stairs, launching themselves on terrified victims and tearing them apart in heartbeats.

I do not want to die! Jorge's mind cried, but he knew that his death was
inevitable. Would the Skraeling eat him after it had killed him? Strangely, Jorge
found that thought even more horribly repellent than the idea of death itself.
An honorable warrior deserved an honorable burial.

"You are right, Jorge," said a voice, and a hand appeared on the Skraeling's
shoulder.

Jorge stared in disbelief at the man who stood before him. How . . . how
did he stand so safe and relaxed among this cursed horde?

Timozel smiled at Jorge, then casually glanced about the room to watch
the Skraelings and Gryphon butcher those few men remaining alive. Finally
he turned his eyes back to the man before him.

"Honorable men deserve honorable deaths," Timozel said, slightly stressing
the first "honorable." "But you and yours hardly fight for an honorable cause.
Do you not fight with the Forbidden, cursed and evil creatures that they are?
And do you not fight for Axis, spawn of the Forbidden?"

"And who do you fight for, Timozel?"

Again Timozel smiled, and Jorge could see the cold cruelty in the man's eyes. "I serve the savior, Jorge. Gorgrael. *I* will see that he triumphs. I will free Achar from the horror that grips it."

Jorge's hands, nerveless with terror at Timozel's words, let his sword clatter to the floor. "Have you gone *mad*, Timozel?" he whispered.

"Not at all, Earl Jorge," Timozel said, leaning down and retrieving the man's sword. "I have come entirely to my senses."

Then, teeth gleaming, he ran Jorge through the belly with his own sword, gave it a vicious twist, and left him to collapse and die on the floor.

As Timozel turned away, Jorge rolled onto his side, knowing from the breathtaking pain knifing through his body that he was dying. He wrapped his hands about the blade and made a half-hearted attempt to pull it out.

But the pain was too great, and Jorge lay still, watching with graying vision as Timozel communed with his nightmare commander.

"Axis," Jorge whispered with his last breath, and this time it *was* a prayer. *Avenge me!*

At the last, Jorge had found his god.

It is done, Master.

Good, Timozel. Was it fun?

Did you not watch, Master?

Ah, yes, I watched and I revelled. But, did you find it fun?

Timozel smiled. *Yes, yes and yes again. I think I will bathe in blood tonight.*

And now you will move south?

Yes. Now I will lay the trap for Axis.

Good, good boy. Pretty boy. You serve me well.

10

RuffleCrest Speaks

Two days later, a Flight of three Wing scouting high over the Western Ranges almost forty leagues above Carlon, saw a black spot drifting slowly over the mountain peaks far below them. The Wing-Leaders, wary that attack from Gorgrael was considered likely any day now, ordered their commands to approach slowly and carefully. They did not want to be lured into a trap.

But as they spiraled down and their far-seeing eyes focused on the spot, their commander, the recently promoted Crest-Leader SpikeFeather TrueSong, gave a wordless cry and beat his wings powerfully to reach his stricken comrade so far below.

SpikeFeather, having survived a Gryphon attack previously, recognized the sight and smell of Gryphon wounds well before the others in his Flight.

They caught Ruffle Crest only minutes before he would have fallen, exhausted, from the sky, and they carried him in turns back to Carlon. There they took him directly to their StarMan, startling him as he sat at supper with the Enchantress in the Jade Chamber. Then they stood back, unspeaking, waiting for the StarMan to weave his enchantments on their dying comrade.

Only because RuffleCrest *was* dying was Axis able to aid him. He gathered the birdman, his torso streaked with crimson and green lines of infection, as he had once gathered SpikeFeather, and he sang for him the Song of Recreation.

Then, as RuffleCrest blinked, surprised, back to life, Axis directed that he be carried to a chamber where he could rest the night. He would speak with him in the morning.

Axis, as Azhure, did not need to speak with RuffleCrest to know what news he carried.

Axis had personally appointed RuffleCrest JoyFlight to lead the single Wing at Jervois Landing.

"Say again what you saw, RuffleCrest."

RuffleCrest bowed his head in shame. He sat at the great circular table in the Privy Chamber, and about him sat Crest-Leaders, Princes, Chieftains, Enchanters and, halfway around the table from him, the StarMan himself, the Enchantress by his side. He had never been in such exalted company before, and he could feel their power keenly.

And, to his utter disgrace, he could hardly remember a thing.

He did not know that much the same had happened to SpikeFeather TrueSong when Axis had re-created him. SpikeFeather and his Wing had been returning to Sigholt from a scouting mission over Hsingard when they had been attacked by a pack of Gryphon, only SpikeFeather and Evensong, Axis' sister, had survived, yet SpikeFeather had been so badly injured that by the time EvenSong had got him home to Sigholt he had been heartbeats away from death. But he had been lucky, as RuffleCrest had been, for Axis SunSoar was there to greet him and to re-create him.

SpikeFeather had remembered nothing of the attack that had all but killed him.

"I can recall so little," RuffleCrest said, and to one side FarSight CutSpur, the senior Crest-Leader of the Icarii Strike Force, leaned forward and motioned irritably for RuffleCrest to speak up.

RuffleCrest's face reddened in mortification, and he repeated his words in a louder voice. "I can recall so little, StarMan." In his lap, hidden by the table, his hands twisted around and about each other. "I can recall Jervois Landing being struck by an ice tempest so appalling that four of my Wing were frozen midair. I can remember day after day huddled about fires, unable even to step outside for fear of instant death in the winds. I remember . . ." his voice faltered and FarSight frowned. RuffleCrest hurriedly cleared his throat and went on. "I remember a sudden calm, and I remember Earl Jorge shouting at me to fly to Carlon with a message for you, but I cannot remember what that message was. I am ashamed to admit my incompetence," he finished on a whisper. "I should have died with my command."

Axis stood up, remembering SpikeFeather's experience. He walked about the table, his commanding presence pulling every eye to him.

RuffleCrest blinked, awed that this powerful man should regard him so kindly.

"RuffleCrest," Axis said as he reached the birdman. "It is hardly your fault that you do not recall. I probably muddled your memory when I re-created you, and if anyone should writhe so in mortification it should be I, not you."

"You saved my life, StarMan."

"Aye, that I did," Axis said, placing a restraining hand on RuffleCrest's shoulder to prevent him from rising. "And because of the life that currently suffuses you, I will be able to recall the memory of what happened for all gathered in this chamber. A small enchantment, RuffleCrest, do not tense so."

But RuffleCrest had tensed in excitement rather than nervousness. He would trust the StarMan with his life—had done so—and if the StarMan could help him recall what everyone about this table needed to know, then RuffleCrest would be indebted to him twice over.

Axis stood behind RuffleCrest, resting both his hands on the birdman's shoulders, and began to sing. All the six Enchanters present recognized the Song of Recall that he sang, but it was sung with such consummate skill and power that most were left agape with astonishment, even StarDrifter. Every time his son demonstrated his power it left StarDrifter almost breathless, sometimes with pride, oftentimes with envy.

The air over the center of the table shimmered and formed a gray haze. Everyone's eyes turned from Axis to the vision appearing before them. In the gray haze appeared the form of Jorge, twisting away from the window as he shouted at RuffleCrest to get his Wing out of Jervois Landing. Every military commander in the room, Axis and Azhure among them, involuntarily winced at the fear and desperation on Jorge's face. Perhaps Jorge had erred in staying by Borneheld's side for so long, but he was an exceptional commander and a brave man, and if so much fear twisted his features and clouded his eyes then it surely meant that Jorge knew his death was close.

Then the view shifted and changed, and the watchers flew with RuffleCrest as he lifted the remaining seven of his Wing out of the building and circled briefly above the town.

"Mother!" Belial cried as he saw what horror invaded the town.

Of them all, only RuffleCrest did not see, for Axis had worked the enchantment so that the birdman would not re-live the horror that had almost killed him.

They flew with RuffleCrest as he led his Wing south, and each and every one of the watchers paled when the Wing was attacked by the Gryphon. As they saw with RuffleCrest's eye the birdwoman explode in a shower of red spray, Axis cut off the enchantment. They had all seen enough.

He glanced at Azhure. Although pale, she, seemed composed.

RuffleCrest looked about the table. "Did it work?" he asked, puzzled by the distress evident on the faces about him.

Axis patted his shoulder. "Yes, RuffleCrest, it worked well. You have done remarkable duty in bringing us this message, and for your bravery I thank you and honor you."

RuffleCrest flushed with pride, but he could also hear dismissal in the words, and knew that the commanders in this room would prefer to discuss his message privately.

He stood, and Axis took his hand and arm briefly. "You will need to rest, RuffleCrest. Your body and spirit still have to heal after the trauma you have endured."

RuffleCrest saluted Axis, then the commanders about the table, then he turned and left the room. All could feel his relief as he finally slipped through the door.

"Well, my friends?" Axis said.

Belial took a deep breath. "Jervois Landing would have been destroyed in under half an hour with the force that invaded it."

"We could all see from the aerial views," Magariz said, "how the canals were frozen and how the Skraelings and IceWorms had invaded the town from just about every avenue. Neither Jorge nor his command would have been able to resist."

"And Jorge knew that," Azhure said. "He knew he was going to die. I am glad for his sake that RuffleCrest managed to get through."

Axis sat back down. "How long ago?" he asked. "How long ago did Jervois Landing fall? FarSight, how long would it take for someone in RuffleCrest's condition to fly south to the Western Ranges?"

FarSight thought. "Perhaps two or three days, StarMan. He would hardly have rested, so desperate would he have been to escape as far as he could from the Gryphon."

"No rest?" Belial was amazed. How could a birdman, almost crippled, fly for two or three days without rest?

"All birdmen have deep reserves of stamina, far more than humans," replied HoverEye BlackWing, one of the senior Crest-Leaders present. "Besides, there would have been a wind at his back. Much of the time RuffleCrest would have drifted in the air currents, almost asleep."

"So," Axis said, focusing everyone's attention back on the critical issue. "Four days ago at most Jervois Landing was attacked and destroyed by a massive Skraeling force. They must have moved—"

"Axis," Magariz interrupted. "Can you recall that vision with RuffleCrest gone?"

Axis nodded.

"There was something about the Skraelings that I saw when RuffleCrest was in the air. Can you recall it?"

Magariz's voice was urgent, and Axis quickly recalled the vision of Jervois Landing and its surroundings, half of the Skraeling force still massed outside the town, the other half penetrating deeply between the houses.

"Yes," Magariz said. "Yes! Axis, my friends. *Look* at the Skraeling force. What is it that is so different about them?"

"Well," Azhure began, "the Skraelings themselves are different. Axis and I saw Skraelings in Hsingard that looked like this. Fully fleshed, almost armored with those bony protuberances. Magariz, we told you about this."

"Yes, yes, I know of that, but this is not what I mean," Magariz said. "Come now, surely you can see it?"

Understanding suddenly replaced the confusion on Axis' face. "By the Stars, Magariz! That is not a *mass* of Skraelings at all. Look, here and here and here," his finger stabbed into the gray vision as it hung over the table, "they are formed into regular units. This is an army under tight discipline, not the chaos that we have been used to previously."

"Yes," Magariz said. "Gorgrael has got himself a good WarLord, it seems."

"I cannot imagine any of his SkraeBolds effecting this remarkable transformation," Axis said, frowning as he thought this through.

Azhure suddenly remembered WolfStar's comment about the Traitor of the third verse of the Prophecy having already made his move. She chewed her lip anxiously. She had yet to tell Axis of the encounter and resolved to do so this evening. Had the Traitor done this? And if so, *who* was he?

"Look!" FarSight cried, living up to his name. "Look to the west. This is not the main force attacking Jervois Landing at all, but merely a detachment from the force that is already moving south into Aldeni!"

Everyone looked to where he pointed. Axis went gray with shock. A massive column (and *column* again, not a seething mass) of Skraelings and Ice-Worms were slowly moving across the frozen system of canals.

"Are there anymore shocks for me?" he asked, desperate to end the hateful vision, but only after they had gleaned all the information from it they could.

For a few minutes longer they stared into the visionary landscape before them, then, one by one, they shook their heads. RuffleCrest had not circled for long; it was a miracle that his mind had stored this much information.

"Well," Axis said as he stopped the enchantment and the vision faded from view. "We march. It is all we can do."

"Where?" FarSight inquired politely, but with a discernible edge to his voice.

"North!" snapped Axis. "And exactly *where* north above the Western Ranges I will rely on your farflight scouts to tell me!"

Later that day, Axis and Azhure stood by the open windows of the Indigo Chamber, the chamber they used as their sleeping apartment. The sun had set many hours ago, but moonlight sparkled across Grail Lake and a soft breeze blew in their faces.

Together with the rest of the commanders they had spent the afternoon and early evening completing the plans to move Axis' army north. Military preparations were already well under way, and in the morning the extended supply column would head for the Western Ranges. Within a day at the most, the ground force would begin their long trek north. A day after that the bulk of the Strike Force would follow; several Wings were to be left in Carlon as a protection force and to assist the Icarii in their move south.

"I will soon be gone," Axis said.

Azhure sighed. "My squads of archers will work well under Ho'Demi's command, Axis. They have trained extensively with the Ravensbund archers these past months, and I trust Ho'Demi more than any other to use them well."

Axis nodded. "Well, you will not lack for company while I am gone. Both Rivkah and Ysgryff can assist you."

Although Ysgryff was a valued commander. Axis did not want to risk every commander he had in the ride north. Besides, Ysgryff could make himself just as useful here.

Now Azhure laughed and Axis frowned at her, puzzled.

"I was just thinking, Axis, here I am being left in charge of a realm when . . . what some two years ago I was but the daughter of the Plow-Keeper of an isolated Skarabost village."

Axis smiled too. Once Azhure had worried that, as a peasant woman, she had no place by Axis' side, but he knew now that she was beyond that old concern.

"I sensed some of your thoughts this morning while we sat in council," Axis said, becoming serious again, and Azhure lifted her head. "You want to tell me something."

Azhure turned away from the view and looked into Axis' eyes. How she would miss him when he was gone! "I will not stay in Carlon for long, Axis."

"I know, Azhure," he said. "You will go to the Island of Mist and Memory."

Azhure started. "How did you know that?"

"You have been fixated on the island ever since you remembered Niah's message to go to Temple Mount to find the answers about your father."

"Yes, but there is more."

"Spiredore?"

She turned away; how could she keep anything from him? Axis caught his breath at the beauty of her profile in the moonlight, and he reached out and lightly touched a tendril of her hair where it drifted about her neck.

"Yes, Spiredore. Axis, I spoke with WolfStar while I was there."

Again, Axis had guessed as much. Azhure had been very introspective since that day she'd spent in Spiredore.

"He told me that I would discover much of my power there." Briefly Azhure informed Axis of what WolfStar had said about the ring and the power it represented.

"Well, I hope you can uncloak some of your mysterious past on the island, Azhure. I hope you discover more of who you are."

Azhure thought back to the expression on WolfStar's face as he stared at the ring. "He was stunned to see me wearing the ring, Axis. Stunned."

Axis put his arm about her shoulders. "I find it reassuring to discover that WolfStar can still be surprised."

Azhure leaned back into his arm, relishing its warmth. "He was also aghast that you—that we—should think he was the Traitor of the third verse of the Prophecy."

Axis frowned. "Do you believe him?"

"Yes," she said. "Yes, I do. I think that the Traitor is the one who has reorganized Gorgrael's armies for him."

Axis did not speak. For so long he had assumed that the Traitor of the Prophecy, the one who would betray him to Gorgrael, was WolfStar. But if not WolfStar, then who?

"He said that the Traitor had already made his move, that he was already with his master, but that he had not yet committed the final betrayal."

Axis shivered, and he wondered what lay ahead for him. "Azhure, Star-Drifter will undoubtedly want to go to the Island of Mist and Memory with you."

"Oh, Axis! Surely not!" Irritated, Azhure moved away from the circle of Axis' arms and into the room. The last thing she needed was StarDrifter making a nuisance of himself.

"Axis," she turned back to look at his dark outline by the window. "I need to be by *myself* on the island. I don't need StarDrifter there!"

As relieved as he was by her reaction, Axis also had to plan for every eventuality. And, if things did not go well in the north . . .

"Azhure, whatever happens you will hardly be by yourself. There are thousands of pirates. There are the Priestesses of the Order of the Stars. FreeFall and EvenSong are at the Temple already."

FreeFall and EvenSong had moved there almost immediately after Axis and Azhure had married. Since his return from death, FreeFall had become increasingly given to the mystical, and EvenSong had been excused from her duties in the Strike Force to go with him. No one wanted to separate them again.

"And there will undoubtedly be scores of Icarii Enchanters, and perhaps ordinary Icarii, who will fly down to the island in the near future. Azhure, it will shortly be as crowded on that island as it is here in Carlon."

"But . . . *StarDrifter!*" Azhure knew that StarDrifter still hungered for her, that he had never recovered from his disappointment and anger when Azhure had chosen Axis on that Beltide night eighteen months ago. He had never ceased to let Azhure know that he still wanted her, and that, should the opportunity arise.

"Azhure." Axis walked over and took her gently by the shoulders. "Believe it or not, I have good reason for wanting StarDrifter to go with you."

He could see by the expression on her face that she did not believe him, or did not want to believe him.

"I will not be there for the twins' birth, my love. And you know that without an Icarii blood relative to talk them through all three of you could die."

All Icarii babies, aware well before they were born, were terrified by the process of birth and needed one of their parents to reassure them and talk them through. Rivkah had almost died in Axis' birth because StarDrifter was not there for them.

"I will surely be in touch with my own power by then," Azhure said. "I will talk them through."

"And if you're not? And even if you are, Azhure, we both know that neither of these babies particularly likes us. Would they listen to you? Listen to *them*, now!"

He paused, and both felt the feelings of resentment and hostility that emanated from their unborn twins. Every day those feelings increased.

"When they were forced to endure what we both went through the day I broke through the block in your mind," Axis said, "they must have been wounded gravely. It twisted their perception of us."

"But why do they dislike *me* so?" Azhure said, her hand on her belly. It was so unfair, she thought, after she had fought to keep them through this long, difficult, lonely pregnancy. How many times could she have just let them slip from her body?

Axis was silent a long moment. "Because you forgave me and because you chose to continue to love me," he finally said very softly. "*That* is why they cannot forgive you."

Azhure stared at him, feeling instinctively that he was correct, but hating the explanation.

"And *that* is why you need StarDrifter, Azhure. Already he spends an hour or two singing to them each day. They like him, they trust him, and they will listen to him. Damn it! I ask you to let StarDrifter talk them through the birth not for his sake, not even for the babies' sakes, but for *yours*!"

Axis cupped her face in his hands. Stars! How difficult this was to say, but how desperately it needed to be said. They might not have much longer together, and Axis could not shake his growing premonition of doom.

"Azhure, you know how much I love you."

Azhure smiled. "You do not need to tell me, Axis, I—"

"Shush, beloved, and listen to what I say to you now. There is a second, far more important reason why I want StarDrifter to accompany you to the Island of Mist and Memory. StarDrifter and I may have had our differences and our envies, but he is my father, and I love and trust him. Azhure, each day I feel a sense of doom growing stronger and stronger within me. No! *Listen* to me. I do not know if I can defeat this force that masses to the north. This morning we both saw its size, strength and effectiveness. If I cannot master my powers before we meet, then I fear that we will be defeated."

"No, Axis!" Azhure breathed in horror, her eyes wide, but he carried on relentlessly.

"Azhure, as enchanting as they are, my powers are pitifully ineffective for what I ride to meet. I could hardly touch the small Skraeling force that Gorgrael sent down the WildDog Plains, and the force I now go to meet is five thousand times that size."

"Axis!" Azhure moaned desperately, hating the shadow of defeat in his eyes. "You have Belial and Magariz and Ho'Demi and the Strike Force—"

Axis laughed harshly. "They will fight just as bravely and they will die just as quickly as Jorge did, Azhure. Now, *if* anything happens to me in the north, if I fail—"

"Then I will have no further reason to live!"

His hands tightened about her face. "No! You *must* go on living, for my sake and for our children's sake and for the sake of Tencendor."

He paused, and what he said next he said only with the greatest difficulty and between clenched teeth. "Azhure, if I die, then let StarDrifter love and support you. He loves you, you are both SunSoar so you will be happy together, and he will be a good father to my children."

"*No!*" Azhure cried, striking his chest with a clenched fist, trying to twist out of his hands.

But Axis was far stronger, and he held her firmly. "Yes, yes and *yes!* You will need advice and help and strength and love, and StarDrifter can give you all of these. Azhure, listen to me," he said, grinding the words out now. "If I die then seek refuge in Coroleas. There you will be safe. There you can plan for the future—whatever that might be."

Azhure wept, not because Axis had planned for the future should he die, but because of the defeat she heard in his voice. Axis *expected* to die!

After a moment Axis gathered her close, and they stood gently rocking under the shadows of the moon for a very long time, the waters of Grail Lake lapping a hundred paces below their feet.

11

The Repository of the Gods

That night the five gathered on the deserted northern shore of Grail Lake: Jack, the senior among them, Zeherah, Ogden, Veremund and Yr.

Yr, who was to visit the Repository of the Gods.

She was the first, and the others envied her, feared for her, and mourned with her. But she was the youngest, the strongest and the most vital, so it was fitting that she go first. She would have the farthest to travel and yet would have the best chance of reaching her destination.

They stood in a line, using rarely touched reserves of power to cloak their activities so that they would not be disturbed.

Jack waited until the moon floated fat and powerful above them. "It is time," he said, and the others sighed.

"Time," Yr echoed softly.

"Time," said a melodious voice behind them, and the five turned to see who spoke.

Yr's eyes filled with tears, honored and gratified that the Prophet should wish to witness her sacrifice.

He stood there in his full glory, such as none—not even Jack—had seen him before. He had assumed his Icarii wings, and they could see that the Prophet was an Icarii Enchanter of such power and magnitude that he would humble all those who sought to oppose him.

He was almost indistinguishable from the moonlight, for he wore a close-fitting silver suit that seemed to have been molded to his body. It was of a material such as the five had never seen before, a closely woven, silvery gray, with glints of blue in its creases and curves that flashed whenever he moved. Behind him glowed great silver wings.

The five bowed to him, and the Prophet himself bowed and acknowledged their service. They had done well, better than he could ever have expected, and his violet eyes were moist with gratitude.

He nodded slightly at Jack—it was time to begin.

"Friend and sister Yr," Jack said, his voice as gentle as the waves that lapped at their feet, his hands folded before him. "There are few words that need to be said at this time. Our entire service has been for this point, which will, in turn, lead us to the final conflagration. We have all served as best we could. We have watched and waited and, since the Prophecy began to walk, we have guided. We have served to the best of our ability."

For some time they were all silent, the Prophet standing slightly behind them.

"I would like to speak some words," Yr finally said. "I harbor a myriad of regrets," she began, her eyes on the moonlight as it skittered across the waters of Grail Lake. "A myriad."

None of the others, and certainly not the Prophet, begrudged Yr her regrets.

"A myriad," she said yet again, almost inaudibly. "I have enjoyed life in this OverWorld, although at times it has been petty and irritating. But I have made friends, friends whom I will now have to leave. Friends whom I may have no chance to farewell as they deserve. Friends whom I will miss and who will miss me."

The others watched, their eyes shining with unshed tears. They shared her regret. They had never, never thought to have made friends on their journey.

"I have even learned to love a little," Yr said. "I shall miss Hesketh, and I regret that in the morning he will wake and I will not be there, and he will never know where I have gone. I fear that he will mourn me for a very long time and that he will spend the rest of his life wondering why I left like I did. Wondering if I was well or in need of help."

Her mouth trembled. "It is unfair to him to end it this way with no explanations and no goodbyes."

The others listened and watched.

Yr took a deep breath, and its unsteadiness betrayed her emotion and fear. "I will miss my health most of all," she whispered.

Jack kissed her gently. "Be at peace, sister Yr. You will be the first among us to share the mysteries of the ancient gods of the stars."

The other three then stepped forward, kissing her and murmuring words of farewell. Tears streamed unashamedly down Ogden's and Veremund's cheeks. They would all see her again, but she would be changed and would continue to change—she would never again be the Yr they had known and loved for so long.

Finally the Prophet came forward, his silvery brilliance making them all blink. He rested his hands gently on Yr's shoulders and kissed her on the mouth.

"You will be beloved always for the sacrifice you now make," he said "And you will always rest in my heart. I could not have asked for better than you."

Yr smiled at him, tears slipping down her cheeks, but they were tears of joy rather than sadness.

"Yr." He smiled, and her breath caught at his beauty. "Yr, tonight you will discover one of the great mysteries of Grail Lake but you will need courage and fortitude to do so. Are you ready?"

"Yes, Prophet, I am ready."

He lifted one hand and ran it through her pale blond hair. "You will need my strength and my breath for the journey you are now about to undertake, Yr."

Then he leaned forward and kissed her again, powerfully.

When he stepped back Yr's tears had dried and she looked vigorous and certain.

"I have loved each of you," she said, then she walked to the water's edge.

She slipped out of her gown and stood naked for a few moments, letting the light of the moon wash over her. Then she raised both arms above her head, stretching her entire body and spreading her fingers in supplication. "Sister Moon," she cried, her voice joyful, "show me the path to the Repository of the Gods!"

Azhure murmured in her sleep and rolled over. Awakened, worried, Axis watched her carefully, but Azhure slipped back silently into her dreams and Axis closed his eyes and relaxed.

For a heartbeat nothing happened, then the moonlight that rippled over the waves flickered, faltered, then coalesced in one spot on the water a few paces in front of Yr.

"I thank you," she whispered, and she dived into the water.

She swam downward for a very long time, following the silver path of the moon. Her hair trailed behind her, glowing silver now itself, and her sharp blue eyes were open wide as she peered into the depths. On either side of her the water deepened from blue to indigo and then to black as she swam deeper and deeper into the mystery of Grail Lake.

She swam deeper than any human could, but then Yr was not human.

She swam longer than anyone had a right to without breathing, but then the Prophet had imbued her with his strength and his breath.

She swam even when others would have given up, sure that they were lost, but Yr believed, and that would see her through.

And always the silvery light of the moon showed Yr her path and guided her into the unknown depths of the lake.

The Charonites spoke of the legend when gods even more ancient than the Star Gods had made a gift of the Sacred Lakes. In a storm that lasted many days and nights, fire rained down from the sky and almost blasted all life from the land. When those few hardy souls who had survived emerged from the deep caves that had sheltered them, they had found lakes where before there were none, and mountains where before there had been only plains. They gazed at the lakes in awe, for then their waters were clearer than they are now, and in the depths they could see the vague outlines of what lay there.

It was said that the ancients themselves lay sleeping in the depths of the Sacred Lakes.

Now these legends were remembered only by the Charonites.

But Yr was privy to knowledge that other Charonites were not, and she believed, and so she swam on.

Just when she thought her strength would finally fail her, she saw lights glowing in the dark far below her. With her goal so near she pushed on with added resolve, despite the fact that her muscles were aching and weak and her lungs screamed for lack of air.

The Prophecy was so close, so close, to achieving fulfilment that Yr swam on, empowered for the final few strokes with the certainty of eventual success.

There!

The Repository lay directly below her, massive, almost totally buried in the silt. Only its smooth spherical top broke the surface of the lake bed, ringed around its outer surface with soft lights glowing in an infinity of different hues. Its skin was smooth and gray, and Yr knew that if it was exposed to strong light it would appear as silvery as the Prophet's suit or her hair as it floated out behind her.

Yr swam over the Repository, searching its immense surface for the opening that she knew must be there.

Ah! This must be it! Yr ran her hands over the smooth surface of the closed entrance, finding a dome of multicolored gems. Drawing on the instructions the Prophet gave her three thousand years ago, Yr carefully struck individual gems with her fingers, listening to the chimes they gave off, revelling in the beauty of the music they made.

Suddenly the music ceased and the dome sank below the surface of the outer skin of the Repository. In the next instant a circular door slid open and a pool of blackness appeared beneath her and, grateful beyond measure that soon she would be able to draw breath again, Yr gave a last powerful kick with her legs and dropped into it.

As soon as her feet had passed the level of the outer skin the circular door closed silently behind her and, praise the Prophet, the next moment the water drained out of the chamber she had entered. Scrambling to her feet, Yr stood for a very long time, hands on knees, gulping in sweet fresh air, her body recovering from its arduous dive.

Now that she was finally here Yr forgot her sadness and her regrets. As her body responded to the air and rest, a sense of sweet excitement filled her.

She straightened and looked about. The chamber was small and plain, but in the wall across from her was cut another circular door. She walked slowly over and spoke in a strange language, which the Prophet had told her was the language of the ancients, and the door slid open. A softly lit corridor stretched into infinity before her and, confident and joyous, Yr began to walk down it.

She continued for a long time and passed many strange things—chambers, caverns, closets and yet more corridors—but Yr knew her destination and she was not tempted to explore these other wonders.

She was going to the great Well of Power in the very heart of the Repository.

After walking some time Yr heard a dulcet song, hummed with almost breathless intensity, and she knew that she approached the Well. The magic that the Prophet had told her the ancient gods had once commanded fueled the Well of Power, but Yr had not thought that it would sing so beautifully.

Or with such deadliness.

She paused before an arched doorway, open and ringed with light. Inside she could hear the Well sing. Not even the Star Gate, she thought, sang this beautifully.

The chamber was circular, as was so much of this Repository, and in the very center sat the Well. Yr was surprised, for she had thought it would be a massive thing, but it was relatively small, about twice the circumference of a thickened body. Its walls stood waist high, and glowed golden with the Power they contained.

She walked over to the Well and stood there a while, staring at the golden Power within it, listening to its music. Then, sighing, she stepped forward so her lower body leaned against the walls, and plunged her arms and face into the Power that called to her.

When Yr surfaced the four watchers thought she had not changed at all. But when she stepped forth, they saw her blue eyes glittering strangely, brilliant with Power.

All longed to touch her, but they knew that to do so would be death. So they smiled sadly, nodded and silently filed away.

Yr, after retrieving her gown, followed at a distance of four or five paces.

They began the slow walk east.

12

Farewell

The crowds had lined the streets of Carlon since early morning. Today the great lord Axis, StarMan of all Tencendor, would lead his army north to defeat Gorgrael the Destroyer. Once he had fulfilled his destiny, all would live great and good lives, and there would be laughter and joy for time without end.

The air of excitement grew almost unbearable. Colorful flags fluttered from houses and shops alike, people leaned out windows, and street musicians attempted, in vain, to keep the crowd entertained.

The army waited in orderly units in the fields outside the city walls. Any air of excitement was notably absent among these men, for most were hardened veterans of the wars fought against Gorgrael and with each other over the past two years. But each and every one was proud to be there, and prepared to fight to the death for his StarMan. The core of the army was the twelve hundred former Axe Wielders who had fought with and behind Axis for many years. Their numbers were augmented by a variety of units, ranging from Ysgryff's mounted knights, the softly chiming Ravensbundmen, the infantry of Achar, militia from Arcen, sundry swords, pike and spearmen, to Azhure's squads of archers. All in all, not counting the Icarii Strike Force that would not fly out for another day yet, the army numbered some thirty-thousand men. All were impressively uniformed in gray, and all wore the blood-red blazing sun on their breasts.

The uniforms, like the emptied laundry hampers, were another of the minor miracles that had swept Carlon over recent days. Axis had always strived to have his men-at-arms clothed uniformly, and ever since Azhure had arrived in Sigholt over a year ago she had been directing needlewomen to sew suitable outfits. But in recent months Axis' army had grown to huge proportions, especially with the addition of seven or eight thousand men who had joined from Borneheld's defeated army, and there had not been the time or the thread to give every man a uniform.

Yet when each soldier had woken this morning, there at the foot of his bedrolls was a neatly folded uniform. Each one a perfect fit, each one a perfect match, each perfectly emblazoned for the rank of the man who would wear it, and each one perfectly unexplainable.

When a messenger, breathless with excitement, brought news of the miracle to the StarMan as he sat at breakfast with the Enchantress, Axis turned and looked at Azhure.

He raised his eyebrows, although he kept his face carefully neutral.

Azhure flushed and stared out the window. After a moment she spoke, her voice quiet.

"I had a dream last night. I dreamed I saw a glittering army arrayed in the fields outside Carlon. I dreamed they all wore perfectly matched gray uniforms, all with your sun blazing across their chests. And in the dream I bewailed the fact that there had not been enough time to fit out the entire army identically."

Axis stared at her for a very long time. "Then pray dream me a great victory," he said finally, his voice hoarse, and Azhure gazed at him, her eyes deep with longing.

"Then pray me the power to *control* my dreams," she said, "and I will do just that."

The Icarii Strike Force, uniformed in black, lined the balconies and parapets of the palace, their faces impassive, their wings extended slightly to ruffle in the breeze. They waited to farewell their Strike-Leader and his ground force, but they would join them soon. Several Wings had already flown to the lower Western Ranges to scout the north as best they could, trying to find the horde of Skraelings that they knew must be in Aldeni somewhere.

Inside the palace Azhure stood with Rivkah and Cazna in the stableyard, the three women waiting to farewell their husbands. Cazna, not yet nineteen and the horror of not knowing Belial's fate at Bedwyr Fort still fresh in her mind, was trembling as she fought to keep her emotions under control.

Azhure reached over and took one of her hands. She was fond of Cazna, and not only because, as Ysgryff's daughter, she was one of her newfound family—Niah, Azhure's mother, had been the elder sister of Ysgryff.

"Come now, Cazna, smile for your husband. You should not leave him with the memory of your tears."

Cazna's mouth jerked in a tight smile. She loved Belial desperately, and was terrified of the danger that he now rode to face. She wondered how Azhure and Rivkah could be so composed.

The other two women had said their private farewells to their husbands earlier; Rivkah was now formally married to Magariz, for they had taken their marriage vows before their friends the day after Axis and Azhure had married.

None of the witnesses had realized that the smile both Rivkah and Magariz wore was not only because of their love for each other, but also because this was for them a renewal of their vows. Long ago, as impetuous teenagers, they had bribed a Brother of the Seneschal to marry them the day before Rivkah's father forced her north to marry Duke Searlas of Ichtar.

Azhure squeezed Cazna's hand reassuringly as the girl composed her face. She was a beautiful girl, greatly resembling Azhure, and would mature into yet greater loveliness. Azhure prayed that Belial gave the girl the love she deserved.

Boots sounded in the doorway a few paces away and all three women tensed. Axis and his senior ground force commanders, Belial, Magariz and Ho'Demi, stepped into the courtyard, cloaks flaring as they pulled on their riding gloves, their faces grim and silent. Arne followed a pace behind them, his eyes on Axis' back. Waiting for them was a small escort of a hundred mounted men-at-arms carrying standards and trumpets—they would make a good enough showing to please the crowds outside.

As Ho'Demi walked to his horse, Azhure glanced at the Ravensbund Chief, envying his wife Sa'Kuya who would be riding into war alongside her husband.

Axis paused by the group of three women. He and Azhure had said all they had to say to each other, but Axis was not going to waste another opportunity to drink in her beauty.

He did not know if he would ever see her again.

"I wish you well," was all he said as he leaned forward to kiss her briefly on the mouth in farewell.

And I you.

Magariz farewelled Rivkah just as briefly, although Belial lingered to murmur to Cazna. She nodded and smiled for him, then Belial joined the others at their horses. They mounted swiftly, the horses' hooves skittering impatiently on the cobbles of the courtyard, and Axis turned Belaguez for a final look at Azhure.

You will *prevail!* she whispered with her mind's voice and Axis stared at her, then nodded briefly.

I cannot wait until I see you again.

Then he swung Belaguez's head for the archway into the streets beyond and dug his heels into the stallion's flanks. Snorting with excitement, Belaguez plunged through the archway, the other riders close behind, the cheers of the crowds already rising to greet them.

For some time Azhure stood there, her heart beating wildly in her breast, then she turned back to the doorway. She would go straight to her apartments, she thought, for she could not bear to watch him ride away.

When she lifted her eyes, Azhure saw that StarDrifter stood in the doorway, staring at her.

13

Upstairs Downstairs

Faraday and Embeth traveled slowly to Tare, seeing only a few sheep and pig herders along the way. Faraday stayed only two days in Tare. Embeth pleaded with her to stay longer, but memories of Axis were too vivid, and Faraday wanted to escape them as soon as she could. Besides, the further east she went, the more persistent became the feeling that she should begin to plant the seedlings from the Enchanted Wood. So Faraday bid a tearful Embeth farewell and set off for the Silent Woman Woods with her two donkeys.

This was the first time Faraday had ever been alone, and, day by day, loneliness became an increasingly crushing burden that she could scarcely endure. Every night, as she sat by her solitary fire, Faraday had to fight not to give in to tears.

"Mother!" she muttered to herself one night. "You will have to spend months planting out the seedlings in the lonely reaches of western Tencendor. Will you fret like a baby for its teat the whole way?"

On the morning of her third day out from Tare, Faraday's isolation was relieved by the unexpected company of three Icarii Enchanters; but even their company proved a two-edged sword.

The Enchanters hailed her from the air, then dropped down to speak with her. Faraday recognized them from the eight days she had spent with Axis in Carlon—BrightStar FeatherNest, StarShine EvenHeart and PaleStar Snap-Wing. They chatted an hour or more, the Enchanters wondering why she was traveling eastward so alone.

"I merely play my part in the Prophecy," Faraday said, and the Enchanters nodded. They knew Faraday was Tree Friend.

The Enchanters were on their way back to Carlon from the Bracken Ranges where they had been involved in the recovery of the Icarii cities, and they extended to Faraday a gracious invitation to stay with the Icarii should she pass through the Ranges—or the Minaret Peaks, as they called the ranges now.

Faraday enjoyed the company of the three Enchanters, but was nevertheless glad when they made their goodbyes and flew west toward Tare. Their presence recalled too vividly the false happiness of those eight days in Carlon and, in the end, they reminded her all too clearly of what she'd lost.

On the afternoon of the fifth day out from Tare, as Faraday approached the Silent Woman Woods, she was gripped by such a black and all-consuming depression she had to consciously force herself on. For the past two days she'd lost all will to eat, and the only reason she had kept moving was because she knew that if she stayed in camp she would roll up in her blankets one night and never wake to see the dawn.

Some fifty paces from the dark tree line, Faraday stood, leaning on one of the donkeys for support, gazing blankly at the Woods. The wind was cold, biting through her cloak, but Faraday scarcely felt it. She was tired, very tired, and she tried to decide whether or not she would camp outside the Woods and enter in the morning, or risk walking through the trees in the darkness. Already the sun was starting to sink into the clouds on the western horizon.

It was the donkeys who decided her. The animal she leaned on put one hoof forward, then another, forcing Faraday to take a step, while the one behind her butted the woman's back with its head, pushing her forward yet another step. So, haltingly, the donkeys hauled, pushed and shoved her into the Silent Woman Woods.

The trees comforted Faraday the instant she stepped beneath their shelter. When Jack had brought her here so long ago the trees had shown her a vision of what she believed at the time to be Axis' death. That vision had horrified her, but the Song the trees now sang for her as she walked down the path toward the Keep was one of joy and compassion, haunting in its beauty yet passionate and full-blooded.

As soon as Faraday heard the Song a smile lit her face and her loneliness and depression dissipated. Within fifty paces her steps became light and she let go the mane of the donkey she had been holding.

"You are beautiful!" she cried, clasping her hands and swinging about in a full circle of delight. "Beautiful!"

One day, she thought rapturously, much of eastern Tencendor will sing like this!

When, as BattleAxe, Axis, his Axe-Wielders and Brother Gilbert had ridden through these woods they had found them dark and close, sharp branches blocking the path to scratch faces and hands, roots humping out of the ground to snag at their horses' hooves. Axis may have been the StarMan, but at that time he was still encased by the lies of the Seneschal, and he was accompanied by the loathsome Gilbert who would never break free of the lies that consumed him. The Woods had only allowed the four men passage after they had seized their axes within a hundred paces of entering them.

But the woman who now skipped down the path toward the Keep was Faraday Tree Friend, beloved of the Mother and of all creatures and beings of the Sacred Grove. So the trees sang joyously for her and the Woods appeared as spacious and as full of light and as mysteriously inviting as the Enchanted Woods themselves.

Axis and his companions had ridden for almost a day to reach the Keep, but Faraday thought she had been walking through the Woods for only an hour or so before she saw the golden glow of Cauldron Lake through the trees.

She paused in wonder at the Lake's edge, leaning down to run her fingers through such magical golden water that left her hand as dry as before she had dipped it in. A quarter of the way around the Lake sat the pale, yellow-stoned Keep, and Faraday smiled, for a warm glow gleamed from the windows and the door stood invitingly open. Even from this distance she felt that the Keep not only expected her, but yearned for her company.

At the Keep, Faraday unpacked and unsaddled the donkeys and they trotted around the back, there, no doubt, to find a warm stable and oats already waiting for them. Faraday stepped into the Keep and stopped dead, breathless with wonder.

Both Timozel and Axis had described its interior to her, and Faraday knew that what the Keep presented to her was vastly different to the interior it had shown the men. The huge, circular room was furnished comfortably with deep armchairs and couches, upholstered and cushioned in jeweled fabrics; tables and chairs, bookcases, chests and cabinets of rich amberwood; lamps and candlesticks of shining brass; patchwork comforters and patterned rugs scattered ankle-deep. To one side was a four-poster bed with a crazily stitched quilt thrown over it and feather pillows piled at its head. On the other side of the chamber a kitchen range glowed, the kettle only just beginning to sing, and a table set for one and laden with food in front of it. In the very center of the room a well-stoked fire crackled cheerfully on a round hearth, the copper hood above drawing away all traces of smoke. To one side stood a large box piled high with pine cones and knots of apple wood.

Faraday wandered farther into the Keep, her hands over her mouth, her eyes wide, and felt utterly and completely loved.

For a week the keep comforted and kept her. It was a time of deep healing, a time when she replenished her courage and fortitude. When she'd arrived that first night Faraday had eaten, then crept into bed fully clothed—so tired she could not be bothered disrobing—and had not awoken for almost eighteen hours. When she did awake it was to find that she was wearing a warm flannel nightgown and pink bedsocks, and that the kettle once again sang atop the range; next to it sat a deep pan of scrambled eggs and bacon warming for her breakfast. Toast and milk and pats of rich golden butter on thick white china plates sat on the table.

That day Faraday had done nothing but eat and sleep—a fresh meal ready for her whenever she awoke from a nap—but subsequent days she had spent in the Sacred Grove and Ur's nursery.

Today, the eighth since she had arrived, Faraday intended to spend luxuriating in the comfort that the Keep provided her. Perhaps she would explore the upper levels and read, if she could, some of the ancient Icarii texts that Ogden and Veremund said were secreted there. Faraday knew she would have to leave the Keep soon. She had now learned almost all the names of the seedlings in Ur's enchanting nursery, and once the last one was committed to memory she would resume her journey east—and begin to plant the Enchanted Wood back into this world.

But for now Faraday squirmed deeper into the armchair and wriggled her toes with sensual abandon before the fire. She slipped into a doze, only barely aware of the Keep about her.

Suddenly she blinked and snapped awake.

She could feel Azhure very, very close.

"Azhure?" Faraday said, rubbing her eyes fully awake. "Azhure, is that you?"

She was puzzled, but not in the least afraid.

Almost as depressed as Faraday had been when she arrived at the Silent Woman Woods, Azhure asked Hesketh, the captain of the palace guard, to row her across to Spiredore. Azhure wanted nothing more than to escape the confines of the palace at Carlon. The royal apartments, so beautiful and comforting when she had shared them with Axis, were now lonely and cold.

StarDrifter had been a constant companion. He was, apart from FreeFall who was already on the Island of Mist and Memory, the most senior of the Icarii present in southern Tencendor and, as such, was involved in much of the discussions and decisions regarding the Icarii nation's move south. As grandfather to Caelum and to the unborn twins and as a powerful Enchanter, StarDrifter also spent time training all three of Axis and Azhure's children. Those hours, in the evening or early morning, when StarDrifter came to the Jade Chamber to sit by Azhure's side, place his hands on her swollen belly and sing to the twins, were uncomfortable ones for Azhure. She would recall Axis' plea that if anything should happen to him she should marry StarDrifter, and Azhure wondered if Axis had said anything to his father. StarDrifter's face and thoughts gave nothing away and always he behaved with the utmost politeness when he was so intimately close to her, yet Azhure could never quite dismiss the thought that StarDrifter somehow hoped that one day his hands might touch her more intimately yet.

All in all, Azhure thought as she drifted across Grail Lake, it would be a pleasure to spend a relaxing afternoon in Spiredore. There was the possibility that WolfStar might appear, but Azhure did not particularly want to see him, and she thought that if she made her feelings known to Spiredore when she first stepped inside, then WolfStar might stay—or be kept—away.

Azhure carried Caelum with her, for over these past days she had not spent as much time with her delightful son as she had wished. The small row boat was also packed with the warm bodies of seven of the Alaunt hounds, including Sicarius. They had padded silently after her down the corridors of the palace and had leaped equally silently, but with discernible determination, into the row boat, eliciting a string of curses from Hesketh—who had then, embarrassed, begged Azhure's forgiveness.

Poor man, Azhure thought as they neared Spiredore's pier, he looks to be in the grip of an even blacker mood than me. A week ago, Yr and the rest of the Sentinels had disappeared and Azhure, as Axis and everyone else close to the Prophecy, had worried about their abrupt and secretive departure. Perhaps Hesketh, deeply emotionally involved with Yr, had worried the worst, and Azhure thought she might ask him to share a midday meal with her one day. Perhaps he only needed to talk.

Perhaps, Azhure decided as Hesketh helped her out of the boat, the Alaunt bounding across the grass toward Spiredore, he only needs Yr.

The interior of the tower was cool and pleasant, and Azhure smiled as she leaned against the closed door. The seven Alaunt were sniffing out every secret corner they could find, and Azhure thought they might find a lot in this most secretive of towers.

Are we going to the rooftop, Mama?

Azhure could detect the faint undertone of worry in Caelum's thoughts. No doubt her son, like herself, had some extraordinarily unpleasant memories of the rooftop of Spiredore.

"Another day, Caelum, but not today. I am too weary to climb all the way to the top."

Then what will we do?

Azhure hesitated. She had thought about this as she lay sleepless in her bed last night. Close to tears from her loneliness in the empty bed, feeling the indifference of the babies within her, Azhure had decided that she would start to experiment with the tower today. See the extent of its power.

She hoped she was doing the right thing. What if she *did* get lost?

She halted at the foot of the first staircase, her hand resting on the newel post, and called the Alaunt to her.

As they gathered about her skirts, Azhure again remembered WolfStar's words.

Decide where you want to go before you start to climb the stairs, and then the stairs will take you to that place.

"I want to go to a place where I will find some comfort," she said, then she started to climb.

The feeling that Azhure was close was now so strong that Faraday leaned forward in the armchair, balancing on its edge, ready to leap to her feet at any moment.

"Azhure? Azhure? Where are you?"

Azhure? Azhure? Where are you?

Azhure stopped climbing the instant she heard Faraday's voice, twisting and turning to peer into the heights above her. The stairs wound between crazily-canted balconies as far as she could see, and Faraday could be anywhere up there.

"Faraday?" she called "Faraday?" What was Faraday doing in Spiredore?

Azhure gathered her skirts in her free hand and climbed as fast as she could, Caelum going red in the face as her arm squeezed tight about him. Sicarius opened his mouth and bayed, his cries echoing through the infinite interior of Spiredore.

Faraday heard Azhure call and now she did leap to her feet. "Azhure!" She thought she could hear the faint baying of hounds.

Breathless with excitement and effort, Azhure reached a wide landing. She paused then spun about, frowning. There were no more stairs leading upward! What was this? A dead end?

"Faraday?" she cried. "I cannot find you. Can you hear me? Where are you?"

She stepped back down the stairs, certain she had missed her way.

Faraday heard footsteps on the circular iron stairway that wound into the heights of the Keep, and she rushed to its foot, laughing in excitement, grasping the iron railing and staring upward.

A great pale hound suddenly leaped down the curve of the steps and brushed past her, followed an instant later by six others. This was followed by a stillness on the stairs, but Faraday could hear the faint fall of footsteps above her.

"Azhure!" and the next moment Azhure, her face alive with amazement and happiness, stepped down into her arms.

Faraday hugged her tight, laughing delightedly, and for the next few moments the women did nothing but laugh and cry.

"How did you get here?" Faraday eventually asked.

"Where am I?" Azhure asked at the same time. *How did I get here? Can Spiredore transfer me from site to site as Axis' Enchanter powers can? Spire . . . Door?*

"We are in the Silent Woman Keep, Azhure. Come, sit by the fire, and we will discover this mystery in comfort." She linked her arm with Azhure's. "See! Already the Keep has laid out tea for us."

As Faraday led her across to a couch, Azhure glanced about the room, noting its comfort and welcome—and also noting that seven bowls of food had been laid out beside the kitchen range. The Alaunt already had their noses buried deep.

Azhure quickly told Faraday of the mysterious powers of Spiredore.

"These magical Keeps must be linked," Faraday said, then smiled. "But let us not waste our time talking of the Keeps. Come, let me cuddle Caelum."

Caelum held out his arms, almost as delighted to see Faraday as his mother was. This was the woman who had healed his Mama when all others had wrung their hands uselessly.

As Faraday cuddled the baby to her, speaking softly to him, Azhure turned to the low table near the couch and poured their tea. *Here we sit as if we were but simple housewives,* she thought, *talking babies and recipes, and no one would guess the magic that surrounds us or the shared love for one man that has brought us both so much grief.*

The Alaunt had finished their meal and drifted back to the fire, stretching out before it, completely encircling the two women.

"Azhure," Faraday finally said, not looking up from Caelum as he nestled in her lap. "Axis. Did he . . . ?"

"He married me that afternoon," Azhure said, making her voice as gentle as she could, yet knowing each word would cut straight to Faraday's heart.

"Ah," Faraday said, and she looked up. "I am glad." Then, utterly surprisingly, a radiant smile broke out across her face. "Glad for all the hearts he must have broken over the years that someone has finally won him."

"Yes. Look, he gave me this ring."

She had wondered if Faraday would recognize it, but Faraday merely exclaimed over its beauty. Yet after a moment she frowned.

"It has the feel of power to it."

"It last belonged, so I am told, to a woman known as the Enchantress, the mother of the Icarii, Charonite *and* the Acharite races." Azhure's mouth twisted sourly. "Now people call me the Enchantress, but I do not know if I like it. I hope that I am not to be submerged in the personality of a woman fifteen thousand years dead."

Faraday patted her hand reassuringly. "I can only see Azhure sitting here before me, not the ghost of some long-dead sorceress."

"Hmm WolfStar told me not to fear that the ring would seek to control me. He said that it sought my hand because it had found one fit to wear it. It has, apparently, come home to me. *He* seemed to fear it, though."

She looked up and started at Faraday's shocked white face.

"WolfStar?"

"Oh," Azhure said, remembering that Faraday did not know of Azhure's connection to WolfStar. "Listen," and she proceeded to tell her of all that had happened since Faraday had left Carlon.

"And so you will leave for the Island of Mist and Memory soon?" Faraday eventually asked.

"Within the week, I think. I cannot wait to find out what secrets it has to offer me." Azhure told Faraday about the fall of Jervois Landing and Axis' march north with his army. "And I think a trip to the island will comfort me. I find the palace a lonely place now that Axis is absent." She paused. "The Sentinels have disappeared, too."

Faraday put her cup down and looked at Azhure sharply. "The Sentinels have *gone?* What do you mean? Gone with Axis?"

"No. They disappeared the day before Axis left to march north. No one knows where they are. No one."

Disturbed, Faraday thought for a few minutes. Had she upset them so badly with her recriminations and tears that they had vanished? She had been sure that the Sentinels would stay with Axis.

Azhure remembered Dru-Beorh's report. "And there is further worrying news, Faraday. Moryson and Gilbert have been seen traveling east. Be careful. I cannot but think that they might prove a danger to you."

And a warning is the best I can do for her, Azhure thought, if Axis thinks an armed escort would be inappropriate.

Faraday, still concerned over the disappearance of the Sentinels, brushed the matter of Moryson and Gilbert aside. "I cannot think that either of them would do much except rant at me, Azhure. But thank you for the warning. Now," she handed Caelum back to his mother and smiled. "I have a wonder to show you and wondrous people for you to meet. But I think you must leave the hounds here by the fire."

As they'd sat talking the idea had slowly grown in Faraday's mind that she might take Azhure to see the Sacred Grove. She wondered if the Horned Ones, or even the Mother, might object, but in the end Faraday decided that it was her decision.

"Come," she said, standing, and stretched out her hand. Carefully stepping over the sleeping hounds, Faraday led Azhure and her son into the Sacred Grove.

*　　　　*　　　　*

Both Azhure and Caelum were transfixed with wonder as Faraday's power then the emerald light of the Mother surrounded them.

Mama! Caelum cried, leaning forward and stretching his hands out as far as he could.

Azhure's arms tightened automatically about her son but otherwise she paid him no attention. While healing Azhure's back, Faraday had described to her the sensation of walking through the emerald light then watching it gradually shift and change until it resolved itself into the trees and sky of the Sacred Grove.

Now Azhure experienced it for herself.

Without knowing exactly when the transition took place, Azhure found herself wandering down a path carpeted with soft pine needles, trees to either side of her, the sky above filled with stars reeling through their eternal dance. She stared at them, thinking she could actually see them move.

Finally lowering her eyes, Azhure glanced to one side and saw that Faraday wore a gown such as she had never seen before. It reminded her of the emerald light as it had darkened and shifted and changed, when Faraday walked, the colors in the gown shimmered from emerald to blue to violet to brown, then back to emerald again.

Faraday herself seemed changed as well. Far more powerful, far more sure, far, far more lovely.

"Are you certain that I should step these paths?" Azhure asked, unsure about her reception here. "The Avar refused to accept me, and their Banes," she thought of the coolness Barsarbe had consistently displayed toward her, "might be furious that I now visit their Sacred Grove. They did not like my violence."

But Faraday did not seem perturbed. "I will accept responsibility," she said. "Now, hush. See? We enter the Grove itself. You will know soon enough how the Sacred Horned Ones regard you."

When Faraday had pulled Axis into the Grove to witness Raum's transformation she had felt almost instantly the resentment that emanated from the trees. They had tolerated him, for Faraday's sake, but they certainly did not like him. But Faraday felt none of this now; instead she experienced the love and exultation that usually enveloped her when she stepped the paths to the Grove.

"Say nothing until you are spoken to," Faraday said, and Azhure nodded, hoping that Caelum would behave himself. Never before had she been exposed to such power as she felt here, and it awed and frightened her. As they stepped into the center of the Grove, giant trees rearing on either side, Azhure felt strange eyes watching her from under their dark branches.

She looked straight ahead . . . and jumped. Walking toward her was the most magnificent—and most frightening—creature Azhure had ever seen. With the splendid head of a stag atop the muscular man's body, this was one of the Sacred Horned Ones, the magical creatures that male Avar Banes transformed into when they died.

Was Raum here?

But this Horned One was not Raum, for he was not a complete stag, but he did have a noble silver pelt that extended over his shoulders and halfway down his back, and Azhure instinctively realized that he was among the senior of the Horned Ones.

"Greetings, Tree Friend," the silver pelt said, and leaned forward to rub cheeks with Faraday.

Azhure started at the sound of normal speech and managed to compose herself only the instant before the Horned One turned her way.

"Sacred One," Faraday said. "I have brought my friend, Azhure SunSoar, to meet with you. I hope you will accept her presence here in the Sacred Grove."

The silver pelt stepped before Azhure and stared into her eyes. His gaze was cold and hard, and Azhure felt herself tremble, but she did not drop her eyes.

She could feel Caelum holding his breath against her body.

"I know who you are," the silver pelt said, his voice puzzled. "I *know* you!"

This was the woman for whom the StarMan had betrayed Tree Friend. But this was not why he was puzzled. Slowly he lifted a hand to Azhure's face and traced his middle three fingers down her forehead.

"You have already been accepted into the Grove and the company of the Horned Ones," he said, with surprise.

"Already accepted?" Faraday frowned. Acceptance was reserved only for Banes of the Avar and those children they brought to the Mother.

"Oh!" Azhure said, memories flooding her mind. Her hand, slowly turning Hagen over until she could see the knife protruding from his belly. His blood steaming in pools on the floor. Shra, the Avar girl Raum had brought back from Fernbrake Lake, scrambling from the bed, dipping her fingers into Hagen's blood and drawing three lines down Azhure's forehead. "Accepted," she had lisped. And none had known what she had meant.

"Accepted," Azhure whispered, remembering, and shared her memory with Faraday and the silver pelt.

The Horned One smiled—and, with his great square yellowing teeth and cold black eyes it was a dreadful sight. "A sacrifice was accepted on your behalf. Be well and welcomed to the sacred paths, Azhure."

Faraday was puzzled by the distress on Azhure's face. "Azhure? Why so concerned? You have been granted a great honor. Few are welcomed so freely to the Sacred Groves."

Azhure blinked at Faraday, then turned back to the Horned One. Her mouth trembled. "Oh, Sacred One, I am aware of the honor that you do me. But it troubles me that an act of wanton violence, violence which has turned many of the Avar against me, should prove the deed that gains me entrance to these sacred paths."

The Horned One lifted a hand and cupped Azhure's face between his fingers.

"Azhure. I was only surprised because I *knew* you, and I only know people who have been accepted into the Grove. Shra, who will grow to be one of the most powerful Banes the Avar have ever birthed, recognized your worth. Hagen's death as such did not make you acceptable to us—"

"Much as it may have further endeared you to us," said a second Horned One who had appeared at the silver pelt's shoulder. Behind him four or five others had materialized from beyond the dark trees.

"—for his death was merely the method by which one of the greatest Avar Banes yet born chose to accept you as worthy to step the sacred paths to this Grove."

"Worthy? Why am I worthy?"

Faraday smiled. Despite what Azhure had learned about herself since she had fled Smyrton, she still found it hard to believe that she was worthy of all the attention, regard and love that had come her way.

"Worthy?" The silver pelt's smile faded and his fingers tightened momentarily about Azhure's face. "Why are you worthy to step the paths into this Grove? You are worthy simply because of who you are, Azhure. You are a Sacred Daughter. You have drunk the blood of the Stag. You have saved the lives of many Avar—despite their ungratefulness. The Sacred Grove thanks you for your actions at the Earth Tree Grove. You saved Raum's life and helped him and Shra to escape the Smyrton villagers. But most of all, Azhure, you are worthy because of the ring you wear and the Circle you complete."

He lifted Azhure's hand and held it for all the other Horned Ones to see. "The Circle of Stars has come home; Shra saw the power within you as well—no wonder she accepted you. Hagen's death was merely a convenient occasion to formally announce the acceptance, it was not the *reason* she accepted you . . . or why *we* accept you. You have great power, Azhure, and deep compassion, and you have aided the Avar and you have aided Faraday and will continue to aid her. Because of all these things, you are beloved and welcomed into the Sacred Grove."

"And," he let go of Azhure's face and hand and picked Caelum out of her arms, "your son is welcomed too. Welcome, Caelum, and may your feet always find the paths to the Sacred Grove."

Caelum, awed but not frightened, submitted to the silver pelt's embrace, overcoming his awe to thrust a curious finger into the Horned One's face so that the silver pelt had to avert his eye to prevent it being poked.

"Caelum!" Azhure muttered, embarrassed, but wondering at the name the Horned One had given the Enchantress' ring; what did it mean? And what 'circle' did she complete? She opened her mouth to ask, but the Horned One forestalled her.

"Your son bears your blood, and he was conceived at Beltide under the Song of the Earth Tree. He will wield much of your power and he will be as compassionate. But, Azhure—"

The Horned One's voice hardened. Azhure paled at the sudden transformation, remembering how the Horned Ones had terrified Axis the first time he had come to the Grove in a dream vision. She realized that these Horned Ones could kill at the snap of a finger and with considerably less effort.

"Azhure, never, *never*, bring those children you carry within you to this Grove. *Their* feet are *not* welcome on the sacred paths."

"But they were conceived at Beltide, too," Azhure said, more puzzled and frightened than defensive. What *was* wrong with these babes?

"They were conceived well beyond the Avarinheim, and they do not share your compassion, Azhure. Beware of them, Daughter, for they may one day do you and yours great harm."

Beware? Azhure paled until her face was almost white, her eyes great and dark. Faraday stepped forward and put her hand on Azhure's arm.

"Now, I have a garden to show you, Azhure," she said, "and two women who would, I think, dearly like to meet you."

At the pressure of Faraday's hand Azhure walked away a few paces, then she turned back to the silver pelt who still stood watching her.

"Thank you for your acceptance," she said, finally finding her voice. "It means a great deal to me." Then she turned and followed Faraday.

That evening, well after the sun had sunk into the west and Carlon was almost frantic wondering what had become of her and Caelum, Azhure walked down the stairs of Spiredore. Behind her the Alaunt snuffled happily. In her absence they had eaten to excess in the Silent Woman Keep.

It had been a wondrous day. The friendship that Faraday had promised Azhure had matured and deepened. She had not only visited, but had been accepted into the Sacred Grove. Faraday had led her past the dark tree line so she could discover the enchanted world that lay beyond—what other mother had ever watched her son play with blue and orange splotched panthers amid the dancing rivulets of a magical stream while diamond-eyed birds fluttered about his shoulders? She had met Raum-that-was, the White Stag, and had cried gently as he let her stroke his velvety nose before bounding away to run unfettered through the Enchanted Wood. And she had sat and talked for hours with two women, one middle-aged and dressed in a soft blue dress with a rainbow sash, the Mother, and one old and red-cloaked, reminding her vividly of Orr. Both women had, in their own way, awed her far more than the silver-pelted Horned One.

They had sat in the warm sun on the garden bench in Ur's nursery, the four women and the baby boy. While the Mother held her hands over Caelum's ears (for such knowledge was not his right), Ur told Azhure the secret of the seedlings.

Moved beyond words, Azhure had taken Faraday's hand, and the women sat for some time, enjoying each other's company, and laughing at the baby as he crawled, serenely oblivious to the significance of what surrounded him, through the pathways of the nursery. In the serenity and comfort of the garden and the company, Azhure set aside her fear at the Horned One's words regarding her twins. All her questions would surely be answered on the Island of Mist and Memory.

"I *have* been blessed," she whispered into Caelum's ear as she stepped forth from Spiredore to greet a relieved Hesketh, half the palace guard, and Star-Drifter, who had been just about to go in after her.

14

Goodwife Renkin Goes to Market

Goodwife Renkin shook out her heavy woollen skirts and sat gratefully down on the stool by the sheep pen. About her the marketplace of Tare bustled cheerfully; this was one of the major fair days in southern Achar—*Tencendor*, she reminded herself—and Tare was full of traders and peasants come to buy and sell and gape and gossip.

The Goodwife leaned back against the stone wall behind her and closed her eyes. She'd set out from her small farm in northern Arcness fifteen days ago, driving her flock of twenty-eight ewes slowly so they could graze the rolling grass plains as they went. Normally her husband would have taken the sheep to market, but he, poor soul, had such bad corns on his toes this year the Goodwife had come instead. She sighed blissfully, and interlaced her fingers across her large belly. It was nice to escape both her husband and her large brood of children. She loved them dearly, but ever since that exquisite Lady had stayed overnight in their farmhouse two years ago the Goodwife had been plagued with odd dreams of adventure and excitement—and there was precious little adventure and excitement in her isolated life in northern Arcness.

So the Goodwife had clucked over her husband's toes, wrapped them in bandages infused with cooling herbs, left instructions with her eldest daughter about the care of the younger children, and set off cheerfully with the ewes. They were good ewes, bright of eye and fat with lamb, and the Goodwife knew she would get a good price for them. Not that she or her husband were desperate for the cash. Ever since the Lady Faraday—may she live in happiness forever—had left them the gold and pearl necklet to pay for the supplies she and her companions took north with them the Renkins had existed in a comfort and security that made them the envy of their neighbors.

"Lady Faraday," Goodwife Renkin whispered to herself, and wondered what had become of the Lady since she had left the Renkins' home.

She opened her eyes and glanced about the marketplace. The square was crowded, and with more than traders and peasants. Now and then the Goodwife glimpsed the bright fabrics and feathered wings of those called the Icarii, and she wondered what the gorgeous creatures could want here.

She sniffed and sat up straight. Life had indeed changed over the past year or so. It was confusing. What was once Forbidden was now welcomed. What was once lost in the dark now stalked the midday sun. The old stories, once told only in whispered secrets on moonlit nights, were now being sung by every passing minstrel—even now a young, gaily dressed man was strumming his lute and singing a song of ancient enchantments to a throng of admiring peasants and their children.

And not a Plow-Keeper or Brother of the Seneshal in sight. Once such a minstrel would have been gagged and dragged away to face charges of incitement to heresy, and there would have been a burning in the morning. But now the people in the market square laughed and clapped as he finished his song, and they tossed copper coins into the hat at his feet. And no one paid overmuch attention to the winged people among them.

The Goodwife, as so many others, decided she rather liked this new world. It was far more colorful, far gayer, far more exciting than the old one. She did not miss the teachings of the Brotherhood of the Seneschal, nor the occasional visit from one of its Plow-Keepers. She did not miss having to glance over her shoulder every time she wandered the pathways of the plains to gather herbs for healing, and she did not miss having to watch her tongue in front her children lest she let slip a whisper of the old stories her grandmother had once murmured fearfully to her.

Life had indeed changed, and it seemed that the changes began the moment the Lady Faraday had graced her poor home with her presence.

"Goodwife Renkin!"

Startled from her reverie, the Goodwife jumped to her feet. Standing before her, a great welcoming smile across his broad face, was Symonds Dewes, a sheep trader from Arcen. He shook the Goodwife's hand enthusiastically, recognizing her from the two occasions he had traveled across northern Arcen to the sheep fairs of Rhaetia.

"Goodwife Renkin, you cannot know how glad I am to find you here. Renkin's ewes are sought-after prizes, and I see you have presented your best stock for Tare's market day."

The Goodwife simpered with delight. Dewes always gave more than a fair price for the sheep he purchased and should he buy all twenty-eight ewes then she would have virtually the entire day to wander wide-eyed about the marketplace with a full purse. She assumed a severe expression. "They are the jewels from our herd, Symonds Dewes, and you shall have to pay a high price if you think to relieve me of their care."

Dewes grinned. Goodman Renkin always haggled at length for the best price for his sheep, and it looked like his Goodwife would do no less. "But they look thin and haggard from their journey, Goodwife. Perhaps you should not ask full-price for half-sheep."

For ten minutes they happily haggled back and forth, the Goodwife resolute, the trader determined. Finally they settled on a price that left both Goodwife and trader convinced each had got the best of the bargain. The gold coins jingled into the Goodwife's outstretched hand and she raised her eyes in delight, about to thank the trader for his generosity, when the words caught in her throat at the sight of two of the winged creatures approaching.

"Symonds!" she whispered, and the trader followed her eyes and looked over his shoulder. Two of the Icarii women, Enchanters by the look of the rings on their fingers and the power in their eyes, were bending and exclaiming over the closest sheep.

"Have you not met any of the Icarii?" Dewes asked, and the Goodwife shook her head, round-eyed. "Well then, shall we ask why they find your . . . *my* sheep so fascinating?"

Without waiting for a reply Dewes took the Goodwife's elbow and guided her over to the two Icarii. Both were dressed in clothes of the most exquisite color and weave that the Goodwife had ever seen, and their wings and eyes glowed with jewellike intensity in the weak morning sun.

The trader bowed and introduced himself and the Goodwife.

The Icarii stood, and the closest of them laughed and held out her hand. "My name is StarShine EvenHeart, and this is my companion PaleStar SnapWing," the other Icarii smiled and nodded, "and I apologize from the depths of my heart if we have upset your fine sheep, Trader Dewes and Goodwife Renkin."

"I am merely surprised," Dewes said, the Goodwife too tongue-tied to do anything but stare at the Icarii Enchanters, "that you should find such mundane creatures so fascinating."

StarShine shook Dewes' hand. "We were trapped for so long in our mountain home, Trader Dewes, that we find pleasure and excitement in what you must consider the most trifling of things. Sheep are virtually unknown to us, and these have such fine ivory wool that we could not resist touching it. And their eyes, full of such liquid darkness, reminded us of our cousins the Avar."

"The Avar?" the Goodwife finally managed. "Who are the Avar?" Instantly she reddened, ashamed to have asked a question of such noble creatures.

But StarShine smiled kindly and took the Goodwife's hand. "They are the people of the Horn, Goodwife Renkin, and they live far away to the north in the Avarinheim. One day they will move south, once the forests are replanted."

StarShine stopped, puzzled, a slight frown on her face, and she gently massaged the Goodwife's hand between her own.

Her companion looked closely at StarShine's expression, then turned sharply to stare at the Goodwife.

"Is there something wrong?" Dewes asked.

StarShine's hands tightened about the Goodwife's, but she shifted her eyes and smiled brilliantly into Dewes' face. Her face assumed such beauty, and her green eyes such power, that Dewes took an involuntary step backward. A hint of music drifted about the small group.

"Have we interrupted your business with the Goodwife, Trader Dewes?"

"Er, no," he stammered. "I was just paying Goodwife Renkin for her sheep when you approached."

"Then how fortunate," StarShine said, "for that means the Goodwife must now be free of her charges. Is that not so?" she asked the woman.

Entranced by the Icarii, the Goodwife only nodded.

"Free," the Enchanter said, "to come sit with PaleStar and myself and tell us stories of your sheep. Would you like to do that, Goodwife?"

The Goodwife nodded once more.

StarShine let the woman's hand go. "Then pick up your pack, Goodwife. Farewell your sheep, and come share some time with us."

So it was that Goodwife Renkin found herself lunching with two Icarii Enchanters under the awning of a food hall next to the market square of Tare. Both the Enchanters nibbled delicately at the fare the proprietor had placed before them; the Goodwife stared at them, her food untouched.

For some time StarShine and PaleStar ate, unspeaking, but sharing unspoken thoughts. Every so often one of them would lift her head and smile reassuringly at the Goodwife, then lower her eyes and concentrate again on her food.

The Goodwife, whose thoughts of adventure and excitement had never gone beyond seeing the market square of Tare, continued to stare at them.

Finally StarShine raised her head and pushed her plate away. "Goodwife, you must tell us something about yourself."

The Goodwife slowly opened her mouth, then closed it silently again. What was there to say about her humdrum life in northern Arcness that might interest these magical creatures?

"Tell us where you come from, my dear," PaleStar said. "It will be a start."

Slowly the Goodwife told the two Icarii about her husband and children in northern Arcen, their lives devoted to sheep and a few meager crops. "This is the first time I have been more than five leagues from my home," she finished on a whisper, certain she must have bored the Icarii Enchanters witless.

However, they looked anything but bored. "And your mother?" StarShine asked gently. "Does she stay behind to watch over your children while you have come to market?"

The Goodwife shook her head. "No. My mother died of the milk-fever three weeks after birthing me."

PaleStar sat back, frowning. "Then who raised you, Goodwife?"

"My grandmother, gracious Lady."

"Ah," both the Enchanters breathed. "Your *grand*mother." All the Icarii Enchanters who traveled south through eastern Tencendor had spent time looking for women such as this. But they were few and far between among the Acharites. The Seneschal had been . . . vigilant.

"She must have been an unusual lady," StarShine said.

"Talented," PaleStar added and lifted one of the Goodwife's hands out of her lap. "Perhaps she told you pleasant stories when you were a little girl."

Very tense now, the Goodwife nodded her head but did not speak. She kept her eyes firmly in her lap.

"You are safe," StarShine said, and laid her hand over the Goodwife's where it rested in PaleStar's. A feeling of peace infused the Goodwife's body, and she looked up. "Safe," StarShine repeated.

"I have never told anyone," the Goodwife mumbled, and now her eyes were full of guilty tears. "Never."

"Of course not," StarShine soothed. "You were good. You had to be."

"They took her away," tears slipped down the Goodwife's cheeks, "when I was eight. And every year for ten years they would come back to ask me questions. I was afraid."

"I have no doubt." PaleStar's voice was edged with anger, but the Goodwife knew the anger was not directed at her.

The Goodwife sniffed, wiping her nose along her sleeve. "They burned her. They told me that."

"They will not burn you," StarShine said, and she impulsively leaned forward to give the woman a brief hug. "You are safe now."

The Goodwife took a tremulous breath, slowly relaxing. "All the Brothers have gone. When I traveled south I saw none, and there are none here in this town."

"No. All the Brothers have gone, and there are few Plow-Keepers left, Goodwife. You are free to do what you like now, free to believe what you like."

"Will you tell me what has happened? I have heard so little—mostly hearsay."

"Of course, Goodwife," and StarShine told her briefly what had transpired in the land over the past two years.

If possible, the Goodwife's face became even more astounded than before. "Then I *am* safe? The Seneschal will not hurt me if I . . . if I . . ."

"You are safe, Goodwife. Do what you will. Do you have a daughter who . . . ?" StarShine let the question trail off.

The Goodwife shook her head. "No. Neither of my daughters have the talent. I was glad, for I thought that they would be safe. But now . . . now I am sad. I should have liked a daughter to carry on." Abruptly the Goodwife realized she had lost her awe of the Icarii and was chatting to them as if they were old friends. She grinned shame-facedly.

StarShine's smile faded and she leaned forward, extending her hand to rest her palm on the Goodwife's forehead. "Shush, Goodwife, I do you no harm. I only want to help you remember."

Bright music flooded the Goodwife's body, and she gasped. "Oh! I had *forgotten* so much!"

"Disuse engenders forgetfulness, Goodwife." StarShine leaned back, looking wan with her effort. That had been a powerful enchantment, and she would have to rest a day or so now before she could fly on to Carlon. "Make sure you do not forget again."

The Goodwife nodded.

"Make sure you make *good* use of what you have remembered, Goodwife, because this new land needs such as you."

She sat for a very long time after the two Enchanters left her, watching the street life with unseeing eyes. Remembering.

When she was a little girl, too young to help in the fields, her grandmother had told her stories. Told her stories and taught her herbs. Herbs and spells. Nothing dangerous, nothing evil, only herbal recipes, that, when used in conjunction with the spells, would ward against hurt or infection, calm tempers, or engender love. Simple things, but enough to have her grandmother seized and burned by the Seneschal.

From the day the Seneschal had taken her grandmother the young girl had lived an unblemished life. She had never (well, hardly ever) used the herbals again, and had *never* spoken the spells again (except a cradle song or two). She had grown to marry the Goodman Renkin and live an exemplary life in their little home.

Exemplary . . . and boring.

It was strange, for the Goodwife had never thought of her life as boring until the Lady Faraday had come to stay so briefly. She had hardly even remembered her grandmother or her grandmother's tales and teachings until then.

But once the Lady had gone, once the Goodwife tried to settle back into her old life, she discovered it to be stupefyingly boring and yearned for excitement and adventure. She had found herself muttering old verses over the stew pot and plucking wild herbs as she drove the sheep along the worn paths of northern Arcness. She had begun to look over her shoulder, remembering the day *they* had come for her grandmother. The pounding of their horses' hooves. The wicked gleam of their axes.

Now she took a deep breath. What was she going to do?

Go home. What else could she do? She stood up and nodded to the proprietor as she wandered back into the street. She had the money for the sheep—and a goodly sum it was too—and she had her pack, and there was nothing else to do.

But would she use her talents if she went home? Goodman Renkin would not tolerate any of that, not when she could be working out in the fields, and none of her children would want to learn the old ways.

But she did not want to live out the rest of her life applying herbed bandages to corn-crippled feet.

The Goodwife stopped in the street just before she reached the market square, uncertainties creasing her homely face. Suddenly she spotted StarShine EvenHeart standing some paces away, her wings folded behind her, staring at the Goodwife.

"Please," the Goodwife breathed as she hurried over. "Tell me what to do."

"You must do as you see best," StarShine said.

The Goodwife stood and thought, shuffling from foot to foot, her eyes on the ground. "Goodman Renkin does not need me as he once did," she said eventually, speaking slowly as she thought it through. "The boys are old enough to take on many of the responsibilities about the farm now, and he has coin enough to hire labor to help with the harvest and shearing. My eldest girl can take care of the tot and the twins."

She smiled as a thought occurred to her and looked up. "Gracious Lady, do you perchance know of the Lady Faraday?"

Truly surprised, StarShine stared at the Goodwife. "Faraday? Yes. Yes, I know her." And how do you know her, she wondered. Did PaleStar and I discover you by chance or by design?

"Do you know where she is?"

StarShine nodded slowly. "She travels east, Goodwife. I passed her on my way to Tare, somewhere just south of the Silent Woman Woods She travels alone with two white donkeys, and she goes east. That is all I know."

The Goodwife's face fell. "East? Alone? Oh, the poor Lady! Oh, goodness! That won't do at all!"

StarShine's face relaxed Whether by chance or by design, it looked as though Faraday would have some company in whatever quest she was engaged in.

And that would be no bad thing at all. Not at all.

15

Three Brothers Lakes

The Three Brothers Lakes had frozen into a crisp corrugated beauty, but none of the thirty-thousand men camped along the edge of the most southern lake spared much time to admire the view. Axis had taken almost four weeks to march his army across northern Avonsdale and then through the gentle passes of the Western Ranges. When they got through, he had expected to be met by Gorgrael's frozen winds hurling sheets of ice.

But all that had greeted them had been an icy calm.

Why? Why? Surely Gorgrael should have struck with all his power, with all his ice, once Axis and his army emerged from the Western passes?

Conditions were so clear that Icarii scouts reported that they could see as far as the mist-encased Murkle Mountains and the still-frozen Nordra and Fluriat rivers.

"And not a Skraeling in sight," Axis whispered as he stood at the northern edge of the camp, gazing into the frozen wastes before him. "Not a Skraeling in sight. FarSight?"

The most senior of the Strike Force Crest-Leaders stepped to his side, his black uniform and wings incongruous in this pristine environment. He'd only just returned from speaking to the last of the farflight scouts he had sent north three days ago.

"How far have the Strike Force scouts penetrated into Aldeni?"

"Not far, StarMan."

Axis frowned, and FarSight hurried on. "There are Gryphon out there, and I will not expose small numbers of scouts to their fury."

"How many? Where? Have they attacked?"

"There are packs of some fifteen to twenty, ranging over most of northwestern Aldeni. None of the scouts have risked attack by flying too close and the Gryphon appear not to have seen them. Our eyesight is better than theirs, I think. All scouts have returned."

"And what have they seen?" said Belial, who joined them.

"Frozen fields and shattered buildings . . ."

Axis shifted uncomfortably, remembering the Skraeling nests that the broken streets of Hsingard had hidden.

"Wagons coated with ice and the stripped corpses of men and cattle, their bones cracked and drained of nourishment."

"The Skraeling force that we saw marching past Jervois Landing in RuffleCrest's vision would have to strip the province bare to feed itself," Axis said, "and yet having fed, they have disappeared Belial? Gather Ho'Demi and Magariz. We will share our evening meal and our thoughts."

The mood was somber that night and the meal eaten in silence in most of the campsites. Axis sat hunched with his senior commanders about an inadequate fire of brush. His mood had bleakened with each day that they rode north until, as now, he was mostly surrounded by silence.

Somewhere out there in the frozen wastes was a massive army—at least ten times the size of his own—and Axis did not know how he would defeat it even if he could find it.

He sighed. Gorgrael had the initiative, and if Axis could not seize it back, if he could not find the power to defeat this writhing mass of Skraelings to his north (or were they east? Or west? Or, Stars forbid, south?) then they were all dead.

At least Azhure would be safe. She must be on her way south to the Island of Mist and Memory by now, Axis thought. Azhure and Caelum. If anything must be saved, they must be. Even if he died, then they could, eventually, fight back.

But for what? For what?

He started, realizing that Ho'Demi had spoken.

"I am sorry, Ho'Demi, my thoughts were elsewhere," Axis said. "You were saying?"

The Ravensbund Chief put down his tin mug. "I can send bands of my Ravensbund warriors north, StarMan. The farflight scouts, while useful," Ho'Demi inclined his head at FarSight but the birdman still glowered at the "useful," "are vulnerable to the Gryphon and dare not range too far north lest they be attacked. The Ravensbundmen revel in these conditions—we are born to them. The snow was our nursemaid as mewling infants and our lover as men. We can use it and manipulate it and the Gryphon will never spot us. Small groups of us can penetrate far north with minimal risk. Use us."

"You would go with them, Ho'Demi?" Axis said. He did not want to risk Ho'Demi. "You could not counter the Skraelings when they invaded the Ravensbund."

"I only suggest scouts, StarMan, not raiding parties. I leave that to you. And . . . yes, I would go with them. I hunger for action against these creatures that have stolen my homeland from me."

"How soon can you organize the scouting parties?"

"By morning, StarMan Where would you have us go?"

Axis looked to Belial and Magariz. "Your advice, my friends?"

"Damn it, Axis," Magariz said. "Where could they have gone?"

"Skarabost?" Belial suggested.

Axis shook his head, catching FarSight's eye. "No, Belial. Skarabost remains free from Skraelings, although much of it lies under a killing frost."

"Then could they have outflanked us and moved south . . . to Carlon?"

Magariz flinched at Belial's words. Rivkah was in Carlon, but then so was Cazna, and Magariz knew Belial would be as worried about his wife as Magariz was about his.

Axis shivered and blew on his hands in a vain attempt to warm them. "We would have known if they had outflanked us. We have scouts and sentries throughout the Western Ranges and so many Icarii now throng the Bracken Ranges that they would sound the alarm if the Skraelings had struck that far west."

"Axis, we should have *some* reports of the Skraelings. Thousands of peasants fled south before the ice while they still could. Has *nothing* useful come from them?"

But Magariz was only speaking empty words, and he knew it. All the peasants who had managed to flee Aldeni before the wind and frost became too lethal had reported Skraelings on every breath of wind, in every puff of snow. If Axis believed everything the fleeing peasants reported, then the Skraelings should have sunk Aldeni into the Andeis Sea by now through sheer weight of numbers.

Belial cursed at the silence about the campfire. "They *must* be in Aldeni."

"And if they are, then we will find them," Ho'Demi finished softly. "If they have dug themselves into pits in the snow then the Ravensbund will find them. I will find them!"

Axis looked up from the flames. "Pray do, Ho'Demi," he said, "before they find us."

Deep in the shafts dim torches glowed, and in the glow teeth and talons crowded.

The SkraeBolds hunched, miserable.

But Timozel was pleased. It was time to call most of the Gryphon in, for there was no further need of them . . . yet. They had kept the Icarii farflight scouts away from his position, and that was all they had to do for the moment.

But he would keep a few in the northern skies.

Axis would expect that.

76

The Island of Mist and Memory

Azhure eased back in the chair sailors had placed on deck for her and wondered if she would ever be comfortable again. Barely seven months pregnant and all she could do was wonder at what point it was that the twins could survive without her—no doubt the twins wondered the same thing. Even now they stirred restlessly, the heels of their feet drumming against the walls of her womb, as if they dreamed of freedom . . . or hungered for escape.

She rolled her head to one side and looked at StarDrifter standing tense and excited in the prow of the ship, his wings bunched behind him as if he yearned for flight. They had been sailing the choppy waters of the Sea of Tyrre for two days now, and surely could not be far from their destination. If he wanted StarDrifter could take to the skies and be on the Island before nightfall, but he had said he would stay with her, and this he did.

They had sailed from Carlon four days ago in one of Ysgryff's private ships, the *Seal Hope*. Azhure had never been to sea before, and if she had not been so unwell she knew she would have found the experience exhilarating. The *Seal Hope* was commodious and comfortable, did not roll overmuch in the waves, and a warm and salty and infinitely comforting breeze blew from the southwest to fill the dusky pink sails. With Azhure came a goodly assortment of court officials and servants, a Wing of the Strike Force, Prince Ysgryff, and Caelum, currently in the care of his nurse, Imibe, below decks.

And, of course, the fifteen Alaunt, who lolled about on the deck and snapped at the waves when they dared splash too close.

Sometimes Azhure found herself listening to the rhythmic slap of waves against the ship and, lulled half to sleep, dreaming of strange shores of rippling sands and rocky beaches.

Rivkah stayed behind in Carlon, serving as the royal presence, although Azhure continued to attend most matters of administration in morning and evening sessions held in the *Seal Hope*'s main cabin Icarii messengers brought what she needed in the way of documents and information from the mainland.

Stars, she now thought in some exasperation, *I cannot wait to discover what I can on the Isle of Mist and Memory, drop these babies, and rejoin Axis as soon as possible.* Although she could feel a faint pull at her soul with each breath that Axis took—perhaps a reverberation through the Star Dance—Azhure had heard very little from him in the past month. Reports drifted down haphazardly, and all they reported was that Axis led his army north, north, north. Azhure supposed Axis must be well into the province by now, and a shiver of fear passed through her. *Live, Axis! Live! Believe in yourself enough to live for me!*

StarDrifter turned from the bow and strode back to where Azhure and Ysgryff sat under a canvas canopy.

"Ysgrvff. How much farther?"

Ysgryff restrained a smile. "We cannot be far, StarDrifter. Really, why don't you leave us earthbound creatures and wing your way there?"

StarDrifter glanced at Azhure. "No. No, Ysgryff, I will stay with Azhure. I promised Axis."

Azhure narrowed her eyes. Exactly *what* had he promised Axis? StarDrifter had behaved with perfect decorum since Axis had departed. Azhure knew it must have been hard for him, for he now spent many hours with her each day, either singing gently to the babies within her or to Caelum. Yet not once had she felt his touch or his eyes to hold anything but restraint, not once had his manners and conversation descended from the heights of good manners and civility.

It was not like StarDrifter at all. Not given the depths of his desires. Azhure wondered if it was her pregnancy that kept StarDrifter at a distance. Maybe, once she was unencumbered of Axis' children . . .

The soft beat of wings broke her thoughts and she sat up in her chair as an Icarii scout landed gently on the deck.

He bowed to Azhure. "Enchantress, there is an Icarii approaching from the south."

"From the Island!" StarDrifter said. "Who? Did you see who it was?"

The scout shook his head. "No, StarDrifter. The Icarii is still too far away."

"Thank you," Azhure said, inclining her head, then smiled at StarDrifter as the scout lifted off. "Peace, StarDrifter. We will find out soon enough."

But even Azhure could not keep her excitement down, and after a few minutes she struggled to stand up, finally taking StarDrifter's hand and letting him pull her to her feet.

"Is it . . . ?" she began, leaning on the railing and straining her eyes to the southern skies where she could just see a black shape emerging from the haze. "Do you think it might be . . . ?"

"FreeFall!" StarDrifter shouted and unable to restrain himself any longer, launched into the air.

Within minutes, FreeFall and StarDrifter had alighted on the deck, the two embracing fiercely before FreeFall turned to Azhure.

"Azhure!" he laughed, hugging her briefly. "You are enormous! Do you carry the entire Icarii nation within you?"

"Sometimes it feels like it." Azhure grinned. "Are you well?"

"Ah, Azhure." Wonderment infused FreeFall's face, softening his violet eyes so that they seemed as blue as the surrounding sea. "I cannot tell you how well! I have seen wonders and mysteries before now, but never such mysteries as I have found on the Island of Mist and Memory."

Azhure stared at him. For a man who had died and who had walked the rivers of death before resuming life in the form of an eagle, the mysteries of the Island must be wondrous indeed to captivate him so.

"And EvenSong?" she asked.

"She is even better than I, except daily her temper has grown worse with her impatience to see you again."

StarDrifter shifted restlessly. "Tell me," he said. "Tell me."

FreeFall glanced at his uncle. "The mysteries of the island will wait another few hours. Words will not describe what should be seen for one's self. Look . . ." He put his arm about what was left of Azhure's waist and turned her to gaze over the railing. "Look."

Faint, so faint Azhure thought it was her imagination, a gray-green line smudged the distant horizon.

"The Island of Mist and Memory," FreeFall said.

For a thousand years the Island of Mist and Memory had been known to the Acharites as Pirates' Nest. For a thousand years the pirates had sallied forth from their island fortress to raid, plunder and burn, and the Barons of Nor, whose task it was to eradicate the pirates from the Sea of Tyrre, had wrung their hands and claimed that the pirates were too vicious and too numerous to do anything about. For a thousand years Pirates' Nest had held onto its secrets, and both pirates and Barons of Nor had cooperated in keeping it that way.

Now the Icarii were returning to claim their island, to worship in the Temple of the Stars and to revere and honor the other, more sacred and far more secret, sites of the island.

But the Island of Mist and Memory held even more secrets than the Icarii counted on.

*   *   *

The *Seal Hope* put into the northern port of Pirates' Town so late in the afternoon that the decision was taken to spend the night in the town before traveling to the temple complex in the morning.

Azhure had been aghast at the size of the island. She had vaguely expected it to be small, a few houses for the pirates, a few more for the priestesses of the Order of the Stars, and the Temple itself, but as they had sailed toward it she saw that it was massive.

"It stretches for ten leagues north to south," FreeFall said softly, moving to her side as the *Seal Hope* docked, "and six east to west. See that peak rising to the south?"

Azhure nodded. The entire island sloped toward the mountain.

"It is called Temple Mount, and it rises almost three thousand paces from the sea. On its plateau rests the complex of the Temple of the Stars."

"My mother lived there," Azhure whispered, "and that is where I was conceived."

"Yes," FreeFall said, "that is where you were conceived, Azhure."

Azhure turned to him. "Have you told the priestesses I am coming? Have you told them who I am?"

FreeFall hesitated. "No. No, I have not. I thought that was for you to do."

"What *do* the priestesses know, FreeFall?" StarDrifter asked.

"They know only that the Prophecy walks, that the StarMan has reclaimed Tencendor, and that the Icarii will shortly return to re-light the Temple of the Stars. EvenSong and I have not told them much, and they have not asked questions. They have waited for a thousand years, and no doubt feel a few more days or weeks will not kill them."

"StarDrifter," Azhure said, "there is no need for you to stay with me tonight. Ysgryff is here, and numerous servants. We will travel to Temple Mount in the morning. You could fly there tonight with FreeFall."

"No." Curiously, StarDrifter seemed to have lost all his impatience now. "No, Azhure. I promised Axis that I would look after you. We will all reach Temple Mount soon enough."

The port of Pirates' Town was situated in a narrow harbor that penetrated deep into the northern shoreline of the island. Over fifteen thousand pirates, their wives, children and numerous cats, dogs and chickens lived crammed into the town; the harbor was crowded with every type of sailing ship imaginable, some built from the forested slopes of the island, some purloined from distant seas and harbors.

The people seemed friendly enough, although their wild eyes, bright scarves and bristling daggers made Azhure hold Caelum close, and many smiled and waved at Ysgryff as he strode through the streets. The Baron found them comfortable accommodation in an inn close to the port, made certain Azhure was settled, then made arrangements for their journey to Temple Mount in the morning.

That night Azhure tossed restlessly, disturbed and irritated by the slightest noise or movement of her babies. Not a sound came from StarDrifter's chamber next to hers in the inn, and she wondered that the Enchanter could sleep this soundly when he was so close to the mysterious Temple of the Stars that he had hungered after for so long.

Finally she fell into an uneasy slumber just as dawn stained the eastern sky, and as she did, she dreamed.

She stood in darkness, surrounded by the slap of waves and suspicious voices and prodding fingers.

"Is this her?"

"It must be—can you not feel the tug of her blood against the shoreline?"

"Her? Truly?"

She moved to one side, away from the prods and the queries, but only met more.

"How can we know it is her?"

The voices sounded angry, disturbed, and she was frightened.

"It would be too dangerous to make a mistake. Too dangerous now."

"Are you dangerous, unknown woman?"

Her hand flew to her throat where a finger had poked painfully and those about her gasped.

"She wears the Circle!"

"She does!"

"What is your name, Circle-wearer?"

"Did you steal it?"

She turned around in the darkness, trying to see. "My name is Azhure. And no, the ring was given to me."

"Azhure!"

"Oh, the name!"

"Azhure!"

"Azhure!"

Her eyes flew open to meet StarDrifter's smiling face.

"Wake up, lovely lady. It is morning and the Temple awaits. Wake up."

"StarDrifter?" Azhure sat up, her eyes bleary with lack of sleep.

"I have called for Imibe to help you dress. What is that?" His fingers traced lazily down her throat. "You have pinched yourself in your sleep, I think. A small bruise, it is nothing. Now, here is Imibe."

Although they started early in the morning, the trek to Temple Mount took most of the day. Most traveled in Ysgryff's hired horses and wagons, but FreeFall left by wing, saying he would warn the priestesses of arriving company but give no details.

This day the island lived up to its name. Soft mist clung to every building and corner and none could see more than a few paces in front of them.

"It is like this much of the time," Ysgryff said, twisting around from the bench where he sat with the wagon's driver. "Yesterday's clarity was the exception. When seen from the sea the island looks like drifting cloud, nothing else. Most sailors tend to stay well clear of it, not only because of the pirates, but because they say creatures of long-forgotten memory lurk within the depths of the mist."

Azhure shuddered and pulled her wrap closer. If she had not seen the island under the kind light of the sun she was sure she too would have been more than a little unnerved by this mist. Even sound faltered and died within a few paces; the bustle of the town was muted, while passing pedestrians were only ghostly shapes, more imagined than real.

"And Temple Mount?" she asked.

It was StarDrifter who answered, his eyes staring ahead into the mist. "Temple Mount is always in the light, Azhure. The mist might cling to its skirts, but the plateau is so high it remains open to both sun and stars."

"You speak as if you have seen it yourself, StarDrifter." Ysgryff's voice was amused.

"The Icarii have never forgotten the Temple of the Stars, Ysgryff. Never." His own voice was flat and expressionless, and after a moment Ysgryff turned back to converse in low tones with the driver.

The road rose as the last hunched shapes of the town's buildings disappeared behind them. For the entire morning they climbed steadily, the road twisting and turning as the gradient became steeper. At noon they stopped for a meal and to water the horses, but they were off again quickly, for Ysgryff said there was still a way to go.

"The last section we will have to accomplish on foot," he grunted, lifting Azhure back into the wagon, and StarDrifter shot him an anxious glance.

The mist cleared by mid-afternoon, and Azhure could see stands of great trees and ferns clustered beside the roadway.

"Much of the southern half of the island is twisted jungle," Ysgryff explained at her querying glance, "and uninhabited. Apart from Temple Mount and the harbor surrounds, most of the island is as it was when first created by the gods; the pirates leave the jungle alone. Who knows, perhaps strange creatures *do* live within the deeper jungles."

Azhure could now see the Mount itself rising before them, its majesty and beauty breathtaking. The sides of the peak rose sharply for a farther two thousand paces, covered with low shrubbery between great granite slabs. The road twisted steeply up its side until, about two-thirds of the way up, it terminated in a wide ledge where the wagons could turn about.

From there steep steps climbed to the plateau.

StarDrifter, his earlier waspish mood forgotten, again locked anxious eyes with Ysgryff.

Azhure did not notice. "We're almost there," she whispered excitedly to Caelum. "That is where my mother lived!"

Despite the memories unlocked when Axis crashed through the barriers she had constructed so many years ago, Azhure still could not recall much about her mother. A kind and beautiful face, a few words, a gentle touch and an even gentler laugh . . . and the blackened corpse crackling almost apologetically on the hearth. But on the top of this mountain she hoped to find answers, not only about her mother, but also about herself. Both Niah and WolfStar had wanted her to come here, where they both had been. This was the only place the three of them had ever been together, even if one of them was only a barely conceived fetus.

And this was the place where WolfStar had told her she could learn, where others could teach her. What others? Azhure frowned as she crooned wordlessly into Caelum's hair. The priestesses? Or those strange voices of her dream?

She hoped she would find *all* answers in this place, because without them, Azhure was terribly afraid Axis would face terrible peril.

The wagons creaked to a halt and Azhure jumped, surprised out of her reverie. She had not realized they'd climbed so far.

She handed Caelum to StarDrifter and let Ysgryff help her out of the wagon. The rest of her retinue, two score of servants and retainers, were climbing out of their wagons and passing down baggage. Azhure turned away from the sheer cliff face before her and gazed out across the island.

From this perspective, and with the now clear sky, the view was awe-inspiring. Far below her the island stretched away to the north and west, and the mist had cleared enough so that she could distinguish the hazy smoke rising from the chimneys of the town about the harbor. To the west lay impenetrable jungle, tendrils of mist still clinging among the leaves of the highest trees. Beyond the western edge of the jungle lay the sea, from this distance as green and mysterious as the trees.

"Azhure?" StarDrifter spoke behind her. "How do you feel? Can you climb the steps, or would you like Ysgryff or myself to carry you?"

Azhure turned. Everyone, wagon drivers and her own retinue, was regarding her silently. Her eyes flitted to the steps before her, and she cricked her neck slightly as she traced their flight toward the plateau; already the Alaunt had bounded up half their height. Did they think she could not manage?

The thought of climbing such a flight *did* concern her, but Azhure's pride was stung by the image of being hauled bodily upward by either StarDrifter or Ysgryff. Damn these babies, she cursed silently. Unencumbered I could have skipped those stairs without losing breath.

"Save your breath for the climb," she said shortly, gathering her skirts to march resolutely to the foot of the steps. "I shall manage well enough."

*   *   *

Within ten minutes everyone knew the lie of her words as she suddenly collapsed, scraping her shins and knees against the stone steps, frantically clinging to the slim iron railing with sweat-dampened hands to try to slow her slide. If Ysgryff had not been directly behind her, Azhure would undoubtedly have slid all the way to the foot of the steps, but he caught her in strong arms and hoisted her up.

"Cursed pride," he muttered, out of breath himself. "No doubt she gets it from both her Nors and Icarii blood."

StarDrifter stepped down and took Azhure's face in his free hand, holding Caelum securely on his hip with the other.

"Can you or a member of the Wing fly her to the top, Enchanter?" Ysgryff asked.

"No," StarDrifter said. "She's too heavy. Will you manage?"

Ysgryff grinned. "When I can't you'll get your turn, birdman. And when she exhausts both of us I'll call forward one of her burly men-at-arms." He twisted his head slightly, trying to see Azhure's face. "Azhure?"

"She's fainted," StarDrifter said. "Come on, man, I have no wish to waste anymore of this day on the side of this mountain. The priestesses can care for her when we reach the top."

They did, eventually, manage to carry Azhure safely to the top of the steps, the final score to the accompaniment of her soft moans as she came out of her faint. Ysgryff, who had taken Azhure back from StarDrifter some ten minutes earlier, set her down gently on the soft carpet of grass and watched the woman who had been waiting for them step silently forward.

"First Priestess," he said. "We have a woman here, ill and pregnant, and she needs your help."

But the First Priestess, gray-haired and gaunt, had eyes for neither Ysgryff or the woman crumpled at his feet.

"Enchanter," she whispered, and bowed low in front of StarDrifter. "*At last!*"

"I greet you well enough," StarDrifter said, "but I beg you to help this woman here."

The priestess finally looked at Azhure, and squatted before her, lifting the woman's head in her hands. For a long moment she stared into Azhure's face, her complexion paling.

"Oh, by the Stars in the heavens," she finally whispered, her hands tightening about Azhure's face, "you are *her* daughter!"

17

Temple Mount

Azhure slept for the rest of that day, throughout the night and well into the next morning. When she did awaken, it was to find a gray-haired woman sitting at the end of her bed, dressed in a white linen robe, a sky-blue sash about her waist and draped over her left shoulder.

"You are awake, Sacred Daughter. Good. Do you know where you are?"

"Temple Mount," Azhure muttered, struggling to sit up.

"Yes, good." The woman lifted a glass from the table. "Drink this."

Azhure took the glass and raised it to her lips, realizing that her mouth and throat were parched.

"It is a strengthening brew, Daughter," the woman said. "You are sadly lacking in strength. But do not worry, your babies are well. They are, I think, what drains you so badly."

Azhure finished the drink and handed the glass back to the woman, glancing about the sparsely furnished room. "Who are you?"

The woman smiled, her face losing its austerity. "I am First Priestess." She paused. "I have no name."

"You know who I am?"

The woman nodded, "Yes, I do, but . . . no! Hush. I do not want to speak of it now."

Azhure's eyes filled with tears and the Priestess leaned forward and cupped Azhure's face in her hands. "You have questions," she said, "I know that. But you have time enough for answers, for I do not think you will be going very far until those babies are born. For now you will eat, then I will bathe and dress you—for that will be my privilege alone—and then we will go and re-assure both the Icarii and the Nors men outside who fret about you."

She grinned impishly, at odds with her apparent age and authority. "Here we are surrounded by some of the greatest mysteries of this world, and all those outside can do is fret about the woman in this cell. But then," her smile dimmed and she patted Azhure on the cheek, "I know who you are and how you were made, and I am not surprised that you command so much attention and love. Come, try some of this fruit. It will nourish you."

After the First Priestess had fed, bathed and dressed Azhure, she brought Caelum in, sitting silently while Azhure cuddled and suckled her son.

"They tell me his father is the StarMan of Prophecy," she said eventually.

Azhure looked up from her son's head. "Yes. Yes, he is."

The First Priestess sighed and fingered the tassel of her sash. "Events and people of great moment walk, Azhure. I hope we may all prove to be worthy of them."

"First Priestess, I did not come here only to discover my mother or the mystery of my conception. I also came here to discover myself."

The Priestess slowly got to her feet, her joints creaking. "As do we all, my child, as do we all. Now, has your son finished? Good. Come, and I will show you the complex of the Temple of the Stars. Questions can wait until this evening."

Outside the room, StarDrifter, Ysgryff, FreeFall, EvenSong and all the Alaunt were waiting, varying degrees of anxiety imprinted across human, Icarii and canine faces alike. Azhure cried out in delight when she saw EvenSong and hastily handed Caelum to his grandfather, hugging the Icarii woman to her fiercely.

"I am well," she said to their queries. "A little tired, but well."

"But not if you keep crowding her as you do," the First Priestess said testily. "I am taking Azhure for a tour of the complex StarDrifter, you may accompany us because I have yet to speak with you at length EvenSong, you may accompany us to carry the baby. The other men must stay behind. I will allow *one* of the hounds."

The First Priestess marched forth and Ysgryff and FreeFall stepped back hastily. Azhure smiled apologetically at them as she passed, Sicarius pressing close to her legs, but she took a deep breath of delight when the Priestess led them into a cloister facing a delightful garden of lavender beds and low juniper trees.

"You were in the dormitory of the priestesses, Azhure," the First Priestess explained, leading them down the cloisters then turning left onto a walkway by a high stone building, "and this is the Temple Library. You can see inside some other time."

"It's where FreeFall spends most of his time," EvenSong said by Azhure's side. EvenSong was softer than Azhure remembered, and it was strange to see her dressed in a robe rather than trousers. The Icarii woman bounced Caelum in her arms, smiling at him, then winked at Azhure. "But I make sure FreeFall occasionally remembers that I am here too, and that not all the wonders of the Temple complex are contained within *stone* portals."

Azhure smothered a laugh, then gasped in utter astonishment as the First Priestess led them across a small bridge and onto a magnificent paved avenue, lined with colonnades of smooth granite columns that straddled narrow, fern-bracketed waterways filled with flashing fish and waterlilies.

"The Avenue," the First Priestess said. She pointed to her right. "It leads from the cliff-face steps to the Temple of the Stars."

Azhure followed the woman's hand. To her left, on a slight rise, appeared to be a large marble-floored circle. Azhure frowned. Where was the Temple?

StarDrifter smiled at the incomprehension on Azhure's face, but he did not say anything.

"Come," the First Priestess said. "There are other places I wish to show you first."

She led them across the Avenue and across another small bridge onto smooth lawns, indicating some smaller buildings farther to their right. "The school houses and children's quarters," she said, and made to walk forward again, but Azhure caught at her arm.

"School houses? Children?"

The Priestess arched an eyebrow. "We are not totally isolated, Azhure. Many of the Nors nobles have their children educated here, as do most of the folk from Pirates' Town."

Azhure and StarDrifter gazed incredulously at each other. How had the secret of the island remained so inviolate if many of the Nors nobility sent their children here for their schooling? And pirates . . . *educated* pirates?

The Priestess marched off through a pleasant garden toward a huge circular windowless building, tight-walled with pale stone.

"Ah," StarDrifter said softly by Azhure's side. "I know what this is—as will you, Azhure, when you see inside."

The Priestess led them under an archway at the foot of the walls, then up some stairs. StarDrifter took Azhure's elbow, and she was not ungrateful for his support as they climbed the stairs and stepped onto an internal open-air balcony halfway up the structure.

"Oh," was all Azhure could say, and she felt StarDrifter's fingers tighten about her arm.

"One day," EvenSong said behind them, "we will all come home to roost here. And when we do, Father, you should be the one to greet us and speak to us the words of arrival and welcome."

Azhure would not begrudge StarDrifter that right. They stood halfway up one of the walls of the Icarii Assembly, circles of seats falling away beneath them and rising into the sky above. The original Assembly, from a time when the Icarii had graced the skies of all Tencendor. It was still in perfect condition, and Azhure was not surprised when she heard, many days later, that every month or so some forty or fifty men and women journeyed from Pirates' Town to weed and polish the stone steps and colonnades.

This Assembly was twelve or fifteen times the size of the Assembly Chamber in Talon Spike and relied on sheer size to inspire rather than intricate or overwhelming carving or tracery. From the circular floor great rings of pale gold stone steps rose into the sky, so far that the lower third of the Assembly lay in shadow. The only decoration Azhure could see was the floor; unlike Talon Spike's Assembly Chamber which was floored in golden-veined marble, the floor of this Assembly had been laid in multicolored mosaics depicting constellations and galaxies—a star map.

There was no roof.

"In the old days, Azhure," StarDrifter said, his fingers gentler now, "the Icarii would float down into the Assembly from the night stars, all carrying torches. They would sing with joy as they came, and they say that some nights the stars themselves accompanied them. I cannot . . ." His voice broke, and he paused to recompose himself. "I cannot wait to see that sight again."

The First Priestess stared at the Enchanter, then shifted her eyes to Azhure. She opened her mouth to say something, thought better of it, then gestured to the steps behind them.

"Come on," she said, "there is yet more to see."

Outside, StarDrifter let Azhure's elbow go and managed a smile. "I did not think the sight of the Assembly would affect me so."

EvenSong took her father's arm, feeling closer to him than she ever had before, and for a time the group walked in silence through orchards and vineyards. Sicarius, relaxed now his anxiety over Azhure was assuaged, sniffed about the tree trunks and grunted at a peach-colored cat quivering high among some branches. Eventually they approached a low dome of strange green stone, about a hundred paces in circumference.

Azhure expected that the Priestess would stop and lead them inside or, at the least, provide some explanation for the structure, but the old woman only muttered, "The Dome," before marching resolutely past, her back ramrod straight.

The Dome of the Stars, Azhure, StarDrifter said in Azhure's mind.

Why does she ignore it so?

The Dome is particularly sacred to the Order of the Stars, to the Priestesses. Only the First among them may ever go in there. StarDrifter paused. *I do not know what they find within.*

Once past the Dome the First's shoulders relaxed and she led the small group to the very cliff face at the southernmost point of the island. Thousands of paces below them the sea crashed against rocks. StarDrifter, Azhure and EvenSong, still holding Caelum in her arms, all stood easily at the very lip of the cliff, their Icarii blood lending them both the balance and the courage to ignore the sheer drop beneath their feet. With them stood the hound, the edge of the cliff crumbling slightly beneath his forepaws.

The Priestess, of human blood, stood prudently some paces back from the lip. "See?" she said, pointing, "see the steps?"

The others looked to where she pointed. A flight of steps, so narrow that only one person could ever negotiate them at a time, dropped from the cliff edge and hugged the cliff face, leading down until they were lost in the upper reaches of the spray of the waves that beat themselves to death against the cliff.

"Where—" Azhure began, but the First cut her off.

"They lead to the Sepulchre of the Moon, Azhure."

StarDrifter lifted his head. "I thought the Sepulchre of the Moon had been bricked up, First Priestess. Forgotten. Disused."

The First stared at him momentarily, wondering at his beauty here in the sunlight as the wind ruffled his hair and the feathers of his wings. How glad she was that she had survived to see this. "It is still open, Enchanter, but it chooses its visitors carefully. Make sure *you* do not choose to visit."

Her voice was harsh with warning, and StarDrifter took a step back from the cliff. EvenSong stepped back too, but Azhure paused, thinking she heard voices amid the crashing waves.

Is this her?

How can we know it is her?

Does she wear the Circle?

Azhure? Azhure? Azhure?

"Azhure?" StarDrifter's voice cut sharply across her mind and she jumped. "Do you want to see the Temple of the Stars?"

She smiled and followed her companions up the grassy slopes toward the Temple on the highest point of the plateau. But the cries of the waves stayed in her mind for a long time.

The Temple was not what Azhure had expected. Her face fell in disappointment as she crested the slight rise and saw the Temple in all its . . . glory?

"I thought Ysgryff said the Temple was well maintained," she whispered. "Intact."

"And so it is, Azhure, so it is," StarDrifter said softly, riveted by the sight the Icarii had been so long denied.

Azhure could not believe him. All she could see was a large flat circle of marble covering the entire top of the rise, perhaps fifty or sixty paces from side to side. The marble wasn't even well polished, merely well swept, and that likely by the wind rather than by human hand. There was not a column, not an altar, not an icon or a single piece of carving in sight.

"Is this it?" she asked. "Is this all there is?"

StarDrifter turned and stared at her, his face alive with power. "A temple can be built of many things, Azhure. Sometimes of stone or wood. Sometimes of brick and mortar. Sometimes of blood and the hopes and fears of those who would worship within it. Sometimes of ideas. And sometimes . . . sometimes a temple can be built of light and music."

18

Niah

That evening, after she had rested and eaten, Azhure sat with the First in her bare apartment. A single lamp burned on the desk between them, the shadows flickering over both women's faces, momentarily lending one the beauty of her youth and the other the serenity she normally lacked.

"Will you tell me of my mother?" Azhure finally asked.

The First paused, then inclined her head. "Yes. I have no choice."

"What do you mean, no choice?"

The First smiled, but there was little humor in it. "Your mother told me that one day you would sit here in this room and ask me questions." She laughed, the sound harsh. "I did not believe her. But I should have. I should have."

Azhure leaned forward, her hands on the desk. *"Tell me!"*

The Priestess' hands stole to her sash and fiddled with it. "Your mother came to the Temple as a child for her schooling, as did so many Nors children. But she loved it here, and asked to stay once her schooling was completed. I was five years her junior, in mid-school as she entered the novitiate of the Order, but I remember those days well . . . as I remember everything about your mother."

"She was very beautiful, and kind, and she loved me."

"Yes to all those. More beautiful than you are now, but perhaps you have yet to grow into your true beauty. Kind, certainly, and she knew how to love. But I see these qualities in you too, and, in these shadows, I think that perhaps it is *her* sitting before me, not her daughter."

"Her name is . . . was Niah."

"I knew of her name," the First said, "but, child, you must know that all priestesses give up their names once they enter the novitiate. She never had a name to me . . . but she was everything to me."

She paused, and when she resumed her voice was heavy with sadness. "She's dead, isn't she?"

Azhure bowed her head. "Yes. She died when I was five. She . . . she . . ."

"I do not want to hear it!"

Azhure's head jerked up, her eyes suddenly hard and angry. "Niah's death has been too long lost in pain and denial, priestess who claims to have been her friend! If you respected her, if you loved her, then witness her death! Do *that* at least for her!"

The Priestess' eyes widened and her hands stilled as she looked over Azhure's shoulder. In the dim recesses of the room she could see movement, hear voices, and then she saw . . . she saw.

She saw the man bent over the woman's struggling form, saw him hold his hands to her throat, saw him shake her and curse her. She saw him thrust the woman's head into the flames, and then saw the flames flicker and burst over the woman's entire body. She heard the woman scream and grunt with pain, and she heard her cry out to the little girl huddled terrified in the corner.

"Azhure! You are a child of the gods. Seek the answer on Temple Mount! Aaah!"
And again the woman screamed.

"Azhure!" Her voice crackled horrifyingly from the ball of flame that engulfed her entire head. "Live! Live! Your father . . . Ah! Azhure. Ah! Your father!"

"Oh gods!" the First screamed, and covered her face with her hands. "*Oh gods!*"

"Thus died Niah," Azhure whispered, her eyes now still and calm. "Thus died my mother. And thus here I am, seeking the answers to why she died. *Tell me!*"

Eventually the First lowered her hands and raised her grief-stained face to the woman who sat opposite her. "She said that she had to leave. But I did not know where she went. I did not know why she . . ." Her voice broke, and she spent some time composing herself. "She never sent word, and I often wondered about her. How she was, what kind of child she had birthed, whether she was happy."

"But you knew she was pregnant when she left."

"Yes." The First's hands fluttered at a drawer in the desk and her face was gray in the lamp light. "Azhure . . ." She took a deep breath and abruptly opened the drawer, withdrawing a sealed parchment. "Your mother left this for you. Read it. I will wait outside. Call me when you are ready."

For a long time Azhure sat and looked at the square of parchment lying on the desk. When she eventually reached for it, her hands trembled so badly that she had to clench them into tight fists to regain some control over their muscles.

She had not expected this. Not this.

She turned the square over. It had a single word scratched boldly across it in dark ink. *Azhure.*

Still trembling, Azhure picked it up, broke the seal, and began to read:

My dearest daughter Azhure, may long life and joy be yours forever, and may the Stars that dance in their heavens dance only for your delight.

I write this caught fast in the shade of the waning moon and, as it fades, so I feel my life falling ever deeper under its shadows. Now I feel the prospect of my death keenly. Five nights ago you were conceived and tonight, after I put down my pen and seal this letter, I will leave this blessed isle. I will not return—but one day I hope you will come back.

Five nights ago your father came to me.

It was the fullness of the moon, and it was my privilege, as First Priestess, to sit and let its light and life wash over me in the Dome of the Stars. I heard his voice before I saw him.

"Niah," a voice resonant with power whispered through the Dome, and I started, because it was many years since I had heard my birth name.

"Niah," the voice whispered again, and I trembled in fear. Were the gods displeased with me? Had I not honored them correctly during my years on this sacred isle and in this sacred Temple?

"Niah," the voice whispered yet again, and my trembling increased, for despite my lifetime of chastity I recognized the timber of barely controlled desire . . . and I was afraid.

I stood, and only my years of training and discipline kept me from running from the Dome. My eyes frantically searched the roof and for long moments I could see nothing, then a faint movement caught my eye.

A shadow was spiraling down from the roof of the Dome and, despite my fear, my mind had a moment of wonder that the god could somehow have squeezed through the delicate lacework of the Dome—but he was a god, and I should not have been surprised.

The shadow laughed and spoke my name again as he alighted before me.

"I have chosen you to bear my daughter," he said, and he held out his hand, his fingers flaring. "Her name will be Azhure."

At that moment my fear vanished as if it had never existed. Azhure . . . Azhure . . . I had never seen such a man as your father and I know I will not again during this life. He took the form of an Icarii birdman, his naked body as alabaster as the statues of the birdmen that they say stand about the great circle of the Star Gate. His wings shone gold, even in the dark night of the Dome, and his hair glowed with copper fire. His eyes were violet, and they were hungry with magic.

Azhure, as Priestesses of the Stars we are taught to accede to every desire of the gods, even if we are bewildered by their wishes but I went to him with willingness, not with duty. I wore but a simple shift, and as his eyes and fingers flared wider I stepped out of it and walked to meet his hand.

As his hand grasped mine it was as if I was surrounded by Song, and as his mouth captured mine it was as if I was enveloped by the surge of the Stars in their Dance. His power was so all-consuming that I knew he could have snuffed out my life with only a thought. Perhaps I should have been terrified, but he was gentle for a god—not what I might have expected—and if he caused me any pain that night I do not remember it. But what I do remember . . . ah, Azhure, perhaps you have had your own lover by now, but do you know what it feels like to lie with one who can wield the power of the Stars through his body? At times I know he took me perilously close to death as he wove his enchantments through me and made you within my womb, but I trusted him and let him do what he wanted and lay back in his wings as he wrapped them about me and yielded with delight and garnered delight five-fold in return.

I do not know your father's name, for he would not speak it, but I have no doubt that he was one of the gods of the Stars—perhaps the sun god, for he burned with fierce and virulent power and his pale skin was hot under my touch.

I feel blessed that he chose me.

Even as he withdrew from my body I could feel the fire that he had seeded in my womb erupt into new life. He laughed gently at the cry that escaped my lips and at the expression in my eyes, but I could see his own eyes widen to mirror the wonder that filled mine. For a long time we lay still, his body heavy on mine, our eyes staring into each other's depths, as we felt you spring to life within my womb.

Even now, as I write, I can feel the fire and the magic of your being within me. My enchanted, sacred daughter—be all that you promise to be.

After a long while your father spoke.

He told me you are to be born in the village of Smyrton, far to the northeast. He told me you are to grow there. He said that there you will eventually meet the StarMan of the Prophecy of the Destroyer—your father said he already totters on baby feet—and that you will be the axis upon which his entire life will turn. Your father said your early life will be one of pain and misery—and I cried when he told me that, but then he wiped away my tears and said that you will walk through the shadows into bright light and find the happiness that I will have to sacrifice.

Your father is gentle for a god.

Before he left he loved me again—and this he did for me, as inadequate thanks for the daughter I will bear him.

I know that I will die in Smyrton, and I know that the man your father sends me to meet and to marry will also be my murderer. I know that my days will be numbered from the hour that I give you birth. It is a harsh thing that your father makes me do, for how will I be able to submit to this Plow-Keeper Hagen, knowing I will die at his hands, and keep a smile light on my face and my body willing? How can I submit to any man, having known the god that fathered you? How can I submit *to a life dominated by the hated Brotherhood of the Seneschal, when I have been First Priestess of the Order of the Stars?*

Your father saw my doubts and saw my future pain, and he told me that one day I will be reborn to be his lover forever. He said that he had died and yet lived again, and that I would follow a similar path.

He said that he loved me.

Perhaps he lied, but I choose not to think so. To do otherwise would be to submit to despair. His promise, as your life, will keep me through and past my death into my next existence.

I hope that Hagen will allow me enough time with you for you to be able to remember clearly how dearly your mother loved you.

Know that I love you and will love you past death and into the forever that your father has promised me.

Niah

By the time she had finished, Azhure was trembling so violently and her eyes were so blurred with tears that she let the letter fall to the floor.

"Damn you!" she cried. "*Damn* you, WolfStar, for lying to Niah so badly!" She leaned her face into her arms and wept.

After a long, long time she sat up and wiped her eyes, picking up the letter and folding it carefully before slipping it into a pocket in her robe.

Outside the First Priestess was waiting. She reached out for Azhure, but the woman stepped back. "What do you know of my conception, First Priestess?"

The Priestess' eyes were bright with compassion. "Only what your mother told me. That a god came to her in the Dome and that he wanted her to leave this isle. That is all."

Azhure's shoulders stiffened. "And when you sit in the Dome, First Priestess, in the fullness of the moon, has a god ever come to you?"

The woman lowered her eyes. "No. None has ever come."

"Then be grateful," Azhure said bitterly, "that you have been so blessed."

StarDrifter started, wakened by the opening door and the soft footfall. "Azhure?"

He heard her take a tremulous breath, and realized she had been crying. He sat up. "Azhure? What is it? What's wrong?"

She sat down on the bed beside him, and for a very long time she did not say anything. He took her hand and stroked the hair from her forehead, and she seemed grateful for the contact.

"StarDrifter?"

"Yes?"

She was quiet for a very long time. "May I stay the night with you?"

"Azhure!"

"Please," she said, tears trickling down her cheeks, and StarDrifter gathered her into his arms and his wings. "Please, just hold me, StarDrifter, and tell me that you love me."

19

Planting

From the Silent Woman Woods Faraday moved slowly northeast toward the Ancient Barrows, finally planting out the Enchanted Wood. Within days she was sore and tired and lonely beyond belief. She was almost constantly nauseous, and at night when she sank to her knees, exhausted, she could hardly force herself to eat. The warmth and comfort of the Silent Woman Keep seemed a lifetime behind her.

She had not thought that the planting would demand so much of her physical and emotional strength.

Each night Faraday spent tossing and turning, spending her dreams between Ur's nursery and dark, uncomfortable places that she could not recognize. Each morning she woke to find herself surrounded by several hundred tiny terracotta pots, every seedling brimming with zest and cheerfulness. Faraday was not entirely sure how they reached her, but she thought that she must spend much of her sleeping hours moving between the Sacred Grove and this world, carrying the pots two by two. No wonder she woke more exhausted than when she lay down to rest. She would struggle up and smile wanly at the seedlings, force herself to eat a few mouthfuls of food, and then begin yet another day of planting.

The morning Faraday had left the Silent Woman Keep, she had walked outside to find only one of the donkeys laden with its saddlebags. The other was harnessed to a small, blue, flat-trayed cart. She was puzzled by this, until the first morning she woke to find herself surrounded by hundreds of tiny pots. If not for the cart, she would never have been able to carry them.

Faraday spent all day and most of the twilight hours transferring the seedlings into mortal land. She moved in a daze, sometimes not truly sure what she was doing, sometimes almost completely disoriented and detached, relying on the strength of the Mother to give her the heart to keep going.

She planted the seedlings far apart, usually at least a hundred paces, in a great swathe from the eastern edge of the Silent Woman Woods. She would stumble along, often holding onto the mane of one of the donkeys with a bleeding hand for support, until instinct and the cry of a seedling told her the time was right.

Calling to the donkeys to stop, Faraday would reach for the seedling that cried out, and sink to her knees on the ground. Her fingers aching with the need to dig, she would set the seedling to one side while she scratched frantically into the hard-packed soil. Then, her fingers bloodied and bruised, she would gently tip the seedling out of her pot, speaking softly to her, calling her by name, encouraging her to find the strength to grow tall and strong, telling her that her wait was ending, and that the final transformation was at hand.

Once Faraday had patted the soil about the seedling she would reach for the wooden bowl which rested on the back of the tray, and was constantly filled with life-giving emerald water. Although where it came from Faraday did not know, for she never filled it herself. Carefully, she would pour a few drops over the seedling and about its base, singing the Song with which she and StarDrifter had woken the Earth Tree so long ago, when the Avarinheim groves had been under attack by the Skraelings.

Faraday prayed the strength of the Earth Tree could reach this far south and somehow infuse will and strength into her tiny daughter. Then, for some minutes, she would kneel and look at the seedling, waving bravely in the cold wind of the northern Tarantaise plains. The plant looked so small, so vulnerable, that she often wondered if the seedlings would survive their first critical months.

And how long would they take to grow? Faraday was no gardener, but she knew that trees took almost a human lifetime to stretch their branches to the sky. Did she have a lifetime to wait for the Enchanted Wood to take root and thrive? Did Axis? Did *Tencendor*?

Then she would sigh and struggle to her feet, and leave the seedling humming quietly to herself as she stumbled farther and farther north.

The end of the day was always the worst. It took Faraday till twilight to plant all the seedlings for the day. Yet when she looked back to the land that she had planted, she could see nothing but the waving grasses of the desolate plains. Somewhere out there were several hundred seedlings, several thousand after two weeks, yet Faraday could not see them, and even their gentle humming had long ago been lost in the lonely plains behind her.

Were they still there? Would they survive the cold nights? The driving rain of the not-so-distant winter? The covering of several handspans of unforgiving snow?

Faraday had thought the planting would bring her more joy. But there were only ever the rolling plains and the constant pain in her fingers and back and legs. And, in the morning, several hundred more seedlings waving gently at her as she opened her exhausted eyes.

Two weeks after Faraday began planting she reached the semicircle of the Ancient Barrows. This was one of the most sacred sites of the Icarii, and Faraday knew that she would likely find an encampment of Enchanters here. It was also where she had first told Axis she loved him, where her mother, Merlion, had died, where Jack and Yr had spirited her away from the man she loved to the husband who had taken so much of her spirit and her youth. It was, she mused, a place of death, and not only because of the tombs of the twenty-six Enchanter-Talons.

For three days she planted in a circle about the Barrows, ignoring the Icarii who flew overhead and who, respecting her wishes and her mission, left her alone. Then, finally, late one evening, she entered the Barrows.

She had not known what to expect. The massive Barrows still stretched in a crescent from south to north, but they had been cleared of much of their undergrowth so that their lines rose even more starkly into the night sky. An aura of power and spirituality hung over them in the twilight, so that the air almost hummed. But what instantly caught Faraday's eye was the column in the very center of the hollow between the Barrows. A slender obelisk of twisted bronze, erected by the Icarii, soared into the night sky, so high that Faraday had to crane her neck to follow its path to the stars. At its apex rested a large shallow bowl, from which seared a blue flame that leaped and flickered in the dark—during the day it was almost invisible.

"Faraday?" a gentle voice said behind her, and she turned reluctantly.

An Icarii Enchanter stood there, his white-blond hair and pale blue wings reflecting the shadows of the blue flame. "My name is StarRest SoarDeep," he said, taking her hands in his. "The Enchantress sent word that you would pass this way and asked us to watch for you."

His eyes darkened in concern as he saw the circles of weariness under Faraday's eyes and felt the scabs and abrasions on her fingers. "You are tired," he said.

Faraday straightened her back with an effort and tried to smile. "As would you be, StarRest, if you spent your days on your knees planting out seedling after seedling."

"It goes well?" StarRest could sense that she did not want his concern or his pity.

Faraday shrugged. "Well enough. I plant where I must, and I sing to the seedlings." She smiled again, more genuinely this time. "They are pleased to finally escape their cribs, StarRest."

He let her hands go and indicated a small campfire close to one of the

Barrows. "Will you share our meal with us, Faraday? And perhaps the Healer with us can look at your hands."

Faraday clenched her hands by her side. "I will eat with you, StarRest, and be glad of the company, but my hands are well enough. They do not need attention."

StarRest did not press the issue. "Then come. We are not many, but we are cheerful enough company."

They joined the small encampment of some ten or twelve Icarii, and Faraday sank gratefully down by the fire after StarRest had introduced her to the other Enchanters. She stretched her hands out to the warmth, and the Icarii winced when they saw them, but, following StarRest's lead, they said nothing. For a while they talked of inconsequential things as they passed bowls of food about, then, as Faraday set her almost untouched bowl to one side, she asked them what they did at the Barrows.

"At the Barrows itself, very little," replied one of the Enchanters, a small birdwoman with exquisite features and flame-colored hair. "As you have seen, we erected the beacon over the location of the Star Gate, and we have cleaned many of the Barrows, but that is all we want to do for the time being."

"My mother is buried here," Faraday said quietly.

StarRest shared a glance of concern with his colleagues. "Really? We did not know. There is evidence of graves here . . . the StarMan once told us he lost a number of his men to a Gorgrael-driven tempest in this place."

"Yes. My mother died in that same storm. She must be buried with them."

"Then we will pray over the graves for your mother, Faraday Tree Friend, and wish her peace in the AfterLife."

Touched, Faraday watched the blue flame flicker far above them for a few minutes, thinking of her mother. "The flame reminds me of the blue shadows that chase across the vault above the Star Gate," she said eventually.

"You have seen the Star Gate?" StarRest asked, startled.

Faraday turned her head toward him. "Yes. Two of the Sentinels took me to the Star Gate two years ago. We went through . . . through . . ."

She looked about her, her eyes straining in the night, then pointed to one of the shadowy Barrows that had collapsed at one end. "We went through that Barrow, then down the stairwell to the Star Gate."

The Enchanters looked troubled. "The ninth," one said under his breath.

Now it was Faraday's turn to look surprised. "That was WolfStar's Barrow?" she asked, and StarRest nodded. Then his manipulations go deeper than any realized, Faraday thought.

"Do you intend to rebuild it?" Did they know that WolfStar had come back through the Star Gate? Had Axis of StarDrifter told them?

Apparently not. One of the Enchanters shrugged, unconcerned "No, I think not. You may not realize, Faraday, but the ninth Enchanter-Talon, WolfStar, is not well remembered among the Icarii. If his Barrow collapses, then none of us truly care. It is well that he be totally forgotten."

An unlikely event, Faraday thought. "And the Star Gate? Have you reached that yet?"

"Yes," StarRest replied, smiling "Yes, we have. If you have been into the chamber of the Star Gate you know that there are many entrances, not only through the Barrows."

"I know. We exited through an ancient tunnel that Jack told me was once your main entrance to the Star Gate. But that collapsed after we had scrambled free. Have you dug it out again?"

StarRest shook his head. "I know the tunnel you refer to. No. That is totally destroyed now. But there are several others that lead down, one of them here among these Barrows that apparently your Sentinels did not know about. It is only small, but we have all been down." He paused. "We have all gazed into the Star Gate."

For a long time there was silence. Faraday remembered the power and the beauty that the Star Gate contained, remembered the multicolored stars and galaxies singing as they reeled across the cosmos. Remembered the lure of the Gate as it called to those who gazed into its depths. "So what will you do?" she asked eventually.

StarRest sighed and stretched his hands toward the fire. "Wait. Wait until more of the Icarii have flown south. Wait until StarDrifter has relit the Temple of the Stars. Wait," he looked at Faraday, "until the Barrows are once more enveloped by the trees. Then we will have a ceremony to reconsecrate this ground. Though I imagine that few but Enchanters will ever see the Star Gate. It is too beautiful . . . too dangerous. You have been blessed, Faraday, to have seen it."

Faraday took a deep breath, turning the conversation away from the Star Gate. If she thought anymore on its beauty and power she would burst into tears. She had been filled with so much hope then, had expected so much. "Have you had much trouble from the Acharites about here?"

"No," StarRest said. "The borderlands between Tarantaise and Arcness were sparsely populated to begin with and, with the signing of the Treaty of the Barrows—"

Faraday's eyes widened. She had forgotten that Axis and Raum had signed the treaty with the Barons Ysgryff and Greville that gave most of this land back to the Avar and their forest at this spot.

"—the few farmers that were here have moved south and west to new farms."

"Yes," Faraday said. "I noticed how lonely the plains are."

One of the male Enchanters leaned forward, concerned. "Faraday, we know what you do here. You are Tree Friend and you replant the great forests. Would you like company? Assistance? This is a hard task for one person, and we cannot help but notice—"

"No," Faraday interrupted harshly. "No," she repeated, softening her tone. "I am well enough, and this is a task I must accomplish on my own."

And I cannot bear to have any Icarii with me, she thought, for your eyes and your power remind me too much of Axis. But thinking of Axis made her ask if they had heard any news of the StarMan or Azhure over the past few weeks.

"Almost nothing, Faraday, and what news we have is old. We know that Axis leads his army north into Aldeni to meet the Skraeling horde and we heard that the Enchantress has sailed for the Island of Mist and Memory with StarDrifter."

StarRest smiled. "Soon this small flame will not be the only beacon lifting into the stars."

From Tare the Goodwife Renkin marched resolutely east. After she had left StarShine EvenHeart in the marketplace, the Goodwife wasted only enough time to entrust a brief message to her husband and the coins from the sale of the ewes with a sheepherder returning to northern Arcness, and restock her pack with food before leaving the town.

Poor Lady, poor Lady Faraday. Fancy traveling into the rolling plains all by herself. What could she be thinking of? What can she be doing out here by herself? I should never have let her leave my home, the Goodwife berated herself. Never let her leave the warmth of my fire.

"She needs a friend," the Goodwife muttered every morning when she rose at dawn and shouldered her pack. "She needs someone to help her."

And as she marched, the Goodwife remembered many things.

First, the recipes and spells that her granny had told her bubbled to the surface. Every day, with every step, another memory resurfaced and the Goodwife was constantly stopping, her eyes round with astonishment. "Oh!" she would breathe, "how could I have forgotten *that?*"

And as she walked, she would spy an herb, and she would pause to touch its leaves, muttering to herself its purpose and the words that needed to be spoken to augment its particular powers.

Occasionally she picked a plant, or plucked a few leaves from it, and placed them carefully into the pocket of her coat. After several days, the Goodwife found she had accumulated such a collection that she spent an entire day drying them before carefully packing them in her pack.

Some of the things the Goodwife remembered she knew her grandmother could never have told her, nor could she ever have witnessed for herself. She remembered struggling out of a cave, with those other few people who had managed to survive, only to see the world they had known devastated by fire that had fallen from the sky—and the great craters they had left in the earth, now gradually filling with steaming water until, within only a few weeks, they were hidden beneath gentle and wondrous lakes.

She remembered standing on a mountain and seeing a great forest, a sea of emerald swaying in the gentle breeze. Bright-hued butterflies fluttered from tree to tree, but when her memory deepened and strengthened, the Goodwife realized that they were not butterflies at all, but more of the beautiful flying people she had spoken to in Tare.

Many fluttered about pastel-colored spires reaching from the forest canopy into the sky.

She remembered a time when flying people were not the strangest folk she could expect to meet in her local market, and when song and music were so widespread that life was lived among their phrases and according to their beat.

She remembered a time when the stars were closer and when there were more gods, more than Artor, who walked the land.

At that memory the Goodwife paused and stamped her foot on the hard soil. "And damn that plow," she muttered, "for it did nothing but wreck my good man's back and keep his feet mired in the mud day after day."

After several days of walking (or was it longer—she had been so mired herself in memories that she'd lost all sense of time), the Goodwife approached the Silent Woman Woods. For many hours she stood at its southern border and stared into its dark depths. All her life she had been taught to hate the forests that had once covered this land, but the Goodwife felt no fear gazing at these trees. The teachings of the Seneschal had receded so far by this stage that she just stood and admired, and thought that the Woods' depths were not so much dark as pleasantly shaded from the sun.

And the trees spoke to her, although she could hear no words.

After a while, the Goodwife nodded, then turned and walked northeast, hefting her pack more comfortably onto her back.

The next day she reached the first seedling.

The Goodwife stood and looked at it for a very, very long time. Poor thing, struggling to survive here in this wasteland, the tough grasses waving three times its height over it. Lost and lonely it was, a little like the Goodwife imagined the Lady Faraday was at the moment.

The Goodwife grunted and scratched her chin, thinking. Shouldn't she do something at this point? Wasn't there something about these seedlings that she should remember? So lost, so lonely, so tiny, struggling for life in this hostile soil.

It reminded the Goodwife of her first child, her daughter, a baby born so small and still that no one thought she would survive. All night the Goodwife had sat in her bed, her husband snoring at her side, holding the baby, willing her to live. Then, as the dawn light had crept through the cracks in the door, the Goodwife—very hesitantly, and making sure her husband was still soundly asleep—had hummed a lilting cradle song over the baby, one of the few tunes she had retained from her granny's teaching. It was a pretty song, and the baby had taken heart from it and had thrived from that morning on.

As her other children came, the Goodwife had hummed that cradle song to them in the first hours of their lives (and always out of her husband's hearing), and none of her children had died from the plagues and diseases that carried off so many of her neighbors' children. Artor's luck, her neighbors said enviously, but the Goodwife knew differently now, and she knew that this dear little seedling also needed that old lullaby to give it the encouragement to take a firm grip on life.

So the Goodwife hummed the song through, bending down to pat the seedling reassuringly on its upper leaves when she'd finished.

"Dear little thing. Your Mother loves you."

Then she walked forward until she reached the next seedling, and the next, and the one after, and always she sung the ancient lullaby over their leaves, stroked them, and told them that their Mother loved them.

And on she went.

And when she woke the next morning she sat up, blinked, and gaped in amazement.

She did not enter the Ancient Barrows, not because she was afraid of the Icarii within, or of the blue flame, or even of the naked power that floated over the Barrows, but because she wanted to reach the Lady Faraday and she sensed that the Lady was only a few days ahead of her now.

But the Enchanters stood atop the Barrows, shocked as they looked at the sight that lay behind the peasant woman tramping through the plains, listening to the sound that reached their ears. So *that* was the music that had been reverberating through their dreams for the past two nights!

The woman smiled up at them and waved, but continued resolutely on.

As she passed, the Enchanters spontaneously broke into a Song of ThanksGiving.

The Goodwife thought it sounded very pretty, but not as nice as what echoed behind her.

Faraday lay still and cheerless under her blankets in the cool morning. She could not bear to open her eyes, for she knew that again she would be surrounded by gently humming seedlings, impatient for her to transplant them. She was exhausted. When would she find time to rest?

Faraday sighed and rubbed her stomach. She felt nauseous again and knew that she should try to force down some food. But even the delicacies that the magical saddlebags could offer didn't interest her. Perhaps later, when the sun was higher and the first seedlings planted out for the day, she would eat.

The wind pushed beneath her blankets, cold and insistent, and Faraday finally opened her eyes. She blinked, then frowned, puzzled. Before her sat, as expected, rows of tiny seedlings, but beyond them . . . beyond them stood scuffed brown leather boots encasing a sturdy pair of ankles, and even sturdier legs that disappeared into a brown worsted country dress.

Faraday sat up and looked at the peasant woman's face. Briefly she thought she was a stranger, then she recognized the woman "Goodwife Renkin! What? How . . ." Her voice trailed off Goodwife Renkin? *Here?*

"My Lady," the Goodwife exclaimed, her face split by a great smile, her eyes shining, her hands clutching among her skirts. "Oh, my Lady! Please, let me stay with you, don't send me away. I'd do anything to help, really I would!"

"Goodwife Renkin," Faraday said again, uselessly, as the Goodwife leaned down to help her rise. As she stood, Faraday looked at the plain behind the Goodwife . . . and realized that the sound of the morning which filled the air was not just the noise of the donkeys grazing or of the tiny seedlings humming.

At the Goodwife's back stood a forest. Great trees, a hundred paces high, reached toward the sun, their branches reaching out fifty paces or more so they embraced the limbs of their sisters. Beneath them the tough grasses of the Tarantaise and southern Arcness plains had given way to low fragrant shrubs and flowered walks dappled with the golden light that filtered through the forest canopy.

And they hummed—a tune Faraday later recognized as the lullaby the Goodwife taught them. It was a breathtaking sound for, although not particularly loud, it was rich and vibrant, full of shadows and cadences, each tree adding her own distinctive voice that nevertheless harmonized perfectly with those of her neighbors and with the sound of the forest. Faraday could feel it vibrating through her body.

What would it be like when they finally burst into song?

The Goodwife looked at Faraday's face, then at the trees. "Don't they make a pleasant sound, m'Lady? They sound like a sea of minstrels, yes they do." One of her booted feet tapped in time with the trees.

Faraday wrenched her eyes away from the forest. "A sea of minstrels, Goodwife?" She took a deep breath of happiness. "Then why don't we call this new forest Minstrelsea? It needs a name, and that will do as well as any other and better than most." She paused. "Goodwife, what *are* you doing here?"

"I have come to help," the Goodwife said quietly, her country burr totally gone, and Faraday, looking deep into the Goodwife's eyes, beheld the eyes of the Mother.

20

Brother-Leader Gilbert

Artor appeared many more times to Gilbert as he hustled Moryson north-ward from Nor, and each time Gilbert's eyes grew a little darker with fanaticism, his mouth a little slacker with ecstasy, and his will hardened. He would do anything, *anything*, to ensure that Artor and the Seneschal regained their rightful place in Achar.

Moryson followed placidly behind Gilbert on a horse the man had grudgingly bought him.

Even though Moryson generally remained quiet and uncomplaining, his presence often irritated Gilbert. Occasionally, but only very occasionally, Moryson would let slip a tart comment that reminded Gilbert too vividly of the days when he had been only a second adviser to the Brother-Leader, and Moryson the trusted friend of forty years' standing. Didn't Moryson realize that Gilbert was in charge now? That Gilbert led the Seneschal? That Gilbert stood at Artor's night hand?

But even more annoying were Moryson's occasional absences. The first time Gilbert noticed that Moryson was missing he entered a fugue of anxiety. The man's horse was there, but not the old man. Had Moryson fallen down a badger's burrow and broken a frail leg? Had he been snatched by one of the flying filth that Gilbert expected to descend on them any moment? Had he lain down to die among the tall grass and neglected to mention it to Gilbert, several dozen paces ahead? For an hour or more Gilbert searched, calling Moryson's name, his face running with sweat. What would Artor think if he lost the fool? At the moment, Moryson was his only follower, and Gilbert, much as he disliked the old man, could hardly afford to lose him.

But just when Gilbert thought that he had vanished altogether, he turned around to see Moryson hobbling across the plain toward him, his face a mask of contrition.

"It's my bowels, Gilbert," Moryson hastily explained. "I am an old man and sometimes my bowels can dribble fluids for hours. Ah, is that my horse behind you?"

Gilbert turned away, his face green, and didn't ask again when Moryson disappeared—usually at night, but once or twice during the day as well. He was disgusted by the old man's weakness. Artor grant me continued health throughout my life, he prayed, whenever Moryson stumbled back into camp, his face pale and damp.

For some time they moved north, and then northeast, as Artor directed. They found another Brother, a displaced Plow-Keeper, ten days after they started on their divine crusade. He was huddled among the grass, crouched as low as he could get, terrified by the approaching horsemen.

Gilbert squared his shoulders and spoke in as authoritative a manner as he could manage. "Get up, man. What is your name? Where are you from?"

The Plow-Keeper, a thin man of middle-age, peered out from underneath his arm, but did not uncurl himself from his protective ball. "My name is Finnis, good master, and I am but a poor sheepherder traveling this plain to market."

Gilbert's lip curled. "Well, good Finnis, where are your sheep? And what is that fuzzy patch I see at the crown of your head—not a tonsure growing out, is it?"

Finnis hurriedly buried his head as far as he could under his arm and gave a muffled squeak.

Gilbert kicked his horse closer. "Get up, Finnis, and behold your Brother-Leader."

Very slowly Finnis looked out from beneath his arm. "Brother-Leader?"

"Brother-Leader Gilbert, man. Now *stand up!*"

Finnis almost tripped in his haste to stand. "But . . . but . . . I thought . . ."

"Well, you thought wrong, you simpleton. The Seneschal has never endured darker days than these, but with the grace and strength of Artor we will walk through them. Surely you know my name. Gilbert? Once adviser to Brother-Leader Jayme?"

Finnis thought hard, staring at the man before him. He was not dressed like a Brother, but then Finnis was only too well aware that to dress like a member of the Seneschal in these days was foolishness personified. Gilbert? Yes, Finnis remembered that name being on some of the orders he had received from the Tower of the Seneschal. He looked behind Gilbert to the old man, huddled despondently on his horse.

"And Brother Moryson," Gilbert said. "My adviser." Until I find better.

Moryson's eyes glinted, but he said nothing.

"What happened to Brother-Leader Jayme?" Finnis asked Gilbert.

Gilbert's face assumed an expression of pious sadness. "Murdered by the foul feathered creatures that block out the sun over the Tower of the Seneschal, Brother Finnis. He died screaming Artor's name."

That was a nice touch, Gilbert thought, not realizing how true it was. "I am Artor's anointed," he made the sign of the Plow, "and I will keep you safe and shall rebuild the Seneschal to its former glory."

Finnis felt the first faint stirrings of hope and he bobbed his head deferentially at Gilbert "Will you tell me what to do, Brother-Leader Gilbert?"

"Gladly, Brother Finnis, but not until we stop for evening camp. For the moment you can scramble up behind Moryson."

After that day Gilbert's band grew until, as they approached northern Tarantaise, it numbered eight displaced Brothers of the Seneschal besides himself and Moryson. After they had stumbled across Finnis, they found a Brother every day or two—Gilbert thought Artor must have directed their steps his way, and the Brothers confirmed this by telling him that Artor had appeared in their dreams. Most were displaced Plow-Keepers who had been ejected by their local village after Axis' army had swung south through Arcness and Tarantaise.

"How is it that the people have accepted the Forbidden so easily?" they asked one after the other as they told Gilbert their story, and Gilbert always replied, "Because of the foul enchantments the creatures fling their way. But do not worry, Artor will save them yet."

Gilbert did not have enough coin to buy every Brother a horse, and compromised by purchasing a cheap horse and cart in Tare. He sent Moryson, well-cloaked, inside the town, reasoning that if the man was caught then it would be little loss. But Moryson reemerged from the town's gates after several hours driving a splintered but serviceable cart pulled by a sway-backed mare who looked as old and sad as the old Brother; and who, Gilbert was disgusted to discover, suffered from much the same bowel condition as Moryson himself.

From that point on they moved faster, Gilbert riding ahead on his horse, Moryson driving the cart with the band of Brothers clinging to its tray.

At the end of the first week of Frost-month they drove past the Silent Woman Woods; they stayed well to the south, for none of the Brothers wanted to go too close. Only Artor knew what demons had reinhabited the Woods in recent months.

"I penetrated deep within those Woods some years past," Gilbert told the Brothers, for once reining his horse back to the cart so he could talk to them. "Not only did I enter, but I led the BattleAxe and two Axe-Wielders, too terrified to lead themselves. They were assaulted by foul creatures who leaped at them from beneath the very earth, but I fought clear, and saved them from a gruesome death. For what purpose, I know not," Gilbert sighed melodramatically, "for the BattleAxe has gone on to betray not only the Seneschal, but Artor himself."

The Brothers jouncing along in the cart gazed at Gilbert admiringly.

"I discovered great secrets in the Keep at the center of the Woods," Gilbert continued, "but at the same time the BattleAxe released into an unsuspecting world two demons who lived there in the guise of Brothers of the Seneschal. I could not stop him, although I tried valiantly. I think that Achar's descent into hell started from the moment those fiends were released."

There were gasps of horror, but Moryson grinned beneath the hood of his cloak.

"I am not afraid of the trees," Gilbert said, "and when Artor tells me the time is right, I shall unleash on them such a storm of righteous anger that they will topple before me. The Plow will win through, and tear the tree stumps out of the earth."

But even Gilbert fell silent in two days' time when they spied the newly planted forest in front of them.

"That wasn't there before," he whispered, "I am sure of it! No one has ever mentioned *this*!"

Moryson pulled the grateful mare to a halt and stared ahead. They had topped a small rise and before them, perhaps a few hundred paces away, sprawled Faraday's forest. It spread across the horizon for over a league, and all could see that it stretched thick and healthy for many more leagues to the north. Far to the north Moryson could just see the Barrows rising out of the center of the forest, a blue flame beckoning.

His companions stared at the forest, eyes and mouths hanging open.

Not even the Silent Woman Woods had trees as tall, as thick, as *powerful* as these. Birds fluttered among branches, and as they watched, a brown and black badger, common to these plains, emerged from its burrow and bounded the fifty or so paces into the tree line.

It had gone home.

"It's disgusting!" Finnis whispered.

One of the Brothers made the sign of the Plow, and the others hastily copied him.

"It *hums*!" Gilbert croaked.

And indeed the forest did hum. Not loudly, and not even with a discernible tune—not at this distance—but all could feel fragments of melody vibrating through their flesh.

"Its name," Moryson abruptly said, blinking, "is Minstrelsea."

The horse lifted her tired head and whickered, her ears flickering forward.

"I don't give an Artor's curse what its name is!" Gilbert cried, too scared to wonder how Moryson knew its name. "Back! Back before it traps us! Moryson, turn the horse about. We'll camp in the hollow behind this rise, out of sight of this demon-spawned aberration."

*   *   *

That night, Gilbert summoned Artor for his band. He had not done so previously, preferring to relay Artor's words secondhand, but he knew that after the horror of the forest they would need the comforting presence of Artor Himself. And it would impress on the men Gilbert's own place at Artor's side.

No wonder, he thought, as he knelt in prayer, his Brothers ranged in a semicircle behind him, that Artor had warned him about Faraday. Was she responsible for this? Had she planted this . . . he tried to remember what Moryson had called it . . . this Minstrelsea? When had *she* been corrupted? Gilbert recalled the looks that had passed between Axis and Faraday across the campfires of the Axe-Wielders so long ago. Perhaps Axis had befouled her with his own corruption way back then.

Well, no matter. Artor would see that Gilbert's commitment would not waver. If Artor wanted this forest destroyed, then so be it.

If Artor wanted Faraday destroyed, so be it.

His head bowed, Gilbert humbly begged Artor's presence. He reached out with his prayers, and summoned the god to his side.

He felt it through his body first, the rhythmic thumping of the plowshare through the earth. Then the labored, maddened snorts of the fury-eyed red bulls reached his ears, and Gilbert lifted his head and flung his arms wide in exultation.

Behind him, the Brothers cowered to the ground in terror. To one side Moryson fought to keep his fear under control, burying his face in his hands.

As Artor urged his plow-team forward, Gilbert scrambled to his feet. "Artor!" he screamed.

My good Gilbert, Artor's voice whispered over the plains and He stepped out from behind. His Plow, His body roped heavy with muscle and power. *Have you seen what she has done? Do you understand now?*

"Oh yes!" Gilbert breathed. "It is foul . . . foul!"

Foul indeed—and yet I can do little without your assistance, good Gilbert.

"Anything, Artor, anything!"

The world collapses about us, Gilbert. The other bitch threatens to open the Gates even farther, but I can do nothing about her. She is too distant. Too powerful.

The other bitch? Gilbert frowned, but did not interrupt his god.

But it matters not. If we can stop this Faraday, then the whole scheme will unravel. Take but one note away, Gilbert, untune that string, and hark! What discord follows!

"Yes, oh Blessed One."

Get her, Gilbert.

"Yes," Gilbert hissed ecstatically.

Get Faraday. You must stop her, Gilbert. Or else I WILL DIE!

Gilbert screamed as Artor's voice ripped through his body, and behind him he could hear the other Brothers screaming.

Then Artor's voice dropped to a whisper. *She moves more swiftly now, and the Enchanted Forest grows. Go to Arcen, Gilbert. Hurry. Stop her before she links these trees with the Shadowsward. If she does that . . . stop her!*

Gilbert, his head bowed, felt Artor step to his side and he trembled, but the god only rested a benevolent hand on Gilbert's shoulder.

Let me lend you power, Gilbert. Let me make you a more effective instrument.

This time, when Gilbert screamed, even the distant trees heard it, and faltered momentarily in their melody.

If you use it well, Gilbert, you will be able to stop her.

"Yes," Gilbert whispered, amazed he could talk at all. He dimly realized he had wet himself when Artor had flooded him with power. Beside him the god lifted his head and surveyed the trembling semicircle behind Gilbert.

Serve him well.

Almost as one, the Brothers screamed that they would.

To one side Moryson descended into terror once more. Pray don't touch me with your hand, Artor, he chanted over and over in his mind, because I don't know what would happen. I don't know how I will react!

Do as he tells you.

Yes!

Destroy her.

Yes!

21

The Sword

A xis stood in what was left of the market hall of Jervois Landing and stared at the frozen corpse of Jorge, Earl of Avonsdale. His eyes, ice now, gazed into whatever eternity he was enduring, while his hands were still wrapped about the blade that had killed him . . . his own.

From the Three Brothers Lakes, Axis had led his army cautiously—oh, so cautiously—north for four weeks. It seemed that he had spent every waking moment, and many a sleeping one, expecting attack. Where were the Skraelings? Where had they gone? Whenever the wind lifted a drift of snow from a low hill Axis would jump, whenever a bird cried behind him he thought it was an Icarii scout warning of disaster.

He had traveled slowly, not only because he expected attack, but because he did not want to lose contact with his supply line. With an army this size, and with territory this useless, he would have to retreat if his supplies could no longer be inched north on mules—no carts could travel through these snow-drifts. Axis worried as much about food as he did about Skraeling attack.

Gorgrael's storms had rendered Aldeni a wasteland. Duke Roland's province had once been one of the main food-producing regions of Tencendor, now it was little more than a bowl of snow and ice. If I ever chase back the Skraelings, Axis asked himself, unable to tear his eyes away from Jorge's frozen agony, if I ever manage to best Gorgrael, will this land ever recover?

"Axis?"

Belial's soft voice sounded behind him, and Axis turned.

Belial stopped as he saw Jorge's corpse, then raised his eyes to Axis' face. "It is the same all over the town. Corpses, frozen in death, litter the buildings. Most have been torn apart. Not like . . ."

"Not like Jorge, Belial? When did you ever know a Skraeling, or an IceWorm, or even a Star-damned SkraeBold, use a sword?"

"Axis." Belial placed a gentle hand on his friend's shoulder. "Perhaps Jorge—"

"No!" Axis' voice was firm. "He was a courageous man, Belial, and he would not have died by his own accord. No." His tone softened. "See the angle. That sword was driven in by another hand."

But whose hand? Did Jorge also have a traitor in his camp?

Belial guided Axis away from Jorge's corpse. "We will arrange a cremation for all who died here. Farewell them honorably into the AfterLife."

They walked slowly out of the building. Outside the air was frigid, but calm, as it had been for the entire time they'd been in Aldeni. Gorgrael was playing games with them.

Axis felt a shiver of premonition. "I don't like it here, Belial. Why didn't the Skraelings stay to feed? These men have been butchered, but they have not been eaten. Not the usual Skraeling way. Someone controls them now, Belial, someone . . ."

Suddenly he twisted away from Belial's hand and punched his fist into the air. "*Where are they?*" he screamed.

They burned and farewelled the dead that evening. For a time Belial had thought they would not find the fuel to ignite the frozen corpses. But, by chance, his men had discovered a cache of oil secreted deep in the cellars of the market hall, and the dead burned with a crispness that partially alleviated the horror of their passing.

Belial and Magariz joined Axis in his tent later; the camp had been set up well outside the town, for none could bear to sleep amid its memories, and Axis could not escape his premonition that the buildings, largely unscathed, remained a trap.

Axis sat on his bunk, head bowed, turning a sword over and over in his hands. It was Jorge's sword; Axis had pulled it from the man's belly as two men carried him to the funeral pyre.

"A well-made sword, Axis," Magariz said as he sat down.

"Yes," Axis said absently. "Well made indeed. Despite lingering for weeks in Jorge's belly it has neither rusted nor stained. See? The remaining blood flakes off." He raised his head. Belial stood before a small brazier that gave off a cheerful glow, if not much heat. "I thought I would keep it, Belial. Wear it, perhaps."

"Axis . . ." Belial began, but Axis dropped his eyes and continued.

"I am not so attached to my own sword that I cannot replace it with one better, and this *is* better. It is an Escatorian blade, sharp and sure, and has a hilt crafted, if I'm not mistaken, in the sweat-riddled forges of Ysbadd. It is a good blade . . . and it yearns for revenge. I shall use it to stick whoever thrust it into Jorge's gut."

Magariz exchanged a glance with Belial, and Axis caught it. "Oh," he said, his mouth quirked lopsidedly. "I am not yet ready to sink into a morass of morbidity, my friends, but I confess confusion and frustration. Where is this army? Who leads it?"

"Can you not use your enchantments, Axis?" Belial asked. "Scry them out, perhaps?"

Axis laid the sword to one side. "No. I have tried, but there is nothing I can do. Gorgrael lends this army the strength of his power, and he commands a power—the Dark Music—that I cannot use. I cannot understand it, nor the enchantments it creates. If he cloaks his army with that power then I will never find them with my own enchantments. We are reliant on strong feet and wings, Belial, and sharp eyes."

Magariz leaned forward, trying to catch some of the warmth from the brazier. "Any news, Axis?"

"No. You have heard the reports of the Icarii farflight scouts. They see nothing but snow and ice stretching across all of Aldeni."

"And Ichtar?"

"Your promised land, Magariz? No, I have not sent them there, Ichtar is too risky, too unknown. Gorgrael has controlled that for almost two years now, and I fear the Gryphon too much to overextend the farflight scouts."

"And nothing from Sigholt? Or Talon Spike?"

"*Nothing*, Belial," Axis said. "They did not even see enough to warn me of the approach of this Skraeling force, let alone inform me where it is now. Come on," his tone became brisk, "give me your thoughts. If *you* were in command of this army, where would you go? What would you plan?"

"A trap, Axis," Magariz said, his fingers unconsciously rubbing the faint scar on his cheek. "A trap."

Axis' mouth twisted bitterly. "A trap, he says. *What* trap, Magariz?"

Magariz shrugged, shame-faced. "Perhaps he wants to draw you north, into Ichtar. Perhaps that's where he has gone."

"No," Belial said slowly. "No. We saw the Skraeling mass moving south past Jervois Landing in RuffleCrest's memory when Axis recalled it for us."

"But perhaps *that* was the trap," Magariz persisted. "Why was RuffleCrest allowed to escape? We all know that those Gryphon could have torn him apart as easily as they did the rest of his Wing. But they let him go. They let him go with his information."

Axis glanced at him sharply. "A good point, Magariz. But what if he's second guessing us? What if he wants us to think that? What if he *does* want to draw us into Ichtar?" He paused, thinking deeply. When he resumed, his voice was very soft. "What if he wants to draw us into Ichtar and then *attack from behind us?*"

"We would be trapped," Belial said. "Nowhere to run."

"All right, all right, let's think this through." Axis stood and paced back and forth. "We know there is a massive Skraeling army somewhere. We know it is now led by a general schooled in warfare, cool-headed, and . . . and who can use a sword." He glanced again at Jorge's blade. "We think—we *know*— that he seeks to trap us Belial, if you were he, and you were *south* of Jervois Landing, where would you hide a large army?"

Belial took a deep breath, considering the possibilities. "The Western Ranges would be an obvious place, but we have too many scouts and troops through the ranges for them to hide there. Eastern Aldeni? In the curve of the Nordra that holds Kastaleon?"

Magariz shook his head. "No. The scouts have covered that territory."

"They could be hiding beneath the snowdrifts," Belial insisted. "Waiting."

All three men shivered at the thought of snowdrifts coming alive around them.

"I pray that is not the case," Axis said. "Anything else?" He looked at his two senior commanders, but both shook their heads after a few moments' thought.

"Well," Axis turned to the brazier. "I am not going to stay around here to be trapped. Alert your commands. We pull out at dawn and move south again. If they want to eat us, then they'll have to come to us."

Axis lay in his bunk, wrapped as tightly in his blankets as he could, dozing lightly. For a long time he dreamed of Azhure, of her smell, of her laughter, of the way she felt in his arms. She rarely left his thoughts, and he wondered vaguely if she would have laughed at the three of them this evening and tossed her head and said that *she* knew where the Skraeling force was. But she was way to the south now, and had StarDrifter to watch over her, and he hoped that within a few months she could join him.

If he was still alive.

He muttered and twisted and forced his thoughts to something else. Un-wanted, a vision of Faraday filled his mind. She looked sick, tired, almost as sick as Azhure had with her twins. But she was smiling at someone, and Axis felt that she was all right. At least she is well out of this, he thought, for there are no Skraelings in southeastern Tencendor to tear her throat out.

The problem of the Skraelings filled his mind again and Axis opened his eyes and stared at the canvas flapping in the wind above his head.

They had to be somewhere. He let his mind drift, let it wander as it would, asking only that it drift across what it knew of the terrain of western Tencendor. They did not have long to hide, he thought. A week or two, and you cannot move a vast army very far in that time. He had Icarii scouts over Aldeni as soon as the weather cleared. He frowned, trying to remember exactly how long

the storms had lasted. Perhaps three weeks from the time they attacked Jervois
Landing.

Where could an army go in three weeks? He had moved reasonably fast
from the Three Brothers Lakes to Jervois Landing, yet that had taken him four
weeks.

Dammit! Think, man!

Ho'Demi was out there. Several parties of the Ravensbund scouts had left
his force at the Three Brothers Lakes and had scattered in different directions.
The only contact Axis had with any of them was the occasional touching of
minds he had with Ho'Demi.

Yes, Ho'Demi was out there somewhere, sworn to serve both the Prophecy
and the StarMan . . . and Axis hoped his sense of loyalty was stronger to the
StarMan than it was to the Prophecy. But Axis hesitated to reach out to him.
Ho'Demi would contact him if he needed to, and Axis did not want to disturb
the Ravensbund chief unless he had something useful to impart.

For a long time Axis' mind wandered back and forth, drifting to Azhure
for a time, then to Caelum. He relaxed toward sleep, imagining that Azhure
was wrapped in these blankets with him, imagining the ways they could find
to pass the night. He sighed and shifted slightly under the blankets. No, there
was no better way to spend a murky night than with . . .

His eyes flew open and his body jerked so violently he almost fell off the
narrow bunk. By the gods themselves, why hadn't any of them thought of that!

Ho'Demi! his mind called. *Ho'Demi, are you there? Where are you? Ho'Demi?*

Ho'Demi?

Ho'Demi cursed as he leaped into full wakefulness and hit his head on the
top of the tiny ice-cave he was secreted in. *StarMan?*

Ah, Ho'Demi, I startled you. Forgive me.

No doubt the StarMan had good enough reason to wake him with such
abruptness. But Ho'Demi could not stop the shortness of his next query. He
had been comfortably asleep for the first time in days. *What is it?*

Ho'Demi, where are you?

In a bloody ice-cave.

Silence.

Ho'Demi rubbed the top of his head, the smear of blood on the tips of his
fingers not improving his temper. *Far west.*

Thank the Stars. Axis could not disguise the relief in his mind. *Are you close
to the Murkle Mountains?*

Yes. A day's march, two at the most.

Ho'Demi. Listen to me. I have had an idea.

"A cursed time to have an idea," Ho'Demi muttered to himself, but he
listened anyway.

*   *   *

Acting only on a hunch, and knowing he and his thirty thousand could be
dead if he was wrong, the next morning Axis gave orders to move west rather
than south.

Toward the Murkle Mountains.

22

Cauldron Lake

None of her companions could doubt that Yr was ill. Her eyes and cheeks were feverish, her skin splotchy, her hair dull, and she was given to bouts of shivering that almost knocked her off her feet when she was walking.

But she would smile sweetly at their gentle inquiries, and say, "I am well enough."

None pressed too hard, and none touched her. All knew that the power would corrupt, and every day the power radiated out of Yr with increased virility. Zeherah watched her keenly; she would be the last to visit the final Repository of the Gods in the Lake of Life, and consequently she would have to bear the greatest burden of care and comfort.

The five Sentinels had walked slowly across the northern Plains of Tare to the Silent Woman Woods. They had taken almost six weeks, for no one wanted to tire Yr too much. They traveled silently and usually at night, avoiding all inhabited areas, their eyes introspective, their mood somber but not sad.

Now they stood at the edge of Cauldron Lake in the Woods. The previous night the Keep had held and comforted the Sentinels as it had previously comforted Faraday. For the first night in weeks Yr had managed a sound and almost pain-free sleep.

Now it was the turn of Ogden and Veremund, and the other three deeply regretted that the corrupting power would undoubtedly consume the brothers' irrepressible humor as it had Yr's tart wit. They all knew and accepted their fate. But they all had regrets.

"I regret the passing of so much life," Ogden said, his hands folded before him, his eyes unblinking on the soft golden lake before him. "I have enjoyed it all so much."

"I never expected to make so many friends," Veremund said beside him. "I did not expect to discover that I would love the StarMan as a friend as well as revere him as the One named by the Prophecy."

The brothers sighed, then spoke as one. "We shall miss riding the open plains, and we regret that we will spend no more evenings about the campfire listening to Axis sing, and watching him smile."

"You will see him again," a gentle voice said behind the small group, and they all turned. It was the Prophet, again in his silvery magnificence, and the Sentinels smiled and bowed slightly.

He stepped forward, kissed Yr softly, then turned to Ogden and Veremund. The Prophet stepped toward Ogden first, took his face in his hands and kissed him as gently as he had Yr.

"You will be beloved for always for the sacrifice you now make," he said. "And you will always rest in my heart. I could not have asked for better than you." Then he repeated the action and benediction with Veremund.

Silent tears slipped down the brothers' faces. As with Yr, they were deeply honored and grateful that the Prophet chose to be with them at this moment.

As the Prophet stepped back Jack moved forward to farewell the two brothers, then Zeherah kissed them and murmured words of farewell.

Yr stayed where she was.

"Are you ready, brother?" Veremund asked, and Ogden nodded and took his hand.

Then the two Sentinels stepped into the golden lake.

They did not have quite the same journey as Yr had in Grail Lake, for the waters of Cauldron Lake had long since evaporated amid its enchantments. But once they reached the Repository, this one clear of silt and thus revealed in its full glory, they went through the same procedure as she had, pressing the jewels in ordered sequence to gain admittance. And, after walking the Repository's corridors, they too found the Well of Power, and first Ogden, and then Veremund, leaned down to receive the Power.

When they emerged from the Lake, their eyes shining feverishly, their lips trembling, Yr stepped forward and hugged them.

"Welcome," she said. "Welcome to the final journey."

23

The Temple of the Stars

"*Azhure?*"

Azhure opened her eyes. "I'm awake, StarDrifter. Come in."

StarDrifter stepped quietly into Azhure's chamber. She was struggling to get out of bed and the Enchanter hurried to lend her his support. His eyes were shadowed with concern, but he said nothing. Azhure did not like any fuss made over her.

She had grown weaker by the day in the month since they had arrived on Temple Mount, as the babies within her sapped her strength and vitality. StarDrifter wondered why, when Azhure had carried Caelum with so little fuss and so much energy, these two should drain her so. Perhaps it was just that there were two, he thought. And perhaps not.

She caught his worried look and smiled reassuringly. "I have rested well, StarDrifter. Truly. Is everything ready?"

"Yes I have wakened you in plenty of time. Come, you'll need something to eat beforehand. It will be a long night."

She let him lead her to a small table. Once she had sat down StarDrifter peeled some fruits for her, placing them before her in small portions, one by one.

"Eat," he said *"Eat."*

Azhure placed a piece of fruit in her mouth to please him and chewed it unenthusiastically. She did not want to disappoint StarDrifter, or concern him anymore than she had to, for tonight would be as hard on him—perhaps harder—than it would be on her. If nothing else, the trip to the Island of Mist and Memory would be worth it for the friendship which had finally deepened and matured between her and StarDrifter. Before his desire for her had always come between them, making her uncomfortable, although, she smiled to herself, doubtless even StarDrifter's persistent desire had faded before her present bulk.

But it was more than that. Since the night when Azhure, distraught over her mother's letter, had come to StarDrifter for comfort, the Enchanter had been almost continually by her side, offering unconditional love and support. The relighting of the Temple of the Stars had been delayed for over ten days because StarDrifter spent so much time with her.

She swallowed and took another piece of fruit. StarDrifter had done nothing but what she asked that night, just holding her and telling her how much he loved her. She had gone to sleep eventually, wrapped in his arms and wings, still weeping slightly, and when she had woken in the morning he had gently kissed her brow and her cheek and let her go.

StarDrifter had comforted her, but he had also done something far more important—he had gained her utter trust, and with it, her friendship.

"Have you thought about what I asked earlier?" StarDrifter said, breaking into her thoughts.

She nodded slightly, and put down a third piece of fruit untasted. "I *have* thought about it, StarDrifter, but . . . oh, I don't know. It would be different if Axis were here . . ."

Tears threatened and Azhure took a deep breath before she continued. "I . . . we . . ." She shrugged and pushed the fruit about her plate. "We are not so close to these children as we were to Caelum," she finished on a whisper, her eyes downcast, her cheeks staining red. It was a shameful thing to admit that you did not love your children.

Despite her fears, StarDrifter could understand how she felt. Every day he spent time teaching the unborn twins some of their Enchanter skills, and though they responded well to him, he knew they spared their mother nothing but indifference and hostility.

If he had to carry such antagonism about day and night, StarDrifter knew he would find it hard to love the babies as well. He did not know why the boy and the girl regarded their parents with such coldness and yet liked him, especially when he had been as guilty as Axis in treating Azhure so badly. And why hate their mother only for loving and forgiving their father?

"Azhure, the babies *need* names. It is hard for me to teach them at this late stage and yet not address them by name."

Azhure finally looked up. "Then you name them."

"Me? Azhure, it is the parents' privilege to—"

"*You* name them," Azhure insisted. "They would accept no name from me."

"And *you* will accept what I name them?"

She nodded.

"Well, then." StarDrifter knew the babies well, and he knew what would suit them. "Azhure, both will be powerful Enchanters and their names should reflect such power, but their names must also reflect their personalities." He took a deep breath, and told Azhure his choice.

Azhure sat back, shocked by the name he'd picked for the boy. "But that is such a powerful name," she whispered, her hand involuntarily on her belly, "even for a male Enchanter Are you sure?"

He nodded and, after a moment, Azhure bowed her head in acceptance. No wonder she felt uncomfortable with these babies.

There was no formality in the procession to the Temple, everyone just walked quietly along the Avenue until a crowd of some eight or nine thousand stood on the grassy slopes surrounding the dull marble circle. Many from Pirates' Town had come, as had five boatloads of people, both nobles and commoners, from Nor and several hundred Icarii who had flown down over the past weeks.

Azhure stood with Caelum in her arms in the center of the circle of the Temple. She was dressed only in a light lavender gown, for the air was balmy even this high up and this late in the year.

She had no idea what was going to happen.

She and Caelum were alone; StarDrifter was conversing with another Enchanter in low tones to one side of the circle, and FreeFall and EvenSong waited in the front ranks of those who watched from outside the circle. As non-Enchanters they would play no role in the relighting.

And so why am I here? Azhure thought. I am hardly an Enchanter, for I can use none of my powers voluntarily. She had used her power the night she talked to the First, but Azhure had no idea how she had done it beyond the fact that her anger and distress had somehow called it forth.

Azhure tilted her head and looked at the firmament above, her arms tightening about Caelum. She would have to wait for the birth of the twins before she would learn more. She knew that WolfStar had said so but, more importantly, Azhure could feel the block they somehow created by their very presence.

She needed to be alone. Totally alone.

"Mama?"

She dropped her gaze and smiled. Caelum was wide-eyed with curiosity and twisted his head from side to side as he watched the crowd grow. "What will happen tonight?"

"I do not know, Caelum. StarDrifter would tell me nothing. But," she kissed the crown of his head, "I am sure that it will be something wondrous."

"I wish Papa were here."

"So do I, Caelum," she said. "So do I."

At some deep, emotional level Azhure could feel Axis, feel his life-force, feel the faint tug of his breathing, but she could do nothing more than that.

Reports from the north remained maddeningly vague, and five days ago a scout had brought her a month-old letter from her husband, but it had said little apart from the fact that he loved her and missed her and thought of her every day. It told her little of where he was, nothing about where the Skraeling army was, and nothing about whether he had found the power within himself to repel them.

"Live," Azhure whispered as she did every time she thought of Axis. "Live."

StarDrifter, Caelum said in her mind, and Azhure turned her head.

StarDrifter strode across the circle toward them, enthusiasm springing his steps and his eyes shining with excitement. He was dressed only in golden breeches; like Azhure, his feet were bare. Behind him his wings were extended, catching the soft light of the stars.

"StarDrifter," Azhure said as he reached them, "I am not sure what Caelum and I do here. What can we do?"

What can I do?

StarDrifter seized her shoulders and kissed her quickly, bending his head to kiss Caelum as well. "You can experience, Azhure. And that ring gives you the right to stand in the center of the circle. Caelum has every right to share with you as his parents' heir. Now," his tone turned businesslike, although his excitement was still patent, "is everyone in place?"

He slowly scanned the extremities of the circle. Among the arriving Icarii had been several dozen Enchanters, and now they stood at the very edge of the circle, spaced evenly, facing inward.

"The Nine?" Azhure asked, looking about for the Priestesses of the Order of the Stars.

StarDrifter indicated to one side and Azhure saw that the Nine stood in a close group behind the circle of the Enchanters, their heads bowed in prayer or meditation.

"They will witness," StarDrifter said, "for only Enchanters can participate in the lighting of the Temple of the Stars.

"Azhure." He looked her in the eye. "Whatever happens, do not be afraid. You will be safe. *Whatever* happens."

She nodded, feeling a thrill of both fear and excitement, and Caelum squirmed anxiously in her arms. StarDrifter smiled and stroked the boy's hair. "You have been born to witness great wonders, Caelum. I hope this will be but the first for you."

Then, abruptly, he left them, striding about the circle, meeting each of the Enchanters' gaze, communicating with them at some level that Azhure could not yet discern.

There was complete silence about the circle and from the thousands of watchers, and Azhure could faintly hear the crashing waves far below.

Azhure? Azhure? Is that you?

Above them the stars reeled.

StarDrifter continued to walk about the circle, but his stride was now slower, and his head was bowed—but still his wings arched behind him. As his steps slowed he walked closer and closer to the center of the circle.

Azhure realized that the encircling Enchanters were singing. The words and music were so soft that Azhure could not distinguish them, although she heard enough to know they sang in the sacred language of the Icarii. It was fluid music, mingling with the cry of the waves below, and for the first time in months Azhure felt revitalizing energy flowing through her. She took a deep breath and smiled.

Caelum looked up at his mother in awe.

StarDrifter's steps were very slow now, his head still bowed, and he was close enough for Azhure to see that his eyes were closed. He was silent, listening, but his fingers flexed slightly at his side, and the muscles of his shoulders and back quivered.

The Song about them deepened, intensified, grew more emotional. Both Caelum and Azhure quivered with its power, and the stars above blurred momentarily.

StarDrifter had stepped behind them and suddenly, shockingly, he seized Azhure's shoulders and gave a great cry that sent waves of power rippling through her. She gasped and would have fallen had it not been for StarDrifter's hands gripping her. Out of the corner of her eye she could see that StarDrifter now stood straight, his head thrown back, his eyes open and staring at the firmament above.

His wings flared behind him, and the brief thought crossed Azhure's mind that he was going to try to lift her and Caelum into the air.

But then a movement about the circle caught her eye and she forgot StarDrifter in an instant. Every one of the encircling Enchanters had spread their wings, their tips touching those of their neighbors, and had thrown back their heads in the same manner as StarDrifter, lifting their arms joyously to the sky.

Then StarDrifter began to sing.

Azhure had heard him sing before, most notably in the Assembly Chamber in Talon Spike, but that had been only a fraction of his power.

Now she heard all of it. Its sheer loveliness rocked her, and she cried out, feeling StarDrifter's fingers bite painfully into her shoulders, feeling his power flood through her. She dimly comprehended that he gripped her for only one reason—to anchor both of them in the torrent of power that he now let free.

Azhure felt his power surround and penetrate her, felt and heard his Song seize and uplift her, and then she heard, and felt, every one of the Enchanters take up the Song also, and let *their* power flood the circle of marble.

She moaned, thinking she did not have the strength to bear it.

Then, just as she thought she could take no more, the Song abruptly ended, although Azhure could still feel power flooding about the circle.

"Wait," StarDrifter whispered behind her. "Wait . . . wait . . . wait . . ."

And then he laughed and let her go, spinning about the circle on feet as light as breath. "Feel it!" he cried. *"Feel it!"*

As quickly as he had left her he was behind her again, although this time he did not touch her.

"Feel it," he said again, his voice now flat.

And indeed Azhure could feel it. A tingling on the soles of her bare feet, a gossamer touch along the skin of her bare arms.

"It lives," StarDrifter said, again curiously tonelessly. "The Temple lives."

The circle of marble, which Azhure had thought so dull and uninspiring, now began very, very gently to glow a deep violet. Azhure could see its faint glow reflected on Caelum's face and on the faces of the Enchanters. When she turned her head slightly, she could see that the glow flowed so smoothly over StarDrifter's pale coloring that he seemed to absorb the light.

Then the marble underfoot disappeared.

She cried out and would have fallen in shock had not StarDrifter seized her shoulders again. There was nothing below her feet now but the violet glow. Not only could Azhure not see anything, she could *feel* nothing below her feet.

"StarDrifter!"

"It is all right," he whispered. "You are safe."

Then the violet glow flickered, dimmed for a heartbeat, and then . . . then the entire circle became a vast cauldron of cobalt light that *throbbed* with power. As Azhure looked down she saw stars circling below her feet, and when she finally looked up, she realized that the circle of light speared skyward in an immense pillar of power . . . and that the stars circled above her and about her as well.

They were standing—or floating?—in the center of a beacon whose power Azhure could not even begin to comprehend, and through this beacon floated the stars.

She wept with the beauty of it. Stars drifted close so close she could feel their burning power although their heat did not singe her. Wind tugged at her hair, and she knew it to be the wind of their passing. Music consumed her, and she knew it to be the full beauty of the Star Dance.

"I have to be so careful," StarDrifter whispered behind her, "not to let it consume me."

She knew what he meant. The power of the Star Dance was so close here that if either had wished it, they could have let its full power envelop them.

For a long time they stood, the other Enchanters floating with them, all participating in the ultimate worship of the Stars.

Here is where we used to come to study and understand and worship, Star-Drifter's voice echoed through her, *and now we can again. Behold, the Temple of the Stars.*

*   *   *

After a long, long while, StarDrifter pulled Azhure and Caelum to the edge of the beacon and they stepped beyond its walls.

Outside the thousands who had come to witness stood, awed, and Azhure looked over her shoulder as StarDrifter led her slowly down the grassy slope. From the outside the Temple was beautiful—although not as beautiful as it was from inside—the great column of light shooting into the firmament, stars dancing in its midst.

"We will let it stand unquenched," StarDrifter said as she halted. "As it did in ages past. Let Gorgrael see it from his cold northern fortress and know the power of the Star Dance. Let the remnants of the Brotherhood of the Seneschal see it and know that the Icarii have reclaimed their homeland."

She trembled and his arm tightened about her. "Will the others go inside?" she asked. She could dimly see the shape of some of the Enchanters floating in the Temple.

"None but Enchanters can go inside and survive the power that the Temple contains," he said.

Azhure's eyes widened. "But I . . . I . . ."

"*I* never doubted you, nor what you are," StarDrifter said. "And neither did the Temple."

All the Enchanters at the Ancient Barrows were looking toward the southwest, their eyes straining, and they could feel, if not see, the great beacon that was the Temple of the Stars leap into the night.

All were above ground, none were present in the Chamber of the Star Gate to witness.

The blue shadows that chased each other across the vaulted dome above the Star Gate swayed, leaped, then intensified in both hue and movement. The alabaster statues surrounding the Gate turned deep purple in the intensifying light. Music so powerful the entire Chamber vibrated coursed from the Star Gate.

And then, as both music and light exploded about the Chamber, seven laughing figures stepped through the Gate. Stepped through from the Stars.

A man first, and he turned to help a woman. Then five others, two women and three men. As the last stepped onto the floor of the Chamber both light and music swelled, then died completely.

"It has been a long time," the first man said, and hugged the woman next to him. The other five looked at each other, then at the first two, and all seven embraced, their eyes glimmering with joy.

"We're back!" one man cried, and then he tipped his head back and screamed. "*We're back, Artor!*"

The first man smiled at his companion's exuberance, but did not reprimand him. Stars knew, they all felt the same.

"Come," he said. "The time draws near. The tides surge and call her name. Soon we will be Eight."

"And then Nine," his wife breathed. *"And then we will be Nine!"*

24

The Fiend

The Goodwife was a gift from the Mother. With the Goodwife beside her, Faraday found the courage and the heart to plant with renewed enthusiasm. That first morning the Goodwife appeared, she cleansed Faraday's hands with soothing herbal ointments and bound them, humming a cradle song all the while. She forced Faraday to sit while she cooked her a good breakfast, and then the Goodwife spent the day at her side, fetching and carrying, and, again, singing the lilting cradle song over each seedling that Faraday planted. In between scolding and healing and cooking and laughing and fetching and carrying, the Goodwife told Faraday of her journey to Tare and her decision to leave her Goodhusband to fend for himself for a few months.

" 'Twill do him good," she said when Faraday quietly questioned the decision. "After fifteen years we need a rest each from the other."

That night the Goodwife cooked with the ingredients she found in the donkey's saddlebag. "Magical, magical," she muttered as she delved yet deeper into the bags, but she smiled, and after they had eaten, she told Faraday of her granny and her granny's stories.

Faraday slept well and when she woke she saw that the previous day's seedlings reached a hundred paces into the sky and their gentle humming filled the morning.

Although Faraday still felt ill from time to time, the Goodwife gave her herbs to ease her stomach, and laughter and companionship to ease her soul, and when Faraday complained that she gave nothing back, the Goodwife smiled and said that Faraday gave her adventure and beauty and music, and they were recompense enough.

And so they planted until they came to the fortified city of Arcen. Their approach could hardly be missed. For many days the townsfolk had watched in wonder as the great forest advanced toward them, and in the two days before Faraday entered their gates, they had stood on the walls and watched the two tiny figures.

Some of the townsfolk had been nervous; it had, after all, only been a matter of months since the Seneschal had held tight sway here. But there were many Icarii present who smiled and reassured them, and said that it was Faraday, Tree Friend, who brought only wonder, not darkness.

"Very soon," one of the Icarii said, "Arcen will be known as the gateway to this enchanted forest, and your market will blossom with the patronage of Acharite, Icarii and perhaps Avar as well. And, see, she plants only on barren land—the trade routes remain well open and the fields free. There is no harm in what she does."

And Faraday *had* been Queen. Many were surprised when they realized that Faraday, Tree Friend, was also the very same Queen Faraday, wife to the late and generally unlamented Borneheld.

"And Lover to Axis," one of the Icarii whispered, and the whisper spread. In her relatively brief tenure as Queen, Faraday had earned a reputation as a fair and compassionate regent. While Borneheld had been occupied in the north, Faraday had virtually run southern Achar, and many traders in Arcen had good reason to regard her kindly, for her favorable decisions had increased the city's prosperity.

And she was so beautiful, the watchers whispered as she and her companion finally stood outside the city gates late one afternoon, that it would be an honor to have her visit.

Mayor Culpepper Fenwicke himself greeted Faraday and the Goodwife at the gates, then escorted them to his own home where he feted and dined them for four days and four nights.

Gilbert led his small band of Brothers northeast, and for weeks the way was barred by a thick line of trees so massive that Gilbert thought they would eventually block out the sun.

And Faraday was responsible for this. Every night Artor whispered in Gilbert's ear, encouraging him to greater efforts, telling him how the foul beings that Faraday daily planted sapped and weakened His own soul.

Daily their whisperings grow, good Gilbert, and daily they ensorcel more and more among the weak Acharites. And there was worse, far worse, to the south, but Artor did not tell Gilbert that.

Destroy this Faraday, Gilbert, and then we can turn our attention to the trees themselves. We will have ourselves a burning, you and I. Kill Faraday, and you may light the match.

So Gilbert pushed and badgered and berated his band, constantly emphasizing to them the disgusting nature of the forest that spread its way across Arcen. Daily the Brothers grew more depressed, how could *they* halt a disaster of this proportion? But when they asked Gilbert, shouting their questions from the back of the cart as Gilbert rode ahead, he only smiled and said he had a Grand Plan, and would reveal it when the time was ripe.

Moryson, sitting cloaked and silent at the front of the cart, the reins of the increasingly sprightly horse loose in his hands, wondered if Gilbert *did* have a plan, or if Artor had yet to fill Gilbert in on the details.

After traveling the southern edges of Minstrelsea for weeks, Gilbert was finally forced to lead his band through the vile forest to reach the city of Arcen to the north. Artor had whispered to him in recent nights that he might catch Faraday here, and the thought that he would finally be able to squeeze his damp palms about the renegade woman's fragile neck gave Gilbert the courage to dare the forest.

Minstrelsea now stretched from the Silent Woman Woods to Arcen, completely enclosing the Ancient Barrows but swinging just south and east of the city itself as it surged toward the Bracken Ranges. Every day, as more and more of the sisters were transplanted out from Ur's nursery, the richness and intricacy of the forest's humming grew just a little more vibrant, and its leaves stretched just that little bit more joyously toward the sun and the stars.

Gilbert, riding behind the cart now (best to let Moryson take the risks in the lead), managed to keep calm only through a supreme effort. This was worse, far worse, than his ride through the Silent Woman Woods with Axis. Those Woods were old, and had seemed slightly faded and tired, but this forest was new and vital, and Gilbert, much as he hated to admit it, could feel its magic. The sky was completely obliterated by the forest canopy, and Gilbert felt as though he had been thrown alive into a dark grave.

The Brothers cowered in the back of the cart as they passed through the forest to the gates of Arcen, but Moryson did not seem overly afraid of the music and fragrance of Minstrelsea. He was an old man, and had seen many strange sights, so even the glimpses of strange creatures gamboling among the crystal waters of rocky streams did not perturb him.

After almost four hours the way ahead lightened and Gilbert spurred his horse gratefully past the cart. "See!" he cried, "I have led you through!"

Arcen was abustle with activity, and Gilbert was appalled. How could life go on with this much gaiety and vibrancy when evil trees loomed not four hundred paces to the south and east?

Arcen was one of the main cities of the country. High-walled and densely packed with tenement buildings, the city boasted a massive covered market, itself a sign of the power of the craft and trading guilds, a town hall that outshone any of the Worship Halls Gilbert had ever seen, and streets that were not only paved, but resolutely swept every morning and evening to keep them free from dust and dung. Almost sixty-five thousand people crowded into its walls, and Gilbert had been stunned when he'd heard the city had capitulated so easily to Axis. Built to withstand a siege of months, Arcen opened its gates and delivered its Earl to Axis in the space of one fine morning.

But Gilbert thought he knew why. The city was evil, yes it was, infected with the filth and lies of the Forbidden. Its noble Earl—who had fought so long and so well for Borneheld and Artor—had been the unwilling sacrifice offered to the traitor knocking at its gates. Now Burdel rested with Artor even though he had found nothing but treachery in this life, at least he has found his just reward in eternity, thought Gilbert as he led his cart of followers through the packed streets toward the market square.

He stopped once or twice to ask directions, then took his band to a small inn situated in a side street just before the great market square. "Wait here," he said, slipping awkwardly from his horse, "while I arrange lodging. Say nothing to nobody."

Gilbert marched inside the inn, the Trader's Rest, trying to look as much like a nobleman as he could. He threw his cloak back over his shoulders and straightened his jacket, proud of its fine cut, even it its rose-pink velvet was a trifle stained by the months spent on the road.

"My man," he said loudly as the proprietor stalked through the crowded tavern toward him. "A room for myself, the best you have, and something suitable for my retainers."

The landlord looked him up and down. By his clothes a resident of Carlon, and a wealthy one at that. The man did not fail to note the fat purse that hung from Gilbert's belt.

"My Lord," he murmured, then gestured about the ground floor tavern. "As you can see, business is brisk. I can let you have a good room for your own person, and the stable loft can be cleared for your retainers, but," he sighed, "I am afraid I shall have to ask premium prices." After an instant's pause he named a sum.

Gilbert glowered. He wanted to haggle with the man—by Artor! he could have had a suite in a palace for that price!—but he felt exposed in such a public place and wanted nothing more than to conclude the business and slink away. He glanced nervously at the faces crowding against the bar—could there possibly be anyone here who knew him?—then nodded tersely.

"If I was not in a hurry, old man, I would sneer at such an exorbitant price. But I have important business to attend, and cannot afford to waste another minute of the day. Very well."

"Half in advance," the landlord said, and Gilbert threw some coins at him in a temper.

"I can only hope that the room is worth it."

*   *   *

Once Gilbert had seen that the Brothers were comfortable in their loft—and, to be fair to the landlord, it was clean and the beds snug—he returned to his room for a wash and a quick meal, then hurried into the streets.

Even though it was late afternoon the crowds were not in the least diminished, and Gilbert had to shoulder his way through in order to reach the market square. Artor had told him he might find Faraday here, and Gilbert felt a knot of excitement in the pit of his belly.

The market square was dominated by the massive stone Market Hall, its roof tiled, Gilbert was astounded to see, in pure gold. The Hall's ground floor was open to the streets, and underneath its archways flourished a myriad of stalls.

Gilbert slipped under one of the arches and stopped at the first stall.

"Excuse me," he said.

The stall-keeper looked up. "Yes?" The man was looking everywhere but at her produce. She narrowed her eyes. Perhaps he was one of those noblemen who haunted the market for women they could lure home for the evening.

"Excuse me," Gilbert said again, even though he had the woman's attention. He didn't like the way she looked at him. "I wonder if I might ask for some information."

"What?" she said curtly.

"Um, I was wondering about the trees."

The woman finally straightened, wiping her hands on the rough cloth covering her hips. She stared at Gilbert.

"I was wondering," he hastened on, "how far north they stretch. You see, I've only just come from the south."

She took a considering breath. Well, the trees were new, and strange to those who had only just seen them. "They go no farther north than this city. They stop just at the northern wall."

Gilbert's face relaxed in a smile Then she *must* be here! "They are unusual," he said, "not what good folk from the plains are used to."

"Unusual enough," the woman said, and wondered what the man wanted. "But we have seen unusual events and even strange people these past months."

"But the trees," Gilbert persisted, "don't they frighten you?"

The woman smiled briefly. "Frighten me? No, good sir, they seem quite appealing. Why, me and my husband think we might spend sixth-day afternoon on a picnic. Down a shaded pathway, perhaps." Her face relaxed in a genuine smile. "The birds sing so, especially in the morning. It makes rising a joy, it does."

Gilbert was appalled by her words, but encouraged by her sudden willingness to talk. "How is it that such great trees grew so quickly? I rode past Arcen, oh, some five or six months ago," he lied, "and there were none here then."

The expression on the woman's face was positively beatific now "Why, good sir, they only appeared some four days ago. With her."

"Her?"

"*Her*," and the woman pointed.

Gilbert followed her finger, and for a moment he could see nothing.

Then he looked straight into the face of Faraday.

She was standing several stalls distant from him, and for one appalling moment, Gilbert thought she had seen him, but in the next heartbeat she turned unconcernedly to a plump, ruddy-cheeked peasant woman by her side and laughed at some pleasantry they shared. On her other side stood a stout gray-haired man, a trader perhaps, but his clothes were rich and he wore a gold chain about his neck.

"You *are* a stranger," the woman said, her tongue guarded again as she watched Gilbert's face, "not to recognize Mayor Culpepper Fenwicke."

"Of course I recognized *him*!" Gilbert snapped. " 'Twas the woman by his side who made me frown."

Then you are a stranger to be suspicious of, the woman thought, her face closing over, if you frown at her. Without another word she bent back to her produce, and Gilbert pushed his way through the crowd.

His palms were positively itching now, and he could hear Artor's voice roaring in his ears.

Faraday had enjoyed her stay in Arcen, but now she wanted to move on. She knew that the country above the Ranges would be cold and snowy, and she would not be able to move as fast through Skarabost as she had through Arcen, yet time was critical. She *had* to have planted Minstrelsea through to the Avarinheim by the time Axis was ready to confront Gorgrael.

Or else he would fail.

"Axis," she whispered, and the Goodwife leaned over and hugged her briefly.

"You should tell him," said the voice of the Mother.

"No," Faraday's eyes gleamed with tears. "No. He does not need to know."

Culpepper, unsure what the two women whispered about but concerned by the expression on Faraday's face, stepped forward. "Have I said something?" he asked anxiously. "Have I tired you?"

"No," Faraday said. "No, not at all. We were frowning over some slight matter, Mayor Culpepper. Now, what fine guests have you invited to entertain the Goodwife and myself tonight?"

Chatting animatedly, Culpepper led the two women toward the archways into the square.

No one noticed the man slipping through the crowds behind them.

*   *   *

Gilbert paused as the three moved away. "Damn!" he muttered, sweat now running down his back. "I almost had her!"

He wasn't too sure what he was going to do once he reached Faraday, but he knew that her sweet, sweet neck would snap with only the slightest pressure. And neither that Goodwife nor the plump mayor looked as though they could rescue a drowning kitten, let alone Faraday. He could easily escape in the subsequent chaos; and then Artor and Achar would be saved, and he could reclaim the Tower of the Seneschal for his own.

He would enjoy redecorating the Brother-Leader's apartment to his own taste.

Culpepper realized that the women would appreciate some time to themselves, so he tried to clear a path through the crowd as quickly as he could. But Faraday was jostled by people wanting to reach out and touch her . . .

"See, Harold, how her eyes gleam so magically!"

"Lady? Would you touch my Martha, Lady? She has a fever."

"Now, Fillipa, if only you could manage such a noble bearing, you too could have any man you desired."

Except the man you truly wanted, Faraday thought, but smiled at the mother and daughter anyway, and touched the feverish baby, and spoke gently to any who called her name.

Her progress through the Market Hall slowed.

"Artor' I'm almost there!" Gilbert whispered, his eyes gleaming feverishly, and any who saw him stepped hurriedly out of his way. Poor man, no doubt he wanted to touch the Lady.

Gilbert surely did, but he wanted a good deal more from Faraday than just a gentle smile and word.

Faraday had told Culpepper she was not tired, but now she felt her weariness crashing about her, and she hoped that she could reach the mayor's house without too much fuss.

She heard a movement behind her, then a hot hand grasped her shoulder.

I have her! Gilbert thought exultantly. Another heartbeat and I'll have her . . . *dead!*

"Take your hand off the Lady!" a voice hissed at his side, and Gilbert, who had recent experience of such things, recognized the sound of power. But he gritted his teeth and tightened his hand. Faraday had to die, and he was not going to relinquish his grip when he was this close.

Surely the power that whispered in his ear, was no match for the power Artor had given him. He reached within himself, seeking Artor's vengeance. His eyes glowed red.

"Release her!" the voice commanded, stronger now, then a heavy-booted foot scrunched suddenly down on his own.

Gilbert gave a squeal of pain, let slip the power within him that he had only barely touched . . . and let Faraday go.

Faraday was turning to see who wanted her with such persistence, when the hand fell from her shoulder and she was free.

"This way, my Lady," Culpepper said. "I shall order that a hot bath be prepared for you as soon as we reach my house."

"Ah," Faraday sighed blissfully. "A bath!" She forgot the crowds still jostling about her and let the Mayor lead her down the path he had cleared.

Gilbert, almost retching with pain, and sure that every bone in his foot had been broken, finally looked up. A heavy peasant woman, coarse-skinned and lank-haired, stood before him, hands on hips, her face suffused with anger.

"*Leave her alone!*" she hissed, and Gilbert heard the power again.

"Do you think you can stop me?" he said, and now power surged through his own voice. "Do you think to stop the great god Artor? Are you *good* enough for that, witch?"

Her face paled and she took a step back. "Leave her alone," she repeated, but now her own voice was not so sure. "The Mother protects her."

Gilbert smiled nastily, and the woman turned on her heel and disappeared into the crowd.

Artor was displeased. Gilbert had been so close, so close!

The bitch would be lying cracked and broken in the gutters of Arcen were it not for your stupidity, Gilbert!

Gilbert cowered in his room in the Trader's Rest, groveling as close to the wooden floor as possible. "She has a helper, Blessed One! A nasty woman. A fiend herself, I think!"

You should have been prepared, Gilbert.

"Oh, I will be now, Lord."

You should have reached into the power I gave you sooner, Gilbert.

"Oh, I've learned my lesson, Blessed One."

If you'd taken your Brothers, she could be dead by now. They could have distracted the . . . fiend . . . while you killed the woman.

"I will use them in future, Great God. She does not frighten me."

Nevertheless, good Gilbert, I shall have to give you more power, I think. I had not counted on the fiend.

"Oh, no!" Gilbert whimpered, his fingernails digging up splinters from the floor.

Good Gilbert Accept my benevolence.

25

Chitter, Chatter

From Jervois Landing Axis slowly moved his army west toward the Murkle Mountains. He would have moved faster, but the thought that if he was wrong, if he committed too fast to the west he would leave both southern and northern flanks dangerously unprotected, kept him hesitant.

He wanted confirmation, and he wanted it fast. But, it seemed he would get neither.

"For the Stars' sake, Axis," FarSight, CutSpur said, wrapping his ebony wings about him for extra warmth as he stood in the knee-deep snow, "tell us what it is you think!"

Axis sat Belaguez silently, hunched deep inside his cloak, his eyes fixed on some distant point to the west.

Belial glanced at Magariz, both men as cold and miserable as Axis, then edged his own horse closer to Axis.

"You *must* tell us what it is you think . . . what it is you plan, Axis," he said. "Dammit! Why lead us west like this?"

Axis finally moved. He gathered up Belaguez's reins. "Meet in my tent tonight," he said, and booted the stallion forward. "FarSight, bring all the far-flight reports from the Murkle Mountains that you have."

The tiny tent was jammed with the three men and the Icarii Crest-Leader, but at least it was out of the wind, and the crowded bodies gave off their own heat. Soon clothes and feathers steamed and men unwound scarves and peeled off gloves.

"I think he's hiding in the Murkle Mountains," Axis said, and raised his eyes to meet those of his commanders.

"The Murkle Mountains?" Magariz asked. "I know little about them."

"Few do," Axis replied, "because few go there. I have some knowledge only because one of my cohort commanders came from a hamlet close to their skirts. Generations ago, perhaps even as long ago as old Tencendor, the Mountains were slightly warmer, and more rain fell. People lived there then. More importantly, for our cause at least, generations of miners tunneled deep into the mountains after opals. Now the mines are abandoned."

"And perhaps not," Belial said. "Axis, what made you think of the Murkle Mountains?"

Axis shrugged. "A trifling thought as I drifted toward sleep, my friend. But listen to me," his voice warmed with enthusiasm, "it would be the perfect hiding place, surely? Those abandoned mine shafts would be enough to hide an army, and Stars knows the Skraelings love dark, hidden places underground."

"And they're the perfect place to spring a trap!" Belial said. "Whether we went south or north from Jervois Landing, our unknown adversary would be able to attack our rear. And it's the last place we would think to look."

"It *was* the last place we thought to look," Axis said dryly. "FarSight. I asked you to send farflight scouts west. Their reports?"

"Not reassuring, Axis. Several scouts have been over the Mountains, but there is nothing but blasted peaks and shadowed valleys. Nothing lives on those Mountains."

"But what lives *inside* them?" Axis insisted. *"Where else can he be?"*

"Axis," Magariz said. "What if the Skraelings *are* in these mine shafts? What do we do? Go in one by one with torches? Or ask, politely, if they would mind coming out to meet us in gentlemanly battle?"

For some time there was silence. None of the commanders envied Axis his leadership.

"Ho'Demi?" Belial finally asked. "Have you heard from him?"

Axis shook his head. "When he needs me to know, then he will contact me. But he is somewhere in the Murkle Mountains. Deep."

Ho'Demi had brought five men, good Ravensbundmen, into the depths of the Murkle Mountains with him. All five were now dead.

Ho'Demi wanted to contact Axis—*had* wanted to contact him for two days past now—but power filtered through these Prophecy-damned shafts and tunnels, and whatever it was shielded Axis' mind from Ho'Demi.

Perhaps it was the cursed rock that hung in countless thousands of tons above him, perhaps it was the dark power of the as yet hidden Skraeling force, but Ho'Demi was not sure.

But home was overrun by Gorgrael's pets, and now Ho'Demi wondered if these shafts were infested with them, too.

After Axis contacted him, Ho'Demi had moved his small group of scouts into the Murkle Mountains. They had found an abandoned mine shaft easily enough and had carefully eased their way down it. Ancient iron ladders still clung to its walls, and Ho'Demi had thought they would snap and kill them all, but the rust had held together, and they'd reached the floor of the first shaft safely. Faint light permeated from the opening far above, but within paces of moving into the first of the tunnels even that was lost. This darkness was so thick, it seemed to *live*, and it moved about them with a fluidity that would do a Ravensbund dancer proud.

None had liked it, but the StarMan had asked them to investigate, and so they dampened their fears and moved deeper and deeper.

Ho'Demi allowed no light. He was sure that the Skraelings' silver eyes would glow, even in this darkness, and that his men would hear their whisperings; Ho'Demi had never known a totally silent Skraeling. So they moved through dark, they *ate* dark and they *breathed* dark, because Ho'Demi wanted the Skraelings to have no warning. He wanted to get his men out alive.

But one by one, his men had been taken, dragged away in utter silence into the perpetual night of the abandoned mines. Those in the front would suddenly realize that the rear man was gone, and none would know at what point he had disappeared.

Ho'Demi had eventually gone to the rear himself, but within an hour the front man had been taken, then the remaining man, and then Ho'Demi had been left alone in the dark. Utterly, totally lost.

If he could, he would have escaped this hell, but at some point he had become so disorientated that now he only crawled through the shoulder-high tunnels. Even death would be a release.

But Ho'Demi was not ready to die. He still had the Prophecy to serve, and he still had Sa'Kuya waiting for him. He rested some minutes, taking a swallow of water from the almost empty flask that hung at his belt, then he moved again . . . slowly . . . slowly . . . expecting death at any moment.

Chitter, chatter. Chitter, chatter.

Ho'Demi's head flew up and, again, he struck it on the roof of the tunnel.

Chitter, chatter. Chitter, chatter.

Ho'Demi realized the noise was in his head, not in the shaft about him.

Chitter, chatter. Chitter, chatter.

Whatever had taken his men was now coming for him. He flexed his hand then closed it about his dagger. If he could not kill these creatures, then he would kill himself. At least, if he died by his own hand, he could die pretending he died on the open ice-fields of the Ravensbund.

Chitter . . . who are you? Chatter . . . who are you?

Ravensbund, his mind replied instinctively, and the creatures that he could now feel crowding the tunnel behind him ceased their chitter, chatter, surprised by the response. *My name is Ho'Demi, and I am Chief of the Ravensbund.*

Chitter . . . doesn't matter, chatter . . . still you can die.

Why? Their need reached him, and Ho'Demi could feel that they needed him to die, but he didn't know why. And he *wanted* to know why. Every man deserved to know why he died.

Chitter, chatter. Why can he speak to us? Others have not. Never, chitter, chatter.

I speak with the mind voice because that is the privilege of the Ravensbund Chief. All Ravensbund people serve the Prophecy, and the Chief more than most. Why do you want me to die?

So you can join us. Don't you want to join us?

No. I want to escape these confines.

(Sigh) *So do we, chitter, chatter. But we need a world crueler than the one we have lost to accept us.*

Ho'Demi felt as though his mind were going to explode. He communicated in the mind voice with Axis, and it did not hurt him, but these creatures drove sharp claws into his head with every word they . . . chittered, chattered. And he was confused. *You need a world crueler than the one you have lost?*

We are lost, lost, lost, chitter, chatter.

The word "lost" echoed through Ho'Demi's mind and sang up and down the tunnel.

Sad, sad, sad, chitter, chatter.

WHO ARE YOU? Ho'Demi screamed into the blackness.

For a long moment there was silence. Then . . . *Our bodies have gone. Lost. Stolen. Ground to dust and pebbles to crown golden rings on graceless fingers.*

Something clicked in Ho'Demi's mind. *You are the . . . souls . . . of the opals?*

Chitter, chatter. Souls, lost. Will you join us? Or can you offer us a world crueler than the one we have lost?

Ho'Demi abruptly sat down in the dust and gravel. It had long been rumored among the people of Tencendor that opals were stones of ill-luck and cruelty, but their incredible beauty still created a market.

If only they knew.

We asked your companions if they knew of a world, a cruel world, that might accept us, but they merely accepted their death, and would not speak to us.

But if they *could* have spoken, then I would wager that each and every one of them could have suggested the world that. I will now offer you, Ho'Demi thought. He shifted slightly in the darkness. *I will offer you a cruel, cruel world, and yet one more beautiful than the one you have lost. No one will come to chase you from this world, nor seek to chisel into its depths.*

He could feel the wild excitement of the lost souls. *Chitter, chatter. Can you? Will you? Where will you?*

A bargain, though. For a world I want freedom from these dark spaces . . . and information.

The souls were suspicious. *Show us this world then. Show us, and do not lie to us with your mind, for we will know.*

Ho'Demi leaned back against the wall of the tunnel, closed his eyes, and formed an image in his mind. Within a heartbeat both the tunnel and his mind reverberated with excited chittering.

Ours, chitter, chatter? You would lead us there? Would you? Would you? Would you?

There are creatures who will gambol about its edges and others who will travel its plains, and you must tolerate them.

But they will not tunnel, tunnel, tunnel?

No.

Ah, chitter, chatter. Then they may gambol. They may travel. It is beautiful. It is cold and hard and it glows with as many colors as our previous world. It is cruel, is it not?

Crueler than you can imagine. The surrounding waters are known among men as Iskruel.

And what is our new home's name, chitter, chatter?

Ho'Demi smiled. *Iceberg.*

They led him, *chitter, chatter*, to the Skraelings. They had not bothered the Skraelings; because they hid deep in a natural cavern to which the lost souls, *chitter, chatter*, felt no claim.

Peering over a boulder at the mouth of a tunnel, Ho'Demi could finally see the soft glow of silver eyes, and the frantic whisperings of Skraelings.

Chitter, chatter. Is this who you seek?

Yes. My friends—and when did I ever think to call those who killed Ravensbund "friends"?—*Can you drive them from here?*

You did say a cruel world, did you not?

Cold and hard and icy. Not like this balmy darkness you currently inhabit.

Oh! Chitter, chatter! When?

At the moment, I and mine are consumed with warring the enemy that whispers beneath us, but when I have time and the opportunity to ride for my homeland, then I will come for you.

You are a true man. We can feel that. Come for us, chitter, chatter.

Ho'Demi edged back from the boulder. *Can you drive them from here?* he repeated.

We can drive anything from these caverns and chambers should we put a mind to it, chitter, chatter.

Then do it.

Axis?

Axis straightened so fast on Belaguez's back he almost fell off. Belial, riding behind, kicked his horse forward.

Ho'Demi?

Axis. I have found them. It was as you surmised. They hid in the mines of the Murkle Mountains.

Axis frowned. *Hid?*

He could feel the wry amusement across the void between their minds. *You have a horrendous enemy, StarMan. They are numerous beyond belief, and the Skraelings are so armored now that a man will have to aim straight and sure if he wants to hit the eye. And the Gryphon . . . the Gryphon will blacken the sky. But they are no longer in the mines. I have herded them for you.*

WHAT?

Ah, but I have had some assistance, chitter, chatter.

Axis cursed the man. Had cold finally tipped his mind beyond sanity?

Ride for the mouth of the Azle River, StarMan. That is where you will converge.

The mouth of the Azle, Ho'Demi?

Chitter, chatter, Axis. Chitter, chatter.

26

Of Ice and Laughter

he fought for a Great Lord, and in the name of that Lord he commanded a mighty army that undulated for leagues in every direction.

Timozel smiled and let the cold seep through to the marrow of his bones. Since he had vowed allegiance to his Great Lord, the cold no longer bothered him. Indeed, he had come to desire it.

The cold wind blew at his back as hundreds of thousands screamed his name and hurried to fulfil his every wish. Before him another army, his pitiful enemy, lay quavering in terror. They could not counter his brilliance.

He turned his head slightly, and saw that, indeed, the Skraeling army undulated in every direction, and every whisper echoed his name. Soon, when he gave the command, they would scream for him.

Remarkable victories were his for the taking.

"Soon," Timozel breathed and looked ahead once more.

It had not eventuated quite as he had planned, but no matter. He would still meet Axis (and how many months, years, had he lusted for this day?) with an army ten times his foe's pitiful force, and he would face Axis on his own terms. Perhaps Timozel could not surprise his former commander, but he could still best him, and best him he would.

A great and glorious battle and the enemy's positions were overrun—to the man (and others stranger that fought shoulder to shoulder with them) the enemy died. Timozel lost not one soldier.

Jervois Landing, no doubt. That had truly been a great and glorious battle, and Timozel had reveled in his victory.

Another day, and another battle. The enemy used foul magic this day, and

Timozel's forces were grievously hurt . . . but Timozel still won the field, and the enemy and its crippled commander retreated before him.

Timozel knew his enemy would be hard to defeat—he could not ignore the fact that Axis was an experienced and battle-hardened commander, as was the army he led—but he hoped Axis would be *dead* by the end of this day. After all, his vision had shown him time and time again how he would prevail. How easily he would prevail.

Timozel had wanted to catch Axis in full retreat. Catch the lightly defended rear of his column as he moved back to Carlon. He had hoped that Axis would think, when he could not find the Skraeling host in northern Aldeni, that they had outflanked him and were heading straight for Carlon. Then Axis would turn south and Timozel could spring the trap from the Murkle Mountains.

But Axis had not fled south, and those cursed . . . *Chatterlings* . . . had worried at his Skraeling host so badly in the mines that Timozel had finally been forced to lead them back into the open air. Now here they were, encamped by the Azle River (frozen over, as were the northern parts of Murkle Bay itself), and Axis' army lay a league and a half to the east.

Today they would meet. Today Timozel would finally show Axis who was the better commander. Axis would not live to defile Faraday again.

His eyes slipped to the slopes of the closest of the Murkle Mountains. Not all those hunched shapes were rocks.

Timozel turned back to the ice-field before him. In the distance he could see his foe's first row of formations darken the snow.

Thank the Stars for Ho'Demi and his strange pact with the lost souls of the Murkle mines, Axis thought, keeping Belaguez reined back as his army slowly moved past him. Without those souls, I would surely have been defeated before I raised my sword to fight.

If the Skraeling host had kept to the mines, there would have been no way to flush them out, and they could have attacked at leisure; perhaps after several weeks of allowing Axis and his men to slowly freeze in this Gorgrael-blasted land.

For the past twelve days, ever since Ho'Demi had contacted him, Axis had moved his thirty thousand toward the mouth of the Azle River. It was not country he knew well, and even had he known it from days when the grass actually grew over this land, he could not have recognized it now. The mountains, plains and river were completely encased in ice. While storms no longer blew, the air remained frigid and the north wind bitter. At night men cried with the cold, and the Icarii suffered most of all. Fires were few and pitiful even when they did flare into life. Supplies had to be packed to the army by mule, and the beasts' backs were already so bent with food that they could not carry fuel as well.

Everyone suffered, and Axis knew his army's effectiveness would be severely compromised by the cold it had already endured and would endure yet. A movement in the sky distracted him, and he shifted his eyes to watch FarSight descend to the ice beside him.

"StarMan." FarSight clenched his fist above his heart, and Axis noticed the birdman's hand was blue with cold.

"Well?"

FarSight shivered, and Axis did not think it was entirely with the cold. "They wait three hours' march from here, StarMan. Hundreds of thousands of them. Skraelings and IceWorms."

"Gryphon?"

FarSight shook his head. "I have not seen them."

"But they *must* be here. Somewhere."

FarSight inclined his head toward the towering Murkle Mountains. "My guess is that they lurk among the rocks and chasms of those slopes, StarMan."

Axis regarded the mountains. His eyes were sharp, their Icarii far-sightedness enhanced by his powers as an Enchanter, but even so he could discern nothing but bare rock, blasted and scraped by ice sliding down from the peaks. But they must be there. On that he agreed with FarSight.

"I do not want to risk the Strike Force unnecessarily, FarSight. Your thoughts?"

"You cannot afford *not* to risk us, StarMan. That Skraeling force is massive, and it sits well-ordered and disciplined. You, we, have faced nothing like this before. On their own, our ground forces will be obliterated within hours."

An overestimate, Axis thought morosely. It should take only an hour for a Skraeling force that size to eat through us. He shuddered, and thanked the Star Gods that Azhure, Caelum and StarDrifter were safe so far south. If the worst occurred . . . then all hope would not be left lying dead in this wasteland.

Belial and Magariz joined them; both men, like Axis, wrapped in felt and blankets under and over their armor. It severely hampered their fighting ability, but a frozen limb would be disastrous in battle.

"Belial," Axis asked, "have you and Magariz had a chance to look at the terrain?"

"Yes. It favors neither them nor us. Flat ice-land in this wide river valley, bordered in the south by the upper Murkle Mountains, and in the north by the low ranges of Western Ichtar."

"The river is iced?"

"Completely, Axis. As is the northern Murkle Bay," Magariz replied. "We shall have no help there."

Skraelings hated open water and Borneheld had kept them out of Aldeni for long months by the series of canals he had constructed between the Nordra and the upper reaches of the Azle. But now Gorgrael had so completely iced in northern Tencendor that all rivers north of the western Ranges were frozen. The Skraelings were no longer hindered by the hateful waters.

Axis chewed his lip thoughtfully, his eyes on the distant mountains. The other three stared at him, waiting for his lead. *Save us, Axis*, Belial thought, *for I have too much life to live yet.*

As if he had caught Belial's thought, Axis shifted his gaze to his friend's face sharply, then abruptly drew the glove off his right hand. He stared at his Enchanter's ring, fingering it gently.

Finally he lifted his eyes. "I have a plan," he said softly. "It is only a fragile plan, but it may work. It had *better* work, because it is all I can think of."

The two armies met as the noonday sun, shining incongruously over this ice-bound wasteland, began its descent toward the western horizon. There was little finesse to the action, for both armies just advanced until they met on the southern banks of the frozen Azle. Axis had pushed his army hard in the final half-league, for he did not want the Skraeling force to advance too far across the Azle. Their lives depended on being able to keep the Skraelings to the frozen riverbanks.

And how do we stop a juggernaut? Axis thought despairingly as he urged his men forward. *How will we manage to push back a force so large it only needs to stand firm to resist us?*

He threw everything he had against the Skraelings. What brands and fuel they had were flourished in the front ranks; but the Skraelings were not the cowardly wretches they had once been, and fire no longer terrified them.

Pikes, lances, spears, arrows—all tried to penetrate the bony ridges sur-rounding the Skraelings' silvery eyes, but the armor was so extensive that men had to keep a cool head to aim precisely, and cool heads were difficult amid the terror that surged toward them. And the Skraelings fought well. They were disciplined and they were ordered, and Axis quickly realized that he could not rely on spooking them into a retreat as he had done occasionally on previous occasions.

Arne did not stray from Axis' back. Wherever Axis drove the plunging Belaguez, there also Arne drove his horse. His eyes were slitted but watchful, for Arne could feel to the very core of his being that treachery rode the north-erly wind this day, and Axis would not die if he could help it.

Within minutes of the attack, Axis could see that his men were already in danger of being overwhelmed, the numbers against them were so fearsome.

FarSight, attack if you dare. Axis did not like using the Strike Force, but he had no choice. Only the winged archers would be able to strike beyond the first ranks of the Skraelings, and Axis needed to keep fresh ranks of Skraelings from his men.

Ho'Demi? Your archers, if you please. Six days ago Ho'Demi had rejoined Axis, and now he led the massed squads of archers, including Azhure's. Their arrows, Axis hoped, would also prevent too many Skraelings from rushing to support their front line. But thirty thousand against three hundred thousand were pitiful, *laughable*, odds, and Axis, as every man in his force, knew it.

Still they fought, bravely and well. Yet many died, overwhelmed, and in some places along the front line more men than Skraelings died.

For a long time Arne and Belial between them managed to keep Axis out of the front rank of the fighting, but eventually it grew so intense, so confused, that Axis found himself engaged with Skraeling soldiers, no thought but to plunge his sword time and time again into a Skraeling eye.

Above them the Strike Force wheeled, and over Axis' head shot flights of arrows so thick that sometimes they blotted out the sun, and Axis thought he could feel the line of Skraelings give way slightly.

He wanted to use his power, but it was not time. Not yet . . . not yet. He needed to husband what he had, because what he intended to do would take all of his ability—and even then he would risk damaging himself with the amount of the Star Dance he would have to manipulate.

Axis leaned down from Belaguez's back and seized a Skraeling by the throat. It had already been mauled by another sword and was easy prey, but its silvery eyes gleamed defiantly even as Axis' sword plunged down.

"Timozel," it whispered as it died.

Axis reeled back in shock, and only Arne's quick action disposed of another Skraeling as it leaped for the golden man's throat.

"Timozel?" he rasped. *"Timozel?"*

Arne seized Belaguez's reins and pulled the horse out of the direct line of fighting. Axis still stared incredulously at the spot where the Skraeling's body had dissolved, now hidden by struggling Skraelings and men. His sword hung limp in his hand.

Arne reached across and slapped his face. "So the traitor strikes, StarMan! You knew he would! Now, *fight on!* Win for us!"

Axis' eyes cleared and his hand firmed about the hilt of his sword. "Timozel!" he said again. "Oh, gods!"

He looked into the sky. *FarSight? Where are we positioned?*

At the banks of the Azle, StarMan. If you are going to do it, then do it now. None of your ground forces will hold out much longer. Already the back ranks of the Skraelings mass forward with renewed purpose. You have ten minutes, perhaps, before they swarm all over you. Do it now!

Yes. Pull back, FarSight. I have risked you enough.

Far along the line to the north Axis saw Belial. He signaled frantically, and saw Belial nod tersely. He turned his head toward Magariz in the south, and Magariz also acknowledged his signal. It would be hard, and some of his own men might well die, but more would die if he didn't attempt this.

Axis backed Belaguez even farther away from the front line, Arne pushing men out of the way behind the horse. He slid the glove off his hand, glancing one more time at what the ring told him, and then emptied his mind of all but the Song he needed to sing.

He hummed, his voice strengthening into music and words, and as the music drifted over the battlefield, his own men cheered, then made sure their footing was as firm as it could get.

Hello, Axis. What pretty music. Shall it be your dirge?

Axis was so shocked at Timozel's interruption—his *ability*—that for an instant the Song faltered. But he forced Timozel's words from his mind, and strengthened his grip on the Song.

I fight for a Great Lord now, Axis, and in his name I shall win great victories. You are pitiful compared to Gorgrael.

Axis' face worked. Damn him! Questions and emotions battled in Axis' mind. More than anything else he wanted to hunt Timozel down, ask him why? Why Gorgrael? But he could not afford to do that. The Song. There could be nothing but the Song. He thought of Azhure's calm smile, and that banished thoughts of Timozel from his mind.

The power of the Star Dance roped through him, and Axis fought, *battled*, to keep it under control. He had never attempted to manipulate so much power before, and he feared its effect on him.

Underneath the feet of the front line, hairline cracks splintered their way across the ice covering the Azle. Men slowly edged backward, even though it meant the Skraelings gained some ground.

Farther beneath the ice, the waters of the great river seethed in response to the Song.

Timozel cursed, watching from halfway atop one of the low hills to the north of the river. He could see what Axis was going to do.

The enemy used foul magic this day, and Timozel's forces were grievously hurt . . .

But what could he do?

"Gryphon," he grated. "I *should* have used them sooner. *Now!*"

And so the Gryphon attacked.

They lifted out of the rocks of the Murkle Mountains where they had been secreted. They stretched their wings on the stiff northerly wind, and screeched with the voice of despair.

There were over nine hundred of them.

They went for the withdrawing Strike Force first, as Timozel had told them, and those units not yet withdrawn to a safe distance were decimated.

Then some five hundred wheeled back and attacked Axis' army, leaving four hundred to murder as they willed among the Icarii, and they wheeled and dived, and every time they dived they carried off a man.

Some were felled by arrows. But not many, for Gorgrael had built his flying pets well, and most arrows glanced uselessly off the creatures' thick fur before dropping in a sad rain to the ground.

Axis did not at first notice the Gryphon attack, nor did he notice how the sky blackened with their bodies. The power of the Song seared through him and he let it rage as much as he dared.

The ice finally splintered apart, shattering in great sheets over the raging waters of the Azle. Tens of thousands of Skraelings, and a few score men, sank instantly, and hundreds of thousands of the wraiths were left seething impotently on the northern bank of the Azle. Over a hundred were trapped on the southern bank, and these were instantly overwhelmed by Axis' force.

Axis came out of his induced reverie amazed that he had actually survived the power of the Song. He looked at the now free and surging waters of the Azle with relief. We will live through this day, he thought, slumping in the saddle, and we will deal with the rest as we may after we have rested and thought some more.

But Axis was denied both rest and thought. Almost as soon as he blinked his eyes back into awareness, Arne seized his shoulder. "StarMan!" he screamed. "Save us!"

Hadn't he just done that? Hadn't he just . . . ?

Then he heard the scream above his head, saw Arne lunge, and felt himself being pushed out of the saddle Belaguez reared and added his scream to whatever it was that reeled out of the sky, and Axis was dimly aware of a great shape that swooped over his head and seized the rider beyond Arne's horse.

"Gryphon," Arne grunted as he hauled Axis to his feet. "Hundreds of them."

Axis finally looked about with cleared vision, and what he saw appalled him. Around him men were dying in their hundreds as the Gryphon swooped, beaks open in screams, eyes blazing with death, talons extended. They were covered in blood, but it was not theirs.

"Get the men to . . ." shelter, Axis was about to order, but there *was* no shelter. The Azle valley was wide and flat, and it would take his men an hour or more to scramble to the nearest rocks in the Murkle Mountains.

And no one had an hour.

Across the Azle the Skraeling mass began to laugh. They stood in their hundreds of thousands, and the sound of their mirth drifted across the surging waters to intermingle with the screams of dying men.

Timozel stood on his hill and roared with laughter.

He shared his thoughts with Gorgrael, experiencing his master's joy, then he summoned his personal Gryphon. He would fly in and dispose of Axis himself. He grinned. Axis' foul magic would not win the day now. Their commander lay crippled, and waited only for Timozel to end his misery.

Axis circled in horror. Everywhere his men were being slaughtered. Gods! What could he do? What Songs of War were there that could destroy these wing-borne horrors?

None. All Songs of War were lost.

He thought frantically, twisting his ring, watching the patterns unfold. *Give me a Song that will destroy Gryphon*, he begged, and for a long, terrible moment he thought the stars would remain obstinately still. But slowly, grudgingly, they formed a pattern, and what they formed horrified Axis almost more than the slaughter about him.

If he sang that it would kill him. There was so *much* power involved . . . no one could wield that much and live. But what choice did he have? He would die anyway, and better that he die saving the remnants of his army, saving them for Azhure, or even StarDrifter, than die uselessly bemoaning his lack of ability.

"I'm sorry," he whispered to no one in particular, then he began to sing.

It was the bravest thing he would ever do.

With the first note he felt the uncontrollable power flood his body. He fought to direct it while he still could, fought to give it meaning, but nevertheless he felt it rope and twist through his body, felt it burn and ruin. Felt himself begin to die.

He had not thought that death could be so impossibly painful.

Arne, standing guard beside the StarMan, turned at the scream that issued from Axis' mouth, and at the same time had to dodge the plummeting body of a twisted and burned Gryphon. All about him Gryphon fell from the sky, but Arne had no eyes for them.

What was happening to Axis?

The StarMan had fallen to the ground and was now convulsing. Wisps of smoke rose from his eyes, and—Arne gagged—they were *burning*!

Timozel snarled as his Gryphon burned before his very eyes. The Gryphon! Frantically he looked over the scene before him, but then he relaxed a little and smiled. Perhaps the commander across the river *had* won the day, but at a dreadful cost.

A dreadful cost.

Timozel laughed again. There were over seven thousand Gryphon young-lings waiting in Gorgrael's Ice Fortress, for these nine hundred who now died had given birth some months previously. Soon the seven thousand would give birth themselves, and when they had done that, then they could fly south to join him.

And the man who had used such foul magic to destroy these nine hundred now lay screaming and writhing on the ground, his eyes burning in his head, his skin rippling and crisping, his fingers smoldering into black claws, and Timozel knew he would never, *never*, wield such power again.

Or any power, for that matter.

"The day is yours," he whispered. "Enjoy your death."

Tomorrow he would find a way across that river and set the Skraelings to what was left of Axis' army. Perhaps the IceWorms could swim across. Yes. Yes, they did not mind the water, and they could disgorge tens of thousands of Skraelings into the pitiful remnants of that foul army.

Timozel laughed again.

Arne dropped his sword and fell to his knees. "Axis," he whispered.

The man's twitching had stopped and he was almost dead. His face—what was left of it—twisted, and from somewhere he found the strength for a last whisper.

"Azhure, I am so sorry. So very sorry."

27

Azhure

Azhure was sitting under a marmalade tree in the orchards of Temple Mount, nursing Caelum and enjoying the sunshine of the enchanted isle, when she felt the fragile link between her and Axis snap.

For several heartbeats she sat unmoving, staring into space, wondering at the sense of complete loss that consumed her. Then, just as she realized what it was, a whisper reached her mind.

Azhure, I am so sorry. So very sorry.

"*Noooo!*" Azhure screamed, and Caelum screamed with her, for he too felt the living link with his father break. She lurched to her feet, running with ungainly strides toward the Temple where she knew StarDrifter was. "*Noooo!*"

He reached her by the Dome of the Stars. StarDrifter had known instantly what had happened, for he remembered the feeling at the moment when MorningStar had been murdered, and this was the same—except now it was his son's life-force that had been snuffed out.

Azhure was sobbing hysterically, and Caelum no better, and StarDrifter managed to quell his own grief in his efforts to calm mother and child.

But Azhure would not be calmed. StarDrifter seized Caelum from her arms and set him down in the grass—there was not much Caelum could do to harm himself there—and wrapped arms and wings about Azhure, trying desperately to stop her writhing and her cries.

She beat at his chest and at his encircling wings, wanting to strike out, wanting to hurt, wanting to deny what that snap and whisper meant. "No!" she kept screaming. "*Live for me!*"

"Azhure," StarDrifter muttered, broken-hearted. His son? Dead? How could that *be*? After having lost him for so long, only to lose him again like this?

"Azhure . . . he's gone. There's nothing we can do. Nothing."

She started to sob, and buried her face against StarDrifter's chest. "No, no, no, no," she muttered over and over again, a litany of denial, and StarDrifter was about to guide her back to her chamber in the Priestess' dormitory when she shrieked, agonized this time, and collapsed to the ground.

"Azhure? Azhure? *What is it?*"

Azhure writhed and clutched at StarDrifter. She stared at him, her eyes wide with agony, but she could not speak as a contraction so violent seized her she doubled over and gagged.

"Oh gods," StarDrifter groaned, and screamed for the Priestesses.

It was a terrible birth.

StarDrifter never left Azhure's side, but neither he nor the three Priestesses who attended could do much to help her.

The twins were intent on escaping her body, and doing it as fast as they could. It was the boy who led, who forced the birth, and nothing StarDrifter could say to him or his sister could stop their headlong rush. Unlike most Icarii babes, they were not scared by the birth, merely so impatient they did not, *would not*, pause to consider the damage they did to their mother.

If they cared about it.

For the final half hour Azhure lay limp and mercifully unconscious, and StarDrifter stopped his efforts to plead with the twins to focus his entire energy on Azhure.

After an indeterminate time he turned to stare at the First. "Gods, Lady, what can we do?"

"Pray, StarDrifter," the First muttered, "that these babies birth themselves soon. She is almost gone."

"*Gone?*" StarDrifter whispered, then stared back at Azhure. Her breathing was shallow, her skin slack and damp, gleaming with unhealthy pallor.

"She has little strength," the First said again. "And I fear she does not want to live. What brought this on?"

StarDrifter told her how he and Azhure had felt Axis' death.

The Priestesses shared horrified glances, but they did not have time to mourn the loss of the StarMan. Not when the Sacred Daughter's life veered so close to extinction itself.

StarDrifter leaned over Azhure and seized her slack face in his hands. "*Live,* Azhure. I could not bear it if you died too."

And so the birth went on, with only the Priestesses sharing a thought for the babies struggling to be born, and then only a sparing one, for the mother was far more important.

As the babies slipped from her body Azhure hemorrhaged, and they almost lost her. As it was she bled so much before the First could persuade her womb to contract and stem the flow that both the First and StarDrifter found themselves covered in blood.

It was left to the two junior Priestesses to take the babies to one side and wash and bind them. They squalled healthily and happily enough, pleased to finally make their own way in the world, and they did not spare a thought for their mother's struggle for life.

It was not until late that night, after five hours of effort and strain and worry, that the First told StarDrifter that Azhure had a chance of life.

"If she does not develop a fever or infection," she said, "and if she still has the will to live."

StarDrifter lifted his eyes from Azhure's face. "If she does not have the will, First, then I will *infuse her with mine! I will not let her die!*"

The Priestess stared at him for long minutes, then she nodded and silently left them alone. Time would tell.

28

hilltop Conversations

Timozel stood atop his low hill, watching the tattered remnants of what had once been Axis' army withdraw to the southwest. He was almost incandescent with rage.

Great Lord We have them at our mercy!

In his Ice Fortress Gorgrael paced back and forth, back and forth. *Nevertheless, I want you to do as I bid.*

Timozel tensed, trying to bring his rage under control, trying to come to grips with Gorgrael's utter stupidity. *Great Lord, I can quash them in a day. Two at the most. When morning comes I can begin to direct the Ice Worms across the Azle.*

No I want you to move north.

Gorgrael had been devastated by Axis' destruction of nine hundred Gryphon. His *pets!* Axis had *burned them!* The fact that Axis had ruined himself in the effort had slipped completely from Gorgrael's mind. His Gryphon were dead!

You have seven thousand with you, Master, and in only six weeks' time they will birth over sixty-five thousand. Master! Hear me! Let me finish them now! Victory is within our grasp!

NO! Gorgrael's voice roared through Timozel's head. *NO! You WILL do as I order! Retreat to the north. Once we have recovered from our grievous loss then we can finish the job. But I will not risk anymore. You said you would win this battle!*

And I bloody well have! Timozel seethed, but kept the thought from Gorgrael. *Retreat may well kill us, Master.*

How, Timozel? How? Is not Axis and his army all but destroyed? I want you north. Now.

Dammit, Timozel thought. In only a day he could wipe out—

Suddenly he was gripped by Gorgrael's power and he arched his back and screamed with such agony that the Skraelings massed below shifted and whispered in agitation.

DO AS I ORDER!

Yes, Master, Timozel whimpered, and turned to give the orders.

"My pets!" Gorgrael muttered angrily. "How could he destroy my pets!" He bent to touch the heads of his remaining two Gryphon, the originals created from the disintegrating mass of dead SkraeBolds. Thank the Dark Music, he thought, that I had these two here to keep me warm at nights. Gorgrael's immediate reaction was to pull his arm back to the protection of the year-long ice and snow, closer to home.

"A brave move," the Dark Man said by the fireplace. "But I see he has not tricked you."

"I had not thought Axis capable of such power," Gorgrael continued to fret. "I had not thought the Star Dance could be used to destroy so easily . . . I had not bargained on this."

"Of course not. You have done the best thing, Gorgrael."

The Dark Man had almost collapsed with relief when Gorgrael forced Timozel to obey his orders. His heart still pounded uncomfortably; he'd thought Timozel might persuade Gorgrael to continue the attack. Disaster had been so close, and even now the Dark Man could hardly believe that Gorgrael could not see it, *smell* it. If he had allowed Timozel to push . . .

By the Stars! the Dark Man breathed silently to himself, keeping his thoughts as well cloaked as his face, thank all the gods in existence he is so obsessed by the Gryphon! The monster is going to give us the time to recover!

If we can.

"And now I cannot feel Axis." Gorgrael stopped in front of the Dark Man and peered unsuccessfully beneath his hood. "Where is he? What has happened to him? Always before now I could feel his hateful tug at my soul. Is he *truly* dead?" His eyes gleamed.

"He is tricky," the Dark Man advised. "He has somehow cloaked his power, hoping that you will think him to be dead." It was the best he could do.

Gorgrael peered uncomfortably a moment longer, then he nodded. "Yes, yes, you must be right. Axis is trying to trick me . . . trick me into throwing my entire host at him. He hides somewhere . . . planning some deception. No, no, I won't fall for that trick."

Gorgrael clicked his claws together as he paced, his thoughts racing beyond the day's events. "She plants," he mumbled. "She plants, and with every seedling that slips into the earth I feel the nasty Song strengthen."

"She has a way to go," the Dark Man said, relieved by the sudden change in conversation.

"But she has done too much already!" Gorgrael hissed.

The Dark Man looked up from his gloved hands. "Nothing is too much until the last tree. If she does not complete her task then even a hundred leagues of forest below the Avarinheim will prove harmless. They *must* be joined."

"Harmless?" Gorgrael spat into the fire. "Harmless, Dark Man? Those trees might not yet sing at their full power, but already they hum distressingly. I have my hands full with Axis, yet I must do something about his Lover and her damned planting." He fidgeted, frowning. "What can I do to stop her?"

"You need do nothing!" the Dark Man said merrily, and Gorgrael frowned even further. "Nothing," the Dark Man repeated, "for Artor himself stalks her."

"*Artor?*" Gorgrael gasped.

"Verily," laughed the Dark Man. "Let that pitiful god do the work for you. He has as much interest as you in stopping the forest."

"He will not harm her?"

"No, merely stop her horrid gardening."

"And then?"

"Why, then you can seize her. Use her as you will."

Gorgrael thought about it. Was there something here he could not see? What was the Dark Man not telling him? But he smiled anyway. "Yes. I shall enjoy that." His smile died. "Going so soon, Dear Man?"

"I will find out what has happened to Axis for you, Gorgrael."

29

Late-Night Conversations

*S*tarDrifter?"

Azhure's weak voice pulled StarDrifter out of his doze and his head jerked out of his arms where they rested on her bed. "Azhure!" He reached out and stroked her forehead "How are you feeling?" It was a stupid question.

She tried a wan smile, but it didn't work, so she sighed and turned her head farther toward StarDrifter's hand. "I am alive, StarDrifter. Let's leave it at that."

"And you *will* live, Azhure."

"Why, StarDrifter? Axis is dead." Her voice broke. "Axis is *dead!*"

"And we are both alive and you have three children to live for, Azhure. Cling to that."

"Three," she murmured and her hand crept down over the coverlets to her belly. "They almost killed me. They tried, I think."

Shocked, StarDrifter opened his mouth to deny her words, then shut it slowly. "The twins are in the next room, Azhure, as is Caelum. Do you want to see them?"

"I will see Caelum in the morning," she whispered, turning her face to stare at the ceiling, "but I am too heartsick now. I do not want to see the twins at all."

For a long time StarDrifter sat and stroked her brow, pleased she was conscious and talking, but distressed by her weakness and despondency. Yet, how else could she have responded to Axis' death? StarDrifter felt as though his soul had been enveloped in cold blackness. Where he had felt the constant contact with Axis' life-force was now nothing but void.

Azhure twisted her head back to gaze at StarDrifter. Dark shadows circled her eyes. "He's won, hasn't he, StarDrifter? Gorgrael has won. There is nothing to keep him from Tencendor now."

"In the morning," StarDrifter murmured. "We'll talk in the morning. Be still now."

There was a knock at the door, and StarDrifter stirred irritably.

"Who can that be?" Azhure whispered.

"Perhaps the First," StarDrifter said. He lifted his head. "Come in."

The door slowly opened, and WolfStar SunSoar stepped into the room.

Both Azhure and StarDrifter froze in shock—StarDrifter had absolutely no doubt who this was. An Enchanter's power—and such power!—radiated from his eyes, and his SunSoar blood called to StarDrifter.

For a long moment WolfStar stared at StarDrifter, as if daring an attack, then he moved to the other side of Azhure's bed, folding his golden wings gracefully behind him as he sat down, smiling at his daughter.

"Azhure. You have endured so much."

Azhure felt StarDrifter's hand clench on her brow, and she shot him a pleading look. "StarDrifter! Please, don't do anything foolish!"

"He would be foolish to even try!" WolfStar hissed, turning the full power of his stare on StarDrifter.

The antagonism between the two Enchanters was palpable, and for the first time since that afternoon Azhure forgot her loss. "*Please!*" she cried. "Please!"

"You murdered my mother," StarDrifter yelled, half rising to his feet, "you murdered your pregnant wife, and you murdered hundreds of Icarii children! Do not think that I will just sit here and pass pleasant conversation!"

Azhure seized his arm, her own hand trembling, and it was enough to make StarDrifter subside. But he did not lower his blazing eyes from WolfStar's, and he bared his teeth in a snarl.

"Reasons governed all of my actions, foolish birdman!" WolfStar snapped "I do not let myself get carried away with petty emotions and passing lusts. I have more responsibilities than you can possibly imagine!"

"And more guilts, too, *I* imagine!"

WolfStar's nostrils flared in anger and he made to rise as well. Azhure could feel the power snap in the air between them.

"Stop!" she cried, her voice cracking with the effort and with her pain, and both Enchanters turned their eyes back to her in concern. "While I am in this room you will behave civilly," she said. "StarDrifter, I will not have you try to avenge all of WolfStar's wrongs. I will *not* have it, do you hear? I do not want to lose you as well!"

StarDrifter nodded stiffly and dropped his eyes to stare at the coverlet.

"WolfStar?" Azhure waited until she had his undivided attention. "WolfStar, you must know how the Icarii feel about you. Can you blame

StarDrifter for his anger? His hurt? Respect that, do not taunt him for it."

WolfStar's jaw tightened, but he, too, nodded stiffly.

"Good," Azhure said wearily. "For I do not have the strength to mourn more than one love tonight."

WolfStar took a deep breath, ill-will simmering at StarDrifter from the corners of his violet eyes, then took Azhure's hand tenderly.

"Axis lives," he said directly, and then smiled slowly. "Axis lives."

If anything, that simple statement overwhelmed Azhure and StarDrifter more than WolfStar's entrance.

"Axis lives?" Azhure asked, so bewildered she found no comfort in the words. "No, he cannot. He cannot. I cannot feel him . . . StarDrifter?"

StarDrifter was shaking his head in as much confusion. "No . . . I mean, yes, Azhure. WolfStar? Neither of us can feel him. He *must* be dead!"

WolfStar continued to hold Azhure's hand, but he looked at StarDrifter. "Sometimes I feel that Death follows me like a shadow. I can rarely shake it off. Tonight, for once, I bring life in my wake." He sighed. "Yesterday afternoon there was a terrible battle at the mouth of the Azle River."

Azhure moaned, and StarDrifter took her other hand.

"Gorgrael's forces swarm, Azhure, and Axis led his army to meet them, even though he doubted the outcome."

"He always doubts," Azhure whispered, and then marveled that she could use the present tense again so quickly.

"Yes, he doubts, but none can fault his courage. Azhure, StarDrifter, Gorgrael's power grows beyond anything I could imagine—"

"Or encourage," StarDrifter said, but Azhure squeezed his hand, silencing him.

WolfStar spared him a swift black look, then continued in an even tone. "Later, StarDrifter, later. Gorgrael has Gryphon. You know of them."

Azhure and StarDrifter both nodded.

"Well." WolfStar's mouth twisted, "he had nine hundred and seven, to be exact, to throw at Axis at the Azle mouth. No wait, I will explain later. For now, let me just tell you about Axis. He had managed to contain the Skraelings, but the Gryphon attacked his force. He had to do something. What he did amazed even me. I had not thought he had the courage."

"You do not know him as we do, WolfStar," Azhure said.

"I know him better than you think!" he snapped, but continued on in a more moderate tone. "He reached for a Song to destroy the Gryphon, which he did, but he virtually destroyed himself at the same time. StarDrifter," he turned his head, "you will understand this. He manipulated an appalling amount of the Star Dance. It almost killed him . . . and now he lies crippled."

Azhure cried out and tried to rise, but WolfStar pushed her back. "No, listen to what I have to say, Azhure. You will go to him soon enough—and, Stars knows, he needs you."

"But we cannot feel him," StarDrifter said, not letting himself hope, not wanting to believe WolfStar. "Why can we not feel him? Why was the link severed?"

"Because Axis has lost all his power. He has lost contact with the Star Dance, and it is through the contact with the Star Dance that members of the same family can feel each other's life force." He shrugged. "He is crippled."

There was worse, but WolfStar did not think Azhure was strong enough to take that yet. She would find out soon enough.

The three were silent for a long time as Azhure and StarDrifter absorbed WolfStar's news.

Stars, Azhure thought, he needs me more than ever now. I *must go to him!* But I cannot, not bed-ridden as I am, not powerless as I am. At least the babies have been born.

Finally, Azhure lifted her eyes to her father. "We need to talk, you and I," she said. "Here I am on the Island of Mist and Memory, and this is where I had to come for the answers. This is where I had to come to find out how to touch my power. WolfStar, you conceal yourself and the truth behind mystery and grief and shadows beyond knowing, but tonight I am going to *demand* answers from you."

WolfStar nodded. "Yes, it is time. But StarDrifter must go."

"No!" he growled, and Azhure felt his hand tense.

"No," she echoed. "StarDrifter stays. You have more people to answer to than me, WolfStar. StarDrifter stays."

WolfStar's eyes glinted, and he threw his head back, but he reluctantly acquiesced. "Nevertheless, Azhure, there are some mysteries that only you shall be privy to." He lifted her hand so that both she and StarDrifter could see the Enchantress' ring. "The ring demands it. Your own power demands it. If you are to grow into what you must become then you will have to do it by yourself. Not even I can attend."

Azhure frowned but WolfStar did not expand. "Well," he said, "your first question?"

She started with the oldest and greatest grief.

"Niah," she said. "Why did you lie to her?"

WolfStar's brow furrowed. "Lie? I do not understand you."

Azhure looked at StarDrifter. "StarDrifter? Could you fetch the letter?"

She had shown StarDrifter Niah's letter the same night she had first read it. Now he fetched it from a box and handed it to WolfStar.

The Enchanter's beautiful violet eyes widened as he read Niah's words.

"She was so beautiful, in soul and form," he said eventually, then raised his eyes to Azhure's. "Lie? I am still perplexed."

"You told her you loved her. Why did you have to lie?"

"I never uttered one lie to Niah," WolfStar answered. "Not *one*. I loved her, and I continue to love her."

Azhure's face twisted. "And *reborn*, WolfStar? Do you mean me to believe that you can actually arrange her rebirth?"

"What exists between Niah and me does not have to be explained to you, Azhure."

"*Yes it does!*" Azhure screamed, half lifting from her pillow, "*because I was the one who had to watch her die!*"

WolfStar flinched, and StarDrifter leaned closer to Azhure, murmuring comfort.

"Yes, it does," Azhure repeated, sinking back down. "Explain to me."

"Niah *will* be reborn, Azhure," WolfStar said quietly, his eyes holding his · daughter's stare steadily. "But it will not be for some years yet. Beyond Prophecy. That is all I can tell you."

Azhure nodded, accepting it, but tears ran down her cheek. She lifted her free hand and brushed them away.

"Why her death, WolfStar? Why the years of horror at Hagen's hands? *Why did you leave me to suffer so?*"

"Why did Niah need to die? Why your suffering? For the same reason, Azhure, all for the one reason." WolfStar hesitated, hating the truth that he would have to speak. "Because you needed to suffer, Azhure—"

StarDrifter leaped to his feet, unable to believe what he was hearing. "No child needs to suffer. How can you sit there and—"

Now WolfStar was on his feet. "Because I *know* more than you and because *I* have suffered. Now, will you let me finish?"

"StarDrifter?" Azhure pleaded, and he subsided as WolfStar sat back down.

"Azhure. You may not believe this, but I wept for you every day you remained with Hagen. When I said that you needed to suffer, it was not because I *wanted* you to suffer. Azhure, I am as bound by the Prophecy as everyone else. Even I must do its bidding . . . although sometimes I did not understand why."

"Enough excuses, WolfStar," StarDrifter ground out. "*Why* did Azhure have to suffer?"

WolfStar sighed and rubbed his eyes. "Because of who you will become, Azhure." He dropped his hand, and when he looked at his daughter neither she nor StarDrifter could mistake the sympathy in his eyes. "You will wield great power one day, Azhure, and that day is not far off. More power than I, *certainly* more than StarDrifter." He shot the Enchanter yet another hostile glare. "Azhure, you needed to suffer because only suffering grants compassion, and without compassion you will misuse the power that will be yours. Suffering was needed to temper the woman you will become."

"And have *you* suffered, WolfStar?" StarDrifter sneered.

"More than you could ever know, StarDrifter," he said quietly.

"Enough, StarDrifter, WolfStar. Father," and this was the first time she had ever called him that, "what do you mean, 'temper the woman I will become'?"

"By dawn you will have your answers, Azhure. I promise you that. But at the moment I can say no more." Not with StarDrifter present.

Azhure nodded, accepting, and returned to the horror of her childhood. "Why Smyrton in particular? Why Hagen? Why send Niah so far north?" She paused. "Suffering can be purchased anywhere."

"Because you needed to be there to meet Axis. And because you needed to be close to Artor. Smyrton is a very special place for Artor, it is his heartland, and it was there you could grow to understand him best and discover his weaknesses."

"What?" Azhure asked. Artor? But WolfStar sat stony-faced and refused to explain.

"Did you come to me there?" she asked.

WolfStar nodded. "I could not ignore you. I did what I could for you."

"Alayne," Azhure said, realizing the extent of WolfStar's manipulation.

WolfStar nodded again, but StarDrifter looked puzzled.

"When I was young, after Niah died," Azhure explained, "a traveling blacksmith came to Smyrton every two weeks or so, StarDrifter. His name was Alayne. I thought him my only friend and he told me many stories." She laughed, bitterly. "He told me the ancient legend of Caelum. The legend I decided to name my son after. And I thought it was *I* who named him. But no. WolfStar named him."

WolfStar tried to explain. "I told you stories of power and kept your own power alive underneath your cloak of fear."

She turned her head away slightly.

"And now *I* have a question," StarDrifter said.

"No doubt," WolfStar replied.

"Why train both Axis and Gorgrael?"

"StarDrifter, you may not believe this but I will tell you anyway I do not control the Prophecy. I am as much bound to it as any other," he said, repeating his words of some minutes previously. "But there were some precautions I could take. Believe me, I want Axis to best his brother, and I will do anything I can to assist the Prophecy to reach a successful conclusion. Axis needed to be trained, and I thought it best that I train Gorgrael as well."

StarDrifter shifted impatiently, but WolfStar ignored him. "It was best that I mold Gorgrael and, in doing so, I have given him the quality that will enable Axis to defeat him."

"What?" Azhure asked sharply, turning her face back to her father.

"Uncertainty in himself. Already his uncertainty has led him to grievous error. One day, I hope it will prove fatal."

"Axis is often uncertain," Azhure said.

"Perhaps it is something bequeathed them by their father." WolfStar could not resist the barb, but he continued before StarDrifter could respond. "Azhure, it will be your task to teach Axis both certainty and joy in himself."

She smiled and nodded, her eyes reflective. She was about to turn the conversation back to her power, but StarDrifter was not yet done.

"And MorningStar? What excuse do you have for the murder of my mother?"

"I do what I must for the Prophecy, StarDrifter."

StarDrifter literally growled. "You use the Prophecy as an excuse, renegade!"

"She saw me in my daily disguise, StarDrifter. I could not risk her revealing me at that point. I do what I must," he repeated evenly.

"As the children you murdered," StarDrifter whispered hoarsely.

For the first time WolfStar had the grace to look uncomfortable, and Azhure wondered if he would again use the excuse he'd offered her—the Enchantress' ring made him do it. But WolfStar startled both Azhure and StarDrifter.

"For that I offer my apology, StarDrifter. I offer it to you, and through you, I extend it to the entire Icarii nation."

Thrown off balance, StarDrifter stared at him. Eventually he opened his mouth to say something, but now WolfStar was looking out the window and he waved StarDrifter into silence.

"Azhure," he said urgently, "time grows short, and there is something I must say before . . . well, there is something I must say. Azhure, Gorgrael has bested me." He laughed shortly. "How I hate to admit that, but admit it I must. Gorgrael has re-created the Gryphon, you know that, but you do not know their dreadful secret." And WolfStar explained that the Gryphon was created pregnant, and that each generation was bearing more and more. "Within months, Gorgrael will have sixty-five thousand Gryphon to throw at Tencendor, and then they will breed . . ."

He let them think about the implications for a moment. "Azhure. It almost destroyed Axis to deal with nine hundred. He will never be able to deal with anymore. That must be your task."

"But how can I—"

"After tonight most of your doubts will be eased. I promised that when you were finally alone many of your questions would be answered and you would be taught how to use your powers. Azhure, are you ready to confront your heritage?"

Suddenly she felt very calm. "Yes."

WolfStar bent down, pulled the coverlets back from Azhure and picked her up in his arms—he was dismayed at how light she was, and how she cried out in agony the moment he lifted her.

"Stop!" StarDrifter shouted, leaping to his feet yet again. "What are you going to do with her?"

"I have had enough of you!" WolfStar snarled, and StarDrifter felt the Enchanter-Talon's power reach out to him, wrap him tight, and hurl him back against the wall.

He blacked out the instant his head hit the stone.

30

The Sepulchre of the Moon

"hush, Azhure," WolfStar soothed as he hurried her silently out of the Priestesses' dormitory. "Your suffering will soon end."

"I don't have the strength for whatever you plan," Azhure began, weeping with her pain.

"You must, darling. You must find the strength from somewhere. Here, wrap your arms tighter about my neck. I will carry you a while."

Azhure whistled for Sicarius as they passed him in an outer chamber, but WolfStar growled at the hound and he sunk back to his belly. "No," he said. "This must be just you and me, Azhure, and then just you. Alone."

The pre-dawn air was cold and Azhure shivered as WolfStar walked swiftly down the Avenue.

"Where are we going?"

"To the Sepulchre of the Moon, Azhure. Be strong for me this night. Be strong for Axis."

Her shivering increased and WolfStar held her as closely as he dared, cursing those babies as he went. They had held everything up, and had then almost destroyed their mother. Their beautiful mother.

"Be strong!" he snapped. "This is no time to succumb to womanly weakness."

That was too much, and Azhure's temper flared as her arms tightened. "You are like all men, WolfStar. You seduce and implant, and then leave the woman to endure the agony! Don't sneer at what you can't know!"

WolfStar smiled to himself, but he did not say anything more until he neared the southern cliffs of the island.

The waves crashed below them.

Azhure?

Azhure? Azhure? Is that you?

Does she wear the Circle? Is it her?

WolfStar, WolfStar, do you bring her?

"Yes," he whispered. "Yes, I bring her. Be patient."

The waves moaned and Azhure cried out, terrified by their wail and by the echoes she could feel in her own blood. She tried to twist out of WolfStar's arms, but he was too powerful. "No!" she cried.

"Yes," he whispered again, and Azhure dared a look at his face . . . and instantly understood why Niah had used the phrase "hungry with magic" to describe his eyes.

Now they stood at the very lip of the cliff, and Azhure clung to WolfStar's arms, afraid he would drop her. The moon was dark, but in the starlight she could dimly see the narrow steps cut into the cliff face that the First Priestess had pointed out so many weeks previously.

The waves shrieked. *Azhure! Azhure!*

She moaned and hid her face against her father's chest, trying to stop her ears with her fists. The wind tore at her inky hair, unraveling it from its knot.

"Azhure," WolfStar said. "I am going to set you down now. Be strong."

"No!" she screamed, clinging desperately to his arms as he stood her on her feet. The lip of the cliff crumbled, and her left foot slipped out into noth‑ingness.

Azhure!

She flattened herself against WolfStar's body, her fingers digging into his flesh, sobbing in terror. Any moment now the wind would tear her from his grip and fling her to her death!

"Azhure," he said. "Survive this night, and death is nothing you will have to fret about."

"WolfStar!"

"Come now, Azhure," and WolfStar's voice was as gentle as a lover's. "You shall have to go on by yourself now. I will wait here for you."

Too shocked and terrified to say anything, Azhure stared at him. His fingers loosened and she tightened her own grip defensively. "I can't . . ."

Go down those steps? In her condition? Those steps in this wind would kill the most sure footed man, let alone her. No. *No!*

"*Yes!*" WolfStar screamed and, tearing her hands from his arms, hurled her headlong down the steps.

For several terrifying heartbeats Azhure tumbled down a dozen of the steps, breaking the skin on her hands and feet as she scrabbled frantically for pur‑chase, battling to stay alive. She ended up facedown against the rough stone, panting with terror, and when she looked back up WolfStar stood calmly at their head.

"Go on," he mouthed, but his words were lost in the wind. *Go on. You cannot turn back now.*

Azhure! Come on! Come!

She pressed her face against the rock, fighting to keep from fainting from pain and fear. Something had torn within her as she tumbled down the steps, and now she realized she was hemorrhaging again.

Azhure! Quick!

Death if you linger!

Death if I rush, she thought, furious now with both WolfStar and whatever cried out to her from the waves. Slowly she turned about so she was sitting on the steps, then eased herself down, first her feet, then her buttocks, letting go with her hands only when absolutely necessary, and then grabbing for the next handhold.

She stayed pressed as close to the cliff as she could, but even so there was only a finger-breadth of stone on her outer side before the void beckoned.

Gradually she eased herself lower.

Now the loss of blood was serious, and Azhure felt her head swimming.

I *am* dead, she thought, for I will never be able to climb these steps again.

Azhure!

Be quiet. I am coming.

Then she slipped again, and slid several paces down the stone steps, ending her slide only by grasping at a protruding stone in the cliff face.

Her legs dangled into a void from the thighs down.

She pulled them back in, her heart beating so violently she could feel it leaping in her throat.

There were no more steps, only the hungry, beckoning waves.

"What's going on?" she sobbed, clinging to the cliff face. *"What's going on?"*

"Azhure," a voice full of loveliness said in her ear, and she started so violently she would have fallen from the steps had not a velvety hand grasped her firmly by the arm. "Azhure. Here is a Door. See? Your hand already grasps its handle."

Slowly, slowly, she turned her head toward the voice. A man was emerging from the very stone itself, and the skin of his face and shoulders were pale and fine and his eyes glowed with complete serenity.

"Who are you?" she whispered, knowing that his hand on her arm was her only hold on life.

"My name is Adamon."

Her head reeled crazily. No . . . no . . . she could not have heard right.

"Come into the Sepulchre of the Moon," the God of the Firmament said, and Azhure felt him draw her through the rock as if it were but inconsequential vapor.

*   *   *

She held her breath, but there was no need, for in the next instant Adamon was helping her to her feet and she saw that they stood in a chamber lit by such a subtle radiance she could not see its source.

The walls were hidden in luminous ivory must . . . was this a dream? Or death?

Am I back in my bed, so weak from loss of blood that I have dreamed this entire night? Or have I slipped out of life into the AfterLife? This was not how she had imagined it to be.

"None of those, dear Azhure," Adamon said. "You have come to visit the Sepulchre of the Moon. See? She sleeps."

It was the dark of the Moon, Azhure remembered, as she looked to see where Adamon pointed. There was a couch to one side of the chamber, and on it lay the form of a sleeping woman, her back to them.

She lay cushioned by thousands of tiny Moonwildflowers.

"She is a representation only, Azhure, of the real Moon who yet lingers in the dark shadows of the firmament, and of the Goddess of the Moon, who yet strides on two feet."

"Enough, Adamon," a musical voice laughed. "For you will confuse poor Azhure, and her questions will choke her!"

Azhure turned to the new voice, too quickly, for dizziness threatened to overwhelm her. When her vision cleared she saw an impossibly beautiful woman standing before her, clothed in a gossamer gown so fine it clung to her every curve.

She held out her hand. "I am Xanon, sweetheart."

"I *must* be dead!" Azhure whispered. Adamon and Xanon were the two most mighty Star Gods, the God and Goddess of the Firmament, yet she could not doubt that these who stood before her were who they claimed.

"Not dead," Adamon said, knowing her confusion. "Not dead, but come home."

Other figures walked from the mist, all as beautiful, all as powerful as Adamon and Xanon. One by one they came to Azhure, took her face in their hands, and kissed her on the mouth.

Narcis, God of the Sun.

Flulia, Goddess of Water.

Pors, God of Air.

Zest, Goddess of Earth.

Silton, God of Fire.

With each touch, Azhure felt life and energy flow back into her. And with each kiss Azhure felt her joy in life renewed. As Silton stepped back, she laughed, reveling in the feeling of health and strength that suffused her.

Now Xanon stepped forward and greeted and kissed her and Azhure felt something deep within her respond to her kiss, to her touch. Xanon smiled secretively, knowingly, but she said nothing, and made room for her husband.

"Welcome home, Azhure," Adamon said very softly, and Azhure turned to him. He took her face and cupped it between his hands. Through his skin Azhure could feel the potency of his power, but she was not afraid. Then he bent to kiss her, more deeply than any of the other six had, and Azhure inhaled his sweet breath, and sighed when he drew back.

She felt whole again, and when she looked down, she saw that her stained and sodden gown had vanished and that she wore a gauzy gown like those of Xanon, Flulia and Zest.

"You are only seven," she said quietly, looking about her. "Yet there are Nine Priestesses of the Stars to match the nine gods. Where are your companions?"

Adamon's face saddened. "We are not complete, Azhure. We are only seven. We want for the Goddess of the Moon and the God of Song to join us. *Then* we will be Nine."

Azhure frowned slightly at his words, trying to remember what she had heard StarDrifter and MorningStar tell Axis about the Star Gods on those afternoons she had attended his training sessions in Talon Spike. There were nine gods, but StarDrifter had said that while the Goddess of the Moon and the God of Song were of the Nine, their names had yet to be revealed. Her frown deepened. In their worship, the Icarii constantly called and prayed to the seven who stood here . . . but never to Moon or Song.

The Goddess of the Firmament held out her hand. "Azhure. Come, sit with us." She led Azhure to a circle of low couches.

"We asked WolfStar to bring you to us," Adamon began as soon as all had seated themselves, "because we have need to speak with you."

Azhure hardly dared ask, but their smiles invited questions. "Is he one of you?" The God of Song, perhaps?

"He is of the lesser variety," Pors answered, his voice as light as the element he commanded. "And of them there are many. But there are only nine of *us*."

"Your hounds are of the lesser, too," Zest said, and laughed at the expression on Azhure's face. "As is Orr and his hidden companions of the UnderWorld."

"As myself," a sharp voice said, and Azhure looked up at the tall and thin woman who stepped into the light. She had a cadaverous face and jet black hair that swayed to her hips. Azhure could not decide if she was the most beautiful woman she had ever seen, or the ugliest crone to walk the face of the world.

"The GateKeeper," the woman said by way of introduction, and sat down on a small stool behind the row of couches, folding her hands awkwardly, as if to keep them still.

"Should you not be on duty, GateKeeper?" Adamon asked.

"It will be a good night, for the dark of the Moon," the GateKeeper said, "and none will die. What will happen here tonight is important. And I would witness."

"As you wish." Adamon turned his gaze back to Azhure. "Azhure, events of great moment move throughout the land. This struggle goes far deeper than you realize. It is not only a struggle between Axis and his brother, Gorgrael, but between gods. Artor now walks the land—"

Azhure shivered, remembering the dreadful deeds committed in his name.

"—and seeks to prevent us from doing the same."

"I thought all gods lived in sky kingdoms . . ." Azhure's voice trailed off. Frankly, she had not thought overmuch about where any of the gods lived.

"We seven have been trapped for over a thousand years, Azhure, trapped in cold and dark spaces, unable to respond to the prayers of the Icarii." Adamon replied. "Of course, we were not complete then—not a full Circle—and so could hardly fight back. But when the Icarii moved south, when they recovered the sacred sites and freed the land from Artor's grasp our prison bars were loosened. And when—" Adamon broke off as his wife grew more excited.

"And when StarDrifter relit the Temple of the Stars we were freed completely!" she exclaimed, clapping her hands like a small child.

Adamon smiled lovingly at her. "Yes, when he relit the Temple of the Stars, we were finally freed from our prison. Of course, soon we will be Nine. That helped, too."

"Although we are free now," Silton leaned forward, his eyes afire with emotion, "Artor seeks to prison us again, and to kill the Mother, whom he has never before succeeded in touching. He seeks ultimate control."

"Faraday!" Azhure breathed.

"Yes, Faraday is in danger, and soon you will have to move to help her . . . but not yet." Adamon paused. "You must help Axis first. He cannot succeed without you, nor without Faraday."

Azhure bent her head. "Axis almost died, and even now he lies crippled."

"He could not die," the GateKeeper said in her sharp voice. "Because he does not have to go through my Gate. He begged," she said shortly, "and he wept, but I would not let him pass."

"You have done well," Xanon said, her eyes huge with relief. "We should all have been lost had he passed through."

The GateKeeper shrugged. "I only did what he asked." When the gods frowned in puzzlement, she explained further. " 'Forever' he said, when he married the Enchantress, and so 'forever' it is."

Azhure lifted her head, refusing to understand the implications of what she'd heard. "No." She twisted the ring on her hand.

"Azhure," Xanon shifted closer to her on the couch so she could wrap her arm about the woman. "You must accept who you are. And your task will be to make Axis accept who he is."

"The StarMan," Azhure said tightly.

There was complete silence.

"Yes, of course," Adamon finally whispered. "Axis. The StarMan. The God of Song."

Azhure stated. "No. It cannot be."

"Accept," Xanon murmured by her side, and turned the woman's shoulders toward the representation of the Goddess of the Moon.

The figure slowly turned in her sleep, and Azhure could see that she had raven-blue hair, and when she had rolled completely over, Azhure saw that the representation wore her own face.

"No . . ."

"Accept," the seven whispered.

"No," Azhure cried, but she let the Goddess cradle her in her arms as she stared sightlessly ahead.

"We are still vulnerable," Adamon said eventually, "and we can still be defeated. Artor is strong. And I spoke only in hope when I said Axis was the God of Song. There are two claimants to the last place among us—Axis and Gorgrael. If Gorgrael defeats Axis—and Gorgrael is the *only* one now who can kill Axis—then he will take the place among the Nine."

"And we would not like that at all," said Flulia. For the God of Song would wield the Dance of Death."

"Azhure," Adamon said, "what you have heard here tonight shall not alter your life very much. But you needed to hear it to grow into your power. Already the Alaunt have sought you out, as has the Wolven. You wear the Circle of Stars, the symbol of unity and completeness—"

"Which was granted to the Enchantress to wear for her lifetime, but which truly waited for you," Pors interrupted.

Azhure shook her head. "No. This cannot be. There have always been the Nine. Always. How can Axis and I now stand forth and claim to be . . . to be . . ."

"Claim to be of the Nine?" Xanon asked. "Those of the Nine have only come together gradually. There was always potential and need for Nine. Gradually the Seven were revealed. But the need for Song and Moon remained. Until now. Soon we will be complete."

Azhure laughed softly, but her laughter was brittle. "No, no. No! This is going *too* far. Two years ago I was a simple peasant girl. Then I became mistress to the StarMan, then his wife and an Icarii Enchanter myself. Now . . . now you tell me that I am a god." She paused, her eyes flitting about the group, wanting them to deny her words. But they kept silent. "It is a dizzying journey from the depths. And I do not think I like it."

Xanon's arm tightened about her shoulders. "Azhure, believe me, we were all human or Icarii at one point. All low-born . . . but all directly descended from the Enchantress. Each of us was Called, and our Calling awakened special powers within us. Low-born," she repeated, winking at Pors, and the god laughed.

"I was a simple marsh man, Azhure, seven thousand years ago. I thought *my* greatest calling was to trap the brown-legged frogs of Bogle Marsh to sell in the marketplaces of western Tencendor. But then . . ." He shrugged expressively and looked at Flulia.

"And I a laundress from the town that once stood in the same site as Ysbadd," she said. "I cared for sheets and starched creases and little else. And yet one day I found that I had a higher Calling I found it hard to accept."

"We all found it hard," Xanon said, "especially those of us who were Called first. But it was a duty we were born into, destined for, and none of us could deny it."

"Azhure, of all the Nine, you have had the highest parentage. WolfStar, a powerful Enchanter-Talon and one of the Lesser Niah, the First Priestess of the Order of the Stars, whose first duty is always to the Moon." Adamon sat back a moment and thought. "*And* you were conceived in the full of the Moon in the Dome of the Stars. How can you doubt your Calling?"

"You were the last chosen, Azhure. Born some two years after the StarMan and the Destroyer. Thus to you the Circle of Stars has come home. Soon we will be Nine. Soon we will be complete."

"But a *god?*" Azhure's eyes were still huge, still frightened.

Adamon reached across and took her hand. "Azhure, you place too much importance on the word *god*. We are only creatures of magic and workers of magic. And you have met and accepted many such creatures before. Have you not accepted the Sentinels?" She nodded hesitantly. "And the concept of the Enchanters? WolfStar? Orr? Axis himself?"

Azhure nodded again, more strongly this time, and Adamon smiled reassuringly at her. "And yet WolfStar has returned from death, and has walked this land for three thousand years. Orr has sat in his ferry for very, very much longer. You welcomed the Alaunt, and yet they are stranger still. You have borne the children of a man who sings with magic. You have taken tea with the Mother and Ur in the Enchanted Wood. Why the difficulty with the concept of 'god'?"

"Azhure," Silton said intensely, "we have our responsibilities, but we do not interfere in the daily lives of men and women. We are creatures of magic, as Adamon has said, except that we exist on a different level than you have encountered previously. Accept."

"Immortal?" Azhure whispered.

Again Pors shrugged. "Who knows?"

For a long time Azhure sat silently. "Would Axis and I have to, ah, spend our time . . . here?"

The Gods looked about at each other, laughing. "Oh, Azhure," Zest said eventually, "do you think that we sit about these misty chambers and look solemn all day long? No. We meet as a group only occasionally. Now that we are free, we will spend our time as we want. If you and Axis choose to walk Tencendor, then that is what you do. If you wish to live in Sigholt or Carlon, well, that is your right. We all live our lives as we please. Of gods you have had experience only of Artor, and he chose to secrete himself from sight and wrap himself in pretensions. None of us are like that."

Such a look of relief crossed Azhure's face that the gods laughed again, and even the GateKeeper smiled. Azhure finally relaxed enough to grin herself. A worker of magic. Yes, she could accept that. "Then will you show me how to use my power?"

"Azhure, it will be our pleasure," Xanon replied. "But you must learn slowly. For now all you need to know is that you do not have to *wield* or *command* power as such. You *are* magic, and eventually your power will come to you instinctively. As your acceptance deepens, so will your ability flower. But we will help."

"I don't have to learn to sing, do I?" Azhure asked with a wry grin, and Adamon patted her hand, restraining his smile.

"No, but one day you will learn more about the Star Dance than any of the Enchanters who surround you."

"And Axis? What can I do for him?"

"Go to him, Azhure, and we will speak to you on the way," Adamon said. "Teach you. And in turn you must teach Axis, and help him accept, too."

"You will grow on the way," Xanon said in a voice so soft that Azhure barely heard her.

"We will all see you again, Azhure." Pors.

"Soon we will be Nine." Flulia.

"Full Circle." Silton.

"And now," Adamon said briskly, standing up, "the sun is ready to rise, and you must return to your children and to StarDrifter, who will have need of your hands if his headache is to be assuaged."

Azhure found herself swaying on the steps cut into the cliff-top. Frantically she leaned in toward the cliff face, but then she stopped herself.

"Instinctive," she muttered, and let her hands fall to her side

Instinctive, the waves sang as the tide surged forward. And Azhure laughed and ran lightly up the steps.

When she reached the top, WolfStar handed her a warm cloak and hugged her. "I may not see you for a very long time, Azhure, but always remember that I love you."

And then he was gone.

*   *   *

She found StarDrifter, his face contorted in pain, leading a band of worried Priestesses and Icarii toward the cliff. Sicarius bounded ahead, and bayed joyfully when he saw Azhure.

StarDrifter couldn't believe his eyes. Azhure had been weak and riddled with pain when last he saw her, but now she almost skipped along, holding a cloak tightly about her, her cheeks flushed with good health and vitality, and her hair streaming out behind her.

When she reached him she seized his head in her hands, kissed him, and leaned back. "Better?" she asked, her eyes mischievous, and StarDrifter realized his headache had completely disappeared.

"How?" he asked, but she laughed joyfully again, and took him by the hand. "Instinctive!"

31

"May We Learn to Live with Each Other"

Ignoring the others who crowded the dormitory chambers, StarDrifter touched Azhure's face, his fingers lingering on her cheek. "Where did WolfStar take you? What . . . what has happened to you?" She was different, and StarDrifter could not quite understand what it was. It was not only her renewed health and vigor; something about her had been fundamentally altered.

Azhure smiled, but she did not answer.

Power, StarDrifter thought. He could see power dancing in the depths of her eyes, and yet he did not recognize it.

"I am well, StarDrifter. I can say no more than that."

And she was at peace with herself, StarDrifter suddenly realized. He had never seen Azhure truly at peace with herself before. As well as power, serenity shone forth from her gaze.

"Ysgryff." Azhure turned from StarDrifter to her uncle. "I have no time to waste. Are the Icarii scouts close?"

Ysgryff nodded, then indicated to one of the Icarii crowding the door of the chamber to fetch them. "Azhure—" he began, but she waved him into silence.

"I have to rejoin Axis," she said. "Fast. Ysgryff, I need to get to Carlon. Can you have the *Seal Hope* prepared for boarding in the morning?"

He nodded, his blue eyes thoughtful.

"Good. You and I shall leave within two hours for Pirates' Town. Axis is hurt, crippled, and needs me."

There were gasps of horror from those assembled in the room, and Azhure realized that StarDrifter had told no one about WolfStar's visit or the information he had brought. She stared levely at StarDrifter.

Should we tell them about WolfStar?

No. StarDrifter shook his head imperceptibly. *Best not.*

"A battle," Azhure said briefly to the others, "at the mouth of the Azle, and Axis lies crippled although he managed to drive back the Skraelings." She spread her hands apologetically. "It is all I know. I'm sorry."

"Can you help him?" FreeFall asked, slipping his arm about EvenSong's waist. Both looked appalled.

Azhure smiled. "Yes, I know I can. Ah, here are the farflight scouts."

Somehow three of the scouts managed to cram into the already crowded chamber. Azhure took a deep breath and spoke to the first. "How fast can you get to the north of Aldeni?"

The birdman shrugged. "It depends on the weather above the Western Ranges, Enchantress. Days, many days, at best."

"Well, do the best you can. I want this message to get through."

"And that message is . . . ?"

"To Axis, or to Belial. Whichever is capable of understanding it." Azhure paused, her eyes steady on the birdman's face "Tell them that I am coming, and not to commit to any course of action until I reach them."

The scout nodded, and slipped from the room. Azhure turned to the other two. "This is the more important task," she said, her tone low and intense. "This message *must* succeed. Fly to Talon Spike. Tell RavenCrest to evacuate *now*. I want every Icarii male, female and child out of that mountain as soon as it can be accomplished, either into the Avarinheim or even farther south. Listen to me, for this is important. Those who can't fly must not go down the ice paths by the Nordra into the Avarinheim. They will have to go down to the waterways and beg, bribe or coerce the Ferryman to take them south. Have you got that? Then repeat it."

Azhure waited as the two scouts repeated the message. Stars, she thought dismally, it might take them weeks to get as far as Talon Spike. Weeks.

"Azhure?" FreeFall's voice cut across her thoughts. "What's going on?"

"Axis' injury is not the only bad news, FreeFall. Gorgrael has Gryphon . . ."

EvenSong paled and shuddered. She would never forget the horror of the Gryphon attack on her Wing.

Azhure glanced at EvenSong but continued. "Many more than we thought." Briefly she explained how the Gryphon bred. "The remade dead, fat with child, will birth abomination," she quoted from the Prophecy, her mouth twisting, "and I fear that Gorgrael will not be able to resist throwing them at Talon Spike."

"The mountain is almost defenseless," EvenSong whispered, and Azhure nodded.

"It is too open, too vulnerable."

FreeFall blanched. As yet the majority of the Icarii were still in Talon Spike. "Pray they get out in time," he said.

"Can we do nothing?" asked EvenSong.

"Not at the moment," Azhure replied. "Nothing but pray. Once I have got to the north, well, then we'll see." She glanced at the scouts, still waiting by the doorway, their eyes horrified by what they had heard. "Go," she said. *"Fly!"* and in a heartbeat the scouts had squeezed out the door. *Fly!*

StarDrifter stepped forward and touched Azhure's arm. He desperately wanted to speak to her alone and only barely restrained himself from shouting at the others to leave the room. "Azhure, what can I do?"

Azhure turned and hugged him. "You have already done more than you realize, StarDrifter. Stay here. Ensure that the Temple continues to shine forth. Revere the gods."

Azhure . . .

I know, StarDrifter. Later. We will speak later.

"And now," she said softly, her eyes shifting to the closed door that led to her private chambers. "I must speak to my children."

The room was quiet and still, and Azhure threw her cloak to one side as she crossed to Caelum asleep on a cot under the window. His eyes were screwed shut as if concentrating on a particularly appealing dream, one fat fist tangled in his black curls, the other lying relaxed and open across his coverlet.

"Caelum," she whispered, and bent down to pick him up.

Mama? Mama! You are well!

Better than I've ever been, Caelum.

Fully awake now, Caelum switched to his speaking voice. "Papa?" he whispered, remembering the events of the previous day.

Azhure laughed, the sound rich and startling in the still chamber. "Papa *lives*, my darling. And your brother and sister have joined us." She glanced over to the twin cribs set carefully to one side of the fire, but she did not move for the moment.

Caelum's eyes widened and he turned his head. "Where?"

Azhure smiled and stroked his cheek, putting off the moment when she would have to walk over to the cribs. "It has been a long night, my love. Your mother has seen and heard many strange things."

Caelum's head twisted back to Azhure and he stared into her eyes. Carefully he raised one hand, although he did not touch her. *Strange things shine in your eyes, Mama.*

"And one day," she whispered against his cheek, "I may tell you about them. Now, shall we welcome your brother and sister into the House of the Stars?"

Slowly she walked over to the cribs. She could feel that both babies were awake and waiting. She took a deep angry breath, remembering the pain—*agony*—both had caused her. She had not given birth; they had torn themselves from her.

But she was well now, and perhaps neither expected that. And she was more than just Azhure now, and *certainly* neither would expect that.

She halted by the first crib and looked down, her face expressionless, her eyes composed.

The baby lay on her back. She had kicked back the coverlet and was waving both arms and legs about. She stilled as soon as she saw her mother.

Her daughter. Azhure had always wanted a daughter, hoping to somehow re-create with her the relationship she'd shared with her own mother. But that would never be possible with this baby. Never.

She shifted Caelum to one hip and reached down and touched the baby's cheek softly.

The baby's violet eyes followed her mother's hand; almost twelve hours old, her Icarii eyes could focus in sharp detail, and Azhure knew her mind was as sharp as her eyes.

Despite herself Azhure smiled. The baby's skin was softer than down, the crown of her head covered with tiny golden curls. She had EvenSong's coloring, Azhure saw, and her fingers ran back through her daughter's fine hair.

The baby twisted her head away and Azhure's eyes hardened. She took another deep breath, composed herself, touched her fingers to her own lips, and then laid them on the baby's brow.

"Welcome, RiverStar SunSoar, into the House of the Stars. My name is Azhure, and I am your mother." Azhure halted, biting down the harsh words that threatened. "And I hope that one day we can learn to love each other." There was not much else to say.

RiverStar. StarDrifter had chosen a beautiful name, and a peculiarly peaceful name, for a child who had caused her parents so much distress. Perhaps he had felt something in the child that was as yet hidden from Azhure. "I hope you will grow into your name, RiverStar," she said briefly, then lowered Caelum so that he could touch his sister's face in greeting.

"Come," she said as she lifted him back into her arms. "There is still your brother."

Azhure had to steady herself before she looked down into the second crib. It was the boy who had generated much of the hostility, who had forced the birth, who had begun the horror and then encouraged his sister in it. She did not know if she could even regard him with equanimity. Even now she could feel resentment rising like a thick cloud from the crib.

Caelum pressed closer into her body, and Azhure smiled briefly at him, loving him for the comfort he gave her.

Then she looked down.

Her second son had WolfStar's coloring. A profusion of dark copper curls covered his head, and his eyes, wide and hostile, were the deepest violet Azhure had yet seen in an Icarii.

DragonStar. Azhure had been rocked by the name StarDrifter had chosen, although, gazing at the boy she knew why. He was powerful, very powerful, and would come into more power. Yet DragonStar was a name that boded only ill.

Caelum trembled, and Azhure hugged him closer. Slowly she lowered her hand into the crib but before she could touch the boy's face he grabbed her forefinger with his own fingers.

Azhure took a quick breath. The boy's fingers squeezed painfully around her own, and his eyes narrowed.

Suddenly Azhure's temper snapped. She had fought long and hard to keep these babies, and if she chose to love Axis despite the wrong he had done her, then that was her business and no one else's.

"Wretch," she muttered, and sent a wave of stinging rebuke coursing toward the baby.

He let her finger go with a squeak of surprise and, Azhure hoped, a modicum of discomfiture. She placed her fingers on his brow. "Welcome, DragonStar SunSoar, into the House of Stars. My name is Azhure, and I am your mother . . . and I am far more than I think you have bargained on. I hope that we may learn to respect and live with each other."

DragonStar stared at her unblinking, and Azhure lifted her fingers. "Caelum?"

Reluctantly Caelum let himself be lowered down to greet his brother, but Azhure could feel his relief as she lifted him back into her arms.

My poor Caelum, to have such a younger brother to torment you. But you are your father's heir, and he will have bequeathed you the power to cope with him.

Brothers, she thought, have given Axis nothing but pain and grief, and I hope DragonStar will bring you more joy. She smiled mirthlessly. I hope.

Relieved that her maternal duty was over, Azhure stepped back from the cribs. "Tomorrow we sail for Carlon, Caelum, and from there I will rejoin your father."

Axis. Azhure sat in an easy chair by the fire and thought about Axis as she nursed her son. The GateKeeper had said that Axis had begged and wept to be allowed through the Gate, to be allowed to die. Only his vow made at their marriage, made with the Enchantress' ring—the Circle of Stars—had kept him from the death he craved. Stars! she thought dismally, his injuries must be horrific if they had driven him to the Gate.

And if he yet lives, then how does he manage to bear such death-dealing injuries? Such pain?

Axis! her mind called, but there was nothing.

32

Command

"A xis?"

Belial bent down and touched the man's shoulder, then leaped back as Axis started violently. "I'm sorry I did not realize you were asleep."

Mother, he thought, how can he sleep through such pain?

"Drifting," Axis muttered. "I was just drifting."

Belial sat back on his stool and glanced at Magariz. Arne stood by the closed tent flap, shifting from foot to foot.

No one knew what to do. How to help. He should be dead, but somehow he would not die. And only in death lay relief from his agony.

Belial rubbed his eyes, still unable to believe what had happened. As the Gryphon had fallen from the sky he had managed to rally those commanders left alive to get their units back in formation and moving back to the east. Arne and Magariz between them had lifted and dragged what they believed to be Axis' dead body over to Belaguez, hoisted it over the horse's saddle, and joined in the retreat.

Now, some two leagues southeast of the Azle, they had made their camp, expecting attack at any moment. But somehow this had never materialized.

A movement at the tent flap caught Belial's eye and he looked up. Ho'Demi, Sa'Kuya and SpikeFeather TrueSong pushed their way in. He nodded at them, relieved beyond measure to see Sa'Kuya, then spoke to Axis.

"Axis, our supply column has caught up with us and Sa'Kuya is here. Let her tend you."

None had known what to do for Axis beyond bathe his injuries in ice-water, and now Belial hoped that Sa'Kuya could somehow relieve Axis of some of his distress. She slipped quietly to his side.

"StarMan," she said. "I have salve and analgesic tea. Here, drink this first."

Arne helped support Axis' shoulders while Sa'Kuya raised a small cup to his lips. He grimaced, but managed to gulp down some of the tea.

"Good," Sa'Kuya said. "Now, let me rub some of this salve into your burns."

Axis' body jerked as she rubbed the salve as gently as she could over his face, and he could not help but moan.

With each of his muffled cries both Magariz and Belial shuddered in sympathy, and Magariz had to wipe tears away from his eyes. Gods, he prayed, please let him die, for how can I bring home this twisted husk to either Azhure or Rivkah?

SpikeFeather, who owed Axis far more than either Belial or Magariz, kept his own dark eyes steady on the man writhing about the bed and wished he could sing Axis the Song of Re-creation as Axis had once sung it for him.

Finally, gratefully, Sa'Kuya was done, and she gathered her jars and bandages and hurried out of the tent. There was no more she could do.

"Belial?" Axis groaned, and Belial reached out a hand and put it on Axis' shoulder.

"Here, my friend."

"Then talk to me, man! Give me something to hang on to!"

Tears slid down Belial's cheeks, but he kept his voice steady. "I have Magariz and SpikeFeather here with me, Axis, and that is Arne's hands you can feel on your arms."

Axis shuddered as he took a deep breath, but it seemed to help him. "Are any of you injured?"

Belial shook his head, then remembered that Axis could not see him. "No," he said hastily. "No. We have all survived with barely a scratch."

"SpikeFeather," Axis said. "Why are you here and not FarSight?"

Silence. Then . . . "FarSight is dead," SpikeFeather said. "As are six of the other Crest-Leaders. Others are critically injured I . . . I am the most senior Strike Force commander left."

"Oh gods," Axis cried, and turned his face away. "I should have been quicker."

"If you had not acted when you did," Magariz said, "then *none* of us would be here."

"Tell me the casualties," Axis said finally.

"Half the Strike Force are gone," Belial said. "The Gryphon tore them apart. Of the ground force, over three thousand were killed by the Skraelings or by falling into the Azle when it broke asunder, and some two thousand were taken by the Gryphon. Another four and a half thousand lie wounded."

Magariz rose and carefully sat on the edge of Axis' bed. "Axis. What happened? What can we do for you?"

For a long time Axis was silent. "I let too much of the power of the Star

Dance flood through me," he said eventually, "in my effort to destroy the Gryphon. Too much . . . I'm sure that you, at least, can see what it has done to me." He paused, licking dry lips, and Arne gave him some more of the analgesic tea Sa'Kuya had left behind.

"I should be dead." He paused again, remembering how the GateKeeper had refused to hear his pleas. The return journey along the River of Death had been worse than a nightmare.

Now he had to live in a body that, by rights, should not be allowed to harbor even the barest flicker of life.

"I should be dead," Axis said, and none present begrudged him the slight touch of anger in his tone. "And I have lost all power. Lost all touch with the Star Dance."

SpikeFeather stiffened. Of all those in the tent, he had the best understanding of what that meant to an Enchanter. "You hear nothing? *Feel* nothing?" he asked.

What was left of Axis' face stiffened in a ghastly parody of a smile; Belial and Magariz both looked away hastily. "I did not know what it meant to live without it, SpikeFeather. Even as BattleAxe, trapped within the lies of the Seneschal, the Star Dance constantly wrapped my soul—although I did not recognize it as such then. Now I do not know how I will be able to live without it. There is no point, and yet I cannot let go."

He twisted his sightless face in Belial's direction. "Belial, why are *any* of us still alive? I thought . . . I thought that *he* would have somehow sent his wraiths after us. How long is it since the battle?"

"Fifteen hours," Belial said.

"Fifteen hours? Has this pain only been going on fifteen hours? I thought I had lived in this . . . this prison for fifteen years. How much longer must I endure?"

Belial's hand tightened on his shoulder.

Magariz cleared his throat. "Axis. For some reason he, ah, Timozel, has withdrawn far to the north."

"I have sent farflight scouts to track his progress, StarMan," SpikeFeather reported. "No, do not worry. The sky is free of Gryphon and the scouts have returned unharmed. The Skraeling host tracks north along the path of the Azle."

"Why?" Belial said. "Why retreat north? He—" as all the others, Belial could hardly believe that Timozel now fought for Gorgrael, "—could have finished us within hours. And yet . . ."

"Timozel only follows Gorgrael's commands," Ho'Demi put in. "And perhaps Gorgrael was unnerved by your destruction of the Gryphon."

"Or perhaps this is yet a trap," Axis said harshly.

Belial exchanged glances with the others in the tent, then lowered his eyes to Axis. "Axis," he said, "I am assuming command of the army."

Axis lay still, then barked in hoarse laughter. "And I am not going to argue with you on that, Belial, for I am useless, useless, useless."

"Axis—" Belial began.

"Gorgrael has won, Belial, for how can I meet him like this? He has withdrawn Timozel to the north simply to toy with us."

"Dammit, Axis!" Belial snapped. "I am not going to give up until I feel my own life fade and die. I fight until there is nothing left to fight for. You still live, and while you live there is hope."

Axis turned his head away, but Belial took no notice. "I have sent word to the south, Axis. Word to Azhure."

Axis' head twitched, and he turned his face back to Belial. "Azhure?"

"Perhaps she can help," SpikeFeather said. "She has her own power."

"She cannot meet Gorgrael," Axis said. "Call back your messenger, Belial, for I do not want Azhure exposed to this tragedy. Besides, she has some weeks to go before giving birth. I," his voice broke, "I do not want her to see *this*."

"Nevertheless," Belial said, "she deserves to know, and she is strong enough to hear the truth. Now, I want advice on where to take this army. Do we follow Timozel? Retreat south? Give me your thoughts."

"We are in no condition to chase the Skraelings," Magariz said, "besides, as Axis says, it could be a trap. Perhaps it would be best to retreat to Carlon."

"It is far too long a march," Belial said. "Every man and horse of us is exhausted, and we have too many wounded to face such a long march."

"Perhaps the Murkle Mountains," Ho'Demi suggested. "There is shelter there, and the Chatterlings would not harm us."

"We would be trapped if the Skraeling host swung south again," Belial responded. "We need more supplies, and we won't find them in there. And besides, those mountains depress me too much."

"Sigholt," Axis whispered.

Every eye in the tent swung back to him.

"Sigholt," he repeated in a slightly stronger voice. "We would be safe there. And the Lake of Life can heal . . ."

His voice trailed off and all looked away from him. As magical as the Lake was, could she heal him?

Belial sat and thought. Of all havens, such as they were, Sigholt *was* the closest. But it would be a long march . . . a long slow march with the injured. And yet, better to attempt something than sit and wait for death.

"Sigholt," he said in a firm voice, his mind made up. "We go for Sigholt. SpikeFeather, fly those of the Strike Force you can there immediately. Keep a wing or two back for scouting duty . . . and keep an eye on the Skraelings. I want to know if they swing south again. Magariz, Ho'Demi, we stay here today and pull out tomorrow morning. The injured will have to be strapped to mules, or stretchered between the beasts if they cannot sit. Axis . . ."

"I will ride Belaguez," he said.

Belial paled. "Axis, you will never manage."

"I will *not* be stretchered, Belial, curse it! Tie me to the bloody horse if you have to, but I will not be stretchered!"

Belial stared at him, then nodded tersely. "So be it, Axis."

After they had all gone, Axis lay in his darkness and tortured himself with thoughts of Timozel.

Timozel. He had been a delightful baby, and had grown into a mischievous but no less delightful child. He had been full of pranks and laughter, the apple of Ganelon's eye.

He had grown into a charming man, but now Axis wondered if some of that charm had been forced. He had certainly developed into a skilful warrior, and Axis had been only months away from giving Timozel command of his own unit when the lad disappeared with Faraday.

And yet, how he had changed. When? Since I began to bed his mother? Axis wondered. Was that it? He writhed on the bed, thinking on it, then cried out in agony as the blanket caught at his corrugated skin. For long minutes he gulped in cold air, trying to keep a grip on his mind, then he forced it back to Timozel.

Who knew what had changed the boy. Axis remembered worrying once how he would tell Embeth if Timozel ever found himself at the wrong end of five handspans of sharpened steel—had he ever in his wildest imaginings thought that it might be he who would push that steel into Timozel's belly as Timozel had pushed it into Jorge's?

And now Axis not only wanted to push it in, he wanted to *lean* on it, *twist* it, feel blade scrape *bone* with it.

"Timozel," he whispered into the dim interior of the tent, "I hope this is the end of your treacheries. How many of those you once called friends have died through your orders? And Gorgrael? How could you turn to *him*? What did I do to you, Timozel, that you should repay me so harshly?"

33

Trap!

O h, Goodwife!" Faraday giggled, "surely not!"

"Surely indeed," the Goodwife nodded sagaciously, pleased to see Faraday so merry. " 'Twas nothing that could be done. Popped out like a greased . . . well, popped out nice and smooth. 'Twas my third, so was easier."

Faraday knelt down and, still smiling, dug into the soft soil with her fingers. Now that they were in the lower Bracken Ranges the soil had more give in it and was easier to work than the hard-packed dirt of Arcness. And it had never been plowed, so it was more receptive to Faraday's touch.

As Faraday dug out the small hole, the Goodwife handed her the seedling. She was quivering in her pot, almost leaping from her crib in her eagerness, and Faraday hushed the sister, singing to her, stroking her tiny leaves. As the seedling calmed down, Faraday gently tipped her into the palm of her hand, then slid her into the soil.

"Thona," she whispered to the seedling. "May you grow tall, and may your voice eventually join with that of the Earth Tree's."

Then, singing the Song of the Earth Tree under her breath, Faraday patted the seedling into the soil and sat back on her heels, remembering Thona's story, the sorrows and laughters of her life, as she had recalled the events of every seedling's previous life as she planted them out.

The Goodwife watched silently. Later she would sing her silly little cradle song over the seedling, the one they all enjoyed so much, but for now she just watched. She was pleased with the girl. She had put on weight and color since the Goodwife had joined her, and took the herbs that the Goodwife pressed on her without complaining. And a good thing I came along when I did, the Goodwife thought. These noble ladies, fine-bred they be, and pleasing to the eye, but they all need a good, stout sensible lass to look after them and tell them what to expect.

Faraday looked up and smiled at the Goodwife's expression. "Nice and smooth-like, Goodwife? Well, I can only hope you're right. Now, lend me your hand . . . I swear my knees have stiffened beyond repair with all this upping and downing."

The Goodwife helped Faraday to her feet and patted her hand. "You've only a few more seedlings for the day, dear. Would you miss me if I wandered up that gully there for an hour or two?"

Faraday looked up at the gully to her left. It was long and narrow and dim, and doubtless held a store of herbs. She waved the Goodwife away. "Off with you, Goodwife. I hope you find something tasty to spice our evening meal."

The Goodwife smiled and bobbed. "And perhaps some more of the claw-leaf mint, m'Lady, for your tea in the mornings?" She patted Faraday's hand again, then walked off.

Faraday watched as the Goodwife wandered away, her boots clumping to this side and that, yet never leaving a mark where they trod.

"Come on, Faraday," she muttered to herself as the Goodwife disappeared behind a thick stand of bracken, "already it grows toward dusk and you've still Meera, Borsth and Jemile to plant out." She clicked to the donkeys behind her, and strode up the long wide valley.

Faraday was more than happy with her progress. From Arcen she and the Goodwife had planted in a swathe directly north then, as they reached the lower slopes of the Bracken Ranges, they'd gradually swung northwest. I'll plant all the way through to Fernbrake Lake, Faraday thought, and give these Icarii cities I keep hearing about some shaded walks for the hot summer afternoons. Over the past week or two an increasing number of Icarii flew overhead, sometimes waving, sometimes dropping down for a chat, and Faraday could hardly wait to see what they had recovered farther to the west.

And from there to Fernbrake Lake and the Mother. Faraday took a deep breath of excited anticipation. She would be there in time for Yuletide and there, she hoped, would be some of the Avar to greet her.

She grinned. What would the Avar make of the Goodwife, and what would she of them? Faraday did not know how the Avar and Icarii would celebrate Yuletide this far from the Earth Tree Grove, but she was sure that whatever they did it would be both beautiful and moving.

She turned back. Her view of the plains was cut off by the low hills behind her, but she could see a faint sheen of green beyond their rise. Minstrelsea, now planted in a great arc across the plains of Tarantaise and Arcness, sung gently to itself. Tomorrow when she rose, Faraday knew that today's seedlings would be full grown and full of song and joy, and soon Minstrelsea would spread deep into the Bracken Ranges.

*   *   *

Whistling cheerfully, the Goodwife wandered along the gully. She had recovered her spirits since that sneaky attack in the market hall of Arcen. That *had* been a nasty surprise, and the Goodwife was sure she'd prevented a murder. Evil-faced man, and with an even more evil touch about him. Artor, the Goodwife thought, for I smelled the same evil when they came to take my gran away.

She sighed. She had not told Faraday about the man, for she did not want to worry the girl, but the Goodwife had been immensely relieved when they finally left Arcen. No more crowded marketplaces to trap her Lady, only the open air and the music of the trees behind them.

The Goodwife browsed for some minutes longer, walking deeper and deeper into the gully. There! The claw-foot mint she had been sure she would see. These hills were full of good herbs, and wasn't it lovely that she should be free to wander and examine them at her leisure? She straightened and peered ahead, then her eyes gleamed. Ah! The willow-waisted endura that would be sure to ease Faraday when . . .

A rock hit her on the back of the head with well-aimed retribution, and the Goodwife collapsed unmoving to the ground. The eight Brothers sprang from their hiding places and leaped down the sides of the gully in ungainly bounds, restraining their cheers and contenting themselves with punching silent fists into the air.

They had got the Fiend!

The Goodwife was only stunned, but she did not have time to rise before all eight reached her, the two largest sitting down firmly on her back.

"Omph!" she cried as another pushed her face into the dirt. Faraday!

"What do we do now?" one of the Brothers asked as the excitement of the capture faded.

The others thought hard. "Wait," one eventually said. "Wait, until the Brother-Leader calls us."

Faraday did not notice Gilbert until she turned to pick the last seedling from the cart. He stood at the other side, his face red and sweaty, his eyes ablaze with fanaticism.

He hissed, and Faraday involuntarily took a step back.

"Gilbert?" She could hardly believe it. She hadn't seen him since . . . when? Before Borneheld died, she was sure of it. What was he doing here? "Gilbert?"

"Witch!"

"Gilbert!" Faraday's voice was strained now, her eyes flickered over the seedling still in the cart. She could feel her distress even from this distance.

"What do you do, Faraday?" Gilbert asked, and Faraday recoiled at the loathing in his voice. And there was something else . . .

What do I do? She thought frantically. Should she tell Gilbert exactly what she did? How could he *not* know! Suddenly Azhure's warning about Gilbert and Moryson sprang into her mind. Faraday had dismissed Azhure's concern then, but now she could feel nothing but danger from the man.

And where was the Goodwife? Her eyes quickly swept the surrounding hills.

"The Fiend has been disposed of," Gilbert said, and Faraday's eyes flashed back to his.

"Fiend?" she whispered. *Disposed of?*

"Now it's just you and me." Gilbert moved around the cart and Faraday breathed in relief, he had not noticed the seedling. "It's time you died, Faraday."

It was the way he said the words, rather than the words themselves, that completely shocked her.

"No." She tried to smile, backing away another step. "Gilbert, you must be tired and hungry. That's all. Why don't you stay and eat with us?" *What had he done with the Goodwife?*

Gilbert edged forward. "Evil, Faraday. That's what you are. Time to die. Artor says it's time that you died."

"Gilbert . . ." She backed away yet another step, her hands clenching her skirts.

Gilbert paused and smiled strangely. "Why did you give up Artor, Faraday? Once you were as pious a girl as He could have wished. A suitable handmaiden to the god. Why did you deny Him?"

"I found other gods, Gilbert," she said. "More beautiful and more compassionate than Artor." She took a deep breath and fought to keep calm. "Let me tell you about the Mother." She reached down for her Mother's power.

And found nothing.

Gilbert burst into a wild cackle of laughter. "Fool! Don't you know I walk with Artor's power now? Your pitiful Mother is nothing compared to Him!"

Now she realized what it was that was different about Gilbert. He wore an aura of power about him that Faraday had seen in others. Axis, StarDrifter, Azhure, Raum, even the Goodwife on occasion. But they wore the power of the stars or of the earth itself, and what now shone from Gilbert's eyes was none of that. It was foreign. Evil. It had cut her off from the Mother.

"*Artor's power!*" he hissed, and stepped forward, his hands extended.

"Can your Artor be all-powerful, Gilbert, if so much of western Tencendor now supports forest instead of dusty furrows?"

Gilbert blinked but didn't hesitate. "Already Artor readies His plow, witch, and soon the trees will lie torn and broken behind His wrath!" His eyes flared, and in their depths Faraday thought she could see red bulls tossing their crazed horns.

She screamed, turned to run, and caught her foot in a rabbit burrow As she hit the ground she heard Gilbert's boot crunch by her ear, and felt his hand grab the back of her dress.

"Bitch!" he grunted, and she felt his other hand fasten around her hair, "Time to die."

He hauled her to her knees, breathless with excitement and with the fear he could see in her eyes, and reached for her neck. This time he would succeed, this time he would not fail!

And felt, instead, hands creep about his own neck.

"No!" he wailed, indignant rather than frightened. "This is *my* time!"

"Right!" Moryson said, and his hands tightened so that Gilbert's cheeks purpled and his eyes bulged obscenely. "Your time to *die*, you senseless idiot! This has gone far enough!"

Gilbert's hands released Faraday to scrabble uselessly at the fingers gripping his own throat, and she scurried back from the struggling men.

Moryson! The old man was even more crazed than Gilbert. His thin brown hair stood on end and his blue eyes blazed with what Faraday assumed to be dementia. His lips were pulled back into a snarl, and his teeth gleamed with thin-roped saliva. He looked as dangerous as a rabid dog.

As Gilbert wheezed and his eyes rolled frantically, Faraday felt the barrier that had prevented her contacting her power crumble. She stumbled to her feet and drew on as much of the Mother's power as she thought she could handle, letting it sear through her body.

Now Moryson and Gilbert were rolling about on the ground, locked together, and in the tumbling bodies Faraday could not see for a minute which was Gilbert and which was Moryson—and if she saved Moryson, would he then turn on her?

There was a sudden wet crack and a whimper, and the struggling ceased. Moryson, old, decrepit and utterly, utterly deranged, scrambled panting to his feet. Gilbert lay dead, his cheek resting beside the last seedling Faraday had planted so that the shadow of its leaves traced peacefully over his cheek.

"Fool girl," Moryson snarled, "wandering about planting your pretty garden. *Watch the shadows!*"

Faraday stared at him The Mother's power vibrated through her but, while she could feel Moryson's anger, she did not sense that she was in any danger from it. Slowly she let the power ease away.

Shockingly, Moryson laughed. "Do you know who I have just killed, Faraday? The last Brother-Leader of the Seneschal! He, he, he! Poor old Gilbert, murdered by his adviser!" He capered about Gilbert's body in a ghastly parody of a dance, then he stopped still and stared at Faraday once more. "Faraday!"

She stiffened, stunned by the command that rang through his voice.

"Faraday, your friend lies trapped under the weight of eight Brothers. But they are a cowardly lot, and should you bear down upon them with the Mother's power blazing from your eyes I think they will disappear faster than Skraelings before emerald fire. But watch!" he said. "Watch the shadows! Artor is not gone, merely his servant, and Artor still wants you dead . . . badly. *Watch the shadows!* Not time to die yet."

He pulled his cloak about him and some of the madness faded from his eyes. "Ask Azhure to help you, Faraday. If Artor comes after you personally, then only she can save you. The Mother's power cannot help you against Artor."

Then he turned and hobbled away.

Faraday blinked, and Moryson was gone.

For several heartbeats she stood and looked at the place where he had been, then she picked up her skirts and ran to find the Goodwife, the power of the Mother blazing from her eyes.

Artor paced behind His Plow and his bulls tossed their heads and roared.

Gilbert was dead . . . by Moryson's hand? *That* feeble Brother? Something was not right here . . . in fact something was very, very wrong, and Artor could not understand it.

And that made Him afraid. Nothing was going right. Gilbert had failed Him, and now those who had been banished walked again.

Artor paced behind His Plow and thought. There was only one chance left. One chance where even if He met this Tree Friend bitch face-to-face, even with what allies she could summon, He would still stop her. Kill her.

The one place left in this land where His power was all-consuming. The place where He had originally made mankind the gift of the Plow. Where the Mother could still be vanquished, as any others who stood to deny Him His right to this land and to these souls.

One place. His place.

Smyrton.

34

Of Tides, Trees and Ice

Azhure pushed against the railing at the prow of the *Seal Hope* and leaned as far into the surging spray as she could, arms spread wide, laughing with the wind.

They were close to the mouth of the Nordra, and soon, two days at the most, she would be in Carlon. And from there to Spiredore . . . and from there to Axis. Two days. She turned to look back along the deck. Only Ysgryff, the children, Imibe and several attendants had traveled back with them, and now Imibe sat on deck feeding one of the twins; Azhure refused to feed them. The Icarii, including StarDrifter, had remained on the Island of Mist and Memory.

StarDrifter had been aghast at Azhure's decision to take the children with her.

"Leave them with me," he had begged, "for their teaching needs to be continued. And they will be safe here."

Azhure had shaken her head firmly. "No, StarDrifter. The children come with me. You will see them again soon enough. And their teaching?" She had shrugged. "Caelum can learn from either myself or Axis, and if the twins refuse to learn from us, then they can stay untrained."

And it would not be such a bad thing, she thought, to leave their training for some time yet. *Training would only give them the skills to make our lives miserable.*

Azhure had told StarDrifter little of what she had learned about herself in the Sepulchre of the Moon. She knew she was changed, and she knew the change shone from her eyes and in her daily demeanor, but she did not feel that StarDrifter—or anyone else apart from Axis—should learn of her true nature immediately. It would, no doubt, be revealed in time.

And in the fullness of the moon. Azhure glanced above her, even though the moon was hidden in the bright sky. It waxed now, growing stronger with each passing hour it floated among the stars, and even during the day hours Azhure could feel its pull in the surge of the tides and the cry of the waves. Even now they called to her, *Azhure! Azhure! Azhure!* and the porpoises that flashed before the prow of the ship danced to the music of her name.

Azhure smiled at Ysgryff who, standing before Imibe, regarded her with some bewilderment. None could understand her amazing return to vibrant health, but all rejoiced in it. Despite the vague news from the north of a disastrous battle, and of Axis' crippling injuries, no one who was with Azhure felt overly despondent.

Not when she smiled and laughed and said, "It will be all right."

The storm had swept down over the remains of Axis' army with the strength of Gorgrael's full vengeance. Despite the decision to make for Sigholt, the driving winds and ice had forced the army to take shelter in the foothills and, eventually, in the mines of the Murkle Mountains.

For three days they huddled in the mines, the healthy sitting, depressed, cleaning their equipment as best they could, the injured lying as still and as sightless as the StarMan himself in the dark tunnels.

At least they were not harried by the Chatterlings. Ho'Demi spent some time with them, for they sought him out, and one day he reappeared from the depths of the mine grasping a rough wooden box.

Belial raised his eyebrows at him.

"I made a vow," Ho'Demi explained, and Belial nodded. Ho'Demi had told him of his peculiar promise to these lost souls.

"I was going to return after the wars were over to collect them," Ho'Demi went on, "but here *we* are and they whispered and argued and drove me to agree to take them with me. So, here *they* are," he held up the box and Belial stared at it in the flickering light of one inadequate brand, "and none must open it but me. None, understand?"

Belial nodded again. He had no wish to open a box full of mischievous lost souls.

Ho'Demi attached the box to the back of his belt where it did not hinder his movement and where, when the dark seemed particularly still, those close to him could almost feel the excited *chitter, chatter* of the souls within.

On the fourth day of their incarceration the storm blew itself out. The scouts reported that the sky had lifted and lightened, although clouds still blanketed the sun. Snowdrifts littered the plains below the mountains, but, with perseverance and determination, perhaps they could begin their way east.

"What do you think?" Belial asked Magariz and Ho'Demi, sitting huddled together for warmth. Axis lay beside them, but he had been silent so long that only the occasional twitching of his blanketed form showed he was still alive.

"I say we leave this cheerless place as soon as we can," Magariz said. "I would prefer to die under the open sky than in these mines."

"Ho'Demi?"

"I concur, Belial. There is no point staying here."

"But what if this is a trap? What if Gorgrael has pulled the storm back to tempt us out? If a storm of that magnitude hit us when we had no chance of shelter we would all freeze to death."

All except me, Axis thought, listening to the conversation wash over him. I would be trapped inside a frozen corpse; alive yet not alive. What must I do to let this life go?

Over the past three days Axis' condition had shifted from the appalling to the abysmal. His flesh was rotting about him, and yet he remained stubbornly alive. And with each passing hour, each passing minute, his pain flowered.

"The choice is yours, Belial," Magariz said.

Belial glanced at Axis and saw the gleam of the man's eyes. It decided him. Axis could not be left to linger in this darkness any longer.

"We move," he said, "as fast as we can for Sigholt."

As Magariz and Ho'Demi left to begin the evacuation, Belial squatted down by Axis. "Are you awake, my friend?"

Axis nodded his head imperceptibly. "I cannot sleep, Belial."

Belial felt helpless. No one could do anything to ease the man's misery. And what of the larger question? What of Gorgrael? What if they *did* get to Sigholt? What then? *Where* then?

"It has all been a dream," Axis whispered, and Belial did not know if he was addressing him, or speaking to himself. "All a magnificent dream. We were teased with a single moment of beauty, of hope, and then we woke to find that it was all a sickening lie. We are finished, Belial, finished."

Belial sat and stared at Axis and tried to convince himself that Axis was wrong. But deep in his heart he found himself believing him.

"It is as you thought, Gorgrael, Axis lives and plans your destruction."

"I knew it!" Gorgrael howled and leaped from his chair. "I was right to pull the army back from the Azle!"

Over the past week Timozel, while still leading the Skraeling host northward toward Gorken Pass, had never ceased to complain about it. Daily he had argued and pleaded with Gorgrael to reconsider his decision, although he was careful never to push his master too far.

While Gorgrael had insisted that Timozel continue north, Timozel's arguments had worried him. *Should* he have pushed while he had the chance? *Had* Axis truly been crippled, even killed, by the power he had loosed on the Gryphon? Gorgrael had been racked with uncertainties, but now these uncertainties were eased. He heard only what he wanted to hear.

"You are sure?" he asked, his silver eyes narrowing at the Dark Man.

The Dark Man bowed his head slightly. "Positive, Gorgrael. What would have happened if Timozel had been allowed to attack as he wanted? Undoubtedly Axis would have loosed more emerald fire on the Skraelings as he did above Gorkenfort."

Gorgrael shuddered, remembering. "Will I never defeat him?"

"Oh Gorgrael," the Dark Man said. "A temporary setback, nothing more."

"I'm sick of these temporary setbacks," Gorgrael muttered.

"You have the Gryphon, and they continue to breed well."

"And look what Axis did to the nine hundred!" Gorgrael said.

"Ah, but can he do that to seven thousand, or seventy thousand? Even Axis' power must have its limits. You need but wait, Gorgrael, and the Prophecy will work its will. Besides, it must come down to only you and him. No matter what your army can do to his, and his to yours, both of you know that it will come down to one thing."

"The final duel," Gorgrael said, his voice calmer now, his eyes introspective. Then his head jerked up, for thoughts of the final battle had made him think of Faraday, and thoughts of Faraday reminded him of . . . "The trees!"

"Ah, yes." The Dark Man moved to stand before the fire, his back to Gorgrael. "The trees. They grow."

"I thought you said that Artor would stop her!" With each passing day Gorgrael could feel the forest growing. With the planting out of Minstrelsea, Gorgrael's hold on the winter was slipping. Not much, but enough to cause him to halt the storm that he had sent down to batter Aldeni. And now he wondered how much longer he could keep the country south of Ichtar caught in its unnatural winter.

"It's all the fault of those SkraeBolds!" he cried, "for not destroying the Earth Tree when they had the chance!"

"Water gone now, Gorgrael," the Dark Man said mildly, turning to face him. "Plan for the future. Timozel can mass and regroup in Gorken Pass—and remember the destruction your army caused there before—and not even Axis with his pitiful army could drive him from that pass. And from there, Timozel can lead Axis to you."

"Yes, yes," Gorgrael let himself be cheered. "There are not enough men in Tencendor to provide him with a force to equal mine. Unless . . . the trees." His mind kept coming back to that. Why did he have to worry about both Axis *and* the trees?

And Faraday. She was a conundrum to drive anyone crazed. He had to stop her planting the trees, for they might yet prove his undoing. Yet he needed her alive, for she was the key to Axis' death.

"Artor will not kill her, will he?" he asked yet again.

"No," the Dark Man reassured him. "Artor may weaken her, but I have that situation under control. She will survive. You will yet have the Lover."

Gorgrael breathed deep. "Good."

They moved cautiously out from the Murkle Mountains, a long column of cold, injured and dispirited men. Above and ahead flew what was left of the Strike Force and what they reported cheered yet perversely worried Belial.

Timozel continued to lead the Skraeling force northward, to Gorken Pass, the scouts thought. There were no Gryphon in the skies. The weather, while ominous, did not look anymore so than could be expected for this time of the year. And hour by hour, day by day, Axis clung to his horse, held upright by blankets and ropes, and stared sightlessly ahead. He was quiet for the most part, but Belial knew that each step Belaguez took, each slip in the snow, sent shafts of agony coursing through his body.

And, Belial could not stop thinking, Axis is the only one who can save us, yet in saving us at the Azle River, he has condemned us to slow defeat.

He thought about Azhure, and wondered if his message had reached her before the storm closed in. And if it had, then what could she do to help them?

35

Rivkah's Secret

Azhure could see the spires and pennants of Carlon hours before the *Seal Hope* finally docked. The ship's approach had been similarly visible, and there was a sizeable crowd waiting. At the front stood Rivkah and Cazna, holding hands, excitement and tension lighting and lining their faces.

Azhure leaned over the deck railing and waved at them, wondering what news they had. She had sent no word ahead to announce her return, and she wondered if the worry on their faces was for her, or whether it was caused by word from the north.

Rivkah let Cazna's hand go and rushed forward to embrace Azhure as she stepped off the gangway. "Azhure! How are you? The children? What's happened? Why are you back so soon? Have you heard from the north? Oh, Azhure!" and she barely restrained herself from bursting into tears.

Azhure hugged her tightly and then embraced Cazna briefly. Now she was closer, Azhure could see that Cazna looked thin and pale, and Rivkah's eyes were bright with unshed tears.

"I'm well," she said, "and the twins have been born. Now, what have you heard from the north?"

"Too little," Rivkah said, holding Azhure's hand tightly. "Far too little."

"Well," Azhure smiled, trying to put both women at ease, "this is no place to share news. Say hello to Ysgryff, and Caelum, and here . . . here are my latest."

"Oh," Rivkah breathed, as the nurses stepped forward, "they are *beautiful!* What have you named them?"

"RiverStar and DragonStar."

Rivkah's eyes flew to Azhure's face. She, as well as any Icani, knew the power of the boy's name.

"And," Azhure continued with a slight twist of her mouth, "yes, they *are* beautiful, aren't they?"

"But come," she said as Rivkah and Cazna both greeted Ysgryff and kissed Caelum; "come. This is no place to talk."

The palace entrance was only a few short blocks from the main gate into Carlon, so Azhure suggested they walk. Human and Icarii smiled and waved at them, but Azhure could sense that the mood of the city was grim. Whatever news had filtered down from the north must be poor indeed. Her eyes slipped briefly to the east, where she could see the top of Spiredore gleaming even in the overcast sky. Soon, she promised herself, soon.

"Enchantress!" Hesketh, captain of the palace guard, was running down the street toward her.

"Enchantress," he panted as he reached her.

"What's wrong?" Rivkah snapped, worried by the expression in Hesketh's eyes.

Hesketh ignored her. "Enchantress, a farflight scout has just arrived from the north. He has a message . . . from Belial."

"Belial?" Cazna cried and seized Hesketh's arm.

"Not Axis?" Rivkah said, her gray eyes apprehensive.

"News for the Enchantress," Hesketh said firmly, and shook Cazna away.

"Shush, Rivkah, Cazna," Azhure said to the two women. "I'm sure we will all know soon enough. Ysgryff," she turned and beckoned to her uncle. "Take Cazna's arm, will you?" and, linking her own arm with Rivkah's, she hurried them along the final few paces to the palace entrance.

As they approached the royal chambers Azhure's apprehension deepened. What had happened during the week she'd been aboard the *Seal Hope?* Had Axis managed to die despite the GateKeeper's opposition? Had he found another Gate to go through? Had he left her?

"Imibe," she said shortly as they paused in the antechamber, "take the children and feed them. Then they will need to rest. Ysgryff, stay with us. Hesketh, fetch the scout. Now," she linked her arms through both Rivkah's and Cazna's, "let us sit in the Jade Chamber and hear what enlightenment the scout has for us."

When the scout did enter, Azhure instantly feared the worst. His wings were tattered and bloody, his clothes stained, his face drawn and exhausted, but he held himself upright proudly, and folded his wings neatly as he had greeted Azhure.

"Enchantress."

"BlueWing EverSoar," Azhure said, recognizing the birdman. "What news?"

"I come from the north," BlueWing said, and the listeners all shifted impatiently. "I have been delayed many days, for a storm of great wrath kept me trapped in the southern Murkle Mountains. Consequent the news I bring is over a week old, and I cannot know what has happened since."

He glanced at Rivkah, and Azhure realized he was reluctant to speak in front of her.

"It is all right, BlueWing," she said. "We must all know eventually . . . and I have some idea of what you are about to relate."

BlueWing nodded. He told of the destruction of Aldeni and, in particular, of Jervois Landing; and Rivkah and Cazna paled when he described Jorge's death. He related the course of the battle at the Azle River, and then even Azhure lost her color, for WolfStar had not told her of the full extent and viciousness of the encounter. BlueWing described how Axis had caused the frozen Azle to splinter asunder, drowning many of the Skraelings and trapping the main part of the force on the northern bank of the Azle.

"We now know who leads the force," he said. "Timozel, once Axe-Wielder and Champion to the Lady Faraday."

Timozel? Azhure frowned, trying to place the name. Ah. Embeth's son. She nodded. "Timozel. Well, at least now we know who it is. Go on."

"We rejoiced," BlueWing continued, "as the Azle broke asunder, because we thought we had survived the day. But then the Gryphon attacked from nowhere, and all seemed lost."

As he described the horror of the Gryphon attack, leaving nothing out, Cazna cried out softly but then composed herself with noticeable effort; Rivkah put one arm about her, her eyes steady on BlueWing, already knowing there was worse to come.

In a much softer voice now, BlueWing described Axis' use of so much of the Star Dance. "The results for him personally were devastating," he whispered.

"Go on," Azhure said, her own voice tight, as BlueWing paused. *"Tell us."*

BlueWing took a deep breath and looked at a distant point over their heads as he continued. "He should have died. Even now no one knows why he yet lives."

Rivkah's free hand flew to her mouth, her eyes enormous.

"Enchantress." BlueWing looked directly at Azhure, his eyes wide and compassionate. "Axis yet breathes, but his soul lives in what can only be described as a corpse. It is as tattered and burned as a rag doll that has been thrown into a fire by a careless child. When it falls apart, I do not know what will happen."

Azhure had expected something of this, but she was not prepared for the horror of hearing it put into such frank words. For an instant she remembered Niah's blackened corpse twisting and crackling on the hearth, and she shuddered. When she spoke she was relieved, yet astounded, to hear how steady her voice was. "And Belial? Magariz?"

BlueWing spoke quickly, grateful for the change in topic. He bowed slightly to Rivkah and Cazna. "They live, and are well, my Ladies Enchantress," his eyes slipped back to Azhure, "Belial sends you this message. 'Axis needs you. I need you. When you are well, join us. Bring your bow and your hounds and your horse and come.' That's it."

For some time there was silence. Azhure sat, close to tears, thinking of Axis' agony, and of Belial's agony watching him suffer.

"And that is what I fully intend to do," she whispered eventually. "Join them as soon as I can."

Cazna raised her pale face. "And did Belial send me word?" she asked, her mouth trembling.

BlueWing shook his head regretfully. "Princess, there was time only for the shortest words. All were desperate. But I'm sure he thinks of you daily."

"And Magariz *is* well?" Rivkah asked. She was not surprised that BlueWing carried no personal messages for them, but she ached for Cazna. The deaths on the battlefield were sometimes not the cruelest wounds of war.

BlueWing smiled briefly. "Yes, Princess Rivkah. He has the devil's own luck on the battlefield."

Rivkah relaxed, grateful for BlueWing's smile; it told her more than words could have.

"And casualties?" Ysgryff asked. All this talk of husbands was trying when there were more desperate things to be discussed.

"Dreadful," BlueWing replied, and told them just how dreadful. Then he explained Timozel's puzzling withdrawal to the north, and the equally inexplicable cessation of the storm after three days.

"Gorgrael constantly surprises us with his inconsistency," Azhure said. "Perhaps it is the advice he receives. Thank you, BlueWing. Have something to eat, and I shall talk further with you once you have rested. Hesketh?"

Hesketh stepped forward from his position by the door as BlueWing left the chamber.

"Hesketh. I sent a farflight scout northward to Axis . . . or Belial. Do you know if he passed through here?"

"Several days ago, Enchantress, but I do not know how far he has got. If there was a storm above the Western Ranges then he may have been delayed."

Azhure bit her lip, wondering about her messengers to Talon Spike. But it was too early for them to have reached the mountain home of the Icarii, and far too early for confirmation of their success. "Thank you, Hesketh. Will you ask the kitchen servants to prepare us a meal? To serve it, perhaps, in an hour or two."

He bowed and turned away but, just as he reached the door, Azhure stopped him with a soft question. "Have you heard from Yr, Hesketh?"

He stiffened, and Azhure had her answer. She nodded, and he left the chamber.

*   *   *

"I am going north," Azhure said after they had sat in silence for some time. "North to Axis."

"I'm coming too," Rivkah said calmly.

"And me!" Cazna cried.

"Oh, by the Stars!" Azhure said, "I cannot be burdened with the two of you. You will stay here."

"Azhure—" Rivkah began, her eyes steely, when she was interrupted by a slight knock at the door. It was Imibe, and she carried Caelum.

"Excuse me, Enchantress," she said, "but Caelum was fretting and wanted to join you. Would you prefer that I kept him away for the time being?"

"No," Azhure said, holding out her arms for her son. "No, he may stay with us. Thank you, Imibe."

She cuddled Caelum close, waiting until Imibe had left the chamber, then stared at Rivkah, her eyes as hard and as determined as Rivkah's own. "Rivkah, I will not take you. You are needed here."

"Nonsense," Rivkah said, shushing Cazna as the girl tried to speak. "Ysgryff is here," she inclined her head to the Prince of Nor, who, amused, inclined his equally as gracefully in her direction, "and can look after the interests of Carlon and whatever of Tencendor remains free of Gorgrael. I *am* coming with you."

"Mama? Where are you going?"

Azhure almost bit her tongue in annoyance. "To Papa, dear. But I must go alone."

"Azhure!" Cazna leaned forward, her eyes bright, ignoring Rivkah's continued attempts to shush her. "We have waited here for months, waited for word . . . and none of us are court-sheltered butterflies who wilt at the first touch of a snowflake. Do you yearn to join your husband? Well, so do we!"

"We were within a day of riding for the north anyway, Azhure," Rivkah said. "Now that you are here, and intend joining Axis, why, you may ride with us," she finished graciously, lowering her eyes to hood their amused gleam.

"Mama, I want to come too. I want Papa."

Azhure fought to keep her temper under control. "The ride is hard, dangerous. It is too much to risk all of us."

"Damn you, Azhure!" Rivkah suddenly seethed. "I am *not* going to be left behind any longer! My son and my husband are in the north and I *damn well will be too*! If you refuse to let me ride with you then I will follow an hour behind. I rode with Axis' army through eastern Tencendor for months, and there's no reason why I can't ride with it again!"

Now Cazna stared defiantly at her as well and Azhure suppressed a curse. She would have to lock these two up if she wanted to leave them behind. "Ysgryff?" she said. "Ysgryff, I will leave you in charge of Carlon."

He inclined his head. "As you wish."

Rivkah looked triumphantly at Cazna, but Azhure was not yet finished.

"You will go north, but not directly to Axis and the army. *And in this you will obey me!*"

Both women blinked at the command and power in her voice. Rivkah had noticed Azhure's added assurance as she stepped ashore, but had thought it only a result of regaining her health after birthing the babies. But this was different. "Where then?" she asked.

"Sigholt. If this Timozel is leading his army north, then Axis will have to follow him eventually. And if so many of the army are hurt then they will need the Lake of Life and the comfort of Sigholt. You will see your husbands soon enough."

"But Azhure," Cazna said, "if we are going to ride north to Sigholt then we will undoubtedly meet with the army in Aldeni anyway."

Azhure smiled and stroked Caelum's curls. "But we are not going to *ride*, Cazna. And," she bent and kissed the crown of Caelum's head, her ill temper now completely gone, "if we go to Sigholt then I may as well take you and the twins, sweetheart." She sighed. "And I suppose Imibe and the nurses shall also have to come along. We shall be quite a party."

Yes, Sigholt was a good idea. She would enjoy going back there briefly, and it would not delay her too long. A few days, perhaps, at worst.

And it will give us time to speak with you, Azhure.

The voice echoed about the chamber and Azhure's head lifted, her eyes stunned. No one else reacted to anything but the surprised look on her face.

"Azhure?" Ysgryff asked. "What is it?"

Time alone in the snow will give you time to grow.

Adamon! Azhure breathed to herself. Yes, perhaps this would be the best plan. To Sigholt first with Rivkah, Cazna and the children . . . and then she could travel southwest by herself . . . alone . . . time to grow.

And, then, when she met Axis . . .

"Azhure?" Rivkah asked. "What do you mean, 'We are not going to ride'?"

Azhure smiled secretively. "We will leave in the morning, Rivkah. Pack a small bag with what you want to take to Sigholt, something you can carry yourself, and then we shall go boating."

"Boating?" Rivkah was getting cross now, suspecting that Azhure was trying to trick her, perhaps leave in the middle of the night without them.

"Spiredore!" Caelum cried, and Azhure laughed and rumpled his curls. "Yes, my love. Spiredore shall take us to Sigholt."

After they had talked some more, Azhure sharing the tale of the birth of the twins (which she glossed over as briefly as she could) and of the wonder of Temple Mount and the Temple itself, and eaten the light meal that the servants carried in, Cazna and Ysgryff left. Imibe took Caelum off for a nap, but Rivkah hung back.

As the door closed behind the others, Rivkah sat closer to Azhure. "Well, Azhure," she said. "What has happened to you?"

Azhure shrugged, wondering how much Rivkah's natural perception had seen. "I have but grown up, Rivkah."

Rivkah smiled. "More than that, I think. You have acquired something much more than maturity. But tell me, what did you find out about Niah?"

"Oh, Rivkah." She took the woman's hand. For so long Rivkah had been the only one who had known of Azhure's yearning for her mother, and now Azhure was happy to share what she had discovered. She told her of Niah's letter and of what the First had said. She told Rivkah of the Temple and of the wondrous jade latticework roof of the Dome of the Stars—which the First had finally shown her—but she did not tell her of WolfStar and of his claim that he truly did love Niah and that she would be reborn. And she did not tell Rivkah of the night she had spent cradled in StarDrifter's arms.

Rivkah wept, and finally hugged Azhure tightly to her. "I am so glad," she murmured, "that you have found so much of your mother, Azhure. Treasure that letter always.

"And now," she leaned back, "tell me of those children. Was the birth as easy as you intimated? I saw Ysgryff shoot you some sharp looks. Tell me what truly happened."

Too perceptive, Azhure decided, but she sat and obediently told Rivkah of the true nature of the birth. "I was pleased to be rid of them, Rivkah, and I hate myself for feeling that way . . . but they were as pleased to be rid of me, too. And, yes, those names—StarDrifter picked them, not I or Axis."

"And how *is* StarDrifter?" Rivkah asked, her eyebrows raised archly.

Azhure laughed. "We have become good friends, Rivkah, finally. Whatever tension was between us has dissipated. Without StarDrifter's love and friendship I would not have managed."

"And . . . ?"

"And *what?*" Azhure said crossly, defensively.

"What about *you*, Azhure?" Rivkah said. "You are changed. Different. But," she grinned, "still the same even-tempered girl I knew beforehand."

Azhure relaxed enough to laugh. "Yes, I have changed, Rivkah, and learned more about myself. But . . . I want to talk to Axis first. Do you mind? This concerns him as well."

"No, of course not. Azhure . . ."

Rivkah's voice trailed off and Azhure looked at her. "Rivkah? What's wrong?"

Rivkah looked at her hands knotted in her lap. She took a breath, then looked up, meeting Azhure in the eye. "Azhure, I'm over three months gone with child."

Azhure felt a bone-sapping chill creep through her. "For a human woman you're too old to be carrying a child," she said finally, tersely.

For a human woman? Rivkah wondered at the phrasing, then decided it was only Azhure's Icarii blood talking.

"Yes," she said, "I am. This child is a gift."

"A gift?"

"After Faraday left you and Axis, the day she healed you, she drew me out into the corridor to say farewell. Azhure, we were close, even though we had not known each other long. We had both been Duchess of Ichtar, and as such we had both suffered, and that pulled us together. And we both loved Enchanters, and suffered because of that, too."

"*And?*"

Azhure's eyes were cold, and Rivkah did not totally blame her. "And Faraday gave me a gift. From the Mother, she said. She kissed me, and when she drew back I felt such a feeling of well-being, of vitality, flood through me that I could hardly breathe. She gave me the strength to conceive this child; that night, I think. Azhure, Magariz deserves an heir. Be pleased for us."

"Axis does not deserve another brother!" Azhure said tightly. "Brothers have given him nothing but trouble and suffering . . . and you would bring *another* into the world to plague him?" Neither doubted that the child would be male.

Both women stared at each other, then looked away, hating the distance between them.

"Rivkah," Azhure said finally, and reached out for the other woman's hand. "I do not begrudge you your happiness, but—"

"But how awkward it is to have a mother capable of still birthing a rival," Rivkah finished for her, bitterly, withdrawing her hand. "Axis thought he was the last of the royal line of Achar. Well, he'll have to think again." She tilted her head back defiantly. "I will do anything to protect this child, Azhure, *anything!*"

Protect him against *Axis?* Azhure wondered, but said nothing. Damn Axis for being so sentimental that he'd given Rivkah the golden circlet and amethyst ring of Achar's royal office. He should have had them melted down for the trouble they were. Now this *legitimate* brother would inherit not only royal blood, but insignia as well, and would prove a natural rallying point for every Acharite unhappy with the new order.

"Damn you, Rivkah!"

Rivkah seized Azhure's shoulders and shook her, her own eyes as fierce as Azhure's now. "Swear to me, Azhure, that you will never harm this child! *Swear to me!*"

Azhure stared at her.

"As you love me, Azhure, *swear it!*"

Azhure's shoulders slowly lost some of their tension. "I swear, Rivkah, that I will never harm this child . . . so long as he does not challenge Axis! If he does, then know that I will stand with Axis and this vow I make to you now will become meaningless."

Rivkah nodded tightly and let her hands drop. "I would not expect you to let the child come between you and Axis, Azhure. I accept your vow."

Azhure relaxed. "Now I know why you were so desperate to rejoin Magariz. He does not know?"

Rivkah shook her head. "It was why I originally planned to ride north, Azhure. But this news of Axis . . ." her face fell and, forgetting the earlier animosity between them, both women wrapped their arms about each other and wept.

"Azhure," Rivkah said finally, wiping her eyes, "do you know that this will be my first legitimate child?"

Azhure blinked, bewildered. "But Borneheld . . ."

Rivkah smiled and told Azhure what she and Magariz had told no one previously. That she had bribed an old Brother of the Seneschal to marry her and Magariz. "We were so young," she said quietly, "and all we had was one night. Poor Magariz, for years he wondered if Borneheld was his son."

"And you told no one of this?" Azhure was aghast.

Rivkah laughed. "What good would it have done, Azhure? The Brother was so old he would have died within a year or two, and there would have been no other way to substantiate the marriage."

"You never told StarDrifter?"

"No. What was the point? It would not have interested him one way or the other."

Azhure laughed. "Poor Borneheld. Not knowing all those years that he, too, was a bastard. And commanding his mother's husband!"

"Azhure," Rivkah's laughter died, "will you stand by me?"

"Yes, Rivkah. Yes, I will."

36

Back to the Sacred Grove

That night, as Faraday traveled back to the Sacred Grove to collect more seedlings, she found Azhure sitting waiting for her in the center of the grassy circle, Caelum playing at her feet, and several of the Horned Ones seated with her, chatting about the intricacies of the Star Dance.

"Faraday!" Azhure leaped to her feet, and the Horned Ones rose gracefully beside her.

Faraday ran and hugged her. "Azhure! Ah, you look so well! And the new babies?"

"They are beautiful children, Faraday, and doing well. I am back in Carlon now."

"You used Spiredore to reach here."

"Yes. I hope I am not disturbing you."

"Nonsense!" Faraday linked her arm with Azhure's. "Let's leave the Horned Ones to watch over Caelum and we shall wander, you and I, through the trees of the Sacred Grove to Ur's nursery."

She winked at the Horned Ones, who did not seem to mind being left so precipitously to child-mind, and drew Azhure toward the encircling trees.

"I can see by the power in your eyes, Azhure," she said after they had left the Grove well behind them, "that you have learned well from your time on the Island of Mist and Memory."

"I am now not such a mystery, Faraday," Azhure replied quietly, and told Faraday of her mother and something of what had happened in the Sepulchre of the Moon.

Faraday laughed, knowing that Azhure withheld as much as she told. "You are more a mystery than ever. But," her smile died, "something is troubling you. What is it?"

"And you," Azhure noted, but did not push. Faraday would tell if she wanted to. "Faraday, Axis is hurt. Badly. Crippled. There was a battle in northern Aldeni."

"Azhure!" Faraday stopped, and her expression reminded Azhure how much Faraday loved Axis. *"Tell me!"*

Azhure told her what she knew, which was not much. "In the morning I will start my journey to him."

"Can you help him?" A living soul trapped in a corpse? Oh Mother, help him!

"I hope so, Faraday, I hope so."

Faraday shuddered, suppressing the impulse to drop everything she was doing to rush to his side. He was bound to Azhure now, and she would have to be the one to help him. If he *could* be helped. "He must survive, Azhure."

Azhure felt a moment's jealousy as she watched the emotions rush across Faraday's face; Faraday had already demonstrated her love and her power by saving Axis' life after the SkraeBold attack at Gorkenfort. Could she do the same? "I know, Faraday. You do not have to tell *me*."

The women continued walking, slowly and silently. About them crazily colored birds and beasts gamboled, and Azhure wondered that so much gaiety could flash about them when they were wrapped in such morbid thoughts.

Her mind drifted to Rivkah. Faraday had enabled her to conceive a future rival for Axis. Why? Simple revenge? Azhure was about to broach the subject when Faraday spoke, driving the thought completely from her mind.

"I have some news of my own to impart," Faraday said. "You were right to warn me about Gilbert and Moryson."

"Faraday! Did they hurt you?"

"Not through lack of trying, Azhure." Faraday told of her encounter with Gilbert, and Moryson's strange intervention. "I have seen nothing like it, Azhure. He was not the Moryson I remembered. He seemed crazed . . . oh, I don't know . . . different. And why strangle Gilbert like that? I'd have thought he would have been as eager to see me dead as Gilbert was. And Moryson has not balked at murder before—Rivkah and, I suspect, Priam have both been victims of his ambition. Azhure," Faraday abruptly switched the conversation away from Moryson, "Gilbert tried to murder me on behalf of Artor, but it was not simple religious zeal that drove him. His eyes glowed with . . . well, with power. Artor's power."

"Faraday, be careful, very careful," Azhure said. "Artor now walks this land." She hesitated. How much could she tell Faraday? "This Prophecy has unleashed more than just Axis and Gorgrael."

Faraday gazed at her. You and me? she thought, and who else? What else?

"Yes," she sighed, lowering her eyes. "None of us will ever be the same. Moryson, strange man, told me that too. He said that if Artor was to come after me personally then I was to turn to you for help."

"Moryson said that?" Azhure frowned. "But he does not know who I am. He disappeared from Carlon well before I . . ." she drifted into silence, thinking furiously, but keeping her thoughts guarded. *Moryson?*

"Well, whatever, why ever, Moryson thought that you would help me."

Azhure smiled and slipped an arm about Faraday's waist. "Never doubt it. Call me, Faraday, and I will come. There is no one more than I who would like to see Artor's damned Plow burned to ashes. But I hope you heed Moryson's warning, as mine. If Gilbert is dead, then there are others Artor can use as instruments."

"Yes, Mama," Faraday said gravely, and Azhure laughed.

"And how goes the planting?"

"Oh!" Faraday smiled happily, glad they had moved to a more pleasant subject. "Azhure, the planting goes so well! All of southeastern Tencendor now sways to the music of the trees of forest Minstrelsea, and I am currently in the Bracken Ranges . . . I will spend Yuletide at Fernbrake Lake. And from there I move to Skarabost."

"And are you looking after yourself, Faraday? You are more than vulnerable at the moment."

"Ah, I have a companion. Let me tell you about her."

For a while longer they walked, talking of this and that, until they reached the gate into Ur's garden.

"Faraday," Azhure said as they paused, watching Ur hobble up the garden path toward them, "how will the trees help Axis?"

Faraday looked at Azhure with her great green eyes. "As they know best, Azhure, as they know best . . . that is all I can say on the matter. We each, methinks, have our mysteries to guard. Ah, here is Ur. Ur, look who I have brought to visit!"

Azhure turned and took Ur's hand, smiling with genuine warmth. Her eyes slipped over her shoulder. The nursery behind her looked far less crowded than previously.

"So much has gone home," Ur said softly, "and yet so much more has yet to go. Perhaps, my dear, you can help Faraday transfer some of the seedlings tonight."

37

"Your Tongue Is Far Too Sweet"!

Azhure hugged Ysgryff. "Thank you, Ysgryff, for so much. Your friendship, your stories to while away the long nights on the *Seal Hope*, and most of all, thank you and yours for keeping the secret of the Island of Mist and Memory for so long."

Ysgryff unexpectedly found himself choking with emotion. He had thought himself too cool and far too calculating to fog up this badly. But then he had never had such a niece before, either. She had done both the House of Nor and Niah proud, he decided, patting her back. "Are you sure you know what you're doing, Azhure?"

She leaned back in his arms and wiped the tears from his cheeks. "No, but that has never stopped me before."

He laughed and let her go. "You look tired, niece. Perhaps you miss the swaying bunks of the *Seal Hope*."

"And perhaps I spent the entire night gardening, uncle," she grinned, refusing to elaborate. "Now, say goodbye to your daughter. When she returns hopefully she'll bring her husband with her."

Ysgryff turned to Cazna, who looked more cheerful than she had for months, and hugged her. His youngest daughter had also done him proud, and Carlon would be a bare and lonely place with both Azhure and Cazna gone. Well, perhaps he would invite some of the Icarii Enchanters to visit him—Stars knew, enough of them were flying the southern skies now to spare him an hour or two for a chat.

The group was standing outside the door of Spiredore in the weak mid-morning sunshine. Everyone, save Azhure, looked mystified, some almost unnerved. How was she going to get them all to Sigholt? The only horse present was Venator his red coat gleaming with impatience, held by a groom to one side. Azhure had greeted the horse with affection. It had been a long time since she'd been able to ride, and she patted his neck and pulled his ear and whispered to him that within the day they would be racing across northern Tencendor.

Cazna stood back from her father and rejoined Rivkah, standing with Imibe and the two nurses. Azhure had hired in Pirates' Town; each nurse carried a baby in her arms. Around their legs wove excited Alaunt hounds, occasionally forgetting themselves enough to bay at the water and the silent tower before them. They could sense the change in Azhure and the magic awaiting them.

Azhure was, for the first time in months, dressed in slim-fitting gray breeches and a deep-red tunic, her hair left to flow loose down her back. She turned for a final look at Carlon, waved at Ysgryff, then inclined her head toward Spiredore. "Are you ready?"

Rivkah stepped forward, then hesitated. Azhure had refused to explain how she was going to take them to Sigholt, and Rivkah couldn't get the faint suspicion out of her mind that this was all a ruse designed to cover Azhure's own plans to travel alone to the north. Was she going to shove them inside the tower, lock the door, then get on Venator and gallop northward?

"Nothing of the kind," Azhure said, and opened the door. "Come," and she stepped inside.

Rivkah glanced at the others, annoyed at having her thoughts so clearly read, then followed Azhure into Spiredore.

She stopped almost immediately, her eyes rising upward, awed by the incredible interior of the tower. Azhure smiled and pulled her gently to one side. "Step over here, Rivkah. There is still a crowd to come."

And a crowd it seemed, once Cazna and the nurses had stepped inside. The Alaunt rushed about the central atrium, and Venator, at Azhure's whistle, trotted through the doorway, trembling slightly at the closeness of both humans and hounds.

Azhure patted him on the neck, quieting him down, and hoped that Spiredore would adjust its risers to his needs.

Behind them the door closed of its own accord, and Azhure wondered if Ysgryff and the servants and even Carlon were still there at all, or if, once the door had closed, there was only one world, and that world was Spiredore.

She grinned at the faces watching her, lifted Caelum more comfortably in her arms, then walked over to the first rise of the stairs. "Spiredore," she said clearly, "I . . . we . . . wish to go to the bridge before Sigholt."

And without another word or explanation, she started to climb.

The horse snorted, then stepped after her, his hooves slipping and rattling on the wooden risers.

"Rivkah?" Cazna said in a small voice, and Rivkah grasped the young woman's hand.

"It will be an adventure, Cazna, and you will love Sigholt. Come on," and she led her forward. The hounds bounded past them up the stairs, and Rivkah looked over her shoulder to make sure the nurses followed.

They climbed for almost an hour until Rivkah could bear no more. Her legs were aching, and she had to shift her small satchel from arm to arm to relieve some of the strain on her shoulder. She touched her belly briefly, worried for the baby. What if she *was* too old to carry this child to term?

"Azhure?" she called. "What are we doing? Why are we climbing into this tower?" She stared upward until the madly tilted balconies made her dizzy. She swayed on the stairs, and as she did so all her fears rushed to the surface and she cried out, frantically grabbing the railing for support.

Instantly Azhure was by her side, her arm about Rivkah's waist. "Shush, Rivkah. All is well, we are almost there. Trust in Spiredore. Come. You too, Cazna, walk with me up the front, and then you will see."

She pulled them up the stairs, brushing past the horse who had his head up and his ears pricked curiously.

"See?" They had reached the head of the stairs and before them stretched a long corridor, a soft blue mist hanging about its walls and ceiling so that the corridor seemed almost circular.

"What?" Rivkah stopped dead. "How can that be in this tower? It stretches farther than . . ." She stopped, stunned by what she saw at its end. Cazna, at her shoulder, likewise stood unbelieving.

"Sigholt," Azhure said proudly, and Sicarius gave a great cry and bounded down the corridor, disappearing into the sunshine at its end.

Rivkah's eyes filled with tears. What kind of magic did this tower, and Azhure, command? There at the end of the corridor, bathed in sunshine, was the bridge that led into Sigholt, behind it rose soft gray walls and, from the darkness of the fortified gate, strode a man, gray and gaunt, but still alive.

"Roland," she whispered, and stepped out of Azhure's arms and ran down the corridor, laughing. "Roland!"

Cazna watched with wide eyes.

"Take the reins of my horse and enter Sigholt, Cazna," Azhure said gently, "and when the bridge asks if you are true, answer with your heart."

Roland was stunned, but enormously pleased to see them.

"Rivkah!"

She hugged him breathlessly. "See who else comes, Roland," and the next moment Azhure's great hounds were baying about his legs, then a young woman who Roland at first thought was Azhure was crossing the bridge leading a horse, stunned amazement on her face as she found herself talking to a bridge. Then Azhure, more beautiful than Roland had remembered her, with three women and three babies, one of whom opened his arms and cried for joy when he saw the old man.

"Roland!"

Roland kissed Azhure on the cheek and took Caelum into his arms. "Azhure! Caelum! What? How? Ah, dammit . . . what *news?*"

"Oh Roland," Azhure laughed. "What news? Have you heard *nothing* since we left to reunite Tencendor?"

Roland was almost quivering with impatience. "News? Here? We are so isolated that we think we live in a world of our own. How many months have passed since Axis led his army from here? How this lad has grown! And these babies? *Yours?*"

Azhure grinned at him. "Roland, where are your manners? Here we are, having traveled unknown leagues in but an hour, and you want to keep us gossiping in the courtyard?"

Roland waved them toward the Keep. "Food and a fire, and then you talk. Tell me, how's my good friend Jorge? Still campaigning as if there's no tomorrow?"

Azhure glanced at Rivkah, then she smiled sadly and took Roland's arm. "Roland, there is so much to tell."

Much later, as twilight embraced the Keep and Lake, Azhure stood alone on Sigholt's roof, wearing nothing but a loose white linen shift, her black hair blowing in the warm breeze that swept off the Lake. She leaned her hands on the ancient stone and closed her eyes, drinking in the warmth and the life and the scent that surrounded her.

When she opened them she turned, half expecting to see Axis standing there, smiling at her, his hand extended, his fingers flaring toward her in love and desire.

But Axis was not there, only the night and the first stars above, and Azhure blinked back tears. Axis was far to the west, perhaps struggling through snow, perhaps lying forgotten amid the ice, and he needed her as he had never needed her before. She could feel that here, could feel his need and his longing reaching out to her, calling, calling, calling, and it was all she could do not to dash down the stairs and rush westward clad only in her shift.

"Axis," she whispered, and turned her face back to the view below her.

Behind its protecting blue mist the hills and town surrounding the Lake of Life had continued to grow apace in the months since she had left. Ferns, wildflowers and deep-swaying trees covered most of the hills, and dividing the thick growth were open glades and mown walks. The scent of the grass and the flowers wafted gently down, and before the sun set Azhure had caught the sound of birds and the cries of children as they played on the slopes closest to Lakesview.

The Lake glinted rubylike with the lingering memory of the sun. Its color had deepened, Azhure saw, in past months. It was beautiful and mysterious and stately, and it throbbed with life. During the day, wrapped as it was about its edges by the blue mist, the Lake looked almost as if a giantess had laid her gown of red silk and blue gauze in the sun to brush it and then, distracted by some great matter, had left it for eternity to enjoy.

At the Lake's edge the town of Lakesview had grown, if not in size, then in maturity, for now all the buildings were faced with stone, and doors, shutters and windowsills had been painted in pleasant greens, dusky pinks and rich creams, complementing the gray slate roofs. Gaily painted signs swung over doorways, and most windows were lead-paned and gleaming. The residents strolled the streets, lighting lamps now, and exchanging news and gossip with their neighbors.

No one had left, Roland told her, for who would want to? The Lake and the hills provided all the food they could require, and the days were long and pleasant, despite the storms they knew howled beyond the mist.

Roland had been devastated by news of Jorge's death. They had been friends for many decades, had fought and wived together, and had somehow both thought they would die shoulder by shoulder in some desperate battle. Jorge had indeed died in a desperate battle, but Roland had been far away, concerned with his own gentle dying here in the mystical realm of Sigholt.

Death was closer now, Azhure had seen that instantly. Where before it had lingered like some half-forgotten shadow in the corners of his eyes, now it stared full from his face. Roland assured her there was no pain, but his hands had trembled at dinner, and he had set his wineglass aside after only a sip or two. A month or so, but Roland would certainly never see his beloved Aldeni again.

And Azhure was glad of that, for the Aldeni that now groaned under the weight of Gorgrael's fury would have distressed him and made his dying harder. Roland was a gentle man, despite his warrior upbringing and occupation, and deserved the sweet fading of the light he now experienced in Sigholt. There would be no rage in his passing.

Did Axis fade sweetly? Or did he spend his nights raging into the darkness?

Azhure shuddered and only barely restrained her tears. Tomorrow she would leave, just herself, her hounds, her horse, and the Wolven, as Belial had requested, and race westward. She did not doubt that she would find him, for the moon now fattened toward her full girth, and she would light the way.

Far beneath her she could feel the tug and pull of the waves at the base of Sigholt.

Azhure

She turned, not surprised or frightened.

Adamon stepped to her side and put his arm about her shoulders, stroking her face and hair with his other hand. His dark hair, so like Caelum's she now realized, curled about his shoulders, and the faint light of both stars and moon picked out the fine lines of each of the muscles of his body.

Do not cry for him.

She shuddered again, and his arm tightened about her shoulders.

He waits for you, and yet is afraid to see you. He sits his horse, a corpse ten days dead, and wonders if you could find anything left to love in it. He fears.

As would I.

Yes. As would we all. None of us have gone through what he has

Azhure leaned against the comfort of his body. *What must I do?*

He fears the power of the Star Dance, Azhure.

It has burned him fearfully.

He misused it. With reason, surely, but he misused it nevertheless. No wonder it bit him.

She wrapped her arms about his body. He was warm, and she could feel his skin quiver against hers. *Help me to help him.*

That is what I am here for. Azhure, can you hear the Star Dance?

Assuredly.

Then let me tell you a secret, a holy secret, about Axis and the Star Dance. And he took her face in his hands and whispered into her ear.

Azhure leaned back, her face shocked.

Imagine, Azhure, what you have held in your arms at night. He felt her shiver. *You have shared much the same relationship, Azhure, as exists between the Moon and the Star Dance. Do you understand?*

She smiled tremulously. *I think so.*

It will become plainer, Azhure. And it is this relationship which will enable you to help him.

I don't understand.

Later, my lovely, later. You have a long way to go, and a long way to grow, before you reach Axis. Many nights in which I will come back to you, and in which the other Six will come to you. But me, mostly.

He let her face go and held her close. *Azhure, has anyone ever told you that your eyes are the same color as the gray blue sea as it crashes against the cliffs of the Island of Mist and Memory? And has anyone ever told you that your hair is the same inky blackness that embraces the stars? And has anyone ever told you that your skin is . . .*

She stood back, smiling. "And has anyone ever told *you*, Adamon, that your tongue is far too sweet and your hands sometimes far too silky?"

He laughed and kissed her, and then he was gone.

When Azhure returned to her chamber she found a set of clothes she had never seen before laid out across her bed. She fingered the material, awed by its beauty.

When she lifted it to her face, she thought she could catch Xanon's lingering scent.

For a long moment she drank in the scent, then abruptly lifted her head and stared about the room, remembering.

A year ago tonight she had been deep in her labor with Caelum in this room. It seemed so long ago—ten years, not one. Then she had only been Azhure. Then MorningStar had still been alive, and Axis still refused to admit his love for her. Then Faraday had been her nemesis, not her friend.

A year ago tonight. Yuletide Eve.

38

Yuletide

Faraday had planted Minstrelsea from Arcen to the Bracken Ranges, then through the ranges toward Fernbrake Lake. Now even Pig Gully, where Jack and Yr had once left Timozel wrapped in enchantment, lay deep in shade and soft song.

For the past three days, Faraday and the Goodwife had been exploring the lost Icarii cities of the Bracken Ranges, with the Icarii as their guides.

Over the past thousand years the Acharites had known the Bracken Ranges as a range of mid-height mountains, mostly so barren the only life they contained was the brown bracken that covered the slopes. But in the days of old Tencendor, and again now, the Icarii had known the ranges as the Minaret Peaks, and even though the recovery of the cities was barely under way, Faraday could well understand why. Every day another of the minarets was disencumbered of the enchantments that had concealed it, and every day another of the spires leaped toward the firmament.

As in Talon Spike, most of the Icarii construction in the Minaret Peaks had been within the mountains themselves; Faraday was astounded to learn that the entire mountain range was riddled with airy corridors and chambers. But the ancient Icarii had built on the outside as well: cloisters leagues long that wound through the passes and arced about the slopes; gentle terraces that provided views of both Skarabost and Arcness; platforms and balconies from where the Icarii could lift into the thermals and descend from the stars; and the minarets themselves, great domes and spires of pale pink, gold and blue luminous stone that reached hundreds of paces into the sky.

And about all of these soon-to-be-recovered terraces, balconies and domes would sway the Minstrelsea. The Icarii showed Faraday where she should plant.

"Once," they explained to her, "the Minaret Peaks stood in the heart of the great forests that covered Tencendor, their spires reaching through the canopy to greet the sun. Now they will again. This is the place where the Avar and the Icarii lived side by side, where both the Mother and the Star Gods walked and sang. Now they will again."

On the day she and the Goodwife crested the mountaintop that cradled Fernbrake Lake, she turned and looked behind her.

"Mother, but I wish I would see this in its full beauty one day," she said quietly, and the Goodwife looked at her in alarm.

"But you will, my Lady," she said. "Of course you will!"

Faraday smiled at her sadly, then took her arm and turned her to face Fernbrake Lake.

"Behold," she said softly, "the Mother."

Below them the Lake glowed gently in the afternoon light, not as beautiful as when it was lit with power, but lovely nevertheless. Faraday had planted up the slopes to the crest, and now she would plant down the trails to the water's edge, linking the ancient stand of trees at the far curve of the Lake to Minstrelsea.

The Goodwife felt her stiffen at her side, and she looked at Faraday in concern. "M'Lady, what's wrong?"

"Nothing!" Faraday laughed. "Look!"

The Goodwife squinted. Several dark shapes were emerging from the trees and pointing to where she and Faraday stood.

"The Avar!" Faraday cried, her hand tightening about the Goodwife's arm in excitement.

Faraday had wondered if any of the Avar had ventured south now that the power of the Seneschal had been broken, or whether they would prefer to wait in the Avarinheim for her to plant Minstrelsea to their home. But here they were, at least five or six of them waving at her, and Faraday was thrilled. She would not have minded spending Yuletide at Fernbrake Lake with only the Goodwife for company, but the Avar's presence made it special.

Of the Avar people, Faraday had only ever met Raum and Shra before, and then only briefly. Now Tree Friend would meet some more people of the trees.

But Faraday did not rush. An afternoon's planting still lay before her, and she did not let her own excitement spoil that of the seedlings who would be lifted from their cribs and planted out this day. Their joy was the more palpable because of where they would finally find their rest; along the shores of the Mother, the seeding ground for the original great forests of Tencendor.

So Tree Friend sang and spoke gently to them as she lifted them from their pots, and the Goodwife clumped behind, humming her cradle song. And behind both of them, careful to keep both hooves and the wheels of the cart well away from the seedlings, trod the white donkeys.

It was late afternoon when Faraday completed her planting and stepped onto the grassy space before the trees. The Avar, six women and a child, had waited patiently as she worked her way down into the crater, and now they stood, some smoothing their long robes or tunics nervously.

But the child had no such reservations. Evading the hand of the leading woman, she ran across the clearing.

"Faraday!" she cried, and Faraday, recognizing her, stepped forward and swung the girl into her arms.

"Shra!"

The child had grown in the two years since Faraday had last seen her. She had more than doubled in height, and had lost most of her baby pudginess. But she retained her friendly grin, and her eyes were still full of the beautiful liquid darkness that Faraday remembered. Shra wrapped her arms about Faraday's neck and gurgled with laughter as the woman spun her about delightedly. The bond that had formed between the girl and the woman when Raum had presented both of them to the Mother had not tarnished during their separation.

"Shra," Faraday said again, but softly this time, and gave the child a final hug before she set her down. The six women had stepped forward until they were only three or four paces from her, and now Faraday caught some of their nervousness.

The leading woman was a Bane, small and delicate, but she exuded the same power that Faraday remembered had surrounded Raum. Despite the apprehension apparent in her eyes, her face was calm and her mouth determined.

"Tree Friend," she said, then bowed, the palms of her hands on her forehead. "I honor you. May you always find shade to rest in, and may the paths to the Sacred Grove remain always open to your feet."

She straightened. "My name is Barsarbe, and I am a Bane of the Avar."

Faraday bowed and greeted Barsarbe in the same manner, then stepped forward and kissed the woman on both cheeks. "Greetings, Barsarbe. My name is Faraday. I am glad to meet you and yours finally."

Barsarbe looked startled at Faraday's kiss, but she indicated the five women behind her. "My companions, Tree Friend. Banes Merse and Alnar, and Elien and Criah, both from the FlatRock Clan, and Relm, from the PineWalk Clan."

Faraday greeted each of them with formal words followed by a kiss, then she turned and waved the Goodwife forward.

"My friend and companion, Goodwife Renkin. She has come to me from northern Arcness."

Barsarbe frowned and spoke before the Goodwife had a chance to greet the Avar. "Tree Friend, I would not have thought that one of the Plains Dwellers would prove a suitable companion."

Faraday's face hardened. "I am a Plains Dweller, Barsarbe, and yet the Mother accepted my service. And I have accepted the Goodwife's service. On many days she speaks with the voice of the Mother, and *every* day she sings to the seedlings and gives them the heart to grow. If I have survived to stand here before you today, then it is in large measure due to Goodwife Renkin."

Barsarbe flushed at the rebuke in Faraday's voice. "Forgive me," she said, lowering her eyes. "We are ashamed that . . . well . . ."

"Faraday, Tree Friend," Alnar, an older Bane, stepped forward. "What Barsarbe means to say is that the Avar are shamed that both Tree Friend and the StarMan bear no Avar blood, yet one of ours birthed Gorgrael. We find it hard. Sometimes our shame makes us say words that we later regret."

Faraday's face relaxed. "Barsarbe, Alnar . . . my friends. The Prophecy bends all of us in strange ways. There was a time when I did not want to be Tree Friend, when I shuddered at the sight of a tree and called on Artor to save me. But I accepted my path, and will continue to accept, and I have found peace. Barsarbe, the people of Plow, Wing and Horn must fight this battle together, and when Tencendor is finally won, then all will walk its paths together. The Mother chooses whom She pleases to serve Her."

Chastened, Barsarbe took a deep breath and lifted her eyes. "Tree Friend," she said quietly, "we have made a bad start." She greeted the Goodwife, offering her the same obeisance and words she had Faraday, and kissing her on both cheeks as Faraday had her. The Goodwife blushed and shuffled, but she managed to return the welcome, and beamed happily at the other Avar.

Shra smiled, and took the woman's hand.

"Let us sit under the shade of the trees," Alnar said, breaking the remaining awkwardness, "and share a meal. There are still some hours before the night is dark enough for us to observe Yuletide and there are many things for us to discuss."

Faraday and the Goodwife unpacked and unharnessed the donkeys, then sat down with the Avar women. Of the Avar foods Faraday had only tasted malfari bread once before, and now she and the Goodwife picked delightedly at the dishes before them, sampling the unusual flavors. On their part, the Avar were astounded by the saddlebag that the Goodwife handed them, drawing out foods they had never even imagined.

"Magic," Criah said, and Faraday smiled at her.

"The donkeys and their bags were a gift from Ogden and Veremund," she explained. "Two of the Sentinels."

Barsarbe nodded, sampling some hot raisin dumplings she had just unwrapped. "Yes, we met them—along with the StarMan—two Beltides previously." She grinned. "They were a friendly pair."

Faraday's own smile dimmed as Barsarbe mentioned Axis; she did not want to talk about him yet. "How did you travel south? Did you encounter any danger?"

The Avar women deferred to Barsarbe, and Faraday thought the Bane must be of significant power to have reached seniority at such a relatively young age.

"We traveled on foot, Faraday Tree Friend," Barsarbe explained, "through the Seagrass Plains, as have all our Banes when they brought our children to the Mother. But we traveled openly, where before we would have traveled secretly, and we walked proudly and confidently."

Even if the power of the Seneschal had been broken, Faraday thought, it would have taken considerable courage for these women to brave the unknown. "Did you encounter any difficulties along the way?"

Barsarbe glanced at her companions, then looked back at Faraday. "Little, Tree Friend. Most of the villagers we encountered were curious and offered us shelter at night." She grimaced, remembering. "But it took us a week or more before we had the courage to accept one of these invitations. Although most of the journey went well, there was one moment . . ."

Alnar patted Barsarbe on the arm and continued. "We met some trouble in Smyrton, Tree Friend."

Faraday looked up, her eyes sharp. The people of Smyrton had condoned Azhure's abuse with indifference and averted eyes. "What trouble?"

The older Bane continued. "They threw rocks at us, Tree Friend, and shouted abuse. Although none of the rocks came close, the hatred evident in their words disturbed us . . . it still does."

"Smyrton is a strange village," Faraday said quietly.

"Yet you will have to plant straight through there, Faraday," Goodwife Renkin said. "Smyrton will have to be abandoned to the trees. It is the only way."

Faraday looked up, startled, as did the Avar. Again the Goodwife's voice had lost its country burr; again it was filled with the authority of the Mother.

"Beware of the shadows," the Goodwife continued, "for there lurks Artor." She put her arm about Shra, as if Artor were about to leap from the shadows at this very moment and seize her.

Faraday shivered, more at the power in the Goodwife's voice than at her words, and she was not the only one.

Barsarbe stared at the Goodwife, then swallowed and looked back at Faraday. "We have come to help you, Faraday," she said. "We could not sit in the Avarinheim, waiting and not knowing. We have come to help."

Faraday reached across and took the Bane's hand. "Thank you," she said. "Thank you."

"Faraday," Merse asked, "do you know what has become of Raum? When he left the Avarinheim . . . well . . ."

"He was transforming," Faraday said. "Yes, I know." She smiled suddenly, brilliantly. "He *has* transformed. I witnessed for him. He is at peace, Merse, and his feet have found the paths to the Sacred Grove. Be happy for him."

They held no ceremony to mark Yuletide, for the rites of the sun would be marked at the Earth Tree Grove and, for the first time in a thousand years, at the Temple of the Stars. But the Avar women would light their own circle of fire, and now five of them, together with Shra and the Goodwife, wandered about the perimeter of the Lake laying out piles of dead bracken. Barsarbe and Faraday sat at the edge of the trees, watching them.

"The Icarii always marked Yuletide at the Temple of the Stars before the Wars of the Axe," Barsarbe explained as the stars came out, "but when they were trapped in the Alps, they flew down to celebrate with us." She paused. "Although there will be a number of Enchanters at the Earth Tree Grove, we will miss StarDrifter's presence this year."

Faraday nodded. "StarDrifter is at the Temple now," she said, her arms about her knees as she stared across the Lake. "Azhure told me he relit the Temple some time ago, and now it sends a great light into the sky. No doubt he will lead the rites there."

Barsarbe blinked. "Azhure? You know her?" She had thought—*hoped*—never to hear of that woman again. Some of the warmth in the night died.

"Indeed, Barsarbe. She has become my friend. Why do you ask?"

"She stayed with us for many months," Barsarbe said.

"You do not like her," Faraday observed.

Barsarbe replied slowly, careful now that Faraday had already said Azhure was her friend. "She was the first Plains Dweller, apart from Rivkah, most of us met. We found her unsettling . . . we found the violence that followed in her wake unnerving."

Faraday turned to gaze at Barsarbe steadily. "She has been as much a victim of violence as your people, Barsarbe."

Barsarbe shuddered, unable to conceive of Azhure as a victim—despite what she knew of the scars on her back. "I am sorry, Faraday Tree Friend, but for some reason I have never been able to like her." She paused. "What has become of her?"

Faraday continued to regard the Bane with steady green eyes. "You will not want to hear this, Barsarbe, but she has married Axis, and has borne him three children."

Barsarbe recoiled violently, her eyes wide and furious. "That should have been *your* right!" she hissed. "Why did she . . . why did *he* do that to you?" Her eyes flew downward. "How could he do this to you? Betray you like this! It must have been her fault! *Hers!*"

"Barsarbe," Faraday interrupted, "fault cannot be apportioned for anything that has happened. There is no blame, nor any ill feeling. There is regret, yes, and sadness, but no blame. There is *no* fault, Barsarbe, that can be apportioned to Azhure."

But Barsarbe was not to be appeased. "The second verse of the Prophecy clearly said that you would—"

"The Prophecy was misunderstood," Faraday snapped. "Yes, I lay with the man who slew my husband, but I did not marry him. And Azhure . . . Azhure is the pain-riddled child who concealed ancient arts. She is Icarii, and an Enchanter, and perhaps far more than that. She wields as much power as do I or Axis, and she has been accepted by the Horned Ones and the Mother, not only for her power, but simply for who she is. Try to do the same."

Barsarbe turned her head away, a muscle in her cheek twitching.

"She is my friend, Barsarbe," Faraday said.

Barsarbe suddenly understood why she hated Azhure so much. It wasn't just the violence that followed her like a shadow—although that was sickening enough in itself—it was the until-now unconscious and intuitive knowledge that Tree Friend loved Azhure. Barsarbe resented that, resented the bond that existed between the two women. Tree Friend was the Avar's, and should belong to no other!

"I belong to no one!" Faraday hissed. "And I choose as my friends those whom I please. Axis needs Azhure, *I* need her, and Mother help you, Barsarbe, if one day you find that you need her as well!"

"I cannot believe he betrayed you for her," Barsarbe said. "Perhaps the Avar should reconsider their pledge to stand behind him."

Faraday battled to control her rage. She could not believe that Barsarbe could not only hate so much, but misunderstand so much. No wonder, she thought, that Gorgrael hates as he does, it is a trait of his Avar blood.

She managed, eventually, to bite back her bitter words. "If the Avar decide not to assist Axis," she said, her voice flat, "then they must be prepared to endure Gorgrael as their lord. Axis' eventual success rests in your people's hands, Barsarbe, for it is Avar power that will make the Rainbow Scepter. The trees will back him, this much I know. Choose as you will, but be prepared to accept your choice!"

It had been a thousand years since the Yuletide rites had touched this much power. In the Earth Tree Grove and on Temple Mount, Icarii Enchanters lit the sacred circles of fire to the accompaniment of Song, and the circles were fueled by the reawakening power of the land, of the trees that Faraday had already planted out, of the Earth Tree, and by the reappearance of the Star Gods themselves.

StarDrifter was inside the Temple of the Stars, ringed by fire, spiraling gently in the center of the cobalt beacon amid the floating stars. Wings and arms spread wide, he let as much of the power as he dared flood through him, and he tilted his head back and closed his eyes, unable to bear the beauty of the Temple. To those watching outside, StarDrifter glowed like a great silver cross as he hovered amid the deep violet of the Temple, the stars drifting by him, yet never touching him.

"I have been blessed," the First Priestess whispered, tears running down her aged checks, "to have been allowed to live to witness this."

"It is a time for great blessing," said a soft voice behind her.

"Indeed," the First said, without turning to see who spoke.

Xanon, her face hidden beneath a deep hood, smiled. "And I count myself no less blessed to have been served by you and yours. I thank you."

Curious now, the First turned, but the woman behind her had disappeared into the crowd standing around the perimeter of the Temple.

The First frowned slightly. The woman had gone, yet there was an unusual scent still clinging to the air, and the woman's voice lingered in her head. *Thank you.*

When she looked back to the Temple and the silver figure floating in the beacon, the First could see that another floated with him.

In the Earth Tree Grove, the Avar and Icarii present marked Yuletide with blood sacrifice, as they had been wont to do for thousands of years. As the circle of flame leaped into life the Earth Tree's Song soared even higher, she could feel the spread of Minstrelsea to the south, and longed for the moment when she could join her Song with theirs. But they were still far distant, and even the power of the Earth Tree's Song could not yet reach them.

About Fernbrake Lake the Avar, assisted by the Goodwife, lit the bracken they had laid out. As it caught alight, and as the fingers of flame touched each other to create the complete circle, the Lake burst into emerald life, and the eight women and the child wept as they beheld her beauty.

Faraday tried to forget her harsh words with Barsarbe, although the thought that the Avar might yet refuse to assist Axis frightened her. The emerald beam speared into the night sky, as it had not done the night that Raum had invoked the name of the Mother, and Faraday thought it looked like a beacon.

Gorgrael writhed and twisted, screaming his fury as the circles of fire were lit across Tencendor. As each flame leaped into life he felt his hold on the ice falter.

"I can feel the fire!" he screeched, capering about his chamber in agony. "It burns!"

But none were there to share his pain save the seven thousand Gryphon.

They scampered across the floor and up the walls and dropped off the roof and seethed through the crevices of the Ice Fortress and across its outer surface, until the Fortress resembled a cake that had been overrun by a myriad of ants.

It would not be long before they gave birth.

As he had four thousand years before, and as he had every Yuletide since he had returned to Tencendor, WolfStar stood at the very brink of the Star Gate. All the Icarii Enchanters were above celebrating Yuletide, he could afford to linger.

One foot resting on the low wall surrounding the Gate, he leaned forward intently, listening and watching.

There was nothing save the lure of the Star Dance.

Back! Back! Come Back!

WolfStar resisted. The Star Dance no longer held the same beauty or lure for him. He looked past it, leaning closer, closer, closer.

"Nothing!" he breathed in relief as he finally stepped back. "There is nothing!"

Azhure shrugged off her linen shift and slipped into the suit Xanon had laid out for her. She stood a long time before the mirror, her eyes solemn, her hands gently stroking the material as it clung to her body.

There could be no name for this material—none like it had ever existed. It glowed raven-blue in the lamplight, as deep a blue as could be without verging into black. Azhure moved slightly, held her breath in wonder, then moved again. Every time she shifted position, even breathed, dark shadows chased each other across the material, now on the curve of her shoulder, now at the swell of her breast, now in the hollow of her back, now sliding down her legs. Dark shapes—representations of the shadow of the moon as it waxed and waned—slid over her body as the shadow of the ever-changing moon slid over the earth.

"Magic," she whispered, pirouetting before her reflection. "I am magic."

And then the tug of the waves caught at her, and her eyes, sliding to the window, darkened.

In the heart of the Temple, StarDrifter opened his eyes to find himself face-to-face with Narcis, the God of the Sun. He floated only a pace away from StarDrifter, and when the god extended his hand, so too did StarDrifter, and their fingers touched in the very center of the beacon.

You have done well, StarDrifter, and I thank you.

"Narcis?" StarDrifter whispered.

The circles burn in an arc around Tencendor, StarDrifter, and the Destroyer's grip loosens.

StarDrifter's fingertips burned where they touched the god's, but the sensation was not unpleasant.

I have been resurrected and I will float over the world tomorrow, StarDrifter.

"I have done my best." And my best has oftentimes been inadequate, the Enchanter thought, but it has been all I have had to offer.

Your best has been more than we could have asked. For the circles of fire, for the Temple, for your fatherhood of Axis and for your care of and love for Azhure, I . . . we . . . thank you, StarDrifter.

For some time they hovered, arms extended, fingertips touching, eyes locked, bodies floating gently among the stars.

Your life will be blessed, StarDrifter.

And with that he was gone, and StarDrifter was left alone among the stars.

The rites were complete and the Avar and those Icarii massed in the Earth Tree Grove relaxed. All the Enchanters present, and some of the Banes, could feel the success of the rites at the Temple of the Stars, and now most drifted away into the tree line.

RavenCrest, SunSoar, Talon of the Icarii, bowed reventialy toward the Earth Tree, then stepped away from the circle of stone, its flames now flickering and dying.

A scout stepped out of the tree line and RavenCrest stopped in his tracks. The birdman's face was lined and exhausted, his wings drooping, his eyes strained yet brilliant with purpose.

"Talon!" The scout saluted smartly, although RavenCrest could see he was ready to drop.

"Yes? What is it?" RavenCrest had learned to dread the arrival of exhausted farflight scouts.

"Talon, I bring a message from the Enchantress."

"Yes?"

"Talon, the Enchantress sends urgent word from Temple Mount. She says it is imperative that you evacuate. Talon Spike. Those who can't fly south must *not* go via the icy paths by the Nordra. She says, 'They will have to go down to the waterways and beg, bribe or coerce the Ferryman to take them south.' "

"*What?* Has she gone mad? Evacuate Talon Spike? Who is *she* to give me these orders?"

"Talon, the Enchantress was desperate that this message reach you. She fears a strike by Gorgrael."

"Bah! Gorgrael has his Skraeling host many leagues to the west. He would not—"

"Talon!" The farflight scout's tone was now urgent. "She fears Gryphon.

Thousands upon thousands of them. I hear tell they have devastated the StarMan's force to the west. The Strike Force most of all," he finished quietly. "Listen."

RavenCrest paled as he listened.

Boots and gloves of matching material waited on the bed and Azhure slipped them on. She could feel the wind calling her name as it whispered beyond the mist, and she could feel the tug of the tides as they lapped the continent of Tencendor, but she swallowed her impatience to be gone . . .

Axis!

. . . for goodbyes needed to be said. She strode toward the door to the central chamber, seizing the Wolven and swinging the quiver of blue-fletched arrows over her shoulder as she went.

She took no cloak, for she would not need it.

And she left her hair free, for she would not need to bind it again.

As she strode, silent shapes rose from behind chairs and by walls and before the fireplace and clung to her heels.

It was time to run. To hunt.

She passed through the central chamber and entered the room where the children slept. Imibe lay asleep, the twins in cribs beside her bed. Azhure ignored them, walking directly to Caelum's cot. He was awake, as she felt sure he would be.

Caelum. Do you know what night this is?

It is Yuletide. The night I was born.

Azhure smiled and gently stroked his face, wishing she could take him with her. *Do you remember that night, Caelum?*

He hesitated. *Yes . . . yes, I do. I caused you great pain.*

No. You caused and cause me great joy, my son. She paused. *I must go, Caelum.*

I know it. Will you bring Papa home?

If I can.

Caelum noticed her hesitancy. *Come home, Mama.*

Azhure's eyes filled with tears. *As soon as I can, Caelum. As soon as I can.* Then she bent and kissed him and was gone.

Rivkah awoke suddenly, knowing someone was in the room. She stiffened, expecting assassins.

"You remember your early years at Carlon's court too well, Rivkah."

Rivkah relaxed in relief. "Azhure?" She strained her eyes in the dark. "What are you doing here?"

Azhure stepped forward into the dim glow of the fireplace embers and

Rivkah gasped and jerked into a half-sitting position. "Azhure! What . . . what is that you wear?"

Azhure was clad in a suit so well-fitting it scarcely crinkled as she moved; indeed, Rivkah could not see a seam or a join anywhere. At first she thought it was of solid deep-blue coloring, but as Azhure walked forward another step Rivkah saw the dark shadows of moons, some quarter, some half, some full, chase each other across her body. "It's beautiful!" she whispered.

"Xanon gave it to me," Azhure said matter-of-factly, and Rivkah's eyes flew to her face. There was a wildness there she'd never seen before.

Azhure sat on the edge of the bed, taking Rivkah's hand. "Do not worry, Rivkah I am still Azhure. Still the girl you befriended so long ago outside Smyrton."

Rivkah nodded "I have never regretted your friendship, Azhure. I sometimes think that you have been more my daughter than EvenSong."

Azhure squeezed Rivkah's hand. "I am starting my journey to Axis tonight. And toward . . ." Her voice trailed off.

"Azhure? What's wrong?"

Azhure shook herself. "Nothing. Will you watch over Caelum for me? He will fret while I am away, and worry about his father."

"We will all fret and worry over both you and Axis," Rivkah said. "Be careful, whatever you do . . . wherever you go."

Azhure nodded, then leaned forward and kissed Rivkah on the mouth.

Outside the mist the wind howled, and at the edges of the continent the tides tangled with the drifting seaweed.

Azhure! Azhure! Azhure!

The circle of bracken had burned now, and clouds had moved in to obscure the stars, but Faraday could feel that the night had been a success.

"This is the year we will break Gorgrael's ice," she said. "It will be the final year of subjection and invasion."

"Faraday." Barsarbe moved to Tree Friend's side. "I am sorry that I spoke so harshly about your friend Azhure."

You are sorry only that she is my friend, not that you spoke of her harshly, she thought, but nodded anyway. By her side the Goodwife watched Barsarbe carefully; again the Goodwife had Shra's hand bonded tight in hers.

"Barsarbe." Faraday caught the Bane's eyes and held them. "You are the senior Bane among your people, and thus you have a fearsome duty. Do not let your personal feelings interfere in your responsibility to your people. Do not let your personal hatreds color any advice you may give them." And by the Mother, she thought, I wish Raum were in your place.

Barsarbe opened her mouth to speak, but Faraday continued, her voice harder. "I have responsibilities, Barsarbe, and they are not only to your people.

I do not belong to you. Bane Barsarbe, listen well. I will plant the trees to the Avarinheim, and do it with gladness. But all that I do after I will do for love of Axis and for love of Azhure, and not through any obligation to your people."

Barsarbe stared at Faraday, unsure what to say or how to say it; how could she have mishandled her first meeting with Tree Friend so badly? But then, who would have thought that Azhure could have worried her way so deep into Tree Friend's heart? "You will not lead us into our new home?"

"Let us wait for the outcome of the Prophecy, Barsarbe. If I am free, then I will be glad to do so. But whatever happens, you will have your leader."

Faraday wanted to explain further, though she felt sure that Barsarbe—as all the other Avar present—knew of what she spoke, but just then she felt a small hand clutch her own and she glanced down. Shra now stood beside her, her young eyes fixed firmly on Barsarbe.

"Accepted," she said clearly "I accepted Azhure, Bane Barsarbe, on behalf on the Avar. The Horned Ones have accepted her, too Faraday?" She lifted her eyes and Faraday smiled at her. "Faraday, do not grieve or fear. The Avar will help Axis. I give you my word."

To one side Barsarbe's mouth jerked angrily.

Faraday stared at the little girl, and she suddenly wondered *who* led the Avar. Barsarbe? Or Shra? A powerful and experienced Bane, or a five-year-old girl? Faraday found herself hoping it was the latter.

The Goodwife looked at the little girl and smiled proudly, lovingly. As she caught Shra's eye, the Goodwife gave a little nod of approval.

After Azhure had gone Rivkah leaned back against her pillow, her eyes reflective. She lifted her hand to brush a stray hair from her eyes and instead brushed her fingers against something soft and delicate on the pillow.

Ever wary, Rivkah started, then relaxed, a mystified expression on her face. Resting on the pillow by her face was a Moonwildflower.

39

The huntress

Azhure paused only long enough to saddle Venator and swing onto his back, then, the Alaunt following like silent shadows, she kicked the stallion through the Keep's gates and across the bridge.

From Sigholt, Azhure angled southwest through the mist, aiming for the western passes of the Urqhart. And from there to Hsingard.

One of the Alaunt bayed, but Sicarius silenced him with a short, sharp gruff.

The enchanted soft blue mist clung for almost a league about Sigholt. Any whom the bridge did not recognize would wander lost and confused for hours until they found themselves back at their original entry point. But Azhure did not get lost, and she rode Venator at a sharp canter through the mist until, close to dawn, they emerged into the western Urqhart Hills.

Beyond the mist, Gorgrael's hold on the winter had not loosened. The winds roared across the hills, whistling through the passes, carrying snow and ice in their wake. As she rode the winds seized Azhure's hair and tugged at her body, but she laughed and tossed her head, and neither horse nor hounds were bothered by the cold or the wind.

"Hsingard," she whispered, and pushed Venator into a gallop.

Sicarius at their head, the Alaunt began to run.

Nine months earlier, Azhure had led a force of several hundred men into Hsingard to discover what it was the Skraelings did there. Gorgrael's force had turned the once proud city into sad rubble and, as Azhure and Axis discovered, had worked the heaps of stone into nests. Massive underground chambers served as breeding grounds for the wraiths.

Now Gorgrael had vast numbers of Skraelings—Azhure could sense them undulating like a great tidal mass to the north—and no doubt they still bred in their remaining comfortable stony chambers below Hsingard.

The last time Azhure had come here she had only barely managed to flee with her life and those of the men she had led. Although she and her men had struck the Skraelings hard, her greatest accomplishment had been in escaping the city with her force largely intact. Now, Azhure was riding back to finish what she had started so many months previously.

She rode through the day, neither rider nor horse nor even the hounds tiring, until, at dusk, she rode out of the final pass toward Hsingard, half a league across the plains.

The hounds streamed out before the horse and rider, the scent in their nostrils, their lips drawn back from their teeth, and both the hunting party and the path before it was lit by a broad moonbeam, shining as brightly as if there were a full moon. But the moon was still waxing, and nothing could explain the occasional violet Moonwildflower that drifted gently undisturbed through the screaming winds to lie in Azhure's wake.

As she passed the moonlight faded and, as it faded, so the wind tore the flowers to tatters.

But Azhure, as horse and hounds, had eyes only for the great piles of rubble that rose twenty paces into the air before them and spread for almost half a league from north to south. Hsingard.

She leaned back in the saddle, unslinging the Wolven from her shoulder and fitting an arrow.

"*Hunt!*" she screamed, and the Alaunt raised voice.

Their pale shapes wove between the shadows of the rubble and slipped into the darkened crevices. Eventually, the entire pack disappeared from sight, but Azhure could still hear the echoes of their hunting clamor reverberate through the underground chambers and around and about the city's dead streets.

Before them the Alaunt drove screaming Skraelings, both parents and hatchlings. The Skraelings tried to turn and nip and bite at the hounds, but they couldn't touch the beasts because they seemed only pale shadows, golden eyes and hot, sharp teeth, and the Skraeling teeth, constantly snapping, constantly missed. And so they ran.

Above, Azhure could hear the Skraelings screech. "To the surface," she cried, "to the surface!" Far below her the Alaunt heard, their lips drew back in savage smiles, and they drove the Skraelings before them.

This is what they had been bred to do. To hunt, and to hunt with the Huntress.

Her stallion dancing beneath her, Azhure raised the Wolven to her face and sighted down the shaft of the arrow . . . and, in their scores and their hundreds and their thousands, the Skraelings surged to the surface, arms flailing, eyes shining in terror, teeth exposed in fulsome voice . . .

And Azhure let fly, seizing another arrow in almost the same movement, and let fly, and seized another . . . and let fly . . .

And the Skraelings died.

They thought there must have been ten thousand archers waiting to greet them as they fled the ten thousand hounds at their back, for arrows appeared out of the nasty, bright moonlight in such thick rain that none could escape their sting. Without fail each arrow flew through the narrow gap between bony protuberances into silver eyes, and soon the sound of bursting eyeballs drowned out the noise of the screaming of those left alive and the rising excitement of the hounds.

And, drifting gently through the night, came a Moonwildflower for each Skraeling killed, and soon the ground was covered with the delicate violet flowers sliding through rivulets of bright red blood.

Azhure did not pause to wonder where the arrows came from, nor where she found the speed and the strength to litter the ground with so many corpses. But while the Alaunt drove the Skraelings forward, she continued to rain her arrows upon them, and the red stallion rolled his eyes and skittered and wondered, in his foggy equine way, if the flowers might be good to eat.

Then, abruptly, it was over. Azhure blinked, and lowered the Wolven, an arrow still notched. She looked about her. She sat her horse in the main square of Hsingard, bathed in intense moonlight, and it was littered with the corpses of Skraelings and the rivers of their blood . . . and Moonwildflowers, some of which still drifted from the night above.

"Stars," she whispered, "what have I done?"

Her shoulders slumping in exhaustion, Azhure slid the arrow back into the quiver, noting dully that it was still full of its blue-feathered arrows, then whistled for the Alaunt.

They emerged from crevices and dark holes, their faces grinning happily, tongues lolling past blood-stained muzzles Azhure swung down from Venator and touched the head of every hound that crowded about her, silently thanking them for the service they had done her. Then she patted the horse, and gazed about the square again.

A flicker of light caught her eye, and she saw that in a sheltered alleyway to one side of the square a man sat at a fire, slowly turning a spit.

He looked up, and even from this distance Azhure recognized the gleam of Adamon's eyes.

You must rest, Azhure, and eat. Come join me.

About them the hounds and the horse lay curled in sleep.

I enjoyed the hunt.

Adamon nodded, handing Azhure another piece of roast partridge. She would need to replenish her energy. Azhure took it and tore into it hungrily, vaguely aware that this must be her ninth or tenth piece.

Why am I so ravenous?

Hunting consumes energy. You will need to rest for a day and a night before you resume your journey west to Axis.

Azhure licked her fingers and eyed the spit. Another three birds were roasting over the flames, and she wondered if that was all.

You will have all you need, Azhure. Adamon's eyes twinkled. *Even such as us can become tired if we expend too much energy . . . too much magic.*

Can I destroy the Gorgrael's host the way I destroyed these Skraelings?

Adamon's eyes lost their amused gleam. *No, Azhure. Do not even try it. Gorgrael's host is three hundred times the size of the number you destroyed tonight. Could you face three hundred times the exhaustion you feel now? Can you face what Axis did?*

Azhure plucked a Moonwildflower from her hair and turned it over in her fingers. *Then even gods have their limits.*

Yes. Even we.

She lifted her eyes. *I enjoyed the hunt so much. Surely I can use that to Axis' advantage?*

You will hunt other creatures, Azhure.

Gryphon?

Yes, Gryphon. And others.

Azhure thought about it. *The Gryphon will be harder to kill. And what others will I need to hunt?*

You will know when the time comes. Now, eat some more, and then rest.

From Hsingard, Azhure rode southwest for several days, skirting the southern Urqhart Hills. This far north the wind and snow still screamed, but Azhure thought she could feel a slight difference. The wind still hated, but it was almost as if there were less . . . vigor . . . behind its blasts. *Plant, Faraday,* she thought, *plant.*

And watch the shadows.

Azhure still worried about Faraday, but the more urgent problem was Axis. Could she help him when she arrived? Would she have the power for that now? How long had it been since he had crippled himself with the use of the Star Dance? Where was he? Azhure did not know if her message to Belial had got through, and as she rode she chewed her lip in thought. If she were leading a crippled army, where would she take it? *Where was it now?*

"Search," she whispered to the hounds before her, and Sicarius turned his head, his eyes questioning. "Search for Axis, Sicarius, and bring me to him."

And the hound lowered his great head to the snow and loped faster.

And so she rode.

Often, she had company.

Azhure, Xanon said to her one day as she ran effortlessly beside Azhure's stallion, her hand tangled in his mane, *let me tell you more about the Star Dance. This you must know, if you are to help Axis.*

Yes. Tell me.

Do you remember the secret Adamon told you?

Azhure felt a shiver of excitement ripple down her spine. *Yes.*

Good. Azhure, all life exists within the Star Dance. All life must listen to it.

I don't understand.

You will. Let us keep silent for a few minutes and, as we run, listen . . . listen for the Star Dance.

I can always hear it.

Yes, you can, but I wonder if you truly hear *it. Let it suffuse you . . . and then listen to the sound of your horse's hooves as they thud in the snow, and to the pitch of the hounds as they pant, and to the throb of your own heart.*

Azhure closed her eyes, her body swaying to the rhythm of the horse as he cantered forward, and let the music of the Star Dance engulf her. Her lips parted, and by her side Xanon smiled.

Once she had relaxed completely within the music of the Star Dance, Azhure slowly let other sounds intrude. The thud of Venator's hooves . . . the pitch of the hounds' breath as they ran . . . the throb of her own heart . . .

. . . the surge of the tide as it beat against the shore . . .

. . . the rise and fall of the moon as she dipped through the sky . . .

XANON!

Xanon tipped her head back and laughed, the music and beat of her laughter adding to Azhure's understanding.

Xanon, Azhure's mind whispered, *all life sways to the Beat of the Star Dance. We all keep time.*

Yes. The Beat suffuses every aspect of life. Good. You understand. Now ride, and as you ride, listen to the Beat of the Star Dance . . . it is the throb of life.

Three days from Hsingard, Azhure rode through Jervois Landing. It stood silent and empty of human or Icarii life, the snow drifting through deserted streets. But the ice and frost that Azhure remembered seeing when Axis recalled RuffleCrest JoyFlight's memory had gone. Now Jervois Landing was still winterswept, but it was not frozen, and in sheltered corners Azhure could see the occasional bird or squirrel crouched, waiting for the thaw.

Perhaps they could somehow feel the spread of the Minstrelsea forest so many leagues to the south.

She camped that night in a small house on the outskirts of the town, and Adamon joined her about the fire.

Adamon, Xanon has shown me how all life sways to the Beat of the Star Dance.

Yes.

Azhure thought for a while, her chin resting in her hands as she stared into the fire *Adamon, I can hear the Dark Music as well. Few Icarii—none, really, save WolfStar—can do that.*

Yes, Azhure. And can you feel its crazy beat?

Azhure shuddered. *Yes. Yes, I can.*

Imagine, Azhure, if that crazed beat became stronger than the beat of the Star Dance. Imagine what would happen.

Life would tear itself apart if it tried to follow the lead of the Dark Music.

Indeed.

Azhure sat up straight, pushing her hair back from her face. *Adamon, stars and sun and moon must be surrounded by both Star Dance and the Dance of Death.*

Both Dances constantly court the heavenly bodies, Azhure. But which do you love?

Azhure smiled. *You know that I love the Star Dance.*

Yes.

Axis.

Yes. Help him.

From Jervois Landing the Alaunt led Azhure west-southwest. Above them and behind them drifted Moonwildflowers, and over them shone moonshine, whether the moon was full or dark.

During those hours when Azhure rode, Xanon, and sometimes Pors or Silton, ran by her side, explaining to her the ways of the gods, deepening her instinct, satisfying her curiosity, letting her grow.

Sometimes, when she rode, the hounds would sniff out small bands of Skraelings, sometimes a nest or two, and then Azhure would let the hounds clamor, and hunt.

During those hours when she stopped to rest and eat, Adamon invariably joined her, and both would share the partridge they roasted above the flames, and divide the bread they baked among the coals.

Azhure was never sure where the fires came from, nor the food. She would be riding one minute, then sitting before a fire the next, the hounds curled in sleep about her and Adamon smiling into her eyes.

Tell me of your fight with Artor, she asked one day.

Adamon sighed, and his handsome face crinkled. He rubbed the furrows on his brow and glanced at Azhure. *Do you really want to know?*

I have to know, don't I?

He laughed, and the hounds stirred in their sleep. *How well you have learned, Azhure. How well you have grown. Very well. I will tell you of Artor.*

He was silent for some minutes, but Azhure did not push him.

The Star Gods are tied to this world—to this earth and water and air and fire, Azhure. This sun and this moon.

She nodded. *You are tied by those who worship you.*

Adamon started. He had not thought her instinct had deepened to this extent. *Yes, Azhure. The worship of the Icarii binds us to this world.*

Azhure thought about that for a while. *Tied. Would you like to . . . travel . . . if you could?*

Adamon smiled, introspective. *Would we? I am not sure. But it does not matter. Azhure, beyond this world, beyond the Star Gate, there are many beings—*

Gods?

Adamon shifted uncomfortably. *Some have godlike powers, certainly. Many of these beings are free, not tied. They seek.*

For what?

For worshipers. Sustenance. Souls.

Artor is one of these beings, isn't he?

Yes, Azhure. He is.

Azhure took a deep breath. *Artor came through space . . . ?*

Through the Star Gate.

Ah. Through the Star Gate. Artor came through the Star Gate, seeking adulation and sustenance, and he managed to imprison you. How?

We were weak then. We were only seven, the Circle was not complete. And Artor is old and very powerful; he is a Circle complete in himself. As the Seneschal cast the Icarii, and the Avar, out of Tencendor and imprisoned them behind the Fortress Ranges, so Artor drove us into the interstellar wastes where we drifted, imprisoned. When Axis re-created Tencendor, when the Icarii came south . . .

When the sacred sites were opened again and the Temple relit, then you were freed. Yes, I understand that. The actions of this world mirror those of the gods.

Adamon reached out and stroked her cheek. *You understand so well, Azhure.*

Azhure let him stroke her cheek for a moment longer, then she gently lowered his hand, smiling. *And why do you think we will be able to defeat Artor now?*

We were weaker, but also we did not understand that to defeat Artor we needed to combine with the force of the Mother.

And this time?

Adamon sat forward, his eyes serious. *Azhure, this time you will have to fight for us. You grew in Smyrton, close to Artor . . .*

Azhure felt a surge of excitement. *WolfStar said I had to grow in Smyrton so that I could be close to Artor, so that I could understand him!*

Yes, Azhure. Of all of us you have been closest to Artor. You know him the best.

Azhure thought about that. *But Axis was BattleAxe. Surely he . . . ?*

No. Smyrton is a place of power. Of Artor's power. Of all people who were born there, you were the only one who managed to resist that power. When it comes time to face him, you will be the strongest. Most capable of facing him and of resisting his power.

And Faraday and I must face him as one. Azhure finally understood. *The power of the Mother and of the Stars.*

Yes.

The farther she rode into Aldeni, the more the wind lost its bite and the more the snowdrifts lessened. It was cold and bitter, but it was only winter, not Gorgrael's calculated evil. Azhure laughed, and kicked Venator into even greater efforts.

Axis was closer, she could feel it, and now the hounds ran with their noses constantly to the ground.

They were silent.

They were tracking.

She and Adamon continued to talk. *Adamon, I have heard of this Fire-Night, from both the Sentinels and from StarDrifter. A night, long ago, when the fire fell from the sky and the Star Gods walked the earth. Their fire created the sacred lakes.*

Yes. Older gods than us, Azhure. Adamon turned yet another partridge on its spit and Azhure grimaced slightly. Truth to tell, she was becoming a trifle tired of roast partridge. *The Nine are yet young; still learning, still developing. The Star Gods who fell during the night of fire crashed and burned. We do not know what became of them.*

He offered Azhure a piece of the bird, but she shook her head and Adamon smiled to himself. She was almost ready. *I am glad you have mentioned Fire-Night. Azhure, you must give Axis a message from me.*

Certainly. If I can help him.

Adamon glanced at her sharply. *You must.*

Azhure sighed. *Yes. What is the message?*

Whatever happens in the next few months, he must be in the Earth Tree Grove for Fire-Night. The Avar still celebrate Fire-Night, held in the third week of Rosemonth.

Why must he be there?

Azhure, the Avar will be instrumental in the making of the Rainbow Scepter, and the Rainbow Scepter can only be constructed on Fire-Night.

Why?

Because the Rainbow Scepter, the single weapon Axis can use against Gorgrael, will be built from the power of those ancient gods who crashed and burned that first Fire-Night.

I understand.

Adamon stood up and threw his uneaten piece of partridge into the coals. "Then ride, Azhure, for Axis lies close to despair, and you have a long way to go."

40

The Beat of the Star Dance

Belial sat before the fire and stared at the tent. They had come to this place ten days ago, and here they had stayed. That was partly due to Axis' condition, but mostly because Azhure's farflight scout had finally caught up with them. "I am coming," Azhure's message had stated, "do not commit to any course of action until I get there."

Where are you, Azhure? Belial thought bleakly. And what are you going to do when you get here? What the scout *had* been able to tell him of Azhure had cheered Belial. She had given birth and was well. She was eager to reach Axis. She would help.

And has she learned of her power? Belial asked the scout.

The birdman had thought about that. She was different, was all he could say, and with that Belial had to be content.

The tent flap stirred and Belial jerked.

Arne stepped forth, his face sallow and creased with deep lines.

"How is he?" Belial croaked with a voice suddenly dry.

"Still there," Arne said. "I have come to refill the water pot."

A pail of melted snow was set to one side of the fire, and Arne ladled water from it into the pot he carried. Axis craved water constantly, and Belial wondered if his internal organs were as charred as his exterior. Gods, he wondered for the hundredth time that day, why can't he die? Why won't you let him die?

Axis' condition had deteriorated so badly that even if Belial had not received Azhure's message, it was doubtful he would have traveled much farther anyway. Axis had started the march east demanding that he ride Belaguez, but as his body further failed him, even the ropes and blankets could not keep him upright, and the day the farflight scout had arrived Axis had slipped twice from the saddle; the ropes meant to secure him almost cutting him in half as he hung down the horse's side, moaning.

Now Axis spent his days and nights inside a darkened tent, wrapped in blankets, sometimes delirious with pain and despair. Arne stayed with him most of the time, Belial taking his place when he had to sleep.

Those hours with Axis, sitting silent in the tent, were driving Belial mad. He had never thought to have to watch his friend suffer this way.

Why couldn't he die? *Why?*

The night was full and dark now, the heavy clouds hiding the silvered disc of the moon floating above. About him the camp was settling down, horses stamped, men spoke quietly, somewhere someone laughed, gear clinked.

It was quiet now, and Belial felt himself drift toward sleep. A horse snorted then whickered, and his head jerked up. But then there was silence, and Belial relaxed again. It was beginning to snow gently, and he wrapped his cloak about him, too tired to get up and search for a blanket or his sleeping roll.

The tent was still and quiet, and Belial hoped Axis had managed to find escape in sleep or unconsciousness.

He jerked out of slumber again. Something soft had tickled his hand where it lay curled about the outer edge of his cloak and he twitched irritably.

But the tickle remained, and Belial twisted his head to see.

Resting on the back of his hand, caught by a snowflake, was a delicate purple flower.

Belial blinked, thinking it a phantasm of sleep, but the flower did not disappear. Wonderingly he reached out with his other hand and lifted the flower to his nose. It had a wild scent, and Belial felt his head spin.

Somewhere a dog barked softly, once, then was quiet.

Belial slowly sat up. There were no dogs in camp. Was this some stray that had survived the ice of Aldeni? He twisted about, looking behind him, wondering if he should investigate, when a rough tongue rasped across his cheek.

"What—" he began, then fell to his back as the hound pushed him over and licked his face enthusiastically.

Sicarius!

"Oh, Mother!" Belial said, tears starting to his eyes, "Azhure!"

"None other," she laughed, and Belial scrambled to his feet. Azhure stood at the other side of the fire, hands on hips, her eyes and mouth soft as she gazed at him.

Belial stared at her. He had always believed Azhure more than beautiful, but now she seemed impossibly lovely. He remembered when she'd arrived at Sigholt, when he had lifted her from her horse. Then he had thought she had gained an aura of wildness; now that aura shone forth a hundred times stronger.

Without thinking he stepped around the fire and folded her in his arms.

Azhure hugged him, feeling his pain, remembering herself what it had felt like to have him hold her. "Shush," she murmured, stroking his hair and kissing his cheek as she would a child. "I am here now. It will be all right."

"Oh, Azhure," he muttered, "Azhure!" and he burst into tears.

For a long time Azhure stood there, rocking him in her arms, trying to comfort him. Her own eyes glinted with tears, for the strength of Belial's despair gave her some idea of the depth of Axis' own nightmare.

She leaned back in his arms eventually. "Tell me," she said.

And Belial did. She did not let him go, and he could feel when her arms tightened in horror even though her eyes and face remained calm. When he had finished she held him close again, gently stroking his cheek, her eyes fixed on some point far distant.

"I thank you, Belial," she whispered, "for what you have done for him."

"Azhure. Can you help him die? Do you love him enough for that?"

"I love him, Belial, and I will do what I have to."

Axis lay still in his constant night and wondered that pain should have become such a valued companion. It was his only link with sanity, for if he held on to the pain, if he concentrated on it hard enough, then the despair receded until it was only a dark shadow lingering in the back of his consciousness.

Pain, and his thirst. His thirst had become almost a living creature in itself, never letting him go, never letting him sleep, always demanding to be listened to, to be sated.

He twisted his head, thinking to whisper to Arne for another sip when he heard the tent flap open, then fall shut. He closed his mouth, wondering if Belial had come in to relieve Arne. Belial was his friend, but Axis did not like Belial sitting with him, he could feel the man's horror and his pity every time he had to come close to him.

Arne's voice sounded, low and surprised, then the tent flap lifted and closed again, and all was silent.

Axis lay, every nerve afire, his ears straining. "Belial?"

But his only answer was a soft footfall. Too soft for Belial. Someone else, then. Perhaps Belial could not face another shift minding this charred corpse and had sent some anonymous soldier. Axis did not blame him. Even friendship must have its limits.

There was the flare of a match.

"No," Axis croaked. "Douse the lamp." He had ordered that no one light a lamp in his presence—he did not need to endure the horrified breaths every time someone caught a good look at him. But he heard the clink as the lamp glass was shifted, then replaced, and could almost feel the warm glow as who-ever it was stood closer to the bed, lamp held high. Did they now disobey him, as well as recoil from him?

Axis twisted in the bed, but his body was now so useless that he could do nothing about this silent inspection. "Put it out!" he rasped. *"Put it out!"*

Then he caught the scent of the person, and his entire body stilled. So warm, so fragrant, and what was left of his hands twitched, as if he could feel her skin beneath his fingers.

"Azhure," he whispered, "Azhure . . . please . . . *go!* Please go! Don't see me like this! Please . . . please . . . GO!"

Belial heard Axis scream and took a step forward.

Then a hand fell on his shoulder. "No, Belial, good man. Leave them."

Belial turned. A man, a beautiful man, stood behind him, his hair dark and curling about his shoulders. He was clad only in the lightest clothes, as if it was but a balmy summer's day. "Who are you?" Belial said.

And yet, strangely, he felt no fear, nor anger.

The man indicated the fire. "Shall we sit, Belial? It will be a long night, I think."

"Very well." But as they sat themselves before the fire Belial turned to the man, his face puzzled. "Who are you?"

"My name is unimportant, Belial."

"Are you a friend of Axis'?"

The man's eyes drifted toward the tent. "Yes. Yes, I am. A friend of both Axis and Azhure's."

Still she did not speak.

He heard her put the lamp down on the stool by the bed, and then, horrifyingly, he felt her reach for the blankets and pull them away from his body.

"No!" he shouted again, and began to cry, his arms twitching as they tried uselessly to cover the ruin of his flesh. Why did she have to see him like this? Why? *Damn Belial for sending for her!*

Then he heard the rustle of fine material and the twitching of his arms slowed. What was she doing? Why wouldn't she speak to him? Why wouldn't she voice her horror? Her rejection?

There was movement in the air, and he heard the crumple of material fall to the ground.

Then she leaned close. "Axis," she whispered so low he almost did not hear it. "Axis," and the word was full of love. "Axis," and she lay down beside him, and wrapped him in her soft, warm flesh.

He thought he would never be able to endure the agony as his skin lifted and tore where she rubbed against him. He arched his back, and opened his mouth to scream. *Why? Why?* But then her movement ceased, and she lay warm and heavy and replete along his side, as if they had just made love, and her flesh no longer tortured, but eased him.

For the first time in many interminable days he could feel warmth suffuse his body.

She lifted her face to his and softly kissed what was left of his cheek, his nose, then his mouth.

"Help me to die," he whispered. "Please."

A cheerful woman, as beautiful as the man, now joined them. Her filmy gown made Belial blush, but politely she pretended not to notice, and gave him her hand to kiss.

"My husband is here already," she said, "and I am late. Well, 'tis ever the way."

She turned to the man. "Are they inside?" and Belial heard the tension in her voice.

Her husband nodded.

The woman turned back to Belial. "Then we must wait. Perhaps we can pass the time with some conversation. Belial, know that we know you."

It was a strange thing to say, and Belial stared at her.

She smiled, and Belial saw some of the same wildness about her eyes that he had seen about Azhure's. He tensed. *Who were they?*

The man replied quickly, sharply. "Friends, Belial. Nothing else matters."

The woman patted him on the arm. "Belial, whatever happens tonight, do not fear. Will you promise me that?"

Belial nodded. "I have seen too many strange things over the past few years, my lady, to jump at shadows now."

"You are a rock, Belial."

"Azhure," he whispered, evading her mouth, "what are you doing here?"

He felt her lips smile against his face, and he wondered that she could bear it. "A strange thing to ask a wife, beloved, when she slips into her husband's bed and seeks to please him with her kisses."

He tried to twist his face away, tried to pull away from her jest, but the bed was narrow, and there was no escaping her persistence. "Azhure," he asked again, "help me to die."

"No."

"What point is there to life like this?" he shouted, startling her enough that she pulled back.

"Axis," she said mildly. "I will show you the way."

"To death?"

"The GateKeeper has already refused you, beloved. Forever, we vowed, and forever it is."

Axis lay still and tried to think, tried to ignore her soft warmth. He had never told Azhure about the GateKeeper. "How do you know?" he asked eventually. Had the GateKeeper been so entertained by his desperate pleas that she had wafted into the OverWorld to share her amusement with his wife?

Azhure smoothed her hand over his head, and tried to remember how soft his hair had been. "I met her, beloved, on the Isle of Mist and Memory."

He was silent, bitter. Why was she here? What could she do?

"The Star Dance did this to you."

She felt him relax slightly under her hands.

"Yes. Azhure, there was no other way! The Gryphon . . . the Gryphon . . . they were blackening the sky, and stealing my army in their talons . . ."

"Shush. I know Belial told me what you did."

"Azhure, I have lost touch with all my power! I *never* thought that life could be so barren." He paused. "I am useless!"

"Axis—"

"Azhure, pray you do not have to feel what I felt that day. The power of the entire Star Dance is a terrible thing. Terrible . . ." His voice drifted off, and Azhure kissed his mouth again.

"Yes, the power is a dreadful thing, especially if you misuse it."

Suddenly, he was angry. "And what would *you* have done, had you been there in my place?"

"I would have watched my army die about me, because I would not have had the courage to do what you did. Now, Axis," her voice became practical, almost brusque, "we must fix this."

"Oh, yes? And how, pray tell, do you intend to do that?"

"By letting the entire power of the Star Dance consume us, my darling."

"*No!*" and she had to wrap her arms tight about him to stop him rolling out of the bed in his terror. "*NO!*"

"Ah, here you are!"

Belial blinked as the woman stood, and welcomed five more strangers to the fire. Two more women and three men joined them, all hopelessly lovely, all clad only in the flimsiest attire.

All of them kissed Belial on the mouth, even the men—an extraordinary liberty he thought, stunned, as the final man drew back—then they greeted the husband and wife and sat down about the fire. The Alaunt slowly crept forth from the shadows and lay at their sides and backs, and the seven smiled and patted the hounds, murmuring their names.

Belial sank back down again, and one of the men, younger than the first and with flaming hair, touched Belial briefly on the arm. "You must excuse us, Belial, disturbing you like this. But—"

"But we have come to witness," one of the women said, her face full of life, "and we would that you witness with us."

"Thank you," Belial said, although he did not know why he said it. "It is an honor to witness with you."

"No," the first man said very quietly. "We are honored that we may witness with *you*, Belial."

And then, as Axis screamed, they all turned their eyes back to the tent.

"NO!"

"Axis—"

"No! Azhure, *do you know what you suggest?*"

"Yes," she replied calmly, "yes, I do."

He wished he could twist away from her, from her touch, her mad suggestion. "It would kill me."

"I thought that was what you wanted!" she snapped.

"I do not want to die," he whispered, and suddenly realized it was true. Azhure was here, and he desperately wanted to believe that she could heal him.

"Are you sure?" Her voice was as soft as his.

"Yes."

She took a deep breath. "Do you love me?"

"Yes," and his voice broke on the word.

"Then trust me."

"I love you . . . I trust you."

"Beloved," she whispered and, cradling his head in her hands, drew his face down to nestle between her breasts. For a long time they lay like that, until she could feel his entire body relax against hers.

"Can you feel my heartbeat?" she asked.

It throbbed against his cheek, its life dulling even his pain, and he did not think he had ever heard such beautiful music. He relaxed further and let its comforting thud lull him toward sleep.

"Axis."

"Hmmm?"

"Listen to my heart. Listen to its beat."

"Yes."

"Listen . . . *listen.*"

And Axis, so close to sleep, thought he could feel something different in her heartbeat. It was . . . slowing . . . yes, that was it. Her heartbeat was . . .

Beat.

. . . slowing. He took a deep breath, drinking in her life and her scent.

"Match yours to mine, beloved," he heard her whisper somewhere leagues above him, and he smiled against her skin. "Match your heartbeat to mine."

Beat.

He thought about it. It seemed such a simple request, but he had never tried to control his heartbeat before. Slow it?

Beat.

Her heart was so languorous now that he could breathe between each of its contractions.

"Slower," she murmured and, so relaxed against her warmth he could deny her nothing, Axis' own heart slowed. Only barely aware of what he did, he felt no fear.

He tried to bury his head deeper between her breasts, tried to burrow closer to her heart, and he felt her fingers press against the back of his skull, encouraging him, loving him.

Beat.

And his heartbeat slowed to match.

A deep breath, and . . .

Beat.

He could feel it, that incredible moment when their hearts met in a single . . .

Beat.

"Listen," said a voice from far away, and Axis listened.

Beat.

"Listen . . . can you feel it?"

"Yes," he whispered, unwilling even to utter that one word, but unable to deny her urgency.

Beat.

And the reverberation of their hearts beating as one threatened to shake him apart. He moaned, but he was not in pain, and he was not afraid.

"Trust me."

"Yes."

Beat.

"You hear our hearts, Axis, beating as one, beating in time to the Star Dance."

He had not thought he'd ever get this close to another person. To share a single heartbeat . . . this was true consummation.

Beat.

"Share with the Star Dance, Axis."

He almost did not hear her, and when the meaning of her words sank into his languor he did not have time to feel afraid, for her heart was so closely bound to his now that it led his deeper and farther until . . .

Beat.

. . . they shared with the Star Dance, and their hearts throbbed in perfect rhythm with the beat of the music of the stars.

"Do you hear it, Axis?"

He was almost weeping. "Yes."

Beat.

"Trust me, Axis. Let it consume you. Become one with the Star Dance, Axis. Float in my arms."

"I am afraid."

"If you become one with the Star Dance, Axis, it will not harm you. Only if you seek to misuse it, will the power harm you."

Beat.

"Revel in the Star Dance, Axis! Let go! Now!"

And Axis trusted her, and let go, and allowed the Star Dance to consume him.

Beat.

Adamon lifted his head sharply and he exchanged quick glances with the others. "Yes!" he whispered.

Beat.

"What is it?" Belial asked. He felt a throbbing, but he could not understand it. He put his hand on the ground, and . . .

Beat.

. . . it leaped beneath him. "What is it?"

"Shush, Belial," Xanon said. "It is all right now. It is the rhythm of life itself that beats beneath your hand and through your body. Feel it!"

Silton took a deep breath and relaxed. "She has done it."

"Yes," Pors said. "She has. He has been reunited."

Belial's eyes quickly scanned the group. All were relaxed and laughing, and he now realized how tense they had been before.

The man who had first walked out of the night leaned across the low fire and took Belial's hand. "My name is Adamon," he said, "and this is my wife, Xanon."

She inclined her head, and the others introduced themselves.

Belial wondered why the names tickled his memory, then the woman Xanon was kissing his cheek and rising to her feet.

"We will go now, Belial. Perhaps we will meet again, perhaps not."

Adamon rose to stand with her, his arm about her waist. "Do not disturb them, Belial, no matter what you see, what you hear, or what you feel. Wait for them."

Belial stood himself, and Adamon gently touched his cheek. "We are thankful for you, Belial. Very thankful. You must remember this night, and when you are old and your grandchildren sit on your knee, you must tell them of the hours you shared about a campfire with the Star Gods."

And then they were gone, and Belial was left with only the Alaunt for company, his eyes staring wildly into the night.

Axis reveled, and by his side his wife exulted with him. They drifted among the stars, borne by the power of the Star Dance, and as its power surged through him Axis understood many things.

He understood why the Star Dance had harmed him. It was never meant to hurt or maim, and it had resented his manipulation of it to kill, even to kill such dark creatures as the Gryphon.

And so it had bitten him.

There had never been any Songs of War, and if there had been, then they must have used some other power than that of the Star Dance. Songs of War? Rumor. Legend. Nothing more.

At his side, Azhure smiled.

He would have to use something different to defeat the Skraelings . . .

"Axis, my beloved," Azhure said, and Axis smiled at her. "The Skraeling host will be defeated by power, but it will not be yours, nor even mine."

"The trees."

"Yes. Faraday and the power of the Mother."

"The power of Tencendor is composed of many things, not just the Star Dance."

"Yes, but these things can wait to be discussed later. For the moment . . . listen . . . enjoy . . . let the Star Dance flood through you."

And so they drifted, hearts linked not only with each other, but also with the Star Dance, and they lost themselves in the throb of the beat.

And eventually she whispered in his ear. "StarMan. I have a secret to tell you."

He smiled. "And what is that?"

"A holy secret, StarMan."

He laughed. "Then tell the StarMan."

"StarMan," she smiled, "you are the Star Dance."

I am? He felt her love and that of the Star Dance throb through him. "Oh."

He could feel her move closer. "And I am the Moon, and all of our days and nights are spent entwined in each other. You sing only for me, and my dance is woven solely for your delight and accomplished solely to the rhythm of your music."

"Ah." None of this seemed very strange, floating here among the stars.

"StarMan," and he laughed, for even here among the stars he could feel the tease of her hands on his body. "Do you know that I prefer you the way you once were?"

"I was prettier then." But here, among all this love and beauty, he did not care very much what his tattered and burned body looked like back in that bed. Then he recalled the shame he had felt when Azhure had pulled the blankets from his body. "But what can I do? How can I change that which has been destroyed?"

"Oh, StarMan!" And her merriment pealed among the stars. "I can remember StarDrifter, filled with pride and love, informing the entire Icarii Assembly that as a baby within Rivkah's womb you sang to yourself the Song of Creation. He said that his seed may have planted you, and Rivkah's womb may have nourished you, but that you made of yourself what you wanted."

"Would you have me create a baby that you could rock in your arms and croon cradle songs to?"

"Oh no," she murmured, "I would have my husband back, and if I would still rock him in my arms, then it is not cradle songs I would like to whisper in his ear."

He laughed and, remembering, began to Sing.

And once he had done so, as they drifted among the stars, they finally consummated their marriage.

Their hearts still throbbed, but now only with barely satiated desire. Azhure sighed and stretched out in his arms, enjoying the feel of his body against hers, enjoying his quick intake of breath as she moved. "Did we couple among the stars or here in this narrow, lumpy bed? I swear I cannot remember."

"Does it matter? But I thank you, Azhure."

She smiled. "Oh, surely it is I who must thank you. I have never felt so—"

"No." He put his fingers to her mouth, stopping her words. "No. Thank you for my life."

She regarded him silently. His skin was pale from lack of sun, but otherwise he seemed unchanged from the time she had first seen him ride into Smyrton. "I could not have lived without you."

He stroked her hair, then tangled his fingers within its depths. "Who are you, Azhure?"

"What?" She laughed, startled. "Who am I?"

He kissed her lightly. "What did you learn on the Island of Mist and Memory that you could have taken me where you did?"

She was silent. Did he recall what she had told him while they lay wrapped in the Star Dance?

"I remember, Azhure. Now tell me."

She took a deep breath, then told him of her encounter with the Star Gods in the Sepulchre of the Moon.

He accepted it faster than she had, and more completely. But then he had been through far more, and the experiences of the last hours had prepared him.

"Song and Moon," he said, then smiled gently into her eyes. "No wonder we were unable to deny each other that night under the Beltide stars, Azhureheart."

His hand moved down her body and she shuddered, but for the moment he only stroked her flat belly. "And those twins?"

"*Those* twins?" She smiled at his tone. "Waiting at Sigholt, beloved, with Caelum." She paused. "StarDrifter named them DragonStar and RiverStar."

His hand stilled. "Powerful names. Especially the boy. Did they hurt you?"

She hesitated, averting her eyes, and Axis had his answer. His face hardened. "Everyone must answer for their actions, Azhure, and one day they will too."

"But for now they are only babes, and perhaps they just need love and care."

He laughed dryly and rolled away from her. "You believe that even less than I do, Azhure. I can feel it. We cannot pretend to each other. Now," his tone softened, and he cradled her back in his arms, "tell me what else you have learned."

For some time she talked: of the First and Niah's letter; of the wonders of Temple Mount and the relighting of the Temple; and, eventually, of darker things.

"Artor walks, Axis," she said quietly, and she felt him tremble.

"Stars! What have we done to deserve *him*?"

She smiled wryly. "We walk, Axis, thus so does he. Adamon tells me that Faraday and I must deal with him eventually."

"Azhure! Oh no! Surely I can—"

"No." Now she stopped his mouth with her fingers. "It must be Faraday and me."

She felt him tremble again.

"There is more."

"Yes. There is more. Gorgrael has more Gryphon."

"What!" Axis raised himself on an elbow, horrified.

She spoke softly, quickly, telling him what WolfStar had told her.

Now Axis trembled, and Azhure realized how deep his pain had really gone; the thought that at least he had rid Tencendor of the Gryphon had helped him endure his agony. "Azhure! Azhure . . . I *cannot* deal with that many. I . . . the Star Dance . . . I can't . . ."

"Hush, my love. I will deal with them. I have my bow and my hounds and I will hunt them down for you."

He studied her. "You *have* grown, haven't you, Azhure?"

She reached for his face. "We are a team, Axis. You and me and Faraday. Together we will defeat Gorgrael and any other who moves against us."

"But in the end, it must be me alone who faces Gorgrael."

"Yes." She paused. "Adamon sends you a message, Axis. He says that you must attend Fire-Night in the Earth Tree Grove this summer."

"Fire-Night . . . it is almost six months away."

"Do you know much of it?"

He shook his head. "No. Only that the Seneschal forbade its observance among the peasants."

"The Avar will be instrumental in the making of the Rainbow Scepter, Axis, and it can only be made in the Earth Tree Grove on Fire-Night. It will use the power of the ancient gods who crashed and burned on the first Fire-Night."

"Azhure," Axis said, "the third verse of the Prophecy warns me that when I meet Gorgrael only my Lover's pain can distract me enough to destroy me. My love, be wary! I do not want Gorgrael to snatch you!"

She laughed, genuinely amused. "Gorgrael snatch *me*? I should like to see him try, Axis. Well," her smile died as she saw how concerned he was, "at least you do not have to worry about the Traitor anymore. At least he has made his move."

"Oh," Axis sighed slowly, understanding. "Timozel."

He was quiet for a long while. "I loved him when he was a boy, but he changed when he grew into a man. I wish I knew what it was that drove him to Gorgrael's service."

"We may never know, Axis. But at least you do not have to worry about shadowy Traitors anymore."

He grimaced. "What you mean is that at least I do not have to tear my friends to pieces in my desperate bid to find him. Yes, you are right. The Traitor has made his move. Now," he cupped her chin in his fingers, "all I have to do is keep you out of Gorgrael's hands."

She kissed him gently. "Axis, there is one more thing I must tell you. It is about your mother."

Belial, Magariz, Ho'Demi, Arne, SpikeFeather and several other commanders had sat about the fire through the night and well into the next day.

"You are *sure* that Azhure was well?" SpikeFeather asked for the umpteenth time, and Belial glared at him.

"And these strange visitors who said you must not disturb Axis and Azhure?" Arne worried yet again. "Are you sure that they should be trusted, Belial? What if they are locked in desperate struggle with unknown fiends within the confines of the tent, and wait for us to save them?"

"Your imagination does you proud," Belial said, although he had played the same scenario over in his mind again and again. Only the strange beat that every so often he could feel in his heart stayed his hand.

"Well," Magariz said for something to say, "at least the weather seems to have improved."

Overnight the clouds had cleared and, although it was still cold, now the sun shone over them so that the snow melted in ever-larger puddles about their feet. Now Ho'Demi eyed his boots morosely; they were damp to his ankles, and he longed for the dry ice-lands of his home.

"I shall have to fly the Icarii out within the hour," SpikeFeather grumbled, "for if we linger among this damp we will all develop wing rot."

"No, SpikeFeather, we wait for a while yet. But if no one emerges from that tent by evening, I will give the order to pull out in the morning. I would almost prefer the driving snows to this soggy melt. We ride for Sigholt."

"And what would you do with me, Belial, when you pull out?" Axis said pleasantly as he poked his head out the tent flap. "Roll me up in this canvas and throw me over Belaguez's back?"

"Axis!" Belial shouted, and behind him the others rose slowly to their feet as Axis stepped out of the tent.

Axis let them look, then he grinned at Belial. "I have been abed, Belial, and now I am up, and I would surely appreciate it if you could tell me where you have put my clothes."

Belial stared gape-mouthed for another moment, then he burst out laughing and stepped over and embraced the naked man.

The tent flap stirred behind them and Azhure stepped out, smoothing her blue suit down over her body. "I thought you might prefer him this way, Belial, than dead," and Belial reached out and included her in his embrace.

Then the others crowded around, laughing and exclaiming, and the hounds bayed and the sun shone and within heartbeats the entire camp knew what had happened.

Belial stepped back, his cheeks wet with tears. "My friend. You can have your command back. I think they are pleased to see you," he said, to the sound of the men shouting out Axis' name.

Axis grinned and whistled, and Belaguez reared back from the horse lines, breaking his halter rope, and galloped to join his master.

Axis seized the trailing rope and vaulted onto the stallion's back, saluting his commanders as they stood watching him.

"Where to?" he called to the thousands that milled about, and about him the roar rose, "Where you lead, StarMan!"

Belaguez reared and plunged, ecstatic to have his master back, well and whole, and Axis laughed for sheer joy. "Where to, Azhure?"

She smiled, her eyes deep with happiness. "I think it is time we went home."

"To Sigholt!" Axis cried, and set his heels to Belaguez's flanks, sending the horse plunging among the ranks of men crowding about. "We ride for Sigholt, and then? Then to Gorgrael's Ice Fortress itself! What can stop us now?"

41

Fernbrake

Thier pace had been, literally, kept to a crawl. Ogden and Veremund had never been as robust as Yr, and with the infusion of the ancient power into their bodies, their physical condition deteriorated rapidly. They could only stumble one or two hundred paces before they had to rest, their faces splotched scarlet and white, their breath wheezing and bubbling in their chests, their hands quivering uselessly at their sides. But Yr had been corrupted by power longer—almost four months now—and there were many days when she could not move at all, when the Sentinels sat in a silent and solemn circle as she struggled to maintain her grip on life.

Jack and Zeherah were quietly frantic as they approached Fernbrake Lake. They had not thought the journey would prove so hard, and they were taking so long! And the two longer stages were yet to be accomplished.

And after tonight Zeherah would be left on her own to cope with the other four.

"I did not think it would be so bad," Jack said to her as they waited at the lip of the crater that held Fernbrake Lake for the other three to catch up. Ogden was hanging onto Yr's arm, but Jack did not know who was supporting whom. Behind them Veremund struggled in his own private hell.

Zeherah leaned against Jack's body, knowing there were only hours left in which she could touch him. "There are only five months before Fire-Night," she said. "Five months."

"We will manage." Jack turned from the struggle below and gazed at Zeherah, knowing and sharing her pain.

"We will have to," she said, and blinked away her tears.

Their journey through the Bracken Ranges had been made doubly difficult by the need to avoid the sharp eyes of hundreds of Icarii who were swarming over the mountains. As much as the Sentinels would have enjoyed their company, they could not afford to be seen. Any Icarii who came close would risk infection by the dreadful power that now radiated from the bodies of three of them; and the Sentinels did not want to risk contaminating the Icarii, nor risk being drawn away from their purpose.

At least they had the trees to cover them from over-curious eyes. This was their first contact with the forest that Faraday had planted, for they had cut directly north from the Silent Woman Woods and had missed Faraday in her eastward sweep. Each of the Sentinels took comfort from the gentle humming of the trees, and the trees lent them sympathy and shelter from the frosty nights. At least, they thought, Faraday continues to plant. Pray to the Prophet that she reaches the Avarinheim unscathed.

Yr and Ogden finally reached the waiting pair, and within a few minutes. Veremund joined them. Jack and Zeherah gave their companions almost half an hour to recover, then they started on the downward path toward the Lake. It was almost dusk, and it would be well into the night before they reached the waters.

Zeherah felt Jack tremble as they turned into the path, and she squeezed his arm gently, treasuring the contact.

The Avar and Faraday were weeks gone, and the Sentinels had the Lake to themselves. They rested an hour after they had finished their descent to its shores, then Jack hefted his staff and stood up.

"Will you want me to carry the staff once . . . once . . ." Zeherah found she could not finish.

"No. I will continue with it. I have carried it this long . . . and no doubt I will need its support once I am through here."

Zeherah could no longer hold her tears in check. "I had not thought this to be so difficult," she sobbed, and Jack leaned down and stroked her cheek. She grasped his hand and kissed it, and Jack battled with his own emotions.

Yr, Ogden and Veremund, lost in their own misery, watched impassively to one side. This was a goodbye in which they could not participate.

"Jack," a voice said, and he looked up. Walking slowly toward him across the grass was the Prophet, silvery and powerful, his coppery hair shining like the late afternoon sun.

The Prophet reached down and laid a gentle hand on Zeherah's hair, and she took a deep breath and swallowed her tears, trying to smile at him. Jack stood straight and tall, determined not to let the Prophet see his own doubts.

But the Prophet saw anyway, and understood. "All goes well," he said, and gazed lovingly on Yr and the brothers. "The Prophecy spins out to its conclusion, and Axis and Azhure have accepted their heritage."

Yr looked up. "Their heritage?"

"We thought that Axis might be . . ." Veremund whispered, "but Azhure?"

"They are the last of the Nine," the Prophet said, and all the Sentinels took deep breaths. So.

Jack sighed and looked toward the Lake. "It is time. Prophet, will you hold my staff while I am gone?"

The Prophet took the staff, his hand closing about Jack's. "You will be beloved always for the sacrifice you now make," he said, leaning forward and softly kissing Jack on the mouth. "And you will always rest in my heart. You have proved far more than I could have hoped."

Jack blinked, then he bent down to Zeherah. "Beloved," he whispered, "there are times when I have wished that you had never accompanied me on that expedition to float down the Nordra, so many thousands of years ago. If you had not, if you had stayed safe in the UnderWorld, then you would never have had to face the dreadful fate you do now."

"And I would have lost you so much sooner," she said bravely, lifting her face to be kissed. "Go in peace, Jack, and go with my love."

The Prophet took the staff and stood back several paces, inclining his head slightly at Jack, and the Sentinel shed his clothes, shivering slightly in the cold night air.

"I have regrets," he confessed, and the others regarded him with compassion. "I never expected to miss life so much."

For one more instant his eyes met those of Zeherah, and then he was gone.

They waited many hours, and it was close to dawn when Jack resurfaced, his eyes glittering with power, the corruption already turning his heart.

Zeherah's jaw clenched, and she lowered her head, almost unable to look at him, but then she straightened, smiled and nodded, and let Yr and Ogden and Veremund greet him and welcome him into their painful community.

Unlike the previous occasions, the Prophet was still with them, and he handed Jack his staff and let his hand rest on his shoulder briefly. Then he gazed at the other three suffering Sentinels. Their bodies were wasted, their strength almost gone. In places their skin hung in narrow strips, and their eyes glittered with as much pain as power. Heat radiated from their flesh and while Yr had lost most of her hair, Ogden and Veremund were now losing theirs in uneven handfuls.

"It is hard on you," the Prophet said. "I understand that, and perhaps I can do something to help you on your way."

He turned and walked down to the Lake until its waters lapped his toes. He did not know if this would work.

He spread his arms wide. "Mother!" he cried. "Hear me! I seek Your aid for my servants who are Your servants too. Did not Jack and Yr lead Tree Friend to You? Did not Yr protect and comfort Faraday during her darkest hours? Have not all five worked as much for Your redemption as for that of the Star Gods?

Mother, hear me. Help them complete their task. If You require blood, then have they not given enough already?"

When the Mother replied it was only the Prophet who heard.

Blood, WolfStar? Who are you to speak to Me of blood sacrifice? Must not My Daughter offer the ultimate—

Mother! I beg You, do not vent Your righteous anger at my actions onto the Sentinels. They have done as much for you and Faraday as they have for me or any other.

"Help them," he said and, without affectation, let tears trail down his cheeks.

His sorrow turned the Mother's heart. She had been indifferent to the Repository that lurked in the depths of Fernbrake Lake, and She had been largely indifferent to the fact that Jack had watched over the Lake for so many years. But She found that She could not remain impervious to the Prophet's sorrow.

She, like so many others, had thought him indifferent to pain or love.

The Lake burst into brilliant emerald light that bathed the faces of those who watched. The Prophet turned to the Sentinels, the trails of his tears clearly evident on his cheeks; and the Sentinels were as much moved by his sorrow as they were by the power of the Mother.

"Bathe," he whispered. "Bathe in the waters, and the Mother will hold you and love you and suffuse you with Her power and strength and courage so that you may continue. You too, Zeherah, for you will have to bear the burden of care, love and courage over the next months."

And so, stumbling with pain and exhaustion, the Sentinels walked into the arms of the Mother.

42

Of Death and Inheritance

They rode through a world in the process of rapid recovery. It was late Wolf-month and thus winter still had a powerful grip on the land, but it was winter only, and Gorgrael's purchase had slipped over much of mid-Tencendor.

The StarMan and the Enchantress led their army, and ranged to either side rode the commanders Belial, Magariz and Ho'Demi, and all who marched behind them were sure that victory was but a month or two away at the most.

Axis turned to Magariz and Belial at his left and laughed. "See, my friends? Gorgrael's hold slips! Soon, perhaps, most of this land will be free of him."

Magariz shifted in his saddle. "Axis? When do we go north to challenge Timozel and his host?"

"Keen to win your lands back, Prince? Well, I don't blame you. I am as eager to see every Skraeling filth wiped from this land as you are. And to finally face this brother of mine," Axis added under his breath. "When?" His eyes briefly scanned the sky. "Spring, I think, or perhaps early summer. I have no more desire for winter campaigning."

"Is it wise to wait so long?" Ho'Demi asked, and Axis gazed at him, understanding. Even more than Magariz the Ravensbund chief was desperate to recover his land . . . and people, if any were left.

"We all need time to heal, Ho'Demi," Axis said. "This army may have had its spirits restored, but it needs its strength. Sigholt will give us the time and the opportunity to recover strength. And, Ho'Demi, look at this land." His hand swept in an arc, indicating the melting snow and the burgeoning greenery. "This process will spread north over the next months as Faraday continues to plant. I cannot defeat the Skraeling host until she has completed her planting, and neither do I wish to. I want this thaw to spread to the Icescarp Alps before

I ride north; it will put the Skraelings at a disadvantage and give us every advantage. Damn it, my friends! I want to win this time!"

He laughed, and his good humor was infectious. His commanders laughed with him, but after a moment, Belial turned away. Mother, pray he is right, he thought. Pray this time of beauty and hope will last, and he lifted his head to smile at his friend. Pray *this* time we have the reality, and not the lie.

Above Jervois Landing, the weather turned bitter, and they rode into a northerly wind that still held snow and traces of ice. But even though Gorgrael's grip still held firm over most of Ichtar, there were signs that a thaw would soon break through. And, as soon as they rode into the Urqhart Hills, much of the wind's bite was blunted, and the ground was generally free of snow.

Within a day or two they would spot the soft mist that hid Sigholt and the Lake of Life, and that meant they would be only a few hours' ride at the most from shelter and succor.

"And your wives." Azhure grinned at Belial and Magariz as they rode through one of the narrow passes early one afternoon. "You two shall have to give up your carefree bachelor existence to resume your husbandly duties. Perhaps you would rather ride straight for the north and Gorgrael's stronghold."

Belial winked at Magariz and laughed. "I cannot wait to see Cazna again, Azhure. All three of us," and he indicated Axis as well as Magariz, "were forced to abandon our wives within weeks of marriage to ride north. Axis has been more fortunate than us in resuming his conjugal burden a little earlier than planned."

They all laughed, but Axis caught Azhure's eye. *Have you told Magariz?*

No. That is Rivkah's right and pleasure.

Axis turned away, and Azhure took a deep breath. He had not reacted well to news of his mother's pregnancy.

The forward scouts spotted the blue mist late that afternoon, and Axis smiled at Azhure, then addressed Belial, Magariz and Ho'Demi. "Well, my friends, do we spend one more night out in the open and ride through in the morning, or do we—"

"Go in now!" Magariz said, his handsome face alive with excitement. "I fancy a warm bed tonight."

It will be warmer than you imagine, Axis thought dryly, then raised his eyebrows at the other two.

Belial laughed at Magariz's eagerness, but he did not try to conceal his own. "Would you camp out for the night knowing Azhure awaited you within, Axis? I think not. I vote we ride."

Ho'Demi nodded. "Sa'Kuya has told me of this magical fortress of yours, StarMan. I will have many things to say to the bridge."

"Then we will have a night ride and a starry welcome, my friends. Arne? Ride back and tell the unit commanders that we'll be continuing for the next few hours, but that at the end lies comfort and a good meal and rest from this wind."

As soon as they entered the blue mist the wind faded, and within minutes the entire army was encased in the eerie haze. Axis pushed Belaguez slightly ahead of the others, relishing the feel of the damp magic against his cheeks.

"Axis?" Azhure rode up beside him. "Will you disencumber Sigholt of her mist now that you're home?"

"Now that *we're* home," Axis said absently, then he smiled at Azhure. The blue mist clung to her form and she looked like an ethereal sorceress who had floated out of myth to tempt him.

It had been his intention to remove the enchantments enveloping Sigholt once he returned, but the sight of Azhure floating through the mist at his side changed his mind. "No," he said. "I'll let Sigholt linger amid her blue skirts for a while longer. Danger still lurks about the land."

Azhure smiled. She did not mind the thought that Sigholt would stay hidden some time yet. She was about to speak when she was halted by a loud, ecstatic voice.

"StarMan! Welcome home! Welcome!"

"The bridge," Axis said, and kicked Belaguez into a gallop.

The Keep and courtyard of Sigholt were alive with excitement as people rushed from beds, pulling cloaks over linen shifts or their nakedness, and milled about as the first riders cantered across the bridge.

About Sigholt the bridge's voice boomed, greeting friends and challenging strangers, but those already across forgot her in their own excited greetings.

Everyone was bathed in brilliant moonlight, and occasionally a fragile Moonwildflower would drift down on a moonbeam and tangle in someone's hair.

"Where is he? *Where is he?*" Cazna cried, her long black hair flying loose about her cloak, her hand gripping Rivkah's arm, frantic eyes searching the men and horses that now crowded the courtyard. "Isn't he here?"

Rivkah started to say something, her own eyes equally frantic, when a horseman rode up behind Cazna, leaned down, and hauled her into the saddle.

"Belial!" she whispered and then found she was allowed to say no more, nor that anymore needed to be said.

Rivkah stared at them a moment, wondering if she could interrupt to ask after Magariz, then decided against it. Neither Belial nor Cazna would hear her, anyway. She turned back to the crowd . . . and came face-to-face with her son.

"Axis."

He had dismounted, Belaguez's reins held loose in his hands, and he just stood, an island of stillness in the excitement about them, staring at his mother.

"Axis," she said, stepping forward, extending a hand, and after an instant's hesitation he took it, then hugged her. She was five months pregnant now, and as her belly pressed into his Axis battled to control his emotions. It seemed somehow wrong, to have a mother this old carrying a child.

And a brother. He could feel it.

Rivkah leaned back, knowing the touch of power. "I'm sorry, Axis," she said, and then cursed herself for apologizing to him.

"Rivkah!" Magariz's voice broke between them, and he unceremoniously shoved Axis aside to embrace his wife.

His reaction was entirely different to Axis'. "Rivkah!" he breathed, his eyes huge. "I . . . I . . ."

"Thirty-five years too late, Magariz," she said gently. "But an heir nevertheless. I hope your arthritis won't prevent you from dangling your son on your knee."

Axis turned away, his mouth tight. He handed Belaguez's reins to a stable boy, and looked about for Azhure.

He found her over by the main entrance to the Keep, Caelum in her arms.

"Papa!" Caelum shrieked, and Axis swung his son high into the air, then hugged him tight. Azhure stepped forward and put her arms about them both.

"A family again," she said, and Axis leaned down and kissed her.

"Roland?" he asked.

"Abed. Apparently he has not left it these past three weeks."

The light died in Axis' eyes; having spent so much time close to death himself, he did not know if he could witness someone else's death this soon. He nodded, then searched the crowd for Belial.

"Belial!" he called, spotting him, arm about Cazna, and waited impatiently as the pair moved over to him.

"Cazna," he said, forcing a smile, "I regret that I will have to take your husband away from you." Her face fell, but she straightened her shoulders stoically. "Belial, order the unit commanders to encamp the army on the grass between Sigholt and Lakesview, then join me in Roland's chambers. He's dying."

"Yes, StarMan." Belial kissed Cazna quickly, then disappeared into the throng, shouting out names.

Axis took Azhure's hand. "Come, let's see Roland."

Roland was one of Axis' last links with a life that was rapidly fading into distant memory. Axis stood for a moment at the side of his bed, staring at Roland, before sitting down on its edge and taking the Duke's hand.

"At least," Roland smiled, as if he knew what Axis was thinking, "I have the grace to die with the old order, and not hang around to clutter up the new."

"You are not clutter," Axis said. Beside him Azhure sank into a chair, Caelum in her arms. As they approached the chamber Axis had asked her the wisdom of bringing Caelum, but Caelum had answered that he spent many hours each day with Roland, and Azhure had met Axis' eyes. *He does not need to be sheltered from death, Axis.*

Roland's smile faded. His face was cadaverous, and his skin shone a dank gray. Axis was well acquainted with the look; the body was dead, but the spirit resisted and clung tenaciously to life. "There have been great battles, Axis, so I have heard."

Axis shrugged. "Battles, yes, whether great or not history will judge. But there are yet to be greater."

Roland's eyes shadowed. "Azhure told me Jorge was dead."

Axis nodded. "He was murdered by a Traitor. Timozel, son of the Lady of Tare."

If possible, Roland's skin shrank even closer against his bones. "Oh, no, Axis! I liked that boy."

"We all did," Axis said softly, "and we were all mistaken." He touched the sword by his side. "I carry Jorge's sword, Roland, the one Timozel used to murder him with, and I vowed on Jorge's body that one day I will sink it deep into Timozel's belly."

Roland looked away. "Perhaps I am not sad to be leaving this world, Axis. No doubt Jorge awaits me in the AfterLife, and will harangue me when I arrive for keeping him waiting."

Axis' eyes filled with tears. "Your children and grandchildren are well, Roland, and Aldeni itself reawakens from its death."

Roland nodded without interest, his thoughts still on Jorge. It would not be long before he saw his old friend again.

Azhure leaned over and kissed Roland softly on the mouth. "We will miss you, Roland. Miss your humor, and your wisdom." She lifted Caelum up so he could say his goodbyes.

The door opened and Belial stepped into the room. He exchanged glances with Axis, then sat down on the other side of the bed.

Roland looked at Belial. "The Enchantress says I am wise, Belial, but perhaps I erred too long in staying with Borneheld. What do you think?"

"I think that even Borneheld appreciated your wisdom," Belial said, trying to smile, "but I do not think he fully understood it."

Roland guffawed with laughter. "For a man who has ridden with the sword for so long, Belial, your courtly manners amaze me."

His laughter died suddenly. "I am afraid, Belial . . . and I think you are the only one in this room who truly understands that."

There was utter silence. Axis opened his mouth to say something, but found that there was nothing to say. Azhure rested her chin in Caelum's hair, her eyes steady on Roland's face Belial took Roland's hand and held it.

"I am afraid," Roland said again, then died.

For some time Axis stood and stared at Roland, then he roused and looked at Belial, still sitting on the other side of the bed, his head bowed "Belial?"

Belial raised his head, and Axis was not surprised to see that his friend's eyes were red-rimmed. "Belial," he said, "Roland is no longer afraid."

Belial shifted his eyes to Azhure, and she gazed placidly at him. "I will fetch the servants, Belial, and attend to Roland myself. There is no need for you to stay. Cazna no doubt awaits you."

"No," he said. "No. I loved and admired Roland too, and he would appreciate it if I stayed to help prepare him for burial and watched the night through to dawn."

As Azhure rose, Axis lifted Caelum from her arms. "Where are they?" he said flatly.

Axis had brought Caelum, not only because he needed the support, but because he thought the twins might react more favorably with their brother present.

Unfortunately, he was wrong.

He paused outside the door to their apartments, his hand on the doorknob, then he turned it quickly, before his courage failed him completely, and stepped through. He did not particularly want to meet these latest children of his, but it was a task that had to be done. Caelum twisted his head toward a door that led to a series of smaller rooms away from Axis and Azhure's main chambers, and Axis walked slowly over. There was a soft light shining from under the door and, when he opened it, he found Imibe leaning over one of two cribs in the first of the rooms.

Axis felt a shiver of premonition crawl down his spine and he berated himself silently; how can you call yourself a great warrior to be so terrified of two small babes?

Imibe straightened and Axis tipped his head toward the door; she curtsied silently and left, closing the door behind her.

Then, as Azhure had done two months before, Axis walked slowly over to the cribs to greet his children. And, as Azhure had, he reached his daughter's crib first. A daughter. Axis tried to conjure up some joy at this thought, for she was indeed a beautiful child, but she lay there and gazed at him with such studied lack of interest that Axis found he could not summon even a single spark of enthusiasm.

He reached down a hand and stroked her cheek. Why couldn't she love him? Why couldn't he love her? But all there was between them was indifference.

"Welcome RiverStar SunSoar, into the House of the Stars. My name is Axis, and I am your father." Much that you care, he thought, almost nauseated by the cold apathy that rose from her flat stare. "May you learn charity and tolerance," he said suddenly, "for your beauty will be nothing without them."

Then he put Caelum down and picked up his daughter, raising her to his face and kissing her brow gently. "I want to learn to love you, RiverStar," he whispered. "Please, let me love you."

But the baby turned her head away, and Axis, his mouth thinning, put her back in her crib and lifted Caelum back into his arms. "And now," he said, "your brother."

If he had felt apathy from RiverStar, then Axis was met with such a torrent of hatred from DragonStar that he took a shocked step back as soon as he looked into the crib.

"By the Stars!" he whispered, and Caelum whimpered, clinging close to his father. "What have I done to deserve this much revulsion?"

DragonStar twisted in the crib and glared at his father and his elder brother. His tiny fists clenched in rage and frustration; he'd hoped his father would never, *never*, come home.

"Why?" his father asked, leaning back over the crib. "Why?"

Because of what you did to my mother.

"There must be more to it than that!" Axis said, trying to control his temper. If that was all that lay between them, then why did DragonStar harbor so much ill-feeling toward Azhure as well?

The baby was silent, but his fists twitched, and Axis suddenly understood that if DragonStar was grown, he would have physically attacked him. As it was, Axis was stunned by the power the baby demonstrated.

I should be first, DragonStar said suddenly, *I should be your heir. With my power, my potential, I deserve to be your heir. Make me first and I will love you.*

Now Axis was even more shocked, and he saw that Caelum had lost most of his color. "No one chooses when or to whom they are born," he tried to explain in as moderate a tone as he could manage, then he repeated what he had said to RiverStar. "I want to love you. Let me love you."

DragonStar narrowed his eyes into tiny slits. *I want to be your heir! I must be StarSon, not that sop-eyed tot you carry in your arms! What quirk of fate seeded me SECOND into Azhure's used womb?*

Utterly appalled, Axis lost his temper. *How can you lie there and berate me for what I did to Azhure, when you tore her almost to shreds in your efforts to be born! You do not deserve her for your mother, and I, at least, am glad that you are not my eldest son! I have every reason to be glad you are not my heir, DragonStar. And I will not welcome you into the House of Stars until you have learned both humility and compassion!*

He took a huge breath, his eyes wide and furious, then he strode from the room.

DragonStar stared at him through the gaps in the wickerwork as long as he could, watching his father stride away, Caelum cuddled tight against his chest, and hated.

I will be your heir, he thought with malevolence surprisingly focused for one so young, *for none deserve it more than I!*

Axis had managed to control his temper by the time he found Azhure and Belial conversing quietly outside Roland's chamber, but anger still coursed through him. Azhure looked up as he approached, and she paled at what she saw on his face.

"I want DragonStar out of our apartments," he said tightly. "I do not want him near Caelum or his sister. If she is indifferent, then it is because of his influence."

Belial opened his mouth, appalled. "Axis? He is but a baby. How can you—"

Axis rounded on him, his temper out of control again. "But a baby? He hates enough for a battalion of Skraelings, Belial! I do not have to live with that, and I do not have to expose my other children to it!"

Azhure placed a hand on his arm, and Axis turned his eyes on her, sharing the memory of what had gone on in the room.

"Axis!"

Belial looked between the two of them, wishing he could understand. "Axis," he said, "do not let this night ruin your relationship with your son." He thought quickly. "If you like, Cazna and I will take him, give you time to think things over. I'm sure that Cazna would like to have a baby to croon over."

"Better to give her one yourself!" Axis snapped, but he nodded curtly after a minute. "As you wish. You can take the boy. But keep him out of my way!"

And with that he was gone, Azhure hurrying after him.

43

Choices

They farewelled Roland at dusk the next day, sending him on his journey into the AfterLife with a great pyre on the shores of the Lake of Life. Almost everyone attended, for Roland had been loved among the people of Lakesview as well as among most of the soldiers in Axis' army. Even the remainder of the Strike Force were there, forming an honor guard as Roland's body was carried from the Keep to the pyre.

The bridge wept as Roland passed over her for the last time, for they had spent many a long hour talking companionably together, and the bridge had come to respect him very much.

Cazna was there too, the baby boy in her arms, still faintly surprised at finding herself so precipitously cast into motherhood. But she smiled and crooned over the baby and remained totally insensitive to the fact that DragonStar directed a constant stream of malevolence toward his parents and elder brother.

When it was done, Axis waved SpikeFeather TrueSong over to him and Azhure.

"SpikeFeather," saluted smartly, then stood ready.

"SpikeFeather," Axis began, "we are worried."

Azhure took over. "Few Icarii have come this way, have they, Spike-Feather?"

"No, Enchantress," SpikeFeather said. "There were some here when we arrived, but most of them had been here since well before the StarMan locked Sigholt in her enchantments. Anyone else coming from Talon Spike would probably be unable to find the place."

"Have you heard word of any movement south from Talon Spike?"

SpikeFeather smiled. "Enchantress. You know how isolated Sigholt has been. If Icarii fly south then they would go through the Avarinheim, then directly south from the Nordra."

Azhure exchanged a worried glance with Axis. "SpikeFeather, you may not know this, but two months ago I sent word to RavenCrest to evacuate Talon Spike. I feared attack by Gryphon—Gorgrael still has many at his command—and you know Talon Spike is almost defenseless."

SpikeFeather's face darkened. "I could fly the Strike Force there within—"

"No," Axis said, raising his hand. "No. SpikeFeather, Gorgrael has over seven thousand Gryphon left . . ."

SpikeFeather blanched so badly Azhure thought he would faint.

"And I don't want you, or anyone else, to pretend that what's left of the Strike Force could protect Talon Spike against the Gryphon."

"We thought we could send you, perhaps with a Wing, north to Talon Spike," Azhure said, her eyes locked onto SpikeFeather's face "Find out what's happening, help if you can."

Azhure could go herself, but she was reluctant. She knew that Faraday would need her within six or seven weeks, and she didn't think she could get to Talon Spike and back with enough time to spare, her instinctive powers did not permit travel between sites as Axis' Enchanter powers did. Her instinct, however, did warn her that to attempt to confront the Gryphon now would be fatal, she still needed to grow further. And Azhure didn't want to leave Axis. Not when she'd just found him again. Or Caelum.

"It will be hard, if not impossible, to evacuate Talon Spike," SpikeFeather said. "There are the young children . . ."

"I sent word that RavenCrest should use the waterways to get the children to safety," Azhure said. "I can see no reason why Orr should refuse them."

SpikeFeather glanced at Axis; he had met the Ferryman two years ago, and he did not think the cantankerous Charonite would accede to anything without great persuasion. The Charonite did not think very highly of the Icarii, and if RavenCrest had gone down there personally and imperiously demanded that the Ferryman take the children . . . SpikeFeather shuddered, and his reaction did not go unnoticed by either Axis or Azhure.

"SpikeFeather," Axis said. "We need to know that the Icarii in Talon Spike are safe. Make sure they are flying to the Avarinheim, or even farther south into Tencendor, but make sure that they are out of there!"

SpikeFeather nodded, saluted, and turned away.

He left at dawn the next morning, a Wing behind him, and flew as hard and as fast as he could. They rested six or seven hours each night in the Avarinheim itself, with one of the Clans if they could find one, and the Avar reported that there had been no large-scale movement south since Yuletide.

One Clan leader had shrugged. "Daily flights of about two hundred for several weeks before Yuletide, and groups of fifteen to twenty every few days since, Crest-Leader, but that's all."

Stars! SpikeFeather cursed, tens of thousands must still be in Talon Spike. That night he gave the Wing only four hours' rest before he hustled them back into the sky.

When they finally arrived at Talon Spike they found the mountain still crowded with Icarii, a discovery that sent SpikeFeather spiraling as close to depression as he had since the virtual destruction of the Strike Force at the Azle.

They had been spotted approaching the mountain, and RavenCrest himself met SpikeFeather at the flight balconies at the very apex of Talon Spike.

"Talon," SpikeFeather said, spreading his wings behind him as he bowed low.

RavenCrest's mouth quirked in grim humor. "Crest-Leader I see, Spike-Feather, by the insignia you wear. Next you'll be telling me that you command the Strike Force itself."

SpikeFeather rose from his bow, and in his dark eyes was such great sorrow that RavenCrest recoiled. "No," he whispered. "It cannot be!"

"Talon," SpikeFeather began, but RavenCrest ignored him.

"I had heard," he said as he half turned away, "that the Strike Force had been devastated by the Gryphon, but FarSight? HoverEye? SharpEye? SpreadWing?"

At SpikeFeather's compassionate look, RavenCrest groaned.

"I had not thought it to be so bad," he said. "SpikeFeather?" He looked back at the birdman. "Is it so desperate?"

SpikeFeather shook his head, wishing RavenCrest would lead them inside out of the wind, "No, it is not. I believe there is still hope. But, sire, you *must* order the evacuation of the mountain No one can defend this mountain!"

RavenCrest finally motioned him inside. "Send your Wing for some refreshment, SpikeFeather, and we will talk."

"Sire," SpikeFeather said urgently, "we spent the night with the Avar, and we are not tired. My Wing can get the evacuation under way. But by the Stars, sire," SpikeFeather could restrain himself no longer, *"why is anyone here at all?"*

"You presume, SpikeFeather!" RavenCrest snapped, drawing himself to his full height and glaring at the birdman from under beetling black eyebrows.

But SpikeFeather was not daunted. "I presume nothing, sire," he said. "I merely ask why you are so lax regarding the survival of the Icarii."

Everyone within hearing distance froze and RavenCrest took a deep, astounded breath. "Crest-Leader," he said, "I will see you in my apartments *now!* As for your Wing, they may await your . . . or my . . . orders in the antechamber."

SpikeFeather could not mistake the threat in RavenCrest's voice, but still he did not back down. "Talon," he said, "I am here on orders from the StarMan and the Enchantress. They believe, rightly, that Talon Spike is facing an imminent threat. I am under their orders to hasten the evacuation any way I can."

If RavenCrest had any doubts concerning his place in the new order, then he was left in no doubt now. "I see, Crest-Leader," he said softly. "But I would still request that we speak privately in my apartments."

SpikeFeather inclined his head. "As you wish, Talon. But I have a great deal to do here and I will not have time for an extended chat."

RavenCrest stared at him, then turned on his heel and stalked toward the closest shaft, stepping into the void and spiraling down on wings stiff with affront.

"Sire," SpikeFeather said when they were alone, "I did not mean to offend. But time is critical."

"SpikeFeather," RavenCrest sighed, "I do understand the danger. But evacuation has been fraught with so many difficulties."

SpikeFeather shuffled in impatience, but RavenCrest ignored him. "I had to take advice from the Elders, and I had to call the Assembly."

Oh, for the sake of the heavens! SpikeFeather thought, you called the Assembly on this? Couldn't you take the initiative just this once?

RavenCrest shrugged. "We were undecided on the matter. Many do not want to go—"

"Then they will die," SpikeFeather said, hoping to shake RavenCrest into some action.

"And I cannot blame them!" RavenCrest retorted, his violet eyes snapping. "We have lived here in safety for over a thousand years, and we do not know what awaits us in the south!"

"*Life* awaits you in the south, RavenCrest!" SpikeFeather shouted. "*Damn you!* What have the Strike Force fought for, died for, if not to win the Icarii back their southern lands? Cities are springing to life, sacred sites are once again open, the forest springs anew, *that* is what awaits you!" He took a huge breath, the tendons standing out on his neck. "Only death waits for you here. It could be minutes away, hours, perhaps weeks. No one knows. But what gives *you* the right to gamble with the lives of our people, RavenCrest? What?"

"He carries many cares, Crest-Leader," a gentle voice said behind Spike-Feather and he whirled about. BrightFeather, RavenCrest's wife, had entered through a silent door and was walking toward him. "And has seen the world he has known disintegrate about him RavenCrest and myself," she walked to her husband's side and took his hand, "are of the Elders now, and we find it hard to accept such sudden change."

"Will you find it easier to accept sudden death?"

RavenCrest rubbed his hand across his eyes. "If I give the order, then where will our people go, SpikeFeather?"

SpikeFeather made a gesture of impatience. "To the southern cities in the Minaret Peaks. To the Avarinheim. To Sigholt, even Carlon, perhaps even the Island of Mist and Memory."

"SpikeFeather, there are many tens of thousands of Icarii in Talon Spike, The emerging Minaret cities cannot yet hold them all, and our friends in the Avarinheim have scarcely enough to feed themselves let alone all of us as well. I cannot let my people fly into such an unknown."

"We will find room for them—"

RavenCrest demurred.

"Then you are worse than WolfStar," SpikeFeather said with icy deadliness, "for you will have the blood of tens of thousands, perhaps the extermination of an entire race, on your conscience. He has but the blood of two hundred children."

RavenCrest and BrightFeather both stared at him, stricken. "You cannot mean what you have just said," RavenCrest began.

"I meant every word of it."

RavenCrest and his wife continued to stare at him. This was not the SpikeFeather TrueSong they remembered.

"Have the courage to lead your people to safety," SpikeFeather said quietly. "Or I will do it for you."

"But where will we go?" fluttered the birdwoman, her great green eyes anxious. "And what will we take? Oh, I think this decision to fly south is far too hasty. I think—"

"I have no time to listen to your qualms, madam," SpikeFeather said. "If you will just follow the shaft to the flight balconies then you can be off. There is no time for baggage. I'm sure your life and the life of your son," he bowed at the adolescent boy, "are far more important." The boy, of a more adventuresome mind than his mother, winked at SpikeFeather and hurried his mother off.

RavenCrest had acquiesced. Once SpikeFeather had the Talon's approval and, more importantly, his authority, he wasted no time. Every minute might mean a life wasted; every hour several hundred at least.

Many of the Icarii were willing to go; they had been eager to fly south anyway. In the five hours since SpikeFeather had left RavenCrest's apartment at a flat-out run, over eight thousand Icarii had managed to leave; for the Avarinheim in the first instance, where all would mass, then for wherever there was room. SpikeFeather hoped the goodwill that Axis and Azhure had generated among the Acharites toward the return of the Icarii would stretch to a sudden invasion of tens of thousands of the birdpeople.

But if the younger generations were ready and eager to leave, the older Icarii exhibited a frustrating inability to make up their minds. There was too much at stake; too many uncertainties lay before them; what would happen to Talon Spike if they left it, and who had counted these Gryphon anyway?

To these queries SpikeFeather had no answer save that he believed the Enchantress when she said that she knew. For many of the Icarii, that was not enough. Eventually SpikeFeather resorted to threat and intimidation. He had no patience with those who demurred. He had seen Wing-mates slaughtered and had felt the grip of Gryphon talons himself. And when he shouted, the Icarii listened. SpikeFeather had been to the borders of death and back, and his experience gave him an aura that, when augmented with fury, quieted most objections and convinced most waverers.

Stars save them, SpikeFeather prayed as he stood on the lip of the flight balcony watching another group of Icarii lift off, if the Gryphon strike them in the air. The thermals to the south were black with wings, but, if anything, their numbers gave them some protection, and as soon as they were within reach of the Earth Tree's Song over the northern Avarinheim they would be safe.

He stood back from the lip and strode into Talon Spike, standing aside briefly for another wave of evacuees to pass by him. The members of his Wing were accomplishing wonders in getting the Icarii out, and he hoped their names would live in Icarii legend for the service they were doing their fellows.

But there was one task SpikeFeather knew he would have to see to personally.

The children. Those who had not yet developed their wings, or those whose wings and flight muscles were still so immature they would not be able to cope with the flight into the Avarinheim. Infants were carried strapped to their mothers' breasts, but toddlers and older would have to walk—or float.

SpikeFeather had ordered that the children be grouped in one of the lower chambers of the Talon Spike complex, then he would take them down to the waterways himself, for he thought the request should be made by someone whom the Ferryman had met before.

And what price would he ask?

SpikeFeather shrugged. That was hours into the future, for he doubted the children would be able to negotiate the stairwell any faster than the adult Icarii. But he underestimated the enthusiasm and agility of the children.

SpikeFeather spiraled down into the chamber where the children had assembled under the guidance of two members of his Wing, and then he hovered, gape-mouthed in astonishment. He had assumed there might be a score of children, perhaps two score, but he had not expected to be confronted with almost six hundred bright and eager uplifted faces.

He slowly settled to the floor and turned to FairEye, one of the Wing members. She shrugged, understanding SpikeFeather's astonishment. "I reacted the same way, Crest-Leader. I did not realize how many children there were."

SpikeFeather turned back to the throng before him. "Stars save me," he muttered, "what is the Ferryman going to say?"

There was nothing for it but to lead them downward. So SpikeFeather waved the two Wing members back to their duties shepherding the adults out of the mountain, and turned back to face the children.

He cleared his throat, then realized he had no idea what he would say. SpikeFeather was not very good with children.

"Ah," he began lamely, "no doubt you're wondering . . ." No, that wouldn't do.

"Um, we're about to embark on a remarkable adventure . . ." Stars! That was even worse!

"Listen," he said eventually, using his normal speaking voice and not patronizing them at all, "Talon Spike faces a terrible danger."

"Gryphon," one tiny child piped up from the front.

"Yes, Gryphon. Gorgrael the Destroyer—you've heard of him?"

Hundreds of faces nodded.

"Well, Gorgrael has thousands of Gryphon, and many fear that he will throw them at Talon Spike."

"We'd be slaughtered if we stayed," one red-haired girl said, her voice practical, and SpikeFeather glanced at her.

"Yes, everyone would die. So I'm here to organize everyone to safety, and because it'd be too dangerous to lead you down the ice paths by the Nordra, I'm going to try something different."

"FairEye said that we're going to go by the waterways!" an excited child cried. "What are the waterways?"

For the next ten minutes SpikeFeather explained about the UnderWorld and the Charonites. He related how he had traveled the waterways with Rivkah, the Enchantress and StarDrifter some two years ago, and that all had traveled safely and with minimal fuss.

"So," he finished, "do you think you'd like to try the waterways?"

A chorus of excited voices assured him that they would, and SpikeFeather could see no child who looked overly nervous about the prospect. Asking the older children each to take a younger child's hand, SpikeFeather shepherded the crowd toward the first of the tunnels.

He led, because only he knew the correct turnings to take, and he had to trust that every child followed obediently. What if one took a wrong turning and the hundreds who followed got lost with him? What if one of the younger ones panicked, and the back ranks refused to go any farther?

But no one took the wrong turning and no one panicked, and all kept up with no complaints. After ten minutes or so one of the children lifted her voice in song, and within heartbeats every child had taken up the melody. It lifted

SpikeFeather's heart, and reminded him that there was hope for the future.

It took them just over an hour and a half to reach the well to the UnderWorld.

Many of the children remarked on the beautiful well that wound down into the earth, and traced the carvings of the dancers in the walls with their fingers. And each stepped eagerly onto the translucent pink marble staircase that wound down about the walls of the well.

And so, softly singing, the children of the Icarii nation walked lightly down into the UnderWorld.

Previously, SpikeFeather had traveled with injured Icarii, and the children made much faster work of the descent than the adults had. They needed no breaks, and every time SpikeFeather paused to look at the staircase above him he could see line after line of children filing down, all singing, all holding hands.

"If I never do anything else in life," he murmured to himself on one occasion as he stood watching the children step down two-by-two, "then I am glad I have seen this. Pray that I am not leading them to their doom."

After several hours they gathered in the stark gray chamber at the base of the well, SpikeFeather making sure that none of the children ventured too close to the lip of the waterway. They were silent now, overawed by the solemnity of the chamber and by the water flowing gently by, stars gleaming in its midst.

As the last child stepped into the chamber, SpikeFeather took a nervous breath and stepped over to the golden tripod that held the bell. He hesitated, then reached out with his fingertips and struck it.

Three clear chimes rang out, and some of the children stirred nervously.

"It is all right," SpikeFeather said gently, turning back to the crowd. "The Ferryman will take some hours before he—"

Then he noticed that the children were not looking at him, but staring down one of the tunnels from which the water emerged.

There was a light bobbing in the distance.

How quick the Ferryman was! SpikeFeather clenched his fists briefly, nervousness raising the dark red feathers on the back of his neck.

A large, flat-bottomed boat glided into the chamber, a cloaked figure seated in its stern, his hands folded, his hooded head bowed. As the boat stopped by SpikeFeather, the Ferryman raised his head.

"Who summons the Ferryman?" he asked in a gruff voice. "Who rings the bell?"

SpikeFeather stepped forward and bowed so low he almost knelt; behind him his wings scraped the surface of the stone floor as they spread out three paces either side of him.

"I do, Ferryman," he said, his eyes downcast, "Crest-Leader SpikeFeather TrueSong, of the Icarii Strike Force."

"What?" The Ferryman's voice sounded surprised. "What, SpikeFeather—and don't think that I don't remember you—no Enchanters this time to harry and annoy me?"

SpikeFeather raised his eyes. "No, Ferryman. None but myself and the innocent children of the Icarii race."

The Ferryman burst into laughter and pulled the hood back from his face, revealing the bald cadaverous features surrounding his incongruously childlike violet eyes. "No children are innocent, SpikeFeather, for the moment they draw breath they draw in the experience of life. Come now, stand up, and tell me what you do here."

SpikeFeather straightened. "Ferryman, I come to ask you a great boon."

"A boon? Surely you know better than that, SpikeFeather."

SpikeFeather licked his suddenly dry lips. "Ferryman, Gryphon threaten Talon Spike and we must evacuate. These children cannot fly, and we cannot use the exposed icy walks by the Nordra Ferryman—"

"No."

"You have not heard my request!" SpikeFeather cried, stepping forward, his hand out in entreaty.

The Ferryman stared at him. "You want me to somehow spirit these children to safety, SpikeFeather."

"Yes, I—"

"No."

"Why not?"

"I do not particularly like children, and this is such a rabble of them!"

SpikeFeather's lips thinned. "They are well behaved and polite, Ferryman, and they deserve the chance of life."

The Ferryman shook his head, and slowly drew his ruby hood over his head.

"Axis sent them to you!" SpikeFeather cried.

"I have fulfilled my debt to Axis."

"And Azhure!"

The Ferryman's hands paused, but then he drew the hood further over his head, shading his entire face. "No."

"I am willing to pay the price."

The Ferryman's sallow face peered out from beneath the ruby hood. "The price?"

"The greatest mystery of all, Ferryman. A life."

Orr stared at SpikeFeather. The birdman stood very tall now, his dark eyes calm, his entire bearing dignified and proud, his dark red wings held out slightly away from his body.

"Whose life?" the Ferryman whispered.

SpikeFeather gazed steadily at him. "Mine."

The entire chamber was silent. Every child's gaze was fixed on Spike-Feather.

"You are willing to give your life for these children, SpikeFeather True-Song?"

"It is a tiny price to pay, Ferryman."

"But you are young, vital . . . courageous."

SpikeFeather was silent, holding the Ferryman's eyes in his own.

"Very well," the Ferryman said, closing the deal, "I accept. Your life for transportation of these children." But he still watched SpikeFeather closely.

SpikeFeather relaxed in relief. "Thank you, Ferryman," he said. "I am honored that you think me worthy the price."

No, I am honored, the Ferryman whispered in his mind, *for few would have offered themselves. Even when I told StarDrifter of the price he glanced about the group he led, never once considering himself. No, I am honored, SpikeFeather TrueSong.*

"Now, where would you like these children to go?"

SpikeFeather's mouth slowly opened. He had thought about everything else but the children's eventual destination. "Ah . . . Sigholt?"

"Easily done, SpikeFeather, for these waters empty into the Lake of Life herself. Now, if the children would like to step into the boat . . ." and he motioned to the first ranks of children impatiently.

"But they will not all fit, Ferryman," SpikeFeather began, then he saw the Ferryman smile and indicate behind him.

"Perhaps you did not notice these, SpikeFeather." Ranged behind the Ferryman's boat, each with its lights glowing gently, were a dozen more of the craft bobbing gently, all connected by ropes.

SpikeFeather nodded, and waved the children forward. Slowly, but with growing assurance, they stepped calmly into the boats. The Ferryman got out of the first boat as the children settled themselves down, waited until all the boats were full and not a single child remained unseated, then turned to SpikeFeather.

"Your life, SpikeFeather," he said, and placed his hand over SpikeFeather's face.

The birdman tensed, but he was not afraid. He did not think the Ferryman would demand a painful death. He waited, holding his breath, but nothing happened.

Exhaling slowly, he finally opened his eyes. Between the Ferryman's outstretched fingers he could see the ancient Charonite's face stretched in a crazy grin.

"What did you think I was going to do?" the Ferryman cackled. "Smite you between the eyes with a hitherto well-concealed mace?"

He dropped his hand and smiled at SpikeFeather. "A life, SpikeFeather, and you thought I meant to *take* your life!"

"Well, what *do* you mean to do?" SpikeFeather said, furious. He had been prepared to meet his death with dignity, and he did not like the laughter with which his gift was greeted.

You are right, SpikeFeather TrueSong. Forgive me.

The Ferryman straightened, sober, and placed his hand back over Spike-Feather's face. "SpikeFeather," he said. "I meant only the use of your life. A life is a priceless thing, but only if it walks and breathes. A life snuffed out is worth nothing at all. Do you understand?"

SpikeFeather nodded slowly under the Ferryman's fingers. "You want me to offer you the use of my life."

"Yes. Good. But your life will still largely be your own. SpikeFeather, I would make use of your life to aid the Charonites. We are few now, and our own lives are bound to these waterways. But we have knowledge, much useful knowledge, and I think that it is time we shared some of it. You are yet a young birdman, but in some years I will summon you back to the waterways. And then I will teach you. Will you accept that?"

SpikeFeather nodded again as the Ferryman dropped his hand. "I accept, but I thought you taught Axis all you knew?"

"I taught him many things that he needed to know," Orr said, "but I certainly did not teach him everything. The rest I will pass on to you, SpikeFeather TrueSong."

SpikeFeather felt his eyes fill with tears. "Thank you for my life, Ferryman."

No. I thank you for your life, SpikeFeather. Then he turned and settled himself in the lead boat, folding his cloak about him.

"Ready?" he called to the children, and they nodded dumbly, overawed by the Ferryman.

"Well, then," he said, "let us go," and the boats moved of their own volition toward the archway in the far wall. As they went, the Ferryman looked over his shoulder, and SpikeFeather thought he could see the gleam of a smile beneath his hood.

As the first boat passed beneath the archway SpikeFeather heard one of the children speak.

"Ferryman, do you mind if we sing?"

"I would be honored," the Ferryman said, and to SpikeFeather's mind, it sounded as if he truly was.

He spiraled up and up, hardly having to work himself, letting the warm wind that rose out of the depths of the world lift him farther into Talon Spike. After reaching the lower chambers of the complex, it was only another hour before he was standing in the all-but-deserted Assembly Chamber of Talon Spike.

Here, seated calmly and quietly, were some eighteen hundred Icarii who, the members of the Wing informed him, refused to leave Talon Spike. The rest had gone.

SpikeFeather strode into the center of the violet-veined, golden marble floor, horrified by the group's obvious intention to die. His eyes circled the Chamber, able to name every face he saw. At the last one he stopped.

RavenCrest SunSoar, Talon of all the Icarii, slowly rose to his feet. He was dressed in the royal violet robes, and he wore the jeweled torc of Talon about his neck. Beside him BrightFeather sat calmly, also in her robes and jewels of office.

"We have decided to die here," RavenCrest said. "We were all born here, and we are all Elders. Here we will also die."

"RavenCrest—" SpikeFeather began, but RavenCrest held up his hand.

"We will not flee, not from the life we have known. There is a new world, a new order out there, but we do not think we want to be part of it. Maybe the Gryphon will come, maybe not, but whatever happens, here we will remain."

"RavenCrest, there is no need for this. All can escape. If you but follow me—"

"No," RavenCrest said, then he reached behind his neck and undid the jeweled torc. "I believe that Axis has handed FreeFall back his heritage. Give this to my son. He will be Talon now, and he will be a great Talon. I wish I could have seen him again, SpikeFeather, but that was not to be."

"Stars damn you!" SpikeFeather screamed, refusing to take the torc. *"This does not have to be!"*

"This is how we want it to be," BrightFeather said softly from her seat. "Don't we all have the choice to do what we will with our lives? If we choose to die, can you stand there and say we are wrong?"

SpikeFeather sobbed, blaming himself for their intransigence, but he could not fault them. Not when he had freely offered his own life to the Ferryman. "Please," he begged, going down on his knees, his red wings spread out behind him. "Do not do this!"

RavenCrest knelt before him and cradled SpikeFeather's face in his hands. "Go, SpikeFeather. Take your Wing and go. Here, take this now," he pressed the torc into SpikeFeather's reluctant hands, "and keep it safe for FreeFall. Kiss him for me, and kiss EvenSong too, and berate them fiercely if they have not already married. SpikeFeather, promise me that when these wars are over, when all the death is done, the Icarii will come back here, and light funeral pyres in our memory, and wipe the blood from the walls and reconsecrate this place in the name of the Star Gods and in the name of those who have lived here and died here and were happy here."

SpikeFeather lifted his head back and screamed, but RavenCrest spoke over the echoes.

"Promise me this, SpikeFeather, promise me that above all others you will reconsecrate this wondrous place, which has nurtured us and loved us, to MorningStar SunSoar, my mother, for above all others, she was beautiful and beloved."

Axis and Azhure were bathing in the waters of the Lake of Life, laughing gently beneath the light of the moon, when they turned their heads, astounded.

Floating toward them across the Lake were thirteen boats, each filled with softly singing children.

The Ferryman was nowhere to be seen.

44

The Clearance of Ichtar

The six hundred Icarii children were boarded out with families in Lakesview. Most families had taken in one or two children, keeping brothers and sisters together; now the children spent their mornings at school with the Acharite children (and there had been a flurry trying to find the desks and stools to accommodate them all) and their afternoons exploring the fragrant hills surrounding the Lake. They did not seem to miss their parents overmuch and never complained. When SpikeFeather arrived back in Sigholt he talked with many of them, and he told Axis that he thought they had been changed by their trip through the waterways of the Under World.

Axis wondered what Orr had said to them, and wondered further if he had *taught* them anything. But the children only looked at him with puzzled eyes when he asked, and eventually he stopped worrying, smiled, and told them to run and play.

Axis had been upset but not entirely surprised by SpikeFeather's news. RavenCrest had never been comfortable with the changes that Axis' presence brought, nor with the knowledge that he lived during the time of the Prophecy of the Destroyer. Axis fingered the jeweled torc that SpikeFeather handed him, his eyes thoughtful.

"Perhaps if I go north myself," Azhure said. "Perhaps I can persuade them to leave."

"No," Axis said, raising his eyes. "No. I cannot spare you. How long would it take for you to travel north and then return?"

"I could find the entrance to the waterways," she said, trying not to believe him but knowing he was right.

"And where is it?" Axis gestured out the window over the Lake. "I do not know, and yet I know more about the waterways than any other here. SpikeFeather?"

"StarMan?"

"I presume you tried to persuade RavenCrest to leave?"

SpikeFeather was silent. How to put into words his frantic appeals? "I tried," he eventually said, and Axis nodded, seeing the pain in his eyes.

"Azhure, you were never particularly close to RavenCrest. If SpikeFeather could not persuade him, then you surely could not. He has made his choice, and those with him." He sighed, and gave the torc back to SpikeFeather. "RavenCrest entrusted this to you, SpikeFeather. Keep it safe . . . for when it is needed. When . . . when we know . . . I shall send for FreeFall. He will have to tear himself from the Island of Mist and Memory and assume his regal duties. There is nothing we can do about Talon Spike. We have warned, and SpikeFeather has saved the majority, but there is nothing we can do."

He sent a silent query to Azhure, wondering if there was, in fact, anything she could do about the Gryphon, but she shook her head and turned away. She would know when it was time to hunt the Gryphon, and it was not yet. Those remaining in Talon Spike would have to cope without her.

If the mountain was attacked.

And Azhure truly did not want to go north at the moment. There was a feeling growing in her blood that she would be needed to the east within a month or two, needed to hunt something . . . something other than Gryphon. Something connected with Faraday.

Artor still lurked to the east, and while the death of RavenCrest, BrightFeather and the other Elders was heart-wrenching, if Artor were to stop Faraday it would be disastrous. So Azhure held her peace. Besides, there was too much work to be done in Ichtar.

From the end of Raven-month Axis embarked on his mission to reclaim Ichtar. He made careful use of farflight scouts to the north to make sure that the Skraeling host had indeed drawn back to the extreme north, then he ordered that the province be cleared of any remaining Skraeling nests. Bands of men some thousand strong were sent on expeditions through the province to scout out nests. Farflight scouts went with them to report on their progress, and by mid-Hungry-month Axis received word that several small nests had been discovered and had, with minimal casualties to the troops, been destroyed. Hsingard had been one of the major breeding grounds for the Skraelings, and Azhure had already cleared it.

Axis remained in Sigholt until the second week in Hungry-month when word reached him that one of the bands of nest-destroyers had stumbled upon a series of nests so extensive they could not hope to destroy them.

"Where?" he asked the farflight scout.

"In the northern Urqhart Hills," the scout replied.

"In the mines," Rivkah said. She had been standing at the window in the map room of the Keep, and now she turned to look at Axis. He kept his eyes firmly on her face, refusing to be distracted by the growing mound of her belly. In the month since he had been home, neither he nor Rivkah had ever discussed her pregnancy.

"The mines there are the most extensive, and the richest, in the entire range of hills, Axis." Rivkah sat down at the table and Axis' eyes relaxed slightly. "Searlas once boasted to me that their shafts stretched into the ground for over half a league, and their tunnels extended many leagues under the hills."

"There could be tens of thousands down there," Azhure murmured, and she glanced at the hound lying at her feet. "The men will not be able to touch them without being eaten themselves."

Axis looked at her, his eyes smiling. "Azhure, it has occurred to me that we have been sitting here safe and warm, cradled in Sigholt's loving mists, when Belial and Magariz brave the dangers and reap the excitement of the Skraeling chase. Soon they shall be the stuff of legends, and we the forgotten heroes."

She grinned. "We are growing fat with idleness, my love."

"Shall we hunt?" Axis whispered, and Azhure felt her blood leap. The northern Urqhart Hills would be only a few days' ride away and the hunt would take but the space of a night. They could be home in just over a week.

Rivkah, watching them, realized they had forgotten the existence of every other person in the map room.

"We hunt," Azhure replied, her eyes locked with Axis', and he smiled slowly. "We hunt."

She sat back in the saddle, feeling the beat of the Star Dance every time she swayed to Venator's stride, and looked over to Axis, loving him. He rode relaxed and easy, clad in his fawn tunic and breeches with the crimson cloak flying back from his shoulders and the bloodied sun blazing across his chest. Azhure thought she had not seen him looking so relaxed and confident nor so vigorous, since the ride south through Skarabost toward Carlon.

Save the Alaunt and their horses, Axis and Azhure were alone.

They had been riding two days now, and the northern Urqhart Hills loomed in the distance. They would reach them tonight.

Mud spattered the horses' legs and bellies, and made for uncomfortable sleeping, but both Azhure and Axis reveled in the mud, for it meant that Gorgrael's hold loosened, and the winter slid still farther north.

Ahead of them the Alaunt streamed, their noses close to the ground.

"Another two hours' ride," Axis said. "Ho'Demi tells me they wait in the first of the passes."

Ho'Demi led this particular force, and if Ho'Demi was not willing to go down those mines then the danger must be great indeed.

Azhure nodded. She had caught the shadow if not the substance of Ho'Demi's thought to Axis. "Has he lost any men?"

"Five or six, apparently among those who were the first to investigate the mines. Azhure, are you sure you can do this?"

Axis' eyes were troubled, and not without reason. From the sketchy reports they'd received so far, it seemed that the nests in the northern mines might prove more extensive than those Hsingard had concealed . . . and Azhure had shared with him her feelings of exhaustion after that particular hunt.

She smiled to herself. "I will be well, Axis. I, we, have both grown in the last month. And," she tossed her head and laughed, revelling in the wind through her hair, "this will be the first time we have fought together in months."

So wrapped were they in each other, neither noticed the black speck circling far above.

Ho'Demi leaped to his feet as he heard the rattle of horses' hooves. "StarMan, Enchantress!" He held out his hand to help Azhure from her horse, but she jumped down even as he stepped toward her.

"Ho'Demi." Azhure took his hand briefly, then stood aside so Axis could greet the Ravensbund chief. Ho'Demi looked behind them, frowning. All he could see were the Alaunt nosing about the campsite.

"Where is your force?" he asked. "These mines are going to take at least five thousand men to clear them."

Axis grinned at Azhure, then clapped Ho'Demi on the shoulder. "Five thousand, my friend . . . or just Azhure and myself."

Ho'Demi's eyes widened. "StarMan, you cannot mean . . . !"

But Axis returned Ho'Demi's stare flatly. "Do you doubt us, Ho'Demi?"

The Ravensbundman dropped his eyes instantly. "No, StarMan. I did not mean to question, but . . ."

"Ho'Demi," Azhure took his arm. "Tell us about these mines. Have your Chatterlings provided any useful information? Do they have cousins awaiting below who could help?"

They sat down before Ho'Demi's fire, the ground mercifully well drained on these slopes. About them the troops huddled at their own fires, but their eyes were riveted on the StarMan and Enchantress, and the whisper quickly spread that the two would clear the mines themselves.

"I am afraid the Chatterlings have been relatively unhelpful, Enchantress. They are of opals only, and they say that the emeralds and diamonds mined here were dead gems, with no heart or soul. Will they help? No. The bargain was that they help in the Murkle Mountains, and now they hunger only for their new home. They will be of no use."

"No matter," Azhure said lightly, and fingered the Wolven by her side.

"Tell us what you know," Axis asked, and Ho'Demi drew a rough sketch of the mines' layout in the earth before them.

"The shafts are not vertical, but slope down steeply for several hundred paces before they branch out into tunnels. There are five mines here, all have one main shaft, and all are interconnected via their tunnel systems."

"So . . . five exits," Axis said. He raised his eyes. "Azhure?"

"Do you know where the Skraelings are concentrated, Ho'Demi?"

"Yes, Enchantress. Here, here, and here." He pointed to the central three mines. "The top tunnels are free, but the lower ones, those over fifteen-hundred paces deep, are littered with hatchlings and eggs."

"And adults?"

"Yes. Many of them. This must be one of the most heavily guarded nest sites."

Axis leaned back and gazed at the Ravensbund Chief. "Give me an estimate."

"Of adults? It is hard to say, StarMan, for none of us lingered to take a census, but I would say there must easily be eight to ten thousand adults, and thirty times more younglings in various stages of growth."

Axis looked sharply at Azhure. "And what did you face in Hsingard?"

"Perhaps eight or nine thousand all told—adults as well as younglings."

"It is too dangerous for you," he said, his eyes on her face.

"I want to hunt, Axis."

"Nevertheless . . ."

Ho'Demi looked between the two of them. "Let me help, Enchantress. I have a thousand men here, many of them archers. Azhure, all of us want to hunt. *Use us!*"

"Azhure?" Axis raised his eyebrows.

She relaxed and smiled, spreading her hands in a gesture of helplessness. "I am outnumbered, gentlemen. Very well, Ho'Demi, I will use your men and thank you for them. Now." Her eyes dropped to the rough map Ho'Demi had drawn and her tone turned brisk. "This is what we shall do."

Azhure and Axis jogged down the steeply sloping shaft of the easternmost mine until they reached the opening of the fourth tunnel that branched off to their left.

"This must be it," Axis said quietly, and felt in the darkness for Azhure's hand. They carried no light with them and Axis did not yet make use of the Star Dance to construct a ball of light as he had in Hsingard. Not wanting to give the Skraelings warning, both relied exclusively on their innate powers to negotiate the shaft; neither had stumbled once during the descent.

At Azhure's side Sicarius whined softly and she reached down and touched his head briefly. The hound was quivering with excitement but she kept him and the other two Alaunt with him back for the moment.

"Axis?"

"Wait," he whispered. *Ho'Demi? Are you ready?*

Yes, StarMan. All is ready.

Axis smiled and Azhure felt it. "Then let us hunt," she cried, her voice ringing through the tunnel before her. "Hunt!"

She gestured with her hand and the three Alaunt seethed forward, the soft sounds of their running disappearing within instants. Music whispered through the air and the ball of light appeared in Axis' hands.

Azhure blinked in the sudden radiance. "Axis . . ."

"I know, Azhure, I know. This light and the ward of protection. That is all." Azhure was worried that in the heat of the hunt Axis might try to use the power of the Star Dance to try to kill the Skraelings, and she frowned, wondering if she should warn him yet again.

"I *know!*" he said sharply, and she smiled.

"I'm sorry, Axis. Let's go," and she turned and strode into the tunnel, lifting an arrow from the quiver on her back to fit to the Wolven as she went.

Ho'Demi and his men had managed to completely block the entrance of the extreme western shaft with rubble and rocks so that no Skraelings could escape that way. And now, if all was going according to plan, Ho'Demi would have divided his force into three groups that each advanced down one of the three central shafts, brands blazing and four Alaunt hunting before them.

The plan was to drive all Skraelings toward a natural cavern at the foot of the shaft to the immediate west of the one Azhure and Axis had descended; there, Azhure had smiled at Ho'Demi, we can all have our fill of death.

And so it was.

The noise, light and hounds accompanying the bands of men advancing down the three central shafts terrified the Skraelings so much that they fled in a whispering mob, unsure about what directions to take, colliding and scrabbling among themselves until many died from the teeth and claws of their neighbors and parents before their enemies had even reached them. Among them leaped the twelve hounds who ran before the men, clamoring and snarling, frightening the Skraelings into a stampede east, filling the cavern and then racing along the tunnel toward the final shaft . . . toward Azhure.

The mob met Sicarius and his two companions first. The hounds were lying in wait for them, bellies pressed to the floor of the tunnel, and as the Skraelings rushed over the top of them the hounds chopped and snapped, and with each bite a hatchling died, its back broken or its head disengaged from its neck.

None of the adults cared. They seethed forward, desperate to escape from hounds and light and noise until . . . until . . . the leading pack of Skraelings lurched to a halt, shrieking, their hands raised uselessly to their faces, trying unsuccessfully to back up against the mob behind them.

Along the tunnel flew an arrow. The Skraelings could not yet see it, but they could feel it. It was straight and true and blue-fletched, it glowed and sparked with death—and it was coming straight for them.

And in an instant they could see it, too. It flew around the final bend in the tunnel, keeping to the very center of the passage, its metal head glowing as bright as a sun, its blue feathers screaming as they slid through the air.

The three Alaunt snapping at the bellies and feet of the pack flattened themselves along the tunnel floor.

The arrow exploded the instant it hit the first line of Skraelings, now turned to face their companions in a futile effort to flee back the way they had come. A flame, at first gold, then orange, then shading into a deep indigo, flared through the ranks of the Skraelings, eating its way back through the tunnel as far as the cavern.

Every Skraeling caught in that tunnel turned to gray ash, and, as the ash drifted to the floor it turned violet, and by the time it settled on the floor it had been changed into Moonwildflowers, and the floor was carpeted in beauty.

Now the tunnel itself was lit with a gentle blue radiance.

Azhure laughed as she strode through the flowers, leaning down and snatching up the arrow as she went. Before her the hounds rose, flowers cascading to either side, and bounded forward to continue the hunt. Behind her Axis walked, extinguishing his ball of flame, an expression of utter wonder mixing with quiet pride on his face.

Then he saw Azhure stumble slightly, and he hurried to catch up.

The Skraelings were trapped in the cavern, screaming and writhing, arrows raining down on them from behind and above and before. The light and the hounds were bad enough, but the woman with the arrows was murderous. And so they died, weeping and fretting and screeching, and soon even the men lowered their bows in awe as they stood and stared at the Enchantress across the cavern, watching as she loosed a flood of arrows into the Skraeling mass, watching as with each Skraeling who fell a flower drifted from unseen heights above them into the massacre below until the floor of the cavern was lost in blood and floating flowers and the disintegrating flesh of the Skraelings.

As the last flower fell Axis tightened his arm about Azhure's waist. The Wolven drooped in her hands, and she leaned her weight back against him.

"You've done too much," he said, feeling her muscles tremble, feeling her gasp for air; knowing that the amount of power she had expended threatened her beyond exhaustion.

"I'll be all right after I've rested," she murmured, but she did not resist when he swung her into his arms.

"StarMan?" Ho'Demi called across the cavern, still dazed by what he had witnessed. "Is she all right?"

"She needs rest, Ho'Demi. Take your men up the shafts and we will rejoin you as soon as we can." He indicated the violet and red mess between them.

"None can cross this. We will all have to use the shafts we came down."

As the Ravensbund Chief turned to go Axis called him. *My friend? My thanks.*

Ho'Demi looked over his shoulder and regarded them silently. *Take care of her, StarMan.*

Sicarius and the other two hounds at his heels, Axis strode back along the tunnel. Now the excitement of the hunt was over he was also feeling the drain of exhaustion, and he thought it would take him two, perhaps three, hours to climb the shaft.

Then he stopped in his tracks, suddenly wary. Ahead of him the the tunnel curved . . . but in this all-consuming blackness he should not have been able to see that. Feel it, yes, but not see it.

Faint light outlined the walls and their ancient chisel marks, and Axis lowered Azhure slowly to her feet. Who was there? *What?*

My love? You will have to stand by yourself a while. There is . . .

The thought was cut off mid-sentence as Sicarius pushed past their legs, the other two hounds an instant behind him, and loped down the tunnel, disappearing around the bend.

"Axis?" Azhure struggled to focus through her fatigue.

Axis opened his mouth, then froze. Footsteps shuffled through the rock dust and a shadow loomed on the rock wall. Axis fumbled at his hip then remembered he had left his sword above ground; he glanced at the Wolven but discarded the thought before it had even formed. Even if he had been able to draw the bow he would not have been able even to hit a comatose cow with an arrow at five paces. Of all weapons, Axis had never mastered the bow.

A bent and ragged figure shuffled around the bend. It was a man, elderly, and clad in the dirty, stained rags of a miner.

"Good sir," he called, "good sir? Will you sit with us a while? We have sweet water and currant cakes, and your lady wife needs sustenance."

Then he turned and shuffled out of sight again.

Axis stared after him, then felt Azhure slump even more heavily against his side.

"Stars," he said, "I hope you are what you look like." He scooped Azhure back into his arms and nervously walked toward the bend; only the fact that the hounds had seemed relaxed kept him from turning and trying to negotiate the bloodied mess of the cavern floor.

Around the bend a small fire glowed in the center of the tunnel; about it sat four men and three women, all elderly, all clad in miners' rags.

The man who had invited Axis waved. "Sit."

Slowly Axis lowered himself to the floor, keeping Azhure close beside him. She roused as she felt the floor beneath her and looked about. "Why—" she began, but the old woman closest to her pressed a flask into her hands.

"Drink, Lady, drink. It will refresh you."

Azhure did as she asked, and indeed she seemed to rouse. She pressed the flask into Axis' hands and he took a sip as well, feeling a warmth like brandy-fire spread through his stomach. Without a word he handed it back to Azhure, his eyes on the seven sitting about the fire.

"Who are you?"

"Currant cake?" Now a man on the far side of the fire leaned forward, and passed a plate around toward Axis: "Just baked, good sir, and still warm."

Axis hesitated, but Azhure murmured at his side, and he reluctantly took the plate. Nine cakes sat there.

"Take one," Azhure whispered, helping herself, "and pass the plate along."

Already she seemed stronger and sat up without any need for support. Axis glanced at her, then took a cake and passed on the plate. Each of the seven miners took one.

Azhure bit into her cake and instantly her back straightened and her eyes flared with life. She chewed, crumbs at the side of her mouth. "Eat," she mumbled about her mouthful.

Eyes still wary, Axis slowly raised the cake to his mouth and bit into it. Almost as soon as he tasted the sweet cake strength flooded through him and he jerked in surprise, managing to keep his mouth shut and chewing only through an extraordinary effort.

"Welcome, Axis." One of the women extended her hand and Axis took it, still overwhelmed by the strength the cake gave him.

"My name is Xanon," she said softly, and Axis stopped chewing and stared at her.

A rag dropped to the floor, and then another. The hand that he held was hard and calloused one moment, smooth and round the next. Her smile broadened, and the creases of her face smoothed out, and Axis realized he was staring into the face of one of the loveliest women he had ever seen.

He swallowed, and Xanon laughed. Half rising, she leaned forward and kissed him.

He trembled, and Azhure shot Xanon a sharp look, but then the others were rising and taking his hand and kissing him on the mouth and murmuring greetings, and about them rags fell to the floor and skin firmed and pallor assumed luster.

As the last leaned back, the Circle of the Stars on Azhure's finger flared into such brilliance all had to squeeze their eyes closed until the light died down.

"We are Nine," Adamon said. "Finally, we are Nine."

*   *   *

They sat for time unknowable, talking, laughing, sharing, until finally Adamon stood and extended his hand to Axis, helping him to his feet. Fully recovered now, Azhure stood beside him and took his hand once Adamon had released it.

"I may not have the chance to speak with you before you move to meet Gorgrael," the God of the Firmament said softly. "Know that we watch and hope. May the Stars shine on you now and forever more."

Axis nodded, unable to speak. He had felt such a sense of homecoming among this group that he thought he could hardly bear it. Azhure's hand tightened about his own.

"When you do meet Gorgrael, none of us can help you," Zest said, stepping forward. "Not Adamon, not Xanon, not myself, not even Azhure. It must be you and he alone."

Narcis laughed and rested his hand briefly on Axis' shoulder. "And make sure you win, Axis. Your place among us is sure *only* if you win. Otherwise . . ."

"Otherwise Gorgrael will take it," Xanon said, keeping her distance this time. "And I do not think Azhure wants to be standing there holding Gorgrael's hand!"

"I have no intention of leaving her, Xanon. I will prevail."

She smiled. "Axis. Be wary. We all have our limits. You have seen tonight how use of her power can exhaust Azhure." Her smile died. "And you have felt firsthand what happens when you exceed or misuse your own powers. Be wary and be thoughtful. That is all I want to say."

Axis nodded soberly, about to say something himself, but then, astoundingly, the seven were gone, and the tunnel was empty of any save Axis and Azhure and the patient hounds.

They looked at each other, laughed, and climbed toward the surface.

When they arrived, it was to find that the night had passed and the sun shone high overhead. Only Ho'Demi's feeling that Axis and Azhure were well had kept him from sending down search parties to find them.

Above them the black dot that had been circling for over a day drifted off on the wind.

45

Gorgrael Considers

Gorgrael sat back in his chair, his feet extended toward the fire, and considered. For hours he had ridden in the Gryphon's mind, watched with the Gryphon's eyes, heard with her ears.

And what he had seen and heard made him wonder if he shouldn't be considering a minor revision in his plans. Had brute force been the correct tack? Would not some subtlety have been more appropriate? Well, maybe so, but it was not too late, certainly not too late.

So he sat back and thought.

And he mostly thought about that raven-haired woman who rode at Axis' side. The Gryphon he had sent scouting was one of the original two and Gorgrael had hated to risk her (the massive pack of Gryphon waiting in the corridors would give birth later this week and soon he would have seven thousand at his disposal), but he had been frantic for information. Timozel had withdrawn so far to the north that any information he could send his master was weeks outdated, or so useless he might as well not have sent it at all.

What was Axis up to?

Where was he?

What force did he have at his disposal?

And how much farther did that *bitch* have to plant before the hated trees were joined to the Avarinheim? Already winter had all but slipped from Gorgrael's grasp below the Gorken Pass, but even that would not matter if he could only use what intelligence he had to cripple Axis' plans.

His Gryphon scout had not been able to garner much—a nest destroyed and some breeding stock massacred—but what little she had seen and heard would prove more than useful.

Who *was* that raven-haired woman?

Who . . . ?

Why had Axis smiled at her with such affection when *Faraday* was his Lover?

What was that bow slung about her neck, and what power was held by the pale hounds who ran before her?

Who . . . *ah!* Gorgrael leaped out of his chair, slipped and would have fallen had not the talons at the tips of his wings caught on the mantelpiece and saved him from an ignominious slide across the floor.

But he did not care, for a memory had quietly surfaced . . . a memory that Gorgrael had buried because he did not think it significant when events of greater moment had surrounded it.

But perhaps *this* was the event of greatest moment.

When Axis had taken Carlon from that fool, Borneheld, Gorgrael had sent a Gryphon to scout over Grail Lake. She had done well, and reported many profitable facts, but she had made a fatal error. She was experienced, experienced in the taste of man-flesh from the trenches of Jervois Landing, and she had thought to taste sweet flesh again when she had seen the unprotected mother and child standing atop the white tower. So she had attacked, and everything she had seen until the moment of her death had been faithfully shared with her master.

Now Gorgrael stood twitching with excitement before the fire, recalling the Gryphon's death. She had angled in from the sun, a good tactic, for the woman had not seen her until it was almost too late. But instead of tearing the woman to shreds, the Gryphon had instead been seized and . . . and unraveled. It was the only word Gorgrael could use to describe the Gryphon's death. The enchantments that had gone into her making had been unraveled, and it had been that woman—the same who now rode by Axis' side—who had done it.

Gorgrael concentrated his thoughts on the woman and child. She was of what the Acharites called Nors blood; that race of women who often followed armies about offering their favors for a meal and a few hours' paltry warmth in a bedroll. Not surprising, then, to see her at the scene of a successful battle, and not surprising to see her cuddling the result of some careless thrust.

Gorgrael fixed the image of the baby's terrified face in his mind. That baby had the features of an Icarii. His mother's coloring, but the face of an Icarii stared out at him.

So perhaps the woman had lingered overlong with one of the feathered beasts.

Gorgrael may once have assumed this, but not now he had seen her with Axis. Not now he had seen Axis look at her with the face of love.

The baby . . . did that baby have the features of Axis? Did it? *Did* it?

Yes!

Gorgrael screamed his jubilation into the ice walls of his fortress until it reverberated for leagues across the tundra. He scrabbled about the room, his hands clenching and unclenching in frenzy, his wings extended, their talons gouging deep wounds into the furniture as he passed.

The woman . . . and the child.

And . . . Gorgrael abruptly halted, his eyes almost popping out of his head with the memory of what had happened the instant after the woman had destroyed the Gryphon. The Dear Man had materialized screaming with fury. *By all the stars in the universe, what have you done?*

The Dark Man had been very upset.

And all over a human woman and bastard Icarii-child?

Apparently so.

Gorgrael sat back down and tried to think it through. What did this mean?

The Dark Man was overly attached to the woman or the child and perhaps both. No . . . no, it had not been the child. It had been the woman. Why?

For most of Gorgrael's life, the Dear Man had imbued him with all three verses of the Prophecy of the Destroyer. It was the third verse, the Dear Man had said time after time, which gave the all-important information. The Lover, the one whose pain would break Axis's concentration enough so that Gorgrael could strike the killing blow.

But what if—for his own reasons and likely connected with that woman— the Dark Man had been trying to mislead Gorgrael?

What if the Dark Man had lied to him?

Gorgrael shrieked again, in fury this time, and tore the hearth rug to shreds. *Which one was the Lover?*

Faraday . . . or this black-haired woman who rode by Axis' side.

Which one could be used to break Axis' concentration?

Which one would be useless?

"And has the Dark Man spent his life lying to me?" Gorgrael whispered as he crouched beside the fire.

Faraday or . . . *her?*

Gorgrael snarled and hurled handfuls of silk into the fire where it charred and burned, sending a sickening odor wafting through the chamber. Then he took a deep breath, trying to calm himself. He could not think while he was so consumed with fury.

"My dear boy," he said eventually, grinning to himself, "why not go for both? What matter so long as both die before him?"

His smile died. Why not? Because Gorgrael had felt the unmistakable aura of power exude from the woman. Gryphon and Skraeling had died at her hand. She was risky. What if he tried to snatch her and couldn't handle her? What if . . .

What if the Dark Man had been training *her* as well as himself? After all, she had used the power of Dark Music to unravel that Gryphon, had she not?

Gorgrael whimpered, curling into a miserable ball before the flames.

The son . . .

He did not at first notice the thin voice that reached out to him.

The heir . . .

Gorgrael blinked and rolled over, slowly rising to his knees.

Vulnerable.

The son. Vulnerable. What did a man feel more for, a Lover or an heir? And whatever Axis may have bequeathed that boy-child, the baby could not possibly be powerful enough to best Gorgrael. Not by any means.

Not if both his parents were absent.

Sooner or later Axis was going to ride north from Sigholt, and the raven-haired woman had already shown she was willing to ride with him.

Surely they would not take the son as well, would they?

No.

No.

46

Gorkenfort

Timozel sat amid the rubble of the Great Hall in the Keep of Gorkenfort and remembered.

Remembered when he had planned here with Borneheld, thinking that Borneheld would be the Great Lord who would propel him into glory.

Now Timozel knew better. Now he served Gorgrael, and Gorgrael had invested him with infinitely more power than Borneheld ever could have.

Yet was Gorgrael as great as he had first thought?

Timozel had spent weeks retreating to the north, then had lingered weeks here at the mouth of Gorken Pass, awaiting orders. He was slightly surprised that Gorgrael hadn't called them all the way back to the Ice Fortress, but maybe Gorgrael felt his host was safe enough here where the winds still screamed and the snow still turned to ice within minutes of touching the ground.

Timozel shifted in irritation. Sooner or later he would have to face what was left of Axis' army—surely it could be little more than a mopping up campaign—and lurking among the ruins of Gorkenfort would not help.

But then there was the problem of the weather.

Timozel's scouts had informed him that several leagues below Gorkenfort the land had virtually thawed; Gorgrael's hand was slipping. Was his power slipping too?

The Skraelings, now fully fleshed, could fight in balmy weather as well as they could in a snowstorm, but they would have little advantage. Part of their success to this date had been that Gorgrael had always prefaced their attacks with numbing cold, severely reducing their foes' ability to fight.

"Damn you, Gorgrael," Timozel muttered, "let me finish the task I have begun so well!"

Timozel?

Timozel started so badly he tore his hand along a jagged stone. *Yes, Master?*

Timozel, I have some news.

Yes?

Axis is not so crippled as we first thought. Even now he rides the plains of Ichtar with . . . well, he rides fully fit and confident.

Timozel cursed foully, long and low. Why hadn't he been allowed to finish the job at the Azle?

Timozel?

Yes, Master?

I shall need you to stop him at Gorken Pass.

Timozel restrained his temper with extreme effort. *Of course, Master.*

Of Course, Timozel. My pets shall be with you soon. They lie about the corridors fat with child, and even now their grunting begins. Then they will be unencumbered and free to join you.

One good piece of news, at least.

Timozel, I think you may be succumbing to despondency alone in Gorkenfort with none but Skraelings and SkraeBolds to keep you amused.

No, Master! Timozel broke into a sweat. *No, my spirits remain high!*

See that they do. Listen to me. Seven thousand Gryphon—look what Axis did to himself trying to dispose of only nine hundred. Take heart.

Yes, there was that. Timozel relaxed, his mouth curving into a smile. The seven thousand would be with him shortly; with those he could decimate anything Axis threw at him.

Timozel, there is something I must ask you. Do you know of a raven-haired woman who rides by Axis' side?

Timozel frowned. *No, Master.*

Do you know if Axis has a son?

Timozel almost laughed. *A son? He undoubtedly has had the opportunity, but I have never heard of a son.*

And what of Faraday, Timozel? When you left Carlon, what of Axis and Faraday?

Rutting on the floor, Master, their passions so feral they could not take the five steps to the bed.

And they were married?

About to be, Master.

Gorgrael thought about this. Timozel had not seen Axis for so long that his information was as cold as the stones of Gorkenfort itself. Why didn't Timozel know about the woman? Why, when it was obvious that well before Carlon she had been sharing Axis' bed?

And if the black-haired witch had married him, that made Faraday the Lover, did it not?

Ah, no matter. Whichever, whoever, Gorgrael still thought he had the better plan. *You have done well, Timozel. I am pleased.*

Thank you, Master.

Seven thousand Gryphon. Axis could never deal with that many Timozel sat back in the Great Hall of Gorkenfort and laughed. "Come on, Axis. Be brave. Come get me. Lead your men. Let me take you."

47

Sigholt

h e's *where?*" Axis hissed.

"Gorkenfort," Ho'Demi replied. "Timozel is in Gorkenfort and his host is ranged about." As he had in Aldeni, Axis had trusted Ravensbundmen to scout the extreme north of Ichtar where the snow still fell.

"Are you sure your spies are right in this?"

Ho'Demi managed not to look affronted; from what he had heard about the battle for Gorkentown and fort it was no wonder the StarMan's face was now creased with concern. He nodded, then folded his hands before him.

Axis and his commanders were seated in the Great Hall of Sigholt in the hour before the evening meal was served. Now Axis glanced across at Belial. "Well?"

Belial considered, then looked at Axis with sympathy shining from his eyes. "It is a good place, Axis."

"Who for?" Axis snapped.

"For him," Belial said. "He would know the memories the place holds for you. The ghosts."

"And he can withdraw into Gorken Pass itself," Magariz added. "Forcing you to follow him. If he plans well, Gorken Pass could become a death trap for us . . . especially if he launches Gryphon from the rocks of the mountains." He finished abruptly. Magariz would rather not fight another battle at Gorkenfort.

"I do not want to hear this," Axis said, but his voice had lost its harsh edge. Gorkenfort. *Damn* him!

Everyone else was silent.

Azhure waited several minutes until she spoke, until the others had begun to shift uncomfortably.

"Well, where else did you expect him to go, Axis? We knew he was moving north, and Gorken Pass is the only route through to the northern coasts . . . unless he wanted to try to move his host through the Icescarp Alps. Surely this cannot be too much of a surprise."

Axis glared at her, but she did not drop her eyes. He'd hoped Timozel might pull his army back all the way to Gorgrael's fortress somewhere in the northern wastes. But it had always been a forlorn hope. He knew he would have to face Timozel again, and it might as well be Gorkenfort or Gorken Pass as anywhere else. After all, Skraelings had died there together with men.

"SpikeFeather? Have your scouts returned from their duty over Ichtar?"

SpikeFeather shuffled his wings, relieved that the StarMan's voice had returned to normal. "Yes, StarMan. It is quiet and denuded of Skraelings from the Fortress Ranges to the River Azle—and possibly beyond, but my scouts did not fly that far. Likewise it is quiet and empty from the Icescarp Alps to the Nordra."

Axis looked at Magariz. "You have your province back, Prince Magariz."

Magariz bowed his head. "Then I thank you, StarMan."

Best thank Faraday, Axis thought, for it is she who has driven back Gorgrael's ice with her trees.

"Fire-Night," Azhure prompted gently, "is only some nine weeks away."

Axis' ill-humor returned and he laughed harshly. "Do you hear that, my friends? Fire-Night is but nine weeks away. By the third week of Rose-month I must have cleared this land of its Skraelings so that I can move to meet the Avar in their groves."

Belial looked bewildered, as did most of the other commanders.

"Axis must be in the Avarinheim groves by Fire-Night so that he can take the Rainbow Scepter with which to destroy Gorgrael," Azhure explained, her eyes still on Axis. "The Avar will be instrumental in the making of the Scepter."

"That does not leave us much time," Belial said, then wished he had kept quiet.

But Axis only waved a hand tiredly. "Then we had better start to move. Belial, what is our state of readiness?"

Belial spoke for some time, occasionally referring a point to one of the other commanders, or querying something with Axis himself. In the eight weeks since the army had been encamped on the Lake of Life, spirits and health had been restored, gear mended and cleaned, and training had continued apace.

"Then when can we ride?" Axis said.

"In two days . . . if the conditions permit it." Belial looked at SpikeFeather.

The Strike Force Leader spoke quickly. "The land is well thawed—"

"And drained?" Belial broke in.

"And drained," SpikeFeather said. "There are still great patches of mud, but the ground forces should be able to ride past them."

Axis lounged back in his chair and stretched his legs out. "The Strike Force, SpikeFeather? Should I take you?"

"Would you have us stay here and mind the children, Axis?"

"If seven thousand Gryphon get to you before Azhure can manage to contain them, then there will be no Strike Force at all."

"We want to fight," SpikeFeather said. "If we die, then so be it."

Axis regarded him carefully. The Strike Force had built itself up so that it now stood at about sixty percent of its previous strength. But SpikeFeather was young and relatively inexperienced. Should he risk them?

They have to fight, Axis. Isn't that what you trained them for in Talon Spike? Did you want them to go home the instant they lost a few members? You gave them their pride, do you now want to take it away from them?

More than a few members lost, Azhure, but Axis conceded the point. "Very well, SpikeFeather. You can start to send the farflight scouts toward Gorkenfort, but be careful!"

"And we fight?"

"Yes. You fight. Ready the Strike Force. You can move out four days after the ground force has gone. Your initial task will be to protect the supply column."

SpikeFeather took a deep breath and relaxed. "Good."

"SpikeFeather, have you any news from Talon Spike?" Azhure asked.

He shook his head regretfully. "I'm sorry, Enchantress. All I know is that the majority of the Icarii made it safely to the Avarinheim. Some have stayed there with the Avar, but many are continuing south to the Minaret Peaks, some to Nor and Carlon, and some to the Island of Mist and Memory."

Azhure nodded. She felt responsible for RavenCrest's decision to stay, but it was his choice, and it was his life. At least most of the Icarii had escaped— and who knew, perhaps Gorgrael wouldn't think to launch his Gryphon on the mountain anyway.

But already she could feel the black surge of Gryphon to the north, a tidal wave of destruction—almost seven thousand, three hundred of them. And their pups, mewling and crawling in an even blacker wave. Waiting. Wanting.

"Well," Axis said with forced lightness in his voice, "so in two days we ride into yet another battle." He reached across to Azhure and took her hand. "Thank the Stars you will ride with me this time."

She gave him a tight, tense smile.

"I can't come with you, Axis."

They were alone in their bed chamber.

He spun to her. *"What?"*

"Axis, please understand, I can't come—"

He seized her shoulders, unable to believe what he was hearing. "Azhure, I *need* you!"

She winced at the strength of his hands and the pain in his eyes but kept her voice soft. "Axis, I will be there in time for the battle, it's just that I'm needed elsewhere at the moment. I'll join you as soon as I can."

"Needed elsewhere?" He laughed incredulously. "Needed *elsewhere?* What? Does RiverStar need to be burped just so? Is Caelum fussing over a tooth? Dammit, Azhure, there's no need to prove to me that you are a good mother!"

"Faraday."

"Faraday?"

She took a deep breath. How could she explain without telling him what Faraday did not want him to know? "Faraday draws close to Smyrton. She is tired, exhausted, yet she faces the greatest danger of all in only a week or two."

"Can't she plant the last few trees by herself, Azhure?"

"Artor waits in Smyrton, Axis. Faraday needs me and I need her. Neither of us can face him alone, and *no one* can ignore him."

"I need you, Azhure," he whispered.

"I know."

"How can I deal with the Gryphon without you?"

"Shush. I'll be there in time," she said.

"I'll fail without you!"

"Axis . . ."

He drew her close to him. "Azhure, I *will fail without you!*"

"We will both fail without Faraday," she said fiercely, trying to make him understand. "I can deal with the Gryphon, but what about the mass of Skraelings? What will you do at Gorkenfort?"

"I dealt with them at the Azle."

"No," she said brutally, "you only bought yourself a few precious hours to retreat in. Don't you want to advance this time? Secure Ravensbund for Ho'Demi as you have secured Ichtar for Magariz?"

He was silent, his face averted. His hands slipped away from her arms and hung at his sides.

Azhure wrapped her own arms about him as tightly as she could, pressing her body against his, maintaining the contact. "The trees will help us, Axis, but only if they are joined to the Avarinheim. If the Song of the Earth Tree can touch them."

"And what will the trees do, Azhure," he said harshly, "pick up their roots and march forth? Can I rely on *them* to get there in time?"

She pressed her face against his chest. "The trees *will* help us, Axis. Faraday has promised."

He was silent long minutes. "She has reason enough to hate me, to lie to me."

"She does not hate you, Axis, and she does not lie to you."

"I lied to her."

Azhure was silent.

"I lied to her," Axis whispered. "I wish before every star in the firmament that I'd had the courage to treat her as she deserved."

Azhure lifted her head and considered him. "Then make sure you tell her that, Axis, when you have the chance."

They held each other quietly, wrapped in their own thoughts. "When will you leave?" Axis asked eventually.

"Tomorrow. For the past two or three days I have felt a growing urge to go to her . . . this afternoon it became almost unbearable. I *must* leave in the morning."

"Azhure . . ."

"I *will* be there for you," she said. "I *will* get to you in time!"

Imibe stood on the roof of Sigholt, the baby girl in her arms, watching with a careful eye as the other nurse played ball with Caelum. She liked to bring her charges up here every morning and afternoon so they could bask in the sun and breathe in the gentle breeze wafting off the Lake.

The stairwell door opened and the StarMan and the Enchantress stepped out. Imibe straightened. The Enchantress had told her earlier that she would be leaving for a week or more. Axis smiled at her, but there were lines of tension about his eyes.

Azhure took the baby girl from Imibe. At three and a half months she was growing ever more beautiful, her hair darkening into a deep corn-gold, her eyes such a dark violet they sometimes appeared almost black.

"RiverStar," Azhure murmured. Since the girl had been separated from DragonStar, Azhure could feel her antagonism lessening with each day; although there was as yet little warmth between them Azhure hoped that one day they could learn to love and trust each other. She felt Axis at her shoulder and turned to smile at him.

"Isn't she beautiful, Axis? She has the SunSoar coloring, this one."

He touched the girl gently on her cheek. He'd been spending an increasing amount of time with his daughter. Although he had not been able to train her while in the womb, now she seemed prepared to accept his teaching.

Caelum clambered over to Axis and clung to his legs. Smiling, Axis swung him into his arms. "And how do you like your sister, Caelum?"

Caelum regarded RiverStar solemnly. "Better when she can run and play."

Axis' smile broadened and the lines about his eyes relaxed. "Small babies are not fun playmates, are they, Caelum? I have no doubt I shall have ample cause to reprimand both of you for your mischief-making when you have grown a little."

A step in the doorway made all turn. Cazna stood there, her cheeks flushing when she realized that Axis and Azhure had joined their children.

She was holding DragonStar.

Caelum twisted and whimpered softly in Axis' arms, as if DragonStar were close enough to pinch his flesh.

"I asked that he be kept apart from my children!" Axis barked, and Cazna's flush deepened. She hurriedly turned and handed the baby to the nurse who followed her, whispering urgently, and the nurse hastened back down the stairs.

Cazna walked over to Axis and Azhure. "I'm sorry, Axis," she said. "I had no idea that either you or your children would be here this morning."

And is DragonStar not "your child" as well? she wondered. Both Cazna and Belial had hoped that Axis' dislike for his son would fade over the weeks, but it seemed as strong as ever. Cazna could not understand it. Drago, as she called the baby (who could look at such a beautiful, cuddly baby and call him DragonStar?), was well behaved and easy to care for. He had learned to laugh early, and Cazna had become addicted to his joyful gurgle whenever she picked him up. Why couldn't Axis and Azhure love him as well? Although Belial wanted to hand Drago back to Axis eventually, Cazna found herself secretly hoping that she could keep him, and she was sure that when her own children came along Drago would accept them easily and joyfully.

And as for Axis' demand that Drago be kept apart from his other children . . . well, Cazna thought that was plain ridiculous.

"I want him kept away from Caelum and RiverStar, Cazna. Do you hear me?"

"Yes, Axis, I hear you. There is no need to repeat yourself nor to speak so harshly."

Azhure glanced at Axis worriedly. His face had hardened at Cazna's tone.

"If you cannot obey me in this, Cazna, then I will have to ask you to leave Sigholt."

"Axis!" Azhure swiftly handed RiverStar back to Imibe and took Axis' arm. She glanced at Cazna; the woman's cheeks were still colored, but with anger rather than awkwardness. "Axis, this was a simple misunderstanding. Please, leave it."

"Nevertheless." Axis took a deep breath and made an obvious effort to clamp his temper. "Cazna, I appreciate what you and Belial have done. Not many newly married couples would be so generous as to take in someone's else's baby. Cazna . . ." he hesitated, not sure how to say this, "Cazna, DragonStar will not be able to stay with you. Certainly not once your own children come along." How to explain to her that he thought DragonStar dangerous? That what Cazna thought was a beautiful baby could well harm other children if he thought them intruders?

Cazna's color had faded, but her eyes were still hard, and Axis knew she did not understand, and perhaps did not want to understand. A dreadful thought occurred to him—could DragonStar manipulate Cazna's mind and emotions without her realizing it?

Azhure, when we come home we shall have to do something about DragonStar.

He could feel her agreement. *There is not much he can do at the moment, Axis. Perhaps once he is weaned we can send him to StarDrifter. He likes StarDrifter.*

Axis' face relaxed completely, and Cazna looked at him carefully. What was going on? Belial had told her that Axis and Azhure, as many Icarii Enchanters, could communicate silently with their minds, and watching them now Cazna believed him for the first time.

"Yes," he said, "that might be best. Cazna, I am sorry for my harsh words, but know that *we* understand DragonStar in a manner that you cannot. Please respect our wishes regarding him."

Cazna nodded and smiled politely.

Axis stood under the fortified gateway of Sigholt and watched Azhure ride across the bridge, the Alaunt already well ahead of her and beginning their run down HoldHard Pass. Back to Smyrton, he thought, back to Smyrton. *What will the villagers think, my love, when they see you ride back into their midst dressed like that and with such wildness shining from your eyes?*

She swiveled in the saddle and gave him a brief wave, letting her love wash through him, and Axis smiled.

"She can look after herself, Axis."

His mother stood by his side, well into her seventh month of pregnancy, and Axis looked at her briefly, awkwardly.

"You should be resting, Rivkah."

"I am not an orchard bloom ready to wilt in the first breeze," she said tartly. "Axis," her tone softened, "Axis, we must talk about this baby."

"What is there to say, Rivkah? The baby is your and Magariz's concern."

"The baby is your brother!" she snapped.

"And I wish he were not!" Axis retorted. "If I had known that you were still capable of bearing a child then I would . . ."

"You would have done *what,* Axis?"

He hesitated, a muscle working in his cheek. "What have you done with the circlet and ring of Achar's royal office, Rivkah?"

"Must you see treachery and black dealing in every shadow, Axis? Must you see this baby as a threat?"

Without another word she brushed past him, her skirts rustling angrily, and

Axis leaned against the warm stone of Sigholt and wondered if Rivkah's pregnancy was Faraday's revenge.

On the roof, Imibe held Caelum so that he could watch his mother ride off.

"Such a lucky baby," she whispered in his ear, "to have such a magical mother."

Caelum laughed in agreement and sent his mother a final message of love. Even at this distance she felt it and sent him love in return. *I will be home soon, Caelum. Wait for me.*

Far below in Cazna and Belial's chambers, DragonStar smiled. Soon both his parents would be gone, and with them, any chance of stopping him.

He would be heir. He *would*!

48

The Lake of Life

They sat on the peak of one of the surrounding hills, cloaked by mist and magic from curious eyes, and watched the exodus of Axis' army. It took the entire day to pass.

"He looked well," Yr remarked, her voice slightly hoarse. About her the kind evening light hid the worst of her sores.

"They all do," Jack replied. Both his hands were wrapped about the staff, the knuckles white. "The Lake has done them good."

Zeherah had eyes only for the Lake. She had not seen it this beautiful for over two thousand years. "It is time to move."

"Will anyone see us?" Veremund asked, his voice thin with pain. The sacrifice had been hardest of all on the two old brothers; the rejuvenating power of the Mother given at Fernbrake Lake was now dissipating.

Zeherah shook her head. "No. Look, the southern shore of the Lake is deserted. It will do us well enough." She rose and turned to watch the other four struggle to their feet. Her eyes lingered on Jack. He had always been so proud, so vital, his shoulders broad and strong enough to carry the cares of all five. Now he trembled and gasped for breath, and though Zeherah yearned to step back and put her arms about his shoulders, she kept her distance and let Yr help him.

Slowly they started down toward the Lake in the dim light, Zeherah several paces in the lead, the others struggling as best they could. Each was careful not to put a foot astray on the slope—a broken limb now might yet mean the breaking of the Prophecy.

*　　　*　　　*

It was full night when they reached their destination and the darkness clung heavily about them. When they finally stopped by the gentle red waters of the Lake of Life they turned to stare at the Silent Woman Keep for some minutes.

"Something is not right," Ogden muttered, clinging to his brother's robe as support.

"Wrong," agreed Veremund.

Even Zeherah ignored the lure of the Lake and scrutinized the Keep carefully. "It has the feel . . . ," she hesitated, furrowing her brow in concentration, "it has the feel of subtlety about it."

"Subtlety?" Jack queried, not sure he had heard aright.

She shifted, trying to put her emotions into words. "When the Dukes of Ichtar inhabited Sigholt, the Keep always had a feeling of wrongness about it, but the wrongness of Dukes of Ichtar was not subtle—it glared forth like the noon-day sun. Whatever is . . . not right . . . about the Keep now is far more elusive. Almost," she paused again to lick her lips, "almost crafty. Shrewd."

"Is it the Keep, lovely lady, or someone—something—inside it?"

Zeherah spun about. Behind her, perhaps three or four paces, stood the Prophet in his silvery beauty. But his brow was as furrowed in thought as hers, and his eyes were fixed on the Keep. She turned back to Sigholt.

"Not the Keep. No, not at all. The Keep is vibrating with health and happiness: It does not feel the wrongness. It does not recognize it."

The Prophet sighed and stood behind her shoulder. "Someone inside, then?"

Zeherah nodded. "Yes."

Who? he thought. Who? It worried him that he could not understand it . . . yet what could he do? If he could not sniff it this close, then he would do no better in the Keep itself . . . and he could not risk the bridge recognizing him. Not yet.

Caelum, he thought suddenly, the realization sending cold ripples down his spine. Caelum is in there! *Be safe, Caelum!*

"We should not be concerned about that now," he said, placing a hand on Zeherah's shoulder. "Tonight we are here to witness for the last of the five. After tonight you will be together again."

"Whole in ill-health and corruption," Yr said.

"Do you wish that you had not volunteered for this task?" the Prophet asked sharply.

"I chose of my own free will," she replied, holding the Prophet's stare.

He was the first to drop his eyes. He had never thought to have been this affected by their suffering. Three thousand years ago it had seemed an adventure, even to him. Now . . .

"I suffer with you, Yr." He raised his head again and met her level gaze.

And yet you will live through it! she whispered in his mind for him alone, and the Prophet winced. He quickly smoothed his expression, then bent and kissed Zeherah on the mouth.

"Zeherah, you will be beloved for always for the sacrifice you now make. And you will always rest in my heart. I could not have asked for better than you."

Fine words, Prophet.

Zeherah nodded, and her eyes swam with tears. "I, like Yr and Ogden and Veremund and my beloved Jack, harbor a myriad of regrets. But most of all," her breath caught in her throat, "I regret that I should have lost so much life trapped in that ruby. That is so unfair."

Unfair, Prophet.

She slipped her robe from her shoulders and stepped to the shore line, hesitating as the wavelets washed her toes, then strode resolutely into the water. Within moments she had disappeared underneath the surface.

Unfair that we should have to suffer so much, Prophet. Was there no other way?

No other way, Yr. Will you go forward with hate in your heart?

I do not hate, Prophet. I merely regret—but regret lies so heavily on my soul that I do not think I will ever smile again.

And to that the Prophet had nothing to say.

When Zeherah walked back out of the Lake, her eyes glittering with power, the other four stepped forward to hug her fiercely.

As they stood together, the Prophet spoke in words of power. "And now you are five again. Whole in your unwholesomeness. United by the corruption that eats at your hearts. From here your only duty is Fire-Night. Be there."

Jack bowed his head, and his grip tightened about the staff. The heavy metal knob at its tip was black with tarnish, but the Prophet thought he could see faint lines of silver tracing across its surface. Soon.

"Be there," he repeated, then disappeared.

"If we bathe in the Lake," Zeherah said, "it will give us the strength for the final journey."

49

Inside the Worship hall

At Faraday's back Minstrelsea swayed and hummed for over eighty leagues in a gigantic arc that swung from the Silent Woman Woods, through western Arcness and Skarabost, until now it waited only a few dozen seedlings' distance from the Forbidden Valley and union with the Avarinheim.

The Forbidden Valley will have to be renamed, Faraday thought as she stared at the last remaining obstacle before her, once it becomes part of the greater forest.

Between her and the valley lay Smyrton. The sun shone overhead, yet some two hundred paces distant the village was gray and dark. There was no one in the carefully tended fields, and Faraday could see no movement within the village, either. Everything seemed gray; the picket fences, once sparkling with white paint, the walls of the houses, once daubed with lime, the mellow thatch quilted thickly to roof beams. Faraday shivered, and the Goodwife put a supporting arm about her.

"Shadows," she said with the voice of the Mother. "Somewhere in there lurks Artor."

Faraday's fear grew. She wished she could plant around Smyrton, leave it unvisited, undisturbed.

"Can't," the Goodwife said. "For that would be to leave a cancer in the heart of Minstrelsea."

Plant straight through, then. Up to this point Faraday had not disturbed any towns or villages or evicted any from their lands. Axis, and then Azhure in her role as Guardian of the East, had made sure that the western parts of Tencendor would be free for Faraday, free for the forest.

All but Smyrton.

Azhure! Faraday thought desperately, where are you? For weeks she had been sending unspoken calls to Azhure, their urgency increasing with every day. Where was she? How was she? Had she managed to rescue Axis from the calamity that threatened him?

Would she be here in time?

"Believe," the Goodwife said, and Faraday's mouth trembled, attempted to smile, then thinned in despondency. She did not feel well, her legs and back were aching, and every movement now was an effort.

Why did she have to plant in this condition? Damn you, Axis, she thought bitterly, for making my life so difficult.

Her hand rested on her belly, and the Goodwife exchanged a worried glance with Barsarbe. In the four months since Yuletide, whatever ill-feeling there was between Faraday and Barsarbe had apparently vanished in the daily ritual of planting; but then, both Faraday and Barsarbe had carefully avoided any mention of Axis or Azhure. Faraday appreciated the company and conversation of the Avar women, and had spent the evenings laughing with Shra and telling the girl stories of her life as Queen.

But Faraday and Shra did more than story-tell. The Goodwife knew that most nights Shra, rather than Barsarbe, accompanied Faraday to the Woods beyond the Sacred Grove to help her transfer the seedlings. Well, the Goodwife thought, that task had finally been completed. Ur's nursery was empty and the last seedlings now waited on the tray of the blue cart, waited for the final union.

The excitement of the forest behind them was palpable. Today, Minstrelsea would be finally joined to the Avarinheim, to the touch of the Earth Tree, or today the chance would be lost forever and the Plow would reclaim that which had been planted out.

And, somewhere among those dank gray houses and streets, waited Artor.

Come on, Azhure! the Goodwife muttered to herself, come on!

The village of Smyrton had changed. It had always been a stronghold of the Seneschal; strangely, some might have thought, considering its distance from the Tower of the Seneschal, but Smyrton held a special place in the worship of the Plow. Many generations ago, well before the Wars of the Axe, this was where Artor had garnered his first souls, where he had first explained the Way of the Plow, and where he had made the gift of the Plow itself to the families who wandered the Seagrass Plains gathering and hunting what they could.

"The Plow will enable you to till the earth," He had explained, "to tame and civilize the earth and thus yourselves. Uncultivated is uncivilized, barren is dangerous, forested is evil. Plow, and you shall reap the rewards."

And so they had. Over many centuries the Acharite civilization had sprouted and flourished in the wake of the Plow, and the Acharites had seen how the Plow gave them comfort and security. Gradually they'd nibbled at the edges of the forest, taking a tree here and a glade there, and the friction that would later grow into war developed apace between the peoples of the Wing and the Horn and those of the Plow.

Artor had also chosen Smyrton as the place where he made the gift of the Book of Field and Furrow to mankind. And though later generations had forgotten the pivotal role that Smyrton had played in the ascendancy of the Way of the Plow, the site itself still remembered. Now that Artor walked again, Smyrton had reawoken out of its long slumber.

And the villagers had changed.

They had heard of the events to the south, and they had watched as flight after flight of the feathered evil had flown overhead. They had witnessed the rebirth of Tencendor, and had bewailed the fact that most of the Acharites had apparently accepted this as easily as they had discarded the Seneschal and the Way of the Plow.

"It is a test," Goodman Hordley, senior man of the village, had told his brethren. "Artor tests us to see how true we are."

And the villagers agreed with him. The troubles had started with the vile murder of Plow-Keeper Hagen by his dark daughter, Azhure. None had ever liked her, nor her mother, and none were surprised that she had been capable of such an act.

From that murder their problems had escalated. The Forbidden pair had escaped, and the BattleAxe—cursed be his treacherous name!—had not been able (or had not wanted) to recapture them. Battles to the north, west and south over the next two years against the invasion of the Forbidden Ones had not resulted in victory for the Seneschal, only disaster.

These days the villagers had grown used to dark news.

But they had also grown used to other things. Lacking a Plow-Keeper since Hagen's death, they had nonetheless gathered each seventh-day in the Worship Hall to honor Artor as best they could. They had sat there quietly, softly mumbling to themselves those words of the Service of the Plow that they could remember, making the sign of the Plow at every opportunity, taking what comfort they could from the icon of Artor that hung over the Altar of the Plow.

But then, five months ago, the icon had begun to talk to them. At first individuals thought they were hallucinating, and did not discuss what they had heard. But then they recognized the fanaticism that glowed in the eyes of every other villager as a reflection of what broiled in their own souls, and people talked, shared . . . planned.

Planned for the bitch they knew was coming from the south.

Planting trees.

Spreading shadows and evil.

Burying the straight and narrow furrows beneath the twisted roots of her forests.

Infecting all who came close.

Lately, Artor had spoken to them in their dreams as well, and for the past four nights everyone in the village had spent their sleeping hours thrashing restlessly as, He had shown them explicitly what threatened; they had dreamed of walks through dark woods where eyes glimmered at them from the unknown and where an old witch clad in a blood-red cloak chased them with spells.

And a woman had also wandered the paths, carrying, two-by-two, the dark seedlings of destruction in her hands.

And so Artor had whispered to them.

Her. Destroy her. Destroy her and we can begin the arduous task of returning this land to its purity. It will take a long time, but her destruction will be the start of the unraveling of all the evil that has infected this wondrous land.

And they listened and believed and planned.

They knew *she* was coming. For days they had watched the dark line of the forest slither closer across the southern plains. Now they waited for her, and their eyes were almost as maddened as those of the monstrous red bulls who drew Artor's Plow.

Their thoughts were even worse.

"Smyrton must make way for Minstrelsea," Faraday sighed. She straightened her back. "Well, we shall have to go in. Barsarbe, perhaps it would be best if you and the others took Shra around the village. There's no need for you to—"

"No," Barsarbe said, and by her side Shra glared at Faraday, daring her to contradict. "Shra and I, and our companions, will come with you. Either we all go, or none of us do."

Faraday nodded, glad of their support, although she worried for Shra. These villagers had already seized and abused the girl—what if they did so again? Would Axis miraculously appear a second time to save her from death?

Slowly she walked forward, feeling the unnatural coldness of the village with each step closer.

Nothing stirred as they approached. Even the crops in the fields refused to sway to the gentle breeze, and shadows hung thick and heavy over the village, although the sky was clear of clouds this fine spring day.

Faraday could feel the humming of Minstrelsea, driving her on, begging her to complete their union and transformation.

How could she fail them?

Behind her walked the Avar and the Goodwife, all calm, all with heads high and eyes shining proudly. In the blue cart the seedlings trembled, desperate to sink their roots into the soil, yet afraid of the soil awaiting them.

In front waited Smyrton.

*   *   *

The streets were deserted as they walked past the first houses. No people, no livestock. The garden plots were bare of flowers or vegetables, but the dark soil lay turned over in neat furrows. Waiting.

Doors were closed, windows tightly shuttered. Silence hung over everything, hiding the village's intentions.

Faraday felt sick. She tried to summon the power of the Mother, but it was tarnished by whatever lurked here, and it sickened and failed even as Faraday touched it. She swallowed. How would she be able to defend herself, defend the forest, without the power of the Mother?

Artor. If Faraday could not touch the power of the Mother then she was sure she could feel *him*. His was not an unknown presence to her, for Faraday had spent the first eighteen years of her life an ardent believer in the Way of the Plow. But that had been before she gazed into the Star Gate and before the Mother's arms welcomed her, and she never, *never*, remembered the sickening, cloying presence she could feel now.

"Watch the shadows," the Goodwife muttered, and Faraday faltered slightly. Watch the shadows? Watch the shadows? And what was she going to do when Artor poured forth from the shadows?

Azhure? her mind screamed, *where are you?*

A man stepped from behind the corner of a house and stood silent, gray, watching the small procession.

Faraday hesitated, wondering if she should call out to him, but his eyes were flat and hostile, and she knew he would not respond. It took all her courage just to keep on walking.

A woman appeared, from where Faraday could not see, holding the hand of a seven-year-old child, and their eyes were as bleak as those of the man's. They stood silently, watching them pass.

And then another stepped forth, and another, until the main street was lined by silent, gray adults and children, unmoving, unmovable.

Faraday and her companions kept walking, and behind them stepped the donkeys, jumping nervously at the hatred in the eyes of the gray people to their flanks.

As they passed, the silent people moved in behind them, following them, blocking their escape.

Faraday kept walking, although she could feel the villagers beginning to mass behind her.

How had Azhure managed to live here so long?

In the village square a small knot of people stood before her. Four men and two women, all gray and silent, madness and devotion lurking about the corners of their eyes.

Faraday stopped several paces from them. "My name is Faraday," she said. "And I have come to plant."

"Witch," whispered one of the men.

"Whore," spat one of the women, her eyes sliding down Faraday's body.

"She is Faraday," said the Goodwife pleasantly, standing a pace behind Faraday's right shoulder, "and she is an Earl's daughter, and a widowed Queen, and beloved of gods and men alike. And she has a task to complete."

Goodman Hordley looked at the peasant woman. "You have been misled, Goodwife," he whispered, infused with Artor's power. "Return to the truth and the Way, and Artor will forgive you."

The Goodwife laughed merrily, and her laughter gave Faraday heart. "Return to Artor?" she said. "I *have* returned, but it is not to Artor. Can you not feel the presence of the Mother, Goodman?"

Faraday shivered as she felt the villagers crowd about them.

The Goodwife's words were brave, but Faraday could sense that she commanded no more power than Faraday did herself. There was no escape. "I must—" she began, but Goodman Hordley stepped forward and his hand snaked out, grabbing her wrist in a malicious vice.

"Artor waits, bitch," he spat, and behind them and about them the villagers stepped forward and seized Faraday's companions. She heard Shra cry out and one of the donkeys bray in terror, and she tried to twist away herself, but Hordley's fingers sank deeper into her flesh. "Are you ready to confess your sins?"

The villagers took them to the Worship Hall, built over the very site where Artor had first appeared to the wandering families of the plains. They tied the donkeys up outside and pushed and dragged and shoved as they took their prizes inside the hall.

It was similar to many Worship Halls that Faraday had visited in her youth, and yet there was something profoundly different about it.

It was a great stone hall, beamed far above with metal rafters specially forged in the ironworks of southern Achar. The walls were thick, with tiny windows set far above, and little light managed to penetrate.

Furniture was virtually absent. When the villagers came to Service they stood in orderly ranks, their hands folded and their eyes downcast in humbleness. All that relieved the starkness was the Altar of the Plow at the eastern end of the hall, a massively oversized metal casting of the Plow itself where young couples gathered to be married, children stood to be admitted into the circle of its safety, and the old were laid out to be farewelled with prayers to their graves. On the wall behind the altar hung an icon of the great god Artor, not gold and silver as those that had once graced the walls of the Tower of the Seneschal and the richer Worship Halls, but bare iron like the altar.

What made this Worship Hall so different to others Faraday had seen was not only the cold power that permeated it, but the mess of blood, torn flesh and feathers surrounding the altar and occupying the floor space beneath the icon of Artor. The sickly-sweet smell of decay wafted through, and Faraday doubled over and gagged.

Wainwald Powle, son of the village miller, regarded her coldly. Women, always weak, always ready to succumb to temptation. Well, they would learn that such weakness would be the death of them.

"Behold," he said, "the fate of those who refuse to admit the light of Artor into their lives."

"Icarii!" Faraday gasped.

"Flying filth!" one of the village women said, "who made the mistake of landing here six days ago and asking for shelter from a rainstorm."

"We have dedicated them to Artor," Goodman Hordley said pleasantly, and he withdrew a long knife from the back of his belt. "Just as we will dedicate you. Now!" he suddenly barked, and those who held the women dragged them toward the altar, tying them to its cold iron structure with cruel ropes. Faraday found that Shra had been tied beside her. The girl's eyes were wide with terror, but she bravely kept silent despite her trembling.

Poor Shra, Faraday thought, to be captured twice by such as these. To her other side the Goodwife lay as quietly as the girl, but with anger simmering from her eyes.

Faraday tried to turn so as to lie more comfortably, but slipped in the blood and feathers beneath her and cried out in agony as the ropes cut deep into her wrists. Where is the power of the Mother? Why cannot I touch it? Mother?

"In Artor the witch-goddess recognizes a power greater than her own," Goodwife Hordley said, squatting down by Faraday's side and wrenching her head back by her hair, exposing her throat. "Husband? The sacrifice is ready."

"Blood to strengthen Artor in his battle with the evil that pervades this land;" Goodman Hordley intoned, and Wainwald Powle took up the cry.

"Blood to strengthen Artor!"

"*Blood to strengthen Artor!*" the assembly screamed, their eyes blazing as red as the blood they craved, hands plucking at the clothes covering their breasts and abdomens in their ecstasy.

"*Blood for Artor!*"

Faraday closed her eyes, knowing all was lost, feeling the cold steel against her throat.

"Why, Hordley, is that Hagen's knife you wield so expertly?"

Faraday's eyes flew open and she felt rather than saw Hordley draw back in surprise. But his wife's hand remained twisted in Faraday's hair, and the blood of the hapless Icarii sacrifices soaked through her gown.

In the doorway, outlined by the light beyond, stood Azhure. Her stance was relaxed, nonchalant, and Faraday could feel if not see the half-smile on her face.

Azhure tossed her head, shaking her hair down her back, and stepped fully into the Worship Hall. The Wolven hung from one hand, unwanted for the moment.

Behind her the Alaunt slunk deep in the shadows, unseen by the villagers whose eyes were riveted on the woman. The hounds' hackles stood stiffly, and silent growls thickened their throats.

Azhure laughed, enjoying the feeling of power that pervaded her body and reveling in the shocked faces before her. "I've come home," she said, sauntering through the hall, the villagers parting like a gray sea before her. She stopped a pace or two from the altar, her eyes meeting Faraday's for an instant, then she reached down and grasped Hordley's wrist where he still held the knife against Faraday's throat. The blade had pierced Faraday's skin, and blood trickled lightly down into the hollow of her neck.

"Why," Azhure said, staring at Hordley, "it *is* Hagen's knife . . . and how well I know it." Her fingers tightened about Hordley's flesh and the man gasped with pain, but he could not look away from Azhure's eyes.

Strange, strange eyes. Blue like the sky one moment, the next rolling gray like the sea that Hordley had once seen beating against Achar's eastern shores.

Azhure's lips parted in a slight smile and she let her true nature blaze forth from her eyes.

Hordley opened his mouth to scream but he never had the chance, for Azhure lifted and twisted the man's arm and plunged the knife, still gripped in his fingers, into his own belly.

"It likes the feel of belly flesh, Hordley," she whispered, "feel how smooth and gentle it glides in?"

At the gentle sigh from Hordley's lips as he did, indeed, feel how smooth the knife slipped in, the Worship Hall erupted.

"Murderess," hissed Goodwife Hordley as she crouched by Faraday, "how practiced you have become!"

Faraday tried to roll away, but was held back by her roped wrists, then she felt gentle teeth about her flesh and the ropes loosened.

Every one of the villagers stepped forward, their gray hands extended, faces slack with hate, red eyes fervent with Artor's power.

Goodman Hordley slipped to the floor, his eyes surprised, his hand still gripping the knife sunk to its hilt in his belly, but he did not die.

His Goodwife pounced at Azhure but grabbed at thin air as Azhure leaned down and kissed Faraday on the mouth.

As Faraday felt Azhure's lips touch hers, the teeth at her wrists finally broke through rope and Faraday was free. The Goodwife rolled clear at the same moment.

"Good doggie," Goodwife Renkin whispered to the hound who had crawled into the spaces of the altar with several of his companions to free the women. She rested her hand briefly on Faraday's shoulder—and whatever bounds had shackled Faraday's contact with the Mother broke asunder and she was flooded with power. Her eyes blazed emerald.

Above her, Azhure leaned over and seized Goodwife Hordley's chin, twisting the woman's face to one side so that she toppled over in the blood and muck where Faraday had rested an instant earlier.

Sicarius, Azhure ordered, *herd.*

And the hounds circled and nipped and snapped, driving the villagers back from Azhure and Faraday and the women, back to the rear of the hall where the door to the cellar stood invitingly open.

Azhure smiled as the villagers, their lips curled in snarls but impotent against the power and anger of the Alaunt, retreated down the steps, and she looked down to Hordley . . .

. . . and recoiled in horror.

50

The hunt

Merciful heavens," she gasped and, seizing Faraday by the wrist, hauled her away. About them the Avar and Goodwife Renkin backed away hurriedly. Goodwife Hordley groveled whimpering—in joy, Azhure thought—at the side of what had once been her husband.

Once, but no more.

Most of Hordley's clothes had fallen away until only a brief loincloth and a short cape about his shoulders remained. His flesh, that had been soft and white, was now darkening as if it had spent years burning beneath the sun, and muscles roped and writhed across his body. His face retained its broadness, but his skin was pitted and scarred. His entire body twisted and then lengthened: twisted again, broadened and yet lengthened some more.

Azhure could hear the screech and grind of his bones as they were reshaped by the power that gripped them.

It groaned, then grunted and convulsed, sweat running in rivulets down the contours of its flesh and then, slowly, jerkily, it raised one arm and tore the knife out of its belly.

The gaping wound rippled, then closed over.

It blinked, clenched its fingers more firmly about the knife, and looked about, looked for the . . .

"Bitch!" Artor screamed, lifting off the floor in one sinuous movement and lunging for Azhure.

One of His great, sandal-clad feet stepped on Goodwife Hordley as she writhed before Him and Azhure heard a crackle and pop as her spine snapped.

Artor took no notice; one hand was splayed toward Azhure's throat, the other slashed with the knife toward her belly, seeking vengeance for Hagen's death.

Faraday took a step forward, but felt Barsarbe grab her arm. "Leave her!" the Bane hissed, trying to haul Faraday away, "she is all he wants. *Leave* her!"

Azhure swayed back, the knife missing her by a finger's breadth, and almost fell as she stumbled to regain her balance. Artor lunged forward, certain. He had her now, then felt small hands grasp His ankle, trying to twist.

Shra, desperately fighting for Azhure's life as Azhure had once fought for hers.

"Argh!" He roared and kicked the frail body away, sending Shra skidding across the floor and slamming into a far wall. At the same moment Faraday leaned around and hit Barsarbe so hard the Bane let go and fell to her hands and knees.

Shra's brief but courageous intervention had bought Azhure time. Now she stepped forward, her face tight and determined, and seized the hand that grasped the knife.

Artor roared again and clenched His other fist, raising it high to smite Azhure in the face . . . then found that grasped too, by fragile hands which wielded the power of the Mother.

And all about Artor and Azhure and Faraday the hounds snapped and howled, unwilling to intervene while the three grappled so close.

"Feel the power of the Mother," Faraday hissed in Artor's ear, and felt the foul sting of His breath as He turned toward her.

"And feel the power of the Nine," Azhure said, her face flushed but calm, and her gray-blue eyes met Faraday's.

"Feel the power of the Earth," Faraday said.

"And the power of the Stars," Azhure whispered, so low her words were almost lost amid the howling of the hounds. On her finger the Circle of the Stars flared into life and it brought with it the strength of the Nine.

As Azhure let the power of the Nine flood into Artor, so Faraday loosed what bonds still restrained the emerald fire and let it surge through the god's body; it had watched for countless generations as the forests died under the Plow, and now it turned the full force of its vengeance upon Artor. He writhed and screamed; Azhure and Faraday struggled to maintain their footing, but both clung grimly to His wrists, knowing they would be defeated if they lost their grip.

Enraged by the sting of both earth and firmament, almost blinded by the Circle that burned in his face, Artor let loose His own power to rope between and about the women. The Avar and Goodwife Renkin screamed and sank to the floor, twisting and beating at their ears. The Alaunt's howls rose, but they kept their feet and snaked their heads, trying to find an opening in which to seize the god they loathed.

Azhure felt His power assail her own flesh and it took all her strength to hang on; Stars knew how Faraday managed. She risked a quick look at the other woman's face. Faraday was as white as snow, and her lip was bloody, where she'd bitten it in her frantic struggle to hang on. But her eyes were wide as they blazed with the power of the Mother, and she opened her mouth to speak.

"Get you gone, Artor." Her words were barely audible, but they trembled and hesitated and then, gaining strength, reverberated about the stone hall.

"We do not want you, Artor," Azhure said, and the voices of both women mixed and fed off each other and soon they roared through the hall with a life of their own.

Artor tipped back His head and bellowed with such an intensity that the very walls of the Worship Hall cracked. Every muscle in His body bulged, and the women had to shift their grip to make sure their hands did not slip in His sweat.

"Go!" Faraday whispered.

"Leave!" Azhure murmured, and their words twisted and writhed among the echoes of Artor's shrieks and roars.

The Worship Hall was filled with a gale of sound, and yet not a breath of air moved.

The Goodwife crawled across to Shra, and she dragged the unconscious girl from the hall. As she passed the Avar women, still writhing on the ground, she caught at Criah's arm. "Get out now," she cried, "before it's too late!"

Criah nodded dumbly, tears of agony streaming down her face, and seized the women next to her, nodding at the door. Soon all the Avar were crawling toward safety.

The three locked in combat did not notice their departure.

Against the power of the Star Gods and the Earth Mother, Artor brought to bear all the power that He could. It shrieked through the interstellar wastes to His aid—and met the combined power of earth and stars. The power was fearsome and it tore and bit at the women, but they were courageous and determined and drew strength from each other.

And Artor was weak, weaker than He had been a thousand years previously. Then He had the power and the belief of the Seneschal at His back; now the Seneschal was broken and belief in Artor had shattered throughout Tencendor.

Where once was plowed plain, now wove forests.

Where once had flourished prejudice and hatred, now laughed Icarii and human as they shared the pain and pleasure of experience and love.

Now earth and stars stood together, as they had not a thousand years ago.

Now the Circle flared complete.

Artor shrieked and writhed and roared and twisted, but the women clung and their words battered at him.

"Go!"

"Get you gone!"

"Leave us!"

"We do not want you!"

Azhure finally managed to twist Artor's arm behind His back and she leaned in against His body as a lover might.

"Let's hunt," she whispered, her lips brushing His ear.

Artor fled, as the Huntress hoped He might. He slipped from the hands that grasped Him and fled into the darkness that surrounded Smyrton.

Faraday dropped back, exhausted, but the Huntress whistled her hounds and her horse to her side and, mounting, set the hounds coursing and the horse chasing, and she lifted an arrow from the quiver on her back and fitted it to the Wolven.

"Let's hunt!" she cried.

And so they did.

They hunted through darkness so complete that it hung in thick curtains about them, but the sound of the Alaunt clamor rose and danced through the spaces and the sound, of the Huntress' laughter crashed about the ears of the quarry.

He drove His bulls hard and fast, leaning over the Plow with strength trebled by terror, and His terror communicated itself to the red and maddened beasts before Him so that their breath steamed hot and bloodied from their nostrils and their horns glinted in great arcs as they tossed and rolled their heads.

Behind them, closer and closer, the Huntress urged on her ghostly pack and her red horse until both horse and hounds could smell the fear before them, and they redoubled their efforts in glee.

The thud of the plowshare and the thunder of hooves echoed about the darkness.

"Hunt!" whispered the Huntress.

"Plow!" screamed the Plowman, and He turned His beasts and His imple-ment to face the threat behind Him.

"Steady," the Huntress counseled as the Alaunt leaped for the throats of the monstrous bulls, and she sat back in the saddle and brought her horse to a dancing halt, sighting along the shaft of the arrow.

She sighed as she loosed it, feeling its loss as keenly as she might feel the loss of a lover's intimate warmth.

It sped through the darkness, fed by vengeance, and in the name of ven-geance for all those slaughtered in Artor's name, it lodged itself in the eye of one of the roaring bulls.

The animal dropped, and instantly its kicking body was covered with hounds who tore into the soft flesh of throat and belly until the bull kicked its life out twisted among the ropes of its own bowel.

The Huntress smiled, and fitted another arrow to the Wolven.

The other bull screamed now, and its scream drowned out even Artor's shrieks, as the arrow twisted through its eye to its brain and the hounds ripped and tore into its belly.

For one heartbeat, Artor stood behind the useless Plow and stared into the eyes of the Huntress.

Her smile broadened and she reached for yet another arrow.

As one, the hounds lifted their blood-stained muzzles from the ruined carcasses of the bulls and stared at Artor, bunching their hindquarters and curling their lips in silent snarls.

"Hunt!" cried their mistress, and they leaped.

But Artor was already gone, fleeing into the darkness.

The hounds streamed after Him, baying their excitement, His sweat-terror scent strong in their nostrils, their mistress laughing behind.

They coursed and they clamored and they screamed.

And they cornered Him, eventually, when even His strength had given out and when His terror and horror made Him miss His step.

Sicarius caught Him first, and his teeth sliced through the vital tendons at the back of the god's right ankle and He crashed to the ground. Another sank her teeth into His left hamstring, and Artor writhed helplessly. As He writhed, yet a third hound dropped to the ground and tore open the sweet flesh of His left armpit and Artor screamed.

"Good dogs," the Huntress said and, reining her stallion to a halt, slid to the ground and strolled over to the crippled god.

"Artor," she said, kneeling beside Him and placing one hand on His shoulder. "Did you smile when Hagen dug his knife into my back? Did you laugh when Niah twisted and charred on the hearth bricks? Did you *feed* off the pain of all those you hounded and burned and murdered in your own righteous name?"

She reached behind her, her arm stilling, then slowly . . . slowly . . . she revealed what she had lifted from the quiver at her back.

Hagen's bone-handled knife.

Artor shrieked and the Alaunt, pacing about Him, lifted back their heads and howled.

Azhure ran her finger experimentally along the blade of the knife.

"For all those who have died in your name, Artor," she said without emotion, then she carefully inserted the blade under the sixth rib on the left side of His chest, slid it in perhaps a finger's breadth to make sure she had the angle correct, then jerked it up and twisted it about, slicing open His heart.

When she withdrew the knife hot blood steamed after it.

She rose to her feet. "Feed," she commanded, and within a heartbeat writhing hounds covered the god's body.

"Feed."

51

The Grave

The Goodwife went back in to see to Faraday, terrified that the Plow god had slain her, but all she found was Faraday, sitting exhausted on the ground, and no trace of the raven-haired woman who had come to her aid.

"M'Lady," she gasped, seizing Faraday's arm and hauling her to her feet. "Are you well?"

Faraday coughed and a violent tremor shook her, but she managed a smile for the Goodwife. "Well enough."

"Where's . . . ?" the Goodwife began, her eyes concerned, but before she could finish the strange woman was there herself.

Faraday grasped the woman's hand. "Is he . . . ?"

"Gone," Azhure said. She leaned forward and hugged Faraday and laughed suddenly. "We did it, Faraday! Now you may complete your planting in peace."

Faraday smiled and hugged her back as tightly as she could. "I thank you, Azhure. You saved my life."

Azhure sobered and leaned back. "And that is hardly thanks for all you have done for me, Faraday. Goodwife," she turned to the woman at Faraday's side, "Goodwife, take Faraday outside and seat her in the tray of that ridiculous cart. Then get everyone out of the village. There is still work to be done here."

"No doubt more murder," Barsarbe said flatly behind them, and Faraday twisted out of Azhure's arms.

"If I had listened to you, Bane," she said, her voice hard, "then we all would be lying dead here this moment, and Artor would have triumphed."

Barsarbe ignored Faraday and stared at Azhure, unable to believe that the woman had walked back into her life. She knew they all owed their lives to Azhure (yet again), but that knowledge only increased her bitterness—how much more bloodshed would the woman bring? Without another word she turned on her heel and stalked out.

Whatever ill-feeling Barsarbe left behind her dissipated the instant that Shra, still shaky from the blow she had received to her head, ran across the floor of the Worship Hall and flung herself into Azhure's arms.

Azhure cried with delight and hugged the child to her. "How you have grown, Shra!"

Shra touched her fingers to Azhure's forehead. "And how, *you* have grown, Azhure."

Azhure smiled and set the girl to her feet. "Later, Shra. Now take Faraday's hand and help the Goodwife get her out of this village."

"Faraday will have to plant through here," the Goodwife said, her tone suddenly heavy with power and authority.

Azhure looked at her sharply, recognizing both voice and power. "She cannot plant while this village still stands, Mother. Let me wipe what remains of Artor from this place."

The Goodwife nodded, then pulled gently at Faraday's arm. "Come, child. You shall rest a little before the final planting."

But Faraday hesitated. "Axis?" she asked Azhure nervously.

Azhure stilled at the expression in Faraday's eyes. "Axis is well," she said gently. "He is well."

Faraday bowed her head and let the Goodwife guide her from the building.

Azhure stood at the door to the cellar, memories flooding through her. Here she had stood at the BattleAxe's shoulder as he had entered the cell that held Raum and Shra; little had she known then how she would come to love him.

Here she had hesitated before climbing down the steps to strike Belial and free Raum and Shra so all three could run to the Avarinheim and Azhure could start the journey that would take her so far.

And now, here she stood again, and there was only one thing she needed to know from the villagers below.

She flung back the door and ran lightly down the steps.

The Alaunt had herded and snarled and snapped until the entire village was trapped behind the iron bars at the rear of the cellar. They were packed in so tightly that several obviously had difficulty breathing.

Azhure spared them no sympathy. They still gazed at her with maddened eyes, their faces gray and fanatical. There was no hope for any of them.

Slowly she paced the length of the iron bars, staring into faces that she had grown up with, that had conspired with Hagen to make her suffer.

One man, Wainwald, reached through the bars and grabbed at her breast. Azhure recoiled, remembering that Wainwald had been the most persistent of the young men who had leered and lusted after her.

"Harlot," he grunted, "with a costume that demands rape to satisfy it. Come here!"

Another man snatched at her and Azhure retreated a step or two. Never had they been this bad, this feral. She walked farther down the bars until she found Goodwife Garland. She was in her early sixties, and she undoubtedly knew where . . . where . . .

"Where is my mother's body?" Azhure said, stepping close enough so that she could sink her fingers into the material of the Goodwife's bodice. "Where did Hagen bury her?"

Goodwife Garland's lip curled, but the next instant her face twisted in horror as Azhure's power invaded her mind with persistent icy fingers.

Where? Where? Where? Where?

The Goodwife whimpered and her face spasmed with the pain.

Where? Where? Where? Where?

"He buried the slut under the floor of the chicken shed." The Goodwife managed a contemptuous smile. "Imagine that. Your mother lies under twenty-five years of chicken shit, Azhure. What better resting place could she have found?"

Azhure let her go and stepped back, her face blank. Goodwife Garland had told the truth, Azhure could feel that, and that was all she cared about. The truth. The insults did not matter.

Not now.

Azhure nodded, letting her eyes travel over the assembled village. Women sneered and men panted, hands itching for her. Even boys of four or five reached out, their eyes hot.

"I wish you all good fortune in the AfterLife," she said, "for you are surely going to need it."

Then she turned and walked out of the cellar.

She had sent the hounds and the horse to wait with Faraday and the Avar, but now Azhure wandered through the village, loosing any livestock she found, opening doors and gates so that all could have the chance for escape. Stars knew, she thought, they deserve escape from this dark dungeon.

She reached the chicken coop last. It was a fair distance from Hagen's house behind the Worship Hall and he must have struggled to drag her mother's body this far; but then, perhaps he had help, and he wouldn't have wanted to be discomforted by the stench of her mother's decay, would he?

She stood outside for a long time, looking at it, and it was only when the wind felt cold against her face that she realized she was crying.

Soft arms encircled her, Faraday.

"Shhh," she crooned, rocking Azhure as she sobbed. "Shhh. Is this where your mother lies? Well, cry now, Azhure, let it all go, and when all is gone, then you and I shall make of this wasteland a fit place for your mother to rest in."

"Oh, Faraday," Azhure sobbed, "she did not deserve this!"

"None of us deserve all that happens to us, and some mothers rest far from the love of their families," Faraday said gently, stroking Azhure's hair. "Come, dry your cheeks. What are you going to do to this village?"

"Destroy it," Azhure said roughly, wiping her eyes. "And what are you doing here, anyway? I thought I told you to wait outside the village?"

"You needed me, Azhure. Now, shall we join the others?"

Azhure nodded, and together the two women walked hand-in-hand through the village.

"This is your childhood you are about to destroy, Azhure," Faraday said as they heard the group of Avar and the Goodwife waiting some distance beyond the village. "Are you sure you want to do it?"

"Never more sure, Faraday."

Just before they reached the women, Azhure turned back to the village, fitting an arrow to her bow. "Azhure's vengeance," she said, then let the arrow fly.

It arced into the sky, catching the noon-day sun, then it turned its head for the ground, and the watchers could see that its rip burned with a feverish flame and it fell so fast that even from this distance they could hear its whispering roar.

It fell straight for the Worship Hall.

"Good," said Shra when she realized its destination, and Azhure risked a fleeting glance and a smile for the child. This was for Raum and Shra as well as for Niah and Azhure.

"Yes," Azhure said, "very good," and the arrow struck.

Fire crackled along the roof of the Worship Hall and then, in the blink of an eye, the hall exploded. Fiery stones flew through the air, and wherever they landed houses exploded and gardens erupted. A hot wind rushed toward the women, and Faraday had to hold on to Azhure's arm as it passed.

It smelled of decay and the fetid breath of the sick, and Faraday wondered what evil had lived under the foundations of the houses and the Worship Hall.

"All gone now," Azhure said. "It's all gone."

And indeed it had, for when the wind and smoke finally cleared, the village had entirely disappeared. Not even rubble remained. Everything, stone included, had evaporated.

And there, tall and proud in the center of the circle of burned earth that had been Smyrton, stood the arrow, its head buried in the earth.

"Will you be able to find your mother's grave?" Faraday asked. Perhaps they should have marked it somehow.

"Don't worry," Azhure said. "Come on, Faraday, an afternoon's planting awaits you."

Faraday and the Goodwife called to the donkeys and they retraced their steps to the last seedling Faraday had planted that morning. When Barsarbe made as if to follow them, Faraday told her to stay where she was. Shra, as the other Avar women, just sat on the ground to wait.

Then, slowly and with the utmost reverence, Faraday resumed planting.

Eventually, after an hour or two, she realized that Azhure was standing before her.

"Here," Azhure whispered, and Faraday looked down at the woman's feet—and drew sharp breath in surprise.

Azhure was standing in a circle of small-leaved plants that had only just broken the surface of the soil. Even as Faraday watched a tiny flower slowly budded and uncoiled; its petals were dark violet and so transparent that they barely cast a shadow. Moonwildflowers. Faraday had only ever heard of them in legend before, but she instantly knew what they were.

She raised her eyes to Azhure's face; it was pale and luminous, her eyes so great and dark, that Faraday thought Azhure was about to faint, but then realized that Azhure had wrapped herself in so much power that some of her true nature shone through.

Very carefully Faraday reached out a hand, intertwining her fingers with Azhure's. "I shall make a grave that will reflect your mother's love and courage," she whispered, and then led Azhure slowly away from the circle of Moonwildflowers, handing her to the Goodwife to hold.

Faraday planted in a great circle about the grave, nine seedlings in all. When she had finished she stood up, brushing the dirt from her hands, her own face pale with exhaustion.

"Nine seedlings for the Nine Star Gods she served," she said quietly, "and now the Nine will stand for eternity to honor the First who died for their sake. Niah's Grove, Azhure."

"A place," the Goodwife said, her fingers tightening about Azhure's, "where the Nine can come to honor her and to dance for her sake and theirs."

Azhure bent her head and wept.

52

The Roof!

Cazna picked up the baby and crooned a little tune to him. The nurse had fed and changed him, and now he lay replete, with a tiny smile for his foster mother.

"Drago," she whispered and held him close to her breast, wishing she could have a baby, as beautiful as this one. Goodness knows why Azhure found it so easy to let Axis dictate to her about the baby; Cazna would *never* let Belial overlook . . . she blinked . . . *disinherit* a son of hers.

Poor baby, poor sweet baby. She rocked him in her arms and smiled and sang to him. Poor Drago. Well, if Axis and Azhure refused to love him then she would give him enough love and attention to make up for it.

The roof.

Cazna sang and rocked the baby.

The roof.

She smiled at him, and wondered how she should fill in the hour before dinner. Since Belial had ridden out with Axis and his army several days past, time hung heavy on Cazna's hands.

The roof.

"Perhaps I shall take you for a walk, little one," she said, bending down to kiss his velvet brow.

The roof, bitch! Now!

"But where to? The courtyard? No, that will be heavy with shadows now and too cool for your skin . . ."

The roof! Roof!

". . . perhaps the hall. But no, for the servants will be bustling about there with the silverware and linen and will not want our eyes to disturb them . . .

Bitch, listen to me!

"Ah! Why not the roof?"

Ahhh!

Cazna thought about it, remembering Axis' warning. Well, she doubted that Imibe would have Caelum and RiverStar there now, and even if she did . . . well, Axis was far away, and who would tell?

"Come!" She laughed, swinging her sweet Drago in her arms, "let us promenade above the bustle of Sigholt, and I shall show you how the blue mist turns to dusky rose where it meets the waters of the Lake of Life."

I couldn't care less, you inane woman. Just take me upstairs. And there . . .

"Let me wrap you in this shawl first, Drago," Cazna said.

. . . I shall gain what should rightfully be mine.

It was time. Gorgrael knew it was time because the faint voice had told him it was so. The parents were both gone, where Gorgrael didn't truly care because all he needed for sweet, sweet victory was that they both be gone from Sigholt.

Gorgrael was nervous about this adventure, nervous because he rarely left his Ice Fortress and nervous because of the magic of Sigholt itself.

But he knew that Timozel had been harboring doubts about his master's courage, and that stung Gorgrael into precipitous action. And the thin voice had told him that Sigholt's magic could be outwitted.

Gorgrael didn't totally trust the thin voice, but he recognized power when he felt it, and he recognized hate when he heard it, and he could feel the truth of what the thin voice told him. So he decided to act on it. If worst came to worst, well, Sigholt wouldn't let him through and he would just have to slink back here to his Ice Fortress and he would never trust the thin voice again.

But something told Gorgrael he wouldn't be slinking anywhere this afternoon.

"Sweetheart," he crooned to his Gryphon, his original, his beauty, and she crawled on her belly toward him. "Shall we take some fresh air?"

Cazna started guiltily. Imibe had indeed brought Caelum and the baby girl to play on the roof of Sigholt, and now the Ravensbund nurse was staring at Cazna with a look that suggested the woman should turn on her heel and haul Drago downstairs again.

But who is the Princess here? Cazna thought, tossing her head, and who the servant?

So she returned Imibe's stare boldly and marched to the far side of the roof.

Imibe glared at the woman's back—surely she could remember the look on the StarMan's face and the tenor of his command!—and then she nervously checked RiverStar and Caelum. The girl lay wriggling on a blanket, but Caelum . . . Caelum was staring at Cazna as though she were about to burst into flames at any minute. His face was pasty white and his blue eyes round and frightened, and Imibe walked over to him, picked him up and cuddled him.

Perhaps it were best if she collected the girl and left.

DragonStar twisted his head around as far as he could and tried to see what Imibe was doing. She had picked Caelum up, that much was certain, but did she walk away with him? He seethed with frustration and writhed in Cazna's arms so that she looked at him in some concern.

Cloaked by his dark magic, Gorgrael rode his Gryphon far above the blue mists that surrounded Sigholt.

Damn his pretty brother for his pretty mists, he cursed. But he could feel the Keep, and he could feel the mind of the . . . Traitor.

It is I. Is all in place?

DragonStar ceased his twisting, and Cazna smiled in relief. *Hurry.*

The bridge . . .

Do not concern yourself about the bridge. She is easily fooled.

Gorgrael smiled.

Imibe put Caelum down as she wrapped RiverStar in her blankets. At least the Nors woman was keeping DragonStar well away, and Imibe ceased her hurrying. She might not be possessed of the ability of the Icarii Enchanters or even of the Ravensbund chief, but she could smell badness from a league away, and there was something about that baby that was just not right.

She put RiverStar, strangely tense now, in her basket and turned for Caelum.

His mouth open in a silent shriek, Gorgrael plunged through cloud and mist.

Are you true? cried the bridge, sending her challenge to meet him.

I . . . I . . . True to what, curse her?

Bridge, it is I, DragonStar, son of Axis and Azhure. Here comes my friend. He is true, bridge. Trust me.

The bridge mulled over this. The stranger should answer for himself, truly he should.

Trust me, whispered DragonStar's mind, and the bridge smiled to herself, remembering the truth of Axis and Azhure and the warmth of their companionship.

Trust me . . .

The bridge thought about sending out her challenge again . . .

Trust me . . .

 . . . but instead she chose to trust. Besides, how could any enemy find its way through the enchanted mists?

Gorgrael plunged straight and true, locking in on the beacon of the baby's mind. That a *baby* should have this power! he wondered, but soon ceased his wondering, for the mist was thinning and there . . . there! was the magical keep of Sigholt and there! there! there was the BOY!

Caelum screamed even before he saw the plunging Gryphon and the horror that clung to its back. He could feel the evil dropping out of the sky, *again*, and he could feel his brother's ecstasy, and he understood.

He understood that he was to be the sacrifice for his brother's ambitions. He was to be the sacrifice that would bring his father to his knees.

And so he screamed.

Cazna spun about, sickened by the sound of primeval terror that had come from Caelum and then confused by the gurgle of laughter that came from the baby she held.

Imibe did not even think. She lunged for Caelum, kicking the basket containing RiverStar into the shadows of the walls.

And then something indescribable dropped out of the sky.

Of them all, Cazna was the first to see it. Her heart seized in terror, and only after a long moment did she think to back up against the wall, as far from the falling shadow as she could.

She had heard tell enough to know that one of the creatures was a Gryphon, but what was that clinging to its back? What could it *be*? "Belial!" she whispered, knowing she was dead.

Gorgrael ignored her, dropping straight to the Ravensbund woman who held the son in her arms.

Yes! Yes! That was he!

He leaped from the Gryphon's back as she swooped low over the roof, and he capered across to Imibe in a half-crouch, wings outstretched, claws extended, eyes and teeth gleaming. Saliva from his protruding tongue splattered across the stone paving. He paused half a pace from her and screeched.

The woman, brave bitch that she was, only held the screaming child closer. She must have known that death was close, but she chose to meet his eyes steadily, and that made Gorgrael uncomfortable.

"Fool!" he hissed, swinging one arm, and raked his talons down her face.

Yet still she held the child close, turning away so that her body protected him, and Gorgrael lashed out in a vicious flurry of fury, shredding her back and flank within instants and, as the dying woman sank to the floor, he seized a mercifully insensible Caelum by one arm and jerked him from the woman's clutch.

He whipped about, Caelum swinging from his grip like a rag doll, and stared at the other woman and baby across the roof.

Far below the bridge screamed. "Woe! Woe! Treachery!"

Gorgrael jumped and the Gryphon swooped.

"Woe! Woe! The roof! The roof!"

But Gorgrael still had a moment to spare, and he was enjoying himself so hugely he thought he might as well make this moment worthwhile. He scampered across the roof, and the woman shrieked in terror and sunk to the floor, trying to curl herself about the baby. Gorgrael grinned. Futile effort. He raised a taloned claw already soaked in blood.

Cease, my friend. She is still useful to me.

Gorgrael paused with his hand suspended ready for the downswing.

And surely it would be best if you had a witness to the kidnap?

"Yes," Gorgrael whispered. "A witness. Yes. Good."

"Woe! Woe! Treachery on the roof!"

"Bitch," Gorgrael snarled, and he turned for the Gryphon. As he swung his leg over the Gryphon's back and felt her welcome fur beneath his buttocks, he looked down at the senseless child still swinging by one bloodied and bruised arm from his claw and screamed his triumph and delight over Sigholt.

"Woe! Woe!" cried the bridge.

But it was already far too late. When the first Icarii arrived on the roof Gorgrael and his Gryphon had disappeared into the mists. All that remained was Imibe's torn body, the hunched and frightened form of Cazna, the screams of the twins, and the memory of Caelum's terror that would linger for days to come.

53

Minstrelsea

Azhure shivered, her stomach suddenly clenching in vague horror, but the moment passed, and she looked at Faraday.

Faraday knelt in the soft earth some fifty paces from the entrance to the Forbidden Valley, and before her the Nordra leaped and roared from the chasm. Behind her the plain stretched almost half a league to the line of trees; seedlings bobbed hopefully across it in between woman and forest. She stared at the seedling she had just planted, wishing it well.

Azhure knelt by Faraday's side, worried. The woman was obviously in terrible discomfort, and every so often would press a hand to her side or back as if she were riven with pain. "Faraday," Azhure asked softly, "are you—"

"I'm fine," Faraday said brightly—far too brightly and far too quickly, and the concern in Azhure's eyes deepened. "Look," she continued, "the Forbidden Valley. I'm almost finished."

Utter silence greeted her words. Azhure struggled for something to say, and raised her eyes to meet those of the Goodwife. Behind the Goodwife stood Shra, clinging to the woman's apron, her eyes as anxious as those of the two older women. The other Avar were twenty or so paces behind them; Faraday had only wanted Azhure, the Goodwife and Shra with her.

"One more seedling," Faraday whispered, and struggled to her feet, swaying alarmingly once she had risen. Azhure caught at her arm but Faraday shook her off. "Please, Azhure. This last I would do on my own."

She reached out and took the final seedling from the Goodwife's hands. "Mirbolt," she said. "The last to die. The last to be planted out."

Azhure stared at the seedling. She'd known the Bane, for Mirbolt had died in the Skraeling attack on the Earth Tree Grove. Mirbolt had also been the one who had conducted the Avar discussion regarding Azhure's request to join them. The Avar had refused her, but Azhure harbored no ill will toward Mirbolt. She had been fair and proud and handsome and had not deserved to die as she had.

"It is fitting that she be the one to connect the forest with the Avarinheim," she said.

Faraday's mouth curled in a gentle smile. "You understand, Azhure. Yes. This will be her right."

"Where will you plant her, Faraday?" Azhure looked at the entrance to the Forbidden Valley. The valley was narrow and its rocky walls steep. The only path beside the rushing river was rock and only a pace wide.

Faraday fingered the seedling silently, her eyes misty. "At the entrance to the Valley, Azhure. That is all I need do." Her face lightened at the expression on Azhure's face. "You'll see."

Then she walked forward, her gait slow and heavy, her pace faltering every seven or eight steps.

"Goodwife," Azhure said urgently. "She's—"

"She's doing what she has to," the Goodwife said, "and we can do nothing for her. Not yet."

"Soon," said Azhure, her voice brittle.

"Assuredly," the Goodwife soothed. "Soon." She gathered her full skirts as if she would follow Faraday, but she paused as she placed one boot beside the seedling Faraday had just planted. She hummed a little lullaby, bending momentarily to stroke the tiny seedling's leaves. Then she straightened and clumped after Faraday.

Azhure, holding her hand out for Shra, hurried after her.

One final time Faraday knelt in the soil, wet here where the Nordra sprayed forth. She paused, her eyes misting with tears. Here. It had all come to this. One final time . . . and then the final journey. One more time, and then Tree Friend's task was done.

"Mirbolt," she whispered, the roar of the Nordra masking her words from the three who had halted two paces behind her. "Mirbolt, take what strength I have left and use it to surge toward the sky. Be joyful, for your time is here and you will be the one to join ancient with replanted. Yours will be the task to receive the Song from the mother tree."

Singing softly under her breath, Faraday dug her fingers into the soil, and then she gently tipped the seedling from its crib and placed it in the hole. "Mirbolt, you are the last, and to you I would entrust my message. Behind you your sisters stretch to the Cauldron Lake, their voices ready to raise with yours. Before you lies the Avarinheim, and the Song of the Earth Tree. Mirbolt, when the time comes I would that neither you nor your sisters nor the mother tree herself hesitate. Axis, the StarMan, will need you. His wife, my sister, will also need you."

She turned her head slightly and indicated that Azhure join her. When the woman had knelt by her side, her face puzzled, Faraday took Azhure's hand and touched her fingers to the top of the seedling. "Mirbolt, this is Azhure— you already know her. Azhure is beloved of myself, of the Horned Ones and of the StarMan . . . and she is accepted among you." She lifted her head. "Azhure . . . do you feel it?"

Azhure nodded, her face filled with gentle wonder. "Yes. I feel it. She accepts me."

"Yes," Faraday said. "She accepts you." She dropped her eyes again. "Mirbolt, when the time comes and Azhure calls, come to her aid, for in doing so you will aid not only the StarMan, but myself as well. Now," her hand tightened about Azhure's, "Azhure and I will secure you together."

And with several deft movements, Azhure's and Faraday's combined hands patted the soil firmly about the seedling.

"It is done," Faraday said, and, glancing into her face, Azhure was horrified to see despair.

"Faraday!"

The Goodwife placed a hand on each of the women's shoulders. "Be still. I must sing to her."

She hummed her special cradle song again, one last time, but Azhure did not hear it. She stared into Faraday's eyes, riveted by the pain, the horror and the sorrow she could see there.

What was wrong? What could she see?

But as the Goodwife ended her song, Faraday blinked and the horror faded from her eyes. Now they were only tired, and if they reflected pain then it was no more than Azhure expected to see there at this time.

"Stand with me," the Goodwife said, extending her hands, "See."

Azhure took the Goodwife's hand, using her other to help Faraday rise, then turned to follow the Goodwife's eyes.

Across the plain behind them the seedlings Faraday had planted that day sprang toward the sky. Neither Faraday nor Azhure had ever seen this process before. Always seedlings had sprung into their full potential under cover of darkness; now they would not wait.

"Faraday," Azhure whispered, her eyes filling with tears. "Faraday!"

But Faraday did not hear her, so enraptured was she by the sight before her.

The seedlings uncoiled—it was the only word that Faraday could grasp to even remotely describe what she saw. It was as if each seedling had encompassed within its tiny form the complete tree; now that tree unwound as if a giant spring had been set free.

The Avar women, some paces distant, all fell to their knees, hands to mouths.

Azhure hugged Faraday gently to her. "Faraday," she murmured into the woman's ear, "look what you have done!"

As she spoke the trees finally uncoiled to their full height, reaching to the first stars glimmering in the twilight. Their branches stretched out each to the other until they covered the ground below with gently swaying shadows.

Whatever memory still lingered of Smyrton was gone forever. In its place wove forest.

Then Faraday gasped and jumped in Azhure's arms, and all three women and the Avar girl had to step out of the way. Mirbolt-that-was now leaped for the sky, and the air about hummed with power and vibrancy and joy as the tree unraveled.

Faraday clapped her hands.

"Look, Azhure!" she laughed, "Mirbolt lives!"

"My Lady," the Goodwife said, "it is almost time for me to leave you."

"Leave?" Faraday cried. "Goodwife, you cannot leave me *now*! I will need you . . . *soon!*"

"Hush, m'Lady," the Goodwife said, gathering Faraday into her arms. "Hush, lovely Lady. Your sister is here. Azhure is here. She has enough experience and she has the hands and the love to guide you through. The path you take now will have little to do with me . . . the planting is done."

Faraday started to cry. "Goodwife . . ."

"Hush, child," the Goodwife comforted. "I have a family to go back to." She hesitated and looked at the wood stretching behind her. "Or perhaps I will wander the forest paths a while. Collect herbs. Recollect the stories my granny told me. Yes. That's what I'll do. Wander the forest paths a while." Her broad face broke into a smile, then it faded a little and she hugged Faraday tightly to her. "No doubt we will meet, my girl, along those paths one day. Wandering. Free. Unfettered."

Faraday swallowed her tears and nodded, understanding. Unfettered. Yes.

"Brave girl," the Goodwife murmured, and kissed Faraday's cheek. "Don't forget the words your Mother taught you."

Faraday sniffed and wiped the tears from her eyes.

"When all seems lost and dead and dark,
Of this I can assure you—
A Mother's arms will fold you tight,
And let you roam unfettered."

The Goodwife sighed in profound relief. "Do not forget them, Daughter, *ever*. Call My name, and I will come."

She turned to go, but caught sight of Shra standing silent to one side. "Girl," she said, and Shra came to stand by her side.

"Girl, you must learn to speak as needed. You are too quiet for your wisdom."

"Yes, Mother."

The Goodwife smiled, her face full of love. " 'Yes, Mother,' that is all she can say. Well, it is enough." She reached out and patted Shra's cheek.

And then she was gone, striding into the woods, waving cheerfully over her shoulder, calling her goodbyes to the Avar women as she was went.

"She *was* the Mother, wasn't she, Faraday," Shra said quietly.

Faraday nodded, her eyes still on the Goodwife's form as it faded between the trees. "At times, Shra, yes she was, but mostly she was just Goodwife Renkin who was my friend."

Azhure's arm tightened about Faraday's waist as she felt the woman tremble. "Faraday, what happens now? The last tree is planted out . . . I would have thought . . ." Her voice trailed off.

Faraday shook her head. "I don't know, Azhure." She grimaced slightly and Azhure glanced at her, her worry for the woman deepening. But Faraday caught her breath and straightened a little. "I don't know. Perhaps there's something I should do."

"You need rest and you need *our* care," Barsarbe said as she joined the three standing under Mirbolt's spreading branches. She looked at Azhure as she spoke and her voice was hostile.

Faraday drew a quick, sharp breath. "I need only—" she began, when Shra pulled at her robe.

"Look!" she cried, pointing down the Forbidden Valley.

The women turned and stared, their eyes narrowing in the rapidly fading light. After a moment Azhure caught sight of a slight movement. A bird, fluttering above the Nordra. It had flown out of the Avarinheim.

"It is an owl," Shra said, her voice subdued now. "The Gray Guardian Owl."

"It haunts the canopy of the Avarinheim," Azhure explained to Faraday, remembering what Pease had told her. "It is rarely seen, but it watches over the entire forest, and at night its soft cry haunts the dreams of sleepers."

Barsarbe stiffened, resenting every word the woman spoke, but before she could speak, the Gray Guardian flew into the topmost branches of Tree Mirbolt.

And the gates opened.

The river spray thickened and yet, conversely, lightened, until the entire valley was cloaked in dense bright mist. In places it bulged, as if strange creatures cavorted within, and it reverberated with the echoes of far more than surging waters. Thousands of unseen eyes stared at them, distorted voices whispering Faraday's name, while power seeped toward and about them. Yet none of the watchers was frightened, while Faraday and Azhure, who knew, broke into laughter.

A shape firmed in the mist, then glowed, and then a great white stag bounded out of the mist and spray.

"Raum!" Faraday cried, opening her arms, and the stag halted before her, every muscle quivering, his eyes rolling slightly. Faraday reached out and gently touched his nose, then the stag leaped past them, almost knocking Barsarbe to the ground, and disappeared into the trees behind them.

"Raum?" Barsarbe muttered. "That was Raum?"

"He has been blessed," Faraday said quietly, staring at the spot where he had disappeared.

"Faraday!" Azhure half cried, half laughed. "Look!"

Hundreds upon thousands of creatures were swarming forth, creatures from the Enchanted Wood beyond the Sacred Grove. Birds and beasts and some that were neither, all rushing toward them in a tide of beauty and joy.

"Faraday!" Barsarbe cried, and tried to pull her out of the way.

Faraday resisted, clinging to Azhure. "No, Barsarbe. They won't harm us. Be still, now."

But Barsarbe would not listen to her. She stared an instant longer, then jumped behind Tree Mirbolt, her hands to her ears as a great euphony of sound and movement swept down the valley. Farther down the path the other Avar women similarly took refuge behind trees.

Faraday, Azhure and Shra stood their ground, allowing the great tide to part and sweep about them, laughing as beasts brushed their skin and then were gone, as birds tangled briefly within their hair and then freed themselves, as soft, hot breath tantalized then vanished.

"Oh!" Faraday cried as she turned with Azhure and Shra to watch the forest absorb the creatures.

"They'll run right through to the south," said Azhure.

"The creatures of the Enchanted Wood have entered their new home," Faraday said, then her smile faded. "Azhure? Shra? Do you hear anything?"

"Save the sounds of the night wakening about us?" asked Azhure.

Faraday frowned, and she glanced at the Forbidden Valley, then at the new forest to the south. "They are joined to the Avarinheim," she said slowly. "Surely the Song of the Earth Tree should have touched them by now? The forest will not truly awaken unless it is touched by the Earth Tree Song. Have I done something wrong?"

Azhure looked back along the Valley—she would never refer to it as Forbidden again. The mist had cleared and now only the spray of the river hung in the air. Soft moonlight—Azhure glanced up and nodded slightly—illumed the valley. The Avarinheim could be seen clearly, and, as she watched a squirrel scamper along the path by the Nordra, Azhure repressed the painful memory of Axis standing at its verge with his sword to Raum's throat.

What about the Earth Tree's Song? Without its touch the forest would be magical, surely, but would wield little power. Gorgrael might be able to regather his forces . . . winter might snatch another bite. All depended on the Earth Tree's Song.

Azhure felt Faraday tremble. "Faraday . . ." she began, searching for some useless platitude when, again, Shra jumped excitedly.

"Hear it?" she cried. "I hear her Song!"

Faraday and Azhure stilled and Barsarbe, whom both had forgotten, slowly emerged from behind the tree. Her face was white; in none of her experiences as a Bane had she seen so many strange things, nor been exposed to so much power, as she had this evening. And yet Azhure stood comfortably by Tree Friend's side as if she were indeed her sister and not her rival and betrayer. Even Shra stood entranced and relaxed, and Barsarbe wondered briefly if she had been ensorcelled by the violent power that Azhure so obviously wielded.

She stepped forward purposefully, determined to see Azhure off once and for all—by the Mother! had she not done enough harm!—when Barsarbe, too, stilled.

There was something moving along the paths of the Avarinheim.

She could not see it, she could not hear it, but she could *feel* it.

Faraday took a step forward, then reached blindly behind her to grasp Azhure's hand, pulling the woman forward as well. *"Listen!"*

No sound was discernible, but, like Barsarbe, Azhure and Shra could feel the presence of the Earth Tree speeding through the Avarinheim toward the new forest.

And Azhure could also feel danger. "Faraday . . . Shra," she said urgently. "Out of the way. *Now!*"

Faraday gave a soft cry of protest as Azhure pulled her backward, but Shra caught the sense of urgency, and between them they pulled Faraday back to Tree Mirbolt. Barsarbe stood undecided for long heartbeats, looking first at the Avarinheim, then to Azhure and Shra, then she too retreated.

"Barsarbe," Azhure said. "We shall all have to share Mirbolt's shade."

Barsarbe glared at her, then looked away.

Faraday clung to Mirbolt's great trunk, not the least perturbed by the feeling of intense power that rushed—surged—toward them down the paths of the Avarinheim.

"Feel her gladness?" she cried, and Azhure did not know to what she referred—Mirbolt or the Earth Tree—but she did, indeed, feel it. It vibrated through her entire body, uncomfortably so.

Then it emerged to flood down the valley.

It was the Earth Tree Song, but sung at such a pitch and with such power and emotion that Azhure could not only feel it, she could almost *see* it.

Anything standing in its path would have been bowled over and flung into the river as it, too, rushed past. And, like the river, the narrow confines of the rocky chasm concentrated the Song until it was almost unbearable and everyone, Faraday included, pressed hands to ears and screwed their eyes shut as the Song of the Earth Tree plunged by them into the forest.

Then silence.

Puzzled, the women slowly, foolishly, loosened their hands.

Silence for one, long heartbeat.

Then the entire forest of Minstrelsea burst, *screamed*, into Song.

Azhure felt Faraday collapse against her, screaming herself, and she wrapped her arms as tight as she dared about the woman, using her own power to try to cocoon them against the sound of Forest Song.

All Tencendor quavered, and people and Icarii cried and clung to the backs of chairs and to table edges and to each other as the Song burst over the land. But the pain did not last. It was only the initial rush that was so devastating. The first burst of Song quickly gathered strength until it moved from sound into pure emotion, and then from pure emotion into even purer power. The Song moved beyond the ability of mortal ears to hear it, but it was still apparent to any who stepped beneath the forest canopy as a feeling of tremendous power that drifted about the trees, and a tremor underfoot that vibrated through the trunks of the trees and caused the leaves to tremble.

Only those who wielded strange powers themselves would ever be able to hear the melody of the Forest Song.

Deep in his Ice Fortress, Gorgrael tipped back his head and shrieked until the sound reverberated about the ice walls and tore through both ice and flesh.

"Bitch! Bitch! Bitch! Both of you!"

At his feet, dwarfed by the great figure arching above him, the baby boy also writhed and shrieked, but terror rather than anger fueled his screams.

Scratches and abrasions lined and shadowed his naked, battered body.

Azhure blinked. What was wrong? Was her sudden presentiment of disaster caused only by the cessation of the audible Song? She opened her mouth to speak but was forestalled by Faraday's action.

Faraday closed her eyes and leaned her forehead against Tree Mirbolt. "Mother, thank you," she murmured. "Thank you."

Now she pressed Azhure's hand to the tree trunk as Jack had so long ago pressed hers to the tree in the Silent Woman Woods. "Azhure, Mirbolt," she said, her voice harsh with power, "know each other, accept each other."

She paused and stared at Azhure.

Azhure, her eyes enormous, nodded once, and she could feel Mirbolt accept as well.

Faraday sighed. "Remember, Mirbolt, when Azhure calls, you must assist her, and bring your sisters as well. Azhure? Azhure, when Axis needs the trees then you must be the one to call them."

"I witness," Shra said clearly, and placed her small hand, over those of the two women.

"Oh, no!" Azhure protested, ignoring Shra. "You are Tree Friend, not I. I . . . I have already taken too much from you, don't make me take this as well."

Faraday smiled. "I have done my task as Tree Friend, Azhure. My task was to plant the trees out—"

"And to bring the trees behind Axis," Azhure said stubbornly. Stars! She didn't want this on her conscience as well!

"You can do that as well as I, Azhure, and I still have to bring the Avar behind Axis. Without them all will yet be lost." She glanced at Barsarbe, then sighed. "But for the moment, until Fire-Night, I will live only for myself and for my—"

She was cut off by a nervous bray.

"Mother!" Faraday exclaimed, "I've forgotten all about the donkeys!"

She turned away from Azhure and Shra and looked into the forest. Trotting toward her were the two donkeys, one burdened with its saddlebags, the other still pulling the blue cart behind it.

"Oh, you poor things," Faraday murmured, stroking them and pulling their ears. "You have worked so well for me, carried me through so much, and I have forgotten you. Here . . ."

She pulled the halter off the first donkey, paused to catch her breath, then undid the girth about its belly.

"Gracious heavens," Azhure grumbled, pushing her to one side as she quickly divested both donkeys of their tack. "You are in no condition to be playing stableboy, Faraday."

Faraday grinned and continued to stroke one of the donkey's noses. "And you're not concerned about your bright red horse, Azhure, and your ghost-pale hounds?"

"Oh, Stars!" Azhure breathed, her face paling.

"Well, no matter," Faraday laughed, "for here they come, too."

And indeed they did, horse and hounds looking slightly bemused by the events of the past hour, but unharmed. Azhure sighed in relief as she patted Venator's nose, then bent down to murmur a greeting to Sicarius.

"At least you didn't decide to hunt the Stag, dog. The Forest is out of bounds for you and your horde. You may only ever hunt on the plains. Remember that."

The hound gave a brief grunt in reply, then nosed Faraday's hand and wagged his tail at Shra.

Faraday smiled, then gave the donkey an abrupt shove. "Go!" she cried, upset to lose them but knowing she would not be able to take them with her. "Go! Run with your magical brethren through the forest! Go!"

The donkey tossed its head and tried to edge closer to Faraday. "Go!" she yelled, her voice breaking, and Azhure took a half-step toward her. "Go!"

The donkeys finally broke loose and cantered away, their heads high and to the side so that they could look at Faraday as long as possible.

"Go!" Faraday whispered as they disappeared into the gloom of the forest. "Go."

Azhure felt like crying. She'd traveled with the donkeys and Ogden and Veremund, too, and she realized it was not just the donkeys that Faraday was farewelling and chasing out of her life.

"Go," Faraday murmured one last time, then she gave a great cry and doubled over, slowly sinking to the ground.

"Faraday!" Azhure was by her side instantly. "Are you . . . ?"

One look from Faraday's great pain-filled green eyes was all the answer she needed.

Then angry hands were about Azhure's shoulders and she felt herself shoved to one side.

"She is in *our* care now," Barsarbe spat, her eyes furious. "*We* will take care of her!"

Faraday reached up with one hand and seized the front of Barsarbe's robe. "No! I am in *Azhure's* care, Bane! I told you that once I had planted the trees all that I did afterward I would do for love of Axis and Azhure. Barsarbe, *you are not welcome on this path!*"

Barsarbe recoiled, stunned. "Faraday!"

"Go back to your people, Barsarbe. I will rejoin you for Fire-Night in the groves."

"Faraday! I'm sorry. I . . . I didn't mean . . ."

But Faraday had twisted her head away and was looking at the little girl. *Shra? I will be back, I shall have to be. Will you want for me?*

Yes.

Shra, I worry about Barsarbe. I should not have been so short with her . . . but . . .

Yes, I know. I understand.

I fear that she will turn the Avar against Axis.

Faraday, concentrate only on your own struggle now. I will see you at Fire-Night . . . and the Avar will be ready to stand behind Axis. To help him.

Shra, I wish you and yours only the best.

And I you, Faraday. Go now, Azhure will look after you.

But Faraday was not quite finished. *Shra? Shra? Thank you for liking Azhure. Thank you for accepting her.*

It was my honor, Faraday. Go now.

Faraday grabbed Azhure's hand, her face white.

"Believe me," Azhure said, masking her worry. "I know."

Then, before Barsarbe's horrified gaze and Shra's understanding one, both vanished.

*   *   *

"We need peace and space," Azhure said as the silver pelt stepped up to her.

"I know," the ancient Horned One replied, "but Enchantress, there is something I must tell you."

"Can't it wait? Can't you see that—"

"Yes, yes," he snapped, and hearing his impatience, Azhure and Faraday paused and stared at him.

"Enchantress, the Destroyer has seized your son."

"What!"

The Horned One grabbed her shoulders. "Gorgrael has Caelum!"

"No," Azhure whispered. "No." She suddenly recalled her vague feeling of horror as Faraday had planted out the last seedling, then the vivid premonition of disaster she'd experienced when the great forest had burst into Song. Had that been Caelum calling to her? Was he even now screaming for her, wondering why his Mama had not come? *Oh Stars!*

Faraday gave her a half-hearted shove. "Go."

But Azhure was not as easy to get rid of as the donkeys. "And who will tend you, Faraday? The Horned Ones?"

"The Mother will—"

"No!" Azhure abruptly hissed. No . . . she owed Faraday too much to leave her now . . . but Caelum? What was Gorgrael *doing* to him? A low wail escaped her.

Now Faraday had her arms about Azhure, trying to give her comfort. "Azhure, go to him."

"No." Azhure had her expression under perfect control now. "Who knows, it may be a trick designed to trap me or Axis. Probably is, in fact. So, no more arguments, Faraday. I will stay."

"Azhure," Now it was the Horned One. "He—"

"I don't want to know!" she hissed. "Can't you see? Faraday needs me now. *I can't leave her!"*

The Horned One took a deep breath and looked at Faraday as if for the first time, then he turned back to Azhure and bowed his head. "When it is finished, Enchantress, then fly. Fly home to Sigholt, and then rescue that boy!"

54

About the Camp Fire

Axis wheeled Belaguez about and reined him in. Stretched out in a column almost half a league long behind him, the army glinted and sparkled in the late afternoon sun. Far above, two Crest of the Strike Force wheeled; apart from several farflight scouts to the north the remainder of the Strike Force waited a league to their west, at the site chosen to camp that night.

They had made good time in the ten days since leaving Sigholt—no snow and ice lay over the ground to slow their progress now. The soil was wet, even sodden in places, and the sky still cloudy this far north, but the Icarii scouted out the best route each morning. Men and horses had found the going easy, and the only complaint was that the northerly night-wind was still bitter enough to frost the blankets. Tonight they would camp at the extreme western edge of the Urqhart Hills, tomorrow they would swing for the north . . . and Gorkenfort.

Gorkenfort. Axis' face tensed. This would have to be the final battle with these damned Skraelings because Axis did not think he could bear yet another indecisive outcome. Though he doubted that this outcome would be indecisive. Either one or the other would have their power broken. And the odds were in Gorgrael's favor.

Before Axis waited a Skraeling host of some three hundred thousand; more, if they had bred in the months since the Azle. The snow and ice still clung to Gorkenfort and Gorken Pass; that would aid the Skraelings and hinder Axis' force. Gorgrael, and Timozel, would have the aid of the seven thousand Gryphon. Axis shivered.

And to meet them Axis had a force of some twenty-six thousand, including the Strike Force.

And Azhure. If she got here in time.

Damn you, Azhure, Axis cursed silently, why aren't you here with me? Why does Faraday need you so badly? Could we not have let Artor run free with his damned Plow for a few more weeks yet?

His twenty-six thousand would die if Azhure did not join him in time. They were good men all, but they would be decimated in half an hour.

"Lady Moon," he whispered, seeing the just-risen disc through a break in the clouds, "be there for me."

But if Azhure hadn't left Smyrton by now, would she be able to catch him in time? Even with her talents, could she move fast enough through either time or space to help him?

And the trees . . . without the trees, Axis knew the Skraeling force would overwhelm him whatever happened with the Gryphon. Azhure might be able to deal with those flying obscenities but she could do little against the Skraelings. For them Axis would need the trees.

Damn those two women! Where were they? What were they doing?

"Axis?"

Belial. Axis made a conscious effort to relax his face. "My friend?"

Belial pulled his bay stallion in next to Belaguez. "Axis, half the column has passed you by while you sit there worrying."

"I was not—"

Belial laughed. "Not worrying? I have known you too long to believe that lie."

Axis sighed. "I was thinking about Gorkenfort. Wishing Azhure was here with me . . . with us."

Belial shrugged. "Either we win Gorkenfort or we lose it, Axis, and sitting on your horse, fretting about it is not going to tip the balance one way or the other."

Axis reached across to grip Belial's shoulder. "You have the soul of a philosopher, Belial."

"Nonsense." Belial grinned. "I am merely trying to shake you out of your fugue so you can order camp to be pitched. It's been a long time since our all-too-brief noon meal, and my stomach is complaining."

Belial sat before the fire and stared at the flames. The meal had been good and there was nothing more to be done tonight than to stretch out and try to think pleasant thoughts. Magariz was inspecting the sentries, Arne checking the gear for tomorrow's march, Ho'Demi was bedded down early with his wife (and wasn't he the lucky one?), and SpikeFeather had joined one of the Crests for his evening meal. Now only Belial and Axis shared the fire, and Belial wondered if he could prevail upon the man to pull his harp from the saddlebags and play a tune or two before they took to their sleeping rolls for the night. He leaned forward, but the words never left his mouth.

For, just as he was about to speak, the world went mad.

A great sound rushed over the plain and enveloped them. Song. So beautiful yet so powerful that it battered all before it. Belial wrapped his arms about his head as the wave of noise hit him, and yet even through its great surge he could hear men shouting and horses screaming. The Song grew deeper and more intense until Belial could feel it pounding through his entire body . . . then . . . then slowly the Song changed, faded, vanished, although Belial could still feel it throb through his flesh and through the ground beneath him for a further minute or so.

"What—" he mumbled, standing up. About him men were similarly scrambling to their feet, their faces puzzled. Others calmed the horses, murmuring to the beasts and petting them with long, soothing strokes.

"Faraday," Axis said, and Belial turned around to look at him.

"What?"

"Faraday," Axis repeated, and said to Belial, "she has completed planting. The new forest has joined with the Avarinheim. What we just heard . . . felt . . . was the initial burst of Song as the entire forest below the Avarinheim joined with the Earth Tree Song."

"And now they no longer sing?"

"They still sing, Belial, but the Song has moved into such realms of power and pitch that most can no longer hear it." Axis' entire body relaxed. "Thank the Stars. Perhaps Azhure can now ride to join us."

He turned aside for a few moments to talk to several unit commanders who had rushed to the fire, reassuring them and asking them to relay his reassurances to the rest of the army. "It was but Tree Song," he concluded, "and it means added power for us. Do not be concerned."

Unless the trees do not fight as Faraday has promised.

Belial slowly relaxed as Axis sank down beside the fire again. As the word about the Tree Song spread men talked in low voices around their campfires; Belial heard occasional soft laughter punctuate the night.

"Good news, Axis."

Axis nodded. "Yes. Gorgrael must have heard that as well. It will virtually negate his hold over the weather."

"And perhaps he worries, too."

Axis laughed. "I shall sleep with that thought tonight, Belial. It shall cause me pleasant dreams."

They sat some time in companionable silence. Belial remembered his earlier thought that he could ask Axis to play a while, but a gentle hand on his shoulder stayed his words; he was fated, it seemed, not to hear the harp that night.

"Belial," a rich voice said, "I am pleased to see you again."

The beautiful woman who had joined him outside Axis' tent the night Azhure had healed him was again standing by Belial's side and smiling at him. Again his face reddened at the filmy robe she wore, and her eyes crinkled in amusement.

"I am here to talk with Axis, Belial, but you may stay. Listen. What I have to say should not be borne by Axis alone."

Bad news, then. The woman stepped to Axis' side and sank gracefully down beside him so that she sat close, her body touching his at hip and breast, her hand on his shoulder. "Axis."

He took a deep breath, unsettled by her appearance and her touch. "Xanon."

She leaned over the distance still between them and kissed Axis on the mouth and Belial stirred, remembering the extraordinary liberties that she and her companions had taken in greeting him that night. The Star Gods, they had called themselves as they had farewelled him. Belial was not truly surprised by anything anymore, not after the shocks of the past two years. Star Gods, perhaps, but the fact that they had said they were friends of Axis and Azhure was more important.

Well, Belial thought as he watched the woman draw slowly back, a smile on her lips, he hoped Azhure didn't mind the liberties friend Xanon took with her husband.

"Axis, I have news."

"The forest sings," he said. "I know."

"Yes, the forest sings. But Azhure and Faraday have done more than join the forests. Axis," her face lit up with pure joy, "Artor is destroyed!"

"Azhure?" Axis asked.

"Azhure is well. Oh, Axis! She is so well! She set her pack to hunt and she hounded Artor through the same wastes where he imprisoned us. He turned to fight, but he was no match. She set her knife, here," her hand pressed against his breast, "and she turned it about in his heart. Artor is no more."

Axis sighed and closed his eyes. "Artor is no more."

Belial sat, staring at them. Azhure had hunted *Artor*! By the Mother, what sort of woman was she?

Axis opened his eyes and smiled at Xanon, gently lifting her hand from his chest where she had let it rest. "And now Azhure comes to join me?"

Xanon stiffened and she turned her face away.

"What's wrong? Xanon, *what's wrong?*"

"Axis." Xanon ran her tongue across her lips. "Axis, Gorgrael has taken Caelum."

Caelum?

Belial did not hear the thought, but he saw the horror ripple across Axis' face and felt it himself. Mother! He dropped his eyes from Axis' face, unable to bear the agony he saw there.

Axis stirred as if to rise but Xanon wrapped her arms about him and kept him down.

"Caelum?" he whispered.

"We do not know how," Xanon said. "How could Gorgrael have snatched the boy from Sigholt?"

"I have to go to him—"

"No!" Xanon's arms tightened and her hands dug into his upper arms. "No, Axis, you can't!"

"I can't?" he shouted, and tried to twist away from her. "Who are you to tell me that I *can't*?"

"I am the voice of reason," Xanon said fiercely. "*Listen to me, Axis!* Why has Gorgrael snatched Caelum? *Why?* To trap you, that's why."

"She's right," Belial said, and Axis threw him a furious glance.

"Listen to us," Xanon continued. "*Listen*, damn you! Gorgrael can feel his power slipping. He's moved to desperate measures. Stars knows the risk he took in snatching Caelum from Sigholt. With the boy he hopes that he can tempt you away from Gorken Pass. Tempt you into making a precipitous rush to his Ice Fortress without the Rainbow Scepter fast in your hand. Axis, if you do not hold the Scepter he will defeat you."

"Caelum," Axis muttered, seeming not to have heard Xanon's words. "Has Gorgrael killed him?"

"You would have felt it, had he died," Xanon said, her eyes bright with compassion.

"Then he lives to be tortured by Gorgrael," Axis said bitterly. "Perhaps death would be preferable. Xanon? What can I do?"

She hesitated, then stroked his face with a hand. "You will have to trust in Azhure."

"Azhure?" Now Axis did manage to free himself from her encircling arms. "*Azhure?*"

"She is the only one who can help him at the moment."

"She is the only one who can be risked, you mean!" Axis snarled.

"You cannot go, Axis! This is *exactly* what Gorgrael wants! To meet you without the Rainbow Scepter in your hands! That would mean instant victory for him."

Axis let Xanon wrap him in her arms once more, and she rocked him gently for a few minutes.

"Will she be in danger?" Axis asked eventually.

"Yes, Axis, I am afraid she will be, but Adamon will help her as much as he can."

"She defeated Artor." Axis tried to find hope.

"Yes," Xanon replied, "but she cannot hope to kill Gorgrael. His power is . . . different . . . to Artor's, and Artor was already mortally damaged by the collapse of the Seneschal and the loss of faith in the Way of the Plow. And

Azhure could use the power of the Nine, the full circle, to aid her against Artor. She cannot hunt Gorgrael."

"She can use none of her skills against Gorgrael? But his power is weakened, too."

"Axis," Xanon spoke slowly, but firmly. "Gorgrael's life is tied to yours by the Prophecy. None can be destroyed unless it be by the other. Yes, Gorgrael's power has weakened, but only concerning his hold over the weather. Otherwise he is as virulent as ever he was."

"Then Stars help her," Axis whispered, "for without her, Gorkenfort will be lost. *I* will be lost."

Gorgrael tilted his head and snarled at the fretting baby. He lifted his taloned hand again, but this time he stayed the blow.

The baby would be no use dead.

But if Gorgrael had known that the baby would fret and whimper and whine night and day then he would seriously have reconsidered the entire plan.

"Silence!" he hissed, and the baby swallowed and tried to halt his ceaseless crying, staring at Gorgrael with eyes wide with terror and pain.

Mama?

"Your Mama will not help you here, wretch." Gorgrael dropped his hand and regarded the baby, his silver eyes merciless. The fact that this baby was his nephew meant nothing to him. In fact, Gorgrael did not know what it was about this limp, constantly complaining lump of flesh that made Axis and his woman love it so much.

Would Axis risk all to rescue it?

Well, he would know soon enough. If Axis was going to try then he would try soon. After all, who knew what the nasty Destroyer was doing to the poor little baby?

Gorgrael smiled and teased the baby with a rough claw down the length of his body.

The boy whimpered despite his attempts to keep silent and Gorgrael's face twisted. Nasty, *nasty* thing! He dug his claw in, to teach the thing to keep still and quiet, and the boy screwed his eyes shut and opened his mouth.

But no sound came out. The scream remained silent.

"Good baby," Gorgrael smiled, and patted the thing on the head. "Good baby."

Perhaps the mewly creature could be trained, after all.

55

The Dream

From the edge of the great forest Azhure flew northwest, across the Nordra and down the HoldHard Pass. Flew almost literally, for Azhure wrapped herself and her horse in so much power that she made the eight- to ten-day journey in under three. Behind her the hounds coursed silently, their breath reserved for running.

Azhure did not stop the entire way, and yet, when she reined up before the bridge into Sigholt, Venator still pranced as fresh as the hour he had begun his run and the hounds milled restlessly about his legs.

"Well?" Azhure demanded as the horse stepped onto the bridge.

"He is gone," the bridge mourned, "and we do not know where, I—"

The bridge had been about to confess her own sin in his kidnap but Azhure had not waited to hear it. Already she was sliding from Venator's back in the courtyard of the Keep and running for the entrance.

Rivkah, sitting morosely with Cazna in the Great Hall after their evening meal, leaped to her feet as the door burst open.

"Azhure!" She held out her arms to hug her but Azhure evaded them. "Well?"

Cazna stood, her face pale. For two days and nights she had remained abed, so terrified she could not rise, seeing again and again as Imibe was torn apart; watching again and again as the horrific creature stood over her, one hand raised to smite her dead, the other clutched about Caelum, dangling helpless at his side.

"The roof," Cazna said, and Azhure swung her fierce glare her way.

"You were there?"

Cazna nodded, then winced and cried out as Azhure seized her shoulders in rough hands. *"What happened?"*

"We were on the roof. Imibe, myself and the children."

"DragonStar too?" Azhure snapped.

Cazna nodded, her blue eyes enormous.

"And?"

"And . . . and a great shadow fell from the sky. A Gryphon, from the description I have heard of them. On its back was . . . a creature fouler than any nightmare, Azhure. He went straight for Imibe, who held Caelum. She . . . she was torn to bits."

Azhure briefly closed her eyes. Imibe had been a friend. Poor Imibe; and yet she had died a warrior's death, protecting Caelum to the last.

And poor Caelum. Twice in his short life to have such horror descend on him from the skies. *"And?"*

"And the creature seized Caelum from her arms," Cazna continued hoarsely, more terrified now by the anger in Azhure's eyes than by the memory.

"And yet you lived? *Why,* Cazna?" Her voice was very soft.

"Would you that I died too, Azhure? Would that make you feel better?" Now it was Cazna who battled with her temper. "The creature turned and came for me. I thought I *was* dead! I cowered on the paving, trying to protect Drago with my body . . ."

Would that he was the one taken, Azhure thought.

". . . but he paused, his talons," Cazna shuddered, "red with Imibe's blood, then stepped back. 'A witness,' he said. 'Good.' Then he mounted his flying creature, Caelum . . . Caelum still caught fast in his claws, and flew away. Azhure . . . Azhure! I could do nothing!"

Rivkah glanced at Cazna, then took Azhure by the arm. "Azhure," she said, "Azhure, who was it?"

Azhure looked at her, confused. What did she mean? She blinked, then realized that the women could not know. "Gorgrael," she said.

"Oh Stars!" Rivkah cried. *"Gorgrael?* Why?"

"Why do you think, Rivkah? For the company?" Azhure's voice crackled across the hall and Cazna stepped backward. Never had she seen Azhure so angry.

"Why, Rivkah? To trap either Axis or myself."

"Azhure, what will you do?"

Azhure stared at her. "I will go after him. I have to. How can I abandon Caelum to Gorgrael?"

"But you just said that—"

"A trap? Yes, it surely is. But better that I be trapped than Axis." Azhure paused. "Better I die than he."

Then she turned on her heel and stalked from the hall.

*   *   *

The roof was quiet, bathed in cold moonlight. Yet Caelum's terror still reverberated here. When Azhure closed her eyes she could *feel* his scream, see with
his eyes as the shadow plummeted from the skies, recoil with him as Imibe's
hot blood splattered across his face.

She lowered her head into her hands and wept. What could she do? She
had virtually exhausted her strength in her mad dash to Sigholt—could she
now do the same to reach Gorgrael's Ice Fortress? No. No, not that. Even with
renewed strength and power it would still take her days, weeks, to reach the
icy tundra.

And by then Caelum would surely be dead. If Gorgrael did not kill him,
the boy would not be able to live so long with this degree of terror. Even now,
even if she could rescue him this night, the experience would scar him for the
rest of his life.

Azhure sank to her knees, then slowly collapsed so that she rested her
forehead on the cold stone paving.

Caelum was dead. If not now, then soon.

She cried until she could cry no more, then she slowly sat up, her face
ravaged with grief. She sniffed, and tried to wipe the tears from her cheeks.

"Here, let me do that for you."

She jumped, even though she'd instantly, recognized Adamon's soft voice.

He knelt down beside her and held her close, cradling her against his warm
body, wiping her face with soft, dry hands.

"Adamon . . ."

"I know, sweetheart, I know."

"Why does Caelum have to be the one to suffer like this? *Why?* Why not
me or Axis?"

"Have not you and Axis suffered enough, Azhure? Why wish more on
yourself?"

"But *Caelum!*"

"Shush," he crooned into her hair, holding her tight against him. "Caelum
yet lives, and he is as strong in body and spirit as his parents."

"But—"

"I know, Azhure. But now you listen to me." Adamon drew back so he
could look her in the eyes. "You were right when you told Rivkah that Gorgrael
wants to trap Axis. But he does not know you. He does not know the strength
of your love, nor the strength of your determination. There remains the slight
chance that you can rescue Caelum."

Azhure seized on the hope he offered. "How? Can I storm Gorgrael's Ice
Fortress? Can I destroy him as I did Artor?"

Adamon risked a small smile, masking his own anxiety. "So many questions! Azhure, to rescue Caelum will take all your courage and cunning and

then more. Gorgrael is not like Artor. He is dangerous . . . far more dangerous than the Plow god, and if he corners *you*, traps *you*, then the Prophecy will be torn apart and Axis will die."

"Why?"

"Because then Gorgrael would have *you*, Axis' Lover; and your death would be Axis' death."

"The third verse . . ." Azhure whispered.

Adamon nodded. "Yes, the third verse. Azhure, you cannot go storming in there with hounds clamoring and an arrow to the Wolven. Gorgrael would laugh at you, rip your hounds apart and break the Wolven over his knee—he may doubt himself sometimes, but never doubt that he is more powerful than you. And once your bow and your hounds were gone, Gorgrael would take you. And he would have many weeks in which to enjoy you before Axis arrived."

Azhure leaned back, her face white and still.

"Knowing all this, Azhure, do you still want to chance rescuing Caelum? Knowing that to fail would mean not only your death and your son's death, but Axis' as well?"

"And if Axis and I survive, how could I look him in the eye, knowing that I hesitated to risk myself—"

"And Axis," Adamon added under his breath.

"—in Caelum's rescue?" She paused. "I have no choice. I gave Caelum life, and I would risk my life to let him live his."

Adamon had expected nothing less from her. "Then listen to me, Azhure. You will have to use all your power, and all that I lend you, to rescue your son. And this power will have to be tempered with even more guile. Now, did you not carry Caelum within your body for nigh on eight months?"

Azhure nodded.

"And is he not flesh of your flesh?"

Azhure nodded again.

Adamon smiled and kissed her gently. "Then listen to me, Azhure. Listen well."

She sat in a shaft of moonlight, letting it surround her, fill her.

She was naked, her raven hair spilling down her back and over her breasts, the moonlight rippling over her ivory skin and sparking blue glints in her hair.

In a corner sat Adamon, Azhure's blue suit in his hands, his eyes fixed on the woman. He sent her all the strength of his power.

Azhure let it flood her, renew her own strength, bolster her courage, calm her.

She put everything from her mind save the beauty of the moonlight and the warmth of its caress. "Lady Moon," she said, and she talked only to herself, "bathe me in your light."

The moonlight flared and Adamon blinked in the sudden radiance. But he did not shift his eyes from Azhure.

"Lady Moon, bathe Tencendor in your light."

And the Moon bathed the land in her light, and across the land, men and women stirred as dream filled their sleep.

"Dream," Azhure whispered, her own eyes wide.

But she did not see Sigholt's roof. Instead she saw the land as the moon saw it. Saw every field and furrow and laneway. Saw every roof and every doorway. Saw, and heard, as dogs sat back to howl their homage. Saw cats slink into shadows and owls blink and tilt their heads in thought.

The shadow of the Moon slid over the land and with it slid Azhure's mind eye. There lay Carlon, people still crowding the midnight streets, pointing to the sky.

She smiled.

There lay the Grail Lake and the Cauldron Lake and the Fernbrake Lake, and they winked at the moon.

Azhure winked back.

There, to the north, lay Axis' army, and moonlight flooded the campsite so that sentries shaded their eyes and all those asleep murmured as dream flooded their minds. They all dreamed of the same thing.

There tossed Axis, half asleep, half awake. He mumbled also, but then his sleep quieted and deepened as the dream caught him. He smiled.

"Dream on," Azhure whispered, and she let her gaze rest a moment.

To east and west and north and south the tides beat and tugged at the shores of Tencendor and with them fluctuated the dream. The Moon, driver of the tides and keeper of dreams.

"North," Azhure whispered, and the moonlight surged northward, a flood in itself, and the northern Avarinheim and Icescarp Alps rippled underneath.

And then . . . then the great northern tundra. Stretching unmapped for as far as the imagination would allow, flat ice, barren soil, lifeless.

Except for the great Ice Fortress that reared in a thousand reflected colors toward the moon. A gigantic prism that was too beautiful for the horror it contained, and yet horror it was, for it was no natural creation.

"Linger," she whispered, and the moonlight lingered.

Watching, Adamon saw her draw a deep breath and close her eyes. She was there.

Courage and daring, Azhure, and good fortune, my darling.

Moonlight bathed the Ice Fortress, and as the light swept down its corridors and across its halls and through its spaces, Gryphon mewed and sighed in their sleep. And they all dreamed the same dream.

Gorgrael twisted in his chair, uncomfortable, half awake yet too languorous to rise and fall to his mat before the fire. He whispered and muttered and . . . finally succumbed to the dream.

He dreamed of a white light so pure he almost cried at its beauty. It called to him. Whispered. "Lover? Lover? Lover?"

"Yes," he muttered. "Yes, I am here."

Deep in sleep, the tens of thousands of Gryphon writhed and trembled across the spaces of the fortress, each seeking her lover.

Azhure tilted her head back and moaned deep in her throat and Adamon leaned forward, sending all that he could without sending the last spark of his life as well. *Courage, my darling.*

And Azhure took courage.

She gazed at the Ice Fortress from her vast height. Then she began to feel. Feel . . . feel the tiny heartbeat that reverberated through the moonbeam toward her.

She knew that heartbeat. Had not her body cradled it for eight months? Had not her arms clasped it to her breast for a year and more after her body had struggled in its birth?

Thump-thud.

Azhure trembled.

Thump-thud.

She moaned.

Thump-thud.

And she grasped it, using it to pull her toward the Ice Fortress.

Thump-thud.

She disappeared from atop Sigholt and Adamon cried out.

Thump-thud.

She descended through the moonbeam, letting the thud of her son's heart pull her to him.

Thump-thud!

Gorgrael dreamed of a woman of such exquisite beauty that his breathing quickened and a moan escaped his lips. She walked the corridors of his Ice Fortress, her hands extended, her mouth open in longing . . . and she walked toward him!

Azhure walked the dreams of every sleeper in the land. Many called her name, many more cried wordlessly, wanting her, reaching for her.

But only in one habitation did she walk in actuality.

Gorgrael moaned again, louder this time, and he writhed in the chair. Never had he seen a naked woman before, never had he thought a woman deprived of her clothes could stir such desires in him. Never! This was a sensation worth reveling in!

His blood surged with the ebb and flow of the tides that beat relentlessly at the edges of the northern ice-cap.

His clawed hands clenched the arms of his chair in time with the crash of the waves.

And still she came. She walked sinuously, invitingly, a smile on her face, gladness lighting her eyes. She stepped about the writhing Gryphon, uncaring, and shook her hair back from her face and off her body and laughed . . . and Gorgrael cried out.

He clung to the dream, for he did not want to lose this. Not now! Not before she had reached him!

She was outside his door now, and it glided open before her.

Yes!

Now she glided, glided across the floor, and Gorgrael's mouth fell open and his tongue unraveled and dripped across his chin.

"I have come only for you," she whispered, behind his chair now, and the next moment he felt her hands on his shoulders, and then sliding down his body, sliding, sliding . . .

His could not help himself and his body convulsed.

"For you only," she whispered, and her mouth brushed his brow.

Oh! she was so exquisite!

"Only for you. Come."

Oh!

"Come."

And Gorgrael's eyes flew open and he turned to grab her, to throw her to the floor and to take her as she so desperately wanted.

But his claws seized only thin air.

Snarling in frustration and desire Gorgrael leaped to his feet and . . .

. . . saw the beautiful woman, naked, aching for his touch, standing with the mewling infant in her hands and cradled to her breast. Moonlight flooded into the chamber and bathed her in light so pure it seemed almost as if she were made from moonlight herself.

"Only for you," she whispered into the boy's hair.

Still trapped by the memory of his dream Gorgrael's solitary thought was to wrest the tiresome infant from her hands and seize her himself. Oh, he groaned, see how smooth the skin, see its sheen, see the curve of hip and breast and the loveliness of her face as she turned toward him.

Yes, tear the baby from her arms and possess her. A moment more, a single breath, and she could be his.

She lifted her mouth from the baby's hair and smiled at him. "Lover," she whispered, and Gorgrael lunged.

And she vanished, and the baby with her.

Gorgrael's arms embraced nothing but the lingering of her scent, and he coupled with nothing but the rough stone floor as it rushed to meet him.

Howling in fury and maddened frustration he scrambled to his feet, his silver eyes narrowed now, his mind fully alert.

And saw nothing but the loneliness of his chamber.

And heard nothing but the heave of his own breathing and the . . .

. . . *Thump-thud, Thump-thud, Thump-thud . . .*

. . . of a retreating heart.

"*Bitch!*" he screeched to the vaults above him, and around the corridors and apartments of his fortress Gryphon rose in a single black cloud.

"*Bitch!*" he screeched yet again, and at first he did not realize the absence of the baby, or its significance. All he knew was that the woman had teased him, flaunted herself in his dreams and in her flesh, and had then denied him the gratification his body demanded from her.

All over Tencendor, men and women cried in loss as the dream wavered and slipped away. Hands clutched at blankets and tears moistened pillows.

Gorgrael's shrieks ended as abruptly as they had begun. Now he remembered where he had seen that face before.

The woman, terrified, clutching the baby to her as the Gryphon plunged.

The woman, riding laughing beside Axis, the bow slung easy over her shoulder.

The power that had emanated from her.

Gorgrael snarled, low and vicious.

And now the baby was gone.

She had snatched him! *She* had deluded Gorgrael in his dreams, invaded, penetrated, and duped.

Promised favors, and then left him lingering with only the floor to embrace.

And she had snatched her son back! The bait was gone!

Now Gorgrael's entire body spasmed with fury, and he let his power ripple forth. Gryphon erupted screaming into the night and surged out of the Ice Fortress in a continually expanding ring, seeking, hunting, tracking.

But they and their master were too late.

The night was dark with thick cloud now and the moonlight had disappeared.

And so had she.

"*Hunt!*" the Destroyer cried to his Gryphon, and their efforts doubled.

"Hunt!" he whispered, and this time he did not particularly care *what* they hunted so long as they *killed!* Ripped apart! Tore limb from limb! Sated!

And then Gorgrael thought of a target.

56

Drago

The moonlight flared and Adamon cried out, turning his head away in pain. "Azhure?" Slowly he blinked as the radiance faded. "Azhure?"

She knelt in the center of the roof, her son cradled against her body, rocking him back and forth, crooning wordlessly.

Adamon rose and hesitantly walked over to her, running his eyes over her body as he did so. She appeared unhurt. But this was more than he could say for her son. Adamon drew in a sharp breath of horror as he saw the lacerations and bruises that covered the boy.

He rested a warm hand on Azhure's shoulder and squatted down besides her. "Azhure?"

She raised her head and stared at him. Her eyes were hard and bright. "Look what he has done to my son," she said.

"Will he . . . ?" Adamon was almost too afraid to ask.

"Live?" Azhure dropped her eyes and nodded. "Yes. None of his wounds are mortal, and with care and rest and love he will mend. His body, that is. Who can say how such an experience has touched his soul?"

The baby stirred and both Azhure and Adamon held their breath.

"Mama," he whispered, and he slowly reached up and grasped a tendril of Azhure's hair where it drifted over her breast. "Mama. You came."

Now Adamon let his own breath out in relief. "He trusted you, Azhure, and you came. That is all that matters to him."

Azhure hugged her son to her as tightly as she dared, her cheeks wet with tears. "Thank you, Adamon."

"I but gave you added strength, Azhure. The power and the courage to effect this rescue was of your doing."

"You told me what I should do."

The god smiled and tenderly stroked Azhure's hair back from her face. He leaned forward and kissed her damp cheek. "And did Gorgrael fall for it, my darling? Did his desire for his dream lover bury his suspicion?"

She laughed. "Fall for it? More than you can imagine, Adamon! It is more than the Destroyer's pride that is bent out of shape this night, I think!"

When Rivkah entered the Great Hall for her breakfast she halted in astonishment.

Azhure was seated before the fire, dressed in a pale gray gown, and asleep in her lap was Caelum.

Rivkah blinked, sure she was mistaken, sure that Azhure held one of her other children, but as she stepped forward, Azhure turned her head and smiled. Her smile was of such beauty, such peace and contentment, that Rivkah indeed knew it was Caelum she held. She stopped several paces away, her heart thumping. "How . . . ?"

Azhure's smile widened. "Did you dream last night?"

Rivkah's cheeks colored slightly. Indeed she had dreamed, but she could not quite remember exactly of what. But she *did* remember the sensations the dream had caused her— what had she been thinking, and in her condition?

Azhure's smile broadened. "Your cheeks stain as prettily as those of the pageboy who served my breakfast, Rivkah. I cannot think what came over you all."

Rivkah gathered her composure and sat down at a sidetable. The pageboy, his cheeks still rosy, laid a platter of fruit and bread before her, then almost stumbled in his rush to retreat to the shadows by the door.

"Caelum?" Rivkah asked softly, ignoring the food and staring at Caelum. He was scratched and bruised, but he slept peacefully enough, and his flesh did not have the flush of fever.

Azhure stroked her son's cheek gently. "He is well, Rivkah. Better than I could have hoped. His fear and his memories will fade over time."

The boy shifted slightly, and roused from his slumber. *I will never forget you standing there in the moonlight, Mama, smiling and reaching for me.*

"But how?" Rivkah asked.

Azhure shook her head. "A dream, Rivkah. Nothing more. The Moon was powerful last night, and she invaded many people's dreams."

Rivkah stifled her cross words, for she knew the tone. She had lived among the Icarii for thirty years and could not fail to recognize their cursed retreat into euphemisms and mysticisims whenever they did not want to explain something.

And whatever Azhure had done, she had bested Gorgrael.

She took a deep breath. "I am glad, Azhure," she said, and Azhure raised her eyes from her son.

"I know, Rivkah. Thank you."

"And now?"

"Now? Now I find out how Gorgrael managed to penetrate Sigholt's defenses." She stood up and held Caelum out to Rivkah. "Come, Caelum, sit with Rivkah for a few—"

She stopped mid-sentence, appalled by the shriek that flew from the boy's mouth. He clung to her desperately and she held him tight against her body, crooning again, her eyes locked with Rivkah's.

"I don't think he wants you to leave him again," Rivkah said gently.

Azhure nodded and, clutching the crying baby closely, she left the hall.

"He is home!" the bridge cried, gladness investing her voice with a boom that echoed about Sigholt.

Well, thought Azhure, now everyone knows. "Yes, bridge, he is home."

"Is he well?"

Azhure frowned at the tone of the bridge's voice—she sounded nervous. "Well enough, bridge, well enough."

Caelum had quieted now and clung to his mother, half asleep again.

"I am glad," the bridge whispered, "for I bear the guilt of his abduction."

Azhure was silent. Waiting. She had come to the bridge for this purpose— how was it that Gorgrael had managed to penetrate its defenses without the entire garrison being alerted?

"I should have challenged the invader, the *snatcher*."

"Why didn't you?"

"My fault," moaned the bridge. "My fault."

Azhure stifled her impatience. "Caelum is home, bridge, and he will eventually grow out of his terror. But he, and I, want to be sure that this will never happen again. Why didn't you challenge Gorgrael?"

"*Gorgrael!*" The bridge almost rocked in her distress. "The snatcher was *Gorgrael?*"

"Surely, bridge."

"Oh! Oh, woe is me! I have failed you, Enchantress, and I have failed the boy who rests so trustingly in your arms!"

"*Why didn't you challenge him?*"

The bridge was silent for a full minute. "Because I trusted him," she whispered eventually.

"You trusted *Gorgrael?*"

"No, no, no," the bridge moaned, "please do not make me tell you, Enchantress!"

"Tell me of your own free will or I will tear the memory from you, bridge!"

"I felt him descending, Enchantress, and I *did* begin to challenge him. But . . . but . . ."

"*But?*"

"But your son told me the visitor was true. A friend. And I trusted him. I trusted his judgment."

Azhure frowned. "*Caelum* told you the invader was true?"

"No, Enchantress. Your other son. DragonStar."

Cazna jumped as the door to her apartments flew open. Azhure strode in, Caelum . . . *Caelum!* . . . in her arms. Behind her hurried Rivkah, slightly out of breath with the rush, Reinald, the ancient and years-retired cook of Sigholt, and Sol Baldwin, the captain of the Keep's garrison.

"Where is he?" Azhure asked, her voice dangerously quiet. In her arms Caelum, fully awake, stared at Cazna, then dropped his eyes to the floor.

"You've got him back!" Cazna cried, genuine relief in her voice, and some of the hardness in Azhure's eyes faded. She had not been sure about Cazna's involvement, but now she understood the girl had been an unwitting dupe of DragonStar's manipulations.

"Yes," Azhure said, "I have him back. Now, where is my other son?"

Cazna smiled. So Azhure wasn't so hard of heart toward Drago as she pretended in Axis' presence. Well.

"I will fetch him for you," she said, and hurried into one of the lesser chambers. She bent down over Drago's crib—and almost recoiled at the expression on the baby's face.

"Drago! What's wrong?"

She reached down for him, horrified at the tension in his little body. Was he ailing for something?

The baby almost growled as Cazna lifted him out, and he extended his arms and legs so stiffly that Cazna had to carry him some distance away from her body as she rejoined the others.

"I don't know what's wrong," she said, her eyes concerned.

"I do," Azhure said. "Cazna, what I am going to do will not be very pleasant, and I do not want to befoul your apartments with the memory of it. But I need you as a witness, as I need Rivkah and Reinald and Sol. Come, we will go to the roof. This will need to be done in the open air."

Caelum cried softly at the mention of the roof.

Either you come with me to the roof, my love, or I will leave you in the care of one of the nurses. Which will it be?

Caelum shuddered, but he feared being left alone more than he feared the memories of the roof. *The roof, Mama.*

What I will do there will be . . . unpleasant . . . but I think you will benefit from the witnessing.

Yes, Mama.

Azhure had already sent a servant to the roof, and when the group arrived they saw that a table had been set out, a snowy cloth laid over it.

The servant had disappeared, but two Icarii Enchanters, visiting from the south, were waiting there.

They nodded silently at Azhure. She had spoken in their minds to call them to the roof, and they had some inkling of what was about to occur.

"Azhure?" Cazna asked, growing more disturbed by the moment. "What's going on?"

She looked at Rivkah, but the woman seemed as ignorant as she. But something bad was about to happen, Cazna was suddenly sure of that, because Azhure's face was set into hard lines and even Rivkah was stiff and uncomfortable. Reinald and Sol, also uneasy, stood behind Rivkah, their hands folded before them, their eyes downcast.

"Cazna," Azhure said, "lay DragonStar on the table and divest him of his wraps and clothes."

"Azhure—" Cazna began.

"Do it!" Azhure snapped, and Cazna jumped.

She walked to the table and laid Drago down, but he screamed the moment she laid a hand to his wraps.

"Azhure!" Cazna pleaded.

"Do it!"

Trembling, Cazna pulled the blankets from around Drago's vulnerable body, dropping them to the paving, then she unbuttoned his soft suit and pulled it over his shoulders and down his body. When she removed the swaddling linens he lay fully exposed to the morning sun and the eyes of the watchers.

"Now collect the blankets and clothes, Cazna, and stand back with the others."

Cazna looked frantically about the roof. Was no one going to help the baby? Her eyes shifted to Azhure. What was the woman going to do? There was death in her eyes.

"Azhure," she said, her voice edged with dread, "do you mean to harm your son? He's but a—"

"Do not even *think* to counsel me, Cazna!" Azhure hissed, taking a step forward. "Your over-soft mind has proved fertile ground indeed for someone with such strength of ill-will as DragonStar. Now, *stand back!*"

Without any further protest, Cazna joined Rivkah, and the older woman took her hand.

Azhure took a deep breath, calming herself. She cradled Caelum gently in her arms; the boy's eyes never left DragonStar. "For what I will do here today I need witnesses," she said, "and for you to understand you will need to hear *all* that is being said."

She exchanged glances with the Enchanters and they nodded slightly, knowing what it was she wanted them to do.

"All Icarii babies are born with minds as sharp as an adult's," she explained for the benefit of the three humans present who, save Rivkah, did not understand these things. "DragonStar's mind is even more acute, because he carries the powers of an Enchanter. He can not only think, but communicate with the mind voice." She paused. "But I want you all to hear what it is he is saying, so that any misunderstandings can be cleared away. My friends," she spoke to the Enchanters, "Axis once told me there was a Song for making the mind voice audible to human ears."

"Yes, Enchantress," one replied, his face grave. "My companion and I can make all that is thought spoken."

"Good. You may commence," she said, and soft music filtered through the air. Within an instant it had disappeared again, but, those with Icarii blood could feel the power that drifted about.

"*Whore!*" DragonStar's voice roared around the roof, "continually offering your body to the man who so abused you!"

Everyone flinched, but Cazna was stunned by the words and voice. Surely the Enchanters were making this up? No baby could be filled with this much bitterness . . . surely?

"I would take that as a compliment," Azhure said calmly, "if I thought that concern for me lay behind its rough language."

"You do not deserve such a son as me!"

"And with that I could not agree more."

"*I* should be the heir, not *he*!"

Azhure remained silent, letting DragonStar damn himself.

"I am the more powerful, the more deserving! I should have the glory and the accolades of heir!" He paused, his hatred and envy rippling across the roof. "Caelum was planted in sweet virgin flesh. *I*? I was seeded in a body tarnished by frequent use."

Utterly repelled by her son's words, Azhure shifted her eyes back to Cazna. "Can you understand why Axis and I did not want DragonStar near Caelum?"

Cazna nodded dumbly, her eyes shocked.

"Stupid bitch," DragonStar remarked casually, and Cazna burst into tears.

Azhure looked back to DragonStar. No wonder her pregnancy had been so troubled, with this much hatred seething inside her. "Do you know who we are, DragonStar?"

"Yes," he replied instantly. "I know that you are Moon, Azhure, and Axis is Song."

His words rocked the two Enchanters. Azhure glared at them, daring them to falter with their enchantment, and after a moment they recovered.

Rivkah stared, her lips parted in astonishment.

"And you are a fool, DragonStar," Azhure said, shocked to find tears in her eyes. She took a breath and composed herself.

"Did you manipulate Cazna to bring you to the roof the day Caelum was snatched?"

"Yes."

Azhure was appalled at his confidence. "And did you call Gorgrael through the musts, and lie to the bridge?"

"Yes."

Far below the bridge stirred. "You were *not* true," she called. "Why?"

"Why?" Azhure echoed.

"Because I know I must be first." He paused, considering. "You are powerful, Mama, if you managed to rescue Caelum."

Azhure closed her eyes. Never before had he called her Mama.

"DragonStar, I cannot let such a crime go unpunished."

Shockingly, DragonStar laughed. "And what will you do to me, Mama? Throw me from the parapets? Smother me before these witnesses? Send me away? If you do that then one day I will return. Only death will stop me. Are you prepared to kill me, Mama?"

Cazna's eyes flew to Azhure's face, fully expecting an affirmative answer.

"No," Azhure whispered. "I cannot do that, although if you were standing here in my place then it is what I would expect from you."

DragonStar laughed again. "Then you will not halt me. You are too soft." He had relied on this, it had given him the confidence to admit his wrongdoing. His heinous crime might well deserve heinous punishment, but no mother could visit such a punishment on the child of her body. And certainly not Azhure, who had suffered so much herself.

DragonStar had planned well.

"By the Stars," Rivkah whispered, "how can a baby have so much ill-will festering inside him?"

Azhure wiped her face of all expression. "DragonStar, listen to me."

He was silent. Confident. All could feel the amusement emanating from him.

"I cannot let what you have done go unanswered. You manipulated Cazna, who only ever meant you well, and abused her hospitality and care. And you planned your brother's kidnap—and murder, for all I know—aware of the hurt it would do Axis and myself. Listen to me, DragonStar."

"Nothing you can do will touch me," he sneered. "You don't have the courage. The strength of will. You are my *mother*!"

"Then you underestimate me. DragonStar, listen to me and answer me true. From where do you derive your power?"

"From the Stars, from the Star Dance," he said, and all could tell he was bewildered at the sudden change in topic.

"Yes, from the Stars. And from where did you inherit your ability?"

"From my parents. From you and Axis." Now his voice was clearly puzzled.

"Yes. From me and Axis. DragonStar, let me be even more specific. You inherited your power from the Icarii blood we bequeathed you. I inherited mine from my father, WolfStar, and Axis from *his* father, StarDrifter."

"Yes, yes." Was she going to punish him by giving him endless lessons in bloodlines? Stupid cow.

"DragonStar," Azhure said, "from the gift of your grandmothers—from Rivkah, here to witness today, and from Niah, whose death you witnessed yourself—you have inherited an equal amount of human blood."

He was silent as his mind raced to try and work out what she meant, what she was going to do.

"You have equal amounts of Icarii and Acharite blood, DragonStar, and in every known case of mixed parentage, the Icarii blood has always proved the stronger."

"No! You wouldn't *dare!*"

"I wouldn't if you hadn't dared to betray, DragonStar. Listen, and hear me well. I will twist your blood order about. From the instant that I have finished speaking your human blood will prove the stronger, and your Icarii blood will lie in subjection to it. I disinherit you of your Icarii blood and I curse you to a human life, DragonStar."

"*No!*" He twisted about the table, his fists stabbing into the air.

"Your wings shall lie dormant, DragonStar, and you shall never fly."

"*No!*"

"Your power shall remain untouched and unused, DragonStar, and you shall never hear the sweet music of the Star Dance again."

Deprived of the Star Dance? He screamed, a thin wail of stark terror.

"You will live out the lifespan of a human, DragonStar, and your sister and brother shall watch you age and die before they leave their youth. Make the best use of your years that you can, for you will not have many of them."

She had to raise her voice now, for the sound of his terror threatened to drown her out. "And finally, DragonStar, worst cruelty of all, I condemn you into the life of a human baby. Your mind shall lose its acumen and you shall live the next few years locked in the dim fogginess of human babyhood."

She stood and stared at him, tears streaming down her face, her hands tight about Caelum, who was also silently crying.

"I strip you of your Icarii name, for you will not need it again."

"*Nooo!*"

She tried to collect herself, but tears choked her voice. "I have finished speaking, DragonStar."

There was instant silence.

One of the Enchanters stepped forward. "There is nothing there, Enchantress, save mild discomfort that he lies so exposed to the breeze."

Azhure nodded, unable to speak for the moment. She handed Caelum across to Rivkah; the boy this time accepting her actions without complaint.

Then Azhure bent and picked the tiny baby up. "Such a beautiful baby," she whispered brokenly. "Welcome home, Drago."

Then, horrifyingly, she tilted her head to one side and stared into the sky. "Hark," she said, emotionlessly. "The Gryphon hunt."

57

Talon Spike

RavenCrest turned from the alps far below and smiled at his wife in the rosy dawn light. They'd never enjoyed a passionate marriage, Bright-Feather was not of SunSoar blood, but they had come to respect and honor each other.

"Are you now regretting your decision?" he said.

BrightFeather smiled and linked her arms with his. The breeze ruffled their hair and lifted their feathers. "I could not leave Talon Spike, nor you. You were right, RavenCrest, when you said that the new world held little for us. But . . . but . . ."

"You regret not seeing FreeFall again?"

She nodded, her eyes over-bright. "Yes, very much so. I could hardly credit when I heard . . . when I heard that Axis had led him back from the River of Death. For two years he has lived in this world, my husband, and for all that time he has not come home to see us."

"He belongs to the new world, beloved," RavenCrest said softly, and BrightFeather turned her face to him, loving him for the rare endearment.

"And to EvenSong," she said.

They stood quietly. "Do you think they *will* come?" BrightFeather asked, her eyes on the horizon.

RavenCrest considered. "Azhure thought they might, but perhaps she was wrong."

BrightFeather shivered and RavenCrest wrapped a wing about her. "Talon Spike seems so empty now, my husband. Empty of the joy and exuberance of the Icarii nation. I miss them."

"Our brethren are undoubtedly spreading their joy and exuberance among the Acharites, BrightFeather. Come. What are we doing here on the flight balcony letting the cold wind whip about us?"

"Enjoying the Alps, RavenCrest," she replied. "As we have for the past two hundred and fifty years."

He briefly hugged her, then they turned and walked inside, and both missed by less than a minute the black line that appeared on the eastern horizon.

They were driven almost mad by Gorgrael's anger and pain. Nothing mattered but that through their actions some of his anger and frustration should be alleviated. His voice roared in their minds and they knew only one thing—destroy.

A cloud seven thousand, two hundred and ninety strong. They had whelped a month earlier and now their young could do without them. They were ready, and they were hungry.

The entrance ways into Talon Spike were many, but they were relatively narrow, and the peak of the mountain was covered in a writhing black mass for almost half an hour as the Gryphon slowly penetrated the ancient Icarii home.

Once in, they slaughtered.

Many died in the Assembly Chamber where they had gathered to reminisce about their lives before the Time of the Prophecy.

Others died in the shafts and corridors of the complex. Still more died in the Chamber of Steaming Water. Many of those trapped there endured a slower and more terrifying death than their comrades in the halls and shafts because they tried to preserve their lives a few minutes longer by diving below water. But they had to surface for air eventually, and when they did they found their faces grasped by talons, and they were hauled, kicking, out of the water and deposited on the granite benches for the predators to feast on.

All died well and, strangely for the circumstances, with peace in their hearts.

RavenCrest SunSoar, Talon of all the Icarii, and his wife BrightFeather died in their apartments. They were among the last to die, for it took the Gryphon some time to reach them, and their deaths were the most terrible because of that. For almost an hour RavenCrest and BrightFeather had to endure the agony of listening to their fellows die, listening to the horror of Gryphon screaming through the complex, before the first of the creatures crawled through the open doorway.

She halted as soon as she saw them, her red, blighted eyes fevered, her breath fouled by those she had already killed. She crouched in the doorway, weaving her head back and forth, wondering which one to attack first.

Then she cried, shrieking with the voice of despair, and her dragon claws scrabbled on the exquisite mosaic floor as she leaped forward.

BrightFeather screamed and fell to the floor, RavenCrest trying, uselessly, to shield her with his body.

BrightFeather felt the comforting weight of his body only an instant, and as she opened her mouth to scream again she paused, horrified, as she saw the Gryphon lift her husband to the ceiling and tear him apart.

Her mouth, still open, collected the blood as it fell in a bright shower from above, and she turned to one side and gagged, numbed with horror.

Thus it was that she felt no pain and even less surprise when the second Gryphon, who had rushed through the door at the smell of blood, seized her and tore off her head with one vicious swipe of her beak.

Gorgrael had expected that his Gryphon would enjoy a massive killing in Talon Spike—unaware that it had largely been evacuated. As the Gryphon clung to the crest of the mountain, screaming their frustration at their inability to get in quickly, Gorgrael had spoken in their heads, whispered of the tens of thousands of Icarii they would find in the corridors and hidden places of Talon Spike.

And so that is what the Gryphon expected to find.

Within an hour of the first Gryphon entering the complex all the Icarii were dead, but the Gryphon did not understand that. They surged through shafts and corridors, howling with hunger and blood-lust and infused with Gorgrael's frustrated anger.

Before them leaped shadows and fancies, designed generations ago by Enchanters to frustrate invaders and deflect them from the ancient chambers in the bowels of the mountain where it had been conceived thousands of Icarii might hide. These chambers were largely empty now (and what they did hide was neither feathered nor alive), but the enchantments still did their task. The Gryphon collided and, in a few cases, tore each other apart, as they chased the shadows down shafts and through corridors.

Deeper and deeper they went, driven by anger, frustration and hunger.

They did not find the well to the UnderWorld, for the Ferryman, hearing the terror filter down, had hidden its entrance with powerful enchantments. Then he had turned aside, tears in his eyes, and drifted silently away.

Gorgrael, and thus his Gryphon, did not know of the more subtle enchantments of Talon Spike. He did not know that the deeper the Gryphon went into the mountain—and every last one flew and scrambled as deep as she could go—the more they would be shielded from his thoughts by both the rock itself and the enchantments that surrounded them.

Cut off from their master's thoughts, the Gryphon received no fresh orders. All they knew was that they had to hunt the tens of thousands of Icarii that *must* be hiding here *somewhere*! They knew they had to avenge their master's anger and frustration by killing, killing and then killing some more.

The anger and frustration with which Gorgrael had filled his Gryphon intensified the deeper they went into the mountain, for they could not find the Icarii, and they screamed and scrambled and shrieked and searched and searched and searched . . .

. . . and so they continued, and when Gorgrael, disconcerted by the lack of contact with his lovely pets, tried to send them fresh ideas, new orders, all he received in return were shadows and fancies that bounced through his mind and sent *him* screaming and shrieking through the corridors of his Ice Fortress.

The Gryphon continued to hunt, rip, destroy and chase the shadows that the mountain itself sent their way, and it would be many days before any of them, exhausted, managed to crawl their way to the surface.

58

Departure

Azhure left that afternoon, knowing that Axis would need her, and that she would have to ride on wings of power to reach northern Ichtar on time. She took Caelum with her. There was no way the boy would be left behind and, truth to tell, Azhure did not want to leave him.

"Azhure!" Rivkah snapped, as she stood by Venator in the courtyard, "you *cannot* take the boy! You will be riding into war—what are you thinking of?"

"I am thinking," Azhure replied, "that when I last left Caelum here in the safety of Sigholt he was snatched by Gorgrael. Where is safety? With either me or Axis. Rivkah," she said, not wanting to leave Rivkah with anger in her eyes, "I will not ride into battle with him. I will find somewhere safe to leave him."

"Safe? In northern Ichtar?" Rivkah muttered. "Very well. Azhure?" Rivkah's entire demeanor changed. "Where will you go once the battle is over? Where from Gorkenfort?"

"I don't know. Ravensbund, I suppose."

"Azhure? Will you be back here in time for the birth of my son?"

"Rivkah," she stumbled, "I don't know . . . it all depends."

Rivkah's face closed over and Azhure quickly leaned down from the saddle, taking her hand. "Rivkah," she said softly, "I will do what I can. You have at least six weeks to go."

"Please, Azhure." Rivkah was almost crying now. "I want you here for the birth."

"Do you trust me to be here, Rivkah?"

Rivkah took a deep breath. "Yes, yes, I trust you Azhure. And I want you here. I . . . I am afraid."

"I will do my best, Rivkah," she said. "That is all I can do."

Rivkah nodded again, jerkily, then stood back. "Then I wish my son and my husband and most of all you, Azhure, the luck and strength of the gods in the battle ahead."

She smiled, her eyes bright with tears. "And make sure you bring that grandson of mine home again."

Azhure smiled then sat up. Caelum was strapped securely to her back, the quiver of arrows now fastened to her waist and hanging down her side. The Wolven rested across one shoulder and the Alaunt milled about Venator's legs.

"Let's run," she said.

One minute she was there, the next she was gone. Rivkah had a faint impression of the horse leaping away and of Azhure's hair flying and obscuring Caelum from sight. She heard a rumble of hooves, a cry from the bridge, and a brief clamor from the hounds, then the courtyard was silent and empty save for herself and the few others who had left their afternoon chores to farewell Azhure.

Again Azhure rode as if her horse had wings at his fetlocks. Through the night, bright moonlight flooded her path and the hounds streamed ahead of her, but even during the daylight hours it seemed as if she were bathed in ivory light.

When she stopped a fire was always blazing and Adamon, and sometimes Pors or Silton, were there to greet her and hand her roast partridge. The horse and the hounds would curl at her back and rest. Even though she woke them as soon as she had eaten and dozed a few minutes herself, they were always as fresh as if they had slept for many hours, and the few handfuls of food that she threw their way sustained them in the dash for Gorkenfort.

Caelum, sweet child, slept virtually the entire way, lulled by the moonlight and the movement of Azhure's body as she swayed to the beat of Venator's gait. He woke only to smile at whichever god sat before the fire, and to accept some food, then he slipped back into dreams that healed his mental and emotional scars. At the same time, his physical injuries faded so that by the time Venator raced westward along the southern line of the Icescarp Alps, Caelum laughed with joy whenever he awoke. And Azhure laughed with him, thanking the Moon that when Axis again saw his son, he would never know the depth of hurt and pain Caelum had suffered.

59

Approach to Gorkenfort

There!" Axis pointed into the sky. "There they are!"

Not having the vision of an Enchanter, Belial had to believe him. "Are they all there?"

"Yes," Axis sighed in relief.

Belial shrugged a little closer inside his cloak and waited for the farflight scouts to land. They were half a league south of the ruins of Gorkentown, although the Keep had survived relatively intact. Earlier this morning, Axis had sent eight Icarii scouting well into Gorken Pass to try to espy the battle formations of the Skraeling army all knew waited there.

In the nine days since Xanon had told Axis of Caelum's capture, Axis had buried his concern for wife and son in activity. He had moved his force hard north for Gorkenfort, although he was careful not to overtire them, nor to outpace their supply column.

The farther north they moved the more bitter became the weather. It was cold for mid-Flower-month but when Axis complained about the wind sweeping down from the north, Magariz grinned darkly and said that even in the warmest of summers the snow barely melted in Gorken Pass.

"And many parts of Ravensbund remain dusted with snow through much of the mid-year," Ho'Demi added.

Axis grumbled, he was tired of fighting through constant winter, but Belial only grinned. "Tencendor lies free, my friend, and even here the sun shines for most of the day. Already Flower-month lives up to its name across Ichtar, and the crops must be close to harvest below the Nordra. If you cannot stand another month or two of snow, driving these wraiths into the sea, well then, perhaps you ought to go home and sit before a fire with a blanket about your knees."

"If I have to spend my time seated before a fire with a blanket over my knees, Belial, then I shall insist that you sit with me to pass the time of day. Perhaps you could knit."

Belial smiled, but he did not continue the repartee, thinking of the reports they had received so far. The Skraeling host had apparently abandoned Gorkentown and fort. They could not all have crammed inside the ruins, and Timozel must have decided that he would prefer to battle in the windswept wastes of Gorken Pass.

"Here they are," Belial heard Axis mutter by his side, and he looked up. With a rustle of wings and a rush of air, SpikeFeather TrueSong settled down into the snow before them. He was followed by two more scouts, the other five flying on to their units stationed at the rear of the ground force.

SpikeFeather bowed. He'd insisted on leading the scouting party, and Axis had acquiesced without demur. Over the past weeks and months, SpikeFeather had grown into his command and, although, like all Icarii, his face remained youthfully unlined, experience and confidence hardened his eyes and mouth.

"StarMan."

"Crest-Leader. What news?"

SpikeFeather drew in a sharp breath between his teeth. "They wait, StarMan, about a league up the pass. They are massed in formation, and they wait patiently . . . well away from the river, which is free of ice."

Axis frowned in thought. Could he use that? "Close to the cliffs of the Alps, SpikeFeather?"

"Not really. They are, oh, at least five or six hundred paces from the cliffs."

Axis exchanged glances with Belial, then turned back to SpikeFeather. "Did you see Timozel?"

"No. He could be anywhere among that mass."

"IceWorms?"

"Yes, but at the back of the force. I cannot think how Timozel would use them."

Axis nodded slowly. IceWorms were useful for breaching defenses and little else. "And Gryphon?" he asked softly.

"None," SpikeFeather replied. "We," he nodded at the two scouts behind him, "flew the entire length of the Pass, only a hundred paces over the heads of the Skraelings and close to the canyons and traverses of the Alps, but we saw no sign of them. We . . ." he faltered a moment, recalling, "we constantly expected attack, but none came."

"You were foolish to risk your lives, SpikeFeather," Axis snapped.

"You had to know, StarMan." SpikeFeather's voice was equally tense. "If we had drawn them out then you would have known where they were."

"Then where *are* they?" Axis said. Timozel undoubtedly had them so well

hidden that Axis' force would not discover them until the moment the abominations landed on their backs.

"StarMan!"

Axis, with Belial and the other commanders, wheeled their horses about
as they heard the shout.

A horseman galloped toward them from the rear of the encampment.
"StarMan," he panted as he reined his horse to a halt, "the Enchantress!" And
he turned and pointed behind him.

Axis dug his heels into Belaguez's flanks and the stallion leaped forward;
within a heartbeat he was gone, galloping across the plain toward the as-yet
tiny figure in the distance.

They met in a flurry of snow and wind and joy several hundred paces south
of the encampment, their horses colliding, the hounds baying about them. Axis
leaned forward and swept Azhure from her horse, his eyes laughing in relief
and love.

Then his eyes widened as he felt the bundle on her back.

"He is asleep," she whispered, "leave him be for the moment."

Axis smiled, tightened his arms and pulled her close.

"How?" he asked eventually, leaning back from her slightly.

She kissed his cheek, and then his mouth again. "Do you remember your
dream nine nights ago?" she whispered, and smiled at the shudder that swept
his body. "I walked with the Moon that night, and I walked into Gorgrael's
dreams and eventually into his chambers. Listen," and she put her mouth to
his ear and whispered.

Axis burst out laughing. "Vixen! I almost feel empathy for my brother, for
you have tortured me ceaselessly since you first walked into my life. But," his
arms reached about her, "Caelum is safe, and you are here, and Xanon tells me
that you battled with Artor and bested him."

"And Faraday has finished the planting and the trees sing—but you must
know that."

She felt him withdraw from her slightly. "And Faraday is well?"

"Well enough, husband. She rests now in the Sacred Grove, with the
Horned Ones and the Mother, for she has been through great travail for your
sake. She will join you for Fire-Night in the Earth Tree Grove."

Axis ignored that. "And the trees will assist in our battle with the Skraeling
host?"

Azhure grinned and snuggled back into his body. "We shall see soon
enough, methinks, when we ride into battle."

Axis said nothing for a few minutes as he reveled in Azhure's warmth and
presence. He had worried constantly about her and about his son, and he had
not realized how much it had affected him until this moment, when both rested
safely within the circle of his arms.

His thoughts turned back to Caelum's kidnap. *How did Gorgrael seize him?*

He felt Azhure shiver, and, as she spoke slowly and softly in his mind, his own body tensed and shook, so great was his fury.

"I will *kill* him!" he hissed.

Azhure's arms tightened. "No. Axis, I was so angry myself.

I have stripped him of his Icarii powers." She outlined the processes she'd used to make DragonStar's human blood dominant. "And now he is just the cuddly, beautiful baby that Cazna thought him all the while. He is back in the nursery with RiverStar, for there is no damage he can do now. Poor baby, I could feel her puzzlement as she tried to penetrate the fog of his mind."

Axis was still not appeased by the measures Azhure had taken, but he was willing to admit she was right. If he had been there . . . Axis knew full well that DragonStar might easily be dead by now. "We shall have to watch him as he grows, my love. I still do not trust him."

"Nor I. But at least his power has been blunted."

Axis nodded and rested his chin in her hair for some time, his eyes on the army spread out before him.

"We cannot find the Gryphon for you to hunt," he said.

She leaned back at that. "Axis . . . when I left Gorgrael writhing out his frustration upon the floor I felt his anger leap after me. He could not catch me, but hours later I felt his rage find new direction. Talon Spike."

"Oh Stars," Axis groaned, "I had hoped that RavenCrest and BrightStar and all those who stayed with them might yet be safe. Are they still there?"

Azhure knew he meant the Gryphon. "I don't know. I have not been able to feel them for many days now. Perhaps I shall have to content myself with sticking Skraelings on the morrow."

Timozel sat in the cave high in the rocky walls of Gorken Pass where he had secreted himself from the far-seeing eyes of the Icarii scouts, and chewed his thumbnail.

Where are they? he questioned Gorgrael.

I do not know, Timozel, and Timozel could feel the fury and frustration and fear in Gorgrael's mind. How could anyone lose seven thousand Gryphon?

No doubt Axis will attack in the morning, Master. I would prefer to have those Gryphon overhead when he does.

Do you think me a fool, Timozel? and the man reeled from the flaming rage that Gorgrael sent his way. *I want those Gryphon to shred his army as greatly as you do. Yet I can do nothing until . . .*

Abruptly his words broke off.

Master? Master?

Timozel! I have them!

*   *   *

It had taken more than eight days for the befuddled yet rabidly angry Gryphon to find their way through the maze of shafts and corridors to the upper reaches of Talon Spike. They had hunted ceaselessly in that time, searching for the Icarii. They could smell them, yes they could, so surely they were just around the next turn, behind the next door. The shadows teased and tantalized them, and the Gryphon crawled through every space they could find.

And they found nothing. Now biting hunger fed their fury, and as they climbed higher and higher in a seething mass, their anger intensified until it glowed from their eyes and steamed with their breath and their shrieks tore through the mountain. Then, as the first of them crawled out onto the flight balcony of Talon Spike, Gorgrael finally managed to touch their minds again.

West! West! Haste! Haste! Where have you been?

Chasing shadows, Master, they whispered back. *Talon Spike is clear . . . we think.*

Then fly! Fly! Fly! Great feeding awaits you in Gorken Pass. Manlings a-plenty mass for the feast—but you shall have to fight back the Skraelings.

We shall eat them, too.

Save your thunder and your anger for the battle, my beauties. Now, FLY!

And the Gryphon, waiting for their fellows to emerge from the mountain, massed about its peak. As the mountain groaned under their weight they launched themselves into the air, spinning about Talon Spike in a maddened black cloud until, as the final few of their brethren emerged from the mountain, they wheeled as one and flew west into the night sky.

Nothing would stop them feasting now.

Dreamers in the Snow

Magariz stood fidgeting in the pre-dawn light as Belial's man fumbled with the buckles on his master's armor.

"Peace, Magariz," Belial said. "I am almost fastened up."

"I admit I cannot wait until this day is over," Magariz said.

"And I, my friend, and I."

All about them men readied for war, and when Belial glanced at Axis and Azhure's tent he could see the shadows of movement within.

Belial's man stood back and Belial straightened and looked at Magariz. "Nervous, my friend?"

"Deathly afraid, more like."

"There is no shame in admitting to fear," Belial said. "I hardly slept myself. But think of it this way, Magariz. Either we will be dead by this evening or we won't. And if we lose the field, if Timozel's forces win the day, then I don't want to be alive to witness the destruction that will sweep Tencendor."

"You sink into philosophy again, my friend," Axis said cheerfully, and Belial turned to look, then started.

Axis had emerged from his tent dressed in his golden tunic with its blood-red sun blazing across his chest. Across his shoulders flowed the red cloak, and the rising dawn light caught golden flecks in his beard, trimmed close to his cheeks, and in his hair combed neatly back into its braid. His hand rested on his sword hilt, and Belial realized that Axis still wore Jorge's sword.

"Perhaps I shall get to stick Timozel with it today," Axis said.

"Have you gone mad?" Belial hissed. "Where's your armor? Axis, you will fall in the first minute if you attempt to ride into battle dressed like that."

Axis' lightness faded. "I want them to know who they face, Belial, and I want them to know where I am. And," his smile returned, "I shall not need armor."

Belial opened his mouth to retort, but just then Azhure stepped out of the tent, Caelum clasped in her arms. She paused to speak quietly with a man-at-arms, then stepped to her husband's side. "Belial, Axis and I have spent much of the night talking. We have revised the battle plans somewhat."

"Oh, *damn* it!" Belial snapped. "We spent hours last night working those plans out to the finest detail, and now you say lightly that you have revised them? Without thinking to consult your commanders?"

"Belial," Axis said, "We apologize for any lack of thought. Yes, we should have consulted you, but it was so late when we had finalized things in our own heads that it would have been pointless waking you."

"I was awake most of the night, anyway," Belial said.

Magariz stepped forward. "Tell us, Axis. What have you dreamed up that makes you leave your armor behind?" Axis always wore armor for major action, as did all his men, and even Azhure wore chain mail when she entered the fray; Magariz could remember she wore as heavy a complement of chain as any man during the Battle of Bedwyr Fort.

"I have sent for SpikeFeather and Ho'Demi," Azhure said. "I want them here."

"And then we will explain," Axis said, taking Caelum from Azhure's arms and laughing with him over some shared thought.

Belial stared at them. When they had sat about the campfire last night, sharing food and ideas, Caelum had almost been inseparable from his father, clambering about his lap or sometimes sleeping quietly in his arms. He shuffled in his heavy armor. It always took an hour or so to get used to, and after eight or nine hours of chafing and rubbing it was a relief to be divested of it. But it was not the weight of his armor that concerned him now.

Why was Axis so cheerful? Belial had fought by his side for many years now, and they had survived more battles together than Belial cared to remember. Always, whether before a march or a battle, Axis was snappy—it was his way of releasing tension—and Belial had never seen him this relaxed before. What *had* those two planned?

"A rout," Axis said softly. "Ah, here's SpikeFeather and Ho'Demi. My friends, today Azhure fights with us and whatever victory we glean will be at her hands. Azhure, will you speak?"

Azhure smiled at him, then turned to the other commanders. "Gentlemen, there are only two tasks to be accomplished today—to rid the skies of Gryphon, and to rid the land of Gorgrael's ice creatures, the Skraelings foremost among them. Simple."

"Simple, Enchantress?" SpikeFeather raised his eyebrows. He was an imposing sight in the early light, his wings again dyed black, his dark red hair and feathers slicked back down his neck, his black eyes snapping with determination. "Simple? There are hundreds of thousands of Skraelings who wait for us. And the Gryphon, well, we do not even know where the cursed Gryphon are."

"SpikeFeather." Azhure's voice was heavy with sorrow, and she stepped forward to rest a hand on his arm. "Even now the Gryphon are massing on the rocks of Gorken Pass. They flew in during the night . . . from Talon Spike."

SpikeFeather gave a low cry and turned away. When he had composed himself, he looked Azhure in the face again. "Enchantress, this I swear," he said. "Every member of the Strike Force will kill two of the creatures before we die ourselves. For RavenCrest's and BrightFeather's deaths, as all those of their fellows *and* of so many of the Strike Force, I pledge to you the Strike Force will do you proud today!"

"Oh," Azhure said, "I *know* you will do me proud. Here."

She lifted the quiver of arrows from her back, pressing it into SpikeFeather's hands. "SpikeFeather, do you remember these arrows?"

Puzzled, SpikeFeather nevertheless smiled with the memory. "Yes, Enchantress, I do. I did not believe you would be able to use the Wolven, which I had flaunted before you, and I wagered ownership of the bow itself and a quiverful of arrows fashioned with my own hands and fletched with feathers from my own wings if you managed to use it."

"And I demanded that you dye the feathers as blue as my eyes," Azhure laughed. "Well, all know the result, and now you hold the quiverful of arrows that you fashioned so long ago. SpikeFeather, tell the members of the Strike Force that they will not need their weapons today. Instead, take this quiver and distribute an arrow to each member."

"But there aren't enough for more than three Wings—"

Azhure placed her hands over his. "SpikeFeather, I think you will find there are exactly enough arrows in this quiver for all the members of the Strike Force, and one left for me."

Captured by the expression in her eyes and the warmth of her hands, SpikeFeather nodded. "As you order, Enchantress."

"And when we step out onto the field of battle, SpikeFeather," she said, "the Icarii will have some measure of revenge for the hurt the Gryphon have done your people."

SpikeFeather took a deep breath. "Good."

Axis, shifting Caelum to one hip, motioned at the fire. "Will someone stoke that fire for me? I have not yet breakfasted, and I do not want to do so before cold ashes."

"But, Axis," Magariz began, then suddenly found himself encumbered with Caelum.

"Here, Magariz, your task today will be to play nursemaid, for Azhure and I wish that our son ride at the forefront of the force. Besides, Magariz, you shall shortly have your own son to bounce on your knee, and you need the practice."

"Axis!" Belial said. "*Will* you tell us what it is that you and Azhure have planned?"

Axis' smile died. "We are teasing you, my friend, and for that I apologize. Come, sit here with me, and divest yourself of some of that armor. Spread the word. I want my men to enjoy a hearty breakfast, for we will not be rushing the field before mid-morning, I think, and I want them to wear only enough armor to make a decent glint under the sun."

Then, as his companions sat down about the fire, Axis spoke.

They rode past the ruins of Gorkenfort and town in the hour before noon, holding tight formation, the Strike Force wheeling above and slightly behind them. Axis shivered as he thought of all the men he had lost there, but he winked at Caelum, riding at the front of Magariz's saddle. As requested, Magariz had divested himself of most of his armor, wearing only a breastplate to gleam under the strengthening sun, and there was plenty of room in the saddle for both man and boy. Caelum was patently excited at being allowed to ride into battle. His cheeks were red and his eyes bright, and he was bundled into a suit of blue-tipped white fur that kept the cold winds from his skin.

Axis turned to his other side. There rode Azhure, the hounds restrained at her side, and beyond her Belial. Belial had recovered his good temper, and had spent much of the ride thus far chatting with Azhure about which oils were best added to the fires used to temper the metal of arrow heads.

From Gorkenfort, Axis swung his column northward, delighting in the sound of the hooves, the jingle of gear and weapons, and the melodious chime of Ravensbund bells behind him. His army was a fine sight, he knew, and he hoped that Timozel would have a moment's doubt when they rode down the pass.

"Gorken Pass," he said under his breath, and urged Belaguez into a long-striding canter.

Timozel sat in his cave and watched them approach . . . and laughed.

"Foolish, prideful man," he chortled, sharing the view with his master. "See how he rides so exposed at the head of his pitiful force. They ride straight for us, and they ride directly to their death. Look! They have left their greaves at home, and their helmets remain unlaced!"

Then make sure you do them death, Timozel. I am tired of the games he and she play.

She? But Timozel dismissed the thought. Gorgrael seemed concerned about this black-haired woman—and, yes, Timozel could see her riding by Axis' side—but Timozel was not worried if Axis' harlot chose to ride into battle with him. She could die as easily as any other.

Then he sat forward, bewildered.

Any good commander would have ranged his force into units to attack those that Timozel had ranged before him (*and* for a league back into the Pass, Timozel gloated). But Axis . . . Axis was dividing his force in two and, even stranger, was directing them so that each half lined the sides of the Pass, leaving the center ground bare. Was he maneuvering for a battlefield . . . or a parade ground? The Strike Force, evil, feathered things, were landing on the snow behind the forward group of commanders, and Timozel was unable to believe what he saw.

Each carried only one arrow, and no bows.

Timozel's hand tightened about the ruff of the Gryphon who lay by his side. The Gryphon had finally arrived during the night, and now they lay secreted among the rocks of the Alps, ready to launch themselves upon Axis' army.

Timozel gasped in surprise . . . was that a *child* one of the forward commanders carried? He grinned. Axis had gone mad after his brush with death. Now he brought babes to fight for him. Or was it only that he brought his family to share his fate? Timozel laughed again.

Axis was waving his commanders away now, until only he and the woman and the Strike Force remained. They exchanged some brief words, then Axis wheeled his mount away to the line of soldiers by the river. The woman dismounted, gestured to the pack of dogs that surrounded her to sit behind Axis, and strode forward until she was some two hundred paces from the first of the Skraeling ranks.

Timozel had to admit she was very beautiful. The Gryphon by his side grunted, and Timozel glanced at her. What was going through her mind?

Slowly, the raven-haired woman turned her eyes to the rocks.

She could feel if not see the Gryphon. They were there, waiting, and Azhure wagered that each and every one of them had her eyes on Azhure. She smiled, and reached with both hand and power, and called softly. "Lover?"

Instantly, every single one of the Gryphon fell back into her dream.

Azhure only wanted the Gryphon to dream, and she directed her power carefully. But she could feel its effect almost immediately, and there was a great collective sigh as each of the creatures closed her eyes and dreamed.

Timozel stared at the Gryphon beside him. She had rolled over onto her side, her eyes closed, and now she twitched and moaned, as if on heat.

He was so surprised he forgot to share the sight with Gorgrael, and his master paced his chamber in frustration, wondering what was happening.

* * *

Azhure smiled and extended both arms now, the power flowing from her eyes and beckoning fingers. "Lover? Are you there?"

An agitated movement came from among the rocks. Gryphon shifted painfully, caught fast by their desires, caught fast by the dream.

"Lover? Come to me. Come."

The soft voice echoed through their minds and inflamed them still further.

"I wait for you, here in the snow," she said. "Come, join with me."

Suddenly a Gryphon burst from her hiding place among the rocks and plunged down the cliff face.

In his Ice Fortress, Gorgrael stirred at the moaning and wailing that arose from the corridors. He flung open the door of his chamber and stared outside. Half-matured Gryphon, their bellies already bulging with the young they carried, writhed and twisted along the floors of the corridor, and a great moaning filled the entire Ice Fortress. Among the masses and spaces of the fortress lay well over sixty-five thousand of the Gryphon, and all were caught by the dream.

Lover? Lover?

Gorgrael stared at them, excluded this time from the pleasure of the dream, and wondered what was going on. Did they all have colic?

"Pretty, pretty," Azhure murmured, and the Gryphon crawled through the snow toward her. "Come to me, Lover. I will give you the fulfilment you crave."

Another Gryphon plummeted from rocks to snow, and then another, and another, and soon the rock face was furred with descending Gryphon and a wave of the creatures undulated across the snow toward her.

"Lover? Lover? Come to me . . . come."

"What?" Timozel muttered, appalled and confused by what he witnessed, and then the Gryphon by his side abruptly leaped out into the swirling air and fell to the snow to crawl weeping and grunting with her sisters toward the woman.

"Sorceress!" Timozel barked, and jumped to his feet.

Soon the snow was thick with Gryphon. They rippled before Azhure, a seven-thousand-strong tide of feathers, tawny fur, tufted tails and eagles' heads weaving back and forth. She rubbed the head of the first Gryphon soothingly, and a great muttering arose from the ranks of the Gryphon behind it.

As Azhure stroked the head of the first Gryphon, so all experienced the ecstasy, and as one they bobbed their heads in time to the movement of her hand.

As one they closed their minds to anything and everything else.

With her free hand behind her back, Azhure motioned the Strike Force forward.

Timozel finally collected himself enough to share his thoughts and the view with Gorgrael.

Bitch! Gorgrael screamed in his mind. *The bitch will betray them as she did me! Gryphon! My pets, heed me only!*

But the Gryphon did not. There was only the Lover, and she stood before each of them, and each of them felt her fingers stroke their heads and their bodies and each of them sighed and moaned and rolled over so that the Lover could rub her hand along their bellies . . . oh! Ah, yes! There! And there!

Listen to me! Gorgrael capered about his chamber, fists clenched, wings outstretched. *Listen to ME!*

Azhure's smile broadened as she felt SpikeFeather at her shoulder. He stared at the sight before him, and thought that no one who could not see this for themselves would believe it.

Azhure touched only the front Gryphon, but as she moaned, so all the Gryphon moaned, and as she rolled and jerked, so all Gryphon rolled and jerked. Now their pale underbellies were exposed to the sun, their bodies twitching, their eyes rolling back in their heads.

Azhure stared at him and SpikeFeather jumped, remembering what she had asked him to do. He held out her quiver, and, as she had told him, there was one arrow left. She took it with one hand, the other still rubbing the Gryphon's belly, and then motioned with her head.

SpikeFeather nodded, and waved the Strike Force forward. Each of them stood ready with an arrow grasped in his or her hand.

"Lover," Azhure whispered, "the moment of final fulfilment is upon you."

As one the Gryphon cried and moaned.

No! Gorgrael screamed in his Ice Fortress as Azhure raised the arrow. *No!*

Azhure smiled at the sound of his voice reverberating in her mind, then she plunged the arrow into the Gryphon's vulnerable belly.

The Gryphon shrieked, and shrieked again, screaming for more, more, *more!* And so Azhure obliged, wrenching the arrow from her belly and plunging it down again and again.

Even as the Gryphon disintegrated she continued to shriek and howl, begging for more.

And in the Ice Fortress, the Gryphon's nine pups shrieked in equal ecstasy . . . and died, their bodies disintegrating into thin air. They left no trace behind.

Among the writhing mass of Gryphon stepped the members of the Strike Force, plunging their arrows time and time again, and every time their arrows pierced the belly of a Gryphon, her pups writhing in the corridors of Gorgrael's Ice Fortress shrieked and died and disintegrated along with their mother.

Gorgrael screamed into Timozel's mind. *Put a halt to this NOW! NOW! NOW! NOW!*

Writhing himself, but with the agony of Gorgrael's shrieks rather than the ecstasy of the dying Gryphon, Timozel ordered the Skraelings forward.

But as they began their march toward the manlings, the snow erupted before them and great sheets of ice speared into the sky. They screamed and backed away. The sight of their comrades plunging through the shattered ice of the Azle was still fresh in their minds, and they had no intention of suffering the same fate themselves. Even the SkraeBolds, wheeling above the Skraelings, neglected to force them forward, horrified by the death of the Gryphon and the ice spears lunging for the sky.

Axis sat on Belaguez deep in concentration. It was a delusion only, and not a very strong one at that. But the ice was enough to terrify the Skraelings, and the sight of the Gryphon rolling onto their backs to be pierced and killed convinced them that powerful sorcery was at work.

Behind Axis, his army watched astounded. Never had the men seen such a rout before.

Azhure stood, the arrow loose in her hand now. The Gryphon before her was dead, her flesh falling away to the grave from whence she had been called. The Dark Music that had gone into her making disintegrated. Within moments at the most, all trace of the Gryphon had disappeared.

Azhure looked up. The Strike Force had worked its way through to the back ranks of the Gryphon, where only a few remained, still writhing in anticipation of the fulfilment they had felt their fellows enjoy, exposing their bellies for the flashing arrows.

Gorgrael slowly sank to the floor, his hands gripping the doorframe.

Before him stretched a corridor filled with congealing blood and little else. His entire pack . . . his entire *family* . . . of Gryphon had been destroyed. Not even a scrap of flesh remained from which he could have reconstituted the pack. Blood in itself was useless. He needed the gray substance. The flesh. All that had gone. Gone back to the ancient graves of the Gryphon, and there was nothing Gorgrael could do to recall them.

But for the moment Gorgrael did not care. He slowly bent his forehead to the floor and wept, his arms over his head. He wept for the loss of his friends. They were his children, and they had gone.

And so Gorgrael mourned. He did not have the heart to watch the Skraeling destruction as well.

Finally, SpikeFeather turned about. His right arm was covered in Gryphon blood to its elbow, his eyes sparkled with satisfaction and vengeance. Azhure waved, and SpikeFeather called to the Strike Force, and in the space of a single breath they had lifted into the air and were winging their way back behind the final lines of Axis' army. Their day was done, and now it only remained for them to stay out of the way.

Axis scanned his army urgently—were they all in place?

Yes. He relaxed, and his eyes swung back to his wife.

Azhure stood alone in the center of the pass. The only sign of the Gryphon's existence was the trampled, blood-soaked ground. She sank to one knee, and rested her face in a hand.

Before her, their courage recovered, the Skraeling host inched forward.

"Mirbolt," Azhure whispered.

Mirbolt.

Mirbolt swayed, her roots sunk deep in the caverns of the earth so she could fathom the mysteries they held, her branches spread to the sky so that the Star Dance could whisper about and between her leaves.

The Nordra leaped and roared, its music a faint undertone to the music that Mirbolt made with her sisters and with the Mother herself, the Earth Tree standing strong and luxuriant in the northern groves.

Mirbolt was content.

Mirbolt?

She stirred, remembering the voice.

Mirbolt, I have need of your assistance.

Yes, Mirbolt remembered that Azhure would ask the trees for aid.

What aid, Azhure? she sang.

Azhure sighed in relief. *Mirbolt, see with my eyes.*

The Skraelings advanced, their fear diminishing. All they saw was the woman kneeling in the snow before them. Her power had gone, and the arrow lay useless beside her. She sat there, patiently waiting for death.

They whispered and laughed and hiccupped.

They seethed toward her.

To one side, Axis stirred in alarm. The Skraelings had now covered over a quarter the distance between themselves and Azhure . . . and Azhure just sat there, terribly vulnerable.

Azhure! Say the word and I will order the attack!

No, beloved. Mirbolt listens and she sees. Be patient.

And indeed Mirbolt *did* see. As the Earth Tree had seen two and a half years earlier, so now Mirbolt. Mirbolt lost her temper and screamed into the sky.

Mirbolt! Stay your anger! Do not let it flood unused! Whisper to your sisters. Whisper, Mirbolt, and show them what you now see. Whisper to the Earth Tree! Ask her for aid. Do this for me, Mirbolt, and for our shared love for Faraday, and for the magical land we both inhabit.

The Skraelings were loping forward, their claws held before them, their teeth gleaming and glinting, their jaws hanging open and slavering obscenely.

See, Mirbolt? See what comes?

Mirbolt saw, and she shared her vision. Anger now rippled through the forests of western Tencendor from the Earth Tree in the extreme north to the Silent Woman Woods in the south.

The Earth Tree saw the threat, and saw the final chance to rid the land of its obscenity. No more would her daughters or the Avar people face slaughter again.

Azhure, the Earth Tree whispered, and Azhure closed her eyes in the face of the Tree's power. *Azhure, you slew the Plowman for me and for my children. For this we thank you. In return, I shall sing for you.*

The Earth Tree changed the note and cadence of her Song. No longer was it the Song of her Making, but . . . something else.

For a heartbeat every tree in the great extended forest fell silent, listening, learning. Then every one of them took a single breath, held it, added their own voices to the Song.

Azhure opened her eyes and smiled in relief. She could hear the panting of the Skraelings, feel their heat pound toward her, and she could feel Axis' anxiety reach critical levels. *Axis! Stay your hand! They come!*

Axis swung away from Azhure to stare south down the pass. All his men turned as well, for all felt it. Horses stirred, and the Alaunt howled and backed away, tails between their legs.

Wrath. It seared across the land in a tide of full-throated vengeance. Song. The Song of the Forest, but altered and rewoven with such ancient anger that it surged in a great wave of death.

The Skraelings halted fifteen paces from Azhure, their laughter and hiccups turning to whimpers.

Azhure, feeling the first stirrings at her back, fell face down in the snow, her body spread as flat as she could make it, her hands extended before her, her fingers gripping the shaft of the arrow, its head pointing directly down the Pass toward the Skraeling host.

The Song roared across the land. It flew over the heads of men and beasts alike, leaving crops quivering and rooftops shaking in its wake. People fell to the ground in terror, but the Song ignored them. It had only one purpose, one destination. The woman lay in the snow, and in her hands lay the arrow, and body and hands and arrow all pointed at one thing—the gray mass of wraiths.

Trapped in the Pass.

The Skraelings tried to run, but their mass was too great to turn easily. Many panicked and fell into the River Andakilsa to be swallowed up by the foaming waves. Others were dashed to death against the rocky walls of the Pass as their fellows pressed frantically against them.

And toward them roared the Song. It swept over the ruins of Gorkentown, and even the solid Keep of Gorkenfort trembled at its passing.

It surged across the plains leading to Gorken Pass, and it funnelled and intensified as it moved between the ranks of the army lining either side of the Pass. It left them unharmed.

All it saw was the woman in the snow, and the arrow in her hands. The Song flowed over Azhure, not stirring a single hair of her head, but she felt it anyway, and trembled at its power.

Then, with the power of the massive reborn forest behind it, the Forest Tree Song hit the milling ranks of the Skraeling army.

As one the Skraeling host broke apart. Limbs fell from torsos and heads rolled from shoulders. Teeth clattered to the ground and jaws wrenched apart.

The SkraeBolds fell from the sky in pieces.

Even the IceWorms, curled waiting at the back of the host, shuddered and split asunder.

In the space of three heartbeats the Song enveloped the Skraeling host and tore it apart.

And, having destroyed, having glutted, the Song vanished.

Far to the south and the east, the forest gently hummed to itself, rustled its leaves, and, in its own way, smiled.

Thank you, Mirbolt. Thank you, Earth Tree. Thank you, forest.

Do not forget us, Azhure.

Axis kicked Belaguez forward and stared at the sight before him. Behind him his army likewise stared.

Where once had stood a vast host, now blew cold wind. Snow drifted almost apologetically over piles of Skraeling teeth, which were the only remaining sign of what had once been Gorgrael's conquering force. After a moment, even the cold wind died, and the Pass was wrapped in silence and stillness.

Azhure had told him that the Earth Tree, backed by her daughters, could do this. It was, she had whispered to him late the previous night, only an extension of what the Earth Tree had done to the Skraeling force in the groves that initial Yuletide attack.

Axis understood this. He just found it impossible to credit that this host which had harried him and his for so long had been wiped out so easily.

He slipped from Belaguez's back and lifted Azhure from the snow. "I honor you," he whispered.

*   *   *

Timozel clung to the rocky outcrop before his cave and gibbered in disbelief. Everything had gone! *Everything* had been lost! His vision his vision . . .

He fought for a Great Lord, and in the name of that Lord he commanded a mighty army that undulated for leagues in every direction.

Yes, and that army had vanished in the blink of an eye.

Remarkable victories were his for the taking.

Yes, and for the losing, apparently.

In the name of his Lord he would clear Achar of the filth that invaded.

Lies, lies, lies, lies . . .

His name would live in legend forever.

Timozel laughed, softly at first, then in great bitter gulps that tore through his chest and throat and rattled out across the still, cold air of the pass.

Axis and Azhure both turned at the sound.

"There," she said, pointing.

"Timozel," he snarled, clutching the sword at his side.

"Too late, Axis. See? He is high in the mountains, and even now he darts behind a rock."

"Heading for his master's den, no doubt." Axis turned to wave the Strike Force into the air, and then halted. "No."

Azhure turned back to him. "No?"

"No. He will run to Gorgrael, and I will doubtless see him there. *I* want to be the one to sink these five handspans of sharpened steel into his belly, Azhure! SpikeFeather and his command have already had their gratification for the day."

Timozel panted, his breath sharp and frosty this high in the mountains. He struggled along the alpine pass, heading for the Icebear Coast. Every third or fourth step he glanced over his shoulder, expecting to see some of the feathered evil descending on him from the heavens.

"Friend Timozel."

Timozel halted. "Friend?"

Scrambling down from a rocky perch was Friend, the one whom Gorgrael called the Dark Man. His cloak lifted and flapped as he leaped from rock to rock, but still Timozel could not see beneath its vast blackness. "Friend?"

"Assuredly, Timozel!" Friend laughed. "It has been some time, has it not?"

"All is lost," Timozel whispered.

"Oh, no, hardly, Timozel. All is still well. A setback or two, I grant you, but all will still be well."

"How can you say—?"

"Timozel." Friend took the young man's arm and Timozel felt warmth and peace flood his body. "All *will* be well."

"Really?" Timozel said.

"Truly. Now, listen to me. All we have to do is regroup at your master's icy palace. Axis has to go there at some point, does he not?"

"Yes."

"And you will still have the chance to save Faraday, young man."

Timozel stirred. "Faraday? Can she still be saved from this disaster?"

"Oh, certainly!" Friend said. "She can still be saved. Helped to find the light. Now, just down this pass a way I have my trusty coracle, and we can launch into the Iskruel Ocean and row for Gorgrael."

"A toast, my friends. To Azhure!" Axis raised his mug and grinned at Azhure across the fire.

"This is the *fifth* toast to Azhure we've drunk," Magariz noted, but he drank anyway. Men laughed, and emptied their mugs.

"Well?" Axis demanded, "who else would you have me toast? Your brave self, perhaps? Clinging to a toddling boy for support? Shame, Magariz!"

Magariz spluttered indignantly. "And who put him there, StarMan? That eighteen-month-old boy was the only impediment to my charge down the Gorken Pass to deal with the Skraelings all by myself!"

Belial laughed and leaned over to Magariz, almost tilting a bit too far and losing his balance. "Magariz, Axis is out of sorts because he didn't get to draw his sword himself." He winked broadly at Axis. "His wife took care of it for him."

"Belial." Azhure's voice was clear and sweet, and it cut across the drunken banter. "I did but win the day—and that was with the help of tens of thousands of trees planted out with Faraday's love and care. You forget that Gorgrael still lurks, and he waits. Axis is the only one who can face him. It will come down, in the end, to a duel between the two brothers. That's the way it will be."

"That's the way it's always been," Axis said, his voice hollow, and he threw the dregs of his mug into the fire.

61

Gorken Pass

"Axis?"

"He knows," Axis replied softly, and Azhure closed her eyes.

Axis sighed and sat up from their sleeping roll, sliding his legs into his breeches. "He felt his death, as he felt MorningStar's, and . . ."

"And as we both felt it when you 'died'?"

"Yes."

Azhure regarded Axis as he pulled on his clothes. He had reached out to StarDrifter in the calm of the early morning, reached out to tell him of the deaths of his brother and sister-in-law and all those who had remained in Talon Spike—as well as the better news of the destruction of both Gryphon and Skraeling armies. Azhure envied Axis' ability to contact his father so far away. It spoke of the depth of both of their powers, and of the bond between them. Azhure, who wielded such a different power, still found it hard to communicate with Axis when long distances lay between them.

"StarDrifter pronounces awe at your role in yesterday's victory," Axis said.

That made her laugh, and Azhure rolled out of the blankets and began to dress. Caelum still slept soundly amid the comfort of his parents' residual warmth.

"Will he meet us in Talon Spike?"

"Yes. And FreeFall and EvenSong. All will need to be there."

"How long will it take for them to fly north?"

"Several weeks at least. They will fly the long way, to the Ancient Barrows, then the cities of the Minaret Peaks, through to Sigholt, the groves of the Avarinheim, and then . . . then to Talon Spike."

Azhure frowned. "Why so long?"

"There is no rush, Azhure, and . . . I want to send the Strike Force from here to clean the complex before they arrive."

Azhure dropped her eyes.

"And StarDrifter and FreeFall want to visit the various Icarii communities on the way. Not only to spread the news about what has happened in the north, but FreeFall is the Talon-Elect, and there are various rituals to be observed as they go."

"And us?"

"Well, that's what we'll have to decide this morning. Come, sweetheart, finish combing your hair and we shall talk to the others. If their headaches permit it."

Faces were drawn, and some eyes reddened, but headaches were only minor, and after everyone had breakfasted Axis called a conference of his commanders to discuss the future.

"My friends," he said, "above all I must thank you for the friendship and support you have given me over the past years. Without you . . . none of this could have been accomplished. I would have lost heart and faded, allowing Gorgrael to move unhindered over this land. But, at long, long last, hope is now stronger than despair. All of us, I think, can afford to smile."

"There is still Gorgrael." Belial remarked.

"Yes, there is still Gorgrael. But it will be just him and me now, and no one here, not even Azhure," he paused to take her hand briefly, "can help me."

"When?" Magariz asked. "How?"

Axis leaned back. "When? Sometime after Fire-Night, five weeks distant. Where? In the northern wastes. You, at least can enjoy the resurgent summer, for I shall have nothing but snow for some weeks to come."

"And us?"

"And you, Belial?" Axis paused. "An army will be of little use against Gorgrael. Belial, Magariz, I want you to return south."

"No!" both cried out together.

"Yes," Axis said. He reached out and took both their hands. "Belial, Magariz, to you both I owe the most. You supported me after the disaster of Gorkenfort, and built me a power base at Sigholt. You have led my army, and you have argued and shouted at me when I would have given up. Now, you can serve me best by moving back south."

He let their hands go. "Magariz, you have a province to reclaim from the devastation to which it has been subject. Go home to Rivkah, wait for the birth of your son. Then rebuild Ichtar."

Magariz nodded, his eyes downcast.

"Magariz?"

Magariz looked up. "Yes, Axis?"

"Where will you construct your home base in Ichtar? Hsingard is in ruins, and yet there is nowhere else."

Magariz stared at him. He had just been informed in no uncertain terms that he could not use Sigholt as his permanent home base in Ichtar. Well, that was no surprise. Axis had claimed Sigholt as his own when he proclaimed Tencendor, and he would want it for himself and Azhure—and their rapidly expanding family—when all was finished.

"I don't know," he began, then smiled. "You know, Axis, the country cupped by the Rivers Azle and Ichtar is rich and fertile. I sometimes summered there when I was stationed in Gorkenfort. I shall build there."

"You and Rivkah, and your son, will be welcome in Sigholt until the construction is finished, Magariz."

"Thank you, Axis."

"Belial, Ysgryff currently holds court in Carlon." Axis' mouth twitched. "I dread to think what he does there. No doubt pirates wrestle in the corridors and clerks and scribes are banished to loiter in the streets. Ysgryff, I think, is disinclined to administration." He paused. "Then again, he has more than surprised me in the past. Belial, will you collect your wife and return to Carlon? Western Tencendor needs its Prince, I think."

Belial took a deep breath. "I'll return to Sigholt, Axis, and go no farther."

Axis stared at him, his eyes sharp.

"I will not return to Carlon until I know the outcome of your battle with Gorgrael. *I will not!*" Belial said. "I have not come this far to be relegated to the sunny south and to the damned clerks and scribes while you battle for your life—and, ultimately ours—in the frozen north with Gorgrael! When I know that you have bested him, when you arrive home, *then* I will leave for Carlon."

"You show a singular lack of faith in my ability to defeat Gorgrael, Belial."

"I show a singular concern for your life, Axis. I can do nothing until I know that you live."

Axis' smile faded and he gripped Belial's hand briefly. "Then wait for me in Sigholt, and when I come home we can share a jug of Reinald's spiced wine and celebrate my victory."

"A deal, Axis. Ysgryff can continue to wreak his havoc on Carlon for a few weeks yet."

"And the army, Axis?" Azhure said.

"Well." He thought about it. "I have an army. What to do with it now?"

Ho'Demi, silent until this moment, spoke urgently. "Axis—"

Axis halted him with a raised hand. "Peace, Ho'Demi. I will get to you in a moment." His gaze shifted back to his other commanders. "There are a large number of volunteers in the army. Men from Skarabost, Arcness and Carlon. They are now free to go home. Belial, will you arrange their journey south? Tell them . . . tell them that pay and compensation will be arranged when you return to Carlon. I can speak to you about it in Sigholt when I arrive home."

Belial nodded.

"There must also be thousands who are career soldiers. Men who were in Borneheld's units or Achar's regular army." Axis grinned suddenly, remembering. "And a thousand or so of the former Axe-Wielders. Magariz, of the regular units you may take half to help you rebuild Ichtar; Belial, you may have a quarter of the remaining to help rebuild Aldem."

Both men nodded.

"And the remaining units," Axis said, glancing first at Ho'Demi and then at Azhure, "the remaining units can go north with Ho'Demi to help him reclaim his homeland from whatever currently inhabits it." He paused. "Under my command."

Do you mind, Azhure?

It sounds like an adventure, Axis. I will be delighted.

"I will be in that quarter," Arne said from the outer ring of those grouped about the fire.

Axis smiled. "I would have expected nothing less from you, Arne. I have forgotten what my back looks like, so long have you watched over it for me." He looked at Ho'Demi. "You do not mind Azhure and myself coming north with you, Ho'Demi?"

"I and mine will be honored, StarMan."

"The honor belongs to me, Ho'Demi," Axis said, "for without the assistance of you and yours the battle against Gorgrael would have been lost years ago. Besides, I have a hankering to see this northern land of yours, and to see the icebergs crash against the Icebear Coast."

"You shall find our land surprisingly pleasant, StarMan. Or should, if the Skraelings have not eaten most of it." Ho'Demi frowned. "I have great concern for those I had to leave behind. When the Skraelings invaded I could only bring twenty thousand of my people south with me. A twentieth of the Ravensbund people. The rest . . ." He shivered.

Axis could understand his anxiety, but for now he turned his mind from the plight of the Ravensbund people. "SpikeFeather?"

"Yes, StarMan?"

"I want several Wings of your command to fly south with the news of the events here. But the majority of your command . . ."

"To Talon Spike," SpikeFeather said.

"Yes. To Talon Spike. It will be a hard task for you, SpikeFeather, but the mountain will have to be cleansed. Do you still have the jeweled torc in your care?"

SpikeFeather nodded.

"Good. StarDrifter and FreeFall will be joining you there, and Azhure and I will move from Ravensbund to Talon Spike by mid-Rose-month. Then the mountain can be reconsecrated and the torc passed to FreeFall."

Axis looked slowly around the circle. "And from there . . . I will move down to the Avarinheim groves for Fire-Night and to meet my destiny with Gorgrael."

The Necklet

The farewells were over-bright and cheerful. Magariz and Belial spoke only in terms of "when we see you again" and not "if." Axis smiled, unable to speak, and embraced them. Azhure stood silently to one side, then she stepped forward and hugged both men herself.

Then Axis and Azhure mounted their horses, Caelum strapped once more to Azhure's back, and Axis waved his command forward to join Ho'Demi's Ravensbundmen farther up the Pass. Only three thousand men now, and he was reminded of the days when he rode at the head of the AxeWielders. He hoped he would never again have to command an army of thirty thousand. He hoped Tencendor would never again *need* an army of that size.

Ho'Demi nodded to his own command, and, as one, eight thousand Ravensbund fighters wheeled their yellow-haired horses for the north. There were almost ten thousand Ravensbund women and children camped about Grail Lake, and soon they would strike camp and move slowly north. Axis had ordered that the riverboats operating along the Nordra be put at their disposal. That, at least, would make the initial part of their journey easier.

Axis and Azhure waited until the Acharite units had joined the Ravensbund, then Axis saluted to Belial and Magariz. Azhure waved, and both swung their horses northward, the Alaunt baying excitedly as they raced to catch the units ahead of them.

Belial and Magariz stood and watched until they were out of sight, and then they turned silently and ordered their men south.

Soon all that was left in Gorken Pass was the drifting snow and the occasional Skraeling tooth. Far above, the remaining Wings of the Strike Force wheeled and dipped, then they too were gone, flying eastward over the alps to Talon Spike.

It was a sadly anticlimactic end to what had been a sometimes grand but often tragic campaign.

They rode through Gorken Pass for many days and the entire way they saw not one living creature save ravens come to fish in the Andakilsa.

They did not see Timozel.

"He would have run directly for Gorgrael," Azhure said one day as she saw Axis absently finger the hilt of Jorge's sword. "Cut straight through to the Icebear Coast."

"Pray the icebears do not eat him before I have a chance," Axis replied, but he dropped his hand, and Azhure knew that he had not truly expected to find Timozel wandering the northern regions of Gorken Pass.

Ho'Demi affected unconcern about the lack of life in Gorken Pass and southern Ravensbund. "None would have lingered here," he said to Axis and Azhure late one night about the fire, "for this was the haunt of the Skraelings. When they first invaded, the wraiths swung south and west about the western tip of the Icescarp. Alps. Any of my people who remained would have made for the extreme north in the hope that the Skraelings were too busy eating their way south to detour after them."

But each day Ho'Demi's concern grew more palpable. There was nothing, nothing at all, and his worst fears seemed confirmed.

It took them a week to ride through the Pass. Cold winds swept the land, and snow lingered, clinging to the tough grasses.

"Sea birds often nest in the rocks of the Icescarp," Sa'Kuya explained one day as she rode next to Azhure. "But none are here this year. No doubt for the past four years Skraelings have been climbing the walls after their eggs. Well, gods provide, the birds will come back one day."

When they rode out of Gorken Pass, the landscape did not alter appreciably. Flat plains spread to the west and north, great expanses still covered in light snow, other swathes where thick grasses had managed to push through the soil.

"The grass can sprout and reach its full height in only ten days," Ho'Demi said. "The growing season is short here, and neither grass nor beast wastes time in reaching for whatever sun there is."

The country seemed as barren and desolate as myth described it, and Axis prepared himself for a long and boring ride north. But, just as he was about to ask Ho'Demi where they should stop for the noon break, he noticed a green line perhaps half a league ahead. It did not reach above the brown grass they currently rode through, so Axis thought that it must be a different variety of grass—perhaps reeds about a marsh.

Ho'Demi had seen Axis squint ahead and he winked at Sa'Kuya. "The hole," he said enigmatically. "We'll stop there for the noon meal, then push hard for the next hole for our night campsite."

"The hole?" Axis said, then probed Ho'Demi's mind, seeking clues. *The next hole?* But the Ravensbund Chief had locked his thoughts about with shadows—or was that drifting steam?—and Axis could not discern the reason behind the man's slight smile.

Within an hour he had his answer. Once they rode closer, Axis could see that the line of green was the tops of trees that grew to the level of the surrounding grasses. The air above them shimmered slightly.

"What?" he began, then Ho'Demi laughed and waved Axis and Azhure to his side. "Mind you stop your great horses when I tell you, StarMan, or else I shall have to waste the rest of this afternoon rescuing you."

Ho'Demi led them forward, then abruptly held up his hand. Axis and Azhure reined their horses back instantly, and Azhure sent a silent command to the hounds. Then she looked down.

They had stopped at the rim of a gigantic hole in the ground. Azhure held her breath and stared. It was, she calculated quickly, easily some two thousand paces across and well over a thousand deep. Worn paths wound their way down the steep sides until they disappeared into the trees that grew up the rocky walls from the hole's floor.

"A small and insignificant hole," Ho'Demi said with studied indifference, but his eyes twinkled as he watched Axis' and Azhure's reactions. "You and your command are the first southerners to see Ravensbund's secret for many thousands of years, StarMan."

Axis, like Azhure, just stared. The hole—if such a mediocre word could describe this remarkable geological feature—contained steaming springs and luxuriant vegetation. Whatever winds and storms swept the flat plains would not reach down into this haven.

"What is it?" he asked eventually.

"A hole, StarMan."

Axis finally wrenched his eyes away from the sight before him. *"How?"*

"How is not an established fact, StarMan, but we have stories. It is said that tens of thousands of years ago, the Icescarp Alps swept even farther westward than they do now. But one day, when the gods were in a playful mood," at this Azhure exchanged a glance with Axis, "they caused a great earthquake, and the final thirty leagues of the Alps sank."

"Sank?"

"Sank, Enchantress, leaving these great holes before us now. Of course," he blew out his cheeks as if he did not believe a word he was saying, "some say it is a fanciful story, but then others say that the hot springs found at the bases of these holes mirror the hot springs that sit in the depths of Talon Spike. Of course, I would not know about that."

Again Axis and Azhure looked at each other, but they did not comment.
"How many of these are there?" Axis asked.

"Perhaps three hundred. They stretch across the center of Ravensbund to the western shores of the Andeis Sea, but they do not extend very far north."

"They must be very beautiful," Azhure said, and Ho'Demi nodded.

"Individually we call them holes, but as a group we always refer to them as the Necklet, because from above they must seem like a jeweled chain about a snowy throat."

"Can we ride down?" Azhure asked.

"Certainly, Enchantress, but not now. It would take this lot an hour at least to descend, and over that to rise. But we will camp in another tonight, and there you will see the true wonders of the individual stones of the Necklet."

Axis looked up. About the hole the Acharite soldiers sat their horses, some dismounting to stand as close to the edge as they could get.

"I think this lot will have some trouble remembering to eat their lunch," Axis said, "although their mouths hang open so wide you might get your Ravensbund men to wander along and push some bread and cheese in."

Ho'Demi laughed, and Axis gave the order to dismount for their noon meal.

That night, all the southerners had the opportunity to indulge their curiosity. Ho'Demi led them to a hole twice the size of the first they had seen, and they spent the last hour of light filing down the steep paths into the haven below.

The hot springs were vast, and supported a wide variety of bird and small animal life.

"The Skraelings didn't bother to come down here then," Axis said.

"No reason for them to," Ho'Demi replied. "If my people had hidden in the holes, then no doubt the Skraelings would have surged down. But the birds are small, and the animals likewise, and all generally live high in the trees. It would not have been good hunting for the Skraelings."

"Your people don't use these holes very much?"

Ho'Demi smiled at him. "We are a strange people, StarMan, and, odd as it may seem, we genuinely do prefer the ice in the extreme north. Although we spend the worst of the winter camped about the holes, for eight to nine months of the year we live among the ice packs."

"And that is where you hope to find your people now."

"Yes, StarMan. That is where I hope to find my people."

63

Urbeth's Joke

But even the ice packs seemed deserted. From the Necklet, Ho'Demi led the force north until, after fifteen days of riding from when they left Belial and Magariz, they stood at the very northern edge of the continent.

Snow lay frosted and compacted on the ground, the fierce winds contained tiny ice drops that stung cheeks and exposed flesh. All save Azhure were wrapped in thick cloaks; ice sparkled among the dark moons as they swept over her blue suit, but she seemed untroubled by the cold. Azhure moved close to Axis' side, and he put his arm about her. Caelum lay snug in a pannier hanging from Venator's back, and all that could be seen of him was a dark, tousled curl.

"It's awesome," Azhure whispered, and Axis had to agree with her.

A thin line of gray-green sea water, perhaps fifty paces wide, stretched between the shore and the edge of the ice pack. There great jagged sheets of ice jostled and ground together, sometimes rearing a hundred paces into the air, sometimes plunging to the depths of the sea-bed in the space of a heartbeat. The ice was yellowish in places, green in others, gray in yet still more, and Axis could not comprehend how anyone could even contemplate risking half an hour on the ice pack, let alone a day or a month.

Yet when he looked over to the ranks of Ravensbundmen standing along the shore he saw nothing but longing on each face. They did not seem to notice the cruelty of the wind's bite, nor the danger of the shifting ice; all they saw was a home long denied them, a place of challenge and companionship, of courage and camaraderie.

He hugged Azhure tighter. There was no way Ho'Demi could persuade him to cross to that treacherous ice.

"No need," Ho'Demi said softly by his side, and he accepted a large conical shell from one of his men. It was ivory on the outside and patterned orange and blue within, and when Ho'Demi put it to his lips it emitted a low but piercing howl. Azhure put her hands to her ears to block out its call, and Axis had no doubts that it could penetrate into the very depths of the ice pack.

"And now?" he asked as Ho'Demi lowered the shell.

"Now? Now we wait."

And while they waited, Ho'Demi told them of the pack ice. "It extends along the western shores of the Iskruel Ocean; and it is a league wide in places, five leagues in others. We hunt seal and sometimes whale from its back, and we have learned to know its sighs and tremblings so that we may avoid being eaten by its jaws. But even we . . ." he paused and contemplated the ice for several minutes. "Even we lose the occasional unwary child."

They took children out there? Azhure shuddered.

"I sent word to the northern tribes to seek shelter from the Skraelings among the ice packs," Ho'Demi continued. "They were to leap in their boats and paddle for the ice, for the Skraelings could not cross the open strip of water between the shore and the pack. I thought that my people would have their best chance of survival on the ice, for they knew it and loved it. But . . ."

He faltered, and Sa'Kuya, who sat by his side in front of the fire, took his hand. "But I had no way of knowing we would be gone so long. For over three years my people have had to fight for their survival among this ice. They were hearty Ravensbundmen and women all, but even I doubt their ability to live that long among the ice without respite."

So they waited. They waited three days, during which Ho'Demi grew increasingly fretful, and Axis and Azhure became concerned about the time that flew by. Soon they would have to be at Talon Spike, and then Axis would have to travel on to the Earth Tree Grove for Fire-Night. How many more days could they linger at the edge of this ocean?

Early on the morning of the fourth day a shout brought Ho'Demi hastening from his bedroll. Were his people emerging from the ice? But all that he could see was a great icebear slipping and sliding as it leaped from ice sheet to ice sheet, one moment apparently in danger of being swallowed by a yawning chasm, the next avoiding being speared by sharp ice only by the merest breath.

Ho'Demi stared and then, with every other Ravensbund man who was awake and watching, he fell to his knees.

"Urbeth," he whispered.

Still wiping the sleep from their eyes, Axis and Azhure joined him, standing at his shoulder.

Axis stared at the bear.

She was massive, the height of a tall man at her shoulder and half as long again as a horse. Her paws had black talons twice as long and thick as a man's fingers, and her teeth, gleaming as she panted for breath, looked almost as wicked as a Skraeling's. Thick fur, yellowing with age, covered her body and, as Axis looked closer, he could see that she had lost an ear.

"Azhure," he began, about to remind her of the icebear he had seen that day they had sat on the ledge at Talon Spike so long ago, but his words were cut off by a gigantic splash. The bear had plunged into the waters and was now paddling toward the beach, only her head and a small island of her back showing above the water.

"Urbeth," Ho'Demi said again in a tone of deep reverence.

Urbeth? Axis asked Azhure, not wanting to disturb the strangeness of the moment with speech. She shrugged, and Axis turned back to the bear.

She was close to the shore now, and she grunted as her paws scrabbled for purchase on the pebbly beach. Water cascaded off her back as she slowly waded toward the watchers, and she shook herself so vigorously that water sprayed over Ho'Demi and all those within ten paces of him.

Axis belatedly wondered if they should be standing so close to one of the fearsome icebears. By the Stars! he breathed, she towers over most here.

"I greet you well enough, Ho'Demi," the bear said pleasantly.

"Urbeth." Ho'Demi placed his hands over his breast and half bowed from his kneeling position. Along the shore line men bowed so that their foreheads touched the beach, and Axis wondered if he and Azhure should do the same.

Us? Azhure smiled at him. *You forget who we are, StarMan.* She inclined her head graciously toward the bear.

"Moon," Urbeth said, and flicked a stray droplet from one of her claws. "I know you, for I gambol among the tides and your light shines over the ice-den where I hide my cubs."

Then Urbeth gazed curiously at Axis. "StarMan," Azhure said by way of introduction, "and Song."

"Well," said the bear, "no wonder I don't know you, for the grating of the ice keeps out all but the low timber of Ho'Demi's horn . . . and the screams of the seals as I sink my teeth deep into their backs."

Axis grinned wanly and pitied the seals.

"I call my people, Urbeth," Ho'Demi interrupted. "Do you know of their whereabouts?"

Urbeth yawned, and abruptly sat down, both hind legs sliding out almost at right angles from her body. "Your people?" She twitched the toes of her hind paws and contemplated one of her fore paws, perhaps wondering if one swipe would be enough to take off a man's head, or if two would be required. "Did I perchance eat them, and forget the fact?"

Ho'Demi stared at her, and did not respond.

Urbeth sighed and put her fore paw down with a slap that sent several pebbles skidding along the beach. "Your people, Ho'Demi. Well. You have left them alone for a long time." She paused and tilted her head, her eyes dark and sharp. "A very long time. Many things can happen in—what is it?—almost four years? But . . ." she turned her eyes skyward, as if consulting deep memory.

"Let me think. Ah . . . yes. They arrived, most of them, although I remember twenty or thirty falling here on the beach with Skraelings clinging to their backs."

Azhure shuddered, and Urbeth dropped her gaze and stared at her. "Not very good to eat," she said. "Not enough salt."

"Oh," Azhure said after a moment. "The Skraelings."

Ho'Demi shifted in frustration. "Urbeth?"

Urbeth sighed again, her breath rippling over the entire assembly. "Your people, Ho'Demi. Yes, well. They scrambled into the ice and there they were safe. For some time. But, oh dear, then the winter storms came, and they were fiercer than they had ever been before. Many froze to the ice, and were swallowed and digested as the ice rose and fell."

She glanced over her shoulder. "They are still there, somewhere, Ho'Demi. Bits of them, anyway, still frozen in the ice. When they thaw out I may taste them."

Axis placed a restraining hand on Ho'Demi's shoulder. Whoever, whatever, this bear was, Axis was afraid Ho'Demi would do something rash.

Ho'Demi relaxed. "You are a tease, Urbeth."

"A tease? A tease?" Axis swore the bear had managed to raise a nonexistent eyebrow. "Ho'Demi, I simply have a sense of humor. Something you should learn to cultivate."

"Good Urbeth," Azhure said, "are your cubs well?"

"Yes, indeed, Moon. Thank you for asking."

"I have my own cub, Urbeth. See? He sleeps, in my blankets by the fire."

"Yes, I see, Moon. He is a fine cub."

Azhure sighed, her eyes somber. "But cubs can be so trying, Urbeth. Sometimes I must rock him and rock him before he consents to sleep."

"Oh, I know, Moon, I know," Urbeth consoled, and Axis wondered if he were dreaming, or if this bizarre conversation was really taking place.

"Such a trouble making him sleep, Urbeth. But you have far more help than I."

"I do?"

"The tides," Azhure said softly, "rock your cubs to sleep in their ice-den, so I think that they cannot be the trouble that my cub is."

Urbeth shifted uncomfortably. "Well, you are right, Moon. And I should thank you for that."

"A boon then, friend Urbeth. I rock your cubs to sleep for you, and in return, I would have you tell Ho'Demi what has happened to his people."

"I would have told anyway, Moon," Urbeth said crossly, and lumbered to her feet. "You did not have to waste a boon on the matter."

Azhure smiled. "I thought Ho'Demi about to stick you, Urbeth, and I sought to prevent a slaughter."

Urbeth chuckled, the sound shocking coming from such a massive beast.

"Indeed you did, Moon, for had Ho'Demi sought to stick me I would have slaughtered all his people standing before me. Well now, Ho'Demi, are you ready for Urbeth's joke?"

He jerked his head in assent.

Urbeth looked sly. "But are you ready for a *walk*, Ho'Demi?" And with that she turned and lumbered northwestward along the shoreline of the Iskruel Ocean.

They had no choice but to follow. Camps were hurriedly struck and horses saddled, then the entire force—eight thousand Ravensbundmen and three thousand Acharites—fell into file behind the great bear as she ambled along, grunting to herself and occasionally pausing to scratch the ruff of her neck.

No one spoke. The Ravensbundmen were either too tense or too awe-struck, and the Acharites were so dumbfounded at what they were doing they could not find the words to discuss it.

Azhure kept the Alaunt slinking in a well-controlled pack behind Venator; she had little doubt that if they tried to play with Urbeth, she would give as good as she got.

Urbeth led them northwest all that day until the dark shapes of the DeadWood Forest loomed on the horizon. Then she sat down, yawned, and curled into a ball to sleep. She had not said a word the entire way.

Men sat in quiet groups huddled about fires that night, and not a few glances were sent toward the great pale shape snoring in the distance.

"Who is she?" Axis asked.

"Urbeth," Ho'Demi replied tersely.

"*What* is she, Ho'Demi?"

Sa'Kuya answered for her husband. "Urbeth is more than a bear, Axis, but we do not know how much more. She has hunted these packs through all the time that the Ravensbund have lived here, and occasionally she has come out to talk with us. We worship her for fear, because we fear that if we did not then she would hunt us instead of the seals."

"I doubt that, Sa'Kuya," Azhure said. "I think Urbeth talks to you because she likes you. I think," and her eyes drifted toward the bear asleep twenty paces away, "Urbeth sometimes gets lonely for companionship and good conversation, so she seeks out one or two of the Ravensbund to chat with. Perhaps she would be pleased if you treated her as an equal, not as a god."

The bear burped violently in her sleep, and Axis laughed at the startled expressions on Ho'Demi's and Sa'Kuya's faces. "I think you should listen to my wife, my friends, for I wager that bear would have many tales to keep you amused through your long months on the ice."

Ho'Demi put his tea mug down. "If she leads me to my people, StarMan, then I shall invite her to be godmother at the naming of my next grandchild."

Azhure leaned over and patted Ho'Demi's knee. "I think Urbeth would like that very much, Ho'Demi."

*   *   *

The bear woke with the sun. She rose and stretched, her grunts waking the entire camp, and ambled toward the forest.

"Tell your men to remain on their feet, Ho'Demi," she called over her shoulder, "for there is no need to disturb the horses."

Ho'Demi muttered as he flung his cloak about his shoulders, his eyes shadowed through lack of sleep. About him the Ravensbund men rose and followed the bear, the chimes tangled in their hair tinkling sweetly in the morning air.

Azhure bundled Caelum in a blanket and held him close, giving him a piece of bread to keep him quiet, then joined Axis as they walked with the others following the bear.

It took them an hour to approach DeadWood Forest, and as soon as they were close a murmur arose among the Ravensbundmen.

"What disturbs them?" Azhure asked.

"The trees," Sa'Kuya answered. "They are alive."

Azhure wondered why the fact that the trees were alive bothered the Ravensbund people. The forest, stretching southwest as far as the eye could see, was of normal conifers, although Azhure could see the blackened trunks of dead trees among the live growth. The trees were a trifle stunted, perhaps, but Azhure was not surprised that they did not grow very tall this far north. That they grew at all was surprise enough.

"Oh," she suddenly said, and Sa'Kuya glanced at her.

"Yes, Enchantress. Dead Wood Forest. For as long as Ravensbund memory stretches, these trees have been dead. A frozen forest at the edge of the icecap. And never this thick."

"Oh," Azhure said again, but now her tone was full of understanding.

Urbeth sat down about twenty paces from the first of the trees, her face bored as she waited for the men behind to catch up. Finally, she barked to clear her throat, then spoke.

"Your people lived for almost eighteen months on the ice pack, Ho'Demi. But it was hard on them. Many died. A growing number, convinced that the end of the world was nigh, refused food or drink, courting death. Many prayed that you would return and lead them back into their homelands, but most felt that you and those who escaped with you had been eaten by the Skraelings who had massed along the shoreline and then seethed south. They debated among themselves about what to do and finally, after many weeks of discussion, they called to me to eat them, and thus end their misery."

Urbeth rolled her eyes. "Their cries annoyed me and woke my cubs. The seals darted away and I lacked food. Although I tried to be patient with their misery, eventually I grew dark with anger. I decided I could not live with them any longer. And finally I *did* answer their calls. I *did* eat them. I swallowed them whole until I could swallow no more, and so I spat them out. Then I ate some more, and eventually spat those out as well. I ate and spat until the dreadful cries were silenced. And where I spat, so grew trees."

She cocked her head and regarded the trees. "I don't like them," she said. "Their greenery disturbs the harmony of snow and ice and gray tides. I think you ought to take them away."

Utter silence greeted her words. Everyone stared at the trees, then at the bear, then back to the trees.

"Urbeth," Ho'Demi said eventually, "there are many of my people in the southern lands who are now wending their way north. Among them is my daughter, In'Mari, married to Izanagi who stands among us now. She is great with child, and when her child is born I would ask that you stand as her godmother."

"Godmother? What is that?"

"Each child born among us has a godmother and godfather bonded to them. They act as spiritual guardians to the child through his or her life. To protect them from demons and to show them the way of the ice."

Urbeth's eyes gleamed. "Oh, I'd like that, Ho'Demi! You are very gracious."

Ho'Demi waited patiently.

"Oh, very well," Urbeth snapped. "Take your people and go. But on one condition."

"And what is that?"

"That you never leave them to drift lonely and sad on the pack ice for so long again. I prefer to sleep soundly at night."

"Done, great Urbeth."

"Done," she muttered, heaved a great sigh, and rose to her feet. She padded over to the nearest tree, considered it an instant, then gave it a great swipe with one of her massive paws.

The tree swayed, then a great crack rent the air. The tree toppled and, as it fell, its upper branches caught those of its neighbor and brought that crashing to the ground as well. As its neighbor crashed to the ground, so it enmeshed *its* neighbor, and the destruction spread among the trees. Soon the sound of cracking timber and the smell of pine resin filled the morning, and pine needles floated thick through the air, causing everyone, even Urbeth, to turn aside and cough and wipe at their eyes.

"A nuisance," she was heard to mutter, "from start to finish."

Gradually people rose from the great tangle of branches and pine needles, in groups of ones and twos to begin with, then in greater numbers. All looked bewildered, all were thin with drawn faces and haunted expressions, but all were alive. As they stared at the bear and the warriors beyond her, their eyes filled with tears and they stretched out their arms, calling softly.

"I would suggest, Ho'Demi," Urbeth said, "that your warriors would be better put to fishing and sealing than standing about with their mouths open. These sleepers will be hungry."

Then, with the utmost dignity, she padded her way toward the sea.

"Urbeth," Ho'Demi cried, "I thank you!"

"Accepted," the bear called over her shoulder, then she paused. "It was a great joke, Ho'Demi, because the Skraelings knew where your people were. They stood about in whispering hordes before this forest for weeks, but they would not approach. Anyone would think they did not like trees."

Then she was gone, plunging into the gray waters and paddling her way toward the ice pack.

64

The Cruel World

Axis and Azhure stayed one more day, then informed Ho'Demi they would travel on to Talon Spike.

"There is nothing for us to do here," Axis said. "As much as I would like to stay and explore the wonders of the Necklet or learn the mysteries of hunting the seal from the back of the pack ice, I must travel eastward."

"I understand, StarMan. Gorgrael still waits. You will prevail."

Axis laughed harshly, and looked away.

"I must say that, and I must believe it," Ho'Demi said, "for if I do not, then there is no hope, and Urbeth will have saved my people for nothing."

"Well then, I must not let Urbeth down. She would be cross if she thought all her effort had been wasted."

"One day you will return, StarMan, and I will teach you to hunt seals."

"Perhaps I will bring my son," Axis grinned, his good mood returning, "and we shall stumble about the pack ice together."

Azhure smiled also, and leaned forward and kissed Ho'Demi gently on the cheek. "And I shall come back, Ho'Demi, and talk some more with Urbeth. She must have great mysteries to explain."

Sa'Kuya stepped forward and gave Axis a package of Tekawai tea; now they had reached the Icebear Coast the Ravensbund people could replenish their stocks. "You will be traveling still farther north, I think, StarMan. Take this tea with our blessing, and when you drink it think of the Ravensbund people whose thoughts will always be with you."

"I thank you, Sa'Kuya." Axis stowed the package in the packs that hung behind Belaguez's saddle. "Ho'Demi, I leave you my three thousand men. Use them if you want, or send them home."

"I shall not keep them overlong, StarMan," Ho'Demi said, bowing slightly in recognition of the gift. "The Skraelings have all gone from the Ravensbund and we live in tents, so there is no rebuilding to do. Perhaps for a few weeks they can help us build up our stocks of seal and fish, but I think they will be longing for their own lands and families. I shall send them back to Carlon."

Axis nodded. "Well, Azhure? Are you ready for Talon Spike?"

She smiled at him. Both were looking forward to the week it would take them to travel to Talon Spike; they had rarely had much time alone in past months. "I'm—" she was interrupted by an anxious voice behind them.

"StarMan! You're not leaving me?" Arne stood there, his face stubborn.

"Arne," Axis said, "I have no further use for an army where I go. After Talon Spike I must travel alone, for what I must do can only be done by me."

Azhure hoped Arne would not make a fuss.

But Arne had every intention of making a fuss. For three years he had been driven by the Veremund-inspired impulse to protect Axis. He had ridden at Axis' back through battlefield and marketplace and snow-field. He had constantly watched for hands reaching to daggers or eyes sliding toward assassins. Every stranger had been a potential traitor, every smile a potential dupe, every mouthful potential poison. The only time that Arne had been away from Axis had been during the months Axis spent in Talon Spike and the UnderWorld, and those months had left him feeling empty and directionless. He had no intent of suffering through such again, not when Axis walked to face his worst threat yet. "I *am* coming with you," he said stonily.

"Arne. I *must* go alone."

But Azhure saw advantages in Arne's presence. "Axis," she said, her voice gentle, persuasive. "What does it hurt if Arne travels with us to Talon Spike and then perhaps even to the Earth Tree Grove with you. And then . . . why, he may not help you in your battle with Gorgrael, but he will prove true company on the way."

Arne shot her a grateful glance.

Axis shot her a glance too, but his was speculative. "Stars above, Azhure, next you'll be saying that you want to come along as well."

There was truly nothing that Azhure *would* have liked more to do, but she knew her presence would mean his death. So she shrugged, and spoke with a light voice. "I would not risk taking Caelum with me, my love, and I will not risk him alone again. Not until Gorgrael lies dead at your feet. Besides, I promised Rivkah I would be there for the birth of her son."

"So while I face the threat of Gorgrael alone, Azhure, you would midwive the birth of yet another brother?"

She flinched at his tone, but she kept her voice steady. "Axis, I cannot come. You know this."

Axis sighed. Yes, he knew it.

Sometime during this conversation Arne realized that his presence with

Axis had been tacitly agreed to. "Thank you, Lord," he said, and a smile lit his normally dark and impassive face.

"Well, get to your horse then, dammit," Axis snapped, and Azhure turned away as well, and mounted silently.

Ho'Demi and Sa'Kuya, flanked by several dozen of the Ravensbund people, stood and watched them ride off.

"He will come back one day," she said.

"Yes," her husband said, "I think that he will."

"Now," he turned and kissed Sa'Kuya. "I have a vow to fulfill. Keep watch for me, wife, and brew the Tekawai when you see me return."

And with that he turned and stomped off to the beach. There were four twin-hulled canoes pulled up on the pebbles, the rest were out with hunters chasing seal. Ho'Demi selected one and dragged it out to the incoming tide, and set off for the ice pack.

But he did not paddle directly for the pack. Instead he sent the canoe sliding through the choppy waters to the south, the bleak landscape on his right, the yellowed ice rearing to his left. Ho'Demi wanted solitude for what he was about to do. The ice, he thought, would never be quite the same again, and he hoped that Urbeth would not mind.

After several hours paddling he finally maneuvered his craft into a stable rift in the ice and moored it solidly. From there he clambered up the steep sides of the ice pack until he reached the top, then he stood, and stared.

"Home," he breathed.

The ice pack stretched before him for leagues, grunting and rolling and whispering as the ice constantly shifted and lifted, only to sink again. In some areas birds hopped across, seeking fish that had been trapped in small inlets as the pack shifted, in other areas icebears—Urbeth's smaller cousins—gamboled, chasing birds or retelling stories of their greatest seal hunts. It was across this ice that the Ravensbund people spent many months hunting seal themselves, and occasionally taking an icebear for its fur. When the seasons and ice were auspicious, they also hunted whale, but that was dangerous, and each tribe generally caught only one per year, using its meat and blubber to keep warm with food and fire, its curved rib bones as frames for their canoes, and its hide for clothes and the hulls of the canoes.

It was a beautiful, magical world, but it was also a cruel one.

Ho'Demi walked twenty or thirty paces into the ice, then he knelt and reached around behind him, freeing the box he had kept at his belt for many months.

Chitter, chatter.

My friends, I have brought you to your new world.

Chitter, chatter. Is it as cruel as you promised? Is it worth the help we provided?

Ho'Demi smiled and undid the thongs that tied the lid firmly in place. *Crueler, my friends. Can you not feel the bite of the wind?*

Yes . . . yes, we can, chitter chatter.

Then revel, my friends, and may you give this place more soul than it currently has.

He tore the lid off the box and leaned back. There was a burst of . . . energy—he did not know how else to describe it—and then the box was empty.

Well, my friends. Do you like it?

We love it! Thank you, Ho'Demi!

Listen to me, my friends. As this pack ice moves and shifts, so you will spread out among the pack and the ice floes that surround it. Others share this ice. My people, as well as the birds and the fish and the seal and whale and all those who hunt them. None will disturb you, and you must not disturb them.

He paused. *Do not pick at their minds.*

Never, never, chitter, chatter.

But if you see those Skraelings again, if they ever touch the ice, then you may nibble at their minds, for they are not wanted here.

Ho'Demi smiled. Few, if any, would realize the presence of these souls, for they only touched the minds of those with the gift. He turned and retraced his steps to his canoe, slipping as the ice moved underfoot, and anticipated the Tekawai Sa'Kuya would have waiting for him.

65

Finger of the Gods

Arne was as unobtrusive as possible, content just to be there, and he rode forty or so paces behind the StarMan and the Enchantress, allowing them some privacy. Axis and Azhure appreciated this, and after the first hour or so each day they forgot his presence. At night, they always blinked in mild surprise when they turned to see Arne setting up his solitary campsite some distance from their own.

Caelum slept. He woke in the evenings and played with his father and listened to the enchantments Axis taught him, and he spent the first hour of each day's ride gazing wide-eyed at the world from Azhure's back, but then he would gently drift into sleep, although his parents' conversations filtered into his dreams, and he learned even while he slept. And the tides spoke to him too, the waves crashing rhythmically into his sleepy mind, as did the wind and the scent of salt and ice along the hundred-league beach of the Icebear Coast. It was an extraordinary landscape, stark but majestic and beautiful. To the south, the alps rose sheer and black, while to the north the gray-blue sea crashed on the pebbled beach, the ice-pack grinding behind it, the sea birds wheeling and crying with eerie voices above.

Sometimes the beauty of the Icebear coast grew so extreme, and the cries of the sea birds so haunting, that Azhure and Axis would kick their horses into a wild and breathless gallop, the Alaunt streaming out to each side and in front of them, adding their cries to those of the birds.

Arne kept his horse to a restrained canter, knowing he would catch them in the end. Even he, dour as he was, was affected by the savage scenery they passed through, and sometimes tears streamed down his face.

Five days out from DeadWood Forest Axis reined Belaguez to a halt late one afternoon.

"Look," he said, pointing, and Azhure saw Talon Spike rearing out of the clouds. They sat for long minutes, staring at the mountain, wondering at its majesty and splendor.

"What will become of it, do you think?" Azhure asked eventually.

"Become of it?"

"For a thousand years it was the home of the Icarii, but now most, if not all, will live in the southern regions. StarDrifter told me that in the days before the Wars of the Axe the mountain was used as a summer residence—a playground for the Icarii." She paused. "It would be a shame if Talon Spike became a playground again. It has seen too much, and meant too much, for that."

"I know what you mean. StarDrifter should be there by now, and FreeFall. We can decide together what we shall do with the complex. Ah, here comes Arne. Arne, see that mountain? That is our destination."

Arne pulled his horse up and stared at the mountain. It was still distant, at least one day's ride away, but the sight took his breath away.

"Come," Axis said. "We shall turn south into the alps here. Say your goodbyes to the Icebear Coast."

"When you come home, Axis," Azhure said softly, "we shall return here and race our horses the length of this beach."

Axis reached across and touched her cheek. "Just you and me, Azhure, on a deep moonlit night. Now," his tone turned brisk, "we shall have some climbing to do."

He took them through several small ravines that led south, then east, the ground rising the whole way. To the north they could hear Talon Spike's glacier grinding and splintering its way to the sea, but soon even that was lost in the labored breathing of the horses.

When they camped that night, Azhure asked Axis if the horses would have to climb much farther. There was little feed here in the alps, and she thought the three horses might be weakening slightly.

"No. One of the things StarDrifter and MorningStar made me learn were the entrance ways and passages of Talon Spike. We will climb another hour or two in the morning, and then we should be able to enter one of the tunnels that lead to the foot of the great peak itself. From there we can bed the animals down in one of the lower chambers and ascend into the complex."

They were in the mountain by noon of the next day. The horses had struggled until they reached the tunnel, which was so smooth-floored and gently graded that they lowered their heads and breathed easy, jogging along with little effort. The tunnel, lit by magical enchantments like all Icarii creations, led into the lower regions of the mountain. Here the riders found stables and fodder for the horses, and once their mounts were comfortable Axis took Azhure and Arne through stairwells and shafts until they reached the higher chambers of the complex.

Axis led Arne to the dining halls where several Icarii sat eating and he left the man in their care. Then he and Azhure continued higher and higher into the mountain. Whatever destruction the Gryphon had wrought had been repaired. The complex was almost empty, and the sounds of the few Icarii who moved through it rang loud and clear.

Azhure shivered, trying to imagine what these corridors must have looked like with thousands of Gryphon crawling through them. For those remaining, the end must have been a horror.

"I wish I could have done something," she whispered, and Axis took her hand.

"You warned them. It was their choice."

"Where is he?" she asked eventually.

"In the Assembly Chamber," he replied, "waiting for us."

They entered the Assembly Chamber from the upper archways, silently, halting at the top tier to stare down to the circular floor below.

StarDrifter was there, lying facedown and spread-eagled in the center of the golden marble.

Azhure gave Axis a gentle push in the back. "Go," she mouthed, and Axis walked slowly down the steps toward his father.

When Axis was a third of the way down StarDrifter raised his head, paused, then rose to his feet. "Axis," he said, and held out his arms.

Axis took the remaining steps at a run and embraced his father fiercely. When Azhure joined them both men's faces were wet with tears.

"I thought I had lost you," StarDrifter whispered.

"You had. Azhure brought me home."

StarDrifter turned and embraced Azhure tightly. "Azhure. You are looking well. I have heard strange stories about you," he leaned back and ran his eyes over her dark blue suit, "and you shall have to spend many hours satisfying my curiosity."

Axis scrutinized them carefully, at first suspiciously and then he relaxed. Whatever desire StarDrifter had carried for Azhure now seemed to have gone. They were at ease with each other, the bonds of their friendship stronger than he could ever have imagined.

StarDrifter lifted Caelum from Azhure's back and hugged him as well. "I heard that Gorgrael had taken him . . ." His voice faltered.

Axis smiled. "Again we must thank Azhure." Then his smile died as realization hit him. "Stars, Azhure," he breathed. "None of us would be here if not for you."

She looked at him quizzically. "Explain."

He took her face in his hands. "You *are* our salvation, Azhure, and you were birthed by a darker power—WolfStar. The last prophecy of the second verse of the Prophecy of the Destroyer has come to pass."

They were all silent for some moments. "Then it is just the prophecy concerning the Sentinels that needs to be fulfilled before I can wield the Rainbow Scepter," Axis said. "Has anyone seen them, StarDrifter? In the events of the past months I had completely forgotten about them."

"No," StarDrifter said. "Wherever they are, whatever they do, they do not seem to want anyone else to know."

"Well, there is nothing to be done, I suppose. I shall have to trust in them to fulfill their part of the Prophecy."

"They have dedicated their entire lives to the Prophecy, Axis," Azhure reminded him, "and the other prophecies have worked their way through without any help or prompting from us. Trust. And try not to worry."

"Yes, you're right, Azhure. StarDrifter . . . have you . . . ?" He couldn't voice the question.

"Within a day of my arrival, Axis. SpikeFeather and the Strike Force had been here two weeks; Talon Spike was clean and the bodies of the dead neatly laid out. Stars!"

His voice quavered and he turned away, his shoulders trembling. Azhure stepped up and placed a gentle hand on his shoulder. "StarDrifter?"

StarDrifter took a deep breath and tried to smile, cuddling Caelum closer. "I'm sorry. But I have never seen such injuries. Not even after the Yuletide slaughter in the Earth Tree Grove." He took another breath, remembering. "We lit a great pyre at the peak of the mount and burned them there. Their souls drifted straight to the stars."

He paused, and Axis and Azhure held their peace. "RavenCrest and I were never particularly close," StarDrifter said after a moment, "for there was such an age difference between us, and our personalities were so different." The reflection in his eyes turned to pain. "RavenCrest so often accused me of being reckless, Axis. Stars, but he was right! It was my own son who ordered this slaughter! My simple lusts brought all this death and destruction down upon my own people."

"Simple lusts, StarDrifter? Then blame yourself for the fact that the Icarii now fly the southern skies again," Axis said fiercely. "Blame yourself for the fact that the sacred sites are now reclaimed. Blame yourself that your simple lusts have resulted in your people's freedom!"

StarDrifter lowered his head. "With great gain needs must also come pain," he whispered.

"Would you rather that the Icarii sit here in the Assembly and mouth useless dreams, StarDrifter? Gods, but I have not been through all that I have to stand here and watch you develop a conscience!"

StarDrifter stared at Axis. Then, unexpectedly, he laughed. "You bring me joy, Axis, and you have brought the Icarii far more joy than pain. Forgive my maudlin ramblings."

Azhure lifted Caelum from his arms. "RavenCrest and BrightFeather and all those who died here have been avenged, StarDrifter."

"Yes, SpikeFeather told me. Accept my thanks, Azhure, on behalf of all Icarii, for what you did in Gorken Pass." He laughed again. "I wish I could have seen it."

Azhure grinned. "No doubt Axis will recall the memory of it for you, when you both have nothing better to do but sit about a fire and cultivate maudlin thoughts."

"Axis? Azhure?"

They turned and saw FreeFall enter from the doorway in the lower tiers. EvenSong was directly behind him. Their greetings encompassed laughter and a few more tears, and Azhure hugged both tightly when she heard that FreeFall and EvenSong had, finally, formalized their union.

"The First heard our vows, Azhure," EvenSong told her, "and she cried even more than you do now."

That made Azhure laugh, and she wiped away her tears. Then she kissed FreeFall again. "Enjoy the SunSoar luck in marriage, FreeFall." She paused, a mischievous twinkle in her eye. "And father a beautiful daughter for Caelum to love."

Both FreeFall and EvenSong reddened, but whatever retort they might have made was cut off when Axis looked to the upper Chamber. "Spike-Feather," he said softly.

SpikeFeather TrueSong stood at the head of the steps, resplendent in his true dark red coloring. But it was not SpikeFeather's red feathers that caught people's eyes.

In his hands he held the jeweled torc of the office of Talon.

FreeFall's eyes grew troubled at the sight of it, and as SpikeFeather stepped down slowly, he shuffled nervously. Axis spared him a puzzled glance—surely FreeFall had anticipated this? As SpikeFeather reached them, Axis looked at Azhure, and without a word they both stepped back, StarDrifter and EvenSong following their lead.

Now FreeFall stood alone and increasingly nervous in the center of the golden circle. SpikeFeather stared into his eyes, then dropped gracefully to one knee, holding the torc extended in his hands.

"You are RavenCrest's son," SpikeFeather said, "and you are his heir, ratified by the StarMan himself. This torc is yours."

"I cannot wear it," FreeFall said, stumbling over the words.

Axis frowned, but it was StarDrifter who spoke. "You will be officially recognized in the Assembly on Temple Mount, FreeFall. When Axis . . . when Axis returns he will conduct the ceremonies there. But the torc is yours, and you can wear it as Talon-Elect from this moment." He paused. "Take it."

But FreeFall still hesitated and SpikeFeather extended his hands farther.

"I cannot," FreeFall said again, but then he seized the torc and held it out to Azhure. "Azhure, this is yours by right."

"*What?*" she exclaimed. "How can you—"

"WolfStar was murdered by his brother who then took the throne as his heir. But you are WolfStar's rightful heir, Azhure, and the office of Talon should be yours."

Abruptly Azhure set Caelum down on the floor and, stepping forward, took the torc. "Damn you, FreeFall!" she snapped. "Must you keep evading your duties? I was not born to the throne of Talon, I have other responsibilities that would never enable me to rule over the Icarii as Talon, and I was conceived *after* WolfStar was murdered!" She paused and took a deep breath. "Damn it, what are you going to do next? Offer it to Axis or StarDrifter or EvenSong? They are all tied by blood and by right to the throne, far more so than I. Now, *take it!*"

FreeFall almost snatched it from her hands, then grinned shamefacedly. "I had to offer it to you, Azhure. Your father was done a great wrong, even though he had done wrong himself. You *had* to have the throne offered to you."

"In a sense, he's right," StarDrifter said. "Ancient Icarii law clearly states that—"

"Curse ancient Icarii law!" Axis growled light-heartedly, then he took Azhure's arm and smiled at FreeFall. "Cousin, when I shared out the honors that shining day beside Grail Lake I gave you little else than your right to the Talon throne back. Now, Azhure and I would give you more. FreeFall, Talon-Elect of all Icarii, I bequeath to you and to your heirs the overlordship of the Icescarp Alps and the Fortress Ranges, as all the eastern regions of Tencendor, from the southern and eastern banks of the Nordra to the southern reaches of Minstrelsea and Widewall Bay, saving those areas that Ysgryff of Nor and Greville of Tarantaise still hold. Your may have those lands, and the rights to a tithe of all rights, customs and duties, save those I have already promised to Greville and Ysgryff and those of the free city of Arcen. This gift carries an awesome responsibility, FreeFall, for you will have Icarii and Acharite and Avar—if they ever return—under your sway, and you will answer to none bar me or Azhure or our heirs. Well? What do you say?"

FreeFall glanced at Azhure. "But *you* are Governor of the East."

She laughed. "Largely an empty title, FreeFall, when I gallivant about the Icebear Coast with my husband. Besides," she continued, "I will have responsibilities elsewhere. To . . ." she glanced at Axis, "to the House of the Stars."

FreeFall took a deep breath, then nodded, his eyes proud. Then he, too, dropped to one knee. Placing the torc on the floor before him he held out his hands to Axis, and Axis took them between his.

"StarMan," he said, "before these witnesses here present, I accept with honor these lands and peoples and the tithe of all the rights, customs and duties that come with them. I give you my pledge and my oath of honor and fealty, that I and my heirs shall serve you well and faithfully all the days of our lives."

Then, surprising StarDrifter and SpikeFeather, FreeFall held out his hands to Azhure and repeated the same oath to her.

As Azhure smiled and kissed him, Axis bent down and lifted the torc and clipped it about FreeFall's neck before he could escape.

"And so you are jeweled and so you are bound, Talon-Elect," he said, and helped FreeFall to his feet.

"Well," Axis said, "will no one offer Azhure, Caelum and me something to eat and drink? We have ridden far and fast to reach you and I, for one, am tired."

StarDrifter took his arm. "Then come, Axis. Now that you are here we can reconsecrate Talon Spike."

"When?"

"Tomorrow night."

They gathered at the very peak of the mountain in the depths of the night. Azhure shivered, half at the cold wind that blew this high, half at the awesome view from the towering pinnacle. Even in starlight the alps could be seen spreading on three sides, while to the north she could see, and feel, the gray sea pounding along the Icebear Coast. She had never been to the pinnacle during her time in Talon Spike; it had been out of bounds to all but the Talon and senior Enchanters. It was, StarDrifter explained to her in quiet tones on the way up, one of the most sacred places of Talon Spike.

"From the peak all of Talon Spike can be touched," he had said, and now Azhure knew why.

The peak was quite large, large enough to hold the several dozen Icarii who had gathered here. In its very center opened the central shaft of the mountain complex, and when Azhure stepped to its guardrail she could see to the depths of the mountain itself. All shafts and corridors opened off the central shaft; here many of the Gryphon had entered, and it was their befouling touch and murders that the ceremonies tonight were intended to eliminate.

StarDrifter led the proceedings. He motioned Azhure back from the shaft impatiently and, chastened, she hastened back to the circle of watchers. Tonight Azhure and the others in attendance wore loose white linen robes that hung in soft, thick folds to their feet. Azhure let her eyes linger on Axis standing partway around the circle. She had only ever seen him in fighting clothes or courtly fashions before, and she thought he had never seemed so powerful, so starkly princely, as he did in his robe.

At everyone's feet lay unlit brands.

"Talon Spike has been corrupted," StarDrifter said, his voice very soft, yet rich and musical. "Fouled by evil bodies and deeds. Tonight we meet to reconsecrate and rededicate this mountain, beloved of the Icarii people. And, in the wishes of Talon RavenCrest SunSoar, who died here, we will reconsecrate it in the memory of the Enchanter MorningStar SunSoar, our mother and widow of Talon RushCloud, who loved our people and this mountain more than most."

StarDrifter's eyes swept the assembled Icarii. "Think of her," he commanded.

He was silent for a few minutes, letting people recall their own memories of MorningStar.

"She was murdered," he said, "far from here. She had been excited at the discoveries to the south, and she was excited most of all by the ancient books we found in Spiredore. Many of these texts the Icarii thought lost, and MorningStar believed that she would have the time and the luxury of being able to study them. Yet that was not to be."

He walked slowly about the circle, the shaft glowing pale golden in the night and lighting his face. "We have already farewelled MorningStar, as those murdered here, in fitting ceremonies. Tonight we cleanse Talon Spike itself and rededicate its spirit. For ancient generations the mountain was a summer pleasure palace for the Icarii, and then it became a safe haven . . . and a goal."

As he walked he reached out to touch the faces of those he passed, gazing deep into each one's eyes, as if he wanted to touch their very souls. As he passed Azhure, running his fingers lightly over her face, she felt his eyes sear into hers, and she inhaled and trembled. In daily life it was too easy, she thought, to forget just how powerful StarDrifter was.

"But now the time has come for Talon Spike to be reborn," StarDrifter continued. "Time for us to think anew about what service this mountain can do us . . . and how *we* can serve *it*. FreeFall SunSoar, Talon-Elect, will you speak?"

FreeFall, the torc about his neck, now stepped a pace out from the circle. Stars, but he is beautiful, Azhure thought. He looks like a god himself with his pale gold hair and violet eyes and those white, white wings at his back.

"Talon Spike waits for a new direction . . . and a new name. StarDrifter has suggested that the mountain complex now be used as a place of contemplation and study, a place where Icarii can come to examine and debate the mysteries. I concur. It will become a fitting monument to MorningStar and to her love of mysteries enlightened. The mountain shall become a place of libraries and halls, of music and enchantments, of tremulous discoveries and lingering silences. And it shall have a new name, for the Talon will now rule from his palace in the Minaret Peaks. Its new name shall be—"

"Star Finger," Axis said to the side.

FreeFall stood with his mouth gaping. It was not the name he and StarDrifter had chosen.

"Star Finger," Azhure said clearly, and her eyes met Axis'.

StarDrifter looked sharply between the two of them, then at FreeFall. "Star Finger," he said.

"Star Finger," FreeFall repeated, and the name was murmured about the circle as tongues and hearts embraced it.

Then FreeFall stepped back and StarDrifter began to sing in the ancient and sacred language of the Icarii. He sang spells and enchantments that would protect Star Finger from further depredations and would encourage all those who worked and lived within her to thrive in her harmony and peace. His voice was sweet and true, not as powerful as the force he had unleashed in the Temple of the Stars, but moving and inspiring nevertheless.

When he had finished he lifted a brand and, in the act of lifting it, somehow lit it. He raised the brand above his head and cried to the stars. "Let the Star Gods witness the cleansing fire!" Then he sent the flaming brand hurtling down the shaft.

One by one the others stepped forward, the brands bursting into fire the moment hands lifted them, and all echoed StarDrifter's cry and sent their brands plunging down the shaft. As they dropped their brands, the Icarii moved to stand in one corner of the peak.

Finally only Axis and Azhure were left, and StarDrifter gestured to them impatiently.

Axis looked at Azhure, then turned to StarDrifter. "You have asked the Star Gods to witness, Father." StarDrifter's eyes widened in shock at the parental appellation. "And so they shall. Will you call them?"

What are you trying to do, Axis?

Call them, Father.

StarDrifter stared furiously at his son, angry that he would upset the ritual. But to argue now would only corrupt the ritual further and risk contaminating it altogether, and so, with obvious bad grace, StarDrifter cried once more to the stars.

"I call upon Adamon, God of the Firmament, to witness the cleansing of Star Finger!"

"And I accept with honor," a deep voice said, and Adamon stepped out of the darkness into the starlight about the shaft. Like all others on the peak, he was dressed in a long white linen robe, but he had a circlet of light in his dark hair, and his eyes radiated with the glory of the stars themselves.

He stood near the shaft and looked at StarDrifter.

StarDrifter stared at him, his chest heaving in great breaths, then he turned his eyes back to the stars.

"I call upon Xanon, Goddess of the Firmament, to witness the cleansing of Star Finger!"

And Xanon, similarly clothed in linen and circlet and power, stepped forth and smiled gently at StarDrifter.

His voice becoming ever hoarser, StarDrifter called in turn on the Gods of Sun, Fire and Air to witness, and Narcis, Silton and Pors stepped forth.

Then StarDrifter called on the Goddesses of Water and Earth to witness, and Flulia and Zest stepped forth.

Now the seven gods stood in an almost complete circle about the shaft. Two spaces remained.

StarDrifter stared at the seven gods, distraught. "The names of the Goddess of the Moon and the God of Song have not been revealed," he whispered, "and I cannot call on them to witness. I am sorry."

Adamon returned his gaze steadily. "You know them well, StarDrifter. Call them to witness and they will stand forth."

"I do not know . . ." StarDrifter began, then he looked at the two empty spaces, and then . . . then he looked at Axis and Azhure waiting patiently in the shadows.

Both were gazing at him, and both had compassionate expressions on their faces.

"I . . ." StarDrifter stopped again, unable to speak. He felt faint, disorientated.

"Speak, StarDrifter," Azhure said, "for you have nothing to fear."

"I call upon Azhure, Goddess of the Moon, to witness the cleansing of Star Finger."

She smiled. "I accept with honor, StarDrifter," and she stepped forward to fill one of the last two remaining spaces. As she did so a circle of light appeared in her hair, and her eyes blazed with the glory of the stars.

StarDrifter dragged his gaze away from her and toward his son. My son, he thought, my son. "I call upon Axis, God of Song, to witness the cleansing of Star Finger."

"I accept with honor, Father," Axis said, his eyes holding StarDrifter's for a moment of such all-consuming love that StarDrifter literally swayed with emotion.

Axis stepped forward to take his place among the Nine, and as he did so the light burned in his own hair. Then the Nine took each other's hands and raised them above their heads, and as they did so fire burned about the shaft, then they brought their hands down sharply and the fire speared into the mountain. Those still inside reported a great light that enveloped the chambers, halls and spaces of the complex—and in that instant Star Finger became a place truly blessed of the gods.

*   *   *

StarDrifter blinked and saw the Nine still there, their hands upraised, the light shining in their hair.

He blinked again and they were gone, and Axis and Azhure were at his side.

"I did not know," he said, "but, knowing you, I understand."

They sat on the rock ledge of the mountain, a cliff at their feet, the glacier and Icebear Coast before them. On one of the distant ice floes an Icebear gamboled; it was missing one ear.

"Do you remember what I asked you when last we sat here?" Azhure said.

The wind caught at her unfettered hair, and Axis smoothed it away from her face. "Yes. Yes, I do. You asked if it bothered me that I would live so long."

"And you said that it did, that it bothered you that you might sit here in five hundred years and not be able to recall the name of the lovely young woman who sat at your side and whose bones now crumbled into dust."

They were both quiet, and Axis turned his eyes back to the view before them.

"And now . . ." He entwined his fingers with hers.

"Now we face a longer and stranger future, but we will face it together."

He grinned, and with his free hand he caught at something floating in the air. It was a Moonwildflower, and he tangled it within her hair. "I promise I will come home to you, Azhure."

Her fingers tightened briefly, painfully, about his. "Come home," she said. "Come home."

He kissed her and changed the subject. "When will you leave?"

"This afternoon, Axis. I will take Caelum and the Alaunt and the horses and traverse the alpine passes to the Icescarp Barren. From there we will ride for Sigholt."

"Ride with the Moon, Azhure."

She nodded, and smiled. "And you?"

He laughed. "Me and Arne? Arne has developed no more respect for me since he has heard some of the whispers about us that are being bruited about the mountain. He grimly tells me that he will attend me for as long as I need him, and so he says and so it will be. There are only a few days before Fire-Night, so I will try to shake friend Arne slightly by taking him to travel the waterways with Orr."

She cuddled closer to Axis. "Perhaps Arne can discuss the mysteries of the Stars with Orr. When will you leave?"

"When we leave this ledge. There is no reason to wait."

Azhure's eyes filled with tears. "Come home to me, Axis."

His hand tightened about hers. "Will you get to Rivkah in time?"

"I think so, although she will be cross that I have tarried so long. Axis?"

"Hmmm?"

"What do you want me to do at the birth?"

Axis was horrified. He knew what she referred to; Rivkah had asked Azhure to midwife the birth—and a talented midwife could make any infanticide look so much like a stillbirth even the mother would not be aware of what had happened.

"Oh, Azhure! Rivkah trusts you. Would you break her trust for me? No!" He looked away. "Do not answer that, Azhure."

He took a deep breath, and turned back to her. "She trusts you, Azhure. I do not want you to break that trust for my sake."

They sat in silence for some time, then Azhure lifted her fingers to his face. "Come home to me, Axis."

He pulled her back against his body and hid her face in his shoulder.

"Come home to me."

And the seagulls wheeling far below them took up the cry and spread it up and down the Icebear Coast.

Come home to me! Come home to me!

66

The Test

"We must consider," Barsarbe said, her eyes sharp, her voice soft, "what to do."

The Avar had assembled in the Earth Tree Grove for Fire-Night. This festival was of only minor importance for the Avar, and usually they would celebrate it in their own Clan groups wherever they happened to be in the Avarinheim. But this Fire-Night would be special. This Fire-Night would see the crafting of the Rainbow Scepter. And so the Avar had gathered in the Earth Tree Grove.

"This will be our last chance to plot our own future," Barsarbe continued, walking slowly around the outside of the great circle of stone that guarded the Earth Tree. "Tomorrow night is Fire-Night. Tomorrow night the StarMan will appear and ask for our assistance. Tonight we must decide whether or not to give it to him."

A confused murmuring rose from among the Avar. Many of the Banes, who sat in the front ranks, stared at Barsarbe unbelievingly. But it was Grindle, leader of the GhostTree Clan, who spoke out.

He stood respectfully. "Bane Barsarbe. I thought there was no question of aiding the StarMan. Surely we wait only for Tree Friend? When she joins us . . ." He hesitated. None of the Avar had seen Faraday Tree Friend since she disappeared the evening the Avarinheim was joined to Minstrelsea. The Avar realized Faraday was in the Sacred Grove, but when would she join them? When would she lead them into their new home?

Grindle abruptly realized that Barsarbe and the entire Avar people were staring at him, waiting for him to continue. "When Faraday joins us she will present the StarMan to us and we will follow her lead. We must unite with the StarMan, as the Icarii have, in order to defeat Gorgrael. This much is clear from the Prophecy of the Destroyer."

"Thank you, Grindle," Barsarbe said. She touched his shoulder, and he sat back down.

Around him the Avar still looked puzzled.

"My people," Barsarbe resumed her pacing. "I am senior Bane among you. Mine is the responsibility for ensuring the Avar step onto the right paths, choose the right fork. No one can deny that tomorrow night we will face a fork in the path. But which is the right direction? Which the road to surety?"

"With the StarMan, surely," someone said, and Barsarbe could see several heads nod.

"My people. I have thought long and hard about our future, and while I traveled with Faraday Tree Friend, I learned of events that disturbed me. They made me see our future path differently. Now is the time that I must share my thoughts with you."

She walked several paces with her head bowed. When she spoke again, her voice was stronger, and harsher. "Avar! Do you know that the StarMan has betrayed Faraday Tree Friend?

"He pretended to love her, but did he not leave her in Gorkenfort to survive or not while he escaped? And now . . . now I have learned that he treacherously betrayed Faraday for another. Azhure. You must remember *her*."

Again Grindle rose to his feet, more cautiously this time. "It was Beltide, Barsarbe. Bonds and promises are set aside on Beltide."

"*Worse* than Beltide," Barsarbe hissed, spinning on her heel to face him. "Far worse! The StarMan has married this woman Azhure and cast Faraday out of his house." Grindle sank down, his eyes on the ground. "Faraday should have married the StarMan. Faraday should have given him his heir!"

She ran her eyes ran over the assembled Avar. None of them moved. "And we can all remember what kind of woman this Azhure was. Violent. Is that not why we refused her acceptance into the Avar? Violence trails after her."

Grindle made as if to stand up again, but Barsarbe stopped him with an angry glance. "Now she has embraced violence fully. Now she walks with bow and arrows, and hounds clamor at her heels. She is a *huntress*! You did not see what she did to her home village, my people. She destroyed it, burned all who lived within it . . . and smiled as she did it."

Shra, seated besides her father, narrowed her eyes, but for the moment she held her peace.

"You said there was a fork in our path, Bane Barsarbe," said Brode of the SilentWalk Clan. As one of the senior Avar, his word would weigh heavily in whatever decision the Avar made.

"Yes, Brode. We have passively accepted whatever the Prophecy told us. The Prophecy says that we must unite with the Plow and the Wing in order to defeat Gorgrael."

She took a deep breath. "But what if we have a different choice? My people, is this *our* fight? We have the Avarinheim, and now we have Minstrelsea to the south. The Earth Tree sings, and the forests sing with her. We are safe. Gorgrael cannot touch us!"

Barsarbe spread her arms wide, hands and voice entreating. "Don't we have what we wanted? So why help Axis? It will surely only bring further pain to our people, and Mother knows we have endured enough. We have what we want," she repeated slowly, lowering her hands. "*I* say we have the choice of refusing the StarMan."

Apart from the Song of the Earth Tree, which the Avar had grown so used to they hardly noticed it anymore, the grove was completely silent. Here and there heads nodded as the Avar considered Barsarbe's arguments.

But Shra had heard enough. Now, as the Mother had told her, was the time to speak.

"You use poisonous words, Barsarbe," she said, and stood up. Shra was small and fragile, even for an Avar child, but her eyes shone with a knowledge that the Avar respected, and her demeanor was far older than her years. "Your mind has been so addled by your spite and jealousy that you can no longer distinguish bright glade from shadowed night."

"Shra." Brode walked forward, and stood by Barsarbe's side. "I think we should listen to Barsarbe. She is, after all, senior among the Banes, and you . . . you are but a five-year-old-girl-child."

Shra stepped out of the crowd so that all could see her.

"I am but a five-year-old-girl-child," she said, "but I have been presented to the Horned Ones and I am training to be a Bane. And even the little I have seen of the events in the world beyond the Avarinheim has been more than anyone else here, even Barsarbe. I . . . I am *appalled*," and she stamped her tiny foot, "at Barsarbe's misrepresentation of the true nature of the events and people that surround us. If it takes the mouth of a five-year-old girl-child to speak the words of truth, then so be it."

To the watching Avar she no longer seemed such a child. She radiated such assurance, and such righteous anger, that even Brode retreated a step as Shra walked to where he stood with Barsarbe.

Had her re-creation when so close to death wrought this change in her?

Barsarbe stared at the child with dark, cold eyes.

Shra ignored her. "As the Earth Tree is my witness," she said, her voice sweet and clear, "I am sick of the Avar reluctance to act, and I am *shamed* by it! Are you proud that such as Axis and Azhure fight for our cause? Are you proud that the Icarii have spilt so much of their own blood on our behalf as well as theirs?"

"We are a pacific people," Barsarbe said.

"We are fools!" Now Shra was truly angry, and it was not only at Barsarbe that she directed her anger. "We cling tenaciously to our creed of non-violence, yct we are ready enough to project violence when it suits us. Barsarbe condemns Azhure for the violence that trails her, but did none of you feel the violence that the trees themselves projected so very recently? Did none of you hear the death that the forests sang . . . led by the Earth Tree who now stands so 'peaceful' behind me?"

"They slaughtered our enemies!" Barsarbe spat.

"So does Azhure!" Shra cried. "How could you stand there and pretend distaste for her actions in Smyrton? She saved *your* life as she saved mine and Faraday's! Avar, listen to me! Azhure slew Artor the Plowman for our sakes, and protected Faraday. If there are forests below the Avarinheim now, then it is largely due to Azhure's help. Have you forgotten the Yuletide slaughter already? Have you forgotten who did so much to save us then?"

"We are safe in our forests, Shra," Barsarbe said, battling to control her temper. All could be lost if she slapped the child as she so richly deserved.

"*Our* forests, Barsarbe?" Shra whispered, tears gathering in her eyes. "We do not *own* these forests, they merely tolerate our presence. If the Avarinheim and the Minstrelsea allow other feet to walk their paths, then who are we to demur?"

"Allow the Plains Dwellers to share our forests, Shra?" Barsarbe grabbed the child's arm, giving her a rough shake. "I have listened enough!"

Grindle sprang to his feet. "Barsarbe, let my daughter go! I have heard her speak, and she has shamed *me*, if not you! Gorgrael is of our blood, and his destruction is our responsibility as well as that of the people of the Plow and the Wing." He put his hands on his daughter's shoulders and attempted to pull her away from the Bane's grip.

But Barsarbe was not prepared to let go. Her fingers sank into the flesh of Shra's upper arm and the girl cried out.

"For the Mother's sake—" Grindle began, but Barsarbe shouted him down, her delicate face contorted with hate.

"She has been left to run too wild and free, Grindle! I shall have to walk with your Clan a while to make sure that she receives the chastisement she so obviously needs."

Grindle let his daughter go and reached for Barsarbe instead. Appalled by both Grindle's actions and Barsarbe's treatment of Shra, Brode stepped between them and hauled the man away. Barsarbe still gripped Shra's arm painfully, and her mouth twisted with satisfaction as Brode pushed Grindle back several more paces.

"The Avar *are* in a pitiful state," she said, turning toward those who sat still and horrified by the scene before them. "We have been contaminated by the violence that Azhure has brought into this forest. It is not surprising that the two who have had so much to do with Azhure—Grindle and Shra—should now so champion her cause."

"This is *all* it is about, Barsarbe," Shra said, blinking back tears of pain,

"Azhure. You hate her so much that you are prepared to lead our people into despair to sate your hate."

"I am prepared to *preserve* our people!" Barsarbe cried. "My people, can you not see that I am right? Can you not see that the best hope for us rests in turning our backs to the pain beyond the forests? We are safe here. Gorgrael cannot touch us here. Let's leave it at that. We *do* have the right to refuse the StarMan when he asks for our help."

To many of the Avar her words made sense. The world beyond the forest was too frightening to risk. Others were more hesitant.

"It was one of our women who birthed Gorgrael," Grindle shouted. "Don't any of you feel responsibility for that? Shouldn't we help right the wrong we have bred?"

Barsarbe ignored him, scanning the crowd with anxious eyes. Whose words would they support?

"If we do not agree to help Axis then he cannot defeat Gorgrael," Shra said, her soft words reaching every ear in the grove. "And if Axis dies then the world will crumble about us. Even the forest will eventually wilt under Gorgrael's relentless onslaught."

"She lies!" Barsarbe shouted. "We will always be safe within the forests!"

"For this generation, and perhaps the next," Shra replied, "but what when Gorgrael's power has grown even stronger than it is now? Should we condemn our descendants to lingering death because we did not have the honor or the stomach to act?"

"Let the trees decide," Barsarbe called with deadly calm. "Let the trees decide the truth."

I have won, she thought exultantly. *I have won!* The trees will never decide for Axis or Azhure. She let Shra go.

"You would put yourselves to a Test of Truth?" one of the other Banes asked.

"Yes," Barsarbe said. "A Test. Do you agree?"

All Avar children who showed the potential to become Banes were administered a frightening test when they were only toddlers, so frightening that many children did not survive it. Despite this, the Avar continued to administer it, because only through this test could they determine which children had the potential to become truly powerful Banes.

But what Barsarbe was suggesting was far worse. The Test of Truth had rarely been administered in Avar history, and certainly not within the past three or four hundred years.

"We are faced with the fork in the path," Barsarbe said. "Let the Test provide the answer for you."

"No!" Grindle cried and reached for his daughter. This time Brode let him go.

"No," he repeated, now down on his knees with his arms about Shra. "There is no need, Barsarbe."

"There is *every* need," she said. "I am certain of the truth, of the path we should take. But I can see that some among you yet demur. This decision is too important to be taken without unanimity. A Test will convince doubters."

"And will kill one of you," Grindle said, his arms tightening around Shra. He had already lost her mother in this grove; he did not want to risk Shra as well.

"Do you fear for your daughter's life?" Barsarbe asked scathingly.

"I am willing," Shra said.

"I agree," said a male Bane after a pause, and the one next to him nodded. "So do I."

"And I."

"I will agree."

And, at first hesitantly, then with greater certainty, the Avar agreed to the Test.

As the last of the voices subsided Barsarbe turned and smiled coldly at Shra. "Let us begin."

They were taken to the Earth Tree, where each stepped out of her robe and, naked, was bound to the tree by ropes. Then, surrounded by the power of the Earth Tree and the Banes before them, they were thrust into the Test.

The forest was calm and quiet, not like it was in the test both had taken as two year olds. Then the trees had crowded them, hindering their efforts to escape the horror that chased them through the forest.

Now the air lay still and heavy with moisture, as if before a storm. Leaves hung listlessly, and every footfall was an affront to the lassitude that gripped the forest.

They walked separately, about forty paces apart. Occasionally one would glance at the other, then her eyes would slide away again. Each wished she were clothed; not through any sense of shame, but because a robe would give her the means to wipe hands moist with apprehension and the warm, damp air.

Neither spoke.

Neither knew how long or how far they walked, but at the same instant both became aware that mist drifted through the trees; each took a last glance at the other, knowing they would never see each other again. Each wondered at her wisdom in suggesting or agreeing to the Test.

Each knew there was no escape now.

The mist thickened and coiled about them until both stumbled blinded into tree after tree, even though they walked cautiously. Bark and rocks scratched at their skin and hair; both quickly suffered a dozen small wounds that stung rather than hurt, worried rather than frightened.

The mist thickened until even the sound of the other's footfalls was lost.

She no longer held her hands out before her, preferring to wrap both arms about her body. The cold penetrated to her bones, and she did not know how much longer she could keep going. Her hair hung heavy and dripping over her shoulders, and her feet were numb.

Where was the Test? When would she be judged?

She knew she was right, despite the way the other had sought to manipulate her people. She knew that to make the wrong decision now would be to fate the Avar to a slow and lingering death.

A footfall sounded to her right and her head whipped about painfully. Was it the other?

But, no. A white form loomed out of the mist and she sobbed gratefully. "Raum!"

She clung to the neck of the White Stag as he nuzzled her head and shoulders, and she sniffed, trying to control her tears.

"Have you come to lead me to safety, Raum?"

The Stag did not answer. He stepped away, but he did not attempt to shrug off the hand she kept on his shoulder.

They wandered until she was almost dropping with weariness. How long would it take him to lead her out of the mist? She must have been tested with some method so sublime she had not even realized she was being tested. Now Raum led her to safety, and the Avar people would be all right.

He stopped so abruptly that she almost fell to her knees, then she gasped, and stepped back hurriedly.

A great chasm yawned at her feet. In front of her were two bridges, each disappearing into the mist.

She blinked and looked at Raum in confusion. Which?

He nuzzled her again, gently, his eyes swimming with love for her.

Your choice, his voice said in her mind, and she turned back to the bridges.

Now neither bridge was so empty.

The bridge to her left resembled one of the fragrant and shaded walks of the Avarinheim. As she watched a bird swooped down over the path, its glad cries echoing and seeming to call to her. At the end of the path was a glade, and figures moved about a welcoming fire. As she watched one of them turned and saw her. He stilled, then lifted his hand so that his fingers flared toward her. It was Axis.

She turned her head.

The bridge to her right resembled a long ice tunnel. Strange shapes cavorted beyond its translucent walls. At its end was a door, and as she watched
it swung open. She gasped, for Faraday stood behind that door, and Tree Friend
smiled and held out her hand for her. Then a shadow loomed behind Faraday
and a taloned hand dropped onto her shoulder, and Faraday turned and, sighing,
walked back into the room. The door closed.

She made her choice. She cuddled against the White Stag, thanking him.

Then she stepped down the bridge toward Axis.

She stumbled through the mist, her hand on the White Stag's shoulder. He
halted so abruptly she almost fell to her knees. In front of her yawned a great
chasm spanned by two bridges.

Your choice, he whispered in her mind.

The bridge to her left led into one of the fragrant and shaded glades of the
Avarinheim. Two tents sat pitched to one side, and a fire crackled cheerfully
in the center of the glade. Several figures sat about the fire. As she watched
one of them turned and saw her. It was the silver-pelted Horned One, and he
held out his arms and called out for her.

She turned her head.

The other bridge led into a storm so severe that at first she could distinguish
no other features. But then a great gust of wind blew the snow to one side and
she could see into the recesses of a strange chamber where warped furniture sat
crazily about the ice walls. A man wrapped in a dark cloak stood before the
fire and she could feel if not hear his laughter. He was standing in a pool of
blood.

She made her choice.

"I thank you," she whispered to the Stag, then she smiled sadly and stepped
toward the man standing ankle-deep in blood.

"Stand back," the woman said, and the Banes who encircled the two still forms
bound to the Earth Tree obeyed. Only a few among them had seen her before,
yet all knew who she was.

Faraday. Tree Friend.

She walked closer to the Earth Tree. She was thin, perhaps as a result of
her effort planting out Minstrelsea, but she was lovely nevertheless, with her
thick chestnut hair waving down her back, and her green eyes serene and sure.
She wore a gown whose fabric reminded all the Banes of the shifting emerald
light when it dappled and shaded into the trees of the Sacred Grove.

She looked, one of the Banes would later remark to the Avar, like the
personification of the forest herself.

Faraday walked to Barsarbe and knelt by her side. She lifted the woman's head and smiled, stroking the woman's hair away from her face.

"A bad choice, my dear," she said emotionlessly, then she looked up at the surrounding Banes, letting the woman's limp head drop back to the ground.

"She's dead," Faraday said, then she stepped about the great trunk of the Earth Tree to Shra.

The girl stirred as Faraday knelt by her side, and the ropes shackling her fell away. Faraday smiled and gathered the girl in her arms. "The saddest choice of all," she whispered.

Humbled, the Avar stood before Tree Friend.

"We will lend Axis the aid he needs," promised one.

"And more," Grindle said fiercely, and Faraday smiled at him.

"You came to Shra's defense, Grindle, and for that both I and the forest thank you."

Faraday turned back to the Avar assembled before her. "Shra will lead you through the mists and into the future. Listen to her. Respect her."

"Will you not lead us, Faraday Tree Friend?" asked Merse, one of the Banes who had accompanied Faraday from Fernbrake Lake.

"I will provide you with the way, Merse. But I will not lead."

"But we thought that . . ." one of the others began, but Faraday silenced him with her smile.

"Legends can sometimes be over-vague. They can be misinterpreted. And we can all be tossed and turned by the tide of events so that none of us can do quite what we would like. I will be responsible for giving you the path. Believe that."

67

Fire-Night

h e stepped noiselessly through the trees, remembering the way as if his last visit had been only weeks instead of years. Arne shadowed him, even more silent and dour now that he had spent hours sitting facing the Ferryman in his magical boat. He was tense and unsure. Arne did not like the darkness that pooled behind the trees, nor did he like the waiting presence he could feel ahead. Axis had made him hide his dagger, but out of sight was also out of ready grasp, and that made him distinctly nervous. Both had left their larger weapons in a dry cache beside the Nordra.

Axis wore the golden tunic with the blood-red sun blazing across his chest. Both breeches and cloak matched the sun, and he knew he was splendid enough to dazzle any court, impress any cynical ambassador. But how would the Avar react? How would *Faraday* react?

And how would he react when he saw her?

He walked into the Earth Tree Grove behind the stone circle surrounding the Earth Tree, motioning Arne to wait at the tree line, and he stepped into silence.

The Earth Tree sang overhead, but somehow her Song did not penetrate into the silence that rose like a dense fog from the Avar people who filled the spaces beyond the stone circle. Every one of them was staring at him, and Axis had to force himself to walk around the stone circle with as firm a pace as he could muster.

Axis may have felt unsure and nervous, but to every Avar eye that watched he looked relaxed and confident, his pace smooth and supple, and he wore his power as easily as he did the cloak that flowed back from his shoulders.

They sat before him in a huge semicircle that stretched into the depths of the Grove. Axis had only ever been here on Beltide before, and that night had been alive with life, music and movement. Now all was silence and stillness and thousands of dark eyes that followed, followed, followed . . .

As he reached the center of the semicircle he slowed, unsure what he should do, or if he should say anything. Just as he hesitated, his eye caught a movement at the stone circle, and he turned.

A small girl walked forth slowly, wearing a robe as blood-red as the sun on his chest. About its hem was embroidered a tracery of leaping white stags. She saw him looking at the embroidery and she smiled. "Axis."

He gazed at her, not immediately recognizing her. Why the girl? She was a pretty little thing, and of great presence for one so young. Then something in the tilt of her eyes and the turn of her mouth reminded him.

"Shra!" Without thinking about it he went down on one knee before her. All he wanted to do was speak to her eye to eye, but the gesture was one of reverence as well, and as one the Avar sighed . . . and relaxed.

"Shra . . . it is good to see you again."

Shra understood what he wanted to say. "It is good to see *you* again, Axis, for I have not yet thanked you for either my or Raum's life."

She took his hand in hers and kissed it softly.

Axis smiled, remembering how good it had felt to hold her tiny body in his arms and suffuse it with life. "You were my first enchantment, Shra. Your suffering was the key that unlocked the gate."

She laughed. "You are as much a courtier as an enchanter, Axis, for you misrepresent the truth so charmingly that it is hard to be cross with you for it."

"And you speak far too well for a child who should still be clinging to her mother's skirts."

Shra's smile faded. "My mother is dead."

"Forgive me, Shra. Azhure told me of your mother's fate."

She patted his hand and motioned him to stand up. "If my tongue is smoother than that of most five year olds, Axis StarMan, then perhaps it is because of the mystical filaments you wove into my re-creation."

He stood reluctantly, wishing he had hours to speak with the girl, but already she was turning to her people. He thought she would speak, and it did not seem strange to him that she stood at the head of the Avar. She was Raum's natural successor, and somewhere in a dark corner of his mind Axis wondered what had become of Barsarbe.

But Shra did not speak. Instead she stood, waiting, eyes fixed into the darkness that had gathered beyond the Avar, and Axis lifted his eyes as well.

A woman walked out of the tree line, and every muscle in Axis' body froze. Faraday.

Oh Stars, he thought bleakly, how could I have betrayed her as I did? How could I have treated her so badly?

His nervousness returned.

Faraday stepped gracefully through the ranks of the Avar, her eyes fixed on the gold and crimson figure before her. She thought she had resigned herself to her fate, but the instant she had seen him step into the grove every doubt and fear she'd ever entertained returned to plague her. But none could have guessed Faraday's inner turmoil as she walked past them. Her face remained serene, her eyes still and calm, her gait smooth.

As she approached Axis and Shra she dropped her eyes to the girl.

"Shra," she smiled, and rested a hand on her shoulder. Then, very slowly, she raised her eyes to Axis' face.

"Axis."

"Faraday." He wondered if every time they met after long absences it would be before large crowds of potentially hostile people. This scene reminded him uncomfortably of the afternoon he had seen her enter the hall in Gorkenfort to stand by Borneheld's side as his wife. Now he did not lust after her as he had then, but he would still have liked to hold her, to embrace her, and to whisper that he loved her.

For he did love her. He could admit that to himself now. It was not what he felt for Azhure—he could never love another woman the way he loved Azhure—but his love for Faraday was like a still, cool lake in the hot, tangled jungle of his existence. He would never remain true to it because he could never be sated by it, but now and again he would like to touch it, to rest by her side, to draw strength from her stillness.

But he could not touch her now, not in front of the assembled Avar, so he merely inclined his head, and hoped that somehow she understood.

She lifted her hand from Shra's shoulder and reached out for his. Her skin was cool, and he was afraid to press her fingers too firmly. She was far more fragile than he had ever seen her before—what had so drained her that it left hollows under her cheeks and her skin so translucent? But her fragility only added to her beauty.

Her fingers trembled in his, and he wondered if she were as calm as she appeared.

"My friends," Faraday addressed the Avar, but she did not turn her eyes from Axis'. "I present to you Axis Rivkahson SunSoar, StarMan of Prophecy. He is the one for whom Plow, Wing and Horn have waited for so long, and he is the one who will heal the hurts that have torn our peoples apart for so long."

Now she did wrench her gaze away from Axis and look at the Avar. "Will you give him the aid he needs to defeat Gorgrael?"

A man stood from the front ranks. He was muscular and swarthy, with graying brown hair, and he wore a tunic with branches embroidered about its hem.

Faraday took one of his hands in hers and nodded at him. The man reached out and took Axis' hand with his, so that the three stood in a triangle; Shra stood slightly to one side of Axis and Faraday.

The man met Axis' eyes without hesitation. "Yes, the Avar will give the StarMan the aid he requires."

Some of the tension left Axis' shoulders.

"Will the Avar give blood to aid the StarMan?" Faraday asked. Startled, Axis' eyes flew to her face.

"Yes," the man said. "The Avar will give blood to aid the StarMan."

No! Axis wanted to cry out, but he said nothing, and Faraday carried on, her voice resolute.

"Will the Avar seek out that which they have created for the StarMan?"

"Yes."

Faraday paused, and now the corners of her mouth lifted in a slight smile. "Will the Avar give that which is needed to form the Rainbow Scepter?"

"Yes, the Avar will give freely to the StarMan."

Faraday leaned over and brushed the man's cheek with her lips. "Grindle, Leader of the GhostTree Clan, I would present you to Axis, StarMan."

Then she repeated the words to Axis, presenting Grindle. "Grindle is Shra's father," she added, and Axis smiled at him.

"Now," Faraday said, "I would present you to the other Clan-Leaders."

As they slowly moved along the front ranks of the Avar, Faraday introduced each Clan-Leader by his name and the name of his Clan, and with each hand that gripped his Axis understood that each man made the same pledge that Grindle had mouthed aloud. It was so different to his last meeting with the elders, Banes and Clan-Leaders of the Avar that Axis felt as if he were in a dream. Any moment now this veil of civility would drop and their hostility would shine forth.

But it didn't. It was then Axis realized that something fundamental had changed among the Avar. Something had been accepted, and it wasn't only himself.

When the introductions were done Faraday and Shra each took him by a hand and drew him back toward the circle of stone, halting some fifteen paces away.

Axis glanced at them both, puzzled, but they motioned him to silence, and then looked at the stone circle.

He followed their eyes. As it had been on Beltide night, torches flickered about the upright stones; beyond he could just see the shape of the Earth Tree looming. Everything else within the stone circle was shadowed. What was going to happen now?

Something moved beyond the stone archways.

Faraday tensed at his side, but Axis did not look at her. Figures were moving slowly about the trunk of the Earth Tree, but even Axis, even with his

Enchanter-enhanced vision, could not make them out. He felt Faraday tremble, and this time he did look at her.

Tears were rolling slowly and silently down her cheeks, but she shook her head slightly when she saw him looking at her.

He turned back to the stone circle, feeling the silence of the Avar behind him almost as a weight.

A figure shuffled into view and Faraday, as Axis, gave a low cry of horror. It was Ogden, but an Ogden so warped and contorted by sickness that Axis took an involuntary step forward.

"No!" Ogden cried hoarsely, holding up an unsteady hand. "No, Axis! Stay back. You must *not* touch us!"

"Oh, Stars!" Axis mumbled, stricken by the sight of the Sentinel. His hair had all but fallen out, only a few wisps clung above his ears. His skin was reddened, covered in running sores, his face so bloated that his eyes were almost swollen shut, and his mouth hung open as he fought to breathe. Even from his distance Axis could hear the breath bubble in his lungs.

Veremund and Yr struggled out behind him, and their condition was, if anything, even worse.

Faraday took a harsh breath and looked away momentarily. Yr was almost unrecognizable—where were the sharp blue eyes, the irrepressible humor, the knowing smile now?

Gone, gone into the same well of pestilence that consumed Ogden and Veremund.

Now Zeherah—and even the stoic Avar silence crumbled when she appeared, and a low moan rippled about the grove. Zeherah could no longer walk, and she had to drag herself from the circle, her fingers clawing into the dirt, her legs dragging uselessly behind her.

"I have to help!" Axis said, appalled, but Shra hauled at his hand as he stepped forward.

"*You must not touch them!*" she hissed. "Let them alone, Axis," she continued more gently, "for they know what they do."

Axis halted, staring at the horror, before him, then he dragged in his gaze around to Faraday. "Did you know?" he whispered.

She shook her head slowly, her eyes not leaving the group before them. "No. I . . . I knew that they were here—they arrived unseen several hours ago and disappeared into the stone circle—but I did not realize . . ."

Axis swallowed and looked back at the Sentinels. Their eyes glittered strangely in the darkness. Golden from Ogden and Veremund, sapphire from Yr, ruby from Zeherah. Glittered with jewel-bright colors.

"Power has corrupted the bright eyes' hearts," Axis whispered to himself, understanding at last.

Then Jack emerged. He walked more upright than the others had, but then he had the staff to support him. Otherwise, Axis was sure, he would have crawled like Zeherah. He struggled forward, stopping to catch his breath where the other four Sentinels rested, then he came forward a few more steps.

"Hail, StarMan," he rasped, and Axis inclined his head, unable to answer.

"We have come a long way," Jack said, and then, unaccountably, he laughed.

It was a horrible sound, feverish and cackling, and Axis could not stop himself from wincing. "What has happened to you?"

"Happened?" Jack's laughter stopped as suddenly as it had begun. "Happened? Why, StarMan, we but follow the Prophecy. Do you not need your Rainbow Scepter?"

"The Prophecy tells me so, yes."

"Yes, the Prophecy tells you that you must wield it against the Destroyer. Well, this is Fire-Night, and this Fire-Night will see the construction of your Scepter."

"I have been told that you will use the power of the ancient Star Gods who crashed and burned the first Fire-Night," Axis said. "Is that what has corrupted you?"

"Yes." Jack paused, his head drooping, obviously debating within himself whether to tell Axis anything else. "StarMan, perhaps I should not tell you this, but I will. I do not want the knowledge to die with us."

To one side Faraday wiped her eyes. She did not want the Sentinels' last view of her to be of tears. She remembered how they had once told her on the Ancient Barrows that no one would have to sacrifice more than they. Well, here stood their sacrifice revealed for all to see . . . and yet Faraday wondered if they were as all-seeing as they sometimes had pretended, or if there was yet a greater sacrifice to be made.

"StarMan." Jack gripped his staff still harder and tottered another step forward. "Be wary of what lies in the depths of the Sacred Lakes. The ancient gods had power that we can only dimly comprehend, which you—yes, even you—should be wary of. Treat the Lakes with respect, Axis, and never think to go exploring."

If what stood before him was the inevitable result of such explorations, then Axis had no wish to go exploring at all. He nodded.

"Good. Now, Axis, you must not interfere with what we do. This will be our ultimate gift to you . . . and we give it willingly and with love. After . . . after we have finished, then it will be the Avar's task to finish crafting the Scepter for you."

Jack looked at Faraday. "Lovely lady, we wish you well in all that you do. You . . ." his voice broke, and Jack had to struggle to master it. "You have done so well, and we are so proud of you. Yours has been the most difficult and the most lonely task of all. Remember *all* that the Mother has taught you, lovely lady, and may you one day find the love and the peace that you deserve."

Faraday could hold herself no longer, and she broke down into great sobs. Axis put his arm about her, and Faraday leaned against him, but she stretched out a trembling hand toward the Sentinels. "I am sorry for all that I said to you in Carlon," she sobbed. "Forgive me. I did not understand."

Now Jack appeared close to tears, and his emerald eyes dimmed. "We have always loved you," he said, then he turned away. "And we always will."

Faraday almost collapsed, and Axis had to wrap both his arms about her to keep her from falling. Shra whispered something in Faraday's ear, and she nodded, took a deep breath, and stood upright again.

"I'm all right," she muttered and, reluctantly, Axis let her go.

Jack had reached the other Sentinels, and now they sat down in a circle. Jack took his staff and, with the last of his strength, struck it into the ground so that it stood upright in the center of their circle.

Then they took each other's hands, bowed their heads, and . . .

"*No!*" Faraday screamed, and Axis seized her again, terrified she would dash to their side. "*No!*"

But the Sentinels did not hear her. As one they chanted, soft and sad, their voices infused with the music of wind and wave.

The staff burst into fire. It flared so bright that Axis had to shut his eyes and turn away. The next instant he felt a terrible heat sear his body and he dragged Faraday back eight or nine steps, shouting at Shra to shelter behind him.

When he found the courage to look back, the five Sentinels were pillars of fire surrounding the burning staff, and he looked away again; not because of the heat, but because he could not bear to watch their deaths.

It was only when he felt the heat die down that Axis turned around. Staff and Sentinels had disappeared, and in their place bright coals were heaped in a glowing pyramid. Occasional spurts of flame shot out, sometimes golden, sometimes ruby, sometimes sapphire or emerald.

The coals hummed, not with music but with power, and Axis stared, unable to look away. Gradually his arms loosened about Faraday and she stood upright, her tears gone now, her face ravaged with grief.

The coals popped and hummed, and very, very gradually their heat dissipated, and the flames lessened. The sense of power about them faded.

Eventually Axis walked over to the coals. The pyramid had crumbled into a heap of blackened ash, still glowing here and there, but cooling rapidly in the night air.

Without knowing why he did it Axis sifted about the ash with a booted foot.

He turned over a pile of ash in the center of the heap and then stilled.

Glowing in what had been the very center of the pyramid was the head of Jack's staff. Previously it had been tarnished, now it glowed bright silver. It was decorated with patterns of swirling lines, and into its body were set five gems—two golden, one sapphire, one ruby and one emerald.

Axis bent down and picked it up. It was cool to his fingers, and about the size of a man's clenched fist, but far heavier.

It was the head of the Rainbow Scepter.

He shifted it in his hands, and its gems sent multicolored rays of light flaring about the grove. The rays hummed with strange power. And in his mind Axis could hear the Sentinels laughing; low and pleasant, as if they had heard some particularly fine jest.

Axis folded his hands about the head of the Scepter and the light died. He took a deep breath and looked up. Every eye in the grove was fixed on him. What now?

"Now," Shra said matter-of-factly, "we will give you a rod with which to wield the gaudy toy you hold in your hands."

She walked past Faraday, past Axis, and into the circle of stone. Beyond the arches she paused. "Father, will you come with me? I shall need your height. And you too, Axis." She considered a moment. "Faraday, come, for you shall sing to the Earth Tree."

Grindle joined Axis and Faraday and they stepped into the circle of stone. Shra had walked over to the trunk of the Earth Tree, and they joined her there.

"Faraday," Shra said, "will you sing to the Earth Tree?"

Sing *what*? Faraday thought distractedly. She had only ever sung to the Earth Tree once, and then she'd had StarDrifter to guide her. Sing what? She opened her mouth—and saw that the other three were staring at her, and so she sang the first thing that came into her head, the cradle song that Goodwife Renkin had sung to the seedlings. At first she only hummed the tune, but then she introduced words that suddenly came to her, and she sang of the sacrifice of the Sentinels and of the creation of the head of the Scepter. She sang of the need for a rod with which to wield it and then, inspired, she sang of the need for the power of the ancient gods—represented in the head of the Scepter—to be welded with the power of the earth and the trees. Artor had been crippled and defeated using a similar alliance, so too would Gorgrael's dark power be overcome.

The tune changed, and the lullaby became a song of victory. The Earth Tree hummed in harmony, and Faraday could hear the other trees of the forests—both Avarinheim and Minstrelsea join in as well.

The sound vibrated up through the soles of her feet and she lifted her arms and face to the Earth Tree, understanding that even in sacrifice there was sometimes life, and that wherever the Sentinels were now, they were joyous and . . .

"Unfettered," she said, and stopped singing.

She blinked and looked at Axis. He was staring at her, his hands still wrapped about the silver head of the Scepter.

"Unfettered," she repeated, and laughed.

Shra smiled at her, then pulled at her father's arm. "Father, will you lift me up?"

Grindle hoisted his daughter onto his shoulder and she reached up the trunk of the tree. Axis dragged his eyes away from Faraday and watched her. He could have sworn that the trunk of the Earth Tree ran smoothly upward at least sixty paces before it branched out, but now he could see that there was a small branch about four paces up.

Grindle lifted Shra as high as he could, and she reached upward with plump arms. For a moment Axis thought that she would still not be able to reach the branch, but just as her finger waved below it, the branch dipped, and Shra grasped it tightly, her laughter tinkling down around them.

The branch came away smoothly in her hands.

Grindle lowered her to the ground and Shra held out the branch to Axis—except now it was not a branch at all, but a slender rod of glossy wood. "Take this with the goodwill of the Earth Tree and the Avar people, StarMan," she said. "It is our gift to you, and it will enable you to wield the Scepter with the power of the Mother behind you. With this rod comes the power of the trees."

Axis took a deep breath and accepted the rod. The power of the ancient gods combined with the power of the trees would create an awesome weapon indeed. He fitted it into the base of the silver head, and he was not surprised to find that it fitted perfectly. When he tried to turn it, he found he could not dislodge the rod.

Rod and head had become one.

"The Rainbow Scepter," Faraday said softly, and Axis, unthinking, lifted it above his head and swung it in a great arc.

Great bolts of light shot into the night sky, and their energy crackled and roared through the grove. Somewhere, unheard, the Sentinels laughed again.

Hastily Axis tucked the Scepter under his arm, slightly shame faced, and covered its head with his hands. "What can I do with it?" he asked, "for I cannot stand about with my hands wrapped around it until Gorgrael steps my way."

Faraday laughed. "Here," she said and, bending down, ripped a length of cloth from her shifting-colored robe. Poor robe, she thought, for I am always tearing strips from you.

She wrapped the cloth about the head of the Scepter and stood back. "Don't take it off until you face Gorgrael," she said.

Axis nodded, and was about to speak when Grindle took his elbow.

"StarMan, the Avar have something more for you."

Puzzled, Axis let Grindle lead him under the stone archways into the grove. Several of the Clan-Leaders stood there and one of them, Brode, now stepped forward.

"StarMan," he said, "I remember that we refused to help you once before when you stood before us in this grove. We were wrong. Perhaps we should have helped sooner. But we *will* help now."

Axis smiled, grateful for the words and the sentiment, but not sure what they could do. He had the Rainbow Scepter, and now all he had to do was face Gorgrael.

"We cannot fight," Brode continued, "but we can do one thing for you."

He paused. "We can find Gorgrael for you."

Axis' breathing almost stopped. "Find Gorgrael?"

"Axis." Brode smiled. "Did you think to walk to the edge of the Avarinheim and there Gorgrael shall be, waiting for you? No, Gorgrael lingers far to the north in his Ice Fortress."

"How can you find it? Have you seen it?"

"No. But Gorgrael's mother was Avar. Whatever else he is, he is also of Avar blood. We can *feel* him, we can track him. Five of us," he waved to the men who stood behind him, "will travel north with you. We will bring you to Gorgrael's fortress."

"No. This is too dangerous, *far* too dangerous."

"We are not afraid of death, StarMan, and we *can* find him. His blood will always call to us, and his enchantments will not be able to fool us with shadows."

Axis was determined to make them see reason. "I am of his blood, too. I can find him."

"Can you feel him, Axis? Can you find him? The Avar blood is stronger at that than the Icarii. And we will be company for you."

"I have company." Axis nodded to where Arne waited shadowed among the trees.

"Yes, we see him and we acknowledge him. Axis, if for no other reason, let us do this for Avar pride."

"You will almost certainly die," Axis said.

Brode inclined his head, but he did not say anything.

Axis let them wait another moment, let them think that he still considered, although he fooled no one. "Very well," he said, his tone gentler. "Come with me, and be welcome."

Faraday stepped to his side and placed one hand lightly on his arm. "I will be coming, too," she said.

"*No!*"

68

Ice Fortress

"You said that Artor would stop her from planting out the last of the trees—and you were wrong! My army is gone! Gone! *Gone!*"

"Now, now," the Dark Man began, but Gorgrael would have none of it.

"Did you not hear the noise of their Song as it ripped my army apart?" he screeched.

The Dark Man flinched, but he held his ground. By the fire sat Timozel, his eyes hooded.

Gorgrael lowered himself into a crouch, his arms curved, his claws flexing. He growled and shook his head.

"It all comes down to—" the Dark Man tried again.

"And now he has the Rainbow Scepter," Gorgrael snarled, his voice low but infinitely more dangerous because of it. He had stilled now, and his eyes were slitted as they watched the Dark Man before him. Gorgrael did not trust him anymore, no indeed he didn't.

The Dark Man saw Gorgrael's expression and prayed he still had some hold over the creature. Azhure was vulnerable, traveling through the Icescarp Alps with her son, and he wanted to keep Gorgrael distracted as long as he could . . . if he could.

"The Prophecy merely works its way through," he said. "You should have expected this, Gorgrael."

Gorgrael cocked his head to one side, his eyes still narrowed. "What do you mean, works its way through?"

"Dear boy," the Dark Man said in as fatherly a way as he could manage. "The Prophecy is not just empty words. It *must* work its way through. I am as unhappy at the situation as you—but, truth told, I am not all that surprised.

The Prophecy has set certain conditions to be met before you can destroy Axis once and for all. Now they *have* been met."

Gorgrael cocked his head still further.

"The age-old souls, long in cribs, will sing o'er mortal land," the Dark Man explained. "The trees. Obviously, the Prophecy felt they *had* to be planted out. As with the Rainbow Scepter. The Prophecy will never work its way through until Axis grasps it."

Gorgrael straightened, but the aura of danger about him did not diminish. "Do you mean that all I have done has been an utter waste?" he said. "That I may as well have sat here and warmed my toes while waiting for my bastard brother to show up?"

"Oh, no, not at all," the Dark Man hastened. "Not at all. Why, the Prophecy has relied on your strength and your power to work its way through. It would have been *nothing* without your help, Gorgrael."

Gorgrael straightened entirely, trying to think.

"It wants you to win," the Dark Man went on. "It likes you. That's why it brings Axis' destruction to your very doorstep."

Finally the aura of danger about Gorgrael dimmed. "What do you mean?"

Behind his hood the Dark Man smiled. "The Prophecy *must* work its way through, Gorgrael. That is why, as Axis comes north through snow and ice, he brings his destruction with him. Faraday."

"Oh!"

"You see? The Prophecy wants *you* to win, Gorgrael."

The Dark Man was gone, and Gorgrael and Timozel sat before the fire. They had drunk several glasses of wine, and were now eyeing each other with somewhat drugged affection.

"I don't entirely trust him," Gorgrael said.

Timozel drained his glass. "He is very dark."

For some reason Gorgrael thought that extremely witty and roared with laughter.

After a moment his laughter died away. "But, untrustworthy or not, I cannot deny the fact that Prophecy brings Faraday to me. She *must* be the Lover. She *must* be!"

Timozel thought about that. "Who else? This dark woman?"

Gorgrael snarled at Timozel, his good mood evaporating under the sun of his uncertainty. "Faraday *must* be, Timozel!"

"The dark woman was very powerful."

Gorgrael growled, remembering the night she had appeared in this chamber.

"And certainly very beautiful. She *might* make a good Lover."

Gorgrael's claws scraped along the armrests of his chair. "She is *nothing* to the Prophecy! Where is she mentioned in it?"

Timozel frowned, reciting the Prophecy in his head. "I cannot think—"

"Quite!" Gorgrael cried. "She's not at all! And yet Faraday is in there at every turn; the woman who planted out the age-old souls from their cribs, the wife who lay with the slayer of her husband. *Obviously* Axis' Lover."

"True. I saw them myself."

"Yes. Timozel?"

"Yes?"

"Timozel, would she trust you?"

"Yes," Timozel answered slowly, "if I gave her enough reason to, then, yes, I think she would."

Gorgrael smiled. "Good."

69

Tundra

Axis shouted, argued, pleaded and even threatened, but Faraday stood quietly and let him rave.

"I am coming, too," she said once he'd finished.

Axis had turned to the five Avar, but they stood quietly, politely. It was Tree Friend's business if she came or not, and it was not for them to dissuade her.

Shra was upset, but neither did she try to dissuade Faraday.

So Axis capitulated, but he was afraid for her.

They traveled light. All had cloaks, but they were a strange sight. Axis strode wrapped in his crimson cloak, golden tunic beneath; Faraday wrapped in a green cloak over the insubstantial robe that the Mother had given her; her only other clothing was some soft leather boots. Arne was the most sensibly dressed, with his stout boots and thick felt clothes, but the Avar men managed well enough in their tunics and leggings, although their boots hardly coped with the snow and ice when they hit the tundra.

Surprisingly, Arne got on quite well with the Avar men. Perhaps there was something in his dour personality that Brode and his companions related to, or perhaps it was that Arne appreciated the woodcraft and tracking skills that the forest men demonstrated. Whatever, he spent most of the days and the evenings talking quietly with one or more of the Avar men.

From the Earth Tree Grove they traveled northeast through the forest. Three of the men carried packs with light supplies of food, but Brode said they could scavenge well enough while in the forest, and once on the tundra there would likely be snow rabbits and birds they could catch for their supper.

At night Arne would help the Avar build two small fires; he shared one with the Avar, Axis and Faraday sat at the other.

For their first evening Axis and Faraday sat in virtual silence. They shared the food Brode handed them, their conversation desultory, and then sat in silence, watching the flames crackle. There was so much that Axis wanted to say to Faraday, but he did not know where to start. He thought about telling her some amusing stories about Caelum, then decided that might not be a good idea. He wondered if he could tell her some of his adventures in the west, but too many of them included Azhure, and while Axis knew that Faraday and Azhure were good friends, he still did not feel comfortable talking of Azhure to her.

I have built so many barriers between us, he thought sourly, pushing at the embers with the toe of his boot. Once we could have talked and laughed . . . but once she believed the lies that I told her.

Damn it, man! he berated himself, *talk* to her! He opened his mouth, but just at that moment Faraday rose gracefully, silently, and walked into the nearby bushes.

Axis dropped his eyes quickly. No doubt she was attending to her private needs and would not appreciate his curious eyes following her. But after half an hour he became worried, and asked Arne and Brode if either had seen which way she went.

Arne shrugged and pointed to the spot in the bushes where she had disappeared. "There, StarMan."

Axis fidgeted, his eyes dark with worry.

"She is of the trees, StarMan," Brode remarked. "She will find her way home."

But Brode's comment did not appease Axis. He paced about the fire, then, his cloak swirling, pushed into the bushes.

He wandered for perhaps half an hour, calling Faraday's name, growing more desperate by the minute. Had she fallen and hurt herself? Had Gorgrael, by some dark art, managed to snatch her from the very forest itself? Then, just as he was about to return and stir the others into searching the forest, she was behind him. "Axis, shush, you will wake half Tencendor."

"Where have you been?" he cried, seizing her by the shoulders.

She tensed, and Axis let her go. "I have been safe, Axis. Do not be concerned for me."

And she would say no more. She returned to the fire, rolled herself in her cloak, and fell asleep.

Axis stood a long time, staring at her deep in sleep. Then he, too, settled down for the night, but it was a long time before he fell asleep. Occasionally he would reach out and touch the Scepter by his side, but mostly he stared across the fire at Faraday, his eyes haunted with memories and guilt.

In the morning she rose early and again disappeared for almost an hour.

This time Axis managed to stay his fears, although he relaxed visibly when she finally returned. She snatched a few mouthfuls of food, then smiled at the men. "I'm ready."

And so they set off.

Faraday did this every morning and every evening. When she returned she always had a small smile tugging at the corners of her mouth, and sometimes the smile broadened when she saw Axis, and her green eyes would gleam with a secret emotion that he could not fathom.

"We all have to eat," she said on the one occasion when Axis managed to force her to say anything about her absences at all.

The journey was easy through the Avarinheim, but cold, bleak weather met them the day they reached the forest's northern border. They stood among the last ranks of the trees for almost half an hour, watching the snow drift across the flat tundra. To their left, the Icescarp Alps rose in waves to the west, and Axis spared them a long look, but to the north and east there was nothing but flat snow land.

"Does anyone know how far this stretches?" Axis asked the Avar.

Loman, of the BareHollow Clan, answered him. "No, StarMan. No one knows. Who would travel this distance from the trees?"

Axis cursed himself for not asking the Ravensbundmen if they had been this far.

"It is just flat snow, StarMan," Brode said quietly. "Flat snow to the north and, if you were to walk far enough to the west or east, rolling gray seas that stretch into infinity."

"And how are you going to find Gorgrael?" Axis thought he could feel an infinitesimal pull at his soul, as if a tiny claw worried at it, but the feeling was directionless and, apart from heading north, Axis had no idea where to go.

"We will know," Brode said, with certainty, but when Axis glanced at him he could see lines of worry about the man's eyes.

When Brode saw him looking, he shrugged, trying to make light of his concern. "It is the trees, StarMan. None of us have ever spent much, if any, time away from them. Only the Banes have traveled south to Fernbrake Lake, and their power enabled them to live for so long without the shade above them."

"Come," Faraday said, "we waste time," and she set off alone into the northern wastes. Axis hurried after her, the Scepter safely in his arm, and behind him came Arne and the Avar.

*   *   *

Gorgrael spied the small group with his mind's eye the moment they had left the trees and set foot on the tundra.

"There they are!" he crowed, and shared the vision with Timozel. "There they are!"

He turned to Timozel standing by the doorway. "Go now, and do not fail me."

Timozel nodded curtly, and then was gone.

And so they went on. The wind was fierce, but it did not hinder them too badly, and the snow was cold, but it was compacted down into a relatively easy walking surface.

The cold and the snow reminded Axis of Gorken Pass.

"We might find Timozel out here somewhere, Faraday," he said.

Faraday blinked. She had not thought of Timozel in a very long time. Poor Timozel. What had happened to him since he had fled Carlon so long ago?

"Why do you expect that, Axis? Have you had word of him?"

"Timozel led Gorgrael's Skraeling army, Faraday, and escaped east after the trees destroyed the Skraelings in Gorken Pass. I have no doubts that I will find him lurking in the snow here somewhere."

Faraday stopped dead and stared at him. *Timozel led Gorgrael's army?*"

"You didn't know? Oh, Faraday." He reached out a hand, but she stepped back.

"Timozel led Gorgrael's army?"

Axis cursed himself. He had forgotten how isolated Faraday had been while she was planting. "Faraday, Timozel has changed. He has . . . he has become the Traitor of the Prophecy."

"Oh, no!"

Faraday had been very close to Timozel in the months leading up to her marriage, and although the closeness had begun to pall once she had married Borneheld, she still liked Timozel. She knew that he had harbored dark thoughts, but this? No. "No!"

The others had stopped now and were looking back at them, but Axis waved to them to keep their distance.

"Faraday, please, listen to me. Timozel is in league with Gorgrael. If you see him out there in the snow, do not talk to him. For Stars' sake, Faraday, *do not trust him!*"

She took a huge breath. "Timozel!"

"Faraday?"

"Yes. Yes, I hear what you say, Axis. I will be careful," she said.

Then she turned and walked toward the others.

Axis stood and let the snow swirl about him for a minute, watching her walk stiff-backed, her knuckles colorless where they clutched at her cloak.

*   *   *

That night Axis found the words to say.

He waited until Faraday had returned from her mysterious walk, waited until she had wrapped herself in her cloak and was preparing to sleep, and then spoke.

"Faraday."

She opened one eye and blinked at him.

"Faraday. You once said that it was too late for me to say anything to you, too late for me to say anything to heal the hurt I have caused you."

She sat up slowly, her hands clutching the cloak tightly about her, her face pale beneath the green hood.

"Faraday, I hope that is not so."

"Axis—"

"No, let me just talk for a while, Faraday. Will you listen? Will you promise that you will not walk off into the night and leave me here alone?"

She nodded.

He fixed her eyes with his own. "You told me that what we once had between us was gone, no more." He laughed, bitterly. "That I was free. Well, our vows were broken, yes, but my conscience was fettered in chains so heavy their singing kept me awake many a long night."

"You do not regret marrying Azhure?"

"No . . . no I do not. If I have a regret it is that she did not walk into my life first, because then I would not have hurt you so much . . . no! No, that was the wrong thing to say. Faraday, I have never regretted falling in love with you. I only regret the way I treated you. You are too remarkable to have been treated the way you were."

He paused, and stared down at his hands. When he looked back up again his eyes were full of pain and self-loathing. "I used to curse Borneheld for being a bad husband—but who treated you worse, Faraday? Borneheld . . . or me?"

"Axis!" Faraday stumbled about the fire and put her arms about him. He had begun to cry, and she rocked and soothed him for several minutes.

"I'm so sorry, Faraday. Oh gods, that's such an inadequate phrase to trot out now, but I am so sorry for all I have done to you."

"You treated me wretchedly, Axis, but I cannot lay all the blame at your feet. Yes, you could have told me about Azhure sooner, but whenever you did it, however you did it, I would have been hurt. Would it have been best to have told me the instant that Borneheld lay dead at our feet?" She smiled. "Imagine, Axis, you turning to me and saying, 'Well, it's been nice, Faraday, good to see you after all this time, but there's someone else.'"

Axis smiled wanly.

"And it *was* I who came to your apartment that night and seduced you.

Poor man. But, oh Axis, I had dreamed about you for so long, hungered for you for so long, that I couldn't wait."

She dropped her hands and shifted in close to his body. She did not think Azhure would mind. Not this once. "There would have been no kind moment to tell me, Axis. No kind way. As it was I had eight days with you. Eight days, eight glorious nights."

She paused, and her mood became somber. "Yes, some fault certainly can be laid at your feet, Axis, but most, I think, can be laid at the feet of the Prophecy and the damned Prophet who penned it. None of us has been able to escape its clutches. It took me, poor simple Faraday, and tore my life into shreds and then cast them to the wind. You, too. And Azhure. And half a dozen others."

"Would you that you were still Faraday, daughter of Earl Isend?"

"Would you that you were still Axis, BattleAxe of the Seneschal?"

They both hesitated, then laughed softly. "No," Axis said, "but I suspect that there are moments when you yearn for the peace of your youth. I have gained more than I have lost. You?"

She waited a long while before she answered. "We both have learned and gained a great deal, Axis. You have given me more joy than I think you realize."

He pushed her face back. "What do you mean?"

"Axis." Her eyes stared fiercely into his. "Axis, if anything happens to me, if . . . if anything happens, promise me that you will go to the Sacred Grove before you go home to Azhure."

"Faraday!" He was appalled by the naked pain in her eyes. "Nothing will happen to—"

"Don't start to lie to me again!" she snapped. "Both of us walk into danger more extreme than either have faced before. *Don't start lying to me again now!*"

"I will protect you—"

"Promise!"

"I promise, Faraday. If anything happens to you then I will go to the Sacred Grove before I return to Azhure."

She sighed and relaxed against his body. "Thank you, Axis."

He started as a thought occurred to him. "Is that where you go in the mornings and evenings?"

"Yes, Axis. But please do not ask me why."

He nodded, and held her close, rocking her now. "What will you do, Faraday, once the Prophecy has let you go? What will you do once your days are again your own?"

Her voice was cold when she answered. "I do not think the Prophecy will ever let me go, Axis. I think I will stay fast in its talons for eternity."

"No! Faraday!" He stroked her face, wiping the tears from her eyes.

She shuddered, then sat up. For a long moment she looked at him, then she leaned forward and kissed him. She let it deepen until she could stand the pain no more, then she pulled away.

"No, Axis," she said. "We can be friends, you and I. Nothing more. You would lie yet again if you tried to be anything more to me. Axis, I wish you well."

She was saying goodbye, and he knew it. "And I you," he said softly. "I have never wished you anything but."

She nodded, knowing he was telling the truth, then stepped around the fire to her sleeping place.

Neither slept very much that night.

He watched them through the day and into the night. He watched as Axis held Faraday under the stars, watched as they kissed, and Gorgrael relaxed for the first time in many months.

"Good," he whispered. "He *does* love her. Yes, yes, yes, the Prophecy brings the Lover to me!"

Far away in his even darker hole of existence, the Dark Man smiled to himself. "Good girl," he murmured. "Good, good girl."

Four days out from the forest the Avar began to die.

It was not so much the cold that killed them, for Axis could wield enchantments that kept them in a small pocket of warmth and with fires at night. It was simple tree-hunger. The Avar could not exist without the love and shelter of the trees.

The first two died on the night of the fourth day, wrapped in their cloaks before the fire.

"They had walked too far from the forest. Their hearts have given out," Brode explained as Axis, pale and shaken, stepped back from the bodies in the chill light of morning.

"Then for the Stars' sakes, man!" Axis said roughly, "take yourself and your companions back to the Avarinheim."

Brode shook his head sadly. "No, StarMan, for then how would you find your way? We can *feel* Gorgrael." He clutched his hand to his breast. "His blood calls to us."

"Damn it, I can find my way, surely? Just tell me what direction to go!"

Again Brode shook his head. "One of our people birthed him, StarMan, and now we would do our part to bury him. We have tarried too long to help in this fight, and I and my companions will not turn back."

"But you will die."

"We knew that when we set out."

The next morning another of the Avar men was dead, and Loman and Brode were gray about the eyes and mouth, and their hands trembled as they shook the night's snow off their cloaks.

Axis stared long and hard at them, but they turned away without speaking and began to trudge slowly north through the snow.

70

"Trust Me"

So they marched on. Brode and Loman led them ever north, then north-northeast. The weather became colder and more bitter and, despite Axis' enchantments, managed to penetrate to their bones.

Axis sometimes heard either Brode or Loman, he knew not which, crying in the night, and his heart cried with them. But he knew he probably would never find Gorgrael's nest without the Avar—or Gorgrael would make sure that he found it only on his own terms. He could have spent weeks out here, wandering until his spirit failed him and despair consumed him—then, Rainbow Scepter or no, Gorgrael would have found him easy meat.

Eight days after leaving the forest they stopped one evening. None of the men had been able to catch any game for two days now, and the last reserves of food had been eaten that morning. There would be nothing to quiet their stomachs when they camped for the night but the snow they could warm at Axis' magical fires.

Faraday sat very quiet, the firelight flickering over her face and her out-stretched hands. Axis worried about her. She'd grown even thinner and more fragile in this march north; now dark shadows circled her eyes and her hair had lost some of its gloss.

"Faraday?"

She rose. "I will be back soon, Axis." She paused as if she wanted to say something more, but the moment passed, and she was gone in the swirling snow.

"Faraday?"

"StarMan. Loman fades," Arne called to him.

Axis stared one more moment into the snow, unaware there were tears in his eyes, then he turned on his heel and strode over to the fire Arne shared with Brode and Loman.

Loman had been growing weaker over the past day; Axis was not surprised that he should sink to the ground and refuse to get up now.

He squatted down beside Loman; Brode the other side, Arne at his head. Loman was mumbling something under his breath.

Brode looked up and met Axis' eyes. The Avar man's own eyes were red-rimmed and sallow, and there were great hollows in the papery skin of his cheeks—Brode was not long for this world either.

"He remembers the pathways of his youth, StarMan, and he seeks now the pathways to the Sacred Grove."

"Will he find them here?"

"Yes, Loman is strong, and his feet will find the paths."

He waited several more minutes, his eyes gentle as they studied Loman, then he looked back at Axis.

"We'll reach Gorgrael's nest tomorrow, StarMan. He is close. Surely you can feel him, too?"

"Yes," Axis said. "All day there has been blackness gathering in the corners of my eyes, and dark notes taint the chords of the Star Dance. He is close."

Brode nodded, and they bent back over Loman.

Faraday walked through the snow, her head bowed, her hands grasping the cloak close. It was cold, yet the ache in her heart was colder. Every time she left the Sacred Grove now she said goodbye as if it were the last time, treasuring every extra moment she shared with him, for she never knew when she would—if she would—be able to go back.

It was almost fully dark now, and Faraday was late. She hurried toward the faint glow of firelight she could see in the distance. She squinted ahead. Axis, Arne and Brode were grouped about a huddled figure on the ground. Loman. Her fingers tightened further about the cloak and she increased her pace. Loman would appreciate it if she were there to see his feet onto the Sacred Paths.

A strange whisper, barely discernible in the night, ran along the edge of the wind.

Faraday paused, the cloak wrapping itself about her body in the wind. Nothing. She hurried on.

There, again, a soft whisper along the wind and, this time, a hint of movement to her right.

She stopped again, every nerve afire. Her fingers pushed fine strands of hair from her eyes, and she concentrated hard, peering through the gloom, listening for any unusual sounds.

"Faraday." A whisper, so soft she almost did not hear it.

A whisper . . . and a soft giggle.

"Faraday."

She stared, hoping it were her imagination, hoping she were wrong.

The flickering campfire caught her eye again, and she looked back. Axis had raised his head and was staring into the snow in her direction, but just as she was about to call out the figure on the ground convulsed and Axis bent down again.

"Faraday."

No mistaking it this time, and Faraday closed her eyes and moaned.

"Faraday? It is I, Timozel."

She mustered all her courage and looked to her right. Timozel was half-crouched in the snow some four or five paces away, his hand extended, his eyes gleaming.

It was not the Timozel she remembered.

"Help me, please," he whispered.

"Timozel . . . go away."

"Faraday, please, help me. *Help me!*"

Don't do this, Timozel, please don't do this! she pleaded in her mind, but if Timozel heard her he paid her no attention.

"He has trapped me, Faraday! Trapped me! Forced me into his service."

"No," she said, but she was unable to look away, unable to call for help. The force of the Prophecy lay like a dead weight about her shoulders; nothing she could do now could alter its abominable course.

The red doe froze, frightened by a movement among the trees.

"Do you know when he trapped me, Faraday?" Now Timozel had crept a little closer. "At Fernbrake Lake when Yr laid me under her enchantment. Yes, yes indeed. While you bathed in the light of the Mother, Gorgrael was sinking his talons into my soul."

"No," she said, louder this time. Not then, oh, please, Mother! Not then!

"Yes, then." Timozel injected as much pitifulness into his voice as he could. "I'm as much a victim as you are, Faraday. Please help me. I want to escape. Trust me."

She stared, her dark liquid eyes enormous, and her entire body trembled.

"Go away," she muttered, and the wind caught at her cloak so that it tore back from her body.

Now Timozel was almost at her feet, and his fingers flattered at the hem of her gown. "Please, Faraday. I want to find the Light again. *Please*, Faraday! Help me. You're my friend. *Help me!*"

No! she screamed in her mind but she could not voice it. Out of the corner of her eye she could see Axis rising from the fire, a hand to his eyes. Then her hair whipped free and, caught by the wind, obscured her vision.

No! But the Prophecy had her in its grip now, and it would not let her go.

The doe lifted one foreleg, her ears twitching, staring with eyes full of frightened memory, then she . . .

"Trust.me," Timozel whispered at her feet. *Trust me.*

No!

"Axis," she cried. "Forgive me!"

. . . turned and . . .

Timozel's hand snatched at her ankle.

"Gotcha!" he crowed.

. . . bounded away through the trees, light dappling her back with gold. She ran free, unfettered.

Axis took a deep breath, then sighed. Sadness overwhelmed him; he had not thought to be so affected by Loman's passing.

"He runs free now, his feet light along the Sacred Paths," Brode said.

"Would you like me . . . ?"

"Yes. Thank you StarMan."

Arne and Brode stepped back and Axis knelt a moment by the body. Then he too stepped back, and Loman's body flared into light and then searing fire.

All said their private farewells.

It was later, much later, when Axis looked up and realized that Faraday had not returned. At first he was not disturbed, for sometimes she spent two or even three hours away in the Sacred Grove. But as the night wore on Axis became frantic.

Arne held onto his StarMan's arm. "Do not let him trap you," he rasped between tight teeth, for it took all of his strength to hold Axis back. "If he has her then we will find her soon enough. On the morrow, Brode says."

"Oh Stars," Axis said. "He has the wrong one. What have I *done* to her?"

Axis would win, he was sure of it—he *had* to be sure of it—but could he also save Faraday's life, or was that already gone?

She was numb with cold and with terror. Timozel held her arm with talonlike fingers, and her delicate skin had bruised hours ago. Now he dragged her down a long ice-tunnel. Creatures leaped and cavorted on the other side of the ice-walls, their shapes distorted by the ice, but Faraday was beyond caring if she saw them clearly or not.

At the end of the ice-tunnel was a door, and Faraday knew what lay beyond it.

"I trusted you, Timozel," she managed to say.

"Fool."

"Doesn't my trust mean something? You promised once to be my Champion, you promised to protect me . . . then what is this you do now?"

Timozel stopped, and Faraday sank to the floor. Her gown had half torn away from her, and her flesh was marked both by the cold and by Timozel's cruel hands.

"You *broke* all the vows that bound us!" he screamed. "*You* broke them and released me to Gorgrael's tender mercy! Don't weep now that I break any trust between us."

He took a vicious breath. "Look at me."

She turned her head even further away.

"*Look* at me!"

She responded to the wrench on her arm if not to his voice, and raised her head slowly.

"Harlot," he said. "If you reap the fruits of your lusts now then so be it."

His fingers tightened and Faraday could not help a small sob of pain.

"Light your face with gladness, Faraday, for before you waits Gorgrael. He will be your true Lord, and we will sit by the fire and drink fine wine from crystal glasses forever and ever and ever."

Her eyes widened at the madness in his voice, but then the door at the end of the corridor creaked and she jerked her head in that direction.

Timozel hauled Faraday to her feet. He swung her into his arms and strode down the corridor toward the open door. Behind it a shadow flickered across the floor.

Faraday buried her face in Timozel's chest, hating even to do that, but Timozel was infinitely preferable to what lay beyond. She tried to reach the Mother's power within her, but that was gone, smothered by the blanket of the Destroyer's dark enchantments. Faraday prayed that in those final paces before the door Timozel would somehow see reason, would somehow remember the friendship and loyalty he had once professed, and would turn and run with her into safety and into the light.

But she knew he would not.

She could feel the temperature change the instant they crossed the threshold. It was warmer here. She whimpered, screwing her eyes still further shut, and tried to contract into as small a ball in Timozel's arms as she could.

"Faraday."

The name was spoken with a sickening hiss and a slap of tongue, as if the creature had trouble with it.

"How I have longed for you."

And then she felt Timozel's stance alter, stiffen, as if he . . .

"*No!*" she screamed, and Timozel passed her into the Destroyer's arms.

She fought as hard as she could, she kicked and bit and scratched (and gagged when she felt the creature's lizardlike skin against her own bare flesh and mouth and fingers), but she made no impression on him, and he laughed and wheezed with triumph.

"Go!" he screamed at Timozel. "*Go!*"

*　　　*　　　*

They sat before the fire, with fragile crystal glasses of fine wine in their hands.

Gorgrael was half asleep, eyes lidded as he looked at Faraday in the chair opposite. She had managed to pull the all-but-destroyed gown about her again, and her hand trembled uncontrollably as she held the glass. Most of her wine had spilled down her arm and lay in a crimson pool in her lap.

Gorgrael was more than replete. He was prepared to be generous. It would be a pity to kill her. A shame. Again he wondered if he might keep her. Perhaps he could dispose of Axis without the need to destroy Faraday in the process. He felt almost tender, certainly protective. She had not been willing, but willingness would come in time.

Timozel sat in front of the fire, between the two. He could feel the comforting touch of vision, and he knew that Gorgrael had won.

The battles were over. Timozel sat before the leaping fire with his Lord, Faraday at their side. All was well. Timozel had found the light and he had found his destiny.

They drank from crystal glasses, sipping fine wine.

They had won.

71

Five handspans of Sharpened Steel

In the early morning light, Brode was clearly dying, but he insisted on taking them to the Destroyer's door.

"I can *feel* him, StarMan," he wheezed. "Not far."

"This is between him and me," Axis said gently. "Brode, you have done enough. Wait here for my return." He looked at Arne standing next to Brode, his arm supporting the Avar man. "You too, Arne. Wait here for me. You cannot protect me against Gorgrael."

Both merely stared at him, their eyes hard with determination.

"Please." Axis tried one more time, knowing it was useless. "Stay here. The snow has cleared. I will leave a fire for you."

They had woken in the pre-dawn darkness to find that sometime overnight the snow had ceased to fall. Even the wind had abated. Axis wasn't sure if Gorgrael still had any control over the weather; if he had, then perhaps he wanted them to walk the last morning in pure light.

So that they could know exactly what they would miss when dead, perhaps.

Axis looked away from Brode and Arne across the tundra. Everything was flat white, sparkling painfully as the first rays of the sun caught the snow crystals.

Where was Faraday? Did Gorgrael have her? Or had she decided sensibly to stay in the Sacred Grove?

Axis knew that Gorgrael had her. He could feel the Destroyer, feel his malignant presence seep like a dark stain over this desolate landscape.

And he could feel its joy. That had changed overnight. Yesterday Gorgrael's presence had been malignant, yes, but it had also been cautious. Now it gloated. It almost *danced* across the snowscape in its glee.

Axis shivered. He bent down and picked up the Rainbow Scepter. He wasn't sure how he would use it, but he had some idea . . . and for that idea he had Azhure to thank. He stared at it for some minutes, stared at the head wrapped in the cloth that Faraday had torn from her gown, then abruptly thrust it into a loop on his weapon belt.

His fingers slipped to the sword resting in its scabbard, and he absently fingered its hilt. Today, he hoped, it would find a different scabbard to rest in.

He lifted his head and smiled at the two men. It was a dazzling smile, full of hope and courage, and the men could not help but respond with smiles of their own.

"Come, my friends," he said. "Shall we go? Brode? Which way?"

Brode nodded northeast and grunted as Arne's arm tightened about him.

Axis glanced at him with concern, but the man picked up his pace after a few minutes, and soon managed to walk by himself.

They walked for three hours. Their eyes hurt from the glare coming off the snow, and after a while they had to pull the hoods of their cloaks close to try to cut down the glare.

Toward noon Axis stopped, and stared to the west.

"What is it?" Arne asked.

"The waves," Axis said. He turned his head. "Can you hear them?"

Arne and Brode both shook their heads.

"The waves of the Iskruel Ocean," Axis continued. "Beating along the Icebear Coast." He paused, remembering, then shrugged and continued the march.

They saw it mid-afternoon, rising in the distance.

"Stars," Axis breathed in awe, "but it is beautiful!"

He had not expected anything like this. He knew that his brother had a bolt-hole somewhere, and he had always imagined it to be dark and festering— nothing like this prism that speared from the snow plain like a pure white hand rising jubilantly from the grave. It was gigantic but graceful at the same time, and the sun glinted off it in a thousand different colors.

"Ice Fortress," Brode gasped, and Axis glanced at him.

But he could not keep his eyes from the beautiful structure rising to the northeast. He did not think he had the imagination to create such a thing himself, and he wondered at his brother who, though so dark and cruel, could still create such beauty.

"Beauty is as beauty does," Arne remarked cryptically.

"You're right," Axis said. "Brode, are you strong enough to continue?"

"I want to see the Destroyer dead before I die," Brode said. "I will be all right, StarMan."

Axis nodded, and without another word the three men crunched their way through the snow.

They took over two hours to reach the Ice Fortress, and they made their final approach through the huge shadow that it spread across the snow plain. It was the shadow, Axis thought, that gave away the prism's true nature. The prism might rise true and beautiful to the sun, but in reality it spread a shadow as dark as a raven's wing over the land. Pristine on the outside, inside beat a heart of darkness.

As they stood close to the ice walls Axis made one final attempt to persuade the two men to wait for him outside. But both were resolute.

"Treachery lurks within," Arne said.

Brode just shook his head, incapable of speech now.

And so Axis nodded. Inside lay their certain death, he was sure of that, but every man deserves to choose the way he dies, and these two had made plain their choice time and time again.

"Let's go," Axis said, and felt a nervous thrill at the thought that, finally, he was to meet his half-brother.

Prophecy.

They entered via a small doorway set in the southern face of the fortress. It was opened and unguarded, and Axis could feel Gorgrael's presence strongly now. It lurked like a foul smell—that was the only way Axis could describe it to himself and, looking at the expression on Brode's face, he knew that the Avar man reacted similarly to Gorgrael's taint.

Arne drew his sword and pushed past Axis; his face was calm, his manner intent. Arne had no doubts about his mission and never thought about whether or not his actions might be foolhardy.

Axis followed, Brode limping determinedly in the rear.

The interior of the prism was a maze. Ice tunnels led up and down and sideways at crazy angles. Steps ended in glassy walls and rose from ceilings. Time and time again they had to retrace their steps as they found themselves in empty chambers and meaningless cul-de-sacs.

Time lost all meaning.

It had been late afternoon when they entered the prism, but the light inside never changed as the hours passed. It shone patiently through the walls, rippled off ice surfaces, scattered along floors and ceilings. It was impossible to tell time except by their own sense of fatigue, and that was no longer reliable.

Brode clutched at his chest, his eyes sunken and gray, and scrambled along as best he could behind the crimson figure ahead of him, and the darker, sterner figure ahead of that. Everything seemed wrong, out of kilter in this abominable construction. He could feel the crazy mind that had constructed it, feel its hatred and its need.

And he could feel its Avar blood, feel its resemblance to himself. Brode had embraced the Avar creed of non-violence his entire life, had believed utterly in it, but now he could see what a sham it was. The Avar were people of innate violence. It might not express itself in physical acts, but in attitude and in way of life. In the violent test the Banes administered to the children of promise; in the tempers and angers that flared to the surface at the slightest provocation; in Barsarbe's reaction to and spite toward Azhure.

In Gorgrael.

He was a child of the Avar almost more than a child of the Icarii. It was his Avar blood that had nurtured so much of his hate, and it was his Avar blood that had created the Destroyer. His Icarii blood may have given him the means to access the power to achieve his ends, but it was his Avar blood that had created the *need* to destroy in the first instance.

Brode moaned and grabbed at the smooth ice wall for support. But his hand slipped down its surface, and he found himself on his knees in the corridor, Axis and Arne already almost out of sight.

A hand grabbed his hair from behind, and Brode felt the prick of a blade in his back.

"Axis," he whispered and, amazingly, Axis heard.

He spun about, his cloak swirling, his sword gleaming in his hand. The light from the ice caught at its blade, and it glittered cheerily, scenting its prey.

Behind him, Axis saw Brode on his knees in the corridor, an expression of utter despair on his face, and Timozel holding him by the hair and by the point of his blade.

Timozel had changed. No longer the carefree boy or the handsome man, his face was gray, and almost as shrunken as Brode's. All trace of good looks had gone. His hair was plastered to his skull by a thin layer of ice. His eyes, once deep blue, were now only rimmed with blue—the rest of his irises were stark white. His teeth were bared in what Axis first thought was a grimace of pain, then realized was a smile.

Axis heard Arne move behind him. "Stay," he ordered. "Timozel is mine," and the sword trembled in his hand.

"Give me your cloak," Arne said, and Axis spared a moment to loosen the ties at his throat and let Arne draw the cloak off his shoulders. Underneath the golden tunic glowed as bright as the first day Axis had unfolded it before Azhure in Talon Spike.

As he felt the cloak lift off his shoulders there was nothing for Axis but he and Timozel. Even Brode, poor Brode, dying on the point of Timozel's sword, was almost irrelevant.

Axis had waited a long time for this.

So had Timozel.

"I couldn't have planned it better," the Traitor snarled, "than to come across you sneaking into my master's house in your gilded finery. He thinks to dispose of you himself, but I have planned this all my life, and I am not to be denied now."

Axis stepped slowly toward him, Jorge's sword weaving gently before him. "Why, Timozel?"

Timozel leaned his head back and roared with laughter, but the moment that Axis took a quick step forward Timozel closed his mouth with a snap and took a firmer grip on Brode's hair.

The Avar man cried out as he felt the point of Timozel's sword slide a finger-width into his flesh.

"Why, Axis? Because even as a toddler I could feel my mother's adoring eyes on you, feel her hot breath as she watched you at sword play in the courtyard."

"Embeth loved your father."

"Liar! Embeth loved no one but you! She betrayed my father with you! When, Axis? When was the first time? When you were eleven and newly arrived in her house? Or did you manage to leave her unsullied until you were thirteen? Fourteen?"

"I never cuckolded Ganelon, Timozel. If your mother and I were lovers, then it was only after your father's death. I respected and loved your father."

But nothing Axis said made a difference to Timozel. All his life he had bottled up his resentment of Axis, of his ability, of his leadership. If only Axis hadn't been there then, Timozel would have been the one to shine. *Timozel* would have been BattleAxe.

"You never gave me the recognition and responsibility I deserved, Axis. I would have died a lowly horse soldier had I remained under your command."

Axis laughed, and his laughter was every bit as harsh as Timozel's had been. "As it is, Timozel, you will die a reviled Traitor under the command of a piece of corruption that should never have been birthed."

Timozel's mouth curled back in a snarl, although no sound left his lips. Brode shifted slightly in his grasp, and Timozel blinked and looked down, as if he had forgotten the Avar man was there.

Axis took advantage of Timozel's momentary distraction to leap.

Timozel reacted instantly, instinctively. He thrust his sword at Axis . . . straight through Brode's body.

The man gave a great shudder, but his lips smiled as he died, and Axis, even caught in his desperate struggle with Timozel, saw shaded forest paths reflected momentarily in Brode's eyes. It distracted him long enough for Timozel to pull his sword free and throw the corpse to one side.

Timozel screamed in pure exultation, flattening himself against the wall to avoid Axis' sword thrust, lunging himself the moment the danger had whistled past. This was his chance to show who was the better, who should have had command in the first instance.

Axis spun gracefully on one foot and parried Timozel's thrust. "I remember once," he whispered, his face close to Timozel's for an instant, "as I lay in bed with your mother . . ."

Timozel howled in fury, and came at Axis with a flurry of blows and strokes that would have decapitated a lesser opponent.

". . . her body entwined as one with mine . . . so warm . . ."

Timozel grunted, his face enraged, his eyes bulging.

". . . how we talked of you . . ."

"Liar!" Timozel raged, and turned his head just before Axis' sword would have sliced off his ear.

". . . and I thought, 'how would I ever tell Embeth' . . ."

Something snapped inside Timozel's mind. He threw all caution and cunning and training to the wind and gave in to his hatred of the man who now stood so close to him . . .

. . . almost as close as your mother once lay with me . . .

. . . and let his sword clatter to the floor, reaching with both hands for Axis' throat.

"I thought," Axis grunted, leaning to one side and letting Timozel step forward, " 'how would I ever tell Embeth if her son was skewered on the wrong end of five handspans of sharpened steel?' "

And he ran Jorge's sword through Timozel's belly.

As soon as he felt the blade break the skin of Timozel's back he released his grip and stepped back.

Timozel let out a great explosive breath of surprise and sank to his knees, his hands clutched about the hilt of the sword rammed into his body.

"Of course," Axis said, his face and voice expressionless, "the question was purely rhetorical, because as far as I am concerned you are now skewered on precisely the *right* end of five handspans of sharpened steel. Do you recognize it, Timozel?" Now his face twisted. "Do you? It is Jorge's sword, Timozel, and I swore as I drew it from his body that I would find it a more fitting resting place."

Timozel slowly tipped over onto his side, steaming blood pooling in widening circles about him.

How could it end like this?

How could it end . . . ?

How . . . ?

Axis stood, breathing heavily, looking at Timozel's body. He had loved and nurtured this man from a baby; had treasured him because he was Embeth and Ganelon's son; had taken as much pride in his achievements as his parents had.

He tried to feel some sorrow for Timozel's death, but could feel none. Timozel had betrayed him . . . and he had undoubtedly betrayed Faraday. Axis looked down the corridor to where Arne stood holding his cloak. "Faraday."

72

The Music of the Stars

he lifted the Rainbow Scepter from his weapon belt and strode toward Arne. Nothing mattered now but that he find Gorgrael—and Faraday.

He brushed past Arne, who fell silently into step behind his StarMan.

The maze of ice corridors no longer confused or disorientated Axis. The Scepter felt warm in his hands, and he thought he could feel a slight pulse grow in its rod. His feet echoed through the Ice Fortress, and somewhere in its depths Axis felt, if not heard, a scream.

It was his brother, calling to him.

The length of his stride increased. Nothing existed except for the need to reach Gorgrael. It was as if Prophecy pulled him through the Ice Fortress, and when he turned a corner and entered a long ice corridor with a massive wooden door at its end he could feel Prophecy reach ice-hot talons into his entrails and tug, pull, *haul* him along the corridor's length.

Only when he stood at the very door itself did Axis remember Arne at his back. He turned so swiftly, so suddenly, that Arne found himself pinned against an ice wall, Axis' hand to his throat, before he could draw breath.

"*Stay here!*" Axis snarled, his face twisted in rage.

Arne knew the rage was not directed at him, but rather at whatever waited beyond that door.

He nodded.

"Stay here," Axis repeated, his voice calmer now. "The Prophecy does not require your presence in that chamber. The Prophecy does *not* require *your* death!"

His voice had risen again, and Arne nodded.

"I want someone to survive this," Axis said, then let Arne go.

Axis took a deep breath, his eyes still locked into Arne's and Arne glimpsed some of the emotion that roiled within the man.

"I will watch the door," he said. "And hold your cloak."

For some reason Axis' eyes filled with tears at Arne's words. "And pray for me and the Lady Faraday. Will you do that also?"

Arne nodded yet again, and tears glinted in his own eyes.

"Yes."

Axis stood before the door, the Rainbow Scepter in one hand, the other on the door handle. He breathed deeply; slowly, calming his thoughts, concentrating. He knew the third verse of the Prophecy. He knew it contained both the key to his destruction and the key to his survival. He *had* the means to destroy Gorgrael, but only if he maintained his concentration.

And Gorgrael knew it too. The Destroyer would do everything in his power to destroy that concentration.

Axis concentrated on the Star Dance, on its beautiful music, and let it ripple through him. He thought of Azhure and Caelum, and of their love, and let it support him.

Then he turned the handle, opened the door, and entered the chamber to meet his brother.

The door swung softly shut behind him.

Gorgrael stood ten or twelve paces away, perhaps standing before a fire, for Axis had a dim impression of some light glowing and leaping behind him.

He was as disgusting as Axis remembered from the cloud in the skies above the Ancient Barrows, and his presence was as evil and as putrid as Axis remembered from the nightmares his brother had tormented him with most of his life.

Gorgrael's face was twisted into a snarl, his lips pulled back from his canine teeth, his tongue lolling over his chin. Behind him, his wings were outstretched, their talons glinting.

Strangely, the overriding emotion that Axis felt seep toward him was envy.

Axis did not understand how he looked from Gorgrael's perspective—how confident, how golden, how princely. He was everything that Gorgrael had ever desired to be, and now he stood before the Destroyer, his faded blue eyes calm, his body relaxed and assured.

Axis did not realize how Gorgrael felt because all Axis could see from behind the mask of his concentration was Faraday.

Faraday—held fast by Gorgrael's clawed hands, one sunk deep into the flesh of her throat, the other clasped tight about her belly.

Faraday—her once-beautiful gown hanging from her in tatters, her flesh marked and bruised.

Faraday—her face toward him, her eyes at first dull with pain and fear and then—to Axis' horror—brightening with hope and pleading and love.

Axis breathed deep, keeping his face calm, maintaining his concentration.

"I greet you well, brother," Gorgrael hissed.

Axis inclined his head, and took a step toward Gorgrael—no farther, because he saw Gorgrael's claws dig deeper at even that one step. "And I you, Gorgrael."

"Finally," Gorgrael said, and his body wriggled a bit. "Finally we meet here, you and I. As the Prophecy said we would."

Axis ignored him, his eyes traveling curiously about the chamber, although he saw nothing. "Is *he* not here to help you?"

"He?" Gorgrael tilted his head to one side. "He?"

"Your friend," Axis said. "WolfStar."

Gorgrael shuffled in his confusion, and he wondered what sort of trick this was. "WolfStar?"

"The man who taught you, Gorgrael."

"The Dark Man?"

Suitable, thought Axis, very suitable indeed. "The man who taught me also."

"No!" Gorgrael hissed, and Faraday moaned involuntarily as his claws tightened. "*No!*"

"Yes, indeed, brother. I walked ready trained into this Prophecy, and it was not my . . . our . . . *father* who trained me."

Gorgrael thought of all the times the Dark Man had gone, disappeared, sometimes for many months. Had he spent that time training Axis? He thought of all the times the Dark Man had appeared, knowing exactly what Axis was thinking, what he was doing. Had he known because he had just left Axis, perhaps after an amusing dinner and light-hearted chat?

And *WolfStar?*

"The most powerful of the Enchanter-Talons," Axis said. "I think he had this planned from the beginning, don't you? When, do you think, did he conceive this Prophecy for his own amusement? When did he begin to put the pieces in place? We are only pawns for his enjoyment, Gorgrael, nothing else. The Prophecy is nothing but idiot gabble for no reason other than babble and confusion."

Gorgrael screeched, and Faraday screamed with him, but Axis let none of this penetrate his concentration.

"The puppets mouth their words, make their moves, all to his direction. Doubtless the old gray wolf watches now, from some safe distance, and claps and chortles."

Axis took another step forward, and this time Gorgrael was so wrapped in thoughts of the Dark Man's treachery and manipulation that he did not notice.

"Who do you think he wants to win, Gorgrael? You . . . or me? What does the script say, do you think? Who has he backed?"

Another step, and Axis' hand firmed about the Rainbow Scepter.

"I do not care," he continued, "because I intend to win—against you *and* against WolfStar, your Dark Man."

Gorgrael's head whipped up and he realized how close Axis had crept.

He hissed, low and sibilant.

Faraday screamed.

Axis' concentration wavered, and for an instant a look of agony swept across his face.

Gorgrael hissed again, this time in triumph.

Axis battled with his emotions, fought with all his being, and rebuilt the wall of concentration about him.

It took all he had, and then some.

Slowly, lest his movements propel Gorgrael into action, his free hand slipped the cloth from the head of the Rainbow Scepter.

Rainbow light swirled about the chamber, and Gorgrael screamed and wept.

He let everything loose then, everything that he could against his golden brother. Dark power, so malevolent that it hissed in its own right, writhed about the chamber, soaking up the rainbow light.

Chaotic music, the music of the Dance of Death, screeched and curled through the air, and both dark power and music coalesced about the form of Axis, masking him in a shadow thick with malice and evil.

Axis could feel it, feel it power toward him, feel all the horror and destruction of the universe thunder about him, seeking him, wanting him, and he closed his eyes and concentrated, concentrated so hard that all thought of Faraday and even of Gorgrael vanished from his mind, and he concentrated on the Star Dance.

He let its beauty and grace flood him, listening for the . . .

Beat.

. . . reaching for its . . .

Beat.

. . . and slowing his own heart so that it . . .

Beat.

. . . in time with the . . .

Beat.

. . . of the Star Dance. And in the . . .

Beat.

. . . of the Star Dance Axis could hear the . . .

Beat.

. . . of Azhure's heart, and Caelum's heart, and of all those who loved him. And he took courage and he took heart and he opened his eyes and hefted the Rainbow Scepter in his hands and let the entire power of the Star Dance flood through him and through the Rainbow Scepter until he could feel it throb with the . . .

Beat.

. . . of the Star Dance and the . . .

Beat.

. . . of his own heart.

Axis stepped forward and raised the Scepter above his head.

Gorgrael screamed with such pure fury and primeval fear that the ice walls of his fortress cracked. With all the energy and potency he could garner he flung the power of the Dance of Death at Axis.

It surrounded the StarMan, clashing with the music of the Star Dance, seeking and invading and penetrating, until the frenetic coupling of the Dances throbbed through the chamber and through the entire Ice Fortress until it thundered across the tundra beyond.

And through the cracked and demented beat of the Dance of Death, throbbed the crazed heartbeat of Gorgrael—itself enough to induce despair in any who heard it.

For a heart . . .

Beat.

. . . the dark shadow surrounding Axis seemed inviolate, seemed as though it was indeed smothering him, as though it was indeed killing through despair, but then a ruby beam pierced the cloud, then a golden one, and another, and then sapphire and emerald broke through, and . . .

Beat.

. . . the full rainbow power of the Scepter flooded through the shadow and about the chamber, fed with the laughter of age-old Sentinels, and gradually, very, very gradually, the Rainbow Light and the laughter absorbed the power of the Dark Music, absorbed the power of the Dance of Death, and the cloud about Axis dissipated into useless fingers that trailed about the chamber until they, too, faded before the relentless . . .

Beat.

. . . of the Star Dance.

And through it stared Axis, his concentration unwavering, his eyes blue and fierce on Gorgrael, and he took one more step forward.

Gorgrael acted. He did the only thing he could. He did the only thing likely to break Axis' concentration . . . the only thing *prophesied* to destroy Axis' concentration.

As Axis took one more step forward, as the cloud and power of the Dark Music faded into impotence, Gorgrael tore Faraday's belly apart.

Something inside Axis tore with it, something railed and coiled and screamed, but he did not let his concentration fail him, not now, not when was so close.

He could not, would not, help her.

As the pain ripped her mind apart, as the last shreds of her sanity disappeared, and with the last breath she was to be allowed, Faraday screamed into the chamber . . .

Mother!

And Gorgrael screamed with Faraday, his voice triumphant, and tore out her throat.

And through it all, as Faraday's torn body sprayed blood about the chamber and his concentration threatened to shatter about him, Axis thought he saw a woman gather Faraday into her arms, gather her close and kiss her mouth with her lips, and that was the only thing that enabled him to keep the shield of his concentration unviolated, but he screamed nevertheless . . .

. . . and somewhere far, far away Azhure lowered her face to her hands and screamed with him as Faraday died in her place and the baby that slithered onto the bed between Rivkah's legs opened his mouth and screamed.

Gorgrael wasn't sure what was happening. Axis had screamed, but the power of the Rainbow Scepter had not faltered, and the rainbow beams continued to sweep about the chamber, chasing down every last filament of darkness that remained.

How much did he have to tear Faraday apart before Axis' concentration faltered?

Gorgrael lifted a clawed hand to shred her some more—perhaps all that was needed was one final swipe. But Faraday was no longer there. Gorgrael's eyes blinked in surprise. One moment her body hung limp in his arms, the next she was gone, and all he was left with was the feel and smell and taste of her blood to remind him of her warmth. And now he shrieked, for Axis strode forth, vibrating with power, and the expression on his face was not one Gorgrael had ever wanted to be faced with.

Axis' concentration had not failed.

Realization hit Gorgrael.

He had shredded the wrong woman.

The Dark Man *had* lied to him. It had been the raven-haired wench who had been the key, the true Lover . . . and Gorgrael had got it wrong.

He had lost, and he knew it.

He dropped to his knees and extended his hands in appeal, his great silver eyes huge with horror, and he gibbered and slobbered and pleaded.

"Axis, I am your *brother*! I am StarDrifter's *son*! Have mercy! I have never had the love and warmth that you enjoyed. I have been trapped, trapped by Prophecy and the Prophet's machinations as much as you. I am your *brother* I am your *brother*! I am your—"

Axis lifted the Scepter above his head, wild light still pulsing from the jewels of its head, and drove its rod deep into Gorgrael's chest like a stave, leaning down with his full weight as Gorgrael fell onto his back, his wings and limbs writhing helplessly, and Axis let the power and beauty of the Star Dance flood into his brother's body and soul.

The wood of the Earth Tree pierced Gorgrael's heart and burst it asunder. Something black and loathsome shuddered through his body, then rippled through the entire Ice Fortress.

And then, with a final convulsion, Gorgrael lay still.

Axis felt such life and vitality flood through him that he staggered, and he would have fallen but for the fact that he still leaned on the Scepter buried in Gorgrael's chest.

But anguish and loss flooded him too, and Axis bent down over the Scepter, over his brother's body, and sobbed.

"*Faraday!*"

Arne staggered to his feet, bleeding from ears and nose, his entire body still shaking from the power and the horror that had flooded out from between the cracks in the panels of the wooden door. He stood, trying to collect himself, trying to believe that he *was* still alive.

And then he heard the wall beside him start to *splinter*.

Before his horrified eyes a hairline crack ran down its length, then it shifted and grew until it was wide enough for him to fit his forefinger into.

And then another crack formed, then another, and soon the entire wall was *breeding* cracks, and they writhed and grew as if they had a life all their own.

"Axis!" Arne swore. They were standing in the heart of a gigantic, shifting, cracking mountain of ice!

"Axis!"

He wrenched open the door, almost tearing his shoulder muscles in his desperate effort, and stared into the chamber.

Against the far wall stood a fireplace, and before it Axis knelt hunched over something dark and loathsome, leaning on . . . a stake?

Arne ran across the room and seized his lord by his shoulders. "Axis! *Get up!*"

Axis raised his head slowly. "Arne?"

"*Get up!*" Arne screamed again, trying to pull Axis away, trying to haul him upright. Was the man wounded? There was blood spattered across the front of his tunic.

"*Get up!*"

Axis blinked and shook his head. His hands were still wrapped about the head of the Scepter, and light still shone between his fingers. Below the head, the rod ran straight until it disappeared into Gorgrael's body—which, Axis was nauseated to see, was falling apart. Already flesh was dropping from rib bones, and rib bones themselves were bending and caving inward.

"Come," Arne said, gently now, "it is over."

Axis sighed. "Yes, it is over." He rose to one foot, every movement an effort, and as he stood he wrenched the Rainbow Scepter from Gorgrael's chest cavity. With that, the body fell apart completely and, as it disintegrated, so Axis felt the floor tremble beneath his feet.

Arne flung Axis' cloak about the man's shoulders and dragged him toward the doorway.

"Faraday is dead," Axis said.

"Then live for her sake!" Arne cried. "If you die here, the Destroyer *has* won. Come. Axis! *Come!*"

Axis finally moved. He took one step, then another, then stumbled for the door, Arne behind him.

As he passed the scrap of green cloth on the floor he bent down and snatched it, wrapping it about the head of the Scepter.

The Rainbow light died, but Axis could still feel the rod pulse in his hands.

"Faraday," he said once more, and left the chamber.

They ran through toppling walls and ice spears that plunged from crumbling ceilings. The maze of corridors buckled and slipped, and Axis and Arne fell time and time again, one helping the other to his feet, one hauling the other from danger and death by his hair or by a hand buried in folds of cloth. Axis never knew how they emerged from the Ice Fortress alive, but emerge they did, to stagger into sunlight.

Sunlight?

Had a whole night passed without his knowing?

Thirty paces from the Ice Fortress they stopped, the breath rasping in their throats in the frigid air, and they turned and looked behind them.

The entire Fortress was collapsing inward; collapsing, Axis realized, toward the central chamber and Gorgrael's body. A sudden and infinitely strange thought hit him—this beautiful ice prism had been the outward manifestation of the beauty that Gorgrael craved within his own person.

And just for the moment that the thought survived, Axis realized the full loneliness and horror of Gorgrael's existence. Sympathy almost flared then, but at that instant the Fortress collapsed completely, and both thought and sympathy disappeared from Axis' mind as if they had never existed.

It was over.

Axis bent to one knee in the snow, his head resting in one hand. Arne stood helplessly beside him, feeling something of the man's grief.

For a long time they stood there, a cold northerly breeze riffling through their hair and fluttering their cloaks, two men frozen into the frozen landscape.

Axis raised his head. He rose to his feet, the movement stiff and painful, and handed the Rainbow Scepter to Arne.

"Here, take this."

"But, StarMan." Arne stumbled, taking the Scepter as though it were red-hot. "What do you want me to do with—"

"Take it," Axis said, his voice harsh. "Take it back to Sigholt and give it to Azhure. She can look after it."

Arne's eyes hardened with determination. "My place is with—"

"*Your place is to do what I tell you!*" Axis screamed, and Arne recoiled a step at the pain and anguish he saw in Axis' eyes.

"There are no Traitors standing at my back now," Axis continued more moderately, regretting the harsh words. "It is *over*, Arne. And where I go now, I can only go alone. Please, take the Scepter and go."

Arne nodded, but he paused. Walk out into this wasteland by himself? He didn't have a horse, he didn't have a pack . . . no food . . . no fuel . . .

"I'll take him," a gruff voice said to one side.

Both men turned.

Urbeth sat seven or eight paces away.

"Urbeth?" Axis said, almost unable to believe what he saw.

She looked at the pile of ice melting in the sun. "It made such a noise crashing down, StarMan, that it woke my cubs. I decided to investigate."

"I apologize for the rude interruption, Urbeth. Can you take Arne? Show him the way?"

She inclined her head. "I like Arne. He has a nice sense of humor. Come, Arne. I can take you as far as Talon Spike, and from there I think you can manage on your own."

Arne turned to Axis, opened his mouth, but found he could say nothing.

Axis put his hand on his shoulder. "I thank you, Arne. Do not fear for me, for I shall see you again."

Arne nodded, and turned aside. He looked at the gigantic bear, now lumbering to her feet, and eyed her back.

"You can *walk*!" she snapped, and turning around she ambled westward.

Without a backward glance Arne followed her, the Scepter tucked safe under his cloak.

73

Of Deceptions and Disguises

Axis watched them for a long time, watched the great pale shape with the smaller darker figure walk into the west, the low rumble of their voices reaching him for almost twenty minutes.

Finally, when he was surrounded by nothing but silence and the light powdery snow that was kicked up by the wind, Axis took a deep breath. It was time to visit the Sacred Grove. Time to fulfill the promise he had made Faraday.

Oh, gods, *Faraday!*

Axis bent almost double as his grief over her hit him anew.

Faraday!

Again he saw Gorgrael, his face twisted with hate, slice open her belly, tear her throat apart. But worse than that was the pain and fear in her eyes, pain and fear that Axis could do nothing to allay.

In order to win, he'd had to let her suffer . . . and she knew it. She'd known she was going to die, and Axis realized she'd known it for a very long time.

"Had she come north with me to offer herself as a sacrifice that I might live?" he whispered.

Had she loved him that much?

He bent his head and wept anew.

When he rose, drained of all emotion, the sun was sinking in the western horizon, and Axis realized he'd spent most of the day grieving for Faraday. Yet even most of one day was not enough. A lifetime would not do Faraday or her love or bravery justice.

He turned, thinking to face east as he sang the Song of Movement, the song that could transfer him to the Sacred Grove, and paused . . . stopped . . . his heart constricting and then racing in his chest.

Across the tundra, striding like vengeance himself, came a black figure. His cloak billowed out behind him like the wings of some great bird of prey, and the hood flapped and ballooned, and yet Axis could see none of the man's features.

But he could feel him smiling.

"The Dark Man?" Gorgrael had asked, puzzled.

Axis knew who this was.

The figure drew closer, and Axis could hear him whistling, whistling some merry ditty, and could see his gloved fingers snapping away as if he were enjoying himself hugely.

The sound of his whistling danced across the tundra toward Axis, and Axis' emotions sparked from grief to rage in the space of a heartbeat.

The Dark Man finally stopped some three paces away, his whistling fading although one booted toe still tapped merrily.

"Well," he said cheerfully, "all's well that ends well, and it *did* end well, did it not, Axis?"

Axis leaped for him. He had no weapons, and he knew that this Dark Man commanded Dark Music, dark power, but he leaped for him all the same. All he wanted was to feel his hands wrap themselves about the Enchanter's throat.

His leap was enough to drive the Dark Man to the ground, but his fingers found no purchase, and the Enchanter-Talon rolled out from underneath him. The next instant Axis found himself pinned to the ground, a black boot to his throat and blackness swirling above him.

"You are Axis Rivkahson SunSoar," the Dark Man said, his voice quiet now, "once BattleAxe, now StarMan, and God of Song, but do not think that you can outmaneuver *me* yet! You still have a long way to go, further yet to grow, and many more paths to travel, before you know what I know, and wield the same tricks I do."

Axis' breath rattled harshly through his throat and he wrapped his hands about the Dark Man's ankle, but he made no effort to try to push the boot away.

"Very wise, Axis," the Dark Man said. "You learn fast . . . but then you always were a quick learner, even as a child."

"Who are you?"

"Me?" the Dark Man cried, the merry tone returning. "Me? Why, I am Dark Man, Dear Man, mentor to Gorgrael himself. Don't you think I did a good job?"

"Who are you?"

"I found him, you know," the Dark Man said, "when he was but a babe. And I held him and cuddled him. I was the only one, apart from those silly Skraelings, to show him any love. Of course, I betrayed him."

Who are you?

"Who am I? In what guise did I come to *you* as a babe and then as a man? Well now, let me think." And the Dark Man's cloak twirled so Axis could see beneath its darkness.

A handsome young man's face laughed back at him, merry eyes and coppery curls.

Axis frowned in puzzlement. "Who . . . ?"

"Ah!" The young man snapped his fingers in contrition. "Forgive me. Thus I appeared to *Rivkah* in *her* youth—a troubadour who sang her songs of such beauty about the mysterious Forbidden races that when StarDrifter alighted on Sigholt's roof she accepted him instantly. I prepared the way, you see. Planned."

Who . . .

The cloak twirled again, and now a middle-aged face haggard with toil and sadness stared down at Axis. Dark hair flopped untidily over features shadowed with a two-day growth of beard. He scratched irritably at his whiskers, and Axis saw his hands were knobbed and calloused with years of labor.

"Don't toy with me. I've never seen . . ."

"Never seen me? Oh! *Oh!*" And he grinned. "Forgive me yet again, Axis. Thus I appeared to *Azhure* in *her* youth."

He bowed in mockery over Axis. "Alayne the blacksmith at your service, m'Lord. I kept Azhure occasional company through her suffering."

Axis' face twisted with anger, and his hands clenched tighter about the boot at his throat, but before he could move or say anything, the Dark Man abruptly threw off his cloak, letting it flutter away in the wind.

Mild blue eyes, thinning brown hair, a form riddled with age and arthritis.

He roared with laughter as he saw the expression on Axis' face. "The *perfect* disguise, BattleAxe! And the *perfect* spot for manipulation!"

"Moryson!"

"Aye, Moryson. I could have been Brother-Leader, but that would have been too obvious and far too dangerous—I could have been exposed there. But as First Assistant . . . ah, that was cunning itself, Poor Jayme. He thought it was he who had the ideas, who formulated the plans, but . . . but I was there all the time, whispering, planting ideas, suggesting courses of action. Advising." He cackled gleefully.

"Why, Axis, why do you think Jayme decided to visit Gorkenfort at the precise time that Searlas spirited Rivkah there to give birth?" Moryson leaned down and rested his hands on his knee above Axis. "And who suggested that, instead of drowning her bastard in a pail of water as Searlas wanted, we take him into the Seneschal instead? Who suggested you would be the ideal choice for BattleAxe?"

"And you taught me as a baby?" Axis' voice was dangerously quiet.

"I rocked you and sang to you for years, Axis, and you lay there and listened. You were an easy baby to teach, as easy as you find Caelum now."

Axis' body tensed under Moryson's foot, and the man laughed. "And *who*, Axis, *who* suggested that you be sent to the battlefront at Gorkenfort via the circuitous route of the Silent Woman Keep and Smyrton?"

"To find the Sentinels and Azhure?"

"Oh," Moryson whispered, "you always were the quick learner."

He stepped back quickly and, as Axis scrambled to his feet, he cast aside the disguise of Moryson and assumed a far older deception.

Axis stopped, stunned by the transformation.

Before him stood a beautiful Icarii birdman, clad in a shimmery silver suit that flashed blue over the curves of his body as he moved. Behind him stretched silver wings, and his face wore an expression of such utter knowledge and sadness that Axis' breath caught in his throat.

"So I appeared to the Sentinels," he said, and Axis blinked at him in confusion.

"As the Prophet," he explained.

"Why?" Axis whispered. "*Why the Prophecy?* What was the point of all this? Tell me before I go mad!"

The Prophet's form shimmered, and WolfStar assumed his true image. "Will you sit with me, Axis, and talk? The Sacred Grove will wait a while longer, and your promise to Faraday will not be compromised by the delay of yet another hour or so."

"Do you know *everything?*"

"Most," WolfStar said. "Yet even so, the Prophecy has managed to surprise me occasionally. Sit, Axis, and talk with me."

Reluctantly, Axis sank to the ground and forced himself to relax. "Well?"

"Well . . . what?"

"Tell me about the Prophecy. Why did you create it? Was it just idiot gabble for your amusement?"

WolfStar sighed and ran his fingers through his coppery curls. "Idiot gabble?" He laughed shortly and stretched one golden wing slightly, then he folded both wings against his body. "Oh, the Prophecy has meaning, Axis, deep meaning."

He settled comfortably. "I did not actually 'create' the Prophecy of the Destroyer, although I *was* the one to write it down." He grinned. "Think, Axis, of when you read the Prophecy in the Silent Woman Keep. The last fingers to trace so closely over that page were mine."

Axis waved a hand impatiently and WolfStar sighed. "There are things that would take me years to explain, Axis, and you have to grow before you can hear them anyway, so I will not attempt to explain them here. I died . . . you know how . . . and I was laid to rest in my Barrow among the others—with my death we were *nine*." His eyes locked with Axis' for an instant. "I walked through the Star Gate and entered another existence."

He stopped, and for some time there was silence between them.

"I existed," WolfStar said eventually, and Axis jumped, for he could see stars circling in the Enchanter-Talon's eyes. "I cannot say more than that. But while I . . . existed . . . there came to me certain knowledges. Knowledges that made it imperative that I reenter this world."

"Wait." Axis leaned forward, and whatever antagonism he had for WolfStar vanished in his thirst for knowledge and understanding. "Some time ago Veremund told me your story."

WolfStar's face remained expressionless, although a nerve twitched in his throat.

"He told me of how you had been fascinated in your youth by the possibility of other worlds beyond this one. You surmised that each sun was paired with a world, perhaps like ours, that circled it, as ours does. You looked at the multitude of stars in the universe, and surmised that a multitude of worlds also existed. The others thought it was crazy, but I wondered. WolfStar . . . *what* did you find beyond the Star Gate?"

WolfStar smiled slightly. "Do you ask if I found other worlds, Axis? Well . . . conceivably. But that is a story that waits for another day. It was," his voice slowed, "perhaps one of the reasons I returned."

He shook himself and the smile died. "Enough. I returned because among the knowledges that came my way was the knowledge that the world I loved and served . . . yes, Axis, I *did* love and serve Tencendor despite my actions . . . faced terrible troubles. A time of turmoil. Of war. An age when it would be torn asunder. Nothing could stop these troubles. But something could be done to help repair the damage."

"The Prophecy?"

"Yes. The Prophecy existed beyond me. I did not create it. It found me and used me as it used so many others. It persuaded me back through the Star Gate and I, in my role as the Prophet, have been its servant ever since. I recruited the Sentinels, I wrote it down, I watched the nation I loved fall apart as the Prophecy said that it would, I fathered Azhure, and I have worked constantly to ensure the success of the Prophecy."

"Manipulated."

"*Yes!*" WolfStar spat. "Manipulated. I will stop at nothing to ensure its success, and I let no trivial emotion or consideration of right or wrong get in the way of the Prophecy!"

"WolfStar," and his hand plucked at his golden tunic.

"Yes?" WolfStar growled.

"Do you see these bloodstains here?"

WolfStar peered, then waved his hand. "Those? Bah!"

And Faraday's blood disappeared.

Somehow that angered Axis more than anything else.

"Does guilt vanish that easily, WolfStar?" he snarled, and he seized WolfStar's forearm.

WolfStar stiffened, but he did not throw Axis off.

"That was Faraday's blood, WolfStar! *Faraday!* Who died instead of Azhure!"

"Yes," WolfStar said quietly.

"Did you manipulate her into Gorgrael's den?"

There was utter silence across the tundra. Far, far away Axis could . . . *feel* . . . the gray waves rolling against the Icebear Coast, but their sound had faded into silence. There was nothing but the featureless snow fields and WolfStar . . . WolfStar staring into his eyes.

"Yes," he said, voice and face calm. "I did."

Axis' fingers spasmed and dug further into WolfStar's flesh, but the Enchanter-Talon showed no response.

"*Yes?*" Axis whispered. "*Yes? You murdered* her!"

"You pitiful fool!" WolfStar shouted, and wrenched his arm from Axis' hold. "Would you rather the entire Prophecy had collapsed at that point? *Would you rather that Gorgrael had Azhure embraced in his talons?*"

Axis stared at the Enchanter.

"Listen to me," WolfStar said, his patience exhausted. "Gorgrael could have won, *would* have won, if he'd had Azhure instead of Faraday. Even as powerful as she is now, Azhure would have been no match for him; he would have overpowered her . . . and killed her. Could you have maintained your concentration, maintained your hold over the Star Dance flooding through the Scepter if it had been Azhure with her throat and belly ripped open before you?"

"And so you murdered Faraday."

"Yes. If you want to put it that way."

"You *sacrificed* her!"

"I fooled Gorgrael into believing that Faraday was your true Lover, and I saved your life, and Azhure's life and the life of Tencendor. That's all that really matters."

"And Faraday died."

"You are *more* than a pitiful fool, Axis." WolfStar's voice was low and very angry. "Why not tax me with Jorge's death? Or HoverEye's? Or any one of the thousands you lost at Gorkenfort? Why not tax me with the loss of Timozel's innocence? Why not? Because of your own guilt that you stood there and watched Faraday die!"

"I had no choice," Axis said flatly. "To try to save her would have been to condemn us both. She had to die."

With those last words his mouth froze open, as if he could not believe that he had said them.

"Yes," WolfStar said, and there was sympathy in his voice now. "She had to die, and in dying she saved you and Azhure and Tencendor, and *she knew it!* That was the greatest gift I could give her in return for her life."

He reached across and took Axis' hand, and when he resumed his voice was very soft. "She knew it, Axis. And she knew there was no place left for her here."

"Stars, WolfStar, what do I do now?"

Even WolfStar had to react to the naked pain in Axis' voice. "You set your guilt to one side, Axis, and you carry out Faraday's last wish and visit the Sacred Grove. Then you go home to Azhure and you rebuild Tencendor into the glory that is its by right and you learn and you grow and you take your proper place among the Nine, and one day I may return and share with you some of the other knowledges I gained beyond the Star Gate. I may even tell you of the worlds I found there . . . I think you would like that. And one day I will have to tell you of the dangers I found beyond the Star Gate."

He stopped, and he squeezed Axis' hand gently.

"Now, go collect Faraday's gift."

Then he rose in one fluid movement and strode away over the tundra.

That was the last Axis saw of him. A figure striding away into the distance.

As he watched, the figure assumed a black cloak that billowed out behind him, and he could hear faint snatches of some merry melody being whistled across the tundra.

74

Faraday's Gift

Axis ran the Song of Movement through his head, and transferred into the Sacred Grove. This was a deeply magical place, and Axis never harbored a single doubt that he would transfer there as easily as he could have transferred to Sigholt.

And so he did.

About him the white tundra flowed into glowing emerald, then that shifted and changed into the trees that lined the paths to the Grove. Axis did his best to still his nerves and strode as resolutely as he could along the path. What would he find? The Horned Ones had never liked him, nor had they ever trusted him—what would they think now? Their beloved Faraday had been torn to pieces before his eyes while he did nothing?

Perhaps that was why they had never liked him. Perhaps they had somehow known.

The path broadened and the trees drew back. Above his head the stars spun in their everlasting dance; the music of the Star Dance was potent here. Before him the Grove yawned in a great, silent circle.

Axis halted at its edge, uncertain. The Grove was very different, but why was not immediately obvious. Axis stood completely still, trying to understand.

The same power still swept it; he could feel it circling, watching.

It was the trees, he finally realized. On the two occasions he had been here previously, once in dream and once at Faraday's behest to witness Raum's transformation, he had felt the weight of eyes watching from the encircling trees.

Now the eyes were largely gone. Oh, some were still there, and Axis could feel them waiting . . . waiting for something, but they were only a fraction of the number that had watched before.

Axis felt more comfortable now that he understood the difference, and he stepped into the Grove itself. Why had Faraday wanted him to come here? What had WolfStar meant . . . "gift"?

He stepped cautiously, unnerved by the silence. Where were the Horned Ones? Always before they had greeted him.

A movement in the grass caught his eye and he jerked to a halt.

Breeze, that's all, he told himself, and took another step forward.

Except there was no breeze.

He stopped again, his heart pounding. He could sense that something very important was about to happen—he could feel the power of the Grove gathering—and the hairs on the back of his neck rose.

Eerie silence crashed about him.

Another step, then another, oh so cautious, and the grass wavered a little more.

Axis stopped again. His heart was beating so hard now that he could feel it leaping into his throat. The sense of *imminence* was almost overbearing, and Axis fought the urge to turn and run.

He looked carefully about. Nothing moved . . . except something in that patch of grass some fifteen paces away.

Why am I afraid? Have I not just defeated Gorgrael? Have I not just *won*? Then why am I so afraid? Afraid like a child lost in a dark wood on a stormy night?

Why? Because here he *was* the child lost in the dark wood.

Axis took several more steps and, when nothing happened, several more. He was closer to the patch of grass now, and he understood that whatever was going to happen would take place there.

Taking a deep breath, summoning all his courage, feeling the icy weight of fate, he stepped over to the gently waving grass.

A tiny naked baby lay there.

Axis wavered with shock, and his face blanched. For several heartbeats he did not breathe.

A tiny baby boy.

No! No! Not this!

He trembled, and his shaking grew so bad he had to sink to his knees.

Beside the baby.

The baby was asleep, and he moved his fists slowly, his fingers kneading, as if he dreamed of his mother. His head was covered with soft blond down, his body was plump and healthy.

He was so small that Axis knew he could not have been more than seven or eight weeks old, if that.

Axis reached down toward the baby, and found that his hand shook so violently he had to clench it into a fist before he could continue. Once he regained control of himself, he touched the baby's head.

The baby woke with a soft cry, and Axis' heart lurched over. The baby turned his head slowly, dreamily, looking for the hand that had woken him, and then he rolled his head completely over and looked at Axis with Faraday's green eyes.

"Oh gods," Axis muttered brokenly, and gathered the baby into his arms.

How could I have done this to her, on top of all the other hurts?

The baby nestled familiarly against his chest, as if he recognized him, and buried one tiny fist in the material of the golden tunic.

The baby's blood called to him, sang to him, and Axis felt his own respond. There was no doubt that this was his son.

Why didn't she tell me? Why? Why? Why?

Axis began to cry, slowly, silently, not wanting to upset the baby. No wonder Faraday had disappeared morning and evening to return to the Grove. She had come to feed their son, and to play with him.

Now she was dead, and her beautiful son would never more know his mother.

Axis bowed his head, and his tears fell on the baby, and he sat there for a very long time, rocking gently, grieving anew for Faraday.

"His name is Isfrael."

Axis blinked, and wiped away some of his tears, but he did not immediately look up.

"She named him that because she thought it resembled a dream."

"A dream?" Axis finally raised his eyes. Standing several paces away was a silver-pelted Horned One.

Utter hostility radiated from him.

"Isfrael," Axis murmured. "It is a beautiful name. A dream?"

The hostility increased. "She would dream of a home and a happiness she knew she could never have. Sometimes, in those dreams, she dreamed of this name."

Axis closed his eyes momentarily against the pain and the guilt.

"She told me to tell you to take him home to Azhure to raise. She said that Azhure would be a good mother to him."

Axis turned his head away, unable to bear the Horned One's stare any longer. Azhure had once feared that Axis would take Caelum from her and give him to Faraday to raise. What ultimate irony. Now Azhure would raise Faraday's son.

"She also said that one day you would give him to the Avar."

"*What?*" Axis looked back at the Horned One and his hands tightened protectively about the baby.

"Isfrael is a gift, StarMan, but ultimately he is a gift to the Avar people. Faraday did not live long enough," and the silver pelt paused to stare at Axis with hard eyes, "to lead them from their exile. Isfrael will eventually do that. He will become the Mage-King of the Avar. You must teach him what you can for as long as you can and, when the time comes, the Avar will take over his care and his training."

No, Axis was going to whisper, but the Horned One forestalled him.

"They died for you as well, StarMan."

Not as many as others, Axis was going to shout, but again the Horned One anticipated him.

"And so did she."

Axis closed his mouth and bowed his head in silent agreement.

Axis?

He raised his head. The silver pelt had disappeared, and by the tree line stood a white stag. He paused, trembling, as if afraid to be caught in the open, and his dark eyes rolled in apprehension at the sky above, but he eventually overcame his fear and stepped daintily, regally, toward Axis and the baby.

Axis?

Raum?

That was once my name, yes.

Have you come to revile me as well?

I would never do that, Axis. I have come to repay my debt to you.

Debt?

Axis, years ago at the border of the Avarinheim you saved both my life and Shra's. For that I owed you two lives.

Yes.

I gave one back to you then. I told you that Faraday lived.

Axis lowered his head, remembering. *Yes.*

Now I give you back the second life that I owe you.

Axis raised his eyes.

Faraday lives.

Axis' eyes widened and his breathing stilled.

But she does not exist in a form that will suit you, StarMan. You may see her occasionally, but you will never speak to her again. You will never touch her again. You will never hurt her again. She runs unfettered, Axis, and she is finally free of you.

The stag paused, trembling again and, as Axis stretched out a silent hand toward him, he bounded away into the trees and was lost to sight.

"No!" Axis cried, and the baby whimpered. "No, come back! *Come back!*"

Epilogue

Nine years later . . .

Papa?"

"Yes?" Axis looked down into Isfrael's green eyes and smiled. He tightened his own hand about that of his son.

"You don't like these woods very much, do you?"

Axis laughed uncomfortably, and glanced back to the forest path they had walked down. To either side the great trees reared toward the sky, but the atmosphere was peaceful rather than constricting, and birds and butterflies frolicked among the sunbeams filtering through the emerald canopy. Earlier in the day, he and Azhure had brought their children to the northern rim of Minstrelsea. They had picnicked by the banks of the Nordra, then Axis and Isfrael had entered the forest alone.

They did this twice a year, as they had every year since Axis had returned to Sigholt with the baby in his arms. Although he could never bring himself to ask, Axis suspected that Azhure sometimes traveled these woods with Caelum or Isfrael or their daughter, and perhaps sometimes all three. There was a deep bond between what-had-once-been-Faraday and Azhure, and Axis wondered if Faraday ever appeared to Azhure in her human form.

The one time he had asked, Azhure had looked at him, and then gently changed the subject.

Axis never asked Isfrael.

"Well?" Isfrael pulled at Axis' hand impatiently.

"I like them well enough, Isfrael. How could anyone not appreciate their beauty? But I feel uncomfortable here, yes. I . . ."

How to explain it to the boy? "The forest and I enjoy different kinds of magic," and Axis suddenly realized that this was the nub of the matter, "and although we appreciate each other, neither of us is truly comfortable with the other."

But Isfrael was persistent. "Azhure loves the forest, and it her."

"She shines over forest and plain and sea alike."

"Yes, I suppose you are right, Papa."

Axis had never ceased to be relieved that Azhure had accepted Isfrael so well or so quickly into their family. They had been blessed these past nine years with a happiness neither could have anticipated or dared hope for. Their hearts had healed well from the tragedies that had enveloped them, and their family had grown about them, leaping and cavorting and laughing through Sigholt's corridors and the shores of the Lake of Life.

His family. His children. Five now, yet Axis only ever really thought of three of them as his. The twins remained on the outer. Drago had grown into a surly boy, silent and withdrawn. Obedient, but Axis thought that rebellion lay simmering beneath the outer fragile calm. He showed no trace of his Icarii heritage—even his face had lost its Icarii cast. He had grown no wings, nor had he demonstrated any Icarii Enchanter powers. He'd paid dearly for his treachery, and yet neither Axis nor Azhure, and certainly not Caelum, ever trusted him. They often sent him to stay long months with Belial and Cazna and their two children.

RiverStar was a reserved girl. She kept Drago company, but they were an odd pair. She had grown into her full Icarii heritage, developing wings and Enchanter powers. She was golden and violet, like her aunt EvenSong, and she smiled and laughed and played and hugged both her parents with apparent love.

But she was still reclusive and sometimes sat quietly for hours on end, refusing to play with the other children. She did not harbor resentment or hostility. Not really, but sometimes Axis caught her looking at him with strange eyes, and a shiver would run down his back. When Drago went to Belial's home in Carlon, RiverStar requested to stay with her grandfather on the Island of Mist and Memory. She got on well with StarDrifter, and he remained largely responsible for her training.

So Drago and RiverStar were absent for long months at a time and, even when there, they were hardly part of Sigholt's life.

Caelum . . . glorious, wondrous Caelum. He was nearing twelve now, and growing into his full heritage. He had never developed wings—had refused to, saying that neither of his parents had wings and he wanted to be just like them—but he was Icarii in almost every other respect . . . save in his overwhelming sense of compassion and humility. He would be an Enchanter like no other, Axis thought proudly.

Now Axis' expression softened even further as he thought of his fifth child and Azhure's fourth. Three years ago she had conceived and birthed a daughter (*another* daughter, he vaguely reminded himself). Azhure had called her Zenith, and she had the look of her mother, but Axis did not realize that one of the reasons Azhure's eyes filled with tears so often when she gazed into her daughter's eyes was because Zenith gazed back at her with the eyes of a reborn soul.

She too would be an Enchanter, but Axis did not think she would have to wield her Icarii powers to enchant a man's soul.

"Will FreeFall and EvenSong join us for Caelum's nameday?"

Again Isfrael's voice sounded a trifle impatient, and Axis tried to rouse himself from his reverie; Isfrael must feel as if he was walking these forest paths alone. It lacked only a week until Yuletide, and the Houses of SunSoar and the Stars often used the excuse of Caelum's birth anniversary, coupled with the sacred rites of Yuletide, to meet as a family.

"Yes." Axis smiled at the boy. "And StarDrifter will join us, too."

StarDrifter had made his home on the Island of Mist and Memory—where Axis assumed he created havoc among the Priestesses of the Order of the Stars. Usually he would have led the Yuletide rites on the Island, but there were other Enchanters who could do so, and this year StarDrifter had elected to join Axis and Azhure in Sigholt for the Yuletide season.

These days Axis spent most of the year in Sigholt. In the two or three years after his final battle with Gorgrael he, as Azhure, had spent a great deal of time at Carlon, as well as traveling about the country, making sure that the new nation of Tencendor emerged strong and vibrant from the chaos and division of the previous thousand years. Most Tencendorians had recovered well after the dislocation of war; the Acharites had settled back into their farming existence, and the Icarii had finally managed to reclaim their beautiful cities amid the waving treetops of the Minaret Peaks. EvenSong and FreeFall, now crowned Talon, had made their home there.

FreeFall, Ho'Demi, Ysgryff, Magariz and Belial managed their territories justly and efficiently, and Axis no longer needed to make his presence felt in Tencendor. He met with the Five formally twice a year, and informally more often, but Axis now spent more and more time behind the soft blue mists surrounding Sigholt, exploring and studying his still expanding powers, talking with the Nine when they came to visit, loving Azhure, playing with their children.

Sometimes Rivkah and Magariz and their son came to stay with them. Magariz had built—and continued to expand—a new town in the fertile plains bounded by the Ichtar and Azle rivers. Severin had taken over from the ruined Hsingard and the rebuilt Jervois Landing as the main town of Ichtar, and his mother and Magariz had built themselves a fine palace on a hill overlooking the town.

Whatever reservations Axis had entertained about Rivkah's son had now mostly disappeared. Zared had inherited his mother's wit and courage and his father's dark good looks and sense of loyalty, and Axis found unexpected delight in his younger half-brother. This time, he hoped, he would enjoy the companionship of a brother rather than suffer his hatred and rivalry.

Azhure's father had never reappeared. No one knew where he had gone— even Azhure professed no knowledge—and Axis did not care if WolfStar never appeared again. Perhaps he had stepped back through the Star Gate, returned to whatever eternity he should have enjoyed in the first instance. Perhaps. And perhaps he plotted mischief elsewhere.

But Axis did not worry about WolfStar. If he ever turned up, Axis would deal with him then.

Axis had never again uncovered the Rainbow Scepter since that dreadful day in Gorgrael's chamber. The rag torn from Faraday's gown still covered it, and the Scepter had been placed in a secret chamber in Sigholt. Eventually, Axis knew, he would have to study it, explore the traces and reminders of the Sentinels he knew still inhabited it, but that time was not yet upon him.

The only cloud in Axis' otherwise sunny existence was cast by the knowledge that one day the Avar would lay claim to his youngest son.

The Avar mostly remained in the Avarinheim, although some Clans spent time walking the paths of Minstrelsea. They would wait until Isfrael grew to his majority, they said, wait until Faraday's son took his place as their Mage-King, before they would move south in significant numbers.

Axis continued to chat with Isfrael about StarDrifter's visit, but the deeper they walked into the forest the more unsettled Axis grew. Each year he found these walks into Minstrelsea with Isfrael increasingly disturbing. Within a few years he knew the Avar would request that Isfrael come live with them, to learn their ways and the magic of the trees—and Axis did not know if he could bear to lose Faraday's son as well as Faraday.

Axis glanced at Isfrael. He was a fey child, and as he grew older Axis could see more of Faraday in him. Especially after their twice-annual visit to Niah's Grove.

They were close now, and Axis and Isfrael fell silent. Even the sounds of the forest were muted, and birds watched still and silent instead of fluttering gaily about the canopy.

There. Ahead. As she always waited for them.

Shra.

She must be fifteen or sixteen now, Axis thought as they approached. She had the dark eyes and hair of her people, and the fine-boned fragility of all Avar women, but was unusually tall and fair-skinned for her race. She commanded immense respect from among the Avar, where she held sway as the senior Bane, as from both Axis and Isfrael. She exuded power, but it was not the threatening power that Axis and Azhure had felt from previous Avar Banes. It was enormously peaceful; Shra was always surrounded by a sense of serenity so profound that Axis sometimes felt like an awkward stable-boy before her.

"Welcome, Axis," she said, and held his hands briefly as she kissed him on the cheek.

"Isfrael." She smiled, and took the boy's face between her own. "You grow another handspan every time I see you." She bent down and brushed his cheeks with her lips.

The boy blushed with pleasure. He looked forward to seeing Shra almost as much as he did his mother. He knew of his heritage, knew that one day he'd live among the Avar, and he knew that it bothered his father. But if all the Avar were as beautiful as Shra, then Isfrael knew he would love living with them.

Shra dropped her hands and glanced at Axis. "You must wait at the edge of the grove."

"I know that," Axis said roughly. Always he waited, unwanted, unwelcome, at the edge—why did Shra need to remind him of it yet again?

She nodded, then she took Isfrael's hand and led him forward.

They always came to Niah's Grove. Axis was not too sure why . . . why Faraday-that-had-been would feel drawn to the site where Niah lay buried. The grove stood as it had since the day Faraday had planted it out; the nine trees ringed it; their branches interlocked, yet bright tendrils of sunshine still dappled the grove itself. Moonwildflowers, Azhure's mark, grew in a thick ring in the center of the grove, and were scattered thinly over most of the grassy clearing.

Shra led Isfrael to the ring of violet flowers, and motioned him to sit inside it. She bent down and talked with him softly for several minutes, then she stood and walked to the far side of the grove. At its edge she paused and looked back, first to Isfrael sitting patiently among the flowers, then briefly to Axis.

Then she turned and was swallowed by the shadows.

They waited, Axis under the ring of surrounding trees, Isfrael in the central circle of flowers. Sometimes they waited only minutes, sometimes two or three hours. But whatever the time, Isfrael always waited patiently, never fidgeting, never speaking. Even as a baby barely able to crawl, when Axis had first brought him here, Isfrael had been patient.

Today she appeared almost immediately.

As always, her appearance was heralded by the White Stag.

Axis, startled, heard a twig snap behind him. The White Stag had walked to within a pace or two of him, his body tense, his dark eyes alert.

He trembled, but he allowed Axis to reach out and touch his shoulder briefly.

Greetings, Raum.

Greetings, Axis StarMan. You are well?

Very well. And you?

The Stag did not reply, and Axis was not interested in trying to continue the conversation. Both turned to look into the grove.

Isfrael sat tense and excited now, knowing his mother was not far away.

His eyes darted about the trees, wondering from behind which one she would emerge.

In the end, stunningly, she stepped out from the White Stag's shadow.

Axis jumped, his heart pounding. Never before had she come this close to him. Stars, but if he stepped forward and reached out he would be able to touch her!

But he stayed still, although the effort cost him dearly. He was terrified that if he touched her she would disappear.

She stared at him briefly, her dark eyes startled, her head and neck tense, the muscles along her back quivering, then, with a single bound, she leaped into the grove and stepped lightly, gracefully, over to her son.

Isfrael gave a low cry of delight and reached out his arms, although he did not rise.

The doe walked up to him and lowered her head, nuzzling the boy's face and neck.

Isfrael rubbed her neck and shoulders, burying his fingers within her deep red pelt, tears running down his face. He was silent, as he always was, but Axis knew that on some deep level he communicated with his mother.

After a few minutes the doe folded her legs and sank down beside the boy, and they sat for over an hour, Isfrael with his arms about the doe's neck, she rubbing her cheek against his.

They were surrounded by dancing beams of sunlight, and multi-colored butterflies fluttered about them, but the forest birds kept reverentially quiet, and the usually constant undertone of Tree Song had completely faded. The forest wrapped itself about them, still and silent.

Axis' eyes filled with tears. The sight never failed to move him deeply, and he yearned, as he always did, to join his son and Faraday-that-had-been in the center of the grove.

But she did not want him there. She only wanted her son. Whatever love she had once borne him had either gone or been buried so deep that it might as well never have been.

She ran unfettered now, unfettered by pain or betrayal . . . or by her love for Axis.

When she rose Axis expected her to bound off into the forest as she always did.

But this day she did not.

Trembling so badly Axis thought her fragile legs would fold on her, the doe stepped back toward where he stood with the White Stag.

Behind him the Stag tensed . . . Axis could feel the entire forest tense.

She halted a pace away from him, and Axis realized he was trembling himself. Slowly, achingly slowly, Axis raised a hand.

Her head wavered, and her dark eyes widened in alarm.

He froze, his hand half extended, his fingers reaching out in appeal. He thought his heart was thudding so loudly its beat would be enough in itself to frighten her away.

Her head jerked, her eyes white-rimmed with anxiety. Yet her nose continued to edge forward, almost unwillingly . . . so near that her warm breath lifted the hairs on the back of his hand.

Oh Stars, Axis thought, unable to breathe himself, she's so close! Another heartbeat and I'll be able to touch her.

But the instant before she nuzzled Axis' fingers the White Stag shifted slightly behind him, and his movement broke the spell.

With a startled gasp the doe gave a single great leap sideways, and the White Stag moved so that his body stood between her and Axis.

"Faraday!" Axis cried.

She paused, her eyes burning with unreadable emotion, then she turned and was away, bounding free through the forest, the White Stag at her shoulder.

Unfettered.

Glossary

ACHAR: the realm that once stretched over most of the continent, bounded by the Andeis, Tyrre and Widowmaker Seas, the Shadowsward Forest and the Icescarp Alps. Now integrated into Tencendor.

ACHARITES: a people of Tencendor.

ADAMON: one of the nine Star Gods of the Icarii, Adamon is the eldest and the God of the Firmament.

AFTERLIFE: all three races, the Acharites, the Icarii and the Avar, believe in the existence of an AfterLife, although exactly what they believe depends on their particular culture.

ALAYNE: a roving blacksmith in Skarabost who once told the young Azhure stories.

ALAUNT: the legendary pack of hounds that once belonged to WolfStar SunSoar. They now run with Azhure. They are all of the Lesser.

ALDENI: a small province in western Achar, devoted to small crop cultivation. It is administered by Duke Roland under the overlordship of Prince Belial.

ALNAR: a Bane of the Avar people.

ANDAKILSA, RIVER: the extreme northern river of Ichtar, dividing Ichtar from Ravensbund. Under normal circumstances, it remains free of ice all year round and flows into the Andeis Sea.

ANDEIS SEA: the often unpredictable sea that washes the western coast of Achar.

ANNWIN: eldest daughter of the exiled and deposed Earl Isend of Skarabost, sister to Faraday. Married to Lord Osmary.

ARCEN: the major town of Arcness.

ARCNESS: large eastern province in Achar, specializing in pigs.

ARHAT: a Ravensbund warrior.

ARNE: a former Axe-Wielder and current cohort commander in the combined army, he often acts as Axis' personal bodyguard.

ARTOR THE PLOWHMAN: the one true god, as taught by the Brotherhood of the Seneschal. According to the Book of Field and Furrow, the religious text of the Seneschal, Artor gave mankind the gift of the Plow, the instrument which enabled mankind to abandon his hunting and gathering lifestyle and to settle in the one spot to cultivate the earth and thus to build the foundations of civilization.

AVAR, The: ancient race of Tencendor who live in the forest of the Avarinheim. The Avar are sometimes referred to as the People of the Horn.

AVARINHEIM, The: home of the Avar people.

AVENUE, The: processional way of the Temple Complex on the Island of Mist and Memory.

AVONSDALE: province in western Achar. It produces legumes, fruit and flowers. It is administered by Earl Jorge under the overlordship of Prince Belial.

AXE-WIELDERS, The: once the elite crusading and military wing of the Seneschal. Its members did not take holy orders but nevertheless dedicated their battle skills to the Seneschal to use as it wished. The Axe-Wielders were the main reason the Acharites managed to defeat the Avar and the Icarii in the Wars of the Axe and, over the subsequent thousand years, enjoyed a well-deserved reputation for military excellence. Once led by Axis as their BattleAxe, the Axe-Wielders are now completely disbanded, their men incorporated into Axis' combined command, fighting with Axis to reunite Tencendor and defeat Gorgrael.

AXIS: son of the Princess Rivkah of Achar and the Icarii Enchanter StarDrifter SunSoar. Once BattleAxe of the Axe-Wielders, now he has assumed the mantle of the StarMan of the Prophecy of the Destroyer. After reforging Tencendor, Axis formed his own house, the House of the Stars.

AZHURE: daughter of WolfStar SunSoar and Niah of Nor. She is married to Axis.

AZLE, RIVER: a major river that divides the provinces of Ichtar and Aldeni. It flows into the Andeis Sea.

BALDWIN, SOL: commander of the garrison at Sigholt.

BANES: the religious leaders of the Avar people. They wield magic, although it is usually of the minor variety.

BARROWS, The Ancient: burial places of the ancient Enchanter-Talons of the Icarii people. Located in southern Arcness.

BARSARBE: senior Bane of the Avar people.

BATTLEAXE, The: once the leader of the Axe-Wielders, he was appointed by the Brother-Leader for his loyalty to the Seneschal, his devotion to Artor the Plowman and the Way of the Plow, and his skills as a military commander. The post of BattleAxe was last held by Axis. See "Axe-Wielders."

BEDWYR FORT: a fort that sits on the lower reaches of the River Nordra and guards the entrance to Grail Lake from Nordmuth. It was the site of the major battle between Axis and Borneheld.

BELAGUEZ: Axis' war horse.

BELIAL: lieutenant and second-in-command in Axis' army. Long-time friend and supporter of Axis SunSoar, now Prince Belial of the territories of western Tencendor. Married to Cazna, daughter of Prince Ysgryff.

BELTIDE: see "Festivals."

BLUEWING EVERSOAR: an Icarii farflight scout in the Strike Force.

BOGLE MARSH: a large and inhospitable marsh in eastern Arcness. Strange creatures are said to live in the Marsh.

BOOK OF FIELD AND FURROW: the religious text of the Seneschal, who taught that Artor himself wrote it and presented it to mankind.

BORNEHELD: Duke of Ichtar and King of Achar. Son of the Princess Rivkah and her husband, Duke Searlas, half-brother to Axis, and husband of Faraday of Skarabost. After murdering his uncle, Priam, Borneheld assumed the throne of Achar. Now dead.

BOROLEAS: an elderly Brother within the Seneschal. Now exiled.

BRACKEN RANGES, The: a low and narrow mountain range that divides Arcness and Skarabost.

BRACKEN, RIVER: the river that rises in the Bracken Ranges and which, dividing the provinces of Skarabost and Arcness, flows into the Widowmaker Sea.

BRADOKE: a senior lieutenant within Axis' forces.

BRIGHTFEATHER: wife to RavenCrest SunSoar, Talon of the Icarii.

BRIGHT SOULS: creatures mentioned by the Prophecy of the Destroyer.

BRIGHTSTAR FEATHERNEST: an Icarii Enchanter.

BRODE: an Avar man, Clan Leader of the SilentWalk Clan.

BROTHER-LEADER: the supreme leader of the Brotherhood of the Seneschal. Usually elected by the senior Brothers, the Office of Brother-Leader was for life. He was a powerful man, controlling not only the Brotherhood and all its riches, but the Axe-Wielders as well. The last Brother-Leader of the Seneschal was Jayme.

BURDEL, EARL: one-time lord of Arcness and friend to Borneheld, Duke of Ichtar and King of Achar. Executed by Axis for crimes against the people of Skarabost.

CAELUM: eldest son of Axis and Azhure, born at Yuletide. Caelum is an ancient word meaning "Stars in Heaven."

CARLON: main city of Tencendor and one-time residence of the kings of Achar. Situated on Grail Lake.

CAULDRON LAKE: the lake at the center of the Silent Woman Woods.

CAZNA: daughter of Prince Ysgryff of Nor, cousin of Azhure, and wife to Belial.

CHAMBER OF THE MOONS: chief audience and sometime banquet chamber of the royal palace in Carlon.

CHAMPION, A: occasionally an Acharite warrior will pledge himself as a noble lady's Champion. The relationship is purely platonic and is one of protection and support. The pledge of a Champion can be broken only by his death or by the express wish of his lady.

CHARONITES: a little-known race of Tencendor, they now inhabit the UnderWorld.

CHATTERLINGS, The: curious creatures found in the Murkle Mountain mines.

CIRCLE OF STARS, The: *see* "Enchantress' Ring."

CLANS: the Avar tend to segregate into Clan groups, roughly, equivalent to family groups.

CLOUDBURST SUNSOAR: younger brother and assassin of WolfStar SunSoar.

COHORT: *see* "Military Terms."

COROLEAS: the great empire to the south of Tencendor. Relations between the two countries are usually cordial.

CREST: Icarii military unit composed of twelve Wings.

CRIAH: an Avar woman from the FlatRock Clan.

CRIMSONCREST: an Icarii male.

CREST-LEADER:commander of an Icarii Crest.

CULPEPPER FENWICKE: mayor of the city of Arcen in Arcness.

DANCE OF DEATH, The: dark star music that is the counterpoint to the Star Dance. It is the music made when stars miss their step and crash into each other, or swell up into red giants and implode. Very few Enchanters can wield this Dark Music—the Dark Man can, as can Gorgrael and, on occasion, Azhure.

DARK MAN, The: Gorgrael's mentor. Also known as Dear Man.

DEAR MAN: *see* "Dark Man."

DESTROYER, The: another term for Gorgrael.

DEWES, SYMONDS: a sheeptrader from Arcen.

DISTANCES:

League: roughly seven kilometers, or four and a half miles.

Pace: roughly one meter or one yard.

Handspan: roughly twenty centimeters or eight inches.

DOBO: a Ravensbund warrior. Now dead.

DOME OF THE MOON: a sacred dome dedicated to the Moon on Temple Mount of the Island of Mist and Memory. Only the First Priestess has access to it, and it was in this Dome that Niah conceived Azhure.

DRAGONSTAR SUNSOAR: second son of Axis and Azhure. Twin brother to RiverStar. (Also known as Drago.)

DRIFTSTAR SUNSOAR: grandmother to StarDrifter, mother of MorningStar. An Enchanter and a SunSoar in her own right and wife to the SunSoar Talon. She died three hundred years before the events of the Prophecy of the Destroyer.

DRU-BEORH: a merchant.

EARTH TREE: a sacred tree to both the Icarii and the Avar.

EARTH TREE GROVE: the grove holding the Earth Tree in the northern Avarinheim where it borders the Icescarp Alps. It the most important of the Avarinheim groves and is where the Avar (sometimes in concert with the Icarii) hold their gatherings and religious rites.

EDOWES: a soldier from Arne's unit in Axis' force.

EGERLEY: a young man from Smyrton.

ELIEN: an Avar woman from the FlatRock Clan.

EMBETH, LADY OF TARE: the widow of Ganelon of Tare, mother of Timozel, and good friend and once lover to Axis.

ENCHANTRESS: the first of the Icarii Enchanters, the first Icarii to discover the way to use the power of the Star Dance. The Icarii revere her memory. This title is now occasionally given to Azhure.

ENCHANTRESS' RING, The: an ancient ring once in the possession of the Enchantress, now worn by Azhure. Its proper name is the Circle of Stars, and it is intimately connected with the Star Gods.

ENCHANTERS: the magicians of the Icarii people. Many of them are very powerful. All Enchanters have the word "Star" somewhere in their names.

ENCHANTER-TALONS: Talons of the Icarii people who are also Enchanters.

EVENSONG: daughter of Rivkah and StarDrifter SunSoar, sister to Axis and wife to FreeFall SunSoar.

FAIREYE: an Icarii birdwoman, a member of the Strike Force.

FARADAY: daughter of Earl Isend of Skarabost and his wife, Lady Merlion. Once wife to Borneheld and Queen of Achar, Faraday now wanders as Tree Friend.

FARSIGHT CUTSPUR: the senior Crest-Leader of the Icarii StrikeForce.

FEATHERFLIGHT BRIGHTWING: a Wing-Leader in the Icarii StrikeForce.

FERNBRAKE LAKE: the large lake in the center of the Bracken Ranges. Also known by both the Avar and the Icarii as the Mother.

FERRYMAN: the Charonite who plies the ferry of the UnderWorld. His name is Orr. Orr is one of the Lesser.

FESTIVALS of the Avar and the Icarii:

Yuletide: winter solstice, in the last week of Snow-month.

Beltide: spring Festival; the first day of Flower-month.

Fire-Night: summer solstice, in the last week of Rose-month.

FINGUS: a previous BattleAxe. Now dead.

FINNIS: a displaced Plow-Keeper.

FIRE-NIGHT: *see* "Festivals."

FIRST, The: First Priestess of the Order of the Stars, the order of nine priestesses on Temple Mount. The First, like all priestesses of the Order, gave up her name on taking her vows. Niah of Nor once held this office.

FIVE FAMILIES, The First: the leading families of the newly created Tencendor: led, in turn, by Prince Belial, Prince Magariz, Prince Ysgryff, Chief Ho'Demi of the Ravensbund people and FreeFall SunSoar.

FLEAT: an Avar woman.

FLEURIAN: Baroness of Tarantaise, wife to Greville. She is his second wife, and much younger than him.

FLULIA: one of the nine Icarii Star Gods, Flulia is the Goddess of Water.

FLURIA, RIVER: a minor river that flows through Aldeni into the River Nordra.

FORBIDDEN, The: name the Seneschal gave to the Avar and the Icarii. The Seneschal taught that the Forbidden were evil creatures who used magic and sorcery to enslave humans. During the Wars of the Axe, a thousand years before the events of the Prophecy of the Destroyer, the Acharites pushed the Forbidden back beyond the Fortress Ranges into the Shadowsward and the Icescarp Alps. Now the name has largely fallen into disuse.

FORBIDDEN TERRITORIES: the lands of the Forbidden, the Avarinheim and the Icescarp Alps.

FORBIDDEN VALLEY: the only above-ground entrance into the Avarinheim from the plains of Tencendor. It is where the River Nordra escapes the Avarinheim and flows into Achar.

FOREST, concept of: the Seneschal taught that all forests were bad because they harbored dark demons who plotted the overthrow of mankind, thus most Acharites had (and some still have) a terrible fear of forests and their dark interiors. Almost all of the ancient forest that once covered Achar has been destroyed. The only trees grown in Achar are fruit trees and plantation trees for timber.

FORTRESS RANGES: the mountains that run down Achar's eastern boundary from the Icescarp Alps to the Widowmaker Sea. The Avar were penned behind these ranges by the Seneschal and the Axe-Wielders.

FRANCIS: an elderly Brother from the Retreat in Gorkentown.

FREEFALL: son of BrightFeather and RavenCrest SunSoar and heir to the Talon throne, husband of EvenSong SunSoar.

FULBRIGHT: an Acharite engineer in Axis' force.

FULKE, Baron: lord of Romsdale under the overlordship of Prince Belial.

FUNADO: a Ravensbund warrior.

"FURROW WIDE, FURROW DEEP": an all-embracing Acharite phrase which can be used as a benediction, as a protection against evil, or as a term of greeting. Largely fallen into disuse with the demise of the Seneschal and the Way of the Plow.

GANELON, LORD: Lord of Tare, once husband to Embeth, Lady of Tare. Now dead.

GARDEN, The: Garden of the Mother.

GARLAND, GOODMAN: Goodman of Smyrton.

GATEKEEPER, The: Keeper of the Gate of Death in the UnderWorld and mother of Zeherah. Her task is to keep tally of the souls who pass through the Gate. She is one of the Lesser.

GAUTIER: once lieutenant to Borneheld. Now dead.

GHOSTMEN: a term used for the Skraelings in the Prophecy of the Destroyer.

GHOSTTREE CLAN: one of the Avar Clans, headed by Grindle.

GILBERT: Brother of the Seneschal; once assistant and adviser to the Brother-Leader.

GOLDFEATHER: the name that Rivkah adopted when she joined the Icarii after Axis' supposed death at birth. She abandoned the adopted name of GoldFeather and resumed her birth-name at the request of Orr, the Charonite Ferryman.

GOVERNOR OF THE EAST: a position created by Axis when he reforged Tencendor and given to Azhure. The Governor of the East is a somewhat temporary office, necessitated by the fact that the old lords of eastern Achar died or were exiled during Axis' march south.

GORGRAEL: the Destroyer, half-brother to Axis, sharing the same father, StarDrifter. Gorgrael seeks to conquer the southern lands. He is a proficient wielder of the Dance of Death, the Dark Music that is the counterpoint to the Star Dance.

GORKENFORT: the major fort situated in Gorken Pass in northern Ichtar. Now deserted.

GORKEN PASS: the narrow pass sixty leagues long that provides the only way from Ravensbund into Ichtar. It is bounded by the Icescarp Alps and the River Andakilsa.

GORKENTOWN: the town that huddles about the walls of Gorkenfort. Destroyed during the initial invasion of the Skraeling army.

GRAIL LAKE, The: a massive lake at the lower reaches of the River Nordra. On its shores are Carlon and the Tower of the Seneschal.

GREATER, The: the nine Star Gods.

GREVILLE, BARON: lord of Tarantaise.

GRINDLE: an Avar man, head of the GhostTree Clan.

GRYPHON: a legendary flying creature of Tencendor, intelligent, vicious and courageous. They were particularly deadly to the Icarii and it took the Icarii many hundreds of years to exterminate them. Now re-created by the Dark Man and Gorgrael. Such was the dark magic worked into their creation that they are born pregnant, and whelp nine pups some four months after birth. All their pups are born pregnant . . . and so on.

GUNDEALGA FORD: a wide shallow ford on the Nordra, just south of the Urqhart Hills.

HAGEN: once Plow-Keeper of Smyrton, husband to Niah, and stepfather to Azhure. Hagen died during a struggle with Azhure.

HANDSPAN: see "Distances."

OHANORI: a Ravensbund elder.

HELM: a young Avar male.

HESKETH: captain of the palace guard in Carlon. Lover to Yr.

HO'DEMI: the Chief of the Ravensbund people.

HOGNI: a young Avar female.

HORDLEY, GOODMAN: Goodman of Smyrton, senior man of the village.

HORNED ONES: the almost divine and most sacred members of the Avar race. They live in the Sacred Grove.

HOVEREYE BLACKWING: an Icarii Crest-Leader.

HSINGARD: the large town situated in central Ichtar, once seat of the Dukes of Ichtar, now totally destroyed by Skraelings.

ICARII, The: a race of winged people, living in the Icescarp Alps. They are sometimes referred to as the People of the Wing.

ICEBEAR COAST: the hundred-league-long coast that stretches from the Deadwood Forest in northwestern Ravensbund to the frozen Tundra above the Avarinheim. It is very remote, and very beautiful.

ICESCARP ALPS: the great mountain range that stretches across most of northern Achar. It is home to the Icarii.

ICESCARP BARREN: a desolate tract of land situated in northern Ichtar between the Icescarp Alps and the Urqhart Hills.

ICEWORMS: potent creations of Gorgrael. Fashioned from ice and snow and shaped somewhat like worms, from whence they got their names, these massive creatures carry Skraelings in their bellies. Rising twenty or thirty paces above men or walls, the IceWorms can then vomit their cargo behind both lines and walls. They were instrumental in the downfall of Gorkentown.

ICHTAR, DUKES of: once cruel lords of Ichtar, the line died with Borneheld.

ICHTAR, The Province of: the largest and richest of the provinces of Achar. Ichtar derives its wealth from its extensive grazing herds and from its mineral and precious gem mines. Now given to Prince Magariz by Axis.

ICHTAR, RIVER: a minor river that flows through Ichtar into the River Azle.

IGREN FENWICKE: wife to the mayor of Arcen, Culpepper Fenwike.

ILFRACOOMBE: the manor house of the Earl of Skarabost, the home where Faraday grew up.

IMIBE: a Ravensbundwoman, sometime nurse to Caelum.

INARI: a Ravensbund warrior.

IN'MARI: a Ravensbund woman, daughter of Ho'Demi and Sa'Kuya, and married to Izanagi.

ISEND, EARL: once lord of Skarabost, a darkly handsome but somewhat dandified lord. Father to Faraday. Isend now lives in exile.

ISFRAEL: a baby boy, a gift.

ISLAND OF MIST AND MEMORY: one of the sacred sites of the Icarii people, once known as Pirate's Nest.

IZANAGI, a Ravensbund warrior, married to Ho'Demi's daughter In'Man.

JACK: senior among the Sentinels.

JAYME: one-time Brother-Leader of the Seneschal.

JERVOIS LANDING: the small town on Tailem Bend of the River Nordra. The gateway into Ichtar.

JORGE, EARL: Earl of Avonsdale, and one of the most experienced military campaigners in Achar.

JUDITH: once Queen of Achar, widow of Priam. Now living in reclusion in Tare.

KAREL: dead king of Achar, father to Priam and Rivkah.

KASTALEON: one of the great Keeps of Achar, situated on the River Nordra in central Achar.

KEEPS, The: the three great magical Keeps of Achar. *See separate entries under* Spiredore, Sigholt, and Silent Woman Keep.

KENRICKE: the commander of the last surviving cohort of Axe-Wielders, left by Axis to guard the Tower of the Seneschal. Now fighting in Axis' combined command.

LAKE OF LIFE, The: one of the sacred and magical lakes of Tencendor. It sits at the western end of the HoldHard Pass in the Urqhart Hills and cradles Sigholt.

LEAGUE: *see* "Distances."

LESSER, The: a term given to creatures of such magic they approach godlike status.

LOMAN: an Avar man of the BareHollow Clan.

MAGARIZ, Prince: once commander of Gorkenfort, now one of Axis' senior commanders and lord of the northern territories of Tencendor. Husband to Rivkah, Axis' mother.

MAGIC: the Seneschal taught that all magic, enchantments or sorcery are evil and the province only of the Forbidden races who would use magic to enslave the Acharites if they could. Under the influence of the Seneschal all Artor-fearing Acharites feared and hated the use of magic, although their fear now dies.

MAGIC LAKES: the ancient land of Tencendor had a number of magical lakes whose powers are now mostly forgotten. Also known as the Sacred Lakes.

MALFARI: the tuber that the Avar depend on to produce their bread.

MASCEN, BARON: Lord of Rhaetia.

MERLION, LADY: wife to Earl Isend of Skarabost and mother to Faraday. Merlion died in Gorgrael's storm at the Ancient Barrows.

MILITARY TERMS (for regular ground forces):
Squad: a small group of fighters, normally under forty and usually archers.
Unit: a group of one hundred men, either infantry, archers, pikemen, or cavalry.
Cohort: five units, so five hundred men.
See also "Wing" and "Crest" for the Icarii Strike Force.

MERSE: a bane of the Avar people.

MINARET PEAKS: the ancient name for the Bracken Ranges, named for the minarets of the ancient Icarii cities spread the length of the mountain range.

MINSTRELSEA: the name Faraday gives to the new forest she had begun planting out-below the Avarinheim.

MIRBOLT: a Bane of the Avar people. Now dead.

MONTHS: (Northern Hemisphere seasons apply)

Wolf-month:	January
Raven-month:	February
Hungry-month:	March
Thaw-month:	April
Flower-month:	May
Rose-month:	June
Harvest-month:	July
Weed-month:	August
DeadLeaf-month:	September
Bone-month:	October
Frost-month:	November
Snow-month:	December

MOONWILDFLOWERS: extremely rare, delicate violet flowers that bloom only under the full moon. Niah once took young Azhure hunting for them under the full moon.

MORNINGSTAR SUNSOAR: StarDrifter's mother and a powerful Enchanter in her own right. MorningStar was the widow of RushCloud, the previous SunSoar Talon. She was murdered by WolfStar SunSoar.

MORYSON: Brother of the Seneschal and friend, chief assistant and adviser to the Brother-Leader.

MOTHER, The: either the Avar name for Fernbrake Lake, or an all-embracing term for nature which is sometimes personified as an immortal woman.

MURKLE BAY: a huge bay off the western coast of Tencendor, its waters are filthy, polluted by the tanneries along the Azle River.

MURKLE MOUNTAINS: A range of desolate mountains that run along the length of Murkle Bay. Once extensively mined for opals, they are now abandoned.

NARCIS: one of the nine Icarii Star Gods, Narcis is the God of the Sun.

NECKLET, The: a curious geological feature of Ravensbund.

NEVELON: lieutenant to Duke Roland of Aldeni, Nevelon died at Jervois Landing.

NIAH: of the once baronial family of Nor, elder sister to Prince Ysgryff. Mother to Azhure, Niah was seduced by WolfStar SunSoar and murdered by Brother Hagen. Niah was the First Priestess of the Order of the Stars.

NINE, The: see the "Star Gods." ("the Nine" can also occasionally refer to the nine Priestesses of the Order of the Stars.)

NOR: the southernmost of the provinces of Achar. The Nors people are far darker and more exotic than the rest of the Acharites. Nor is controlled by Prince Ysgryff.

NORDMUTH: the port at the mouth of the River Nordra.

NORDRA, RIVER: the great river that is the main lifeline of Achar. Rising in the Icescarp Alps, the River Nordra flows through the Avarinheim before flowing through northern and central Achar. It is used for irrigation, transport and fishing.

OGDEN: one of the Sentinels, brother to Veremund.

ORDER OF THE STARS: the order of nine priestesses who keep watch in the Temple of the Stars. Every priestess gives up her own name upon taking orders.

ORR: the Charonite Ferryman.

OSMARY, LORD: husband to Annwin, Faraday's elder sister.

PACE: *see* "Distances."

PALESTAR SNAPWING: an Icarii Enchanter.

PEASE: an Avar woman killed in the Yuletide attack on the Earth Tree Grove. Mother of Shra.

PIRATES' NEST: for many centuries the common name of the Island of Mist and Memory and still the haunt of pirates.

PIRATES' TOWN: the town in the northern harbor of Pirates' Nest—or the Island of Mist and Memory.

PLOW, The: under the rule of the Seneschal each Acharite village had a Plow, which not only served to plow the fields, but was also the center of their worship of the Way of the Plow. The Plow was the implement given by Artor the Plowman to enable mankind to civilize themselves. The Seneschal taught that use of the Plow distinguished the Acharites from the Forbidden; neither the Icarii nor the Avar practice cultivation.

PLOW-KEEPERS: the Seneschal assigned a Brother to each village in Achar, and these men were often known as Plow-Keepers. They were literally the guardians of the Plow in each village, but they were also the directors of the Way of the Plow and guardians of the villagers' souls. Many Plow-Keepers still remain in Tencendor and many still adhere to the Way of the Plow.

PORS: one of the nine Icarii Star Gods, Pors is the God of Air.

POWLE, WAINWALD: a young man, son of Miller Powle, of Smyrton.

PRIAM: once King of Achar and uncle to Borneheld, brother to Rivkah. Murdered by the consortium of Borneheld, Jayme, Moryson and Gilbert.

PRIVY CHAMBER: the large chamber in the royal palace in Carlon where Achar's Privy Council once met. Now used for a similar purpose by Axis.

PRIVY COUNCIL: the council of advisers to the King of Achar, normally the lords of the major provinces of Achar. This council has been replaced in Tencendor by the Five, the leaders of the First Five Families.

PROPHECY OF THE DESTROYER: an ancient Prophecy that tells of the rise of Gorgrael in the north and the StarMan who can stop him.

RAINBOW SCEPTER: a weapon mentioned in the Prophecy.

RAUM: once a Bane of the Avar people, now the sacred White Stag.

RAVENCREST SUNSOAR: the current Talon of the Icarii people.

RAVENSBUND: the extreme northern province of Tencendor.

RAVENSBUNDMEN: the inhabitants of Ravensbund, once loathed by the Acharites as barbarous and cruel, but now widely respected for their fighting abilities and their loyalty to Axis.

REINALD: retired chief cook of Sigholt, undercook when Rivkah lived there.

RELM: an Avar woman from the PineWalk Clan.

RENKIN, GOODWIFE: a peasant woman of northern Arcness.

RETREATS: many Brothers of the Seneschal preferred the contemplative life to the active life, and the Seneschal had various Retreats about Achar where these Brothers lived in peace in order to contemplate the mysteries of Artor the Plowman. Many still remain.

RHAETIA: small area of Achar situated in the western Bracken Ranges. It is controlled by Baron Mascen.

RIVERSTAR SUNSOAR: third child of Axis and Azhure. Twin sister to DragonStar.

RIVKAH: Princess of Achar, sister to King Priam and mother to Borneheld, Duke of Ichtar, and Axis. Now married to Prince Magariz.

ROLAND, DUKE: Duke of Aldeni and now in residence in Sigholt.

ROMANA: daughter to Duke Roland of Aldeni.

ROMSDALE: a province to the southwest of Carlon that mainly produces wine. It is administered by Baron Fulke.

RUSHCLOUD SUNSOAR: father to RavenCrest and StarDrifter. Once Talon of the Icarii.

SACRED GROVE: the most sacred spot of the Avar people, the Sacred Grove is rarely visited by ordinary mortals. Normally the Banes are the only members of the Avar race who know the paths in order to find the Grove.

SACRED LAKES: the four magical lakes of Tencendor: Grail Lake, Cauldron Lake, Fernbrake Lake (or the Mother) and the Lake of Life. According to legend, the lakes were formed during Fire-Night when ancient gods fell through the skies and crashed to Tencendor.

SA'KUYA: a Ravensbundwoman, wife to the Ravensbund Chief, Ho'Demi.

SEAGRASS PLAINS: the vast grain plains that form most of Skarabost.

SEAL HOPE, The: a ship belonging to Prince Ysgryff of Nor.

SEARLAS: previous Duke of Ichtar and father of Borneheld. Once married to the Princess Rivkah. Now dead.

SENESCHAL, The: once the all-powerful religious organization of Achar. The Religious Brotherhood of the Seneschal, known individually as Brothers, directed the religious lives of all the Acharites. The Seneschal was extremely powerful and played a major role, not only in everyday life, but also in the political life of the nation. It taught obedience to the one god, Artor the Plowman, and the Way of the Plow.

SENESCHAL, TOWER of: once the headquarters of the Brotherhood of the Seneschal, it has now been revealed as one of the ancient Keeps of Tencendor, Spiredore.

SENTINELS: magical creatures of the Prophecy of the Destroyer.

SEPULCHRE OF THE MOON: rumored to be on Temple Mount, the Sepulchre was used so rarely, even when the Icarii still flew the southern skies, that most Enchanters believe it has fallen into total disuse.

SEVERIN: the new town that Magariz builds as the replacement capital of Ichtar.

SHADOWSWARD: the Acharite name for the Avarinheim.

SHARPEYE BLUEFEATHER: A Crest Leader in the Icarii Strike Force.

SHRA: a young Avar child. Daughter of Pease and Grindle. She was bonded to the Mother with Faraday, and shows promise of becoming a great Bane. When captured and beaten close to death by the folk of Smyrton, it was Axis, then still BattleAxe, who saved her life by singing the Song of Re-creation over her still form, and Azhure who ensured her escape from her prison with Raum.

SICARIUS: leader of the pack of Alaunt hounds. One of the Lesser.

SIGHOLT: one of the great magical Keeps of Tencendor, situated on the shores of the Lake of Life in the Urqhart Hills in Ichtar. Axis' home.

SILENT WOMAN KEEP: one of the magical Keeps of Tencendor, lies in the center of the Silent Woman Woods.

SILENT WOMAN WOODS: the dark and impenetrable woods in southern Arcness that house the Silent Woman Keep.

SILTON: one of the nine Icarii Star Gods, Silton is the God of Fire.

SKALI: a young Avar female, daughter of Fleat and Grindle. She died during the Skraeling attack on the sacred Earth Tree Grove at Yuletide.

SKARABOST: large eastern province of Achar which grows much of the kingdom's grain supplies. Currently administered by the Governor of the East, Azhure.

SKRAEBOLDS: leaders of the Skraelings.

SKRAEFEAR: senior of the remaining SkraeBolds.

SKRAELINGS: (also called wraiths) creatures of the frozen northern wastes who feed off fear and blood. Once insubstantial wraiths, they are assuming far more solid forms as Gorgrael's magic grows.

SMYRTON: a large village in northern Skarabost, virtually at the entrance to the Forbidden Valley.

SONG OF CREATION: a Song which can, according to Icarii and Avar legend, actually create life itself. StarDrifter claimed that Axis sang it to himself while still in Rivkah's womb.

SONG OF RE-CREATION: one of the most powerful Icarii spells which can literally re-create life in the dying. It cannot, however, make the dead rise again. Only the most powerful Enchanters can sing this Song.

SORCERY: see "Magic."

SPIKEFEATHER TRUESONG: an Icarii Wing- and Crest-Leader.

SPIREDORE: one of the magical Keeps of Tencendor. Now owned by Azhure.

SPREADWING RAVENCRY: a Crest-Leader in the Icarii Strike Force.

STAR DANCE: the source from which the Icarii Enchanters derive their power. It is the music made by the stars in their eternal dance through the heavens.

STARDRIFTER: an Icarii Enchanter, father to Gorgrael, Axis and EvenSong.

STAR GATE: one of the sacred sites of the Icarii people, situated underneath the Ancient Barrows and very hard to access.

STAR GODS: the nine gods of the Icarii, although only seven of their names have been revealed to the Icarii. *See separate entries under* Adamon, Xanon, Narcis, Flulia, Pors, Zest and Silton.

STARMAN: the man who, according to the Prophecy of the Destroyer, is the only one who can defeat Gorgrael—Axis SunSoar.

STARREST SOARDEEP: an Icarii Enchanter, one of those who helps to recover the site of the Star Gate.

STARS, HOUSE of the: Axis' personal House.

STARSHINE EVENHEART: an Icarii Enchanter.

STRAUM ISLAND: a large island off the coast of Ichtar and inhabited by sealers.

STRIKE FORCE: the military force of the Icarii.

SUNDOWN CROOKCLAW: one of the Icarii Strike Force killed in the Skraeling attack on the sacred Earth Tree Grove at Yuletide past. EvenSong SunSoar filled his place in SpikeFeather TrueSong's Wing.

SUNSOAR, HOUSE of: the ruling House of the Icarii for many thousands of years.

TAILEM BEND: the great bend in the River Nordra where it turns from its westerly direction and flows south toward Nordmuth and the Sea of Tyrre.

TALON: the hereditary ruler of the Icarii people (and once over all of the peoples of Tencendor). Generally of the House of SunSoar.

TALON SPIKE: the highest mountain in the Icescarp Alps, the home of the Icarii people.

TANABATA: a Ravensbund elder.

TARANTAISE: a rather poor southern province of Achar. Relies on trade for its income. It is administered by Baron Greville.

TARE: small trading town in northern Tarantaise. Home to Embeth, Lady of Tare.

TARE, PLAINS of: the plains that lie between Tare and Grail Lake.

TEKAWAI: the preferred tea of the Ravensbund people, made from the dried seaweed of the Icebear Coast. It is always brewed and served ceremonially and is drunk from small porcelain cups bearing the emblem of the blood-red blazing sun.

TEMPLE MOUNT: the plateau on the top of the massive mountain in the southeast corner of the Island of Mist and Memory. It houses the Temple Complex.

TEMPLE OF THE STARS: one of the Icarii sacred sites, located on the Island of Mist and Memory.

TENCENDOR: once the ancient name for the continent of Achar before the Wars of the Axe, and, under Axis' leadership, the reforged nation of the Acharites, Avar and Icarii.

THREE BROTHERS LAKES, The: three minor lakes in southern Aldeni.

TIME OF THE PROPHECY OF THE DESTROYER: the time that begins with the birth of the Destroyer and the StarMan and that will end when one destroys the other.

TIMOZEL: son of Embeth and Ganelon of Tare, and a member of the Axe Wielders. Once Champion to Faraday, Timozel's soul has been seized by Gorgrael.

TREE FRIEND: in Avar legend Tree Friend will be the person who will lead the Avar back to their traditional homes south of the Fortress Ranges. Tree Friend is also the person who will bring the Avarinheim behind the StarMan. The unfolding of the Prophecy of the Destroyer has revealed Tree Friend to be Faraday.

TREE SONG: whatever Song the trees choose to sing you. Many times they will sing the future, other times they will sing love and protection. The trees can also sing death.

TYRRE, SEA of: the ocean off the southwest coast of Achar.

UNIT: see "Military Terms."

UR: an old woman who lives in the Enchanted Woods. For aeons she has guarded the transformed souls of the Avar female Banes.

URBETH: a bear of the northern wastes.

URQHART HILLS: a minor crescent-shaped range of mountains in central Ichtar.

VENATOR: Azhure's war horse.

VEREMUND: one of the Sentinels, brother to Ogden.

WARLORD: a title once given to Borneheld, Duke of Ichtar, by King Priam in acknowledgment of Borneheld's de facto command of the armies of Achar.

WARS OF THE AXE: the wars during which the Acharites, under the direction of the Seneschal and the Axe-Wielders, drove the Icarii and the Avar from the land of Tencendor and penned them behind the Fortress Ranges. Lasting several decades, the wars were extraordinarily violent and bloody. They took place some thousand years before the time of the Prophecy of the Destroyer.

WAY OF THE HORN: a general term sometimes used to describe the lifestyle of the Avar people.

WAY OF THE PLOW: the religious obedience and way of life as taught by the Seneschal according to the tenets of the Book of Field and Furrow. The Way of the Plow was centered about the Plow and cultivation of the land. Its major tenets taught that as the land was cleared and plowed in straight furrows, so the mind and the heart were similarly cleared of misbeliefs and evil thoughts and could consequently cultivate true thoughts. Natural and untamed landscape is evil; thus forests and mountains were considered evil because they represented nature out of control and because they could not be cultivated. According to the Way of the Plow, then, mountains and forests must either be destroyed or subdued, and if that is not possible, then they must be shunned as the habitats of evil creatures. Only tamed landscape, cultivated landscape, is good, because it has been subjected to mankind. The Way of the Plow was all about order, and about the earth and nature subjected to the order of mankind. Many Acharites still adhere to the Way of the Plow.

WAY OF THE WING: a general term sometimes used to describe the lifestyle of the Icarii.

WESTERN MOUNTAINS: the central Acharite mountain range that stretches west from the River Nordra to the Andeis Sea.

WHITE STAG, The: when Raum transformed, he transformed into a magnificent White Stag instead of a Horned One. The White Stag is the most sacred of the creatures of the forest.

WIDEWALL BAY: a large bay that lies between Achar and Coroleas. Its calm waters provide excellent fishing.

WIDOWMAKER SEA: vast ocean to the east of Achar. From the unknown islands and lands across the Widowmaker Sea come the sea raiders that harass Coroleas.

WILDDOG PLAINS, The: plains that stretch from northern Ichtar to the River. Nordra and bounded by the Fortress Ranges and the Urqhart Hills. Named after the packs of roving dogs that inhabit the area.

WING: the smallest unit in the Icarii StrikeForce consisting of twelve Icarii (male and female).

WING-LEADER: the commander of an Icarii Wing.

WOLFSTAR SUNSOAR: the ninth and most powerful of the Enchanter-Talons buried in the Ancient Barrows. He was assassinated early in his reign. Father to Azhure, Enchantress.

WOLVEN, The: a bow that once belonged to WolfStar SunSoar. Now in Azhure's possession.

WORSHIP HALL: the large hall built in each village where the villagers go each seventh day to listen to the Service of the Plow. It also used for weddings, funerals and the consecration of newborn infants to the Way of the Plow. It is usually the most well-built building in each village.

WRAITHS: see "Skraelings."

XANON: one of the nine Icarii Star Gods, Xanon is the Goddess of the Firmament, wife to Adamon.

YR: one of the Sentinels.

YSBADD: capital city of Nor.

YSGRYFF, PRINCE: lord of Nor, brother to Niah and uncle to Azhure.
YULETIDE: *see* "Festivals."
ZEHERAH: one of the Sentinels.
ZENITH: a girl child.
ZEST: one of the nine Icarii Star Gods, Zest is the Goddess of Earth.